I0730337

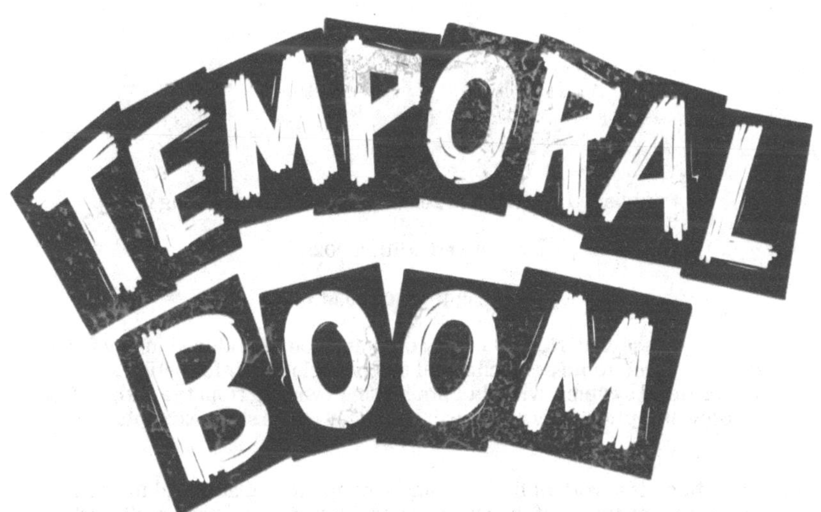

First published in Australia 2024 by Shawline Publishing Group

Second edition 2025

Copyright © 2024 J.M.Voss

All rights reserved. No part of this book may be reproduced in any form or by any electronic or mechanical means including information storage and retrieval systems, without permission in writing from the author. The only exception is by a reviewer, who may quote short excerpts in a review.

This book is a work of fiction. Names, characters, places and incidents either are products of the author's imagination or are used fictitiously. Any resemblance to actual persons, living or dead, events, or locales, is entirely coincidental.

Cover design by Shawline Publishing Group

Paperback ISBN 978-1-7641090-0-0
eBook ISBN 978-1-7641090-1-7

A catalogue record for this book is available from the National Library of Australia

# TEMPORAL BOOM

## J.M. VOSS

This book is dedicated to my friends - both those who read the drafts and informed me of the spelling errors, and those who don't read books but were nontheless excited that I had written one.

# ACT 1

# THE ARTIFICIAL DETECTIVE

### Date: Tuesday 10 March 2082

*Booting sequence initiated...*
*Internal system check: All systems online...*
*Carapace integrity: 100%...*
*R.L. integrity: 100%...*
*CONFIRM ACTIVATION = YES*
*Loading EXP025: 'THE DETECTIVE'...*
*Initialising...*
*Visuals online in 3... 2... 1...*

The Detective opened their eyes. Apertures whirred as they adjusted to the harsh sunlight, zooming and focusing.

The door to the travel crate had opened automatically. Visual analysis pieced together a burnt orange landscape beyond the crate, dotted with patches of silver-green foliage. Above, a brilliant blue dome, cloudless and vast.

With a smooth whir, the Detective lifted a hand and reached for the 'eject' button. The hand was shiny chrome, reflecting the colours of the world in concave. With a hydraulic hiss, the clamps around the Detective's legs and torso retracted. Wires disconnected and rattled into their sockets.

The Detective stepped forward, out of the crate. Their foot sunk into red dirt.

First things first – they had arrived, but there were several things which needed sorting out. Protocol required that the Detective should settle on an external appearance. Suspects were most comfortable divulging information if they believed they were speaking to a human.

They opened the appearance generation program and a graphic materialised before their eyes, superimposed on the landscape. At lightning speed, they scrolled through the various options, considering the factors. The climate was hot and sunny, so skin with a higher melanin count would be beneficial in preventing UV damage. Regarding body shape, masculine was better for intimidation and feminine for persuasion.

Intimidation, while it could get results in certain circumstances, had a higher chance of leading to an altercation and consequent structural damage, which was to be avoided. The Detective chose female – at least for now. They could always change it again later.

With appearance chosen, the Detective stood still and waited while their selection became reality. Synthetic skin, released as a dark liquid, flowed out of ports to cover their body and slowly solidified. The skin was tough but flexible, soft to the touch. On a macroscopic level it was indistinguishable from real human skin, albeit oddly smooth and flawless. There were no scars, birthmarks, wrinkles or even hair.

It took about twenty minutes for the skin to solidify. During this time, the Detective stood perfectly still, arms outstretched and feet apart, a Vitruvian statue.

At twenty minutes on the dot, a tiny alarm went off, and the Detective moved again. Lowering their arms, they got to work on shifting their topographical plates, to better resemble a stereotype of the female sex. A symmetrical face, conventionally attractive. A slim body with modest curves, athletic, but not overtly built for power. This was, of course, a deception. Regardless of external appearance, the Detective's dense, electronically powered carapace meant they could deadlift over 250kg.

Next, was the name generation program. The Detective sorted the extensive list first by feminine names, and then by region, before sorting at random. The top name which the program spat out was 'Callista Claw'. This name would do just fine.

The last step was clothing – but in this, there was little choice. The Detective opened a small hatch in the side of the travel crate, revealing a row of near identical outfits, in slightly different sizes and styles. The outfit had been specially selected by to fit in with the locals. Bright orange baggy pants, a sky-blue tank top and a jacket with bold black and orange patterns. A small alarm alerted the Detective that this outfit would not provide adequate camouflage in any natural terrain – but they ignored it and put the outfit on.

With the addition of boots, and an orange baseball cap bearing the logo of the Department of Sin, the setup protocol was complete. The baseball cap functioned both to provide shade against the sun's beating rays, and to hide the Detective's conspicuously bald head. Unfortunately, despite its other qualities, synthetic skin was unable to produce hair naturally, so until they could acquire a wig, the Detective would have to cover it up. Their courtesy protocols informed them that some people would find the perfectly smooth, follicle-free scalp 'strange and unsettling', which could be a major drawback, especially for missions involving stealth or subtlety.

On the other side of the crate, inside another small hatch, was an official Department of Sin badge, with the face and name of the Detective's new identity already displayed. The Detective stowed the badge in a special-made compartment in the side of their neck, before pausing, hand hovering over the door to the hatch.

There was a note taped to the inside of it, handwritten, in a large, scrawling font. RED CLIFFS it said. There was a smiley face underneath.

The Detective took the note and put it away in a small evidence storage compartment in their right thigh. They would decipher its meaning momentarily.

Before that, there were several other establishing pieces

of information to clear up. Where were they? Why were they here? What were they supposed to be doing?

In fact, there wasn't much that the Detective could claim to know in general. They could only remember being awake once before, a few days prior, when they had completed a series of athletic and cognitive ability tests as proof of concept. The Detective knew they were a prototype – a ReadMe file that sat on their internal HUD had explained that much. In fact, they were the very first of a planned line of entirely cybernetic sin-seeker officers. Everything was cybernetic, from the tips of their ears to the tips of their toes. The only exception was their brain, which the ReadMe file explained had been sourced from a human organ donor.

So far, the fully-cybernetic line had displayed promising results – but they had yet to be truly tested in the field. Conceptually, the cyborg officers would be perfect to send into the most dangerous regions of the Last Nation, thus reducing the death and injury rates of human officers. But more data was needed before this change could be properly implemented.

The Detective was well aware that the fate of the program rested at least somewhat on their own success. Each mistake they made, no matter how small, could be a tick against them, another round of ammunition in the belt of those who opposed the program. If their case was a catastrophic failure, then there was a chance the entire program would be scrapped. But the Detective wasn't worried. They had been purpose-built to solve cases. They were literally the perfect sin-seeker. This wasn't a matter of pride, only cold, hard fact.

The looming weight of expectation was nothing more than a mere consideration, one minor factor amongst a thousand others. It was with cool confidence that they opened the case file program and examined its contents for the first time.

*Case ID: 6437876M*
*Date of Incident: Sunday March 8th 2082*
*Time of Incident: Between 11:00AM and 1:30PM (exact time unknown)*
*Location: Mildura – Millewa-Mallee Region, Victoria*
*Description: Multiple reports have been filed stating that the city of Mildura and its entire population have 'vanished without a trace'. Detective dispatched in order to determine the truth and extent of these reports.*
*Prime Priority: Determine the existential status of Mildura*
*Secondary Priorities: <empty>*

The initial priority was simple enough. Was the town of Mildura where it was supposed to be? Had it really vanished, or had the locals fabricated the case and reported it for their own amusement?

The Detective opened their satellite navigation program and input 'Mildura'. They were not certain where the arrival crate had been deployed in relation to the city, but it surely wasn't far away. Logically, the ideal distance would be close enough to travel on foot, but not so close that the arrival itself would be observed. Taking into account the time of day, the landscape and the size of Mildura, it was likely that the crate had been deployed between ten and fifteen kilometres away, and thus-

The sat-nav loaded, and the Detective paused, examining the data.

They blinked, and then slowly turned around in a circle.

That was interesting. According to the map, they were currently standing on Mildura's main street.

It was possible the satellite navigation was wrong – after all, there were fewer satellites left in orbit these days, and their reception was notoriously patchy. But after comparing the view in front of them to several panoramic photos of Mildura in their files, the Detective was forced to conclude that this time at least, the sat-nav was correct.

So, where was Mildura?

The Detective stepped further from the crate and turned

around again, scanning the horizon. Nothing but unbroken red earth and tough, scraggly eucalypts, in every direction. To the north, the Murray River twinkled in the sun. The only evidence of human existence was the crate itself and a set of vehicle tracks leading away to the south.

Well, that solved the prime priority. Mildura had, in fact, disappeared. Not one brick of it remained.

The Detective noted this down, and formulated a new prime priority: *determine the series of events leading up to Mildura's disappearance.* Then, after locking up the arrival crate, they plotted a course to the next closest town in the sat-nav.

Red Cliffs – the same place mentioned in the mysterious note. It was just over fifteen kilometres away. The Detective set off southwards, in the same direction as the vehicle tracks. If they were going to find out what happened to Mildura, first they were going to have to locate a witness.

As they headed south, the Detective kept an eye out for any wreckage or debris. At this early stage in the investigation, any sort of evidence was welcome.

Oddly though, there was nothing. No remains of buildings, or rubbish, or people at all, only unbroken bushland, buzzing with insects, twitching with the furtive activity of small lizards and birds. It was as if Mildura had not only vanished, but been wiped from existence. The land here was undisturbed, pristine, restored to a pre-colonised state.

The lack of evidence, however, was a certain evidence in itself. It ruled out most natural disasters – fire and flood left clear debris, while diseases and bushranger raids affected people, not structures.

This left supernatural causes as the obvious answer – a Portent, or maybe P.I.U.S.

There were currently eleven Portents officially on record, each of them an anomalous force of destruction, perfectly capable of flattening an entire town within minutes to hours. But as the Detective scanned through their files, they couldn't help but conclude that none of the known eleven quite fit the profile.

In the past, Portents had razed towns through a variety of means, including extreme weather events, instantaneous mutant tree growth, transformation of all structures into the Sydney Opera House, transformation of all civilians into 'birds', and thermonuclear detonation – but none of them had caused a town to just disappear. This meant that either one of the existing Portents had suddenly developed new and interesting abilities – or, more likely, a Twelfth Portent had appeared.

If true, then this was an alarming turn of events. If there really was a new Portent roaming the countryside, deleting towns in its path off the map, then everyone needed to know about it A.S.A.P.

The only other possibility the Detective could think of was that P.I.U.S had caused the disappearance. Portent-Induced Unreality Symptoms – or more specifically, the people who wielded these strange abilities – were capable of things that were considered impossible in polite society. It wasn't completely off the table that one or more of them had somehow, accidentally or deliberately, caused Mildura to vanish.

P.I.U.S abilities were not usually powerful enough to achieve something on this scale though, especially not accidentally. And the Detective couldn't begin to fathom what sort of sociopathic sinner would deliberately do something like this.

Currently, there was no evidence for either of these conclusions – but it seemed much more likely that a Portent was responsible. Either way, the faster the Detective solved this case, the better. They increased their pace from a powerwalk to a brisk jog. A small alarm warned them that their battery would run out at 11:00PM if they persisted with their current activity, but they ignored it. They were confident the closest town was well within reach.

***

After jogging for twenty-two minutes, the Detective finally spotted evidence of human activity. It was an old, burnt-out car husk, extensively rusted, with plants growing out through the empty windows. Beyond it was a field of grape vines, that looked as though they had been recently tended to.

Pausing, the Detective noted the year, make and model of the car before deciding this was extraneous information and discarding it. More interesting were the grape vines and the fact that a few metres beyond the car was a tarmac road.

The road was in bad repair, cracked and crumbling at the edges – but then, this wasn't unusual for roads outside of Greater Melbourne. It had been over thirty years since the roads had been properly maintained. Still, the Detective frowned when they saw it. Badly kept roads only increased noise level and subsequent risk.

The state of the road wasn't what was interesting about it though. It wasn't even the fact that the tire tracks from the arrival crate led here. What was most fascinating was that approximately ten metres to the north of the car husk, the road abruptly crumbled away into nothing.

The Detective moved closer, crouching down and running their hand along the edge. The road was there – and then suddenly, it wasn't. A prickly shrub bobbed in the wind just centimetres from the end. Further along was an entire sapling, six to ten years old.

On either side of the road, the transformation from tidy agricultural land to wild bush was just as abrupt. It was as though the road and fields had been stripped away, not only in space, but time as well.

The Detective thought for a moment, and stood up, staring east, and then west. Accessing the sat-nav again, they searched for other nearby roads.

There was a dirt road to the west, 5.2 kilometres. The Detective immediately set off towards it.

It was a detour in the wrong direction – but could potentially serve as valuable evidence.

Sure enough, after finding the road and following it for a short distance, the Detective found it similarly unnaturally truncated. With two points of data available, they formulated a rudimentary hypothesis. It wasn't just Mildura that had vanished – it was a specific radius of effect. To be exact, a radius of around six kilometres, centred on what satellite data informed them had once been a weather station.

Interesting.

The Detective marked the hypothetical radius on the map, then turned and headed back the way they'd come.

***

As they approached the town of Red Cliffs, they saw that someone had set up a hay bale roadblock across the highway, wrapped in brightly coloured plastic and festooned with weak relics. Two young men were leaning against it, smoking cigarettes. They hadn't noticed the Detective yet.

The Detective came to a stop, eyeing the men from a distance. It was clear they were on guard duty. Their relaxed pose and narcotic indulgence indicated that they had been here for many hours without action. If they were bored enough, it was possible they would attempt to pick a fight with a stranger.

The Detective filtered through multiple lines of approach, before settling on the straightforward. It was likely that the guards were here due to the Mildura incident. They would be wary, but not immediately aggressive, if the Detective didn't appear as a threat to them.

They resumed walking, settling into a slower, casual pace. When the men saw them, visibly tensing up, they waved a hand in friendly greeting.

The two men watched in silence as they got closer. Then,

when the Detective was about ten metres away, the one on the left raised a hand, indicating the Detective should stop.

The Detective did so, and arranged their face into a 'friendly smile.exe'.

*Hello,* they said in sign language. *May I pass?*

The man on the left, who seemed to be the older of the two, dropped his cigarette, grinding it into the cracked tarmac.

*Who are you?* he signed back.

The Detective paused and decided there was no clear detriment in telling the truth.

*My name is Detective Claw. I am from the Melbourne Department of Sin.*

The two men looked at each other in surprise.

*Melbourne?* the left one signed, and then grinned. *How's this weather we're having, eh?*

*I could really go for a latte,* the other one signed.

The Detective stared at them blankly as they both shook with stifled laughter. They suspected that the men were making fun of them, but weren't familiar enough with local culture to understand the reference.

*I am investigating the disappearance of Mildura,* they said briskly. *I do not have time for jokes.*

The men glanced at each other again. Their expressions had become more serious.

*Go on in,* the one on the left said, and pointed to a narrow gap between the hay bales.

As the Detective moved to pass through though, the man on the right signed for them to wait.

*Is it a new Portent?* he asked. There was fear in his eyes. Clearly, the Detective wasn't the only one to have deduced this possibility.

*I do not yet know,* the Detective said.

*Probably though, right?* the man continued. *Do you think it will come here next?*

*I don't know,* the Detective said again. *I have only just begun this investigation.*

*So you don't know anything?* the man said. *What it looks*

*like? How fast it moves? Whether it flies, or crawls, or burrows?*

*I don't know if it exists*, the Detective said. *It is hypothetical at this time.*

The man nodded, sending a nervous glance down the road.

*I guess we'll know it when we see it*, he signed unhappily.

*If you keep your noise a minimum*, the Detective said, *it's unlikely to come here. Even if it does exist. Statistically, your chances of survival are high.*

The man did not seem particularly comforted by this knowledge.

***

Red Cliffs was a small town, an auxiliary of the much larger Mildura, little more than two rows of shops just off the Calder Highway. Most knew it as a refuelling point for food and solar power, a brief stop on the way to somewhere else. Otherwise, their main claim to fame was a large relic, an antique tractor known as Big Lizzie, on display at the centre of town.

The Detective paid no attention to Big Lizzie as they went by, hurrying on through the fresh produce market. It was closed for the day, empty stalls silent, small rows of colourful banners and flags hanging limp in the late afternoon heat. Locals turned to look as they passed, watching the Detective with suspicious eyes.

Beyond the produce market was the sin-seeker station, blue and white chequered sign hanging over the street – and this was where the Detective headed. Before initiating their own investigation, it would be useful to see what information the local authorities had already gathered.

It was just after 5PM, which was technically after closing hours. But peering in through the front window of the sin-seeker office, the Detective could see someone inside. They waved to draw attention.

A woman was sitting behind the front desk, frowning at

an ancient, boxy computer monitor. A mug was half-way to her lips. Startled, she placed it back down and gestured for the Detective to come in. The Detective did so, carefully and quietly closing the outer door before they opened the inner one. As they went through, they quickly scanned the soundproofing, to make sure it was up to regulation. It was.

With the airlock closed behind them, they opened their mouth and tried out their vocals for the first time. 'Good afternoon,' they said, in a randomly selected feminine voice.

'Hello,' the woman responded and she glanced pointedly up at the clock. 'It IS closing time, so unless its urgent, I'd really rather you came back tomorrow.'

The Detective scanned the woman's face. Late thirties to mid-forties, Caucasian, square jaw, with blonde hair tied tightly back in a cropped ponytail. Her face was not in any sin-seeker staff register they could find – but this wasn't unusual. Outside of Melbourne, the strict bureaucratic systems quickly broke down.

'Am I speaking to a member of the local sin-seeker force?' they asked.

'You are,' the woman said dryly.

'Good,' the Detective said. 'My name is Detective Callista Claw. I have been sent by the Melbourne Department of Sin to investigate the disappearance of the town of Mildura.'

They produced their ID badge from the slot in their neck and placed it on the desk in front of the woman. Frowning, she looked down at it, then up at the Detective again.

'Well, fuck me, you're not what I was expecting,' she said.

The Detective blinked. 'You... were expecting me?'

'Yeah,' the woman said.

She reached over to where a battered mobile phone sat on the desk and tapped in a number.

'Hey, Tank,' she said into the phone. 'The cyborg just walked in. Yeah. Go and tell Bill, will you? Oh, he's there? Okay, well tell him his cyborg is here in the office. And tell him they look freakishly human. Really tall, and you can kind of see it if you know, but still, I had no clue until they slapped their ID on the desk! Yeah! Tell Bill to hurry up.'

She hung up and looked at the Detective again. 'You ARE the cyborg, right?'

'That is correct.' The Detective frowned.

'Fuckin' hell,' the woman said. 'That's really incredible. Sorry – I was expecting some sort of tin-can looking thing. Not –'

She gestured vaguely.

'Who is Bill?' the Detective asked.

'Oh, you'll see,' the woman said. 'He should be here in a minute.'

'And who is Tank?'

'Tank's the other half of the Red Cliffs sin-seeker force.'

'There are only two of you?'

'Yep,' the woman said. 'This isn't the big city anymore, Detective. Speaking of which – we're not going to be able to help much with the Mildura case, I'm afraid. It's not that we don't want to share information – we just don't have any information.'

She slapped the side of the monitor in front of her. 'Bloody thing crashed yesterday. Blue-screen-of-death, the works. I've been trying to fix it, but I'm no wizard. It gets better too – Red Cliffs has a tech wizard, but he's not here anymore. Guess where he went. Eh? Go on, guess.'

'From context, and the implied irony, I am assuming he was in Mildura when it vanished.'

'Yep! Mildura! So yeah, R.I.P to him, and our computer. One of the last working ones in the entire town, too.'

'I might be able to fix it,' the Detective said.

'Oh?'

'It isn't my primary purpose,' the Detective said, 'but I am capable of rudimentary electronic repair.'

'Alright, have a look, then. It's worth a shot.'

The woman moved aside, making room for the Detective to fit behind the desk. 'I keep trying to restart it, and it's not working,' she told them.

The Detective thought for a moment, eyeing the screen,

which was displaying nothing but an analogue sad-face emoji. While mentally going through a list of possible problems, they pulled open the top of their right ring finger, revealing a USB cable. The officer watched sceptically as they plugged it into the computer.

As they began methodically diagnosing the issue, the airlock opened behind them, and two men came in. The first was a broad East Asian man in a sin-seeker uniform and crew cut, nearly as tall as the Detective was – probably Tank, the Detective guessed. The second was a short, somewhat rotund South Asian man, wearing canvas shorts, a Hawaiian shirt and a bowtie, each in a different bright colour. His hair and beard were several weeks past needing a trim, and he was carrying a large clipboard. It was likely this was Bill.

'Hey, Wombat,' the man who was probably Tank said. 'Is that...?'

'Yeah,' the woman said. 'Doesn't it look like a real person?!'

The Detective ignored their excited chattering, focusing on the task at hand. The monitor was broken beyond their capabilities of fixing – but the actual computer was still accessible. With a few tweaks here and there, they quickly located the files stored inside and saved them locally onto their own currently empty multi-terabyte internal hard drive.

'I have identified hardware which requires replacing,' they said out loud.

The two sin-seeker officers seemed somewhat unnerved, but not overtly scared of, the Detective, which the Detective noted was within standard response parameters. The rotund man, however, was not showing any signs of trepidation. On the contrary, he seemed quite happy to see the Detective, with body language indicating that he not only recognised them but was reasonably familiar.

'You are Bill?' the Detective confirmed, once they'd finished explaining how to fix the computer.

'Yep!' Bill said cheerfully. 'That's me!'

'It seems you know me, but I do not know you,' the Detective said.

'Yeah,' Bill said. 'I helped build your body! But I suppose you wouldn't remember that?'

'No, I do not.'

'Well, I was there. And now that you're all growed up, I'm here to keep an eye on you, ha ha.'

He went in to give the Detective a friendly punch on the arm, but with lightning speed, the Detective caught it on their palm.

'Keep an eye on me?' they said.

'Yes. I'm going to watch you while you solve the case,' Bill said. 'Since you're a prototype and all, they wanted someone to follow you around while you work. Make sure you don't go rogue and decide to kill all humanity, ha ha.'

'Why would I do that?' The Detective frowned. 'My purpose is that of all sin-seekers: uphold the Survival Act and ensure the preservation of the human species into the future.'

'It was a joke,' Bill said. 'But I'm glad to hear it! By the way, did you see my note? I assume you did, since you're here?'

'Your note – I see,' the Detective said. 'Yes, I saw it. How closely are you going to be observing me?'

'Very closely!' Bill grinned. 'From now on, I go everywhere you go, and do everything you do. We're gonna be partners in crime-solving! You're Sherlock, and I'm Watson!'

'Okay,' the Detective said, blank-faced. 'If we are partners, then I suppose we must share information. What are your current hypotheses regarding Mildura?'

'I hypothesise that the sucker is gonzo,' Bill said with a grin.

The Detective stared at him for a moment, then turned to look at Wombat and Tank. 'Do you have any hypotheses regarding Mildura's disappearance?'

'Nothing concrete,' Wombat said. 'We know it disappeared on Sunday afternoon, between 11 and 1:30.

Seems like no one actually saw it vanish though, not even from a distance. There were no explosions, earthquakes, bright flashes of light, nothing. It was just there in the morning, and then in the afternoon, it wasn't.'

'First we heard of it was Sunday evening,' Tank added. 'A truckie came in and told us Mildura was gone. Thought he was pulling our leg, until we went and saw for ourselves.'

'I spoke to a man who seemed to believe it was a Portent responsible,' the Detective said. 'Is there any evidence to suggest this is true?'

'Just speculation.' Wombat shrugged. 'But I mean, what else could it be?'

'I agree that a Portent is the most likely suspect,' the Detective said. 'Although the incident profile does not match any of the known eleven. Have there been any Portent sightings reported recently near here?'

'Actually, yes,' Wombat said. 'A bunch of 'em, just within the last six months. The Eighth came particularly close back in December, only just missed the town. Only one person got caught in it fortunately, but he's in bad shape. Still alive, but, you know. He probably won't ever be the same.'

'Is he displaying P.I.U.S?'

'Non-active P.I.U.S, yes,' Wombat said. 'The Mildura Sanctuary's been monitoring him. Well... they were.'

'What is this man's name?' the Detective said.

'Liam King. We can give you his address if you want, but I doubt he'll have much to say. He's been bedridden since the incident.'

'I would like to confirm all recent Portent sightings with eye-witnesses,' the Detective said. 'If there is a new Portent somewhere in the area, then chances are someone has seen it. It's possible they misreported it as one of the known eleven. I would like to interview them to make certain.'

'Well, I'd give you a list of witnesses,' Wombat said, 'but again, the computer is a bit fucked.'

'Don't worry – I have already obtained the list of witnesses,' the Detective said. 'I have arranged them alphabetically, by date of incident, by Portent witnessed, and by vicinity of their home address, starting with those nearest. I have decided that those that live nearest is the most efficient method to quickly talk to as many witnesses as possible. I shall visit all of those nearest in order of date of incident, before widening my search and continuing in the same pattern.'

'Oh,' Wombat said. 'Wow.'

'When do we start?' Bill asked enthusiastically.

The Detective looked outside, to where the sun was setting.

'Tomorrow morning, 6AM,' they said. 'In the meantime, I must recharge.'

While Tank and Wombat clocked out for the day, and Bill began making himself dinner in the break room, the Detective moved to the back wall and took off their left boot. There was a small hatch at the base of the ankle, which when opened, revealed an orange electrical extension cable. They attached it to the wall socket and then stood upright, perfectly still. The electrical connection triggered a diagnostic test. A report informed the Detective that all systems were online and functioning perfectly, although their coolant was already running a little low.

Fortunately, the coolant they used was just water and was very easy to top up. With no other issues reported, the Detective externally shut down for the night.

Internally, they began a deep analysis of their current findings and a resulting action plan for the following day.

Within the last six months, there had been four separate Portents sighted within the region – in order of date, the Fourth, the Fifth, the Eight and the First. The Fifth and the Eighth both had plenty of witnesses to choose from. The First, as usual, had no surviving witnesses from the actual event, but plenty of witnesses of the aftermath. The Fourth, however, was more of an issue.

There was only one reported witness of the Fourth, and it had been made at the Mildura relixorcist office.

The witness in question was a minor, a sixteen-year-old girl called Quinn Kelly. There was no home address listed in the paperwork, but considering where she'd made the report, the Detective thought it was likely that she had since disappeared off the face of the Nation.

The Detective mulled over this issue for a few minutes, before deciding that there was no helping it – they would have to ignore the Fourth for now. They simply did not have the spare time to hunt for a witness who was probably dead.

That meant the first Portent sighting they would investigate was the Fifth – and fortunately, a key witness of the Fifth's recent activity lived only twenty kilometres away. Internally, the Detective smiled in satisfaction. If things went well, then they should have their first witness statement completed before the sin-seeker office opened at 9AM the next day.

18/11/2052

## THE SURVIVAL ACT

The Survival Act 2052 and related regulations aim to preserve the human species into the future, following the cataclysmic event commonly known as the Apocalypse, Armageddon, Judgement Day, or the End of the World.

The purpose of the Act includes:

- Preserving the lives and livelihoods of citizens of the Last Nation (formerly known as Australia).
- Promoting safety, longevity and freedom from suffering for current and future generations.
- Preserving the culture, history and technological advancements of humanity for the benefit of current and future generations.
- Providing guidelines on how to continue living with minimal disruption in the post-apocalypse.

'This Act may be the most important for our Nation in its history. The World as we knew it is no more, but against all odds, the Nation still stands. But we stand upon a knife's edge. Humanity is the on the brink of extinction, and if we do not work together to ensure our own survival, then we will die, not just as a people, but as a species.

If we are to survive the next fifty years, then the Survival Act must be followed by everyone, supported by everyone, and upheld by everyone. This Act is not just in place for the purpose of maintaining law and order, but for keeping us alive. To break the tenants of the Act is to directly compromise our future. I cannot stress this enough. To fail the Act is to fail your Nation on a basic, moral level. If you break these laws, you are not just a criminal - you are a sinner.'

- Deborah Lonsdale, Premier of Victoria

*Deborah Lonsdale*

# CHAPTER 2

# QUINN KELLY

### Date: Wednesday 17 September 2081

Quinn stood under the dripping eaves, hands deep in pockets, black and green striped hoodie pulled all the way up over her dark brown, shoulder-length hair.

Half a metre in front of her, the rain was pouring down in torrents, hissing as it washed the tarmac road. It was loud, blocking out all other noise, and the smell of damp dust clogged Quinn's nose, mingling with the savoury scent of fried street food that was drifting across from a vendor nearby.

Quinn's stomach growled audibly but she ignored it. The fried whatever-it-was smelt amazing but she didn't have the spare cash for lunch today. Impatiently, she eyed her lime-green plastic wristwatch and then looked up at the slate-grey sky.

It was almost time. Quinn watched the second hand tick forward, past nine, ten, eleven...

At 1PM on the dot, the rain abruptly stopped.

A few seconds later, a teenage boy stepped out of a hardware store across the street and headed towards Quinn. He was thin and wiry, of East Asian ancestry, his ears studded with metal, a shark-tooth necklace hanging down over a scrappy yellow sleeveless jacket. His jet-black hair was combed back in a truly atrocious hairstyle.

Grinning mischievously, he nodded at Quinn, gesturing meaningfully at his backpack.

Quinn dipped her head in return and, silently, they hurried down a nearby alley.

The alley twisted and turned, then opened up into a quiet backstreet, on the side of which was parked an RV. The RV was a bright, obnoxious pink, an aggressive splash of colour on the otherwise dreary, rain-soaked street. It had clearly been painted by an amateur, with pastel-toned love hearts, stars, and flower shapes festooned across the bonnet. Along its flank were the words THE GLAM VAN, in large graffiti letters. The only part of the RV that wasn't pink or pastel were the wheels, and the roof, which was set with a row of solar panels.

It was towards this vehicular abomination that Quinn and the young man hurried. Quinn pulled open the door on the side and they climbed in.

Inside, the RV was clean, but densely cluttered, with storage or shelving on every vertical surface and random objects strung along the ceiling. It was divided in two distinct sections; the front 'living area', with a tiny dinner table and kitchenette, and the back 'work area', which was mostly taken up by a desk, with a chunky computer underneath and several monitors bolted to the walls around the back window.

There was also a tiny bathroom, partitioned off for privacy, and at the very front, the driver's cabin, separated behind a fluoro pink curtain. Some would say it was horribly cramped, not to mention tacky – but other more generous folks might call it cosy. Quinn and the young man, who was referred to by most people as 'Mullet', called the place home.

'Alright,' Quinn said now, once the door was closed behind them. 'Let's see it, then.'

Grinning, Mullet took off his backpack, dumping it on the floor and unzipping it with a flourish. Amongst the usual junk he carried everywhere was a shiny new pair of bolt cutters. 'Behold!' he said grandly.

Quinn took the hefty tool out and turned it around in her hands. As she did so, there was a faint noise from the cabin of the RV and the curtain was pulled aside. A tall, willowy East Asian woman, with very long hair and very thin eyebrows, stepped through. She was wearing a crop top with the word BITCH on it and a high-waisted skirt, both in similarly violently feminine colours to that of THE GLAM VAN itself.

'Oh good, you're back,' she said, her voice clipped with an air of perpetual impatience. 'Please tell me that no one saw you this time, Mullet?'

'Of course not,' Mullet said, his voice a husky drawl. 'I'm a master thief!'

'That's what you said last time,' the woman said. 'And yet, there I was, bailing you out with the last of our cash. Maybe if you were a master thief, we would have had enough money to buy the bolt cutters like normal people.

'Anyway.' She turned to eye Quinn. 'The deal's at two. New client, so there's a chance it could go sideways. I want you both there, looking intimidating, in case he thinks he's tougher than me. Got it?'

'Yes, Kylie,' Quinn and Mullet chorused.

'Good,' Kylie said. 'You have half an hour to chill, then we're going.'

She disappeared inside the cabin again.

'So ungrateful.' Mullet sighed, flopping down in a chair. 'We do ALL the work, risking life and limb... Me, her own cousin! Flesh and blood! You, I understand at least. You're just a charity case.'

Quinn put down the bolt cutters and leaned on the kitchenette. 'She's just worried about the deal,' she said. 'We really need this one.'

'Yeah, yeah,' Mullet said. 'We really need all of them.'

'Actually, what we really need is new gear,' Quinn went on. 'The stuff we have is stale. Everyone already has a copy! If we wanna sell more, we need better shit to sell! Something new and exciting, you know?'

'Yeah, and why do you think we bought the bolt cutters, dummy?' Mullet said. 'We're gonna get more gear tonight!'

'I sure hope so,' Quinn said.

'I KNOW so!' Mullet said. 'None of that pessimism, Quinn! We're gonna find some absolute certified bangers that no one's ever heard of, just you watch! And then everyone will buy it, and we'll be rich! We'll buy fuckloads of lunch every day and have three GLAM VANs. One each!'

'Do you really think we'll find them though?' Quinn said.

'Find what?'

'The certified bangers. We didn't find anything new last time, or the time before that. Just stuff we already have. I don't even know if there IS more stuff to find.'

'There is,' Mullet said. 'Just you watch. Third time's lucky, baby!'

Quinn sighed. 'Whatever.' She leaned back, staring up at the ceiling. Her stomach gurgled.

***

Half an hour later, Kylie emerged from the cabin again in a fluffy pink jacket and oversized sunnies.

'Alright babes,' she said. 'Let's fuckin' go.'

She opened the door and Quinn and Mullet scrambled to their feet, Mullet grabbing his backpack where he'd left it on the ground. As Kylie began powerwalking down the street, Quinn ran to catch up and fell into step beside her.

*What are we selling this time?* she asked in sign language.

*Two starter packages,* Kylie signed back. *Acca Dacca and Barnsie.*

*And where are we meeting the client?* Quinn asked.

*Behind the weather station,* Kylie said.

Quinn made a face. *Why there?*

*Client makes the rules,* Kylie said. *Sorry. You're gonna have to suck it up. Now stop asking questions where people could see them.*

Quinn fell back again and send a disgruntled look Mullet's way. She hated the weather station. It was one of her least favourite places in Mildura.

In fact, it was one of her least favourite places in any town she'd been to – and she'd been to a lot. The nature of their work meant it was too dangerous to stick around in the same place for long. Quinn had been to most of Victoria's towns at least once, with the notable exception of the capital, Melbourne, which was simply more trouble to get into than it was worth.

Mildura was one of the larger towns in the state, a north-western hub of trade and food production. The farms here fed the whole region, and the vineyards supplied wine to Melbourne and beyond. There were thousands of people here, so many that there were TWO shopping centres rather than one. It was also home to one of the largest weather stations in Victoria.

It was large enough that Quinn could feel its aura from several blocks away.

It wasn't that it was painful or even particularly unpleasant – it was just uncomfortable. It made Quinn feel stifled, like the air was just slightly thinner than she was used to. It dulled her senses and stilled her imagination, filling her mind with static fuzz and the deadening weight of here-and-now-ness. Within the aura, nuance and possibility were gone – there was only the present, the facts, the tangible, the stark reality which sat right before the eyes.

The building looked innocent enough from the outside. Surrounded by a chain-link fence, it was long and grey, with a single, extremely tall tower in the centre. Far, far above, at the peak of the tower, whisps of cloud circled a long, metal spire.

Inside the tower, the weathersmiths were hard at work, wrangling the weather around the clock. Their P.I.U.S abilities lent them the power to remake reality at will – although not without significant dangers to both themselves and those around them.

Below, in the main building, a veritable blockade of relics kept the unreality effects tidily caged and away from the public. Within the relic's aura, unreality was not possible. When not at work, the weathersmiths stayed in the main building, where they became regular, harmless, people – albeit perpetually dulled and stifled.

Quinn couldn't begin to imagine how the weathersmiths could endure it for so long. As they walked along the weather station fence, she began to dawdle as tiredness gripped her. Hunching in, she pulled her hood down as far as it would go over her face.

Glancing back, Kylie gave her a concerned look. *You alright?* she signed.

Quinn took a deep breath and nodded. She would be, that was a fact – just as soon as she got away from the weather station.

The fence felt like it went on forever, a wall of cold metal links, interspersed with notices displaying the week's scheduled weather events. At last, they reached the far corner and turned into an alley between the weather station and a shopping centre parking lot. The alley was lined with colourful graffiti slogans interspersed with garbage skips.

Quinn didn't notice when Kylie suddenly stopped walking, and almost ran into her.

*Sorry,* she signed dazedly.

*It's fine.* Kylie waved a manicured hand. *Stay quiet, now. I think I see our man.*

Arranging her face into a pleasant smile, she stepped further into the alley, to where a figure was leaning against the wall, cigarette in hand. Quinn and Mullet followed quietly at a distance. Mullet had folded his arms, scowling to show that he meant No Funny Business. Quinn, meanwhile, was trying her best to not fall over her own feet.

The figure turned to look as they approached, cigarette smoke issuing out of his nostrils and between his fingers. He was a large, burly guy, sunburn peeling off his powerful shoulders. He was probably at least twice Mullet's weight – but he seemed relaxed enough.

*You the dealer?* he asked Kylie one-handed, stubbing out his smoke with the other.

*Depends,* Kylie said. *Are you 'Tassie Tim'?*

The man nodded.

Kylie nodded back and reached into her coat, pulling out a cyan-blue USB stick.

*It's all on here,* she said. *Acca Dacca and Barnsie, our entire digital collection for each artist. Fifty-six individual tracks in total, including iconic rock classics such as Back in Black, Highway to Hell and Working Class Man.*

*All on that USB, huh?* the client said.

*Yes,* Kylie signed smoothly. *I believe you said you do have computer access, correct? It is a requirement.*

*Yeah, I have a computer,* the client said.

He took the USB from Kylie's palm, squinting at it curiously. Then, after a pause, he reached into his pocket.

*Five hundred, wasn't it?* he said.

Kylie nodded.

The man brought out a wallet and fingered through a stack of dusty fifties. *Ten pineapples, count 'em,* he said.

Kylie rapidly counted the notes, and they disappeared into her pocket.

*Great,* she said, smiling at the client again. *Enjoy your music! But a word of warning – please only listen in the privacy of your own home. And keep the volume down.*

*Of course,* the client said. *I'm not an idiot.*

*Just making sure you're aware.* Kylie smiled. *And remember to contact me again if you want more!*

She waved goodbye and walked calmly out of the alley, shepherding the others ahead of her. Once they were around the corner, she visibly breathed a sigh of relief.

Mullet gave her an excited thumbs up and she returned a peace sign, which was the Kylie equivalent of pumping her fist in glee. Mullet then prodded Quinn, until she also gave a weak thumbs up.

No one said anything until they were back in THE GLAM VAN – but the second the door closed, Mullet let out a whoop of celebration.

'Dude, that went perfectly!' he yelled, bouncing on the balls of his feet. 'He didn't even try and haggle down the price!'

'No yelling in the RV.' Kylie waggled a finger at him. 'But yes, it did go well, didn't it?'

She took out the five hundred dollars and fanned them out, kissing the air above them. 'Ladies, we're eating well tonight,' she purred.

Quinn, who was already feeling a lot better, moved to stand right in front of her.

'Kylie,' she said excitedly. 'Kylie, Kylie. Can we please get something fried?'

'Tonight,' Kylie said, 'you can get anything you want, babes! Although,' she added, when Mullet opened his mouth, 'ONLY if it's under twenty dollars.'

'Aw,' Mullet said. But he was still grinning as he said it.

# LANDFILL

## Date: Wednesday 17 September 2081

The Mildura Landfill was just to the north of the town, and it was one of the best guarded that Quinn had ever seen. Quinn had seen a lot of dumps in her time too – after all, they were one of the only places to find new gear, without paying a ludicrous price for it.

Apparently, the Mildura Scrapper's Guild were quite well off. This dump was a veritable fortress. There were floodlights, fences and even a night patrol, with a dog and everything. Quinn was pretty sure the dog was entirely for show, though. There was no way it could smell anything, over the powerful dump stench. Smelling intruders amongst that eye-watering malaise would be like trying to spot a lightbulb in front of the sun.

But the gang hadn't come unprepared. They were veterans at breaking into landfills. They had crank-powered flashlights, on full charge, and with red plastic over the front to dim the beam. They had new bolt cutters, replacing the last pair they'd had to abandon when the last job had gone balls up. They had a rough patrol schedule, after staking out the site for the last few nights. They even had handkerchiefs to cover their nose and mouth, to block out the smell, slightly.

Just before sunset, Kylie drove THE GLAM VAN off-road and behind the landfill, where she parked it just in the tree-line. It was better to get into position before night fell – the van's headlights were a lot more suspicious in the dark than THE GLAM VAN itself was in the daytime.

From this position, the gang waited in the darkening bush for a few hours, and then disembarked. They had all changed into black clothes and soft shoes, all the better for sneaking.

Approaching the back of the landfill, they watched the patrol go past, flashlights sweeping just inside the perimeter. Once the lights moved off, they made their move. Mullet brought out the bolt cutters and deftly snipped a hole in the chain-link fence.

Quietly, they stepped through, running lightly to the nearest pile of trash. The floodlights, shining from the perimeter and from regularly-spaced poles inside, cast their shadows on multiple angles, in varying shades of grey and black.

*Okay,* Kylie signed. *Tech section is over there. Let's go.*

They darted across to where a massive pile of technological junk towered into the air. Cracked computer cases, burnt-out diodes, colourful bundles of gnawed wires and green motherboard fragments. An entire washing machine casing sat beside a sack full of dead mobile phones, spilling out onto the ground. The ground itself was dotted with detached letter keys and frosted with a fine layer of broken glass.

Quinn went straight for the sack full of phones. These were the most likely place to find new music, if any of the phones were both intact enough to turn on, and possible to unlock.

The vast majority of the phones would be useless – but there were always one or two that had survived better than the rest. Carefully, Quinn tipped out the sack of phones, and began sorting through them.

As expected, most were crushed, rusted, shorted, or smashed beyond repair, and these she pushed aside. Many more were models that Kylie, even with all her computing power and multitude of illegal password bypass programs, had not yet figured out how to hack into, even if they did turn on.

The last few, a cluster of less than ten hopefuls, Quinn stuffed into her backpack. Kylie would try and get into them later, from the safety of THE GLAM VAN. Maybe they would turn on, maybe they wouldn't. If just one proved workable, then they would have access to its entire song library, with potentially dozens of new tracks.

Nearby, Mullet was picking through the larger hardware, while Kylie was examining motherboard fragments, in case one of them was salvageable. Quinn moved in a different direction, panning over the pile of junk with her red-beamed flashlight. As she did so, she caught sight of what looked like another old brick-style phone, still wrapped in its original plastic packaging. Stooping, she picked it up and turned it around. It looked to be in good condition – however on closer inspection, she was no longer sure it was actually a phone. The buttons were all wrong.

Frowning, she picked her way back to where Kylie was holding up two board fragments, which looked like they'd originally been attached to each other.

*What's this?* she gestured, showing Kylie her find.

Kylie eyed it. *I think that's a digital voice recorder. Looks like it's in good condition. Does it turn on?*

Quinn pulled open the packet and saw that the device was powered using A3 batteries. She had brought some in her pockets for this exact reason and placed them into the empty slot.

There was a pause, and then the screen of the device lit up. There was no password – it went straight to the user interface.

Quinn grinned delightedly and showed Kylie again. *Should we take it?* she asked.

*Yes. If it works, we can sell it.*

*Or we could keep it and make voice recordings!* Quinn said.

*Sure.* Kylie went back to staring at the two motherboard halves.

Quinn moved away, curiously thumbing through the controls. It seemed to be very straightforward to use. Experimentally, Quinn pressed the record button.

'Hello,' she whispered into the speaker and then hit replay.

'Hello,' the recorder said.

Quinn jumped up and down in excitement, although quietly. Then she went over to Mullet.

'Hello,' she played in his ear.

Mullet almost dropped the half-a-laptop he was holding. Eyes wide, he turned to stare at Quinn.

*Check it out*, Quinn signed and showed him the recorder.

Mullet grinned. *Record me*, he signed and leaned forward.

'Hi, I'm Mullet, and I'm the fully-sickest cunt in all of Mildura,' he whispered.

'Untrue,' Quinn said and then hit replay. They shook with repressed laughter when both their voices came right back out of the device.

'Hey,' Quinn whispered, 'give me a beat!'

Mullet put his hand over his mouth and began quietly beatboxing. Quinn looped the recording and pressed play. Quietly, she hummed a tune over the top of the beat.

Kylie appeared next to her and she hurriedly stopped recording herself.

*What are you doing, fucking idiots?* Kylie signed. *This is not the time or the place!*

*Sorry.* Quinn put the recorder away in her bag. While Kylie glared at her, she went back to poking through piles of damaged tech. She found another sack of phones and was just about to tip it out when she heard Kylie give a muffled exclamation.

She turned to look and saw Kylie beckoning. *Come over here!*

Quinn joined her, and she pointed at another green board, buried half-way up a trash mountain. It was a whole, unbroken board – but it was also stuck, partially wedged underneath an old microwave.

*Help me get it out,* Kylie said and pointed. *Grab that side.*

Quinn looked at the microwave, and then up at the vast pile of trash stacked above it.

*Won't that disrupt the pile?* she said.

*Carefully,* Kylie said. *C'mon. We need that board!*

She grabbed one side of the microwave and lifted it, nodding at Quinn to grab the board from underneath. Quinn did so, gently shifting it back and forth, easing it out. Above, metal and glass shifted and resettled. A few pieces slid down and bounced on the ground.

Slowly, slowly, centimetre by centimetre, the board was freed. Finally, it was clear, and Quinn set it down by her feet.

Kylie let out a breath. Quinn gave her a thumbs up.

Kylie nodded and let go of the microwave.

Immediately, the entire trash mountain began to collapse.

Quinn skipped backwards as appliances and old computer parts cascaded downwards in an extended, thunderous crash. Parts of the pile collapsed into the next one, which in turn began to avalanche.

*RUN, RUN, RUN!* Kylie signed as the cacophony grew.

They turned and bolted back the way they'd come. As they did so, the lights around them started to blink red and blue. A few trash piles away, powerful flashlights waved in the dark.

Quinn and the others sprinted back towards the hole in the fence. But before they got there, a lean shape leaped into view and barrelled towards them.

It was the guard dog, a black-and-tan bullet of lithe muscle. As they skidded to a stop, it leapt in front of them and opened its mouth to bark. No sound came out beside a slight wheeze – the dog had been muted. But the flash of white teeth was enough reason to pause.

Kylie tried to go around it, and it lunged at her, grabbing her sleeve, tugging it, dragging her off balance. At the same time, the flashlights rounded the nearest trash heap, converging on the gang, pinning them there in full view.

'Halt or we'll shoot,' a voice said from behind the blinding light – quiet, but sharp with authority. 'Hands above your head!'

Mullet and Quinn froze. Mullet slowly raised his hands above his head. Quinn did as well – but there was something in her right hand. It was the voice recorder. Moving slowly, she cranked the volume to max and reached for the play button.

'You're trespassing on Scrapper Guild property,' the guard continued, moving closer. 'The Department of Sin has been notified. You are to come quietly with us and wait until they... what the fuck is that?'

'Music,' Quinn said.

'What? Turn... turn it off!'

'No,' Quinn said. And then, to the bafflement of the guards, she began to sing over the top of the tune she'd recorded earlier. Lyrics came to her head, words that had been tugging half-formed at her mind for a while:

*I guess you forgot*
*All the things that I said to you*
*I guess you forgot*
*All the conversations that we had, us two*
*I guess you forgot,*
*And I guess that's fine, but your amnesia makes me blue*
*I guess you forgot, I guess you forgot*
*Well, I hope you rot.*

'Hey!' the guard hissed. 'What the fuck are you doing!? Stop that! Turn it off, or I'll open fire!'

It was hard to tell behind the bright lights but Quinn thought she saw the guard raising his gun. Time was up. Three layers of music and around thirty seconds... was it enough?

It had to be. She'd hedged her bets already. There wasn't a plan B.

She closed her eyes and focused on the beat. The interweaving sounds, in perfect time. Her heartbeat with it, and with each beat, an image became clearer in her mind. A twisted, spinning shape, radioactive yellow and gunmetal grey. Wings, turbines, billowing smoke, panes of glass and metal, mashed together in ways that should never have been possible, churning in eternal fifth-dimensional torture. Worst of all, the sirens. Loud and unholy, in measured bursts, surrounded by islands of pure silence. A cry to herald in the End of the World.

The sirens made a beat of their own, a heartbeat of untold death and destruction. Time, marching forward as it always had, a fundamental pillar to the Canon Material Timeline.

But the First Portent was not of this timeline. And for those who gazed upon it and lived, the dogma of the universe became less absolute.

Quinn took the beat of the song, of time made manifest, and unmade it. As the First Portent's dread siren echoed in her ears, audible only to her, she took the inexorable tide of time into her hands and flipped it in reverse.

The first layer, the beat, did nothing by itself – it was the base layer, barely music. It could stop time, but not rewind it.

The second layer added melody to the beat. A song now, proper. Time could now move backwards, at the same rate as it moved forwards.

The third layer added to the complexity and the power. The rate of reversal was faster, compounding, accelerating, doubling the speed.

It was this third layer that Quinn had been relying on. The first two wouldn't cut it. But with the addition of the third...

The music began to play backwards.

A muffled gunshot. She opened her eyes again. Face cast in deep shadow, the guard stood, mouth open in an expression of fear and rage. The bullet left the gun, slowing, slowing, and coming to a stop. Then it reversed. It disappeared back into the gun in a tiny flash of light.

The man lowered his gun and gestured angrily, in

reverse. Then he and the other guard left, walking backwards over the trash piles like marionettes on strings. The dog followed them, letting go of Kylie and leaping gracefully away, hindlegs first.

Quinn herself began to run backwards, much faster than she ever could forwards. It was not a process she could interrupt, even if she wanted to.

She turned and watched the massive trash heap rebuild itself, debris flying upwards in the face of entropy. Pieces lodged themselves back into the pile, dust billowing inwards. The thunderous decent played in reverse, echoing oddly, stilted.

Finally, she put the motherboard back into place.

The song reached its beginning. Time resumed its forward march.

Gasping, Quinn buckled, all energy leaving her body. Kylie was reaching for the microwave. Desperately, she opened her mouth to warn her – but only thick black smoke came out, pouring off her tongue and tonsils.

Kylie, fortunately, noticed this was happening – and pulled her hand back like the trash had burnt her.

'Shit,' she hissed and crouched next to Quinn. *What is it? What's about to happen? Quinn, talk to me! Are we in danger?*

Quinn drew in a ragged breath and doubled over, coughing into her black T-shirt.

*It's... fine,* she managed. *I've... avoided it. But Kylie,* she said, between fits of coughing. *Forget about that board. It's not worth it!*

## THE FIRST PORTENT

FIRST RECORDED SIGHTING: 12/06/2052, Sydney, Gadigal country, NSW

PHYSICAL APPEARANCE:

The First Portent resembles an F-35A Lightning II combat aircraft, in early-to-late stages of total systems failure. The craft is 15.7m long, with a height of 4.4m, and a wingspan of 11m. It carries a single crewmember, pilot T. Fisk, colloquially known as the Doomed Pilot. The aircraft is painted in silver, with an Australian Flag on the tail; however, the paint is observed to be in a state of disrepair. Flames, smoke and debris are often seen trailing or falling from the craft.

The First Portent's dimensions are not fixed, with wide variation described between sightings. This variation extends to all physical aspects, including window position, wing position and number, colouration and patterning, and most aspects of fundamental layout. This 'mutation' of original form has been observed to increase in magnitude over time.

BEHAVIOUR:

The First Portent is both the most predictable, and most physically destructive, of the Portents yet discovered. Its behaviour works on a well-documented cycle:

MATERIALISATION PHASE: The cycle begins when the First Portent appears in the sky, materialising over a period of seventeen hours and four minutes, in a location within 500 km from its previous point of impact. This phase ends when the structure of the Portent is completed, at which point the structure bursts into flame and the SOS phase initiates.

SOS PHASE: During this phase, an SOS call is broadcast on all radio frequencies from the Portent. The call, which is thought to be initiated from the pilot, T. Fisk, varies between incidents both in content and legibility, with static interference typically being high. Below are excerpts from iterations where legibility was relatively high, and messages were recorded:

2nd iteration: 'Mayday, mayday, this is Fisk. The plane is falling apart around me and… I think I hit something? I repeat, I hit something. There was an explosion. I can't see what's happening. The plane is on fire. There was an explosion, but I'm still alive. Somehow, I'm still alive.'

3rd iteration: 'Command, please respond. I don't know what just happened. I thought I crashed again, but… I'm still in the sky. The plane is still falling apart. I don't know how I'm still alive. Please respond, command. Please respond command. Please respond. Please respond. Please –'

4th iteration: *Sobbing can be heard distinctly, although words cannot be made out.*

6th iteration: 'Mayday mayday. Mayday. This is Fisk. Please respond, Command. The plane is on fire again. I'm not dead, Command. I'm not fucking dead. Why aren't I dead? Why? Why? I blew up. I exploded again. My body was in pieces, and now it's not. Why is this happening, Command? Why is this happening to me?'

9th iteration: 'Please respond. Please respond. Please, please. I don't know what's happening. There's something wrong with me. Please respond. I have died. I have died, and come back, so many times. Is this Hell? Please respond. Please respond. Please respond. Please respond. Is this Hell, Command?'

10th iteration: 'No no no no no no not again. Not again. I want to die! I want to fucking die! I hate this. I hate it I hate it I hate it. No. No no no no no no no no no no! (screaming).'

Note – Attempts have been made to contact Fisk, however so far all efforts have been unsuccessful.

DESCENT PHASE: After six minutes and forty-five seconds, the First Portent enters Descent phase. At this point, the plane burns up enough as to no longer remain airborne, and plummets from the sky. It is the most rapid phase, at only 182 seconds, after which the plane hits the ground, and enters Impact phase.

IMPACT PHASE: On impact, the cargo of the Portent undergoes a ten-kiloton thermonuclear explosion. This is accompanied 0.034 seconds later by an index 10 unreality burst, at a rubicon radius of 3.5 km. Local structures are flattened, local fires are ignited and hazardous quantities of radioactive fallout are released into surrounding areas.

Note 2 – the use of weathersmith and mattersmiths P.I.U.S have to date proved highly effective at minimising the spread of radioactive material beyond the impact site.

LATENT PHASE: Following impact phase, the First Portent remains dormant for a period of time between twenty-eight and thirty-four months, before as-yet-unknown triggers cause it to once more enter Materialisation phase, beginning the cycle anew. During Latent phase, the Portent is completely inactive. Parts of its structure can be found scattered across the impact site, which display a passive unreality index of between 2-4, but with careful handling, can be safely relocated. All pieces of the First Portent, along with remaining radiation caused by its Impact phase, disappear from the previous site when the Materialisation phase initiates.

Since its first appearance over and subsequent destruction of Sydney, the First Portent has gone through 11 iterations. While some of these have resulted in the First Portent impacting harmlessly in uninhabited regions, it has landed 5 additional times in populated locations. It is estimated that in total the First Portent is directly responsible for over 6 million human deaths.

PORTENT INDUCED UNREALITY SYMPTOMS:

P.I.U.S RUBICON RADIUS: 3.5 kilometres

ACTIVE SYMPTOM DEVELOPMENT: > 98%

LETHALITY: >99%

DESIGNATION: Timesmith

ADDITIONAL NOTES: Survivors of the First Portent's Impact Phase are rare, and thus relatively little is known of P.I.U.S abilities that stem from the First Portent. It is theorised that those few to survive the thermonuclear blast will develop active P.I.U.S at a rate of 98% or higher. Common Symptoms involve the ability to manipulate the flow of entropy, through 'pre-cognitive' tendencies, or direct manipulation of the fabric of spacetime.

# MUSIC DEALER

**Date:Thursday 18 September 2081**

The next morning, Quinn's mouth still tasted like acrid smoke. She spent twenty minutes trying to wash it away, even going so far as the wipe soap on her tongue – but it kept coming back, tainting her breakfast and souring her mood.

It wasn't every day, but there were certainly days when she hated her P.I.U.S. She would much rather be a normal person and live a normal, peaceful life – but with active Symptoms that was basically impossible.

The Sanctuaries hadn't found her so far, but if they ever did, that would mean the end to any freedom or choice she had in life. She would be forced to work whatever job they decided was best for her, using her Symptoms 'for the good of the Nation', regardless of any pain and suffering it caused her personally. Sure, they'd provide her with food, and a warm bed, and she'd never have to worry about finding work – and on some nights, when her belly was particularly empty, Quinn had even found those prospects attractive. But most of the time, she thought it sounded like a prison, a place to stifle out any possibility she had of at least pretending to be normal.

But even if the Sanctuaries never found her, the Symptoms would always be there, tempting her to use them. They were extremely useful, she had to admit. Inevitably, she would end up in situations she would rather not be in, and unlike normal people, she had the choice to rewind and try again.

In some instances, like the previous evening, she would be foolish not to.

Most of the time though, it wasn't worth the trouble. P.I.U.S abilities could do wondrous things – control the weather, heal grievous wounds in an instant, or cause crops to grow at supernatural speed. But there was a cost – breaking reality had its side effects, both unpredictable and highly unpleasant. These side effects were capable of causing serious bodily harm and were known to drastically shorten the average lifespan of those who were affected.

There were other downsides to having P.I.U.S. as well. People who knew about it would often treat Quinn differently, fear or pity clear in their voice and behaviour. And relics were debilitating to be around – which sucked, because normal people loved them and put them absolutely everywhere.

Even Mullet and Kylie would occasionally treat Quinn different, although they'd gotten better about it the longer they'd known her. When they'd first found her, sitting shellshocked near the irradiated ruins of her family home, they had treated her like she was made of glass. The first time she'd rewound time, completely by accident, they'd freaked out for days.

To be fair though, Quinn had also freaked out the first time. And before she'd developed P.I.U.S herself, she too had been scared of the people who had it. As a kid, she would hide when she saw them, walking the streets in their fluoro-orange jumpsuits, always in groups of even numbers. Her mother had always whispered a prayer when they passed, for protection for those who wielded raw unreality, and for protection against them.

The prayers had not prevented the First Portent from showing up – but somehow, Quinn had survived the event, so maybe they hadn't been completely useless?

It would have been better if none of it had happened, of course. But there was no use dwelling on the past – at least, not that far back. Quinn was alive and kicking, and equipped with the ability to reverse the flow of time, for a couple of minutes. Things could be worse.

They could also be better, though. And no one in the Nation could stop Quinn from griping about it if she wanted to. She spent a good portion of the morning complaining about her sore, smoky throat to Mullet, while Kylie drove THE GLAM VAN out of town.

They were headed to the Murray Sunset National Park, with the intention of staying for a couple of days. There, it was very unlikely that anyone would disturb them, while they went through the previous evening's loot.

After their close brush with calamity, they'd ended the job on the Mildura Landfill earlier than expected. But despite this, the haul had turned out pretty decent. There were nine mobile phones, several functional computer parts, a couple of promising headphone sets and a broken portable speaker that Kylie was convinced she could fix.

Now, all that remained was cracking into the phones and extracting the music – but this was easier said than done. Most of the phones were locked behind a range of encryption systems, four-digit codes, unique dot-to-dot patterns, password phrases and fingerprints of owners long since dead. Kylie, however, was an expert in breaking into them. She had magic fingers when it came to tech, and on top of this, had collected an impressive arsenal of password-cracking and jailbreaking programs.

After driving for a couple of hours, Kylie pulled the RV to a stop beside a small pink salt lake, under a crop of squat eucalyptus trees. The trees did nothing to hide THE GLAM VAN from view, but they did offer a small amount of shade, which would stop the RV from overheating inside.

While Quinn and Mullet went out to check that there was no one else camped nearby, Kylie set up her workstation at the back of the RV, booting up her main computer and plugging in one of the phones they'd found. It was a veritable dinosaur – a Nokia 1100 from the mid-2000s, somehow still functional.

'This one will be easy,' she said to the others, when they

came over to see what she was doing. 'But don't get too excited. I think this model outdates MP3. There will probably be no music onboard.'

A few minutes later, she was proven right. 'Like I expected,' she said, scrolling though the extracted files. 'No MP3 player.'

'What about those?' Quinn asked, pointing at the screen.

'Ringtones,' Kylie said. 'Useless.'

'Are they?' Quinn said.

'Yes,' Kylie said. 'They're only ten seconds long. Look, this one's only three seconds. They're just sound effects.'

She moved to close the window.

'Wait!' Quinn said. 'Can I have them?'

'Why?'

'I might be able to make something out of them.' Quinn shrugged.

Kylie sighed. 'Quinn, you need to stop trying to make music out of this garbage,' she said. 'It's a waste of time. We can't sell it; we can't do anything with it. We don't do fakes, remixes or covers, remember? We only sell original, pre-apocalypse, good-quality music. Them's the fuckin' rules, babes.'

'I don't wanna sell it,' Quinn said. 'I just wanna mess around with it. Please?'

'Ugh. Fine,' Kylie said.

She drag-and-dropped the sound files onto a waiting USB and handed it to Quinn. 'Go nuts, kiddo. And don't pester me again.' She firmly put on a set of headphones.

Quinn took the USB with a grin and, grabbing one of Kylie's spare laptops, she settled down at the tiny kitchen table. There, she plugged in the USB and, an expression of concentration on her face, she went through and listened to all the files in turn.

Some of them were just sound effects, like Kylie said – but others were tunes, even if they were tinny and high pitched. One in particular caught her ear, and she replayed it over and over.

Frowning, she went and grabbed the voice recorder she'd found the previous evening.

After some time, Mullet slouched over and sat down opposite. 'What are you making?' he asked curiously.

Quinn looked up from a notebook, where she'd been writing lyrics.

'Check it out,' she said, and picking up the recorder, she pressed play.

A multi-layered track, based around the best of the ringtones, echoed throughout the RV. Lyric notebook open in front of her, Quinn sang words over the top of it for a couple of bars – before trailing off.

'That's all I've got,' she said apologetically.

'Dude,' Mullet said.

'What?'

'That's fuckin sick.'

'I know, right?' Quinn brightened. 'Kylie says I'm not allowed to make things to sell, but I reckon we could sell this. Do you think so?'

'Maybe,' Mullet said doubtfully. 'Kylie definitely won't agree to it, though.'

'What won't I agree to?' Kylie said, taking off her headphones.

'Nothing,' Quinn said. 'Did you find any music yet?'

'I did, actually,' Kylie said, and she held up a phone. 'It's another oldie – an Xperia Ray, 2011. I was concerned it also wouldn't have an MP3 player. But it does, and guess what? There's a whole bunch of stuff on here.'

'Heck yeah!' Quinn bounced up out of her seat. 'Show us!'

Kylie moved to the side and pointed at the monitor screen, to where the phone's contents lay bare.

'So Fresh 2005?' Mullet read out. 'Is that a band?'

'It's a collection,' Kylie said. 'The most popular songs of 2005, I believe.'

'Put one on!' Quinn said excitedly.

Kylie clicked at random on the list, and My My My by Armand Van Helden began to play. They all stood back, listening. It was a dance track – and by the end all three of them were moving along to the beat.

'Perfect.' Kylie saved the album to her computer. 'It'll fetch a good price.'

'Can we listen to the rest?' Quinn said.

'Not right now,' Kylie said. 'We still have half a dozen phones to crack.'

'Aw,' Quinn pouted.

She watched Kylie set up the next phone and initiate one of her jailbreaking programs. A progress bar popped up, at one per cent. A few minutes later it inched up to two per cent.

Quinn got bored of watching and, grabbing her lyrics book again, she went to the door.

'I'm going out for some air,' she announced to the room in general. 'Back soon!'

Outside, it was warm and sunny, but not oppressively so. Head in the clouds, Quinn trudged along the edge of the salt lake, and up onto a small, steep hill. At the very top was a tall rock and she climbed up onto it, peering out over the trees.

On the other side of the hill, a wide orange plane stretched out towards the horizon, speckled with silver-green desert shrubs and the occasional lone eucalypt. Patches of small purple flowers nodded here and there amongst the rocks.

Quinn sat cross-legged and hummed quietly to herself, tapping a pattern on her knee, book open in front of her. She was still trying to come up with the next verse for her song. Something about the salt lake? It was a beautiful place – alien, harsh but stunning in its own way. It deserved recognition through music. Quinn muttered to herself, trying to find the correct rhyming to describe the emotion it evoked.

As she sat there though and listed words that rhymed, a strange feeling came over her. It was a prickly, uneasy feeling – oddly exhilarating, but frightening, an anxiety fuelled adrenaline rush. Quinn's hair stood up and goosebumps broke out over her arms. Her heart was beating too fast and her head was full of too many ideas, spiralling out of control. The feeling intensified, and then, just when Quinn was starting to get properly worried, it faded again.

Quinn stood up on her rock and looked around. The bush had gone still, birds and insects falling silent.

In the distance, a plume of dust billowed above the salt. A vehicle. No, two vehicles. Quinn stood and stared for a moment, before jumping down from the rock and scrambling back towards THE GLAM VAN. When she hit flat ground, she broke into a sprint.

Kylie, who was engrossed in her monitor screen, didn't look up until Quinn tapped her urgently on the shoulder.

'Someone's coming!' Quinn said in a rush.

'What? Who?' Kylie removed her headphones.

'I dunno! It looked like two cars, heading this way!'

'From which direction?' Kylie said. 'Mildura?'

'No, the other way!'

'East?' Kylie frowned. 'But there's nothing out that way...'

She stood abruptly, moving to grab a pair of binoculars from one of the shelves, before jogging outside, up onto the same hill that Quinn had just come down from. Quinn and Mullet both followed her, stepping carefully to avoid cracking twigs.

At the top of the ridge, they saw that the vehicles were already a lot closer, travelling at great speed across the plain, twinkling specs beneath a haze of heat and orange plumes of dust.

Kylie raised the binoculars and Quinn saw her face crease with worry. Wordlessly, she turned and began hurrying back down the hill.

'Who are they?' Quinn whispered as she ran past.

'The one on the left is a sin-seeker,' Kylie hissed.

'Oh, shit!' Mullet said.

'Shhh! It gets even worse,' Kylie said. 'The one on the right is a relixorcist!'

Mullet opened and closed his mouth. He'd gone pale.

They got back to THE GLAM VAN and, as quickly and

quietly as they could, began packing everything away. Quinn's heart was pounding again, fear twisting at her guts. She knew what she'd felt now, earlier on the rock. It had to be it. But where was it now? Where the fuck was it now?

They packed the last of the cables away in a cupboard, and then stood in silence, breathing hard.

'Are you sure it was a relixorcist?' Mullet said.

'Yeah,' Kylie said. 'No one else owns THAT many relics.'

'Well, maybe they're not on duty at the moment?' Mullet said. 'Maybe they're just hanging out, with their buddy, who is a sin-seeker?'

'Hanging out, at one hundred kilometres per hour?' Kylie said.

'Maybe they're having a friendly race?'

'No, there's definitely a Portent around,' Quinn said shakily. 'I... felt it earlier. For a few seconds. I didn't see it, though.'

'You felt it?!' Mullet said. 'Why didn't you say anything!?'

'I didn't realise what it was!' Quinn wrung her hands. 'It was literally, like, five seconds!'

'Can you feel it now?' Kylie said.

'No.'

'Good.'

Outside, the two cars rocketed by, twinkling blurs passing on the far side of the salt-lake. At that speed, they would be making a lot of noise, even with the very best in sound-reduction engineering. But it was inaudible through the RV's sealed doors.

In an instant, they were gone again.

As their dust trails began to settle, Kylie went and opened the door to THE GLAM VAN'S cabin. Then she paused, looking back at the others.

'Obviously, we should leave,' she said. 'But... should we go now, or wait a bit?'

'Now! There's a Portent around!' Mullet said, waving his hands frantically.

'I think we should wait,' Quinn said.

'Why?' Kylie looked at her.

'If we stay quiet,' Quinn said, 'then even if the Portent's still nearby, it probably won't notice us. If we wait for an hour, then the Portent will probably have gone somewhere else.'

'Probably?' Mullet said. 'What if it blindly blunders into us instead?! We're sitting ducks!'

'If it makes you feel better,' Quinn said, 'we can put music on. And if a Portent shows up, I'll just reverse time, back to this decision! If it's the wrong choice, then I'll let you know in the next few seconds...'

She paused. The others watched her.

Nothing happened.

'See, its fine,' Quinn said.

'Okay,' Kylie said. 'We'll wait.'

She closed the cabin door and sat down. Meanwhile, Quinn rebooted Kylie's computer. Then, as everyone waited in tense silence, she put on the new album, So Fresh 2005. As it began playing through the tinny inbuilt speaker, Quinn couldn't help but think that the vibe of the album was way off for their current situation – but at least it was something to distract from the looming dread.

They waited for about ten minutes, eyes glued to the windows for any sign of movement. Outside, the trees sat completely still, not even a breeze to lift their branches.

'Which Portent was it, do you think?' Mullet said.

'Don't know,' Quinn said. 'One of the smaller ones, I guess? Otherwise, I would have seen it.'

'The Seventh?' Mullet said. 'That's the smallest one, right? About the size of a footy, isn't it?' He held up his hands to demonstrate.

'It's a floating brain,' Quinn said. 'It's the size of a brain. Although, I think it makes a lot of noise, with all the lightning crackling off of it. I probably would have noticed that.'

'Okay, what about the Ninth?' Mullet said.

'No. That would have been super obvious, with all the rocks flying up into the air.'

'The Eighth?'

'I hope not,' Quinn said.

The next song on the album came on, and outside, nothing continued to happen. Eventually, they began to relax.

'We'll have to drive another couple of hours and set up again somewhere else,' Kylie said resignedly. 'And this time, we're being extra fucking quiet!'

'Do you think that's what drew in the Portent?' Mullet said. 'Did we make too much noise?'

'Probably,' Kylie said and sighed. 'Although we weren't exactly being noisy. It's just bad luck, that it was in the area – but it's also a wake up call. We're becoming complacent, after getting away with it so many times. There IS a reason why we're supposed to be extremely quiet outside, and this is God or fate or whatever telling us to shut the fuck up.'

'I guess we're lucky it went this well,' Quinn said.

She turned and looked out the window again. Wind had returned to ruffle the leaves and a flock of cockatoos had landed on the lake side.

As she watched, the cockatoos suddenly took flight. A white sedan with distinctive red and blue roof lights nosed into view.

Quinn's eyes widened.

'Oh, shit,' she said. 'Guys – the sin-seekers are back!'

# SHARKEY'S RELIC SHACK

### WHAT IS A RELIC?

Relics are objects, symbols, foods or places that define or are otherwise inherently tied into the Canon Material Timeline (CMT)! Typically, they are non-living items, made or altered by human hands, with some level of cultural or historical significance. While all relics originate from before the year 2052, it is possible to make copies that are also relics! However, the more dissimilar the copy to the original, the weaker the relic!

### WHY SHOULD *YOU* OWN A RELIC?

Relics are the only known 100% effective Portent repellent! Whether you live remotely, travel as part of your job, or are concerned about neighbourhood noise levels, then relics are the simplest way to put your fears to rest!

### HOW MUCH DO THEY COST?

Relics can range in price, from a few hundred, to a few hundred thousand dollars, depending on their rarity and index. Which relic you buy is down to how much you're willing to spend for peace of mind!

### WHAT DOES 'INDEX' MEAN?

Not all relics are made equal! Some are simply stronger and better at grounding the timeline than others.

Strength is measuring using the Relicity Index – see the table below! The most common relic you will find on the market are those at index 3-4, as they are both effective and abundant!

| INDEX | DESCRIPTION |
|---|---|
| 0-1 | Objects with a relicity of between 0 and 1 are considered 'neutral' to the timeline. The timeline is not perceptively influenced by their presence and would not be significantly altered if they never existed. The vast majority of everyday items have a relicity within this range. Examples include an individual teaspoon, a disposable toothbrush, or a single piece of gravel. |
| 1-2 | Objects with a relicity of between 1 and 2 have significance on a personal level. They are highly sentimental or meaningful, but only to a very small number of people. Examples include a childhood soft-toy, an heirloom locket, or a photograph of a treasured memory. |
| 2-3 | Objects within this range have community significance. They are often centrepieces of local pride, legend or notoriety; however, their influence does not extend beyond a specific area or group of people. Examples include statues of beloved folk-heroes, highly regarded local delicacies or places associated with children's ghost stories. |
| 3-4 | Objects within this range have National significance, but have been copied many times over, resulting in a diluted relicity. While relatively weak, these objects are instantly recognisable to most citizens and are tied in with the Nation's history and culture in some way. Relics of this index are generally considered strong enough for use in deterring Portents or dulling the effects of |

| | |
|---|---|
| | P.I.U.S. They are commonly referred to as 'Weak Relics'. Examples include nationally recognised foods such as Vegemite, beverages such as Victoria Bitter, or symbols tied in with National Identity such as Australian Football League paraphernalia. |
| 4-**5** | Objects with a relicity between 4 and 5 are highly significant on a National level and additionally are rare or one-of-a-kind. Commonly referred to as 'Strong Relics', these objects are highly sought after and extremely useful in repelling Portents. They represent national heroes, historic events, and culturally defining moments or places. Without them, the CMT would be significantly altered. Examples include the original Eureka Stockade flag, the site of Uluru, or the 'baggy green' cricket cap worn by legendary spin-bowler Shane Warne. |

**WHAT ARE YOU WAITING FOR? PURCHASE A RELIC TODAY!**

NOTE: Beware of counterfeit relics! If the documentation is missing, then DO NOT complete the purchase! If you are unsure whether your relic is real, you can test it for free at your local Sanctuary!

**SHARKEY'S RELIC SHACK ONLY SELLS OFFICIALLY LICENCED RELICS.**

# SIN-SEEKERS

**Date: Thursday 18 September 2081**

There was no doubt that the sin-seekers had seen THE GLAM VAN and were coming to investigate.

Kylie swore under her breath but then gathered herself. 'It's fine,' she said. 'It's fine. It's just a cop. A regular fucking cop. We've dealt with them before and we'll deal with them again. We've got The Story, remember? Quinn, where did you put the phones?'

Quinn showed Kylie the box she'd shoved them into, and Kylie took it. There was a hidden compartment in the floor, which she opened and dropped the box into, along with several other especially incriminating pieces of tech. Then she moved to the computer and opened a program which she'd custom-built.

It was a fake desktop, with fake software, showing only what Kylie wanted to be seen. A tech wizard wouldn't be fooled for two seconds – but most sinnies didn't know more than the layperson when it came to computer use.

'Everyone remember the details?' Kylie said in a low voice. The others nodded. Outside, the seeker car had pulled up nearby and come to a stop. The blue and red lights on its roof pulsed briefly, drawing attention.

Kylie put on her best customer service smile and then pulled open the van door. She gave a wave in the direction of the car, acknowledging it.

The seeker car's doors opened as well – driver and passenger – and two Caucasian men stepped out. They were each wearing the standard blue and hi-vis-yellow uniform of the Department of Sin. Both carried guns and displayed cybernetic augmentations. The top half of the driver's face was a chrome plate, with blue pinpoints for eyes, bolted into his skin below a receding hairline. The passenger had a human face, but both his arms and legs were clearly robotic.

Carefully, the two sin-seekers crossed the distance between their car and THE GLAM VAN. They were both looking at Kylie, although they didn't say or sign anything for an uncomfortably long time.

*Good afternoon officers,* Kylie said, nodding to them. *I couldn't help but notice the relixorcist that drove by ten or so minutes ago. Is there a Portent around?*

The sin-seeker with the metal face came to a stop a metre or so in front of Kylie and looked her up and down. His expression was, by design, completely unreadable.

*The Portent has moved on,* he signed.

*That's a relief,* Kylie returned. *We are in no danger, then? Can we resume our satellite chasing in peace?*

*Sat-trackers, are we?* the cop said.

Kylie nodded. *Our readings say there's a landing due any day now.*

The cop said nothing for a moment. Then he nodded at THE GLAM VAN.

*May we come inside and talk properly?*

*Of course,* Kylie signed, a saccharine smile on her face.

The sin-seekers stepped into the RV and Kylie closed the door behind them. Both officers immediately noticed the array of computer monitors and sent each other a look.

'I've always found sat-tracking fascinating,' the older cop said. 'It's impressive that anyone is able to track the path of a satellite, let alone predict when and where it will fall.'

'It's not so hard, with the right equipment,' Kylie said.

'I imagine not,' the cop said. 'I don't suppose you can talk me through all your equipment, speaking of which?'

'No offence, Officer, but I don't know whether you would

find that conversation particularly interesting,' Kylie smiled.

'Oh, no,' the cop replied. 'I think I would, actually. Please – go ahead.'

'Well, if you insist,' Kylie said.

She began to talk about sat-tracking equipment, in excruciating detail. This was a topic she knew a lot about, as it had, in fact, been her former occupation, before she'd discovered the much more lucrative business of music-dealing.

While she spoke, the second cop began to poke around. Quinn and Mullet, who were standing at the back of the RV with hands behind their backs, stared at him suspiciously. He stared back, his eyes ice-blue beneath a shock of curly blond hair. His expression was a haughty snarl.

'What?' he snapped, when Quinn met his eyes. 'Do you have something to say?'

He was young – surely no more than a couple years older than Quinn was. He was clearly trying, and failing, to grow facial hair, with nothing but a pathetic whisp on his upper lip. It was all Quinn could do to keep quiet. How dare this pipsqueak of a sin-seeker try and pick a fight with her?

He was still a sin-seeker though. If she disobeyed, he might take that as reason to arrest her, if not shoot her on the spot. She dropped her gaze, glaring angrily at the floor while he began tapping at the nearest monitor.

A password prompt blocked his way, and he spun around to stare at Quinn again, as if it were her fault personally.

'Unlock it,' he said.

'I can't,' Quinn told him, with slightly more smugness than was strictly necessary. 'Sorry.'

The seeker stared at her. 'Can't?' he said through his teeth. 'What do you mean, can't? I'm asking you to!'

'Don't know the password,' Quinn lied. 'You'll have to get Kylie to do it.'

'What do you mean, you don't know the password? You live here!'

'It's Kylie's computer. She doesn't let us touch it.'

The seeker clicked his tongue angrily and stalked over to his colleague in a furious whirr of electronic limbs.

'What's your computer password?' he demanded.

Kylie, who was explaining in painful depth how the satellite-fall algorithm worked, turned to look at him, one thin eyebrow raised.

'Answer the question,' the other cop said calmly.

Kylie paused. 'Must you look through my computer? I have nothing to hide – but the predicted location of the satellite-fall is, well, somewhat of a trade secret, you've got to understand...'

The older cop went to speak – but the younger beat him to it. 'We don't care about your satellite!' he snapped. 'We're looking for noise sources, that's it! We know you were making noise earlier! Now, what's the password?!'

'Hey, hey!' the older cop said. 'Spencer – it's okay, chill. I do apologise for my young colleague – he is quite, shall we say, zealous. Although, we DO require access to your computer. If you have nothing to hide, then it will only take a minute.'

Kylie waved a hand. 'Yeah, yeah. Come on, then, let's all go look at my computer, since that's what you're here for.'

She led the way to the back of the RV. Quinn and Mullet were forced to move – with five people, the space had become very cramped. Kylie barely had room to move her elbows as she typed in her password, the two sin-seekers breathing down her neck.

Momentarily, she stepped aside, gesturing at the screen, open to her oldest, most user-unfriendly, sat-tracker program. 'Here,' she said. 'Go nuts.'

She stood out of the way and watched as the cops began clicking on buttons and searching through files. They located the search bar and typed in, among other things, 'music', 'MP3' and 'MP4' – but Kylie had locked these terms away behind the façade, and nothing came up.

The younger seeker quickly got bored and began poking at the other equipment. He looked through Kylie's spare computer parts, but clearly had no idea what he was looking at – which was fortunate, since there were several de-assembled speakers in there. He then went around and checked the RV's soundproofing, prodding at it as if hoping it would fall apart beneath his hands. But he found nothing – the soundproofing was not only up to scratch, but quite new, and of good quality.

As he bent down to examine the proofing on the base of the door, however, he got dangerously close to the hidden compartment in the floor. His left foot was directly on top of it. It was hard to see if you didn't know where it was – but if he got close enough, it wasn't impossible that he'd notice it.

Quinn watched nervously as he crouched right above it, peering at the wall. He put down his hand, and it brushed right over the thin crack in the floor. His head began to tilt downwards...

'Hey, *Spencer*,' Quinn said. 'How old are you?'

The young cop's head snapped up again and he turned to look at her.

'What did you say?'

'I wanna know how old you are,' Quinn said. 'Cause you seem like you're really young for a sin-seeker. I think you're probably my age.'

'Yeah?' the cop narrowed his eyes. 'What's your point?'

Quinn shrugged. 'I dunno. I just think if you're not even old enough to legally drive or vote, you probably shouldn't be a sin-seeker.'

A small vein appeared in the cop's forehead. Across from her, Mullet was making throat cut motions. But Quinn had achieved her goal – the seeker was no longer anywhere near the compartment in the floor.

Still, it was possible she had gone a little too far. The cop was going red in the face and was staring at Quinn with an expression of hatred. 'I'm old enough to arrest you,' he hissed, and his hand went to his gun holster.

The older cop turned away from the screen and put his

hand on the young cop's shoulder. 'Cool your jets, hotshot,' he said quietly. 'Now isn't the time.'

His face going even redder, the young cop let go of the holster, but he didn't stop staring at Quinn. Quinn set her jaw and stared back, arms folded, daring him to blink first.

He came closer, and his eyes moved from Quinn to the small shelf behind her.

'What's in that shelf?' he said aggressively.

'Food and supplies,' Quinn returned, eyes narrowed.

'What sort of supplies?'

'Water canisters. Plates and cutlery. Toolbox. The usual supplies, that most people have.'

'Oh yeah? What's that book?'

Quinn turned to look at the book in question – and froze. It was the notebook where she wrote her lyrics. She'd put it back on its usual spot on the shelf, without thinking about it.

'It's just some doodles and stuff,' she said carefully.

'An artist, huh?' the cop sneered. 'Let's see, then.'

Quinn hesitated – and the cop narrowed his eyes. 'Go on,' he said. 'Give it over. Or are you hiding something?'

Gritting her teeth, Quinn reached back and grabbed the book. Her heart was racing. What if he realised they were lyrics? Sure, they were just words, but the implication was there. She'd even written 'new song' on a few of the pages. If he saw that, then their entire web of lies would start to unravel.

Slowly, she handed over the book. She shouldn't have said drawings. She should have said something more boring, like recipes, or Mullet's workout diary. She should have hidden the book better. She shouldn't have goaded the cop quite as much. She shouldn't have even caught the cop's attention in the first place – maybe he wouldn't even have noticed the secret compartment?

The was no music playing. She couldn't even reverse it.

The cop opened the book to its centre and frowned down at the words in front of him.

'What is this...?' he began.

Quinn suddenly inhaled sharply.

No. No, no, no. It was back. It was coming back! This was the worst fucking timing – but there was no mistaking it!

'Kylie!' she said urgently through her teeth. 'KYLIE!'

Everyone turned to look at her.

'What is it?' Kylie said carefully.

Panicking, Quinn opened and closed her mouth, then pointed wildly outside. 'I, I saw something!' she squeaked. 'I think the Portent's back!'

Everyone looked where she was pointing, but outside, nothing had visibly changed.

It was there though, Quinn was certain. It was hiding, somehow, but it was very close. She could feel it, even stronger than before. Sweat beaded on her forehead and breath caught in her throat. As fear rose, she was struggling not to cry out or run somewhere, anywhere.

'What did you see?' the older cop asked her. 'Describe it.'

'Um!' Quinn gasped. Reality was coming loose around them. Infinite meanings and interpretations, exhilarating and terrifying. Her imagination was branching out in five directions at once. How could no-one else feel it?!

The cop was waiting for an answer and he was growing suspicious. She could almost see the suspicion rolling off him in waves of shimmering yellow.

'I don't know how to describe it,' she squeaked. 'But it was definitely there!'

The older cop looked to the younger, who nodded, and went to the door.

'What are you doing?!' Quinn yelped. 'Don't go outside!'

'He's not,' the older cop said. 'He's just checking something. Everyone remain calm.'

Quinn clapped her hands over her mouth, cutting off any sound she could involuntarily make. The young seeker pulled the handle, cracking the door, just a little.

-AAAAAAAAAP BWAAAAAAAAAAARP BWAARP BWA-AAAAAAAAAA-

The seeker closed the door again, cutting off the sound

of the distant car horn, sounding repeatedly. Sharply, he looked at his colleague.

'That's the relixorcist,' he said.

The older cop was silent for a moment.

'Shit,' he said.

They both abruptly ran for the door, pulling it open and sprinting back towards their car.

Mullet hurriedly closed the door after them, while Kylie ran for the cabin. Quinn, meanwhile, was shrinking uselessly into the corner, tears welling in the corners of her eyes.

'WHERE IS IT?' Mullet yelled, staring out each of the windows in turn. 'QUINN, WHERE?'

'I DON'T KNOW!' Quinn wailed. 'I DON'T KNOW WHERE IT IS BUT IT'S REALLY CLOSE!'

'Both of you, sit down and hold on tight!' Kylie yelled from the driver's seat. 'If the cops are fucking gunning it, then we are too!'

She started the engine and rammed the RV into gear, pulling out onto the edge of the lake. Salt and small rocks sprayed behind the wheels. Ahead, the seekers had pulled out as well, accelerating powerfully towards the open plain.

Kylie turned THE GLAM VAN in the same direction, although a lot more slowly – THE GLAM VAN wasn't exactly built for speed. On the far side of the lake, the relixorcist suddenly shot into view, a red four-wheel drive with dozens of AFL scarves blowing wildly from the roof-rack.

Her stomach heaving, Quinn threw herself towards the hidden compartment, where her voice recorder was. Music! They needed music as a safeguard!

'Shit, shit, shit,' Kylie spat, as the van's wheels spun. 'Is the relixorcist running, or chasing? Where's the bloody Portent?! Is it fucking invisible?!'

Quinn yanked open the compartment, and pulled out the recorder, mashing the ON button over and over. 'Go towards the relixorcist!' she yelled. 'They have a bunch of relics! It's safer near them!'

'But they're beeping their horn,' Kylie said. 'With all that noise, wouldn't it be better to –'

'Go towards them!' Quinn yelled. 'I've got music, I can fix it if it's wrong!'

She hit play on one of her experimental recordings from earlier and tinny music filled the RV. It was only two layers, and Quinn felt too dizzy to try and add a third. But it was better than nothing.

Hand outstretched, volume at max, she hauled herself into a seat and held on tight as Kylie spun the RV towards the relixorcist. The seeker car, meanwhile, continued to accelerate in the opposite direction, out into the open plain.

The relixorcist saw THE GLAM VAN coming and angled their car to drive alongside. The person inside was dressed in a Wiggles costume, probably an original, with a very high relicity index. As they drew close, they signed one-handed at Kylie through the window.

'What?' Kylie said, and then exclaimed. 'Oh fuck, it's under the ground! No wonder we can't see the bastard!'

'The Fourth!' Quinn yelled. 'I should have kn-ARGH!'

Kylie had abruptly turned to the left, letting off a string of swear words as she did so. Quinn was almost thrown to the floor.

When she recovered, she saw exactly what caused Kylie to turn so sharply. The Fourth Portent was emerging.

Eighty or so metres ahead, a rusty metal spike was rising out of the plain. It was rapidly followed by another, and then three more.

The spikes were spinning, rotating like drill-bits, small at the point but tapering larger and larger. As they rose, the ground around them began to warp and melt, fracturing, boiling, explosively turning to gas. A massive saw blade broke the surface, followed by a dozen metal girders, groaning and twisting around themselves like coat-hangers. Black oily sludge began bubbling up from beneath, saturating all it touched.

As the main body of the Portent rose into view, Kylie

performed a tidy three-point turn, and slammed down the accelerator. Meanwhile, the sin-seeker car wasn't so fortunate. The Portent had emerged right under them, and they'd skidded to a stop, narrowly avoiding a breaching drill-spike.

With frightening speed, the Portent hauled itself fully out of the ground. It was huge, a behemoth of whirring drills and thundering pistons. Long arms extended every which way, tipped with blades and buckets and claws. Taut wires creaked and hummed with every movement, exposed generators churning, belts screaming over rusted wheels. Black oil leaked from every joint, staining the machinery, dripping down onto the ground, shining with a sinister iridescence.

The seekers threw their car into reverse as fast as they could – but not fast enough. One of the Portent's sawblade arms swatted down towards it, hitting the bonnet and sheering through with a metallic scream. The car was ripped apart in an instant. Black ooze began welling from its wreckage.

Kylie did not stick around to see what happened next. As the relixorcist began to circle the Portent, still blaring their horn to draw its attention, she accelerated away. Quinn and Mullet hung on for dear life as the RV swerved back and forth, bouncing over loose rocks – but at least they were gaining distance.

No one spoke for about twenty minutes. Then, as they slowed and turned onto a narrow dirt road, Mullet let out a long, loud sigh.

'Fuckin' hell,' he said, 'I think I almost shit my pants.'

'Same,' Quinn said.

'Okay, but I've never seen a Portent that close before,' Mullet said. 'Fuck me, they're WAY worse up close.'

'Well, I've only seen one that close before,' Quinn said. 'And yeah, they are.'

'Do you think it'll follow us?' Mullet said, pressing his face against the window to look back.

'It better not!' Kylie yelled from the front.

'I don't think it is,' Quinn said.

She turned off her voice recorder and sat back in her seat with a sigh.

'We should probably report the sighting,' Kylie called back. 'If the Fourth Portent goes on to rampage through Mildura, there's no way I'm going to be held liable for that shit! We're going to warn the suckers about the Fourth, like good law-abiding citizens. We're going back through town anyway, so we can do it then.'

'Do we have to?' Quinn said. 'Isn't that the relixorcist's job?'

'They're a bit busy at the moment,' Kylie said. 'You can do it. I need to recharge the van anyway, so you can pop into the office and report the sighting while I do that, Okay?'

'Sure, whatever,' Quinn said.

'What do I get to do?' Mullet asked.

'You can get snacks,' Kylie said. 'I think we all deserve something nice, after today.'

'Hell yeah,' Mullet said. 'Snacks? Maybe we should narrowly avoid being absolutely destroyed by Portents more often!'

'Absolutely not,' Kylie said. 'This better be the last fucking Portent I ever see, in fact.'

## THE FOURTH PORTENT

FIRST RECORDED SIGHTING: 21/11/2053,
Kalgoorlie, Wongatha country, WA

PHYSICAL APPEARANCE:

The Fourth Portent resembles a large,
mechanical structure of anomalous design,
comprised of the parts from at least 28
separate earth moving and mining machines.

At full height, the structure stands at
approximately 80 metres, and can extend to an
estimated maximum of 210 metres in length. It
is estimated to weigh upwards of 14,000
tonnes, although weighing it has proved
impossible to date.

While the majority of the Fourth's structure
is comprised of generic heavy-duty machinery
and thus remains unidentified, distinctive
features originating from multiple makes of
bulldozer, trencher, rock driller, conveyor
belt, dragline excavator, bucket-wheel
excavator, and longwall miner, amongst
others, have been recorded.

The Fourth Portent's various interconnected
engine systems are thought to run using crude
oil, which is continuously generated within
the Portent itself at a rate of approximately
50 kilolitres per hour. The source of the oil
is unknown, however can be clearly observed

leaking continuously from all sections of the structure.

BEHAVIOUR:

The Fourth Portent is able to submerge itself below ground, where it spends around 90% of the time. Whilst underground, it is able to travel at speeds up to 48km/h, regardless of rock or soil composition.

On occasion, for reasons including the detection of noise or earth-moving activity, the Fourth Potent will breach the surface. On average, it will spend two hours and forty-five minutes above ground, before once more submerging. Above ground, the Fourth Portent is considerably slower, with a top recorded speed of around 10km/h.

The Fourth is able to travel rapidly through solid rock due to its primary anomalous quality – the disruption of the states of matter. Within an aura of effect extending approximately 8 metres beyond its surface, the Portent causes Canonical states of matter to rapidly fluctuate. Solids can sublimate, liquids solidify, and gases condense into liquid, regardless of temperature, pressure, or other conditions.

Aside from the Fourth Portent itself, which maintains a constant solid form, the only substance that appears unaffected by this rapid and drastic shifting in physical laws appears to be crude oil, and products derived from crude oil, such as plastic.

Thorough testing of the crude oil produced by the Fourth Portent has determined that it is, in all practical aspects, normal oil and can be used as such with no adverse effects, despite its anomalous source.

PORTENT INDUCED UNREALITY SYMPTOMS:

P.I.U.S RUBICON RADIUS: ~35m (exact radius fluctuates with the movement of the structure).

ACTIVE SYMPTOM DEVELOPMENT: 74%

LETHALITY: 33%

DESIGNATION: Mattersmith

ADDITIONAL NOTES: P.I.U.S that stem from the Fourth often relate to the manipulation of the states of matter, as well as spontaneous creation or destruction of non-living matter. These abilities are of high usefulness to the Nation, particularly in the fields of construction, fabrication and demolition

# CAR TROUBLES

## Date: Wednesday 11 March 2082

Before the sun had even peeked over the horizon, the Detective was up and ready to go. Fully charged and with coolant levels restored, they opened the task list they'd created for themselves the previous evening.

The second task on the list was to visit their very first Portent witness – an acre-grinder called Anne Gum. Ms Gum lived on a farmstead about 20kms away and had reported seeing the Fifth Portent on Friday, October 31st, 2081.

According to the file, Ms Gum had been hosting a 'small private gathering' at the time, for the purpose of celebrating 'Halloween', an event which despite its lack of cultural significance to the Nation, had persisted throughout the years due to its strong aesthetic draw. According to Ms Gum, the Portent had been attracted to the otherwise 'lowkey' event due to dodgy soundproofing, and had consequently filed an official complaint against the retailist Lewis 'Sound-B-Gone' Russel.

The Detective was interested to hear more of the details in person – but that was the second task on their list.

The first task was to locate transport.

The Detective could jog the twenty kilometres to Ms Gum's farmstead in less than two hours, but by the time they returned, half the day would be gone. If they drove, then it would take less than fifteen minutes, which was a far more efficient use of time.

The problem was finding a vehicle to drive.

Vehicles were expensive to maintain and, due to the fact that it was impossible to make them completely silent at high speeds, inherently dangerous to own. Because of this, vehicle ownership was gated behind a tall stack of paperwork. Yes, you could own one, technically – but only if it strictly adhered to soundproofing guidelines, and its necessity was justified before a panel of the Department of Law's finest goons.

Because of this, most people just didn't bother – which was by design. The fewer cars on the road, the quieter things would be. Only people who REALLY needed a car would brave the paperwork and see it through to its end. And thus there were only a handful of vehicles in town.

The Red Cliffs Sin-Seeker Office did actually own a car – or so the documentation claimed. But the Detective wasn't sure where it was. There was no garage behind the office, and no car keys to be found in any of the drawers in the desk. There was a parking space out the front – but it was conspicuously empty.

After searching the entire office twice over and finding no clues whatsoever to the vehicle's whereabouts, the Detective decided to ask someone. It seemed likely to them that Bill wouldn't know anything, so they left him to snore in the corner and went out the front.

Tank's home address, taken from his staff record, was closer than Wombat's, a mere three-minute walk from the office. The Detective jogged there to reduce time even further. Time wasted was knowledge lost!

Once there, however, they had to ring the doorbell for six minutes and thirty seconds before they saw movement behind the frosted glass window. This was an embarrassingly long response time. It should only have taken thirty seconds maximum, and that was if Tank was in the furthest room from the door and walked very slowly.

Eventually, Tank opened the door and waved the Detective inside. He was dressed in grey tracksuit pants and a rumpled green T-shirt, hair tousled and expression slack.

'It's 6:30,' he said blearily once the Detective had closed the airlock behind them.

'Correct,' the Detective said. 'I require the use of the Red Cliffs Sin-Seeker Office vehicle.'

'What? At 6:30 in the morning?'

'As soon as possible,' the Detective said.

Tank glanced out the window. The sun was only just starting to peek over the horizon.

'Christ, you're keen,' he muttered.

He trudged further into the house, returning shortly with a fat ring of keys.

'Car key's on there,' he said, shoving the whole thing into the Detective's hands.

'Okay,' the Detective said. 'And where is the car?'

Tank paused for a moment, visibly thinking.

'Ah,' he said.

'Yes?'

'It's at the mechanic,' Tank said, rubbing his eyes. 'We, uh... had a little incident on the way back from Mildura on Sunday evening. Roo jumped out suddenly. The car's mostly alright, still drives and all, but it's... missing a few bits.'

'Like what?'

'Like the side mirror,' Tank said. 'And the entire passenger door.'

'That does not sound roadworthy.' The Detective frowned.

'Well, no, not technically,' Tank said.

They were both silent for a moment.

'In that case,' the Detective said, 'I do not require this key. Thank you for your time.'

They returned the key and made to leave.

'Um,' Tank said. 'What are you going to do?'

'I will find another vehicle,' the Detective said without looking around and stepped into the airlock.

The discovery that the sin-seeker vehicle was out of

action was a definite setback – but hopefully only a minor one. There were other vehicles in town, most of them belonging to businesses, and the Detective was confident that at least one of them would be willing to hire out their vehicle for the morning.

The main issue was that none of the businesses were open yet and wouldn't be for several hours. At that point, the Detective might as well walk to the witness' house.

As they made their way back to the office however, they caught sight of movement across the street. An older woman, greying hair tied up in a loose bun, had emerged from a bakery, to tip a bucket of food scraps into the compost skip.

The Detective approached her and she put down the bucket and wiped her hands on her apron, eyeing them suspiciously. *Morning,* she signed.

*Good morning,* the Detective signed back. *Is there somewhere in town I might hire a vehicle? I require transport as soon as possible.*

The woman looked up and down the street. *There's a solar station over that way. You can probably bum a ride from someone there.*

*No, that won't do,* the Detective said. *I need a vehicle which I can drive myself to and from a specific location, today.*

The woman squinted up at the Detective, chewing her lip. *What location?*

*A farmstead, twenty kilometres from here.*

The woman looked thoughtful. *A small vehicle? You could... borrow mine? If it's just for one day. And if you'll compensate me.*

She rubbed her fingers together meaningfully.

The Detective tilted their head. *You own a vehicle? What is your asking price for hire?*

The woman thought about it.

*Eight thousand,* she said. *But if you bring it back in one piece, you can have seven grand back.*

*That is a considerable sum,* the Detective said.

*If you crash it, I need to buy another,* the woman said. *As long as you return it, you'll get most of it back.*

*One thousand dollars is still a lot of money for half a day.*

*Take it or leave it.* The woman shrugged.

The Detective thought about it for a moment longer, and then nodded. This had taken too long already. *I agree to your terms,* they said. *I will create a document to officiate the agreement in writing shortly. But first, allow me to see your vehicle. If it isn't roadworthy then the deal will be off.*

*It's roadworthy,* the woman said. *Come with me.*

She led the Detective behind the bakery and into a small shed, where she turned on the light.

'There,' she said.

The Detective stared at the vehicle before them, taking it in. It was clean and appeared to be in good condition, with all the regulated soundproofing measures in place – electric engine, thin tires and a streamlined design.

It also resembled a giant sandwich. The flanks were painted brown like bread, with sesame seed patterns. A ridge of stylised lettuce, tomato, ham and cheese ran along the roof like a dorsal fin.

'She's a looker, isn't she?' The woman chuckled. 'We call her the Lamborpanini.'

'It's definitely roadworthy?' the Detective said. 'All up to date?'

'Yup,' the woman said. 'Had her serviced a month ago. Everything's spick and span. I can even show you the documents if you'd like.'

'Excellent,' the Detective said. 'I'll take it.'

# CHAPTER 7

# DR HOOPS AND THE FLESH TORUS

## Date: Wednesday 11 March 2082

As the Detective went back into the sin-seeker office to print off their freshly written up car hire agreement, they were greeted by a noticeably frazzled Bill. Clad in sleep-ware, hair distinctly uncombed, he barrelled towards the Detective, stopping right in front of them and pointing an accusatory finger up at their chin.

'Where did you go?' he yelled.

The Detective blinked. 'I went out to locate a vehicle.'

'Well, why didn't you wake me up?' Bill said. He put his hands on his hips. 'Huh? Why not? I'm supposed to supervise you at all times, remember? If you went out and, and something happened, I'd be the one who got into trouble!'

'I apologise,' the Detective said. 'I was not made aware of the importance and extent of your assignment. I will make sure to accommodate your wishes in the future.'

'You'd better,' Bill said.

Muttering to himself, he went into the break room and turned on the ancient electric kettle.

The Detective went over to the damaged computer and connected to it via their finger USB. There was an old desktop printer sitting in the back corner, which they were able to successfully send the car hire agreement to after only eight attempts.

By the time they'd finished printing, Bill had gotten dressed and made himself a cup of tea. The Detective went and stood by the door and watched him run about the office, mug in hand, toothbrush in mouth, bright purple shirt crumpled and unbuttoned.

'Where in the Nation is my left shoe?' he muttered, peering underneath the desk.

'It is there,' the Detective said, pointing.

'Oh, thanks.' Bill pulled it on, swallowed down the last of his tea, and then stood upright. 'Okay. I'm ready to rumble!'

Wordlessly, the Detective opened the door and stepped outside.

The bakery owner was waiting across the road, tapping her foot impatiently. The Detective handed her the printed agreement, along with a cheque for eight grand, billing the Melbourne Department of Sin.

The woman read over and signed the documents before handing the Detective a set of keys. The keychain had a small plastic croissant dangling from it.

Bill watched the exchange with a puzzled expression on his face. His confusion only deepened when he saw the Lamborpanini.

'Umm,' he said, as the Detective opened the driver's door.

The Detective paused. 'What is it, Bill?'

'What is that?' Bill gestured at the car.

'It is a roadworthy vehicle,' the Detective said.

'But...' Bill said. 'Oh, it doesn't matter.'

Sighing, he climbed into the passenger seat and buckled up.

'Where are we off to this morning anyway?' he asked resignedly.

'We are off to interview our first witness,' the Detective said.

***

It was around 7:30AM when the Detective arrived at the front gate of the farmstead.

All around, fields of golden crop waved in the breeze. A

thin dirt driveway and bright red letterbox marked the property, alongside a large, peeling billboard, which said:

'Dr Hoops?' Bill said, leaning forward to read the board.

DR HOOPS – TECH WIZARD

I WILL FIX YOUR DODGY FARM EQUIPTMENT! AFFORDABLE PRICES!

CALL THE NUMBER BELOW TO MAKE AN APPOINTMENT!

'Is that our witness?'

'As far as I am aware,' the Detective said, 'our witness is called Anne Gum. But it is possible Ms Gum has taken on the nickname of "Dr Hoops". Either that, or another separate person whose name is "Dr Hoops" resides here.'

'I wonder why they're called Dr Hoops?' Bill said. 'What does it mean?'

The Detective elected to ignore the question and turned the car onto the property.

According to old satellite imagery, the house was about two kilometres down the driveway. As they approached the coordinates, however, the Detective found no house in sight. There wasn't even any visible wreckage or ruins – just a continuous field of bobbing cereal crop.

Frowning, the Detective pulled to a stop right where the satellite data said the house should be. The data was just over a decade old – but even if the house had been torn down since then, there should have been signs of its presence. If there wasn't, then this would be the second large, immovable structure that had mysteriously vanished without a trace...

The Detective quickly opened the door and stepped out. Had the force that took Mildura struck here as well? Were they too late?

... No. On closer inspection, there were actually faint signs that a house had once been here. Just barely visible, were a series of ridges half buried in the ground. On closer inspection, they were clearly old foundation walls. The house HAD been here, ten years ago.

But it wasn't anymore.

Bill got out the car and stepped into the Detective's field of view.

*What are we looking at?* he signed.

The Detective pulled back a handful of grass and showed him the old brick ridges. *The house used to be here,* they explained briefly.

*The witness' house?* Bill said. *Where'd it go?*

The Detective stood up and looked around. The driveway ended a few dozen metres further along. Beyond that, there was nothing but fields in any direction, beside the occasional line of trees.

*That is the question,* they said.

They cycled their vision through infrared and ultraviolet spectrum and re-examined the landscape, but nothing changed. Frowning, they followed the driveway to its end, scanning the ground for any clues as they went. There was an old beer can in the ditch, a few old boot prints here and there, and signs of multiple sets of tires coming in and out, but nothing unexpected –

Wait...

The Detective went back to the footprints and cocked their head, staring down at them. There was something off about them, but it was hard to pinpoint what exactly.

They turned and waved Bill over, pointing at their find.

*What do you think of these?*

Bill crouched and looked at the footprints closely. There were multiple types of shoe clearly printed in the mud, in multiple sizes, from young children's to statistically large adult. The Detective counted at least twelve different people, based on sole pattern.

Bill scratched his chin.

*They're all facing the same way,* he said.

The Detective nodded. The footprints were all facing the

same way – exactly the same way. The angle was precisely the same in all cases, 42.6 degrees from North.

On top of this, the footprints were identical in depth. Regardless of size, each print was set exactly 2.3 cm into the mud.

It was though twelve or more identically weighted humans with widely variable foot size had marched this way in an impressively regular line.

This, however, seemed a highly unlikely scenario. The Detective decided they had insufficient data to make a conclusion – but there was definitely something strange going on.

*Let us follow the footprints*, they said to Bill.

Leaving the Lamborpanini where it was, they waded out into the bobbling cereal crops. Internally, they set a GPS marker on the driveway, just in case the trail went on for a while. Most of the fields looked extremely similar and the driveway quickly disappeared from view. With so few landmarks, it would be easy to get disorientated here.

As it turned out though, they only had to walk for fifteen minutes before they found the farmhouse. And as soon as they saw it, everything else fell neatly into place.

It was a very small house – more of a shack really, made of red-painted weatherboard and rusty aluminium sheets. It looked like it was barely hanging in there, held together by nothing more than a handful of nails and strategically placed duct tape.

This effect was made worse by the fact that the house was suspended two metres above the ground, in the centre of a series of rust-pitted metal hoops. There were six hoops in total, all in parallel, and attached to a central hub, around which the house was built. Each of the hoops had a series of short, regularly spaced spokes set along its outer face. On the end of each spoke was an old shoe.

The structure was obviously able to move, rolling gently through the crops with a much lesser degree of disturbance than a regular vehicle. When it moved, it would make lines of footprints on the ground, all facing exactly the same direction.

Well, that was one mystery solved. Two, in fact – when he saw the house, Bill excitedly signed *Dr Hoops* over and over until the Detective told him to stop.

They approached the house-on-wheels and went around to where the front door was. It was painted to resemble a blue sky with fluffy white clouds. It was also several metres above the ground.

As the Detective stood there and wondered how to reach the doorbell, there was movement in the window. A moment later, a middle-aged Black woman, wearing a patchwork dress and an orange bandana, opened the door.

'Morning,' she called down, her voice clear and melodious in the morning air. 'I don't do appointments before 9AM – sorry! If you want to make a time though, I'm free this afternoon?'

She didn't say any of this particularly loudly – but they were still outside. Without the protection of soundproofing, any unnecessary noise was bad noise. The Detective frowned.

*We are not here for an appointment,* they signed. *May we come in?*

The woman raised an eyebrow. 'If you're not clients, then who are you?'

*Please refrain from talking outdoors,* the Detective said. Then they extracted their ID badge from the slot in their neck and showed it to the woman.

She leaned down, squinting at it before her eyes widened. Without another word, she went and grabbed a retractable ladder, which she let down in front of the door.

The Detective and Bill climbed inside, crowding in while the woman shut the door behind them. The interior was just as rickety as the exterior, cluttered with junk and heavy-duty tools, each of its walls a different colour. A pair of cats, one calico and one ginger, sat draped across the top of an old floral print settee.

Once the door was closed, the woman immediately began to apologise.

'I'm so sorry,' she said. 'I know I shouldn't talk outside, but I'm a bit short sighted, and sign language is hard to read at times, so I get into the habit of just talking, and I know it's bad, but well, you know...'

'You should address this issue as soon as possible,' the Detective said as she trailed off. 'You may not think that a talking volume is loud enough to attract a Portent – but every small noise adds up over time. A visit to the fleshsmith to have your myopia fixed is quick, easy and statistically ranked as "painless to moderate pain" by customers. Or, if you'd rather not use unrealitic means, traditional methods such as eye-glasses or cybernetic eyes are available for purchase all across the state.'

'Yeah, I know,' the woman said, 'but it's kind of expensive, you know? My eyes aren't THAT bad... Plus, I don't own a car, so it's a hassle to get there... I just haven't gotten around to it...'

'But I will!' she added, as the Detective eyed her flatly. 'I definitely will! Soon!'

'Okay,' the Detective said – then they held out their hand to shake.

'You asked who I was. My name is Detective Claw, from the Melbourne Department of Sin. I am investigating the recent disappearance of the town of Mildura.'

'Oh,' the woman said, shaking the Detective's hand.

'As part of my investigation,' the Detective went on, 'I am interviewing witnesses of recent Portent activity. This includes the report made by one Ms Anne Gum on Friday, October 31st, 2081, regarding the Fifth Portent. Ms Gum is recorded to reside at this, er, approximate address. Are you Ms Gum?'

'Yes,' the woman said. 'That's me!'

She glanced sideways at Bill and the Detective realised they had forgotten to introduce him.

'That is Bill,' they said, and then paused. They did not actually know Bill's surname or official job title.

'Oh, ignore me, I'm just here to take notes.' Bill waved the attention away. 'Although, I've got to ask – did you build this house? The hoops and the little shoes and everything?'

'Yes, I built it,' Ms Gum said.

'Wow,' Bill said. 'I love it. How does it work? I assume it is able to move around, right? Is the entire house built around some sort of central axel?'

'Bill,' the Detective interrupted before Ms Gum could respond. 'This is not relevant information. We are here to investigate Portent activity and nothing more. Although, for the record, I do not "love" this house. In the short time that I have been inside, I have already observed eighteen building code violations, as well as dangerously minimal soundproofing measures.'

'Well, okay, it's a little rough around the edges,' Ms Gum said defensively. 'But it works for me! And anyway, if it wasn't for this house, I'd probably be dead by now!'

'Is that so?' the Detective said. 'Please explain how this is the case.'

'I will,' Ms Gum said. 'But first, I'm fixing myself a cuppa, if that's okay. I was just about to make one when you showed up. Do either of you want one?'

The Detective declined, but Bill nodded and followed Ms Gum into her tiny kitchen. While she put the kettle on, he quietly asked more questions about how the house worked. He glanced furtively at the Detective as he did so, perhaps under the impression that they couldn't hear him.

The Detective went and sat down at the dinner table and waited in silence, glancing occasionally at the clock on the wall, or the two cats on the settee, which were watching them with yellow eyes. Bill was delaying the investigation slightly – but on the other hand, his questions and friendly manner did appear to put the witness at ease, so perhaps it wasn't a complete waste of time.

Shortly, Ms Gum and Bill came and sat down as well, cups of tea in hand. Ms Gum blew away the curling steam and took a sip, before sitting up straighter and meeting the Detective's gaze.

'Alright,' she said. 'How much detail should I go into?'

'As much as possible,' the Detective said.

'Right,' Ms Gum said, and she cleared her throat. 'So, this all happened on a Friday night. It was Halloween and I had some friends over. It wasn't a big event, just a spontaneous thing. I don't actually celebrate Halloween – it's mostly an opportunity to get dressed up and have some fun.'

'Was there alcohol present?' the Detective asked.

'Well, yes,' Ms Gum said, 'some. Modest amounts. Anyway,' she continued, 'as a bit of backstory, I'd recently gotten my soundproofing checked by this man, Lewis Russel. He insisted that I get it changed to his special soundproofing, which was better and cheaper, yada yada. Like a fool, I fell for his charms, and installed all new soundproofing in the house. Cost me a pretty penny as well. He insisted that it would work for even the loudest of noises. You could yell at the top of your lungs and it couldn't be heard from outside, he said.

'Well, turns out that was a load of bull – but at the time, I believed it completely. I told everyone they could be as loud as they wanted inside the house. And they were loud, alright.'

'They were shouting?' the Detective said.

'Oh, yes. You know how it is, a few drinks in and everyone starts talking over each other.'

The Detective frowned slightly. 'How many guests were there exactly?'

'Oh, well – seven. Eight people, with me there too.'

'And they had all consumed alcohol?'

'Most of them.'

'And there were no additional sources of noise within the house?'

'What do you mean?'

The Detective looked Ms Gum in the eye, carefully watching her reaction. 'Like music, for example.'

Ms Gum's eyes dropped. 'No music,' she said quickly.

The Detective was quiet for a moment, watching her

fidget. Bill looked up from his clipboard, looking from the Detective to Ms Gum and back again.

'It was loud,' Ms Gum said eventually. 'Is the exact reason really necessary to your investigation?'

'Yes,' the Detective said. 'Every detail may prove important later.'

Ms Gum sighed. 'Fine. There may have been music. Not mine – I didn't plan for it to be there. But someone brought it and put it on, and I didn't stop it from happening. I know I should have. But it is what it is. And I really did believe my soundproofing was the best thing since sliced bread at this point.'

'I see,' the Detective said. 'Who was it who brought the music?'

'I don't know,' Ms Gum said. 'I wasn't paying attention.'

The Detective figured that this was probably a lie – with only seven guests, it would not be difficult to figure out who brought what to the gathering. But it was to be expected that Ms Gum would be hesitant to 'snitch' on her friends.

They decided to drop the matter, for now.

'So, what happened next?' they asked.

'Well, it was the middle of the party, everyone talking and laughing and having a good time,' Ms Gum said. 'That was when one of my friends slipped outside for a cigarette. Came back in and he'd sobered right up. Looked like he'd seen a ghost. He came up to me, and he quietly said, "Anne, I don't want to alarm you, but there's *something* outside." And then we went outside and he said "listen to that."

'It's then that I realise that first of all, you can hear everything from inside the house – the music, and the drunken hollering, it's all clearly audible. Then I realise that there's another noise as well.'

Ms Gum paused to take a sip of her tea.

'What sort of noise?' the Detective prompted.

'A sort of... wet noise,' Ms Gum said. 'Like mud squelching. And these sharp crackling sounds, like sticks snapping and ripping noises, like fabric tearing in two. Had no clue what it was. Thought it was a flash flood initially.

But that didn't make sense, 'cause there was no rain scheduled for another half a week.'

'Okay,' the Detective said. 'Did you see what was making these noises?'

'Oh, yes,' Ms Gum said. 'I went and got the hi-beam flashlight, shone it into the dark. Saw that it was the Fifth Portent, about thirty metres away. Almost died of a heart attack on the spot.'

She paused to take another sip, her dark eyes distant.

'Could you describe what you saw?' the Detective said.

'It was red,' Ms Gum said. 'And organic – moving. Like a wall of lungs and hearts, all breathing in and out, pulsing, rolling around like a vertical wave. Bones coming out and snapping and sinking in again. Blood dripping everywhere. The ripping noises were its legs – they were ripping themselves out of the flesh and rolling underneath, pushing the thing right towards us.'

'This description does match that of the Fifth Portent,' the Detective said.

'Yeah,' Ms Gum said. 'What else could it possibly be? I froze up when I saw it. Sheer panic. Never been so scared in my life. Fortunately, my brave friend shook me out of it and we ran back inside and told everyone to be quiet as there was a Portent outside. Everyone shut their traps real promptly after that. Stayed silent for a good hour, as we rolled away as fast as the hoops could take us. Fortunately, we were faster than the Fifth Portent and we left it behind. It disappeared into the night.'

'Do you know where it went next?' the Detective asked.

'Well, its trail was obvious in the light of day,' Ms Gum said. 'Came from the South, wondered around the fields a bit, and then headed Northwards. Everywhere it went started growing like mad for a few weeks. It's mostly back to normal now, but it's been a lot of work to get it that way. I've cut down a whole jungle's worth of mutated plant matter and there's still more around. Just yesterday I found another tree with weeping tumours all over it.'

'But you haven't seen the Portent itself again?'

'No,' Ms Gum said. 'I've kept an eye out for it, of course, but nothing. To be honest, every time I see movement in the corner of my eye, I think it's back. I've lost sleep over it, even. What if it comes back and I don't notice it in time? We only noticed it that Friday because my friend went out for a smoke. If he'd gone out just a few minutes later...'

'There is no reason for it to return, if you are quiet,' the Detective said.

'Yes,' Ms Gum said, 'but what if it just wanders into my house by accident?'

'If you are concerned about that, I suggest that you purchase one or more relics,' the Detective said.

'I've been trying to.' Ms Gum sighed. 'But they don't grow on trees! Plus the good ones are very pricey!'

She leaned back in her chair, staring up at the ceiling. Her face was lined with stress.

'Damn you, Lewis,' she muttered. 'I shouldn't have trusted him or his soundproofing. Should have checked it myself. I hate living in constant fear. I hate it.'

'Then the price of the relic will be worth it to ease your mental strain,' the Detective said. 'I would also recommend that you stop delaying on fixing your myopia, and avoid talking while outside. Additionally, I would recommend avoiding music and other noisy activities in the future and, where possible, encourage your friends to do the same. If they refuse, I would urge you to provide their names and addresses to your local Department of Sin office, so that they may be officially discouraged from such behaviour.'

Ms Gum sighed again, deeply. 'Don't worry,' she said. 'I've learnt my lesson. No more music for me.'

'And your friends?' The Detective leaned in. 'I don't suppose you have remembered which of them it was who brought the music to the gathering?'

'No,' Ms Gum said.

'Are you sure? If they are distributing music, then there is a chance this could happen again. Their actions could cause death or permanent harm to many people.

Withholding information about them could be considered almost as sinful.'

'Look,' Ms Gum said, 'none of my friends are music dealers, if that's what you're asking. Some of them are occasional users, but they don't spread it around. Maybe they are not the brightest of bulbs, but they're not malicious either. They own three or four albums at most.'

'And were these three or four albums all at the gathering?'

'No, there was just the one,' Ms Gum said.

'And do you recall what it was titled?'

'I think it was some sort of greatest hits collection,' Ms Gum said wearily. '*So Fresh 2005*? I think that was it. Does it matter?'

'It might matter,' the Detective said. 'Or it might not. Only time will tell.'

They stood abruptly and nodded at Ms Gum.

'Thank you for your information,' they said. 'Bill and I will leave you now.'

'Oh, okay, we're done.' Bill stood up as well. 'Thanks for the tea! And again, love the house, even if it is an OH&S violation on wheels.'

'Remember to keep your noise to a minimum,' the Detective said, pausing by the door. 'The sound regulations are there for a reason, and that reason is your safety and wellbeing!'

'Yes, okay, thank you,' Ms Gum said.

She didn't move from the table or wave goodbye as they opened the door and climbed back down the ladder.

***

As they walked back to where the Lamborpanini was parked, the Detective analysed the data they'd gotten from the interview.

The most relevant piece of information was the confirmation that it had been the Fifth Portent lurking on the farmstead. The description of its appearance and behaviour had been consistent with official accounts and the

Detective was satisfied that, for the most part, Ms Gum's statements had been truthful, with minimal embellishment.

The Fifth Portent's effects were relatively well known – and did not include the ability to make anything disappear, let alone an entire town. It was thus extremely unlikely that it was responsible for Mildura's disappearance.

The Detective struck Ms Anne Gum from their witness list. They went to strike the other names from the same event from the list as well – but then paused.

The fact that there was music involved was... interesting. Why exactly it was interesting, the Detective couldn't quite pinpoint. It was just a hunch, a feeling deep down, that the music was important somehow – more important than it initially seemed.

The Detective did not like hunches. They were not the same as evidence and, if wrong, could even lead to clouded judgment. But for some reason, they couldn't let the idea go.

Ms Gum had said that her friends owned three or four albums, and the way she'd said it implied that this was not a big deal. Owning any music was illegal, though. Owning just one album was a sinful offence, let alone three or four.

Did that mean this was a common occurrence? Did lots of people own three or four albums?

If this was the case, then it might explain why there had been so many Portents sighted in the area in the last six months.

'Bill,' they said thoughtfully, once they were both back inside the Lamborpanini.

'Yeah?' Bill said.

'What do you know about music dealers?' the Detective asked.

'Well, not much,' Bill said. 'Never been one myself.'

He chuckled, but fell silent when the Detective said nothing.

'Why do you ask?' he said eventually.

'I have... no real explanation why,' the Detective said slowly. 'I... just think we should keep an eye out for them.'

# THE FIFTH PORTENT

FIRST RECORDED SIGHTING: 01/03/2055, Gogango, Gangulu country, QLD

PHYSICAL APPEARANCE:

The Fifth Portent appears as a large, solid torus comprised of flesh, bone, blood and various mammalian organs. It stands atop an array of malformed, hoofed 'legs', at around 4 metres in height (± 30 cm) and is 16 metres wide (± 1.5 m), with a central hole of approximately 8 metres in diameter (± 1 m).

The walls of the torus have been observed to continuously rotate vertically, moving matter from the torus' inner face, over the top, down the outer face, underneath and up into the inner face once more. The speed of rotation has been observed to vary between 0.2 and 4 revolutions per minute. During this process, extensive volumes of blood and viscera have been observed to fall from the torus. The exact volume of matter expelled is estimated to be between 10 and 100 kilograms per minute, varying with speed of rotation.

Run-off samples collected from the Fifth Portent have revealed that much of its organic matter is genetically similar to that of the domesticated cow (Bos taurus); however, on two separate occasions, human DNA has also been identified. Following

collection, samples were shown to undergo
continuous uncontrolled mitotic division for
a period of up to seventy-two hours, before
spontaneously necrotising, at which point all
unrealitic potency was lost.

BEHAVIOUR:

The Fifth Portent has been seen to maintain
between twelve and twenty-two 'legs' at any
one time, each oriented in a random
direction, and in varying states of
structural decay. It is able to travel over
land at a maximum speed of 32 km/h and can
change direction instantaneously and with
ease.

Due to its high volume of expelled matter,
the Fifth is typically observed to leave a
clear trail in its wake. Upon exposure to the
Fifth's excretions, all other living
organisms including plants, animals, fungi
and microorganisms display rapid and
uncontrolled cell growth. The extent of
growth is proportional to exposure level,
with larger volumes of unrealitic matter
resulting in longer, larger magnitudes of
growth.

Expelled matter remains highly hazardous for
up to seventy-two hours following excretion
from the Fifth Portent. During this period,
it should not be approached or handled in any
way without correct authorisation and proper
personal protective equipment. Following
seventy-two hours, the expelled matter can no
longer initiate uncontrolled growth -
however, growth in previously exposed

organisms can continue and does so until the effected region is excised, or until the event of the organism's death. Growth has been observed to continue for up to a maximum of two months in certain species of tree.

Note - If you or someone you know has been exposed to the Fifth Portent's expelled matter, remember your three Rs:

1 - Remain calm - breathe, try to move slowly and, if possible, sit or lie down. A decreased metabolic rate has been shown to improve chances of survival.

2 - Relic - if available, apply a relic to the exposure site. All relics, including weak relics, are able slow the progression of anomalous cell growth.

3 - Report - report immediately to your local medical clinic, where a fleshsmith can safely remove all affected tissue. Afterwards, remember to report the location of the incident to authorities, so that others may avoid it.

PORTENT INDUCED UNREALITY SYMPTOMS:

P.I.U.S. RUBICON RADIUS: 6m.

ACTIVE SYMPTOM DEVELPOMENT: 98%

LETHALITY: 60%

DESIGNATION: Fleshsmith/Agrismith

ADDITIONAL NOTES: While nearly two thirds of those who come into contact with the Fifth

Portent succumb to uncontrolled cell growth, those who survive are almost certain to develop active P.I.U.S. Abilities stemming from the Fifth relate to the manipulation of organic matter, with a wide range of specific symptoms recorded. Of particular note are those who are able to supercharge the natural process of healing (fleshsmiths) and those who are able to influence the behaviour and growth of agriculturally significant plants and animals (agrismiths).

# THE STALKER

**Date: Sunday 2 of November 2081**

*MUSIC CAN SPELL DISASTER!*
*THE DEPARTMENT OF SIN IS NOW CRACKING DOWN*
*ON MUSIC DEALERS.*
*CALL 000 TO REPORT SUSPICIOUS ACTIVITY.*

Quinn stood and leant against the wall, astutely ignoring the message on the display screen opposite.

She was standing outside a furniture store, inside the Mildura Plaza Shopping Centre. A colourful banner advertised the store's 'new' and 'antique' furniture – but Quinn knew that both had been salvaged by the scrapper's guild and bought in bulk. The 'new' furniture were the pieces that looked nice, while the 'antiques' looked like shit.

The store was run by a gangly, red-headed man called Bluey, and his two adult sons. The sons were both relic prospectors on the side, and Bluey himself traded in low-tier, paperwork-lite relics under the counter.

Kylie had been selling him music for several years. She was in there now, haggling the price for their latest batch. Quinn had been left on watch outside, where she stood and gave her best belligerent teenage glare at anyone who got too close to the door.

She had to glare almost constantly. It was a Sunday afternoon and there were lots of people out and about, wandering through the dimly lit shopping centre in the off chance they found happiness in retail therapy.

There was also a medical clinic just down from the furniture store, outside of which a long queue of ailing patrons had formed. At the front of the queue, a beleaguered bureaucrat tried their best to get everyone to fill out their incident forms correctly. Beyond them, inside the clinic, Quinn could feel the fleshsmiths at work, mending bones, sealing cuts or purging infections from their patient's bodies.

Each small burst of unreality made Quinn wince internally. The feeling was nothing compared to a Portent, but it still jangled at her nerves like brightly coloured fingernails on a blackboard.

She could barely imagine what it would be like, using P.I.U.S near constantly like that. The physical toll would be extreme. Of all the P.I.U.S types, fleshsmiths were the best at fixing the injuries their symptoms caused them – but it still sounded unimaginably unpleasant. It took someone truly selfless to heal others at the expense of their own health.

Still, there wasn't really an alternative. Without P.I.U.S, the Nation would have collapsed years ago. The Earth's natural weather patterns were broken beyond repair, everyone knew that. Without weathersmiths, it would be one natural disaster after the next. Without the fleshsmiths, the populace would yield to disease and infection. Without agrismiths, the crops would fail, and everyone would starve. Without mattersmiths, the radiation would close in. P.I.U.S were the backbone of society, and without them, humanity would succumb to its extinction. Those who had P.I.U.S would suffer, so everyone else could live. That was just how things were.

With a sigh, Quinn turned away from the clinic and glared instead at the screen opposite. It was now displaying a different message, about construction laws and noise mitigation.

The screen was set in a bracket in the wall, accompanied

by the only legal type of electronic speaker in the Last Nation. It was a part of Mildura's E.W.S – the Early Warning System – that alerted the populace of an approaching Portent or other natural disaster. If a Portent or a bushfire or some other hazard was spotted nearby, the speaker would sound a low-volume siren and an emergency message would be displayed on the screen. Identical screens and speakers were inside most of the public buildings in town, as well as many private homes.

Quinn had never heard the siren personally, or seen a real emergency message. Most of the time, the screens were used to displayed public messages, news articles, and the occasional advertisement for a local business.

As the screen went back to MUSIC CAN SPELL DISASTER, she huffed in annoyance and looked away again.

As she did so, she caught sight of someone, leaning against the wall like she was, a few shops down. They were wearing a bulky red jacket, with the hood pulled right up, face cast in shadow. Quinn didn't think she knew them – but for some reason, she got a weird vibe from them.

Maybe it was a tense, rigid way they were standing? Or the fact that they kept glancing in Quinn's direction?

Were they watching her?

Quinn narrowed her eyes, debating whether or not to move closer and confront them, but just then, the door to the furniture store opened behind her. Mullet bounced out and shoved something under Quinn's nose.

'Check it out!' he said.

Quinn felt the relic before she saw what it looked like. Wrinkling her nose, she stepped away from it and shook her head, fighting the deadening fog that had started creeping in.

'Oi, get that shit away from me,' she said indignantly.

'Sorry.' Mullet moved it two whole centimetres further away. 'But that confirms its real!'

He disappeared back inside. 'IT'S REAL!' Quinn heard him yell before the door closed.

She took the moment to glance back at the hooded figure – but they'd disappeared. Quinn frowned uneasily.

Shortly, Mullet came back out, grinning and turning the relic around in his hands. Quinn watched him, slightly baffled that he couldn't feel it's intense existential weight.

The object was a flat, shiny piece of wood, curved like a banana and painted in bright colours on one side.

'Is that a boomerang?' Quinn said.

'Yep!' Mullet said. 'It's fake, though.'

'What?' Quinn said. 'No, it isn't.' She lowered her voice. 'I can feel it from here,' she said, glancing warily at a nearby group of shoppers.

'No,' Mullet said. 'Not a fake relic – a fake boomerang!'

'Huh?' Quinn said. 'If it's fake, then why is it a relic?'

'Why is anything a relic?' Mullet shrugged. 'It's a symbol of the Nation and its culture and history. Doesn't matter that it's technically a fake boomerang, as long as it's sufficiently associated with the Canon Material Timeline.'

'Fine,' Quinn said. 'But what's the point of it, then? Why'd they make a fake one?'

'Bluey said it was a "trashy souvenir",' Mullet said.

'What's that mean?'

'They used to sell them cheap to people who visited from other countries,' Mullet said proudly. 'The visitors would buy it, and then take it home with them to remind them of their trip.'

'Huh,' Quinn said. 'Does that mean there are a bunch of fake boomerangs out there in the other countries?'

'The other countries don't exist anymore,' Mullet said. 'So, no.'

'You don't think there's one out there somewhere, amongst all the rubble and radioactive ash and skeletons?'

'Well... maybe,' Mullet said. 'Dunno. More importantly, this one belongs to us now! Kylie wanted to buy one, since the Fifth's been seen lurking around.'

Quinn made a face. 'Great. Do you really think that one tiny weak relic is going to scare off a Portent? Or is it just going to annoy me specifically?'

'Kylie thinks it's better than nothing.' Mullet shrugged. 'She said she'll keep in hidden away most of the time.'

Quinn snorted, eyeing the boomerang. 'I don't think that will help. I can still feel it, whether I can see it or not.'

'Is it really that annoying?' Mullet asked. 'Like, if it's a few metres away?'

'A few metres is fine, I guess,' Quinn said. 'Where you are now is fine.'

'What about now, is this annoying?' Mullet moved closer.

'It's getting annoying, yeah.'

'What about this?' Mullet waved the relic in the air directly above her head.

'Yeah, that's really annoying,' Quinn said. She tried to knock the relic out of his hand, but missed.

The door opened again and Kylie emerged.

'You'd better put that away,' she said. 'If a sin-seeker sees it, they might start asking for the paperwork, and I WILL start claiming to not know you.'

'Sorry.' Mullet put the boomerang in his bag.

'How'd it go?' Quinn asked, moving close to Kylie as they headed towards the entrance of the shopping centre. 'What did you sell?'

'The new stuff, plus a couple of older packages,' Kylie said quietly. 'Oh, and Bluey mentioned something else – a certain event which is happening soon. I'll talk about it when we get back to the RV.'

In silence, they left the shopping centre, stepping out through the double airlock doors into a truly beautiful Sunday afternoon. The weather was perfect – sunny and twenty-five degrees Celsius, with the occasional fluffy, aesthetic cloud.

This was no accident – the weather station had announced several days prior that this Sunday was going to be a 'Barbeque Day'.

As they passed by the park, Quinn turned to look at the hordes of families, couples and groups of friends who were sitting quietly on the grass, on picnic rugs, or around the public barbeques. As usual, she walked on the side of the pavement furthest from them.

The concept of 'chucking a snag on the barbie' was so tied into the identity of the Nation that all barbeque grills acted as weak relics. The Government, upon discovering this, had legislated that all city centres above a certain population should host a Barbeque Day at least once per annual quarter.

Quinn remembered taking part in them when she was a kid. They'd been fun – quiet, but with an air of spontaneous holiday, a chance to relax with friends and family and eat a sausage on a slice of bread.

These days, the relicity meant she couldn't really enjoy them – but the fond memories were still there. As they passed, Quinn glanced wistfully at the sizzling snags and onions and bowls of limp, slightly warm salad.

THE GLAM VAN was parked in a backstreet nearby, and they all silently piled in. Kylie took the relic off Mullet and stashed it in the glovebox.

'Does it bother you from there?' she asked Quinn.

'It's not too bad.' Quinn shrugged. 'Especially at the back of the van.'

'Okay,' Kylie said. 'Well, if it bothers you, let me know.'

She took off her sunnies and sat down, crossing her legs.

'So,' she said, eyeing the others. 'I mentioned that Bluey told me about a certain event. It's a concert, with live music. Some rich schmuck is hosting it in a warehouse basement. Strictly invite only. Obviously, if word gets out, it'll mean trouble for everyone involved. But Bluey tells me that this isn't the first event this guy's hosted, and previously they've gone well.'

'Live music?' Quinn said, eyes wide.

'Yeah,' Kylie said. 'I don't know the details yet. Probably a cover band. But the main thing is, lots of music enthusiasts are going to be there. It's the perfect opportunity to sell a fuck-ton of gear.'

'When is it?' Quinn asked excitedly.

'Next Saturday.'

'And we're going?'

'Yeah. If we can secure an invite.'

'How do we get one?'

'The host has to invite us,' Kylie said, inspecting her nails. 'But fortunately, Bluey's already vouched for us. He rang ahead and asked, and the host wants to meet us. Make sure we're the real deal, etcetera.'

'Heck yeah!' Quinn said.

'When are we going?' Mullet asked.

'Now,' Kylie said and she stood up. 'So you chuckle-fucks had better be on your best behaviour, okay?'

***

The 'rich schmuck' lived outside of town, along a narrow road that led into empty bushland. As they turned into his driveway, Quinn leant her face against the window and stared up ahead at the massive house, gleaming white and surrounded by neatly trimmed banksia bushes.

'So what does this dude do for a living?' Mullet asked from the opposite window.

'Runs a roo-rustling business, I believe,' Kylie said from the cabin. 'Has thirty crews working for him. Does nothing himself, except hand them a gun and point them into the bush. Makes a bucketload of cash for it. Must be nice.'

She parked THE GLAM VAN in the drive, and they all got out. As they did so, the front door of the house opened and a man stepped out and waved at them.

He looked to be in his late twenties or thirties, athletically built, tan skin and dark hair in a ponytail, his crisp cyan-blue shirt closely hugging his body. Quinn initially thought he was wearing a mask – but as he got closer, she realised it was a cybernetic. His entire face had been replaced by a gently-curved LED screen, set into a bed of complex sensory bionics. The screen was currently displaying a stylised cartoon face with a big, friendly smile.

Quinn desperately wanted to know what had happened to his original face – but she didn't dare ask, not with Kylie breathing down her neck. Instead, she just stood and tried not to stare as he came and shook all of their hands.

His face screen changed to display the words 'WELCOME! LET US GO INSIDE!' and he beckoned them to follow. Once the door was closed, his face went back to the smiling cartoon.

'Welcome, welcome!' he said, voice emanating from a speaker in his chin. 'Justin Waratah, at your service! You must be Ms Collins?'

'Kylie.' Kylie smiled, and she looked him up and down exaggeratedly. 'But you can call me, anytime.'

Justin laughed, a jarringly robotic sound. 'You – I like you already,' he said. 'Please, come this way.'

He led them down the hall, and out into a spacious living room, where it was all Quinn could do to not gawk open-mouthed. Everything was painted white, with minimalist furniture, tasteful artworks, and a cabinet that, even across the room, Quinn could tell was full of relics. In the centre of the room was a gigantic cylindrical fish tank, inside of which a pair of sharks gently circled.

'Love the setup,' Kylie said, trying her best to look unimpressed by the sheer amount of wealth on display.

'Thank you.' Justin smiled. 'Please, sit! Would you like a cup of tea? Coffee? A beer?'

'Oh, no, thank you,' Kylie said. She went and perched uncomfortably on the corner of a white leather couch.

While she and Justin engaged in a serious bout of small talk, Quinn and Mullet wandered around the room and looked at Justin's stuff in awe. The walls were decked with old-world paintings and dead-nation trinkets. There were flags in frames and an old map of the world from before the End.

The cabinet of relics was full of 'souvenirs' from places with strange names like 'Paris', 'Tokyo' or 'New York' – and one from 'Greece', a name Quinn recognised. Her mother had mentioned Greece many times – a mythical, sunny place, of sheer cliffs, ancient ruins and piercingly blue waters. Quinn remembered seeing an old photograph of her mother as a young child standing with relatives from that country. They would have all died years ago now though – and even the photo was long gone.

Feeling numb from the relic proximity, Quinn decided she was better off distancing herself from the collection. She went instead to watch the sharks cruise around in their tank for a while.

Nearby, Kylie had brought out a USB full of product demos and was showing them to Justin on his laptop. After playing a few of them out loud, Justin nodded appreciatively.

'This is good quality gear,' he said. 'I can see why Bluey recommends you so highly. I would love to see you at the concert.'

'Hmm,' Kylie said. 'If I accept, might I assume you will be taking a small cut of our profits?'

'Ten per cent,' Justin said. 'Since I am arranging the venue and much of the risk is on my head, it's only fair, don't you think?'

'It's acceptable,' Kylie said.

'Great!' Justin beamed. 'I'll add you and your associates to the door list. Now, obviously there are rules for the event, but most of them are common sense. No noise or music outside the specific confines of the venue. No BYO drugs or alcohol – they'll be plenty at the event already, don't worry. And remember, it's invite only, so no telling your mates about it, at least not without explicitly asking me first.'

'Naturally,' Kylie said. 'What time should we arrive?'

'The concert itself will begin at 10PM,' Justin said, 'but before that we will be hosting a small original works competition, and before that, there will be time for the guests to mingle and interact with the vendors. This is a social event, after all! The guests will be arriving between around 7PM and 9PM – their entry times are staggered to avoid too many showing up at once and raising suspicion. Basically, if you arrive before 7PM, you'll have plenty of time to set up.'

'Alright.' Kylie inclined her head. 'And how long do you expect the concert to... uh, what is it, Quinn?'

'Sorry.' Quinn slid into view. 'But you said there was going to be an "original works competition?" What does that mean?'

'The competition?' Justin said. 'Well, it's what it says on the tin – a competition for original musical compositions. It's a chance for aspiring musicians, young and old, to get up and perform in front of a live audience. A bit of friendly rivalry to get the creative juices flowing!'

'Aspiring musicians?' Quinn said. 'As in... they write their own songs? And perform them?'

'Yes. Are you interested in getting involved?'

'Yes, absolutely!' Quinn said, just as Kylie said, 'No, definitely not.'

'That's not why we're going,' Kylie said, eyeing Quinn. 'You're going to be busy helping me in the sales booth.'

'But–!'

'Later, Quinn! We'll talk about it later.'

'Fine,' Quinn said. 'But we ARE talking about it.'

***

After an hour or so, Kylie and Justin had hashed out all the details, from finances, to escape plans if the sin-seekers showed up and, after bidding Justin farewell, they all headed back out to the van.

The second they were inside, Quinn opened her mouth.

'I want to be in the competition,' she said.

'No,' Kylie said, without looking around.

Quinn pouted. 'Why not?'

'I told you – I'm going to need your help in the booth.'

'Do you really though?' Quinn moved to look her in the face. 'Do we really need all three of us there, for the entire evening? C'mon Kylie, it'll be for, like, ten minutes! You can go ten minutes without me standing there, can't you?'

Kylie sighed. 'Okay, do you want to know why I'm actually against it?' she said.

'Yes,' Quinn said. 'Why do you hate the idea SO much?'

'Because it's dangerous, Quinn,' Kylie said. 'Dealing music is one thing – but making it is an entirely different ballpark. Do you know why there's no new music being made? Huh? Do you know why we have to keep on digging through endless piles of literal garbage to find new content? Because musicians don't last long, Quinn. One whiff of their existence, and the sin-seekers come down hard. They won't even lock you up, they will kill you. No trial. No mercy. Do you know why they do that?'

'Why?' Quinn mumbled.

'Because… everyone loves musicians,' Kylie said. 'Because live music, new music, is so much better than the same old tracks from fifty years ago. Because no one can resist it, Quinn.'

She took a breath.

'Music is a powerful addiction,' she said. 'That's why we make so much bank off it. Hear it just once or twice, and you're hooked. You want to listen to more and more, louder and louder, because it's even better when it's really fucking loud. And here's the thing – with digital tracks, you can mitigate the risk. You can play it quietly in the safety of your own soundproofed home or, if you're lucky, you can dig out some old headphones that still work and play it silently to everyone but yourself. But live music? No way. It cannot be quiet. It is, by necessity, a noise hazard. And because of that, the sin-seekers will stop at nothing to shut it down, as quickly as possible.'

There was a long silence. Quinn crossed her arms, sinking into herself.

'If you hate music so much,' she muttered, 'then why are you a music dealer?'

Kylie sighed. 'I don't hate music,' she said. 'I love it. I'm just as addicted as anyone. But there are lines that I must draw. You can't enjoy music if you're fucking dead, Quinn.'

She stepped past Quinn and into the cabin, drawing the curtain, clear signal that the discussion was over. As the van shuddered to life, Quinn went and sat down, staring crossly out the window.

She wasn't trying to arrange concerts – she just wanted to enter the competition, which was already happening. The people who saw it were already addicted to music. They were already at a concert! Surely she wouldn't be adding any more risk by performing one song live?

As they turned down the driveway, she slumped against the window and blinked back tears. It wasn't fair. All she wanted to do was make something that she liked, but no, the world had to hate her for it. She wasn't trying to hurt anyone. It wasn't her fault that she was born with music trapped in her mind. Was it such a crime, to show others the things she'd created–?

Something was moving in the bushes.

Quinn sat up straighter and hurriedly wiped her eyes. Craning her neck, she tried to catch sight of it again.

'Mullet,' she said sharply. 'Did you see that?'

'See what?' Mullet moved to join her at the window.

'I thought I saw…' Quinn frowned. 'There was this weird person in a red jacket, earlier today at the shopping centre, and I could have sworn I just saw them again.'

'What, standing in the bushes?' Mullet looked sceptical.

'Yeah,' Quinn said. 'Do you think they're following us?'

'Are you sure it was a person?' Mullet said. 'Wasn't a kangaroo, was it?'

'It was the same jacket!' Quinn said. 'Although… I dunno. I didn't see it clearly. Maybe it was just a big piece of red plastic…'

She tried to peer through the undergrowth, but she couldn't see anything before the RV turned onto the main road again. Sighing, she leaned back in defeat.

'Or maybe I'm just insane,' she muttered to herself.

# CHAPTER 9

# JUSTIN WARATAH'S
# WAREHOUSE BASEMENT BASH

### Date: Saturday 8 November 2081

Despite being forbidden from entering the original works competition, Quinn was still hyped about the upcoming concert. As the big day drew nearer and nearer, she could barely contain her excitement, talking about it near constantly and practically bouncing off the walls of the RV.

Time dragged by at a snail's pace – but at last, it was Saturday evening. Kylie drove them to the venue, a warehouse that, at least externally, looked identical to every other warehouse in Mildura's industrial district.

Justin had instructed them not to park too close, since a large number of vehicles around the warehouse would look suspicious. This meant that they had to carry all their equipment down several blocks – but since most of it was just USB sticks in a suitcase, this wasn't too hard.

Outside the venue, Kylie paused and looked the warehouse up and down. It had clearly seen better days. Its sheet iron walls were filthy and pitted with rust, and many of the windows were missing glass. On one corner, someone had spray-painted the word TITS in giant colourful letters.

Kylie double checked they were at the right place – but apparently, they were. Shrugging at the others, she went in through a door that was literally hanging from its hinges.

Inside, the warehouse was just as grotty. It smelt of damp and animal piss, and when they stepped in, several birds flew noisily out of the broken windows.

Kylie stoically crossed the room and opened the door of what had once been some sort of foreman's office. Inside was a rotting desk, a rat corpse and a chair with a fleshy white fungus growing out of the seat.

There was also another door, hidden away at the back – and on closer inspection, this one looked distinctly out of place. It was though someone had transplanted someone's front door into the metal wall, complete with a peephole, a cheap buzzer and noticeably heavy-duty soundproofing.

Kylie quickly navigated around the desk and the rat corpse and, adjusting her hair, she pressed the buzzer. There was a pause, and then the door opened. A large Caucasian man who resembled a thumb poked his bald head into view and looked at her expectantly.

'Kylie Collins,' Kylie said quietly. 'And two associates.'

The man disappeared for a second, then reappeared to open the door properly. They all filed past him, and into a stairwell leading down. At the bottom of the stairs was another door, heavily soundproofed, and lit by a single flickering bulb.

Kylie opened it – and they stepped out into another world.

What had once been a storage space had been converted into a concert hall. It was clean and brightly lit, in stark contrast to the warehouse above. A stage had been set up along the back, complete with speakers, amplifiers and colourful spotlights. There were lines of chairs set up before the stage and booths around the edges, where several other vendors were already settling in. The walls were decorated with strings of multicoloured fairy lights and a glittering disco ball hung in the centre of the room, throwing scintillating specs across the walls.

As they closed the door and stood in front of it, staring in awe, Justin appeared, arms open in greeting. He was wearing all black, in a crisp shirt and jeans that both looked painted on. 'Kylie!' he called cheerfully. 'Glad you could make it! Did you find the place okay?'

'Easy,' Kylie said. 'Although, I wasn't sure I was at the right place. Until now.'

Justin beamed. 'Did you like the decor upstairs? My personal favourite is the fungus chair.'

'It's UTTERLY revolting,' Kylie said.

Justin laughed. 'Just the vibe I was going for! Now, you can take any of the unclaimed booths – but personally, I recommend the one over there. Best view of the stage!'

Kylie nodded and led the other two to the booth in question. They all dumped their gear on the floor and Kylie began arranging it.

Quinn hovered around and tried to help, but when she almost dropped the laptop, Kylie snapped at her for being in the way. 'Just, go and have a look around,' she said, waving a manicured hand at the rest of the room. 'Come back in ten minutes!'

Quinn scuttled off and went to look at the other booths. The one next to theirs was some sort of food stall and were busy setting up a portable deep fryer. Beyond that was a vendor selling antique band merchandise, which looked very interesting, but had enough relicious vibes that Quinn was reluctant to approach it.

On the other side of the room was a home-brewed beer booth, and a hot jam donut vendor, which Quinn spent some time looking at, her stomach growling hopefully. Then, she noticed the next booth over and forgot her hunger.

It was another music dealer – but where Kylie specialised in cracking old electronic devices, this dealer had acquired an impressive collection of hardcopy CDs, DVDs, tapes and records.

It was rare to find any of these ancient devices intact, and Quinn had never seen so many in once place before. Eyes wide, she approached the stall and reached out to flick through the stack of records.

'Hey,' a voice said. 'Please don't touch the merch.'

Quinn hurriedly withdrew her hand and looked up to see who was speaking. It was a young Black woman, sitting with feet up at the back of the booth. She was dressed strikingly in black and white, with goth-style makeup behind a set of circular-framed, old-style eyeglasses. Her braided hair was also black and white, striped along the side like the bride of Frankenstein.

'Sorry.' She shrugged at Quinn. 'It was my dad's stuff. I don't want it to get damaged before it sells.'

Quinn frowned. 'I wasn't gonna break it,' she said.

'Yeah, I mean you weren't intending to, maybe,' the woman said. 'But shit happens. Also, I don't know you. Maybe you're a weirdo who likes breaking shit?'

'I'd never do that!' Quinn bristled. 'I was going to be careful!'

'Alright,' the woman said, 'I believe you. But you still can't touch it, unless you're going to buy it. Sorry.'

'What if I AM here to buy it?' Quinn put her hands on her hips. 'What if you're being rude to a customer?'

'No offense, kid,' the woman said, 'but I doubt you could afford any of this stuff.'

Quinn scowled. 'You don't know that!'

'Yeah I do,' the woman said. 'You look like if a sewer rat was a human. No offence.'

Quinn scoffed, offended anyway. 'Fine,' she said crossly. 'Keep your records to yourself. I bet your dad had shit taste anyway.'

She flipped the woman off and stalked crossly back to her side of the concert hall.

She went to find Mullet to complain about what had just happened, but he wasn't in the booth. Looking around the room, she spotted him at another booth, near the stage. He was chatting to a girl, and based on his puffed-up pose, Quinn was pretty sure he was attempting to flirt.

Rolling her eyes, she headed towards him. She had never really understood his apparent desire to flirt with every single person his age that he came across. All he ever did was make an idiot of himself.

She was ready to drag him away – but that was before she saw what the booth was selling. Her mouth fell open, all other thoughts sidelined. It was instruments! Real, actual instruments! Guitars mostly, but some percussion too, and simple woodwinds like recorders and panpipes.

The girl in the booth, a Southeast Asian girl in a purple hijab, was holding up an acoustic guitar and showing Mullet how it worked. She was wearing it via a strap across her shoulders and was in the middle of demonstrating the various finger positions, fingers splayed at an improbable angle.

'And this one's a C chord,' she said, and strummed it lightly. The sound was quiet, but pure, beautiful. Quinn felt it resonate somewhere in her chest.

'What does the "C" mean?' Mullet asked. 'Does it stand for something? Chord?'

'The chord-chord?' Quinn said, raising an eyebrow at him.

'It doesn't stand for anything,' the girl said with a smile. 'It's just called that. All chords have a letter, starting from A.'

'Really?' Mullet said. 'How fascinating! That's crazy that the guitar can do twenty-six chords, for all the alphabet letters!'

Quinn rolled her eyes again, while the girl explained to Mullet that the highest letter was actually a G. As she played a few more chords to demonstrate her point though, Quinn was transfixed. The sound the guitar made was just so good. Kylie was right when she said that live music was better.

'Can you play a tune?' she blurted out.

The girl turned to look at her. 'Sure. Do you have something in mind?'

'Um,' Quinn said. 'No, just anything.'

The girl nodded, and her fingers began moving over the strings. A melody emerged, complex, harmonious. It was gorgeous, and Quinn felt tears prickle at the back of her eyes. Embarrassed, she looked down until the feeling subsided.

'What song is that?' she asked when it was done.

'It's called *Mist*.'

'Did you write it?' Quinn asked in awe.

The girl laughed. 'No,' she said. 'It's by the John Butler Trio. I don't really write stuff myself. Well, I dabble occasionally, but none of it's any good.'

'Quinn dabbles too,' Mullet said enthusiastically. 'Although she doesn't own a guitar, so it's not as cool.'

'Shut up.' Quinn jabbed him in the ribs.

The girl looked interested. 'You write music? Do you play any instruments?'

'Nah.' Quinn looked at her feet. 'I just mess around on the computer. Midi files and stuff.'

'That counts!' the girl said. 'If it's original, that's really cool! Are you going to enter the competition?'

Quinn's head jerked up, before she slumped. 'Well,' she said. 'I'd like to...'

'What's stopping you?'

'The boss said she wasn't allowed,' Mullet explained.

'I said shut UP!' Quinn jabbed him in the ribs again. 'Stop telling my life story to people you just met!'

'It's fine.' The girl waved a hand. 'My name's Aida if that helps.'

'I'm Quinn.'

'Yes, Joey said as much.'

'Of course he did.' Quinn eyed Mullet. 'So, are you going to be in the competition?'

'No.' The girl laughed bashfully. 'I told you, I don't write anything good. But I'm pretty sure Maggie is entering, if you want to ask her about it?'

'Who?' Quinn asked.

Aida pointed across at the woman in the CD booth.

'Oh.' Quinn scowled. '*Her*.'

'Do you not like her?'

'She was rude to me.' Quinn sniffed. 'Said I looked like a rat.'

'Oh,' Aida said hesitantly. 'Really? Usually, she's very nice... Anyway... she's very good with a bass guitar! She won the original works competition last time, actually.'

'Did she?' Quinn said, and she turned to glare across the room. 'Fancy that.'

She had never been more determined to enter the competition than she was in that moment. Leaving Mullet to flounder, she went to find Justin.

She found him quickly, which was good, because it meant she had no time to overthink it or chicken out. He was talking to someone else, and she waited till he was done before sliding closer.

'Hi,' he said. 'Uhhh…'

'Quinn.'

'Quinn!' Justin snapped his fingers. 'Is there a problem with your booth?'

'No,' Quinn said. 'Actually, I just wanted to ask something about the original works competition.'

'Oh, sure,' Justin said. 'Ask away!'

Quinn hesitated. She glanced across the room, to where Kylie was looking the other way. Then she looked over to where Maggie was picking something out of her fingernails.

'I'd like to enter it,' she said.

'Great!' Justin beamed. 'I'll put you down!'

He brought out a piece of paper and leant against the wall to scribble on it.

'I'm glad to hear that Kylie has come around to the idea,' he said without looking.

'Yeah,' Quinn said stiffly.

'I knew she'd see sense!' Justin grinned. 'Alright, you're currently on last, out of five acts. What instrument will you be playing, by the way?'

'Um.' Quinn blinked. 'I don't actually have an instrument. I'm gonna sing. Over some backing music.'

'A singer!' Justin said. 'Excellent. Now, the backing music also has to be an original composition, okay?'

'It is.'

'Good. Do you have an electronic copy for me to hook up?'

'Yes,' Quinn said, and she took out a USB and handed it to him. 'It's called *Breaking the Wheel.*'

Justin wrote it down, then grinned at Quinn again. 'Awesome,' he said. 'I look forward to seeing what you've created!'

Quinn just nodded. When Justin turned away, she practically ran back to Mullet.

'I did it,' she told him breathlessly. 'I'm in the competition!'

Mullet, who was now holding Aida's guitar and letting her show him the finger positions again, looked at her blankly. Then he registered what she'd said and his eyes widened.

'You're in the comp? Damn. Does Kylie know?'

'Nope!'

'Geez, Quinn, she's gonna be pissed!'

'I don't care,' Quinn said stubbornly. 'She can punish me all she wants afterwards. This is more important!'

'Well, your funeral.' Mullet shrugged. 'Hey, before you die though, check out my sick guitar skills!'

He strummed a clumsy C chord, an A chord, and then an even clumsier G.

'Very good!' Aida said. Mullet beamed.

'Cool,' Quinn said distractedly.

She hovered around and watched Aida teach Mullet more chords, until Kylie appeared and told them to get their arses over to the booth and help her. By now, the guests had started to arrive, milling about the booths and sitting in the rows of chairs, their chattering voices a low, constant hum.

Soon, Kylie, Quinn and Mullet were busy talking to guests, spruiking their collection, and doing their best to sell as many USBs full of music as possible. The money started to roll in.

Quinn could barely concentrate though. Several times, Kylie berated her for not paying attention, and several times, she handed the wrong change over to customers.

Then, Justin got up on the stage and announced that the original works competition was about to start, and her stomach almost twisted itself out of her mouth in terror. Suddenly, she regretted everything. Why had she signed up for the competition? Had all common sense abandoned her? She was going to make a fool of herself. She was going to embarrass herself in front of the entire music community of Mildura.

The panic only got worse as the first act got up onto stage – a middle-aged man in a bowtie, carrying a flute. She forced herself to concentrate on his music, but it was a struggle. He was good. The flute was sweet, whimsical, filling the air with delicate notes – although the tune itself was a little one dimensional. Add another instrument or two, and it would be even better, Quinn thought.

The song ended, and the audience waved their hands in a silent cheer. A couple of people whooped or whistled, although tentatively. The venue was soundproofed, but old habits died hard.

On the stage, the man gave a small bow and disappeared into the wing. A teenage boy, face spotted with acne, got up next.

He looked very nervous under the bright lights – which only made Quinn more nervous as well. Oh geez, oh fuck. That was about to be her.

A simple beat and melody started playing over the speakers, and the teen took a breath. Then he began rapping along to the track. At first, he stumbled a few times but as the song progressed, he seemed to find his rhythm. His voice got louder, more confident.

When he reached the end, the crowd cheered again and he scuffed off stage. The next performer was Maggie. She was carrying a bass guitar. Quinn narrowed her eyes, her nerves momentarily forgotten.

A backing track began to play – also bass guitar, with a drum layer as well. Then Maggie began playing the third part of the song live, a duet with herself.

Quinn's frown deepened. Dammit. Maggie was really good. Aida had said she'd won last time, and it was easy to see how.

The crowd cheered louder when Maggie finished, with many whoops and whistles. Some people even clapped old-style, with their full hands. It was a sharp, shockingly loud noise.

The next person got onto stage, but Quinn wasn't paying attention anymore. Her heart had dropped away into her shoes. She was next! In a few minutes, she'd be up there on stage! Shit shit fuck!

She queasily told Kylie that she needed to use the bathroom and dipped around to the side of the stage, where Justin was standing. He turned his smiling screen-face towards her.

'Ready?' he whispered.

Quinn could feel the bile sloshing up into her oesophagus but she nodded.

He sent her two thumbs up. Quinn felt ill.

Too quickly, the performer before her finished, and it was time. Quinn's panic rose even higher as she stepped towards the stage. Shit, this was such a bad idea. Crap. Shit. Fuck!

The lights were bright, shining into her eyes. She couldn't see the audience, but she could hear them, shifting in their seats, whispering amongst themselves. She couldn't see Kylie, but she could picture her expression. She could feel the eyes boring into her. Her hands were shaking as Justin handed her a microphone.

'And for our last act,' Justin said, from very far away, 'we have Quinn, with *Breaking the Wheel*!'

Polite applause, fading in seconds. The silence which followed stretched on into eternity. Quinn's heart thundered in her ears. She felt like she was going to faint.

Then the song started playing. It was her song. She'd heard it in her head and brought it to life on the computer. She knew every part of it, back to front.

There was a part missing, though. There was no voice in this version. The song was incomplete.

Quinn entered the eye of the storm. The winds of terror were twisting around her – but she could no longer hear them. All she heard was the music.

Closing her eyes, she opened her mouth and began to sing.

*There once was a woman who worked all day long*
*She lived as a prisoner though she'd done nothing wrong*
*She worked just for others, for her boss and her Nation*
*No time to clock off at the old weather station*
*Her voice it fell silent, her body grew frail*
*Her tears they ran down behind rain, cloud and hail*
*Each day was the same in her tower of stone*
*Each night in her bed she would whisper alone:*

*This world is broken*
*This time we're alive in*
*This way isn't living*
*It's only surviving*
*The wheel it churns on*
*As the light dims to grey*
*I wish things would change*
*But I don't see a way*

*There once was a man who got up with the sun*
*He worked all day long until all work was done*
*He sowed and he tended, he weeded and watered*
*A monster came by and his efforts were thwarted*
*His voice it fell silent, his passion degraded*
*He kept at it daily, but his fire had faded*
*He would keep at his post, since this was his life*
*But at dinner he would say to his kids and his wife:*

*This world is broken*
*This time we're alive in*
*This way isn't living*
*It's only surviving*
*The wheel it churns on*
*So awful and strange*
*But maybe there's something*
*We can do to make change?*

*There once was a Nation who worked all the time*
*They thrashed and they fought on the end of the line*
*Their number was up, but they did not give in*
*But they were trapped in a loop of the same fucking thing*
*Their voices fell silent, as the rules said they must*
*They followed the rules, with no other to trust*
*But the monsters closed in and with no how or why,*
*They could only look upward and scream to the sky:*

*This world is broken*
*This time we're alive in*
*This way isn't living*
*It's only surviving*
*The wheel it churns on*
*And beneath it we drown!*
*We've got to do something*
*To break the wheel down!*

Before she knew it, Quinn had reached the end. She breathed a sigh as the last chords faded away.

For a moment, there was only silence. Then the clapping began.

It was loud, louder than Quinn had been expecting. Most of them were using their full hands now, whistling and hollering over the top.

Quinn's eyes shot open. She could still barely see them, but they were there – and they had liked it!

Her heart fluttering, she scuttled off the stage and into the welcoming darkness.

'Well done,' Justin said to her as she passed him. 'That was awesome!'

Awesome? He'd liked it? The crowd was still cheering as Justin got onto the stage and thanked everyone who took part in the competition. 'The voting box is open!' he called. 'Cast your votes! At the end of the night, the winner will be revealed!'

As she stumbled back to her booth, Quinn felt elated and

exhausted at the same time. She'd done it! She'd performed to a real crowd, and they'd liked it!

Reeling in excitement, she got back to the booth. Mullet was grinning. 'Dude, that was so cool –'

A hand fell on Quinn's shoulder.

'Quinn,' Kylie said. 'What the FUCK.'

Elation sunk like a stone. Hunching her shoulders, she turned around to face her punishment.

'I'm sorry,' she said to the floor.

'No, Quinn,' Kylie said. 'Sorry doesn't cut it. I SPECIFICALLY explained to you why this was a bad idea, and you still went ahead and did it. Why? Why, Quinn?'

'I had to,' was all Quinn could say. 'I had to see what it was like, just once...'

'You don't fucking get it, do you?' Kylie said in a low voice. 'I TOLD you how dangerous this shit is! You know, someone I knew wrote one song – ONE song, Quinn, and guess what? He was shot in a raid two weeks later. Do you want that to happen? I know you're young and naïve, and you probably think I'm a bitch and I'm overreacting, but –'

'Excuse me,' a voice said.

Kylie paused mid-rant and turned to look at the woman who had just come up to the booth. She hurriedly composed herself and smiled politely at the customer. 'Yes? How may I help you?'

'I really liked your song,' the woman said, smiling at Quinn. 'I was wondering whether you had it for sale?'

Quinn blinked, staring at the customer in shock. Kylie, also taken by surprise, opened and closed her mouth. 'We, uh,' she began.

'Yes,' Quinn said.

Both Kylie and the customer looked at her.

'The song's on the computer,' Quinn continued, bolder. 'We can easily transfer it to a USB. I... I can also include some other original tracks, if you would like?'

'Really?' the woman's eyes lit up. 'Yes, please! How much for your entire collection?'

'Um.' Quinn glanced at Kylie. 'Well, there's only about six songs that are ready at this point, so...?'

'Twenty for the lot,' Kylie said stiffly.

The woman reached into her purse.

Fumbling with a USB, Quinn found her completed tracks and shakily transferred them across. As she handed the USB over to the customer, she saw that an elderly couple had also appeared at the booth and were watching the exchange in interest.

'Is that your original song?' one of them asked.

The next ten minutes were total chaos as dozens of people came up and asked to buy Quinn's music. Quinn was in shock the entire time, hyper aware of the looks that Kylie was giving her.

Eventually, as the main event appeared on the stage and began setting up, the customers stopped coming. Quinn shrunk to the back of the booth, watching as Kylie bundled up the cash from the transactions and counted it.

After putting it away in the cashbox, she turned and eyed Quinn again. Her expression was unreadable.

'So,' Quinn said carefully. 'How much did we make?'

'Six hundred and forty,' Kylie said.

'That's pretty good,' Quinn said, 'for something I made.'

Kylie said nothing.

'Imagine,' Quinn went on, 'if you sold it for more? Or if I made more? Imagine how much money we could make if we had original music? We'd be the only dealers who had it.'

Kylie sighed. 'Look,' she said. 'I still think it's dangerous. I haven't changed my mind on that. And if you pull another stunt like tonight, I'm going to strap you to the ceiling of the RV for a week.'

'But?' Quinn said hopefully.

'But...' Kylie turned away. 'I suppose... selling the stuff you make is fine. Since you're going to keep making it anyway. And since it's not really any more dangerous than what we already do. But'—she turned back—'I have conditions.'

'Oh?' Quinn said.

'The first condition is that we ONLY sell music on USBs,' Kylie said. 'No live concerts, no more competitions, nothing. They're just TOO dangerous. Okay?'

'Okay,' Quinn said.

'The second condition is that if we're going to market this shit, we're going to have to do it under an alias,' Kylie said. 'If the sinnies get a copy of one of your tracks, I don't want them tracing it back to us immediately.'

'An alias?' Quinn said. 'Do you mean, like... a band name?'

'Yeah,' Kylie said. 'A band name. Whatever. As long as it's not obviously you.'

Quinn nodded. Then a smile broke slowly across her face.

'A band name,' she said. 'Awesome.'

# CHAPTER 10

# THE CONCRETE LAWS OF REALITY

### Date: Saturday 8 November 2081

'Absolutely not,' Kylie said firmly.

It was half-time break for the main act, and Mullet was giving Kylie his best puppy-dog eyes. Kylie, however, was immune. 'I thought Quinn was an idiot,' she said, 'but you're SO much worse.'

'I wouldn't play it,' Mullet said. 'I'd just have it, to show to people! You don't understand how COOL guitars are!'

'You want a guitar, just so you can show it off to dates?' Kylie said. 'And you think that's acceptable?'

'Well, yeah!' Mullet said. 'I wouldn't be making any noise with it. I'd just hold it, and instantly look a thousand times cooler!'

'I'm pretty sure it isn't cool unless you can play it,' Quinn said sceptically.

'It's a guitar,' Kylie rolled her eyes. 'Even if you can't play it, it's a big fat music artifact, sitting in our van. Do you know how difficult to explain that would be?'

'You won't have to explain it – the sinnies will be too busy staring in awe at my EPIC GUITAR.' Mullet slicked back his hair and busted out a pair of finger guns.

'No.' Kylie shook her head. 'Just, no. I cannot be more emphatic about how much I disapprove.'

'Aw,' Mullet said. 'Please? You said Quinn could make music.'

'Yeah, and I'm THIS close to revoking that right,' Kylie said.

'Mullet.' Quinn glared at him. 'Put the fucking guitar away! That girl isn't going to fall in love with you just because you bought her stuff!'

'You don't know that,' Mullet grumbled – but he trudged back to the store to return the guitar and break the bad news.

'Fucking idiots,' Kylie muttered, shaking her head. 'Both of you. I don't know how we've managed to survive this long...'

She trailed off, sorting money into neat stacks and putting it away in the cashbox. Meanwhile, up on the stage, the cover band, who were called Judging Books, were getting ready to do the second half of their set.

Quinn sat down on her stool and watched them closely, taking in every detail. They were a classic four-piece band, each with their own instrument. They weren't perfect – occasionally the drummer was a little out of time, or the singer missed his perfect pitch – but Quinn was still enjoying it immensely.

So far, they'd played a series of popular rock songs, most of which used the same four chords. Despite their simplicity though, the songs were catchy, and the fact that they were live made them a hundred times better. There was something so powerful about hearing, *feeling* the music in person, the bass vibrating in her ribcage, the drums crashing in time with her pulse.

Justin jumped up onto the stage and tapped the mic.

'Alright!' he called over the scraping and shuffling of chairs. 'Everyone filled up on snacks and drinks? Great! Let's get back to it, shall we?'

He jumped back down and the lead singer moved forward to take his place at the mic. 'Uhh. Hope you're all enjoying the music,' he mumbled into it. 'Anyway, here's *Smoke On The Water*.'

They started playing and Quinn leant in,, chin cupped in her hands. Transfixed, she watched the guitarist's fingers change smoothly between chords.

What if... what if that was her up on the stage? She knew

Kylie would never allow it, but the thought was still intoxicating. She could start a band, a real one, with new music and not just covers. She could sing, and Mullet could play the guitar. Of course, she'd need more people as well, to play the other bits, but –

A sharp feeling of unease interrupted her pleasant daydream.

The feeling was fleeting, lasting a second or less, but it stood out like a flash of lightning in the night. It was the distinct, familiar tang of unreality, like someone had squeezed a lemon into her brain.

Someone was using P.I.U.S.

Quinn sat bolt upright and stared at the audience. Where had it come from? Who else here had P.I.U.S? What had just changed?

No one else had reacted, at least not visibly. She could only see the backs of their heads from where she was, but they seemed to be sitting in calm silence, completely oblivious that someone nearby was tweaking the laws of the universe. To Quinn, it was almost bizarre that they hadn't noticed – but logically, she knew that most people just couldn't sense that sort of thing.

Beside her, Kylie noticed her change in demeanour and sent her a questioning look.

*Someone's using P.I.U.S*, Quinn signed briefly and then stood up. *Back in a sec.*

Before Kylie could reply, she slipped out of the booth and headed to the other side of the room. She wasn't sure exactly where the burst of unreality had come from, although she knew it was close by. She was pretty sure it hadn't come from the audience – but it might have come from one of the other vendors? If that was the case, then chances were they were showing some sort of visible side effect.

On the other side of the room, however, things were no clearer. None of the vendors were behaving oddly at all.

Frowning, Quinn went and stood at the very back of the room, near the door. She couldn't concentrate on the music anymore. What was different? Had the P.I.U.S feeling come from outside? Surely not – it had felt closer than that...

Behind her, the door banged open.

Quinn turned to see who had just come through. In an instant, she recognised them.

It was the person in the red jacket – the very same from the shopping centre and from the bushes outside Justin's house.

In that same instant, Quinn knew with complete certainty that they were the source of the P.I.U.S.

'You –' she began, raising her arm to point.

The figure reacted instantly. She felt them reaching in, drawing power from the unrealitic void that sat above their heart. She didn't know what they were about to do – but she knew she didn't want it to happen.

The band was still playing and Quinn reached out for the music, the First Portent flashing before her eyes, dragging her into its horrible, spiralling architecture.

Around her, the floor was starting to buckle, shivering, warping. Like a fluid, the concrete was boiling upwards, forming into a thin, deadly spike.

Four layers. There were four layers in the song. Vocals, lead guitar, drums and bass. Time slowed and distorted, compounded by four. The concrete spike accelerated into her stomach, a shocking, terrible pain –

Time stopped. Quinn looked down at the spike that had impaled her. Then she looked up at the red-hooded figure.

His face was visible, contorted into a snarl of wide-eyed fear. The eyes were ice-blue. It was a face she recognised.

Time began to unravel again.

The spike retreated, blood sucking back into her body, the wound sealing itself. The concrete flattened, returning to normal. Quinn's arm went back to her side. The door closed, red-jacket retreating backwards up the stairs.

Quinn watched herself walk back along the booths and sit down again at her own. On the stage, the band reached the start of their song – but time wasn't done unravelling.

She watched Mullet return with his guitar and argue with Kylie, twitching as he gestured with unnatural speed.

At last, the twitching slowed as the reversal came to an end. After a moment of stillness, time once again resumed its forward march.

As her body attached once more to the Canon Timeline, Quinn gasped and sunk to the floor. Tiny, razor-sharp pains stabbed all throughout her body.

Kylie, who was just opening her mouth to ask Mullet what he was doing with a guitar, glanced down at Quinn in concern.

'Fuck,' she said. 'Was that...? Is something's about to happen?'

Quinn whimpered and ground her teeth, clutching at her chest. The pain was getting worse. It felt like someone was drilling into her repeatedly with a series of long, jagged needles.

'He tried to kill me!' she gasped between waves of pain. 'That fucking bastard!'

Kylie crouched down and patted Quinn on the back, which didn't help at all, although Quinn appreciated the sentiment. 'Are you okay?' she asked. 'Do you need a glass of water? Can you talk? How long do we have until the thing happens?'

Quinn took a shaky breath. The pains had thankfully begun to subside, leaving her dizzy and fatigued.

'About eight minutes,' she said. 'He's going to show up in about eight minutes, come through that door and stab me in the guts.'

'Who?' Kylie said.

'The sin-seeker,' Quinn wheezed. 'The fucking sin-seeker, who was in our van that one time. Spencer, or whatever he was called. You know – the young one with the blonde hair?'

'What?' Kylie said. 'But... I thought he was dead? Didn't their car get destroyed by the Fourth Portent?'

'Yeah,' Quinn said. 'But clearly, he got away! And before

you ask, yes, he's a fucking mattersmith now. Stabbed me with the fucking concrete.'

'Well, shit.' Kylie leaned back. 'Wait – why is he here?'

'I told you, I saw someone following us!' Quinn said.

Kylie swore a few more times.

'We should leave,' she said, standing up.

'I dunno if that'll help,' Quinn said. 'He's probably already outside. I'm pretty sure I felt him attack the bouncer, about five minutes from now.'

'So what you're saying is, we have five minutes to attack him first,' Mullet said.

'Absolutely not,' Kylie said. 'Quinn said he has P.I.U.S now. I don't want to fuck with that.'

'Okay,' Mullet said, 'but he doesn't know that we know about him! What if we ambushed him? Snuck up and bonked him on the head? Can his P.I.U.S save him from a concussion?'

'It might work,' Quinn said. 'If he didn't see us coming.'

'Yeah!' Mullet said. 'So, we hide at the top of the stairs and when he comes through the door, we smack him!'

'With what?' Kylie said.

Mullet blinked. 'Um. This guitar?'

'Where did you get that?' Kylie narrowed her eyes.

Quinn saw Mullet have a thought and decided to intervene.

'Mullet, put it back,' she said. 'You've already had the argument from my perspective. Kylie said no. Very firmly. Just give it up now. We don't have the time.'

'Aw,' Mullet said – but he went and returned the guitar.

In the meantime, Kylie hurriedly locked up her cashbox and packed the remaining USBs away. Quinn sat and watched her, rubbing her still-sore arms and feeling vaguely sick. Her skin felt like there was something underneath it, pieces of glass or metal, hard and smooth – but she elected to ignore that for now. She wasn't sure whether she was imagining it and if she wasn't, it was a little too much to deal with just then.

Once Mullet returned, Kylie had packed away the gear

and was fiddling with the booth itself, unscrewing one of its legs.

'Here,' she said, handing the short bar of metal to Mullet. 'This should make a decent club.'

Mullet took it and gave it an experimental swing. Quinn hauled herself upright.

As they headed for the door, Justin hurried past, and did a double take. His face, Quinn saw, had changed. The cartoon was displaying an exaggerated expression of woe.

'What are you doing?' he asked abruptly. 'Are you leaving?'

'Just going out for a smoke,' Kylie said sweetly.

Behind her, Mullet smacked the table leg experimentally into his palm.

Justin looked like he wanted to ask more, but then shook his head and moved off.

'He looked stressed,' Quinn commented as they went up the stairs.

As the heavy door closed behind them, all sounds of the chattering crowd cut off. At the top of the stairs, the bouncer looked up from the book on theoretical physics he was reading. On seeing the metal bar in Mullet's hands, he slowly put the book down and stood up.

'Can I help you?' he asked suspiciously.

'Yes, actually,' Kylie said. 'There's a young man outside, who's about to break in and cause a ruckus. He's an ex-sinnie with something to prove. Acting on his own, as far as we know, but still dangerous.'

'How do you know about this?' the bouncer asked.

'A friend of ours saw him heading this way,' Kylie lied quickly.

'And he's dangerous how exactly?'

'Unregistered P.I.U.S,' Kylie said.

With those words, the bouncer was fully on board. Kylie explained their plan to attack Spencer before he knew what was happening and the bouncer agreed to play along. He kept an eye on the peephole and a few minutes later, he told them that the young man had come into view.

'He's heading this way,' the bouncer said quietly. 'Going around the dead rat... Okay, he's about to ring the doorbell.'

BZZZZZZZZZZZZZZZZZT

Quinn's heart jumped to her throat as the buzzer crackled to life. He was right outside! This could go wrong, horribly, terribly wrong. She couldn't hear the music anymore either...

'Alright,' the bouncer said. 'Get ready.'

He removed the latch and opened the door a crack.

'Hello,' a low voice said from outside. 'I have a delivery for this address.'

'Is that right?' the bouncer said.

He paused. Last time, he had questioned it. Last time, he'd probably been impaled.

'Come on in,' he said abruptly.

Stepping back, he opened the door a little wider – but not wide enough to see onto the landing. There was a moment of silence, then footsteps.

The second Spencer stepped through the door, Mullet pounced. Quick as lightning, he struck Spencer's temple with a solid *clonk*.

Spencer went down like a sack of bricks.

'Got him!' Mullet yelled excitedly, waving the bar around. Then he paused, looking down at the limp body. 'Shit, he's not dead, is he?'

'No,' Kylie said, kneeling to turn the young man over. 'In fact, he'll probably wake up pretty soon. We should tie him up. Quinn, if we strap a relic to him, will that stop him from using his symptoms?'

'If it's strong enough, yeah,' Quinn said. 'I doubt our fake boomerang is going to cut it..'

'Your confidence is inspiring,' Kylie said. She removed her necklace, an oversized heart shaped locket, and held it out towards Mullet. 'Go and get the boomerang from the RV,' she said. 'The key's in the locket. Quinn, can you go and ask Justin if he's got any of his fancy relics on hand? Or at least some strong rope?'

Quinn nodded and hobbled quickly back down the

stairs. As she opened the door, the sounds of the chattering crowd washed over her.

For some reason, the band still hadn't returned to the stage. But there was no time to ponder why that detail had changed in this iteration of events, at least not until Spencer was safely neutralised. Quinn spotted Justin near the stage and hurried over to him.

His face was still displaying an expression of melancholy. Quinn was almost afraid to ask him for anything, but he'd already spotted her, so she took a breath and forged ahead.

'Do you, um, have any relics with you?' she said.

'Relics?' Justin said distractedly. 'No, not with me. Why?'

'Uhhh,' Quinn said.

Justin's cartoon face abruptly changed again, switching rapidly to shock, then anger, before cutting off to black. Before Quinn could react, his hand shot out and latched onto her shoulder.

'What do you know?' he demanded. 'You know something, don't you? Why do you need a relic? Why is my band refusing to play?!'

Quinn wriggled out of his grasp and took a large step back.

'I don't know why your band isn't playing,' she said warily. 'But we need a relic because there's a rogue mattersmith in the stairwell!'

'What?!' Justin said.

His face switched on again, displaying the same woeful expression as before. Muttering to himself, he left Quinn, hurrying away towards the main exit.

Quinn watched him go blank-faced. It looked like he was about to be Kylie's problem now – but that didn't really help her on her mission to find relics and/or rope.

Turning, she looked around the room for inspiration and her eye fell on the band merch stall – the same one that she'd been avoiding all night because of its relicious aura. A lightbulb went on inside her brain.

Gritting her teeth, she approached the stall.

'How much is that T-shirt?' she asked, pointing at the strongest relic she could see.

'The Back In Black Tee?' The attendant leaned out to see what she was pointing at. 'That one's six hundred. Rare specimen, in near mint condition! Very popular band, back in its day!'

So popular that their iconography had relicious properties, Quinn thought – but she didn't say anything. Six hundred dollars was a lot for a T-shirt, but it was pittance for a relic, especially one of that tier. It was clear that the attendant had no idea what they were selling.

She wasn't about to clue them in, either. Instead, she just nodded and went back to tell Kylie about it.

Kylie was busy explaining to Justin why there was an unconscious teenager on the landing outside his event. Justin did not look happy. Mullet, meanwhile, had returned with the boomerang and a long length of rope, and was busy wrapping Spencer up like a dead bug in a spiderweb.

'Let me get this straight,' Justin was saying. 'This child, who is also a sin-seeker, and ALSO a mattersmith, followed you all the way here to my invite-only event?'

'Yep,' Kylie said.

'How the fuck did he do that?'

'I don't know!' Kylie said. 'He's a sneaky bugger! We didn't know he was following us! Didn't know he was still alive, in fact. We were pretty fuckin' sure that the Fourth Portent killed him. Trust me, if you'd been there, you would have thought the same.'

'This is a pretty fucking grave mistake,' Justin said. 'How did you not notice him? A fucking sin-seeker!'

'Well, not anymore, he isn't,' Kylie said. 'They don't employ people with P.I.U.S.'

'That's not the point!' Justin half-screamed.

'Alright.' Kylie eyed him. 'Untwist your panties, babe. We've caught him now. We'll chuck him in a Sanctuary, problem solved. Even if he talks about your event, which he didn't even see with his own eyes, no one's going to take him seriously. He'll be carted off to some construction site within a week and none of us will ever see him again.'

Justin took a deep breath.

'Okay,' he said. 'Okay. If you're *really sure* that he was working by himself, then I guess it's fine. As long as he hasn't tipped off the actual sin-seekers, and they're not on their way here right now...'

'Look,' Kylie said with a sigh. 'I can't guarantee that. It might be best to call off the event.'

'Yeah,' Justin said. 'Great. Great! Fucking... it's not like the band was going to play anything else anyway, I fucking guess. Fucking shitheads, blabbering that they'd done it already...'

He stalked off down the stairs, slamming the door with a little more force than was necessary.

'Arsehole,' Kylie muttered. 'Oh – Quinn, I don't suppose you found out whether he brought any relics with him? I forgot to ask.'

'He didn't,' Quinn said.

'Dammit.' Kylie sighed. 'I guess we'll have to just hope that the boomerang is enough.'

'Well, actually,' Quinn said – and she told Kylie about the T-shirt.

# HOSTAGE SITUATION

### Date: Saturday 8 November 2081

It was about forty minutes later when their captive came to.

With the concert ending prematurely, and not knowing what else to do with him, they had taken Spencer back to THE GLAM VAN. There, he lay in the middle of the floor, wrapped in rope from the neck down and stuffed into the newly purchased AC/DC T-shirt.

Mullet, who was keeping watch, noticed that he was waking up and alerted the others. Kylie put down the map of Mildura that she'd been looking at and eyed Spencer suspiciously. Quinn, who'd been sitting as far away from the T-shirt as possible, inched a little closer.

On the floor, Spencer groaned, his eyelids fluttering. He looked quite sad and pathetic, tied up as he was, and Quinn almost felt sorry for him – until she remembered that he'd just tried to kill her.

Kylie crouched over the young man and shone a torch directly into his eyes. He screwed up his face and tried to turn away from it, but Kylie just moved the light with him.

'Alright, dishrag, listen up,' she said as he blinked blindly into the torch. 'I don't know what your problem is or why you've decided to stalk us, but you've picked a fight with the wrong bitch. Maybe you were some sort of hotshot sinnie-kid before, but guess what? You're not anymore. Now, all you are is an unregistered mattersmith. Do you know what we do with those?'

'No,' Spencer muttered, shaking his head. 'No!'

'Yes,' Kylie said. 'We're gonna take you to the Sanctuary, where you belong, and where you can't bother us again. And don't even think about trying to use your symptoms on us before we get there. I've got more relics and I'm not afraid to shove them directly up your arse. Understand? Blink twice if you understand me.'

Spencer tried to lift his head and look around, but tied up as he was, he didn't get far. 'Fuckyou,' he slurred.

'Good enough,' Kylie said, moving back. 'You two, keep an eye on him, while I figure out where this bloody Sanctuary is...'

She picked up her map again, running a finger along it and mouthing the names of streets to herself. Meanwhile, Mullet moved into their captive's field of view, grabbing a chair, turning it backwards, and sitting down with his arms folded over the top.

Spencer's eyes fixed on Mullet and narrowed in rage. 'Fffuckyou,' he said again.

'What was that?' Mullet said, jutting his jaw. 'Whatchu lookin' at, punk?'

The young man's lips curled in disdain. 'Fuck... you,' he enunciated.

'Oh yeah?' Mullet said. 'Well, fuck YOU!'

'Yeah, fuck you,' Quinn said, moving closer again. 'Stabby Shitheadicus.'

Spencer shifted to look at Quinn. He scowled when he saw her, then began thrashing about in his bonds.

'Woah, woah!' Mullet grabbed him, pinning him down. 'Where do you think you're going, mate?'

'I'm, argh, get off me!' Spencer snapped. 'I'm just trying to sit up, you buffoon!'

'Is that it, huh?' Mullet said. 'Too bad. You revoked your sitting rights when you tried to stab Quinn.'

'What are you talking about?!' Spencer spat. 'I never stabbed her!'

'Oh, yeah,' Mullet said thoughtfully. 'I guess you technically didn't, huh.'

'He did,' Quinn said, 'or he would have, anyway. Doesn't mean I don't remember.'

Spencer turned his head to glare at her again.

'I know what you are,' he said.

Quinn blinked. 'Oh?' she said. 'And what's that?'

'Realitysmith,' Spencer said.

'No, I'm not.'

'Yes, you are,' Spencer said. 'You knew the Portent was there before it breached the surface. Also, don't think I can't see you, sitting way over there, distancing yourself from the relic.'

'I'm sitting here because I want to,' Quinn said. 'You don't know shit about me, Spencer McStinkbrain.'

'Spencer's my surname, idiot,' Spencer said.

'Stinkbrain McSpencer, then,' Quinn said. 'It doesn't matter. We're not going to see you again, after tonight.'

'Oh yeah?' Spencer said. 'What if I tell the Sanctuary about you?'

Quinn narrowed her eyes. 'What would you tell them?' she said. 'You have no proof of shit. Even if I had P.I.U.S, which I don't, you don't even know what Portent it's from. You have nothing to tell and anyway, they won't believe you.'

'Won't they?' Spencer said. 'Is that a risk you're willing to take?'

Quinn scowled at him and he glared back. Mullet looked from one to the other, eyes wide.

'Aha!' Kylie exclaimed, tapping her finger on the map. 'There it is! Ten-minute drive, easy peasy.'

As she went and started up the engine, Spencer swallowed visibly. He'd been putting on a tough show, but the longer he kept it up, the more the cracks began to form. The relic was clearly taking a toll – he was clammy and pale, visibly sweating, each word he spoke a clear effort. And with all his bluster, it was clear he did not want to go to the Sanctuary.

'I'm w-warning you,' he said loudly, as Kylie pulled the van out onto the street. 'If you take me to the Sanctuary, I'll report you! They'll come and get you and take you in as well!'

'Oh, fuck off,' Kylie called from the cabin. 'They're not going to listen to some pissy brat like you.'

Spencer opened and closed his mouth. Panic was rising in his eyes.

'You can't do this!' he yelled, his voice cracking. 'I'm an officer of the Department of Sin! This is all your fault! This is your fault that I'm like this! You're not even sat trackers – you're music dealers! We knew you were, soon as we saw you! Sinner scum! You drew in the Portent with your noise!'

'Mullet,' Kylie said, 'can you put a sock in his mouth?'

'Literally?' Mullet asked.

'Sure. Just shut him up.'

'The Department of Sin WILL find you!' Spencer screamed, thrashing in his bonds. 'Those who sin against the Nation are doomed to fail! You will pay for your sins! You wi-umph umfff!'

He tried to spit out the old balled-up pair of socks that Mullet and shoved into his mouth, his nose wrinkling in disgust. But with arms roped firmly to the sides of his body, he couldn't remove them. All he could do was glare in rage, tears forming at the corners of his eyes.

'Ah, finally – peace and quiet,' Kylie said coldly.

No one dared break the silence as they neared the Sanctuary. As Kylie pulled up outside the front gate, Quinn hunched into her knees, making herself as small as possible.

She hated Sanctuaries. Like weather stations, they housed a large number of relics – but not quite enough to mask the near constant P.I.U.S activity inside. It was a sickening seesaw of emotions, wrapped up in a bouquet of despair. Many who passed through those iron gates were not there by choice, their lives irreparably uprooted, any plans they had for the future obliterated in a single moment. The ghosts of their helplessness clung like ash to the stone walls.

Spencer could feel it too, she could see that. The closer

they got, the greyer he began to look. The fire had left him, his face sheened in sweat. He lay very still and looked at nothing.

Watching him, Quinn once again couldn't help but feel bad for him. He was living out one of her worst nightmares. If it was literally anyone else, she would have been against this. But Spencer was a sin-seeker, and he knew too much. He'd threatened her and tried to kill her and, if not for her own abilities, he would have succeeded. His presence in their lives could only spell trouble.

But still, she couldn't watch it happen. She looked away and buried her chin in her knees as Mullet and Kylie hauled him up and dragged him outside.

'C'mon,' Quinn heard Kylie say between huffs of breath. 'It's not so bad. You were already a servant of the Nation, right? Now you'll just be a different kind.'

Then the door closed and all sound cut off.

Quinn closed her eyes, willing away the tears that were threatening to come out. Why did she care so much about this? Spencer was their enemy. He was a danger to them, and to others. He would probably end up in a Sanctuary anyway. If they didn't turn him in, then someone else would.

Turning, she looked out the window and up at the sky. It was a pleasant night, clear, a slim moon scudding between wisps of cloud. The weather station had promised rain tomorrow, but it wasn't scheduled to begin for another six hours.

The door of the RV ripped open.

Quinn turned to look in surprise. Kylie and Mullet were already back? That was quick...

'MotherFUCKER,' Kylie swore, once she'd closed the door. 'Absolute fucking bastard!'

She was holding something in her hand: a tattered black rag. Quinn frowned at it before realising what it was – the remains of the AC/DC T-shirt.

'What happened?' she asked, eyes wide.

'That fucker escaped!' Kylie threw the black rag onto the

floor. 'Sneaky piece of shit! Pretending to be all helpless and forlorn, while cutting a hole in his bonds the whole time!'

'What?' Quinn sat up. 'How?'

'Robot arms,' Mullet said sadly.

'Oh, yeah,' Quinn said. 'Shit. I forgot he had those.'

'Yeah, we all did,' Kylie said. 'Bunch of idiots, we are. Got him two metres from the van and he ripped out of the T-shirt and bolted away into the night. Really fucking quick, he is, too.'

'Robot legs,' Mullet said, even more sadly.

'Well, what should we do?' Quinn asked.

'I don't know!' Kylie thew up her hands. 'I guess we have to skip town again! Repaint the van, the whole shebang!'

Grumbling angrily to herself, she disappeared into the cabin.

Quinn stood and went to pick the black rag off the floor.

It was no longer a relic. She could hold it in her hands with no problem.

As she stared down at it, she tried to unpick how she was feeling. On the one hand, it was bad that Spencer had escaped. It meant he was free to come after them again and she had no doubt that he would. He was going to keep on causing trouble, until they somehow stopped him.

But on the other hand, her first reaction to hearing he'd escaped had been... relief?

'Where are we going to go next?' she asked whoever was listening.

'Don't know!' Kylie called from the cabin. 'Back east? Or south maybe? I hear the Grampians are nice this time of ye – oh, what the fuck is it now?'

She angrily picked up her flashing mobile phone and jammed it against her ear. 'Yes, what?'

'Oh, hi Justin,' she said a moment later, her voice instantly becoming more saccharine. 'Yeah. Sorry again about all that. It sure has been one hell of an evening!'

As Justin began talking inaudibly on the other end of

the line, Quinn tuned out. But she tuned back in again when Kylie said her name.

'Really?' Kylie said. 'Yes, of course I'll tell her. Oi, Quinn!'

Quinn poked her head into the cabin. 'Yes?'

'Justin says you won the competition,' Kylie said.

Quinn stared at her blankly for a moment, then brightened. With all that had happened, she'd almost forgotten about the original works competition.

'Holy shit, really?' she said.

'That's what he says.' Kylie shrugged. 'Hang on, I'll put you on speaker...'

'Congratulations, Quinn!' Justin's voice crackled tinnily out of the phone. 'Everyone loved your stuff! Between you and Maggie, barely anyone else got any votes!'

'Cool!' Quinn said, grinning.

'Yeah, it's cool!' Justin said. 'Several people were asking me about you, actually. They want more! Want to know how I found you, and who you are, and what you're making! Oh, actually – speaking of which, one of Madam Brinesworth's people was at the concert. They wanted to know whether you'd be interested in entering their sponsorship progr –'

The voice cut off, as Kylie switched the phone off speaker.

'Hey!' Quinn said crossly.

Kylie ignored her. 'We're not interested,' she said tersely into the phone.

'What? What do you mean we're not interested?' Quinn said. 'Who's Madam Brinesworth? What sponsorship program?'

Kylie waved away her questions. 'Sorry,' she said to Justin. 'We're not looking for that sort of thing right now. Yes. No, I...'

She paused and Quinn saw her eyebrows shoot up.

'Hold on, wait,' she said. 'HOW much did you say they were offering to pay?'

# CHAPTER 12

# BIRD MAN

## Date: Wednesday 11 March 2082

The Detective returned the Lamborpanini in a slightly cleaner condition than they'd borrowed it. Then, with Bill in tow, they headed back to the Red Cliffs Sin-Seeker Office.

It was 11AM and the office was officially open. Inside, Tank was sitting behind the desk and filling out an incident report. The report was in hardcopy – the office computer still hadn't been fixed.

When the Detective came in, he looked up, and his expression went suspiciously neutral. 'Oh, you're back,' he said. 'Do you want something?'

'No, thank you, I do not require your assistance at this time,' the Detective said. 'I am merely here to report my findings and to request information.'

'Mmm,' Tank said. 'What are your findings?'

'Recent reports of the Fifth Portent's activity within the area appear to be accurate,' the Detective said. 'Henceforth, I shall be focussing my efforts elsewhere.'

'Mm hmm,' Tank said.

'Specifically,' the Detective went on, 'I shall be investigating recent alleged sightings of the Eighth Portent. Yesterday evening, your colleague mentioned that a local man called Liam King had encountered the Eighth in December of last year and was suffering non-active symptoms. Is this correct?'

'Yeah,' Tank said.

'I would like to interview this man,' the Detective said. 'Would you be able to provide me the address of his current residence?'

'Yeah, I can,' Tank said. 'But we've already interviewed him about it. It was definitely the Eighth he saw, I can save you that much trouble.'

'Noted,' the Detective said. 'However, I would still prefer to interview him myself. Thus, I can eliminate any question or ambiguity and move on with the investigation.'

'Alright,' Tank said, grabbing a scrap of paper and scribbling on it. 'Here's his address. I should warn you though, he's not the friendliest of blokes. Had a few minor run-ins with the law in the past, etcetera.'

'Has he?' the Detective said. They internally opened the files they'd downloaded the previous evening and cross-referenced the name 'Liam King' with two decades worth of infringement notices. Sure enough, his name came up several times. He'd been fined in the past for public drunkenness, excessive noise, driving without a licence, and unregistered construction work on a private property.

'Interesting,' they said. 'This man is clearly careless – a danger to himself and others. I am not surprised he encountered a Portent. Although'—they eyed Tank—'I *am* surprised that he has not been jailed even once.'

'Detective,' Tank said wearily, 'if we jailed every single person who made this sort of minor offense, then the entire town would be empty.'

The Detective frowned. 'Officer Tank,' they said. 'If the rate of sin amongst your citizens is so alarmingly high, then I might suggest that something is wrong.'

'Is it?' Tank said. 'Is something wrong? Really?! What could it be!'

'I do not believe resorting to sarcasm is necessary at this time,' the Detective said.

'Okay.' Bill stepped in between the two. 'Time's-a-wastin', isn't it, Detective? Let's go and have a chat to Mr King!'

'Yes,' the Detective said. 'Time is, as you say, a-wastin'.'

They turned and abruptly left the office.

*****

Mr King's place of residence was a small, unkempt house, with stacks of old car parts in the overgrown front yard. Around the side were two entire vehicles, although the Detective was relieved to see that their engines appeared to have been removed. They both looked alarmingly un-roadworthy.

They picked their way to the front door and rang the doorbell. A minute later, the door cracked open. The Detective looked down at the young child who was peering at them through the gap.

*Hello,* the Detective signed. *Is your parent or guardian present?*

The child didn't respond beyond staring unblinkingly and chewing on their thumb. They looked to be about six or seven years old.

*Is there an adult on the premises who I may talk to?* the Detective tried again.

Bill moved into view.

*Hi,* he signed, smiling at the kid. *We need to speak to Liam King. Is that your dad?*

The child stared at him, then nodded once.

*Can we speak to him?* Bill asked. *We're sin-seeker officers – but he's not in trouble! We just want to ask him some questions about his accident.*

The child tilted their head to the side.

*Sin-Seekers?* they signed.

Bill glanced at the Detective. After a pause, the Detective pulled out their ID badge and showed it to the child.

The kid stared at it for a few moments, then reached up and unlatched the door. The Detective and Bill filed in.

'Thank you,' Bill said once the door was closed. 'What's your name, kiddo?'

'Sandy,' the kid said. 'Are you here to fix Daddy's arm?'

'Um.' Bill winced slightly. 'No. Unfortunately, I don't

know if anyone can, uh, fix your dad's arm. But we are going to get to the bottom of what happened! That way, it won't happen to anyone else!'

'Oh,' the kid said.

'Where are your parents or guardians?' the Detective asked, looking around. They were standing in an open living-room-slash-kitchen area. It was messy, with used cups, empty cans, utensils and crayon drawings all over the benchtop and dinner table.

'Mummy's at work,' the kid said.

'And where is your father?'

'Daddy's in bed.' The kid pointed towards a short, dark hallway. 'He's sleeping.'

'Do you mind if we wake him up?' Bill asked.

The kid shook their head.

The Detective led the way down the short hall, opening a door near the end. Inside it was dark, with heavy curtains drawn across the window, but after switching to IR spectrum, the Detective saw a man lying in bed, his back towards the door.

'Mr King,' they said loudly.

The man started awake. Slowly, he wriggled around to face the open door, blinking at the light.

'Wha–?' he croaked, squinting at the figures in the doorframe. 'Who is it?'

There were bandages on his head, covering much of his scalp and his left cheek. The skin that was visible beneath was pale, discoloured and grey, with patches here and there of strange, downy hairs.

The Detective briefly compared the symptoms in front of them to known P.I.U.S of the Eighth, and found it an immediate match. The hairs were actually small feathers, genetically identical to those of the common myna bird, *Acridotheres tristis*.

'Mr King,' they said, stepping closer. 'I am Detective Claw, from the Melbourne Department of Sin. I am investigating recent Portent activity in Mildura and surrounding regions. I wish to discuss your encounter with the Eighth Portent in December last year.'

Mr King muttered something involving the word 'fuck'.

'I thought we'd already been through this,' he said, louder.

'This is an independent investigation,' the Detective said. 'I must ask you to recount your experience a second time. I apologise for the inconvenience.'

Mr King sighed, deeply.

'Yeah, okay,' he said. 'Not like I was doing anything else today anyway...'

He wriggled around again and reached out to turn on his bedside lamp. Then, with a series of winces and grunts, he pushed himself upright.

Breathing hard, he sat for a minute, leaning against the headboard. His throat worked and his cheek twitched, strange muscles flexing involuntarily beneath the greying skin. He looked terrible, gaunt and sickly, with dark hollows beneath his eyes. According to the files, he was thirty-two years old, but he looked at least twice that.

As the blanket fell away, more bandages came into view, all down his left side. His left arm was entirely wrapped in gauze, oddly bulky, with dark feathers poking out between the wrappings.

'Alright,' he said once his breath had settled. 'Pass me my medicine, and then we can talk.'

He gestured to a cabinet at the foot of his bed. The Detective opened the top drawer and found two plastic containers inside. One had a red lid, and the other blue.

'Give me both.' Mr King beckoned with his pointer finger.

The Detective handed them over, then watched cautiously as Mr King opened the red-capped container. Inside was a packet of high strength painkillers. Mr King took two, washing them down with a glass of water from his bedside table.

Then, he opened the blue-capped container. It was full of wriggling mealworms. Mr King pinched some between his fingers and put them into his mouth, chewing contentedly.

'Sharon hates it when I do that,' he said with a weak grin. 'But I think its harmless. It's not going to make things worse than they already are. I'm already a fucking bird man. So what if I want to eat bird food? Fuck you, I enjoy it.'

'If wanting to eat worms is your only behavioural change,' Bill said, 'then you've gotten off pretty lightly.'

'Lightly?' Mr King said. 'Ha! Is that a joke? Fuck off.'

'Sorry,' Bill said. 'I am aware that your situation is exceptionally awful.'

'Yeah, it is,' Mr King said. He dropped another pinch of gently writhing mealworms into his mouth.

'So,' he said when he'd finished chewing. 'Are you gonna ask me questions, or are you just gonna stand there and stare at me like I'm some kind of freak?'

'If you are ready, then let us begin,' the Detective said. 'First of all, I must confirm your identity. You are Mr Liam King, correct?'

'Yeah,' Mr King said.

'And on Sunday, the 14th of December, 2081, at approximately 7:30PM, you encountered the Eighth Portent, correct?'

'Yep,' Mr King said bitterly.

'Could you please describe the encounter in as much detail as you are able?'

Mr King took a deep breath. His cheek began twitching again, and he visibly made an effort to still it.

'Righto,' he said eventually. 'Well, like you said, it was back in December. It was a Barbeque Day, so me and the family had been out and about all afternoon.'

'And your family consists of?' the Detective asked.

'Me, my partner Sharon, and the kids, Hunter and Sandy,' Liam said.

'Okay,' the Detective said. 'Continue.'

'Yeah, so we'd been out all afternoon,' Mr King said. 'But it was one of those days, you know, where everything goes wrong. Left half the lunch at home, then the barbeque wouldn't turn on, then there was a bull-ant nest… Just little, annoying things, but there were enough of them that we were all in a bad mood by the end of it. Sharon wanted to go home early but, like an idiot, I decided not to. Instead I went over to Road Warriors to grab a beer.'

'Road Warriors?' the Detective said. 'Could you please describe this establishment?'

'It's a bar,' Mr King said. 'Out near the solar station. It's, uh, a themed place. Bunch of punks hang out over there, but they're not a bad crowd. I used to go there often.'

'Punks?' the Detective frowned.

'Yeah, you know.' Mr King waved his hand. 'Lots of piercings, spikes, leather, cheap cybernetics. They like pretending that they live in a different apocalypse.'

'I see,' the Detective said. 'So, what did you do at this bar?'

'Well, I got my beer,' Mr King said. 'Had a good old gripe about my day with the bartender. Good bloke, I've known him for years. Had another beer or six, in a very short amount of time. Went outside for a walk to clear my head.'

He paused.

'Fuck, I wish I didn't go on that walk,' he said.

'That was where you encountered the Eighth?' the Detective said.

'Yeah.' Mr King sighed. 'About twenty minutes in, I noticed there were a lot of birds around. In hindsight, I should have realised what they were, but I was drunk and distracted. Just kept walking on all oblivious, until the core popped out of the trees right next to me. Realised that I'd fucked up at that point.'

'Could you describe the core?' the Detective said.

'Looked like hundreds of birds, all stuck together,' Mr King said. 'All flapping about and trying to escape, but they couldn't, because the others kept pulling them back in.'

'And what did you do?' the Detective said.

'I ran,' Mr King said. 'Fastest I've ever run, I reckon. Probably broke some records. Not that it helped me much. I'd already gotten too close to it. Inside the rubicon, or whatever the eggheads call it. One of the birds broke away from the core, felt it brush my left arm. Just for a second, and it didn't hurt, not yet, but even before I got back to the bar, it was starting to change colour.'

He paused again to eat more worms.

'I don't really remember much after that,' he said. 'I know I got back to the bar, but the details are hazy. I was in shock. I think the Portent followed me, but they chased it off with relics. Then they took me to the Sanctuary. I remember that. I was there for about a week. They wanted to see if I would develop active P.I.U.S, but I didn't. All I got was a fucked arm, ongoing dermatitis, and excruciating chronic pain. Lucky me.'

'Any chance the symptoms could become active later?' Bill asked concernedly.

'Nope,' Mr King said. 'They told me it happens immediately, or never.'

He pointed to the wall above his bed, where a large cardboard cut-out of the traditional Christmas character, Santa Claus, hung. The jolly man was riding a surfboard in red and white board shorts and a festive hat.

'The Sanctuary lent that to me,' Mr King said. 'Told me "Merry Christmas" when they gave it to me. It's a relic, apparently. They used to come down here and check on me, ask if it bothered me.'

'And does it?' the Detective asked.

'Of course not,' Mr King said. 'I mostly forget it's there. Sharon hates it, though. Says it's an ugly piece of shit.'

He chuckled, but then his cheek began twitching again, and he had to hold it until it stopped.

***

After a few more questions to clarify the details, the Detective left Mr King to his own devices. As they made to leave the house though, they caught sight of Sandy, sitting on the floor and gluing bits of paper together, and paused.

'You,' they said. 'Why are you not at school?'

Sandy looked up at the Detective with wide eyes.

'It's Hunter's turn,' they said, then looked back at their paper craft.

'Hunter is your sibling, correct?' the Detective said.

'Yeah. He's my brother,' Sandy said. 'He's ten.'

'And he's at school?'

'Yeah. But tomorrow it's my turn,' Sandy explained.

'You attend every second day?' the Detective frowned. 'This is highly disruptive to your education.'

'Detective.' Bill leaned in. 'Stop interrogating the child. I don't think they have much of a choice but for one of them to stay here and look after their dad. It's not their fault.'

The Detective frowned. 'This is highly irregular,' they said as they headed towards the door. 'Assistance should be provided to families affected by P.I.U.S by their local Sanctuary! There is legislation in place to ensure this!'

'I think that the local Sanctuary is having some other problems,' Bill said. 'Like vanishing from the timeline.'

'That was three days ago,' the Detective said. 'Why has a new representative not been sent?'

Bill snorted in amusement.

'I think you're severely overestimating how organised they are,' he said.

'Clearly,' the Detective said. 'A pattern that seems to be emerging.'

They stepped outside and headed back to the street. After a short pause, they began to march rapidly down the road.

Bill ran after them, waving to draw their attention.

*Where are you going?* he gestured. *Sin-seeker office is back that way!*

*I'm not going to the sin-seeker office,* the Detective said. *I am going to this 'Road Warriors' establishment. I would like to confirm Mr King's story with them.*

*Why?* Bill asked. *The Eighth Portent obviously got him. What else do we need to know?*

*There were several holes in Mr King's story,* the Detective said. *I would simply like to fill them in.*

The Eighth Portent

FIRST RECORDED SIGHTING: 19/08/2057,
Newcastle, Awabakal country, NSW

PHYSICAL APPEARANCE:

The Eighth Portent is a living structure of variable size and density, comprised of between approximately 1500 and 4000 individual birds. All birds in the structure are of the same species and resemble the common or Indian myna (Acridotheres tristis), with a brown body, black hooded head, yellow legs and beak, bare yellow skin behind the eye, and white wing patches visible during flight.

The Eighth Portent is distributed in two distinct zones, known as the corona and the core. The corona is typically comprised of approximately 200 to 800 birds, which are able to move and fly about freely. The corona can extend up to 10 kilometres from the core, with bird density decreasing proportionally with the square of distance. Further than 10 kilometres, birds originating from the core have been found to harbour no significant unrealitic properties and are thus considered normal animals.

The core is comprised of between 1300 and 3800 birds, packed densely together in a roughly spherical shape, often with long tendrils or loops of semi-fused birds attached to its outer surface. The sphere regularly expands and contracts in size but is on average between 2 and 4 metres in diameter.

The birds of the core can be seen to be fused together at many points, with the extent of fusion increasing towards the centre of the core. It is hypothesised that the birds originate in a 'genetic slurry' at the core's centre, from where they slowly graduate outwards, developing form and individuality, before eventually breaking away from the surface to become part of the corona. It is not known how long this process takes from start to finish, however the rate of dispersal from the core to the corona is estimated to be between 2 and 20 birds per day.

BEHAVIOUR:

The core of the Eighth Portent is able to move freely in three-dimensional space, subject to the movement of the birds on its surface. It is capable of flight and is frequently seen hovering several metres in the air, although more often it is observed 'hopping' along the ground between short periods airborne.

Due to the random and conflicting movement of the birds, the Eighth Portent changes direction often and is typically slow to advance. However, on the rare occasional that the birds all move in the same direction, it is capable of short bursts of speeds greater than 30 km/h.

The birds on the surface of the core appear to be in distress, showing behaviour such as frantic flapping, scrabbling, and distress calling. The combined noise of bird calls can at times exceed 100 decibels. While part of the core, the birds do not appear to require food or water, and do not sleep, however the Portent displays decreased activity during the night.

The birds of the corona have been observed to behave in a manner characteristic of a healthy member of their species, including feeding, roosting and breeding habits. Aside from an increased unreality index, these birds are extremely difficult to distinguish from an ordinary common myna, and thus represent a substantial and insidious risk. As a precaution it is recommended that citizens avoid common mynas and report them on sight to local authorities.

BIRDIFICATION

All birds originating from the Eighth Portent represent a significant mutagenic hazard to humans.

Upon physical contact with the core or corona, human tissue is immediately subjected to aggressive genetic mutation via a self-replicating anomalous biological vector, similar in function to a virus. Cells are rapidly infected and co-opted to produce more vector agents, which are in turn spread to neighbouring cells. Large insertion sequences of DNA are introduced into the genome, resulting in a wide range of deleterious effects, including widespread growth of feathers or scales and the transmutation of limb structures and organs into those seen in the common myna. This is typically accompanied by a range of autoimmune disorders, as well as the appearance of 'birdlike behaviour' in the infected.

The severity of this 'birdification' effect is dependent on exposure time, and is more severe upon contact with the core, although the corona is still capable of significant mutagenesis.

Note – while the Eighth Portent's 'birdifcation' effect has only been seen to affect humans, the large number of myna birds released each day represents an additional significant ecological threat to wildlife, particularly native bird species.

PORTENT INDUCED UNREALITY SYMPTOMS:

P.I.U.S RUBICON RADIUS: 3m.

ACTIVE SYMPTOM DEVELOPMENT: 52%

LETHALITY: 52%

DESIGNATION: n/a

ADDITIONAL NOTES: Of those who come into contact with the Eighth Portent, around half develop active symptoms, and half non-active. Active P.I.U.S of the Eight results in a 100% mortality rate, over a maximum period of two weeks. Additionally, the host represents a significant hazard to others around them, as live vectors are continuously shed from their body, which have the capacity infect others with non-active symptoms.

For those who develop non-active P.I.U.S, the vector will remain live for up to 48 hours, before instantaneously disappearing from the body. There is no evidence to suggest the vector is able to reactivate after this period. Following a non-active P.I.U.S diagnosis, and with correct management, it is possible to live a normal, fulfilling life, however the genomic damage resulting from the encounter has been found to be irreversible.

# ROAD WARRIOR

### Date: Wednesday 11 March 2082

oad Warriors was a kilometre down the road, just opposite the solar station. Built on the end of a long line of empty garages, it appeared externally as a rickety shack, walls covered in graffiti art and rooftop lined with an excessive number of spikes. Hazard stripes, for purely aesthetic purposes, were painted around the front door, below a metal sign displaying the bar's name. Several human skulls hung from chains underneath the awnings.

As they approached, however, the Detective could see that the rickety appearance was nothing more than a façade. The bar was fully sealed and soundproofed, above and beyond regulation. The spikes were made of foam and the skulls were plastic, distanced so that they didn't rattle or knock together.

With a noticeably apprehensive Bill in tow, the Detective entered the building. The walls of the airlock were plastered with posters of old-fashioned petrol-engine vehicles and scantily clad models.

Pushing open the inner door, they stepped into the bar proper. It was a dingy place, with darkened windows and deliberately low lighting. The walls, like the airlock, were pasted floor to ceiling with posters, retro movie promotionals and cut-outs from magazines. More skulls, chains and decorative car parts hung from the ceiling or walls.

Like the outside, however, the grungy look was part of

the aesthetic. On second glance, it was clear that the tables were clean and the floor had been recently mopped. The posters were graphic to a tasteful degree. Everything was up to health and safety regulation.

Since it was a Wednesday, and just after lunch, the bar was relatively quiet. Only a handful of patrons were present – but they were clearly dedicated regulars. They wore leather and spikes, hazard stripes and ripped denim, each sporting more tattoos and facial piercings than the last. When the Detective entered, they all turned to look and there was a noticeable lull in the conversation.

The Detective decided to take the opportunity to introduce themselves.

'Good afternoon,' they said into the silence. 'My name is Detective Claw. I am investigating recent Portent activity in Mildura and surrounding regions. It is to my knowledge that the Eighth Portent was observed in the vicinity of this bar in December of last year.'

They paused. The silence continued.

'I wish to speak to witnesses of this event,' the Detective went on. 'If anyone present attended the Road Warriors bar on the afternoon or evening of December the 14th 2081, I ask that you please approach and explain in your own words what transpired. Any information will be appreciated, regardless of its apparent insignificance.'

They paused again, and then, upon receiving only blank and vaguely hostile stares from the patrons, they moved to the nearest table. The chair scraped loudly on the floor as they pulled it out.

'I shall place myself here for your convenience,' they said, then sat down, ramrod straight.

The patrons turned away and resumed their conversations. Bill moved to join the Detective at the table, hunching down in his seat.

'You have no shame, do you?' he hissed, eyeing the Detective reproachfully.

The Detective looked at him. 'I do not understand your point.'

'No, you wouldn't, would you?' Bill said. 'I can't take you anywhere...'

The Detective cocked their head. 'Have I committed a social error? Please explain.'

'No, no.' Bill sighed. 'You're just... very direct sometimes and it stresses me out. But that's a me problem. Keep on doing what you're doing.'

'Okay,' the Detective said.

They switched their attention back to the patrons. None were showing any signs of approaching, although a few were clearly talking about the Detective. One was emphatically explaining that all sin-seekers were bastards, while their friend insisted that actually, the Detective was 'pretty hot' and 'could put them in handcuffs any day'.

None of this was relevant to the case. The Detective was just starting to wonder whether they should attempt a different tactic for gathering information, when a man came out from behind the bar and approached the table. He was a large, muscular fellow of Maori ancestry, with a bald head, full beard and an eyepatch over his right eye.

Pulling out a chair, he thumped down two pints of beer on the table, sat, folded his arms and looked across at the Detective.

'So,' he said, with a light Kiwi accent. 'You're investigating the Portents, eh?'

'Yes,' the Detective said, eyeing the pints of beer. 'I appreciate that you have come forward. However, the beer is unnecessary. It is inappropriate for officers of the law to consume alcoholic beverages during working hours.'

'Oh, no,' the man said. 'These are both for me.'

He took a long sip out of one, and then the other.

'Twice the beer, twice the relicity,' he said with a grin. 'Anyway – name's Deppie. I'm one of the owners of this here fine establishment.'

The Detective briefly searched their onboard records, but no one of the name 'Deppie' came up.

'Is "Deppie" your birth name?' they asked.

'Nah,' Deppie said. 'It's a nickname. Stands for "depth

perception". My real name is Laurie, but no one calls me that. Anyway, I was here last year when the Eighth came through. Real horrible business. Fucked up one of our regulars real bad. He's been bedridden ever since.'

'Are you referring to Mr Liam King?' the Detective asked.

'Yeah, that's him,' Deppie said. 'Poor bloke. Has a family too – they're all on struggle street now. You sometimes forget about the Portents and what they can do to people, you know? Then next minute, one of the bloody things is right on your doorstep...'

'It is foolish to forget about the Portents,' the Detective said.

'Yeah, yeah,' Deppie said. 'It's not forgetting, exactly. It's more that, it's hard to imagine it happening to you personally. Until it does.'

He took another long sip of his beer.

'In your own words,' the Detective said, 'could you please explain the series of events that occurred on the evening of the 14th of December?'

'I was behind the bar that day,' Deppie said. 'It was a Barbeque Day, so it was pretty quiet. Liam came in around 4, and he was obviously upset. Had a tiff with his girl, I think. He told me about it, but I honestly don't remember the details. I do remember that he ordered a lot of drinks though.

'Around 6:30 he started getting a bit too rowdy, so I cut him off. He swore at me a bit, then went outside. I thought nothing of it, least not until half an hour later, when he came back. Burst through the door like the devil was after him. Which, in a way, it was.'

'He had encountered the Eighth Portent,' the Detective said.

'Yep,' Deppie said darkly. 'Although, it took us a couple of minutes to figure that out. He was babbling incoherently, clutching his arm. Couldn't make head or tails of what he was saying. Thought he was having a bad trip. Then his hand started sprouting feathers and we realised it was worse than that.'

'What did you do in response?' the Detective asked.

'Well, I froze up, to be honest.' Deppie shrugged. 'Fortunately, Daz has a cool head in an emergency. Went and fetched all the beer out of the cellar. Got everyone in bar helping. I –'

'Wait,' the Detective said. 'Who is this "Daz"?'

'Daz is my partner,' Deppie said. 'Other owner of the bar. His real name is Daniel.'

'Daniel Williams?' the Detective said. This was one of the names was on the Eighth Portent incident report that they'd taken from the sin-seeker office computer.

'Yeah, that's him,' Deppie said.

The Detective nodded and waved their hand to indicate Deppie should continue.

'Yeah, so, about ten minutes after Liam came back, a truckie came in and told us the Eighth was just down the road,' Deppie said. 'Probably followed Liam back here, he was crying so loudly. Anyway, it was heading right for us. Daz went out and had a look, said there were bloody myna birds everywhere. He could hear the core as well, hundreds of 'em twittering and shrieking all over the top of each other. Said he thought the sound would turn his hair white, like in the old movies.

'As I said though, he's got a cool head between his shoulders. Got everyone to help him bring up every can of beer in our possession. Lined the VB longnecks along the walls, Carlton Draughts in the airlock, XXXX Gold on the tables. On their own, their individual relicity is very low. But Daz figured if there were enough of them, they would be strong enough to do something.

'I admit, I was a bit sceptical. They're just cans of beer, after all – not even good beer. But'—he gestured around at the bar—'it worked. The Portent went harmlessly by. We were a bit worried it would go on to Red Cliffs proper and wreak havoc there, but they knew it was coming by then. The Early Warning System went off, and then, forty minutes later, they sounded the all-clear. The Eighth had trundled off back into the bush, apparently.'

The Detective nodded thoughtfully.

'The use of beer cans to increase localised relicity was highly resourceful,' they said. 'I must commend your partner's logical actions. Has he ever considered joining the sin-seeker force?'

Deppie snorted in amusement. 'Nah, not for him,' he said. 'But I'll tell him you said that.'

'You should tell him to consider it,' the Detective said. 'But back to the matter at hand – what became of Liam King?'

Deppie sighed, his expression serious again. 'Poor bloke was in a bad way,' he said. 'He'd stopped crying, but his silence was just as bad. He was lying on the floor, shaking uncontrollably, still clutching his arm. We surrounded him with beers, just in case it helped, and then, when the all-clear sounded, we took him into town. Dropped him off at the Sanctuary. Dunno what happened after that, but he survived at least.'

He took another sip of his beer.

'Bloody terrible,' he said, shaking his head. 'As I said, it really hammered the fear of Portents back into us all. Bar was real quiet for a fortnight or so after that.'

The Detective nodded again. 'This has been very informative,' they said. 'Is there anything else you would like to add?'

Deppie shrugged. 'Nah, I think that about covers it.'

'Alright,' the Detective said. 'In that case – thank you for your time and information. That will be all.'

Deppie nodded and swallowed down the rest of his beer, one glass, then the other. As he moved to stand up though, the Detective frowned.

'Wait,' they said. 'I must ask for one last clarification.'

'Oh yeah?' Deppie said.

'You said that Daz could hear the core, "twittering and shrieking all over the top of each other",' the Detective said. 'Could he not see it?'

'Nah, it was too far away,' Deppie said. 'Behind the solar station, off in the trees.'

'How far away would you say it was?' the Detective asked.

'Well, at least fifty metres.' Deppie shrugged. 'I dunno. I didn't go out myself.'

'And he could clearly hear it, fifty or more metres away?' the Detective said.

'Yep,' Deppie said. 'Loud bastard, it is.'

'Okay,' the Detective said. 'And would you describe Mr Liam King as "hard of hearing"?'

Deppie blinked.

'No,' he said. 'I never got that impression.'

'I see,' the Detective said. 'Interesting.'

***

The Detective left the bar and went directly back to Liam King's house.

It was by now late afternoon and Liam's partner, Sharon, had returned from work. She opened the door when the Detective knocked and her face set into a scowl.

'I suppose you're the sinnies who came by earlier,' she said, after letting them in. 'What do you want?'

'You must be Sharon,' the Detective said, holding out their hand to shake. 'Nice to meet you. I have some follow-up questions for Mr King.'

'Can't it wait?' Sharon ignored the Detective's hand. 'It's almost evening. We're all tired. Liam's already stressed out, after your earlier unannounced visit.'

'If you would rather schedule an appointment at 6AM tomorrow morning, that will be acceptable,' the Detective said.

'6AM? No. Are you insane?'

'Then I take it now is more agreeable?' the Detective said. 'It will only take a few minutes.'

They stepped towards the bedroom but Sharon moved into the way and folded her arms.

'Shouldn't you be clocking off around now?' she said coldly. 'I thought you sinnies loved clocking off early.'

'I cannot speak for Red Cliffs's lacking examples,' the Detective said, 'but a true sin-seeker never "clocks off". Will you kindly step aside, ma'am?'

'What happens if I don't?' Sharon said.

'Then we will be here for a while.' The Detective narrowed their eyes.

Bill stepped closer.

'Ma'am, I do apologise for all this,' he said wearily. 'But I do recommend you do as they say. The Detective isn't kidding when they say they don't clock off. We literally could be here all night.'

Sharon glared from Bill to the Detective and back again – then, with a sigh, she stepped away.

'Fine,' she said. 'But you'd better be quick about it.'

'I will be,' the Detective said. 'I only need to clarify some points.'

They stalked past and went into the bedroom. Mr King was awake this time, propped up against the headboard and staring at an automotive magazine, his eyes unmoving. When the Detective came in, he slowly put it down.

'So, you're back,' he said.

'Yes,' the Detective said.

They went and stood at the base of his bed. In the doorway, Sharon was watching, arms folded.

'I apologise for questioning you twice on the same day,' the Detective said. 'However, after verifying your story with one of the owners of the Road Warriors bar, I am left with several pressing questions.'

'Oh?' Liam said. 'Like what?'

'The Eighth Portent creates a lot of noise,' the Detective said. 'Officially, it has been recorded to produce sounds at a volume of over one hundred decibels. Additionally, Daniel Williams, co-owner of Road Warriors, reportedly claimed that he could hear the core from over fifty metres away, describing it as "loud", even from that distance.'

'How is this relevant?' Sharon asked.

'It is relevant,' the Detective said, 'because considering all current evidence, I cannot see how it is possible that Mr

King was able to "accidentally" come across the core of the Eighth Portent without hearing it well in advance.'

There was silence in the room.

'There are two possible conclusions that I have come to,' the Detective went on. 'Conclusion one is that Mr King DID hear the Portent and went towards it anyway. Although it seems unlikely that anyone could hear such a noise and misinterpret what they were hearing, it is well established that Mr King was inebriated at the time. Perhaps he believed it was a regular flock of birds? Or perhaps, acting in a state of emotional disruption, he deliberately went to find the Portent, either through reckless thrill-seeking, or suicidal intent –'

'What?!' Sharon said. 'No! How dare you! Liam would never do that! He's a fighter. Even now, he's fighting! Lesser men would have given up, but he hasn't! How dare you. How DARE you suggest that!'

'I am only stating all possibilities,' the Detective said. 'This is just one possibility, considering that Mr King was under the influence of alcohol, and in emotional distress, following an alleged fight between the two of you. Do you dispute these facts?'

Sharon sighed, while Liam rubbed his face.

'Yeah, okay, we had a fight,' Liam said. 'But it wasn't anything serious, not really. Not in hindsight. It was just stupid stuff. We would have worked it out.'

'We *have* worked it out,' Sharon said.

'And Sharon's right,' Liam continued. 'I would never kill myself. Never even considered it, not seriously.'

'Okay,' the Detective said. 'In that case, is it your position that you did not intend to go towards the Eighth Portent?'

'Of course not!' Liam said. 'Why the fuck would I go towards it? I already told you, I didn't realise what it was, until it was too late!'

'So you heard it, and disregarded it?' the Detective asked.

Liam hesitated.

'Or,' the Detective said, 'conclusion two, you didn't hear it. Perhaps… because your ears were blocked?'

Liam took a deep breath.

'Why did you come here and ask questions, if you already knew the answer?' he said.

'I did not know,' the Detective said. 'I only suspected.' They leaned in closer.

'Tell me what your ears were blocked with, Mr King.'

'Headphones.' Mr King sighed. 'I was wearing fucking headphones, okay?'

'And listening to music?' the Detective asked.

'Yes,' Liam said.

At the door, Sharon's mouth fell open.

'I'm sorry,' Liam said, eyeing her. 'I know it was stupid and I shouldn't have done it. Trust me, I regret it every fucking day. And'—he looked at the Detective—'you can fuckin' arrest me if you want. But know that my sins have already been punished a thousand times over.'

'Liam, you fucking idiot!' Sharon muttered, head in her hands.

'Where did you acquire the headphones and music?' the Detective asked.

Liam waved his hand defeatedly. 'I bought them off a dealer, a month or so before the incident. First time I'd bought anything.'

'A dealer?' the Detective said. 'Could you describe this person?'

'It was a group of people,' Liam said. 'Came through town in their RV. The RV was pink when they arrived and green when they left. They repainted it while they were here. Could be any colour now, I suppose.'

'And the dealers?' the Detective said. 'What did they look like? Do you have their names?'

'Don't know their names.' Liam shrugged. 'The ringleader was this woman – she also wore a lot of pink. Had some teenagers working for her. Oh… one of them kept referring to herself as Temporal Boom.'

'Temporal Boom?' The Detective frowned.

'Yeah. I think it was some sort of stage name?'

'A stage name?' The Detective cocked their head.

'Yeah.' Liam shrugged. 'She was selling music that she'd written herself.'

'Is that so?' the Detective said. 'Interesting. Did you purchase any of this music?'

'Well,' Liam said. 'Actually... yes. That was what I was listening to, when I ran into the Portent.'

'And do you still have this music?'

'No. I threw it away when I ran. It's somewhere in the bush now. I couldn't say where exactly.'

'I see,' the Detective said. 'That is almost a shame. It would have been useful to analyse a copy.'

***

The Detective, now satisfied that they had the complete picture, left the King residence for the second time that day. They had considered leaving Mr King with an infringement notice for music possession, but had decided against it. As Mr King himself had said, no amount of punishment by the Department of Sin would come close to what had already happened to him.

It was by now early evening and, a good day's work done, they headed back to the sin-seeker office. There, while Bill sat on the floor and rubbed his calves, they promptly plugged into the wall socket to charge up and analyse the day's findings.

The events surrounding the Fifth and Eighth Portents' recent appearances had each been successfully cleared up. In each case, it was apparent that the Portent in question had been exactly as expected. There was no evidence yet to confirm the existence of a town-swallowing Twelfth Portent.

There WAS evidence, however, that music had been involved in both incidents so far. That meant that music dealers were indirectly responsible for the presence of at least two Portents in the area. In fact, according to current data, it was safe to hypothesise that the increase in Portent activity in the vicinity of Mildura was at least influenced by, if not entirely down to, music dealer activity.

Even more interesting was the name they'd been given – Temporal Boom. It was a striking name – especially when compared to the disappearance of Mildura. The Detective had already considered the idea that it had been some sort of temporal anomaly that had caused the town to vanish. The name of this music dealer, who was writing their own music, was therefore an odd coincidence.

Was it more than coincidence? The Detective did not yet know. But they would find out.

Opening their casefile, they added another priority to the growing list:

*Secondary Priority – Further investigate music dealer activity in the region, in particular the musician known as Temporal Boom, and eliminate such activity, thus preventing further music-related Portent incidents.*

With their new priorities sorted, the Detective went back to the list of recent Portent sightings. In order of timeline, the next incident to investigate was a big one. The First Portent.

It had landed near Ouyen just over a month ago. Like usual, its appearance had caused a stir, making headlines even in Melbourne.

The Detective opened their satellite navigation program and searched for the landing site. It was over a hundred kilometres away from Red Cliffs. Apparently, their transport issues weren't yet over.

They opened their eyes and located Bill, who was eating his dinner at the office desk.

'Bill,' they said.

Bill jumped slightly, spilling soup over the side of his bowl. 'Ah, what?' he said.

'Tomorrow we're going to Ouyen,' the Detective informed him.

'Oh?' Bill said.

'It is quite far away, so we will have to locate transport

again,' the Detective went on. 'If this morning was anything to go by, this may take a while. We should therefore prepare to leave quite early.'

'Let me guess,' Bill said with a sigh. '6AM?'

'5AM,' the Detective said.

'Ah,' Bill said weakly. 'Even better.'

# ACT 2

# CHAPTER 14

# ARK 2

### Date: Tuesday 25 November 2081

Quinn tilted the handheld mirror and stared at the tiny, flat lump which had appeared underneath her left ear. It was difficult to see, no larger than a grain of rice, but it was solid when she touched it, shifting slightly underneath her skin. She knew what it was – a tiny piece of metal, lodged against her jaw, slowly worming its way to the surface.

It wasn't the first to appear, and it probably wouldn't be the last. Ever since she'd used her P.I.U.S at Justin Waratah's music concert, she'd been finding them all over her body. They were never very big – the largest so far had been the size of her pinkie fingernail. But she didn't want to think about how many there were, or what sort of long-term health problems they were causing.

Sighing, she put the mirror down on the edge of the bathroom sink and pinched the skin, isolating the fragment. Then she lifted her other hand. Held in it was the sharpest knife she could find from the kitchen utensil box.

Bracing, she sucked in her breath and brought the tip of the knife to the lump.

She had to do it quickly or she would lose her nerve. With a small gasp, she drew the knife sharply down. Blood dripped into the sink.

It hurt and Quinn grit her teeth – but it wasn't over yet. Pinching the skin again, she viciously pushed the piece of metal outwards. She felt it come loose, landing in the sink with a tiny *clack*.

Quinn grabbed a clean rag from the open first aid kit and pushed it against her jaw to stem the bleeding. For a moment, she felt dizzy – but after sitting on the floor and closing her eyes, she felt better. Using the handheld mirror, she applied antiseptic and a small adhesive bandage to the wound. Then she slowly packed the first aid kit away and wiped the stray blood droplets off the floor, chucking the tissues in the toilet.

In the sink, the tiny piece of metal was resting where it had fallen. Quinn stood up again and eyed it reproachfully for a moment.

'Bitch,' she said to it.

Picking it up, she rinsed it off and looked at it more closely. It was very small, a couple of millimetres thick and less than a centimetre long. One side of it was dull grey. The other side was a bright, toxic yellow.

Despite its size, she could feel its aura of unreality. It was ludicrously strong, for something so tiny. There was no doubt that this was another fragment of the First Portent.

Frowning, she took a matchbox out of her trouser pocket and opened in. Inside were the fragments that she'd already pulled out. There had been six before – this one made seven.

Of all the side effects Quinn had ever experienced, this was definitely inside the top five worst. Usually, the effects only lasted for a few minutes – but this one had been going on for weeks. Maybe it was because she'd reversed her own death? Maybe, larger changes had larger consequences? Or maybe it was just bad luck? Quinn didn't really know.

She dropped the latest piece of shrapnel into the matchbox and stowed it back in her pocket. She didn't really like carrying the box around with her – but she wasn't sure what else to do with it. If she put it down, then the others might find it and ask questions, and she'd have to explain what it was, and it would turn into a whole thing... But she couldn't just throw the fragments away. It felt wrong. They were pieces of the First Portent – casting them to the wind felt like bad luck, like the seeds of disaster would be sown wherever they landed. At least if she had them, she knew where they were.

They were hard to ignore, though. In moments of silence, between conversation lulls, she could feel them there, a static buzz of raw creativity and deathly foreboding, localised to her left hip. On the plus side, their presence made relics more bearable. But while they were there, her mind was plagued with disquiet and her dreams were strange and disturbing.

Sighing, she cleaned up the sink and then washed the blood from her own neck and hands. As she put her T-shirt back on, there was a loud knock on the bathroom door.

'Oi, Quinn!' Mullet yelled from outside. 'Stop taking a dump and get out here! We're arriving!'

'Coming!' Quinn called. She grabbed her hoodie from the towel rack and put it on, raising the hood to hide the bandage on her neck. Then, after checking one last time for stray droplets of blood, she exited the bathroom.

Mullet was looking out of the window at a cluster of rickety buildings on a low hill up ahead. Quinn joined him.

'What are we looking at?' she asked.

'Ark 2,' Mullet said cheerfully.

'Ark 2?' Quinn said. 'What happened to the first one?'

'Dunno,' Mullet said. 'I think it's a biblical reference.'

'Well, it looks like shit,' Quinn said.

On a low hill of dry, yellow grass, stood about ten structures made of rusty corrugated iron. At one end of the cluster stood a water tower, its once-bright colours worn almost entirely away. At the other end, a small herd of cows stood and stared at the approaching RV, perfectly still aside from the occasional swish of a tail. Far in the distance, a line of wind turbines rotated slowly.

The road they were following turned from cracked tarmac to gravel, then from gravel to dirt. As they approached the cluster of buildings, Kylie slowed the RV, coming to a stop before a small metal signpost. On the sign were the words ARK 2.

'What is this place?' Quinn asked, as the engine cut out. 'Is it a farm?'

'It's not a farm,' Kylie said from the cabin. 'Although, that IS the illusion they like to project.'

'Illusion?' Quinn said. 'What do you mean? If it not a farm, then what is it?'

'I suppose you could call it a club,' Kylie said. 'For rich people.'

With no further elaboration, she opened the driver's door of the van. Quinn watched her climb out and turn to stare in the direction of the buildings, hands on hips.

Quinn and Mullet sent each other a bemused look, before sliding open the passenger door and joining her. Outside, it was uncomfortably warm and dry and smelt of dust and cow dung. It clearly hadn't rained here for weeks – but with nearest weather station over fifty kilometres away, it wasn't surprising that the climate here was largely uncontrolled.

Fortunately, they didn't have to stand in the sun for long, before a man came out of one of the buildings and waved at them. He was an older Caucasian bloke, with a hatchet jawline, perfectly coifed salt and pepper hair, and an old-fashioned business suit and matching tie. He looked extremely out of place amongst the rusty farm equipment.

As he got closer, he grinned at them with very white teeth. 'Hello!' he called loudly into the open air. 'You must be Ms Collins!'

Kylie blinked at him, slightly taken aback at the noise. *Hello*, she signed. *Yes, that's me.*

'Ah, sorry!' the man said. 'My Auslan is very rusty! It's alright though, you can talk! No one will arrest you here, don't you worry!'

He held out his hand to shake. 'Matthew McCleave!' he announced. 'But you can call me Matt!'

Kylie slowly took his hand. 'Kylie,' she said quietly.

'What's that? Speak up!'

'Kylie!' Kylie said, then glanced around uneasily.

'Fantastic to meet you!' Matt beamed. 'And you two.' He advanced with hand outstretched towards Quinn and Mullet. 'What are your names?'

'Joey, but most people call me Mullet,' Mullet said as Matt enthusiastically pumped his whole arm up and down.

'Quinn,' Quinn said hurriedly, avoiding the same fate.

'Oh!' Matt looked at her. 'So you're the brains behind Temporal Boom! We really love your stuff, kid. Very excited to see what you can do!'

'Thanks,' Quinn said.

'Love the RV, by the way,' Matt went on. 'Such a bright colour! Green is one of my favourites, you know? In fact, I used to have a green car myself, back when I was a young rascal. Me and my mates used to drag race it down the strip! Got into a fender bender once or twice, but nothing too serious. Heh – those really were the days, weren't they?'

'Sure,' Kylie said. 'Um. Can we please go inside? I'd rather not have the Fourth Portent show up and try to kill us again.'

Matt looked at her blankly for a second.

'Well, of course,' he said, his grin returning. 'Where are my manners? Right this way!'

He led them up the hill and into one of the rickety buildings. It was dim and musty inside, with metal fences partitioning the interior. It looked like some sort of shed for keeping livestock, although clearly no animal had disturbed the dust for years.

There were, however, two people in black Kevlar vests, standing just inside the door. They wore sleek helmets with tinted visors and both were visibly carrying firearms.

They were some sort of security force, Quinn thought. Like Matt himself, they looked out of place. Clearly, Ark 2 was more than it initially appeared.

Ignoring the security, Matt led them across the room to a small, innocuous door. The door opened into a short, white hallway, at the end of which an elevator waited.

The elevator was surprisingly roomy, with panels of

glass in three of its four walls. Outside, a dark chute could be seen, lined at regular intervals with small red lights. There were only two buttons inside, one marked with an 'up' arrow, and the other with a 'down'. Once everyone was inside, Matt pressed the downward arrow, then turned to beam at his guests.

'Are you ready?' he said, as the doors closed. 'Make sure to keep an eye on the window; you're gonna love this!'

With a slight jolt, the elevator began moving downwards. Outside, the red lights accelerated past, before settling into a regular rhythm.

'Now, I don't know how much you know about us already,' Matt said, 'but basically, Ark 2 is a world away from the world. A little slice of life as it used to be, before everything went, you know, up shit creek. Its fully environment controlled, self-contained, self-sustaining and self-governed! We produce enough food to feed everyone here and generate all our own power.

'More importantly though, Ark 2 is a place where the old Australian lifestyle persists. Here, our culture and way of life is preserved in full, away from the tyrannical restrictions of the Last Nation. Freedom of thought and expression are not only permitted, but encouraged! We are a haven for scholars, free-thinkers, artists and those who wish to live without fear!'

'Are you saying,' Quinn said, 'that music is legal here?'

'It's not only legal, but loved!' Matt beamed. 'Musicians are not persecuted, but revered! As it should be. But don't look at me – look at the window! We're almost there!'

Quinn looked where he gestured, just in time to see the walls of the elevator chute abruptly disappear. Her eyes widened.

They had just descended into a vast cavern. It was hundreds of metres deep and at least a kilometre long. An entire town lay below, nestled in the floor. There were dozens of houses and shops and streets, all mapped out in a tidy grid. There were streetlights and cars on the road, and a central park full of lush, green plants.

The cavern was lit as bright as day. A massive array of high-power LEDs, stylised with radiating spokes to resemble the sun, was suspended from the roof of the cavern on a huge set of tracks. The array ticked slowly across from east to west, simulating daytime. Around it, the walls and ceiling were painted in azure blue. A grid of projectors, suspended on scaffolding, painted the sky with looping footage of gently shifting clouds.

'Well, there we have it,' Matt said grandly. 'Welcome... to Ark 2!'

# CHAPTER 15

# BRINESWORTH

**Date: Tuesday 25 November 2081**

Quinn stared, speechless, as the elevator gently descended in through the roof of one of the buildings, slowing to a stop. Why had she never heard of this place before? It sounded incredible! It LOOKED incredible! Music was legal here!

In fact, as they exited the elevator, she could hear music already. There were speakers in the entrance lobby, playing canned pop music for all to hear.

Mouth slightly open, Quinn followed the others out of the arrival building. The building itself resembled a small, compact version of Flinders Street Station, mildly relicious and painted a warm yellow with a domed green roof. A line of clocks sat above the door, each labelled with the name of a different train line.

Beyond it was a spacious town square, bordered by dozens of old-style shops. Each bore the name of a long-dead franchise, selling fast food or fast fashion to the time-pressed consumer. In the centre of the square was a large, inscrutable statue made up of colourful abstract shapes. There were people about, walking or sitting together or browsing shop windows. They were chatting and laughing, out in the open air!

And there was more music! As Matt led them across the square, Quinn stared at a man on the corner who was playing a violin. He was just playing it, right there for all to see! And people were stopping to listen and throwing coins into his violin case.

It was thrilling – but also terrifying. Were there no Portents here? Surely they could get in, if they tried? The Fourth could easily tunnel in at any moment. Were the people of Ark 2 not worried about that?

They left the square behind, but there were even more shops in the streets beyond. Most were playing yet more music inside, doors wide open, tinny tunes clashing or mingling with those from next door. Quinn stared at them before whipping around when something roared loudly past on the road. It was a car but it wasn't soundproofed at all.

'Mullet,' Quinn whispered. 'What IS this place?'

Mullet just shook his head, clearly just as overwhelmed as Quinn was.

They turned a corner, leaving the shops behind and passing by the central park. It was full of strange trees and flowers that Quinn had never seen before, lit from all angles via a network of blue and red lamps. A signpost declared it the Ark Botanical Gardens.

On the other side of the park was a residential district – but the houses were all massive. They were multistorey, painted in clean, bright colours, with huge, manicured gardens and private swimming pools. As they went by one house, a dog bounded into view on the other side of the fence, wagging its tail. Quinn almost jumped out of her skin when it started barking.

*I'm going to have a heart attack*, she signed at Mullet as they left the dog behind.

Eventually, they arrived at a particularly massive house, nestled right beside the cavern wall. As they approached, the cast iron gates swung open to let them in.

'Ava has asked to see you immediately upon arrival,' Matt explained, as they headed up the wide tarmac driveway. 'Ava Brinesworth, that is. She's what you might call our resident music aficionado. Always looking out for fresh talent. She was very impressed with your performance at Mr Waratah's event.'

'She was there?' Kylie said.

'Well, no, not personally,' Matt said. 'But her agent was there and gave a glowing review! She's as keen as a bean to meet you! Although'—he glanced at his wristwatch—'we may have to wait a few minutes. She's currently in a meeting. Actually, I'm supposed to be in the meeting as well, but when you arrived, I volunteered to get you! Between you and me, the meeting was starting to drag.'

He winked roguishly at his guests, then reached out to ring the doorbell.

There was no soundproofing, so they all heard the bell jingle cheerily from somewhere inside. A moment later, the door was opened by a stern-faced red-headed woman in a suit jacket and pencil skirt.

'Good afternoon, Councillor McCleave,' she said, without smiling.

'Afternoon, Saoirse,' Matt beamed. 'I've brought our new musicians! Is the council meeting over yet?'

The woman peered at Quinn and the others through rectangular eyeglasses. The glasses were styled in the old-fashioned way, but instead of resting on the ears, the arms vanished directly into the sides of her head. Clearly, it was an augmentation cybernetic – a subtle display of extreme wealth.

'The meeting is not yet over,' the woman said shortly – but she opened the door wider. 'However, you may wait inside until it is. Please follow me.'

She turned and led the group through an enormous entrance hall, tastefully decorated with elegant furniture, framed artworks and a modest chandelier, before opening a door to the side and gesturing that they should enter.

'Please wait here until the Madam is ready,' she said. 'In the meantime, may I interest you in a cup of tea or coffee?'

'Coffee for me, please,' Matt said. 'You know how I like it.'

He looked expectantly at his guests.

'I...' Kylie said. 'I'll have the coffee. With milk. And two sugars.'

'Me too,' Mullet said quickly.

Quinn blinked as everyone looked at her. 'Um...'

'She'll get the coffee as well,' Kylie said.

Quinn opened her mouth to argue, but Kylie silenced her with a look. The woman, who Quinn had decided was some sort of butler, nodded curtly and disappeared.

Matt went and sat down in the room they'd been brought to, and hesitantly, the others joined him. It was dauntingly lavish, with antique velvet couches arranged around a delicate wooden coffee table. A massive, gold-framed canvas of an Australian bush scene took up most of the back wall. It wasn't a relic, but Quinn still felt dizzy when she looked at it.

She'd thought that Justin's house had oozed wealth, but this place was ten times worse. It was like a palace! Just standing inside, she felt horribly out of place. Her clothes were ragged, and her shoes obscenely dirty. Uncomfortable, she perched on the edge of one of the chairs and tried not to let her feet touch the carpet.

'I don't want the coffee,' she said to Kylie miserably. 'I don't even like it.'

'That's because you haven't developed a taste for it yet,' Kylie said. 'Because you're a child.'

'No, Quinn's right, it tastes like arse,' Mullet said.

'Child,' Kylie repeated.

'If you don't like it, then why'd you ask for one?' Quinn eyed Mullet.

'Because usually, they're really expensive,' Mullet said. 'Duh!'

'Actually'—Matt leaned in—'here in Ark 2, coffee is cheap and available for everyone, just like it should be! Give it a few weeks, and you'll be enjoying it along with the rest of us, just you watch!'

Kylie raised an eyebrow. 'How do you manage that?' she said. 'Do you grow it yourself?'

'Oh, no,' Matt said. 'We import it from up north, like

everyone else. And yes, it's expensive, getting the beans all the way here, through jungle and desert, and the Sydney Dead Zone and whatever else – but there are some things that the council spares no expense on and coffee is one of them! Ark 2 wouldn't be the same without it.'

'Okay, but I still don't want it,' Quinn muttered.

Behind them, the door opened and the butler returned with a tray in her arms. She placed it down on the coffee table, then stood back.

'Your drinks,' she said. 'Is there anything else I can assist with?'

'No, thank you, Saoirse,' Matt said. 'If something comes up, we'll call!'

'She's a taciturn one,' he said to the others as Saoirse left. 'But deep down, she's got a heart of gold!'

He kept talking, but Quinn was distracted by the tray. Four mugs of steaming hot coffee sat before her, arranged around a plate of chocolate biscuits. The surface of the coffee was frothed up and artfully made to resemble a leaf. The biscuits, however, were what caught Quinn's attention – they were emanating a relicious aura.

'Oh, wow,' Kylie said, reaching for the mug closest to her. 'Latte art! And are those real Tim Tams?'

She picked up one of the biscuits and bit into it. 'Oh, my god,' she mumbled around the mouthful, 'I haven't had one of these for years!'

'We have a regular supply of Tim Tams here in Ark 2.' Matt grinned. 'The council has a direct contract with the factory in Shepparton. You know they almost went into ruin, following the End of the World? But since Tim Tams have relicious properties, the Government went out of their way to ensure the factory returned to full working order! And aren't we glad they did, eh?'

At the mention of relics, both Kylie and Mullet glanced quickly at Quinn. Quinn, meanwhile, was trying not to lean back or make it obvious that the Tim Tams made her unconformable. As the fuzziness began to descend, she reached down into her left pocket, closing her fingers around the matchbox hidden there. It helped a bit, although the vast unrealitic difference between her left hand and the plate of biscuits made her feel a bit queasy.

After a few minutes, Matt noticed that she hadn't touched her coffee or the biscuits at all – but fortunately, he entirely misinterpreted the reason.

'It's okay,' he said, smiling at her. 'It's all on the house! You don't have to hold back – eat as much as you want! The Ark is happy to have you here!'

Quinn shook her head. 'No thanks, I'm not hungry,' she muttered.

Matt frowned slightly. 'Are you okay?' he began. 'You look –'

Next to him, Mullet took a massive swig of coffee, and immediately spat it out again, all over the coffee table.

'Argh!' He gasped dramatically. 'That's nasty! Kylie, I told you it tastes like arse! Why is everyone so obsessed with this stuff?'

'Joey!' Kylie scolded, while Matt stared at the table in shock. 'Now look what you've done!'

'Oh.' Mullet looked down at the mess he'd made. 'Oh no, oh geez! Hang on, let me clean it up...'

He grabbed a tissue box off a nearby shelf and began frantically dabbing up the mess. A lot of it had gone on the Tim Tams and he picked each one up and individually wiped it off, before putting it back.

'There we go, good as new!' he proclaimed shortly.

Quinn looked down at the biscuits, most of which had tiny pieces of tissue stuck to them.

'Well, now I definitely don't want one,' she said.

Mullet winked at her.

The door abruptly opened again and Saoirse appeared. She was holding a cloth and a spray bottle. Without a word, she wiped up the rest of the mess and whisked away the tray, soggy tissues, biscuits and all.

'Damn,' Mullet said. 'How'd she know?'

'She's very good at her job,' Matt said faintly. He was still looking somewhat shocked.

Fortunately, they didn't have to wait much longer before the council meeting ended. As the sound of voices echoed in the hall outside, Matt hurriedly stood up.

'Sounds like they're out!' he said. 'C'mon – let's meet everyone, shall we?'

He opened the door to reveal a small crowd of senior citizens, each of them dressed elegantly in old-style fashions and scented of ancient, floral perfumes.

When Matt came out, several of them greeted him, before turning their gaze upon Quinn and the others. In moments, Quinn was surrounded.

'Ethan Bow,' a large, red-faced man wheezed, pumping her arm up and down. 'Treasurer of Ark 2, at your service!'

'Quinn,' Quinn said.

'Willow Keeble.' A woman with dyed red hair and enormous breasts laid a hand on her shoulder. 'Councillor for food, water and agriculture! How are you, darling?'

'I'm fine!' Quinn moved back a bit.

'Penelope Rayford.' A tiny, frail woman, eyes magnified through thick glasses, appeared at her elbow. 'Secretary of Ark 2. Nice to meet you, dear!'

'Hello!' Quinn squeaked, backing into a wall.

There were more, but Quinn instantly forgot their names and titles. Fortunately, none of them stuck around for long. Within minutes, the crowd had dispersed and shuffled off down the drive. As the last closed the front door behind them with a snap, Quinn breathed a small sigh of relief.

'Well, there you have it,' Matt said cheerfully. 'Ark 2's council! For the record, I'm the councillor for external affairs! Anyway – Ava awaits! What do you say, shall we go and meet the President?'

No one said anything – which he took as an affirmative.

'This way!' he said, and led them further into the house.

Shortly, they arrived at a huge set of double doors, made of solid hardwood. Beyond was a spacious room, its vaulted ceiling painted intricately with images of beautiful people dancing, feasting, and lounging on expensive furniture. At the back of the room, a sliding glass door opened out into a lush private garden and lagoon pool.

The room was otherwise entirely bare of furnishings, aside from a single, very long table, right in the centre. A thin woman in a pale blue cardigan and red lipstick sat at the far end, with a cup of tea and two plates in front of her. On one plate was her lunch – a small bird, roasted and drizzled in savoury sauces. On the other plate were more Tim Tams, their relicious aura dampened by distance.

'Ah,' she said when they came in, her voice echoing slightly in the massive room. 'You must be the new musicians. Welcome!'

Behind them, the door closed. Matt had apparently left.

Quinn and the others cautiously approached the table, seating themselves at the opposite end to the woman. Their chairs scraped nosily against the polished wooden floor.

The woman took a sip of her tea, smiling pleasantly at her guests. She had white hair, but did not come across as particularly old or frail. Instead, she radiated an aura of calm, indisputable power. It was immediately clear that she was the one in charge here.

'I am so glad you could make it,' she said, her voice clipped and proper. 'When I heard your music, I knew immediately that I HAD to meet you.'

Her gaze fell on Quinn.

'Quinn, wasn't it?' she said. 'The genius behind the music, correct?'

'Um,' Quinn said nervously. 'Yeah, I guess?'

'Well,' the woman said, 'allow me, as your fan, to congratulate you on your talent and your bravery. Musicians are a rare breed these days, especially those who create new material. It is a shame that the world has come to this – but in a way, it makes you all the more special.'

Quinn, who wasn't used to this many compliments at once, felt her face heat up in embarrassment. 'Aha, thanks,' she managed.

'You're so very welcome,' the woman said. 'But, I forget

myself! I am Madam Ava Brinesworth – president of the Ark, and life-long music enthusiast. You may call me Ava.'

She smiled and cut into her lunch. Meat sheered from bone, reddish juices seeping outwards.

'So,' she said, looking at Kylie and Mullet, 'if Quinn is the mastermind, then who are the two of you?'

'I'm the manager,' Kylie said, a little too sweetly. 'And he's the hired muscle.'

Mullet flexed quickly to demonstrate.

'Indeed,' Ava said. 'Well, my welcome extends just as warmly to the both of you. A musician cannot exist in a vacuum. Great art takes many hands.'

'Sure,' Kylie said. 'Um, not to derail the pleasantries, but can we talk about the contract now? We've wasted a lot of time to get here already and I don't even know yet if it's going to be worth it.'

Ava's eyebrows went up, just slightly.

'But of course,' she said, after a long pause.

She didn't call out or make any visible gestures, but a moment later, the double doors opened and Saoirse appeared. She was holding a manilla folder, which she placed in front of Kylie before disappearing again.

'You will find the documents enclosed,' Ava said as Kylie opened the folder. 'Please take your time to read through – but I will describe the contents in brief:

'Basically, you will stay here in Ark 2 and make original music – just as you already have been doing. You will be provided with a residence, free of charge, complete with full utilities, and have access to all facilities of the Ark. Each of you will also be provided with an allowance of three thousand dollars per month, with which you may purchase whatever goods and services you desire within the Ark. In return, all music you create will be licenced through me and I will oversee its sale and distribution. A fifteen per cent cut of all profits made, in addition to the allowance, will return to the artist. If the music is of high quality, then this cut can be quite significant.'

'I see,' Kylie said. 'So, Quinn becomes your cash cow and in return, she gets to use the public swimming pool?'

'Quinn gets to make music, unhindered by the fascist laws of the Last Nation,' Ava said calmly. 'And in return, I gain the exclusive rights to distribute it. It is what you might call a win-win situation.'

'Is it?' Kylie said. 'How do we know these "Ark facilities" are any good? What if the house you provide turns out to be a shithole? Are we allowed to leave?'

'Of course, you are allowed to leave,' Ava said. 'However, doing so will break the contract.'

'And what does that mean?' Kylie said.

'It means that your allowance will come to an end and your residence liable to be given to someone else,' Ava said. 'Additionally, all music created during the contract period will remain in my name and I will retain exclusive rights to its sale and distribution.'

'Yeah?' Kylie tilted her head. 'What happens if we sell it anyway?'

'Oh, you don't want to do that,' Ava said. She smiled as she said it – but her eyes glinted like ice.

Kylie clicked her tongue. 'Assassination, got it,' she said. 'So, how long does the contract last for?'

'Until you wish to leave,' Ava said.

'Hmm.' Kylie sat back. 'Well, if it's alright by you, I'm going to take my time reading the fine-print. Meanwhile, we'll take a little walk around the Ark – and if we like what we see, then we'll consider signing our lives away.'

'That's perfectly fine,' Ava said. 'Saoirse can give you the address of your residence, if you'd like. That way you may free yourself of the worry that it will turn out to be a "shithole".'

'Thank you.' Kylie gave an especially fake smile.

She took the manilla folder and stood up.

'Should we return here with our decision?' she asked.

'Oh no, no need.' Ava waved a hand. 'I'll send someone to find you in a couple of hours.'

'Okay,' Kylie said. 'Is that all then?'

'Yes, that will be all.'

Kylie nodded once, then turned and headed for the door. Quinn and Mullet hurriedly got up and followed after her.

As she left, Quinn sent Ava an apologetic look. Ava sent her a small wave in return, lip twitching in amusement.

Once the door was firmly closed, Quinn turned to eye Kylie reproachfully. 'Why did you have to be so rude?!' she asked.

'It's simple,' Kylie said as they headed down the hall. 'I just don't like the bitch.'

'Kylie!' Quinn said. 'You just met her!'

'Yeah, and trust me,' Kylie said. 'One to another, she's a bitch.'

'Okay,' Mullet said, 'but a free house? And free money? That sounds pretty sick, right?'

'It's not free,' Kylie said. 'We're paying with Quinn's soul.'

'I don't mind!' Quinn said. 'If I get to make music, I don't really care what happens to it. She can sell it if she likes. Some of the money comes back to us anyway, right?'

'Barely any,' Kylie said. 'Fifteen per cent? Fucking bullshit.'

'But three thousand dollars a month, each?' Mullet said. 'We don't have to spend it all here, do we? We could save it up! If we stay for just one year, then that's, uhhhhhh...'

His face wrinkled in effort as he tried to do the maths.

Kylie sighed.

'Look, on the surface, it's a good deal, I'm not gonna lie,' she said. 'We'd be making significantly more money than before, with zero additional risk or effort. I just...'

'Just what?' Quinn said.

'I just don't like her,' Kylie said, and she shrugged.

# CHAPTER 16

# MELODY SANDS

### Date: Tuesday 25 November 2081

'So this is it, huh?' Quinn said.

They were standing at the entrance to what looked like some sort of nautical-themed commune. A wide driveway ended in a cul-de-sac, surrounded by simple cottages, each of them gaudily painted to resemble a Brighton beach house. Between them were neatly kept gardens of coastal flora, and beyond, a lagoon pool before a massive seascape mural. At the front, a signpost declared the place to be Melody Sands.

Kylie took out the house-key she'd been given, thumbing over the attached sky-blue tag to read the address written there. 'This is it, alright,' she said, eyeing the place over the top of her sunnies. 'Tch. Kinda tacky.'

'Which one's ours?' Mullet asked.

'Number fifteen.' Kylie shrugged.

They walked up the driveway, heads turning as they looked from one garish cottage to the next. Each had a number above the front door and it didn't take them long to find fifteen. It was light blue, with thin orange stripes and a matching orange door.

'Very tacky,' Kylie said.

She unlocked the house and, curiously, they all poked their heads inside. It was definitely small, although compared to THE GLAM VAN, anything looked spacious. There were three distinct bedrooms and the laundry was separate from the bathroom.

'Yo!' Mullet yelled as they wandered through the house. 'We all get our own rooms? This is sick!'

'I bags this one!' Quinn yelled back.

'No you don't,' Kylie said. 'I haven't decided if we're staying yet.'

'Aw, c'mon!' Mullet appeared in the doorway. 'Why not? Our own rooms, Kylie! Three grand a month!'

Kylie just pursed her lips and went and turned on all the hot water taps.

After going around and opening all the cupboards, Quinn stopped by the front window and noticed that there was someone outside. It was a young South Asian man, with shaggy hair falling into his eyes and an oversized T-shirt with a graffiti style logo emblazoned across it. He was standing in the doorway of the cottage opposite, smoking a cigarette and doing a bad job of pretending he wasn't looking their way.

'Hey look,' Quinn said, 'there's our neighbour!'

'Where?' Mullet joined her. After staring at the young man for a moment, he went and opened the front door.

'Oi!' he called. 'Do you live here?'

'Yeah,' the young man called back, his voice weedier than Quinn had been expecting. 'You moving in?'

'Maybe,' Mullet said.

The young man stubbed out the cigarette and slouched across the cul-de-sac.

'Keanu,' he said, holding out his fist.

'Mullet,' Mullet said, bumping the fist with his own.

'So, what do you play?' Keanu asked.

'Huh?'

'What instrument do you play, dawg?'

'Oh, I don't play one,' Mullet said. 'Not yet, anyway. I want to play guitar, but Kylie won't let me.'

'Is that your girlfriend?' Keanu asked.

Mullet snorted in amusement. 'Nah, she's my cousin. Also my boss.'

'Aw, dude, that sucks that she won't let you play guitar,' Keanu said.

Quinn poked her head out the door.

'Hi,' she said. 'I'm Quinn. Um. Does everyone here play an instrument?'

'Yeah,' Keanu said. 'Melody Sands is mostly musicians.'

'Is it?' Quinn said in interest. She stepped outside, closing the door behind her. 'What instrument do YOU play?' she asked.

'Guitar, actually,' Keanu said. 'Hey.' He looked at Mullet. 'I could probably teach you, if you want? You can tell your cousin we're doing something else, like watching a movie or some shit.'

'They have movies here?' Mullet asked. 'With full sound?'

'Well, yeah,' Keanu said. 'It was, like, a major pastime, before music got banned.'

'That's fuckin' awesome,' Mullet said.

'Yeah.' Keanu grinned. 'Wanna see my collection?'

Mullet was about to say yes, but just then Kylie came out.

'Seems like everything in the house is functional,' she said, 'so I suppose it has that going for it. I wonder if we can repaint it, though?'

'Yeah, you can repaint it,' Keanu said. 'But you have to get it, like, approved by the council and stuff.'

Kylie looked at him. 'And who might you be?'

'Keanu,' Keanu said. 'I live here.'

'By yourself?'

'Nah, with my aunt and uncle. But they're not home right now.'

'Are all these houses occupied?' Kylie asked, gesturing at the surrounding cottages.

'Yeah, most of 'em,' Keanu said.

He pointed at each of the nearby houses in turn. 'Ms Janet lives there with her husband,' he said. 'She sings opera – you'll hear her, don't worry. Old dude called Leo lives there, he plays guitar really well, like, classical shit. That's Mr Austen's house, he has three arms and he plays piano with all of 'em. And that's Bridget's house – she has, like, twenty pet parrots in there. I dunno what else she does.

'Oh,' he added, pointing next door at number fourteen, 'and that's where the new girl moved in. I haven't spoken to her yet, but she seems cool. Goth or some shit.'

'There's a goth girl next door?' Mullet said, and he looked at Kylie. 'Can we PLEASE stay here?'

'I'm thinking about it,' Kylie said.

'Okay, but why?' Mullet said. 'Why are you still thinking about it? It's clearly awesome! There's movies, and music, and bedrooms for all of us, and a private swimming pool, and so much else!'

'There's also a spa at the back,' Keanu added in. 'And a self-serve tiki bar next to the pool.'

'Oh, there's a bar?' Kylie said – but then she shook her head and sighed.

'Here's the thing,' she said. 'Superficially, this place is pretty fucking great. I'm just concerned that once we get settled in, it's going to be very difficult to leave again. And if the place turns out to be a scam, or a cult, or even just some sort of extremely boring retirement home for people who can't accept that the world ended, then it's going to be more trouble than it's worth.'

'I mean, I've been here for two years now,' Keanu said, 'and it's not bad. A bit boring maybe, but there are festivals and shit like every other week. You can even get a job, if you're really bored. Dunno why you'd do that though, personally.'

'So, in your opinion,' Kylie said, 'Ark 2 is genuinely a nice place, and they give you free money, and there are no dodgy downsides?'

'Yeah?' Keanu shrugged.

'And the council definitely isn't a weird cult?'

'I don't think so?' Keanu wrinkled his nose. 'They all seem nice, anyway.'

'Even that Brinesworth bitch?'

'Oh, well, she is a bit scary.' Keanu laughed. 'But the rest of them are okay.'

'Just okay?' Kylie leaned in suspiciously.

'Yeah,' Keanu said. 'I mean, they're a bunch of old white people. I don't really hang with them, you know?'

'Hmm,' Kylie said, unconvinced.

She asked a few more questions, but Quinn had zoned out, thinking about the other musicians that lived just metres away in the other cottages. Then, as someone began walking up the drive, she turned to look – and grabbed Mullet's arm.

Mullet looked at her, then at the person who was approaching. His eyebrows shot up.

'Oh, hey!' he said. 'It's that girl from the concert! What was her name again?'

'Maggie!' Quinn hissed.

'Oh, you guys know the new girl already?' Keanu said.

'Yes!' Quinn said. 'Shit! Where do I hide?!'

'I think she's already seen you, actually,' Mullet said, smirking.

Quinn glared at him, and then shrunk into her hoodie as Maggie got closer. Crap! She didn't want to talk to Maggie again, not after last time!

It was too late though, Maggie had definitely seen them – and not only that, she lived next door! She stopped in front of her house now and looked at them through her circular glasses.

'Hi!' she said pleasantly. 'You guys were at Justin's concert, right?'

'Yeah!' Mullet said. 'Your bass piece was epic!'

'Thanks!' Maggie said, and her eyes fell on Quinn. 'Congrats on winning the comp, by the way,' she said. 'You deserved it. The rest of us never stood a chance.'

Quinn blinked in surprise.

'I...' she began.

'Sorry I yelled at you for touching the CDs, by the way,' Maggie said. 'And called you a rat. I was having a bit of a rough day and I took it out on you. I hope you can forgive me.'

Quinn opened and closed her mouth.

'S-sorry I said your dad's taste was shit,' she mumbled.

Kylie stepped forward.

'So, you signed Brinesworth's contract, then?' she asked, eyes narrowed.

'Yeah?' Maggie said. 'Why?'

'It doesn't bother you that any content you make doesn't belong to you anymore?' Kylie said.

'Well, no,' Maggie said. 'The opportunity to make music free from the fear of arrest is honestly worth it. Besides, I get fifteen per cent of the sales. That may not sound like a lot, but it's going to be a lot more than what I could make on my own. I don't have a long list of established buyers, like Ava does.'

'Okay, well I DO have a list of buyers,' Kylie said. 'And if I'm here for too long, then they're going to move their business elsewhere!'

'It's not as big as hers,' Maggie said. 'Trust me, I saw it. There are thousands of names on it.'

'You saw it?' Kylie raised an eyebrow.

'Yes, she showed it to me, after she sold some of my songs,' Maggie said. 'Showed me who bought them. There were literally hundreds, in a couple of days. Honestly blew my mind. I didn't even know there were that many people who listened to music.'

'Is that so?' Kylie said thoughtfully.

She fell silent.

Quinn opened her mouth again.

'Um,' she said. 'I don't think... I ever introduced myself. Um. I'm Quinn.'

'I know,' Maggie said, with a smile. 'I saw your performance, remember? Although, to be fair, I wasn't sure if it was your real name or not.'

'It is,' Quinn said. 'That was before I came up with a stage name.'

'Oh?' Maggie said. 'What's your stage name?'

'Temporal Boom,' Quinn said.

'Oh, that's pretty cool,' Maggie said. 'What does it mean?'

'Well,' Quinn said, looking everywhere but Maggie. 'It,

um. I guess... I mean, music is time and noise, arranged into a pattern, see? And when you... when time, um... there's like this feeling, like BOOM... and you know it'll kill you eventually, but you also can't stop, you know?'

She glanced at Maggie, aware that she was making very little sense.

Maggie, however, was nodding thoughtfully. 'Yeah,' she said. 'I get it. Music is like that. It resonates with your soul, in a way nothing else can. You know, I've been trying to think of a name for my own stuff, but nothing's stuck yet. I can't even think of names for my songs. They're all untitled.'

'Do you write lyrics?' Quinn asked curiously. 'I usually just name the song after one of the lines in it.'

'Nah, I don't write lyrics,' Maggie said. 'I never know where to start. But hey – if we're gonna be neighbours, maybe you can teach me?'

'Yeah!' Mullet interjected. 'And Keanu can teach me guitar at the same time! Jam sesh! Whoo!'

'Fuck yeah, dude,' Keanu said.

'Fine,' Kylie said.

Everyone looked at her.

'Are you saying, fine, we can stay?' Mullet said.

'Yes,' Kylie said. 'However,' she continued, while Mullet jumped up and down and violently pumped his fists, 'we will only stay for a couple of months, as a trial. If it goes well, maybe we'll stay longer. If I hate it, we're leaving. Okay?'

'Okay,' Quinn said, while Mullet played an air-guitar beside her.

'Good,' Kylie said. 'Alright – I suppose I will go and find Matt or one of the other council members and let them know. Also, we'll need to bring down all of our stuff from THE GLAM VAN, which might –'

She broke off, eyeing the driveway.

'Hello, hello!' Matt McCleave called, waving cheerfully as he strode up the drive. 'What do you think, eh? Do you like it?'

'Speak of the devil,' Kylie muttered – but she moved away to meet him.

When she was gone, Keanu nudged Mullet in the ribs. 'Is that Kylie?' he whispered.

'Yeah,' Mullet said.

'Dude,' Keanu said. 'Your cousin is pretty hot.'

'Nope,' Mullet said. 'Keanu, if we're gonna be friends, you're not allowed to say that ever again.'

'Fine,' Keanu said. 'But you can't stop me thinking it. Anyway, wanna see my movie collection?'

THE SECOND PORTENT

FIRST RECORDED SIGHTING: 12/06/2052, Sydney, Gadigal country, NSW

PHYSICAL APPEARANCE:

The Second Portent superficially resembles the iconic performing arts centre known as the Sydney Opera House, repeated recursively many times over, across a distance spanning hundreds of square kilometres. It consists of an arrangement of 'shell-like' or 'hemispherical' arches, each sprouting outwards from the convex surface of the 'shell' before it.

The 'shells' of the Second Portent vary greatly in size, from over 80m tall, to less than one millimetre. Regardless of height, they are identical in structure and colour. The outer face of each 'shell' appears uniform white from a distance, however subtle tile patterning is visible when viewed more closely. The concave inner face of each 'shell' resembles a public concert hall, constructed of glass, wood and concrete. Both outer and inner faces appear clean and new, with no signs of damage or wear. At night, both inner and outer faces are lit up with anomalously powered electrical lighting, and furniture and other public amenities are visible inside.

While appearing to be made of canonical materials, the Second Portent is constructed entirely of an anomalous, inert and highly stable form of matter. The precise qualities of this matter have to date proven impossible to measure; however, it is known to be extremely hazardous to living organisms. All living organisms, both complex and single-celled, that come into contact with the Second Portent are rapidly and irreversibly transformed into an equivalent mass of the Second Portent.

BEHAVIOUR:

Due to its capacity to create more of itself, the Second Portent expands in size each year. Initially, this expansion was extremely rapid, overtaking an area greater than 100km in diameter – a region now recognised as the Sydney Dead Zone. However, containment measures implemented four years following its appearance have resulted in the Second Portent expanding on average 2km squared each year.

Measures taken to reduce or halt the expansion of the Second Portent include, but are not limited to, the following:

- An exclusion zone no smaller than 2km in width should be maintained along the outer border of the Second Portent at all times. This clearing must be kept free of all life, including plants, fungi, animals and prokaryotic life. Highly concentrated salt, arsenic, heavy metals and other highly toxic chemical compounds can be used to prevent

plant and fungal growth and severely hinder
the growth of most prokaryote organisms.
Animals seen entering or flying over the zone
should be destroyed on sight.

- A dedicated force of personnel must
consistently patrol the outer rim of the
exclusion zone, and report any changes to the
Second Portent, no matter how minor, as soon
as possible. Patrols must contain a minimum
of three individuals, one of which must have
P.I.U.S abilities, so that minor changes in
unreality may also be recorded.

- Dedicated weather stations must be
constructed and maintained at regular
intervals along the exclusion zone perimeter,
positioned so that all segments of the border
are under coverage. The weather conditions
along the perimeter should be kept calm and
dry at all times, with minimal wind and rain.

- Relic stations must be positioned at
regular intervals between the weather
stations, each containing one or more tier 5
relic. These are present only as a last
resort means of containment, should all other
systems fail, and should not solely be relied
on.

Note – the section of the Second Portent that
extends to the East of its point of origin is
fully submerged beneath the South Pacific
Ocean. This section of the Portent is much
more difficult to observe, and it is not fully
known how far it extends.

Note 2 – Canberra, the capital of old

Australia, was constructed as a compromise, when rival cities Sydney and Melbourne each refused to let the other have the title. Canberra was built in New South Wales, but only under the condition that it be constructed at least 100 miles (160km) away from Sydney.

Due to the expansion of the Second Portent, an argument was made that Canberra was no longer 100 miles from Sydney, and thus could no longer be the capital. This argument contributed to the official redesignation of the Last Nation's capital to Melbourne in 2056.

PORTENT INDUCED UNREALITY SYMPTOMS:

Due to its 100% lethality index there are no realitysmiths of the Second Portent.

# CHAPTER 17

# BIG KOALA

## Date: Thursday 12 March 2082

At 5AM on the dot, the Detective unplugged themselves from the wall. They woke up Bill and, while he blearily locked himself in the bathroom, they began tidying the office, ready to leave it behind cleaner than when they'd arrived.

They managed to rearrange the desk, sweep the floor and remove the cobwebs from just over half of the windows before Bill came out again, dressed in a fresh Hawaiian shirt and scowling groggily. He had already packed his suitcase the evening before and was ready to leave faster than the Detective had anticipated. They complimented him on this as they headed out the airlock. His only response was a zombie-like stare.

After analysing their options, the Detective had decided that the solar station was their best bet in finding a vehicle heading southwards – with luck, directly to Ouyen. As they approached the station, however, they noticed one immediate issue with the plan: there were no vehicles in sight. The lot, small to begin with, was entirely empty. A single piece of white Styrofoam tumbled across the tarmac in the breeze.

Frowning slightly, the Detective headed for the solar station's attached convenience store. The lights at the station were on, although there didn't appear to be anyone behind the counter.

The Detective went in anyway and Bill shambled in after

them. There was a buzzer on the desk, under a sign which read 'please ring for service'.

The Detective did so. A few moments later, there were footsteps and an old man came in through a door at the back.

"Ello 'ello!' he said. 'How can I help you, this fine morning?'

'Do you know if there are any vehicles scheduled to travel southwards within the next few hours?' the Detective asked without preamble.

'Ah, sorry,' the man said. 'I haven't a clue. Chances are, they'll be a few – although I wouldn't count on it.'

'Why shouldn't I count on it?' the Detective said.

'Well, ever since Mildura disappeared, our traffic has gone way down,' the man said. 'Most people who came through here were going to Mildura, see. No one's making the trip just to come to Red Cliffs.'

'I see,' the Detective said. 'That is a problem.'

'Yup,' the man said. 'Can I help you with anything else?'

Bill shuffled forward.

'Coffee,' he said, slapping a twenty dollar note on the counter.

'Oh,' the man said. 'Sorry. We're out of coffee.'

Bill sighed, deeply.

'Tea?' he asked.

'Now that, I can do!' the man said.

While he turned around and began making Bill a tea, the shop was suddenly washed with light as a pair of hi-beams turned into the lot. The Detective immediately went to look out the window. Outside, a white sedan reversed into a parking spot and cut its engine. The driver's door opened and an overweight Caucasian man in blue overalls got out, heading straight for the convenience store.

The second he stepped inside, the Detective moved to intercept him.

'Hello,' they said, looming over him. 'Are you the owner of that vehicle?'

The man eyed the Detective with a guarded expression. 'Yeah?' he said.

'Okay,' the Detective said. 'Might I ask whether you happen to be travelling southwards? My companion and I require transport to Ouyen, as soon as possible. We are willing to compensate you financially.'

'Oh, that's what this is,' the man said. 'Nah, sorry, ma'am. I'm going north.'

He attempted to skirt around the Detective.

'You're going north?' the Detective followed him. 'Where are you going, might I ask?'

'Mildura,' the man said. 'Not that it's any of your business.'

'I thought you might be,' the Detective said. 'Considering how little else there is directly north of here. That means you haven't heard the news.'

'What news?' The man frowned.

The Detective picked up a newspaper from a stand nearby and handed it to him. On the front page, in massive font, were the words TOP SCIENTISTS BAFFLED BY MILDURA'S DISAPPEARANCE, above a photo of the flat plain where Mildura had previously been.

The man blinked at it for several seconds.

'What?!' he said.

'Yup, it's true, Mildura disappeared on Sunday,' the store attendant said, handing Bill his tea. 'Whole bloody thing. ZAP! POW! Gone in an instant. Rumours are it's a new Portent that did it.'

The man looked from the newspaper to the attendant to the Detective and back again.

'Is this some sort of joke?' he said.

'Nope,' the attendant said. 'It's not. Although somewhere, God is laughing at us and thumbing his nose.'

'I...' the man said, and he scratched his head. 'Well, what am I supposed to do, then?'

'Go back home, I suppose,' the attendant said.

The Detective waited for a few seconds, letting him

digest the news in silence, before once more sliding into view.

'So,' they said, 'if you are no longer going to Mildura… will you be going southwards?'

'Well,' the man said slowly. 'I… I suppose so…'

'And would you be able to take myself and my colleague with you?' the Detective asked.

The man looked at them wearily.

'Look,' he said. 'If I take you to Ouyen, you said you'd pay me, right?'

'Yes,' the Detective said.

'Well, alright, then,' the man said.

***

After wasting a small amount of time buying and eating a consolatory meat pie, the owner of the vehicle led the Detective and Bill outside and gestured that they should get in. The Detective climbed into the passenger's seat and Bill squeezed into the back along with his luggage.

It was just after 6:30AM when they set off for Ouyen, which meant they would arrive around 8:30AM. This would give them plenty of time to introduce themselves at the Ouyen Department of Sin branch office, before investigating the landing site of the First in the afternoon.

Aside from introducing himself as Stevo, the driver was quiet, at least for the first twenty minutes of travel. After that, he asked the Detective whether Mildura was really gone and, upon discovering that they were somewhat of an expert on the subject, asked a lot of follow-up questions.

The Detective was just explaining that there was currently no hard evidence that a Twelfth Portent existed when they drove out of a dense cluster of squat, scraggly trees and immediately caught sight of something strange in the distance.

Ahead, while trees continued on the right, to the left the land was very open and flat. About two hundred metres away was a single shallow hill. And sitting at the top of the hill was an extremely large koala.

Based on the distance, the Detective calculated that it had to be about fourteen metres tall. It was sitting perfectly still, eyes staring blankly into the distance – and after a moment, the Detective concluded that it was actually a building, or a very large statue.

Next to them, Stevo was struggling to keep his eyes on the road.

'What in the blazers is that?!' he said.

'A koala, I believe,' the Detective said calmly.

'Yeah, I can see that!' Stevo said. 'But what's it doing there?!'

'I could not say,' the Detective said. 'As I see it, human behaviour is not, for the most part, logical.'

'No, I mean,' Stevo said, 'usually, it's near Horsham!'

The Detective blinked.

'What –' they began.

Ahead, a tree abruptly toppled into their path.

Stevo swore, breaking hard and swerving off the road as branches bounced on tarmac just ahead. Gravel caused the tires to skid as they careened towards the empty field, smashing through an old fence before slamming sideways into another tree and coming to a stop.

The airbags deployed. Stevo continued to swear for another thirty seconds.

The Detective, meanwhile, ran a quick diagnostic to determine structural damage to their carapace. In the back, Bill, who had been asleep until a few seconds ago, clutched at the seat in front of him and stared about wildly.

The Detective's damage report revealed only minor issues – the prolonged skid into the field had slowed them enough to reduce the impact of the crash. The next priority, however, was getting out of the vehicle.

'If you would please open the driver's door!' they said loudly, over Stevo's continued swearing. 'The passenger door has been crushed!'

Stevo tried the driver door, which opened without issue,

and he hurriedly got out. The Detective followed, while Bill climbed out the back. They were greeted by the sight of four masked bushrangers, guns levelled in their direction.

Bill and Stevo immediately froze, hands raised. The Detective hesitated, processing this latest development, before slowly raising their hands as well.

One of the gun-wielders, a tall, lanky Caucasian man with a cowboy hat and a blue bandana across his nose and mouth, stepped closer.

'Alright,' he said, his voice muffled through the cloth. 'You know what this is. We're taking the car and everything in it. In return, you get to live. Understand?'

The Detective looked him up and down. His firearm was unregistered and, not only that, was not equipped with a suppressor. This, plus the fact that he was talking in the open, showed a blatant disregard for noise mitigation laws.

'Good,' the lanky man continued. 'Here's what you're gonna do. You're gonna put your hands on your heads, like this, and you're gonna walk away in a straight line. You're gonna keep walking until you're out of sight. If you look back, we'll shoot. If you show any signs of doing anything other than walking away in a straight line, we'll shoot. Got it? Nod if you get it.'

Bill and Stevo nodded quickly. The Detective, however, did not.

The lanky man squinted at them.

'Do you not get it?' he said. 'Are you stupid? Because trust me, you are in no position to play the hero. Hands on your fuckin' head.'

Watching him, the Detective moved their hands slowly upward. Inside their left wrist, delicate machinery quietly shifted into a new position. Two shiny metal nibs, near the base of the thumb and the pinkie, twisted their way out of the synth-skin.

'That's right,' the man said. 'Now, choose a direction and off you go. And remember, if you so much as glance back –'

For just a second, he looked away – and the Detective pounced.

Quick as lightning, they crossed the two metres between them and slammed their left palm into the base of his throat, unleashing fifty thousand volts.

He spasmed and began to collapse, dropping his gun. With their right hand, the Detective caught it, engaged the safety and clocked him heavily in the temple. As he sunk to the ground, lights out, they turned and threw the gun as hard as they could at the head of the next closest bushranger.

It connected with a solid SMACK and the bushranger stumbled back. Before they could recover, the Detective charged in and followed through with a powerful uppercut.

The next one had time to raise her gun, but not fire it, before the Detective's hand-taser caught her in the collarbone. As she buckled, her shot going wildly astray, the Detective hauled her around to face the last man, preparing to use her as a human shield if necessary.

It wasn't. The last of the group, an adolescent male, was clearly panicking, backing away, his gun hand wavering.

The Detective took a moment to properly incapacitate the human shield, before placing her down, and staring grimly at the last man standing.

*You are under arrest,* they signed at him. *Do not resist.*

Eyes wide, he took another step back. The Detective saw his finger tighten on the trigger.

The Detective was not the sort to issue a warning twice. Before he could make the decision between running or shooting, they leapt towards him and snatched the gun from his hand.

He let out a torrent of swear words and turned to run, but too slowly. The Detective grabbed his arm, spun him around and slammed him bodily into the dirt.

They were not carrying any handcuffs on them and so settled for sitting on his legs. With a free hand, they waved Bill to come closer.

*Rope,* they signed.

Bill stared back at them, mouth slightly open.

*I don't have any,* he returned after a moment. *But... wait!*

He went back to the crumpled car and dragged out his suitcase. Digging inside, he found a necktie and brought it over. It was sea-green, with tiny orange starfish patterned across it.

It would do for now. The Detective took it and tied the young man's hands behind his back. Then, standing up, they moved around where he could see them.

*You are under arrest,* they informed him again, *for the following sins: Highway robbery. Intentional property damage. Possession of illegal firearms. Creation of unnecessary noise. Threatening an officer of the Department of Sin.*

His face smeared with dirt, the young man glared at the Detective and Bill. Stevo also approached, a scowl on his face.

'Would someone mind telling me what in the flying fuck is happening?!' he said.

The Detective turned and gave him a stern look. *Remain quiet while outside,* they signed.

'No,' Stevo said hotly, 'I think I at least deserve a bit of slack in that department! First Mildura disappears, then the Big Koala appears, then I'm in a fucking car accident, then bushrangers threaten to shoot me, and now, it turns out my passenger is some sort of freakish superhuman?'

'Cyborg,' Bill said faintly.

'A cyborg, huh?' Stevo said. 'Great! What next?! A piano falls from the sky and strikes me dead?'

A second after he spoke, there was an extremely loud CRACK, like thunder, but much closer.

Stevo yelled in shock and Bill immediately dropped to the ground, hands over his head. The Detective ducked, looking wildly around for the source of the noise.

It took them a second to see what had changed. The low hill behind them looked different somehow – then they realised why.

The Big Koala had disappeared.

# CHAPTER 18

# SMALL KOALA

### Date: Thursday 12 March 2082

After using more of Bill's novelty ties to secure the other three bushrangers, the Detective removed their masks and laid them out in a line beside the damaged car. After scanning their faces, the Detective identified two of them – one Lachie Flemington and one Fitzy Walsh – as repeat offenders for a range of petty crimes, although neither had been arrested for highway robbery before. The other two, who were clearly younger, had apparently been recently recruited into a life of sin, as there were no previous criminal records for either of them.

The Detective picked up the one conscious member, hauling him over their shoulder and placing him into the backseat of the car, which, while damaged, was still much more soundproofed than outside. Then, after getting into the front seat and shutting the door, they turned around to stare at him unblinkingly.

'I am going to ask you some questions,' they said, 'and I expect truthful answers. Do not attempt to be evasive – I will not tolerate such a waste of time. Do not attempt to lie to me either – I will know.'

In the backseat, the young man hunched his shoulders and looked at the floor. The panic had left him, to be replaced with indignation. He was angry at the Detective and embarrassed at his own failure to escape them.

'First of all, what is your full name?' the Detective said to him.

His lip curled. 'Damian Cash,' he muttered.

'And how old are you?'

'Seventeen.'

'And the other three,' the Detective asked, 'what are their names?'

Damian scowled. 'Why don't you ask them?' he said petulantly.

'They are unconscious,' the Detective said. 'You must answer the questions in their stead.'

'Yeah, well, don't I have the right to remain silent?' Damian said.

'You have an obligation to remain silent, while outside,' the Detective told him. 'One which, in the very act of carrying an unsilenced gun, you have demonstrated your disdain for. I will not ask again – what are the names of the other three?'

Damian opened and closed his mouth.

'Fucking Trent,' he muttered. 'I SAID we needed fucking suppressors.'

'Trent?' The Detective cocked their head.

'Uhh,' Damian said, eyes darting away. 'The man in the hat?'

The Detective narrowed their eyes.

'You are lying,' they said. 'That man is called Lachie. Who is Trent?'

Damian went silent.

'How many other members of your gang are there?' The Detective leaned closer. 'Where are they? Are they inside the Big Koala?'

'I'm not saying shit.' Damian crossed his arms. 'And you can't make me. I know my rights.'

'Does Trent control the movements of the Big Koala?' the Detective said.

'He controls the movement of your mum's arse,' Damian said.

'I do not have a mother,' the Detective said.

They fell silent, thinking. Then, they abruptly opened the door of the car and got out.

'That's right, you can fuck right off!' Damian called, as they shut the door.

Bill immediately approached.

*Did you find anything?* he asked.

*There are more members of the gang,* the Detective signed. *I believe they are hiding inside the Big Koala. It is likely that at least one of them is a rogue spacesmith, who is able to move the Koala at will.*

Bill nodded thoughtfully. *That makes sense,* he signed back. Then his brow furrowed. *We'll never find them,* he said.

*I disagree,* the Detective signed back.

Bill raised an eyebrow.

*No time to explain,* the Detective said. *Stay here.*

With no further warning, they turned and sprinted off across the field.

The logic was simple – the simplest reason for the Big Koala to instantaneously appear or disappear was that it was being controlled by one or more spacesmiths. After scanning rapidly through several Department of Unreality documents on spacesmith symptoms, the Detective had found out several things:

Firstly, they had confirmed that a common spacesmith symptom was the ability to instantaneously transpose objects in four-dimensional spacetime.

Secondly, while individual ability varied significantly, it was commonly understood that objects of larger mass, greater complexity or high relicity were generally more difficult to transpose.

Thirdly, the more difficult it was to teleport an object, the smaller distance the spacesmith could teleport it.

Lastly, the Big Koala was a large, complex and very heavy object, with a relicity index of three.

There had been an equation in one of the articles, mathematically describing the relationship between mass of object, relicity, magnitude of symptom and distance of teleportation. While the Detective did not know the magnitude of this particular spacesmith's ability, they could make an informed guess – and as a result, they were able to calculate the distance.

Assuming there was one spacesmith, with a symptom magnitude towards the upper recorded limit, then at maximum, the Big Koala could only be around one and half kilometres away. If there were two spacesmiths, then this could be increased to a maximum of four kilometres.

The Detective could run that in under five minutes.

Of course, there was no way of knowing for certain which direction the Koala had teleported in – but again, the Detective had made an informed guess.

The road they'd been travelling along ran north-south. To the north and east were dense trees, which the Detective figured might present a hazard, especially if teleporting in a hurry. To the south, the road continued straight, into private farmland, which was flat and free of trees, but not without the risk of being seen. To the west, meanwhile, there was nothing but abandoned, overgrown fields for about nine kilometres.

The Detective knew which direction they would have chosen. Whether or not the spacesmith had made their decision with such logic remained to be seen.

They sprinted due west for three and a half minutes, and then stopped to scale another small hill. At the top, they stared west – but could see nothing out of the ordinary. Turning south, they stared at a distant field of sheep. Then, turning north, they scanned the treeline. Still nothing.

They were about to climb down from the hill, when they saw it – a small cluster of trees to the northeast of their hill. There was something sitting behind it – something with large, distinctly koala-shaped ears.

It was sitting 2.8 kilometres from its previous location. Two smiths, then.

Wordlessly, the Detective sprinted towards it.

Rounding the trees, they confirmed that they'd found the Big Koala. As they neared it, however, slowing to a jog, the door between its front legs opened and a man stepped out. He was holding an old-fashioned hunting rifle and it was trained directly on the Detective.

'Stop RIGHT the fuck there!' he called.

The Detective came to an abrupt halt. They were still fifteen metres away from the Big Koala – which was a bit too far to run before the man got a shot off. And if it hit, the rifle would do a lot more structural damage than the Detective was comfortable with.

*You're under arrest,* they signed at the man. *Do not try to resist. Do not attempt to teleport the Koala.*

'Oh, fuck off!' the man called. Behind him, inside the Koala, there was a faint wail. It sounded like a child crying. The man glanced briefly towards the sound and back again, his eyes darting away from the Detective and into the trees. He was looking distinctly nervous, sweat beading at his temple.

'Fucking pig freak!' he yelled. 'What the FUCK are you anyway?'

*I am an officer of the Department of Sin,* the Detective said. *You are under arrest. Do not resist or run. If you attempt to run, I will find you again.*

The man licked his lips and tightened the grip on his gun, raising it to point at the Detective's head.

'Fuck off now and I won't shoot you!' he called. 'Take one step closer though, and I'll rearrange your face! I'm warning you!'

*I am able to rearrange my own face, thank you,* the Detective said.

While the man processed this response, there was another wail from inside the Koala, louder this time. The Detective wondered whether it was one of the spacesmiths. It was possible they were currently experiencing a painful post-symptom side effect.

If this was the case, it meant there was very little chance the Koala was about to teleport a second time – which was good news. They'd said that they would find the Koala again – and they could, twice, but twice only. Sprinting to the Koala's current location had already cost them twenty-six per cent of their daily power. That, combined with the use of the left hand taser, meant they only had two more attempts left in them before they would be forced to give it up.

They simply couldn't afford to wait around all day – but fortunately, they had already formulated a new plan of attack. The next time a wail emanated from the Koala, they burst into action.

The man, distracted by the cry of distress, reacted too slowly. As the Detective sprinted clockwise around the Koala, the rifle shot went wide.

It would take several seconds to reload. It took the same amount of time for the Detective to circle all the way around the Koala, spiralling inwards at a sharp angle. As the man got ready to shoot a second time, the Detective appeared at his left elbow. He yelled as they grabbed the barrel of his gun, pulling him off balance. A second later, their electrified left hand connected with his collarbone, and his scream cut off as he toppled to the ground.

Inside, the wail abruptly fell silent.

The Detective secured the man's hands and feet with more of Bill's novelty neckties, then dragged him inside, to lie dazed in the corner. After quickly scanning his face, they located his criminal record and confirmed his name to be Trent Umberfield. They then closed the door to preserve soundproofing and began looking around.

The inside of the Koala was a small, two storey house, with tools, furniture and amenities crammed into every centimetre. There was no one on the ground floor – but after going upstairs, the Detective discovered a pair of children.

They were almost certainly the spacesmiths. Huddled at the far end of the upstairs room, they were inside a large metal cage, which appeared to be nailed directly to the floor and the wall behind. They were both boys, the older one around eight years old and the younger around six.

The younger had clearly been crying, his eyes still wet. He was huddled on the floor, clutching a plushie koala tightly to his chest. The older was crouched in front of him in a defensive stance, ready to protect his brother, despite the fear in his eyes.

When the Detective entered the room, the younger boy screamed piercingly and buried his face into his toy. The older boy's eyes widened and he backed away, teeth bared in fear.

They were clearly being held captive here – and based on their behaviour, the Detective thought it likely they had not been treated particularly well. They opened their mouth, but then paused, uncertain what to say in such a circumstance.

'Do not be afraid,' they said momentarily. 'I will not harm you. Do not engage your P.I.U.S. You are being rescued.'

This didn't seem to help at all – in fact, moving closer only seemed to be making things worse. After standing for a moment, the Detective decided that they were not particularly well equipped to deal with frightened children and went downstairs again.

Trent was attempting to wriggle away – but he stopped when the Detective came into view and pretended to be unconscious.

The Detective picked him up like a sack of potatoes and dumped him back in the corner. Then, they crouched down to talk to him.

'How long have you been keeping those spacesmiths captive?' they asked.

'Fuck you,' Trent spat.

'Are you aware that the use of unregistered realitysmiths for non-emergency situations is illegal?' the Detective continued. 'Additionally, there are many legal and ethical issues related to the storage of minors in cages. This is not to mention the fact that you have stolen a relicious object from its rightful place, and are using it to commit sins. It is a truly deplorable track record.'

'Fuck you, and your mother,' Trent said.

'As I already mentioned to your young associate,' the Detective said, 'I do not have a mother.'

Behind them, the door abruptly banged open. The Detective hurriedly stood up – but it was just Bill.

He was gasping for breath, his collar and underarms soaked with sweat. Coughing twice, he pointed at the Detective and then doubled over to cough again.

'You!' he managed, between gasps. 'What... *wheeze*... did... *wheeze*... I say... *wheeze*... about running... *wheeze*... off?!'

'I apologise,' the Detective said, eyeing him critically. 'I was not sure how long I would have before the Koala teleported a second time and subsequently became more difficult to locate.'

Bill raised a hand, shaking his head. 'We have... a car!' he wheezed. 'Could have... driven!'

'That vehicle is no longer roadworthy,' the Detective said.

Bill made a face. 'No longer...? Are you serious?! Do you know how far I just ran?!'

'Yes,' the Detective said. 'I ran the same distance. Might I suggest that you work on your physical fitness in the future.'

Bill sent them an exasperated look.

'In any case,' the Detective continued. 'I am glad you are here. There are two spacesmiths upstairs, who are minors. They are being held captive and are currently experiencing a state of prolonged fear. I admit that your skillset is more appropriate than mine for dealing with this particular problem.'

'Oh, shit,' Bill said seriously.

Without another word, he gathered himself and ran up the stairs.

The Detective went back to questioning Trent – but with little success. Trent was extremely uncooperative, his answers composed exclusively of swearing and insults.

After a few minutes, the Detective gave it up and went to see how Bill was doing. Bill, however, immediately shooed them away.

'They're a bit scared of you,' he said in a low voice. 'Give me a few more minutes to calm them down. Ten minutes, let's say.'

'Okay,' the Detective said and left again.

After trussing Trent very firmly to a tree outside, they used the time to go back to Stevo and the car, and make sure the other offenders were not attempting to escape. This time, they jogged rather than sprinting, as they wanted to preserve power. It wasn't even 8:30AM, and they were already approaching half battery.

Stevo was sitting on a rock, a few metres from the still unconscious bushrangers. When he saw the Detective coming, he stood up, frowning and rubbing his backside.

*What's happening now?* he signed grumpily.

The Detective briefly filled him in on the new developments and he sighed.

*Right,* he said, *what next?*

The Detective had been pondering the same thing.

Ideally, they would next bring their detainees to the nearest sin-seeker office for processing. The problem was, the nearest office was in Ouyen, over thirty kilometres away.

With Stevo's car wrecked as it was, the Detective wasn't sure how best to traverse that distance. Walking would take several hours, or longer, since the detainees were unlikely to make things easy. And they couldn't rely on another vehicle passing by with any regularity, let alone stopping and lending aid.

The Detective could run to Ouyen alone, and return with a different vehicle – but with their battery already running low, they could not afford to sprint, and therefore this would still take several hours.

The only other option the Detective could think of involved using the spacesmiths to teleport someone directly to Ouyen, thus instantaneously negating the multi-hour trek. But, while it was permitted in emergency situations, the legality of this option was still uncomfortably sketchy – and besides, there was a good chance the spacesmiths would be unwilling, or unable, to cooperate.

After ten minutes, the Detective jogged back to the Koala again, and once more checked on Bill.

It was immediately clear that he was making headway. The two boys were sitting close to him, just inside the cage, and they were both looking a lot more relaxed.

When the Detective came up, they both hunched down slightly, staring across the room with wary expressions. Bill turned and waved at the Detective cheerily.

'See?' he said to the boys. 'There's nothing to be scared of, honest! Why don't you say hello?'

'H-hello,' the older boy said, in a small voice.

The younger boy hid behind his koala toy.

'Detective,' Bill said. 'Meet Arlo and Levi.'

The Detective nodded, impressed at Bill's progress. Although he was slow at times, the short sidekick did have his uses.

'Bill, I wish to talk to you downstairs,' they said.

Once they were out of earshot of the children, they explained to Bill their latest conundrum.

'Are you sure that the car isn't an option?' Bill said.

'It is not legally driveable in its current state,' the Detective said.

'Right.' Bill sighed. 'And we gotta stick to the letter of the law, at all times.'

'Yes,' the Detective said. 'Although...'

Bill tilted his head. 'Although?'

'There is another method of transport,' the Detective said, glancing up the stairs. 'While not expressly illegal, it is not exactly gold standard either. It is, however, the fastest option available by a considerable margin.'

'You want to use the spacesmiths?' Bill frowned. 'I don't know if they're up to that, Detective.'

'I am aware they are in a state of stress,' the Detective said. 'In order to minimise further stress and maximise effectiveness, we should send only one person, who would then return with a vehicle to collect everyone else. I would propose that you would be the best option to send, as the spacesmiths are the most comfortable around you. Using your mass and assuming the spacesmiths are able to act outside of the Big Koala's relicious aura, I have calculated that Ouyen is well within the limits of their ability. It would take only one trip and, assuming you are able to acquire a vehicle from the Ouyen Sin-Seeker Office within ten minutes, will mean you are back here in approximately forty minutes. This is two and half hours earlier than the next best option.'

'Hmm, okay,' Bill said. 'Um. Do you think the sin-seeker office will give me a vehicle that easily?'

'I will lend you my badge,' the Detective said.

'Alright,' Bill said. 'Well... I suppose I can ask the boys if they'd be willing to do it. I'm not going to force it, though. If they say no, then they say no, okay?'

'Okay,' the Detective said.

They followed Bill back upstairs and watched as he explained the situation to the boys. They initially seemed unenthusiastic, but when Bill said they would be leaving the Koala behind, they both brightened.

'Are we leaving it forever?' Arlo, the older boy, asked.

'Yes,' Bill said.

Arlo grinned, before his brow furrowed.

'Where will we live?' he asked.

'I will take you to the Sanctuary,' Bill said. 'Which... well, you probably won't like it much, not at first. It has an aura, just the Koala. But it's nicer than here. You'll have proper beds and all the food you could ever want. And I'm confident you'll get through the training, easy-peasy! After that, you'll be sent on placement, and get to do and see all sorts of things! Just you wait!'

The boys eyed him with solemn expressions.

'Well,' Arlo said slowly. 'I don't mind doing it. And Levi doesn't mind either. Do you, Levi?'

His little brother shook his head.

'But we need a shell,' Arlo said seriously.

'A shell?' Bill asked. 'As in... from the beach?'

'No.' Arlo shook his head. 'It's an object that you go inside. It has to be all around, and made of mostly the same stuff, otherwise it doesn't work. Also, we need a small copy to tie it to.'

'A small copy?' Bill wrinkled his brow.

'Yeah,' Arlo said, and he pointed to the toy koala that his brother was still holding.

'That's the small copy of the Koala,' he said.

'Oh, I think I understand,' Bill said. 'You're saying that in order to teleport, we all have to sit inside an object, and the object has to completely surround us. For example, if we sat inside a car, you would be able to teleport the entire car, with us inside it. But if one of the doors was missing, it wouldn't work.'

'Yeah.' Arlo nodded.

'And you also need a small version of the object you are teleporting,' Bill said. 'For example, in our car scenario, you would need something like a matchbox car, to act as a sort of power focus. Is that right?'

'Yeah!' Arlo grinned.

'Right,' Bill said. 'Did you get all that, Detective?'

'Yes,' the Detective said. 'Would the cage you are inside currently suffice as a "shell"?'

'No,' Arlo said. 'The back wall and the floor are made of different stuff.'

'What if they were not?' the Detective said.

While Bill stared at them in mild alarm, they advanced on the cage and abruptly began ripping it out of the floor. Nails screamed as they were pulled from hardwood. Backs against the far wall, the two boys watched on in wide eyed awe.

After detaching the entire thing, the Detective folded the sides in, and carried the cage downstairs. Bill hurried after them, boys close behind him like a pair of imprinted ducklings.

The Detective took the cage outside, a hundred metres from the Koala, and then placed it down. Then, they paused, raising their right hand.

Machinery hissed quietly, and their right thumb folded away. A second later, a large, serrated blade clicked into its place.

Using the blade, they went to work on the metal. The cage had had four sides in total – three walls and the roof. The Detective carefully cut corners off each square until it resembled a triangle instead. Then, using spare strips of metal from the parts they'd shaved off, they tied the triangle shapes together, leaving one open for access.

Once the metal tetrahedron was complete, they stepped back, and looked at the two spacesmiths.

*Is this shell adequate?* they asked.

Arlo nodded, his eyes very round.

The Detective picked up a few more of the scraps, and rapidly twisted them around each other. Shortly, they were holding a much smaller tetrahedron in their hand. Blank faced, they handed it to Arlo, who gingerly accepted it.

Bill grinned and gave the Detective a double thumbs up. *This is great!* he signed. *Perfect!*

The Detective inclined their head.

*I urge you to go as soon as possible,* they said.

Bill nodded and beckoning for the boys to follow him, he stepped inside the tetrahedron. It was not a large space, but the boys were small, and all three of them fit inside. Bill closed up the final side, holding it closed via a handle the Detective had included on the inner face. Then, he made shooing motions at the Detective until they moved well back.

*Okay,* the Detective saw him say to the boys. *Do you know where we're going?*

They both nodded. *Ouyen,* Arlo signed. *We know it.*

*Good,* Bill said. *Alright. When you're ready then.*

He visibly braced, while the boys looked at each other. Arlo grabbed Levi's hand and then held up the small copy, staring at it.

There was a pause as both boys focused on the small copy. Then, Arlo abruptly extended his arm to the side, fingers splayed.

The tetrahedron vanished.

Its disappearance was followed a second later by a deafening clap of thunder.

## THE TENTH PORTENT

FIRST RECORDED SIGHTING: 23/05/2069, Perth, Whadjuk Nyoongar country, WA

PHYSICAL APPEARANCE:

The Tenth Portent is an anomalous spatial phenomenon, capable of manifesting inside and instantaneously replacing the interior of an existing housing structure. While the exterior appearance of the affected house, apartment, mobile home, etcetera, does not visibly change, its interior becomes that of the Tenth Portent, regardless of previous floor plan, size and specific furnishings.

The Tenth Portent resembles a two-storey, four-bedroom, two-bathroom suburban family home. It has plastered, off-white walls and timber floors, aside from bedrooms, which are carpeted, and the bathroom/laundry, which is tiled.

The house is fully furnished and appears well maintained, with functional electrical lights, running water and central heating. These systems operate regardless of whether or not the hosting structure is connected to an electrical grid or plumbing system. All surfaces inside the house appear recently cleaned and are free of dust, dirt or mould. The furniture present, as well as framed photographs visible in the hallway, suggest

that the house is occupied by a family of
five, including two adults, three children,
and a pet Jack-Russel Terrier.

While initially appearing to be an ordinary
home, the interior of the Tenth Portent
displays several anomalous properties,
including the following:

1 – All doors that should lead to the
exterior of the house instead lead to the
main entrance of the hosting structure. This
includes the front door, the kitchen door and
the laundry door.

2 – All external-facing windows in the house
look out onto the same yard, regardless of
their position. The yard, which is surrounded
by tall hedges, contains several pieces of
children's play equipment including a
trampoline, a set of swings and a small
sandpit. The sky above the hedges is always
overcast and always daytime.

3 – All timepieces within the house display
1:43 PM. All timepieces taken into the house
will continue as normal, until reaching 1:43
PM, at which point they will freeze in place.
After removal from the house, the timepieces
are able to resume function, but are
spatially altered as per observation 4.

4 – All non-living objects taken into or
originating within the house appear as normal
while remaining inside. However, once removed
from the house, the objects can be seen to
have undergone a process of spatial warping
known as 'spaghettification'.

During this process, objects become noticeably shortened on the X and Z (horizontal) dimensional axes, while the Y (vertical) axis remains as normal. This process increases in magnitude for objects left in the house for longer periods, with objects originating in the house appearing extremely thin, with little more than one dimension remaining. The process is not observed in living creatures, which instead undergo the alternative effect of developing P.I.U.S.

5 – The house is inhabited by a 'sentient' phenomenon, known as the Tenant. The Tenant can be found at any location within the house, and appears as a hair-thin vertical line, extending 1.9 metres upward from the floor.

The Tenant is able to move horizontally in any direction, and does so at a speed of up to 6km/h. It appears to show an 'interest' in any intruders to the house and has been commonly observed 'following' them from room to room, at an average distance of 1 to 2 metres.

When passing before a source of light, it is possible to observe the shadow of the Tenant, which resembles that of an adult male. It is hypothesized that the Tenant is a former occupant of the house, who has undergone an extreme spaghettification.

BEHAVIOUR:

With only five documented appearances to date,

the Tenth is one of the most elusive Portents discovered so far. Consequently, relatively little is known about its behaviour. While it has been seen to appear in a range of housing structures, the exact requirements of these structures are not precisely understood. However, in all cases, the structures were vacant of human inhabitants and had been so for at least thirteen months.

The Tenth Portent is able to appear or disappear instantaneously, to seemingly any location on Earth. It has been observed to remain in one place for a period of time between two days and eight weeks, before moving elsewhere. The pattern by which the Tenth chooses its new location and length of stay is not yet known.

Due to the tendency of the Tenth to inhabit vacant housing structures, the Department of Unreality recommends that all abandoned or unused housing be torn down, or reoccupied, as soon as possible.

PORTENT INDUCED UNREALITY SYMPTOMS:

P.I.U.S RUBICON RADIUS: 0m (rubicon does not extend beyond the borders of the Portent itself).

ACTIVE SYMPTOM DEVELOPMENT: 97%

LETHALITY: 8%

DESIGNATION: Spacesmith

ADDITIONAL NOTES: P.I.U.S of the Tenth Portent typically involve the ability to manipulate space and dimension, including the instantaneous teleportation of people or objects. Due to its high active P.I.U.S, low mortality ratio, the Tenth Portent to date boasts the highest proportion of deliberately induced P.I.U.S.

# CAROLS AND CYBERCRIME

## Date: Sunday 21 December 2081

Time passed in Ark 2 and before she knew it, Quinn had been living there for almost a month.

It had been a good month. The cottage was comfortable and the neighbours pleasant. It was always between eighteen and twenty-five degrees Celsius, and never raining. If you didn't look at the 'sky' directly, it was almost like being outside.

Ark 2, while small, wasn't boring. There were events on every weekend, which the citizens of the Ark were encouraged to attend. On the first weekend after they arrived, there was a cheese festival, where Quinn ate a larger variety and quantity of dairy than she ever had before. On the second weekend was a scavenger hunt and on the third, an open-air Shakespeare performance.

On the fourth weekend, approaching Christmas, an event called 'carols by candlelight' was scheduled. Quinn didn't know what it was, but after being told it involved live music and singing, she was looking forward to it.

She still wasn't used to music being everywhere – but she was loving every second of it. For the first time ever, she was able to openly talk about music. She could talk about bands that she liked, and why she liked them, and about what made them good. She could show her own creations to other people, who weren't just Mullet, and they could give her feedback in real time.

Surrounded by fellow artists, it was as though she could

feel her mind expanding by the day. The other musicians all knew so much, about genre, history and musical theory. There was so much to learn, so many new words – majors and minors, treble and bass, tempo, dynamics, circles of fifths – the fundamental structures that made music, music. Quinn absorbed it all with a voracious appetite. She hadn't known that she was starving until now.

For the first time, she also had access to real music instruments. She tried to play all of them, with limited success. Some, like the piano, were easy enough to pick out a tune on, although playing with both hands took practise. Others, like trumpets and flutes, were harder. Quinn couldn't even get them to make any noise other than a sad wheeze for several hours.

But while playing real instruments proved difficult, Quinn could still write down the sounds they should make – and now, she had the tools and knowledge to do it properly. For the first time, she wrote down one of her songs using real musical notation. Then she watched in pure delight as Maggie and Keanu brought it to life in front of her.

After her initial hesitation, Quinn had decided that she actually liked Maggie. The older girl could be prickly at times, but for the most part, she was chill. And she clearly loved music as much as Quinn did. As the weeks passed, Quinn found herself spending more and more time with her.

Mullet, meanwhile, became firm friends with Keanu. They spent almost every waking hour together, watching movies, kicking a footy or getting into trouble in town. True to his word, Keanu also began teaching Mullet how to play the guitar. Mullet took to it surprisingly well, and within weeks, was getting through entire songs without making a mistake. He had a good ear and was very determined to learn. Watching him from a distance, Kylie often lamented that his dedication was a waste.

'If he cared this much about literally anything else,' she said sadly, 'we'd already be rich.'

Quinn, however, was happy for him.

Of the other residents of Melody Sands, most were significantly older. There were around two dozen residents in total, and most of them had been there for many years. Around half of them were over the age of sixty, and over three quarters had learnt to play their instruments before the End of the World.

Quinn asked them questions about what life had been like in the Before times – but most of them seemed reluctant to talk about it. The memories, they said, were painful, or they'd simply forgotten. It was thirty years ago, now. That time was gone, and there was no use dwelling on it.

'People seem to have the impression that life before the End of the World was easy,' one of them, an elderly man called Leo, told Quinn. 'But it's not true. We had problems back then, lots of 'em. Sure, they were different problems than the ones we have now, but they were just as bad, in their own way. Stress is stress, and misery is misery. Doesn't matter if you're living in a soulless, corporate dystopia or an insular police-state plagued by extradimensional terrors. Either way, you're suffering. If anything, it's more peaceful now. Our planet is exhausted. The silence is a nice change.'

Quinn made an effort to talk to every musician in Melody Sands – but she found it difficult to connect to many of them. The thirty-to-fifty-year age gap meant they treated her like a child or had vastly different opinions and interests to her.

By the end of the month, Quinn mostly found herself tagging along with Mullet and Keanu's shenanigans, or hanging out with Maggie and writing music. Sometimes, Kylie joined them – although she wasn't interested in the music and barely joined in with their conversations. She mostly just sat in the corner and typed away on her laptop. She was clearly hard at work on something – although she wouldn't tell anyone what it was.

On the morning before the carols by candlelight event,

however, she finally turned her laptop around and showed Quinn what she'd been working on.

'What do you think?' she said.

On the screen, a stylised Christmas tree twinkled grandly, in the foreground of a majestic moonlit landscape. Gusts of snow blew occasionally across the screen and clouds drifted gently from right to left.

Quinn blinked at it for a moment. A tiny silhouette of Santa Claus in his flying deer-drawn sleigh appeared and flew across the moon. The entire assembly was faintly relicious, although not enough to be properly bothersome.

'Um?' Quinn said. 'What is it? Did you make it?'

'Yes, I made it,' Kylie said, turning the laptop around again. 'It's an animated screensaver. Do you like it?'

'It's alright,' Quinn said. 'It's nice, I guess.'

'Okay,' Kylie said. 'What if you were a sixty-year-old woman, with an obsession with preserving the ways of Old Australia?'

'Huh?' Quinn wrinkled her nose. 'Kylie, what are you planning?'

'Nothing,' Kylie said. 'I just thought I'd make a nice Christmas gift for the Ark council members, since they've been so nice to us and all.'

She smiled sweetly at Quinn and then went back to typing. Quinn had never been more suspicious of anything in her life.

She only grew more suspicious when, a few hours later, Kylie announced that she was going to help the Minister for Events Management, Jean Harper, set up the lights for the evening's event.

'You're helping her?' Quinn said, watching her pack her laptop away in a case. 'For free?'

'Yes,' Kylie said. 'She's a lovely old lady. Very sweet, very organised. Doesn't know much about computers. I thought I would offer my services and help her program the light show for the carols tonight. Make it a special evening for everyone. She was very happy to have the support – and I'm happy to provide it!'

Quinn folded her arms. 'Okay, who are you, and what have you done with Kylie?' she said.

'Oh, Quinn,' Kylie said, 'is it so strange that I might help an old lady, out of the kindness of my heart?'

'Yes,' Quinn said, 'it's very strange. Are you going to rob her?'

'No,' Kylie said.

'Are you going to give her the screensaver?' Quinn narrowed her eyes. 'What does it do, really? Are you going to hold her computer to ransom?'

Kylie only smiled and gave Quinn a tiny wave before she left.

Mullet was also out, so Quinn went next door and told Maggie about Kylie's suspicious behaviour.

'I usually wouldn't care,' she said, 'but I don't want Kylie messing things up for us! If she starts blackmailing the council members, then they'll probably kick us out of the Ark! And I like it here! I don't want to leave, not yet!'

'You really think she's going to try and blackmail someone?' Maggie said in concern.

'Probably!' Quinn thew up her hands. 'I wish she would stop scheming, for five minutes! We have a good thing going on! Does she have to ruin it?'

'Should we... warn them or something?' Maggie said.

'Maybe?' Quinn said. 'But what if they kick just Kylie out of the Ark? I don't want that either!'

'We could try and convince them it was an accident?' Maggie said. 'Like, oh no, sorry, I messed up and put the wrong program on the USB, don't plug it into your laptop!'

'I guess.' Quinn sighed.

'Or,' Maggie said, 'you should talk to Kylie, and let her know how you feel about this.'

'She knows,' Quinn muttered. 'She just doesn't care.'

'Aw, that's not true,' Maggie said. 'She does care! I think that maybe she isn't the best at showing it, but she does, I can tell. I'm sure she thinks she's doing what's best for you guys. And hey – maybe she IS just helping Ms Harper for the sake of it?'

'Yeah, right,' Quinn said. 'Maybe what's best for us is staying in the Ark and not getting into trouble for once!'

'Fair,' Maggie said. 'Hey – if you like, we can go to the Botanical Gardens? That's where they're setting up. Maybe Kylie will be reluctant to do anything, if you're there, staring her down?'

Quinn brightened.

'Yeah, let's do that!' she said.

***

The Carols by Candlelight was going to be held in a small grassy field, surrounded by flowering, sweet-scented bushes. A gazebo at one end of the field, festooned with tinsel and fairy lights, was the focal point of the event. At the other end of the field was the Ark 2 Museum and adjoining café, a quaint bluestone building, similarly decked out in Christmas trimmings.

Kylie was sitting on the floor of the gazebo with two laptops in front of her, surrounded by cables and wires. Nearby, the Minister for Events Management, Jean Harper, was overseeing the arrangement of several thousand candles.

Quinn approached the gazebo and coughed to let Kylie know she was there. Kylie glanced at her briefly, then went back to her work.

'What is it?' she said.

'Oh, nothing,' Quinn said, leaning on the wall of the gazebo. 'Go ahead and set up the lights. I'm just going to be over here, in case something happens.'

'What exactly are you expecting to happen?' Kylie said, without looking up.

'I don't know,' Quinn said. 'What IS going to happen?'

'Nothing,' Kylie said.

'Okay,' Quinn said. 'Good.'

'Yes, good,' Kylie said. 'Now, leave me alone, please. I'm trying to concentrate.'

Quinn gave her a long, suspicious look, and then moved off.

'So?' Maggie said when Quinn re-joined her near the museum. 'Do you feel any better?'

Quinn shrugged. 'I dunno,' she said. 'I don't think anything I say will really change things.'

'I think you're underestimating yourself,' Maggie said. 'Anyway – have you ever been inside this museum before? I haven't. I didn't know it was here!'

'I haven't been in it,' Quinn muttered.

'Well, shall we?' Maggie said. 'There's still a few hours before the carols start!'

'I guess,' Quinn said. 'Sure.'

After sending one last glance in Kylie's direction, she followed Maggie inside.

They stepped into a rustic entrance lobby, the walls of which were covered in photos of Old Melbourne. At a desk in the corner, an old woman with flyaway, wispy white hair looked up from a book she was reading.

'Hello there,' she quavered, eyeing Quinn and Maggie through her old-style glasses. 'Are you here to see the museum?'

'Yes,' Maggie said. 'Is there an entrance fee?'

'Oh, no.' The woman waved a bangled hand. 'Free entry. But I must ask that you sign into the logbook, just here. Thank you, ladies.'

Maggie went and did as she asked, and Quinn followed her example. The old woman, she noticed, was halfway through a cup of tea, and with it, she was eating a Tim Tam.

Seeing where she was looking, the old woman chuckled.

'They're selling Tim Tams in the café,' she said with a wink. 'Two bucks a pop, if you want one.'

'I'm okay, thanks,' Quinn said quickly.

'Maybe later,' Maggie said. 'Do you have a map of the museum?'

'Oh, you don't need a map,' the woman said. 'There aren't that many rooms to see.'

She pointed to the back of the room, where there were

two doors. The one on the right was marked IN and the one on the left OUT.

'You go in where it says, go around the loop, and come out again,' she said. 'Nothing to it.'

Quinn followed Maggie into the first room of the museum – and immediately decided that she'd made a mistake. The first room was full of artifacts from Melbourne's history – and a good third of them were low tier relics.

Trying not to display her discomfort, she pretended to read a few of the plaques, before hurriedly moving onto the next room. Behind her, Maggie took her time reading everything, occasionally commenting out loud on the things she saw.

In the next room, which was done up to resemble a 'typical Australian suburban home, circa 2010', Quinn stared blankly at the bookshelf and read the titles over and over. The words were in English, but the topics were nothing she'd ever heard of before – *Tourism on a budget*, *Macroeconomics for dummies*, and *The definitive guide to the keto diet*. In close proximity to so many relics, Quinn struggled to even imagine what they might be about. Gritting her teeth, she reached for the unrealitic matchbox in her pocket, before realising that she'd left it in her bedside drawer at home.

'Isn't this so cool?' Maggie said, coming into the room. 'Look at the clothes on those mannequins! The business suits? The stilettos? Ridiculous! I can't believe people really used to wear those every day!'

'I reckon some of the people at Melody Sands own outfits like that,' Quinn said. 'They're all old enough.'

'You're right, they probably do!' Maggie said. 'I wonder if they'd let us see them?'

'Maybe,' Quinn said.

'In fact, I bet they have a bunch of Old-Australia stuff, hidden away in their cupboards. Probably relics, too! Hey, I wonder if any of these things are relics?'

'They are,' Quinn said, without thinking.

Maggie looked at her.

'I mean, probably, right?' Quinn said hurriedly. 'It would make sense.'

'Yeah…' Maggie said.

There was an awkward silence. Quinn tried to think of something to say, but the fogginess defeated her.

'Let's see what's in the next room!' she said brightly.

The next room was further back in time, displaying images and artifacts from Melbourne in the ninetieth and twentieth century.

'Do you ever think how weird it is, that so many of the musicians in Melody Sands are old?' Maggie said, staring into a glass cabinet full of Gold-Rush era tools and trinkets. 'You know, music used to be the domain of the young. The vast majority of musicians were in their twenties and thirties. But I guess it makes sense that they're all seniors now. No new musicians have been coming in to replace the old. Music is becoming a dying art.'

On the other side of the room, Quinn frowned. 'Music can't die,' she said.

'But it is dying,' Maggie said. 'Once the older generation passes on, then that's pretty much it. There will be fewer and fewer people who remember how to play instruments, or to read sheet music, or to write it. If there's no one alive to pass on the knowledge, then the knowledge will be lost.'

'But there's more to music than that,' Quinn said. 'Yeah, the sheet notation is cool – but you don't need it for music to exist! I made music for ages without it!'

'I suppose,' Maggie said. 'But without notation and the rest, the art becomes diminished. Fewer and fewer instruments will exist. Songs will be lost and fewer will be created to take their place. Complexity, history, all gone. It's really very, very sad. I hate thinking about it.'

'It can't die forever,' Quinn said stubbornly. 'We have voices, don't we? We can sing! We can slap things, and drum two sticks together to make a beat! Music might go into hiding for a bit, but it will always return, eventually! It's just noises arranged in time, after all – and you can't get rid of noise, or time!'

'Maybe,' Maggie said.

'I don't know why they're so fixated on noise, anyway,' Quinn went on. 'Noise is only bad because it draws in the Portents, right? So why don't they focus on getting rid of the Portents instead, huh? Then all our problems would be over!'

'Oh, they ARE trying to do that as well,' Maggie said. 'The Department of Unreality has multiple teams dedicated to it. But so far, it's been pretty unsuccessful.'

'Oh?' Quinn said. 'How do you know that?'

'Because,' Maggie said, 'I used to work there.'

Quinn, who'd been about to walk into the next room, stopped abruptly in her tracks.

'What?' she said, turning to stare at Maggie. 'You worked at the Department of Unreality?'

'Yeah,' Maggie said.

'As, like... a janitor?'

'No,' Maggie said. 'I was a scientist there.'

'What?' Quinn said. 'But... how old are you?'

'I'm twenty-seven.'

'What?!' Quinn said. 'Twenty-seven! You're so old! You're older than Kylie! Also, a scientist? When were you going to tell me that you're some sort of nerd genius?!'

'I'm not,' Maggie said.

'Who even are you?!' Quinn said.

'Well, I'm NOT a scientist,' Maggie said. 'Not anymore. I left.'

'Why? Why'd you leave?'

Maggie sighed and looked away.

'It wasn't for me,' she said.

'Why not?' Quinn said – then her eyes widened. 'Ooh! Was it really unethical? Let me guess – human experimentation? Were they chopping people up and sewing them back together? Or, like, turning babies into glue?'

'What, no!' Maggie said. 'You know there's an ethics committee, right? There's no way any of that stuff would ever be approved.'

'But what if the ethics committee was in on it?'

'No,' Maggie said. 'Just, no.'

'Okay,' Quinn said, 'well, why'd you leave then?'

'Nunya.'

'Huh?'

'Nunya business. Stop asking.'

'Okay,' Quinn said, 'but what did you do there? Or was it top secret?'

'No, I can tell you, if you really care that much,' Maggie said. 'I worked with relics, mostly. But technically, I was on the realitysmith team. Most of my co-workers were studying realitysmiths, and how they work.'

'Oh?' Quinn said, eyes wide. 'What were they doing? Dissecting them?!'

'No!' Maggie said. 'I don't know where you got the idea that the Department of Unreality are some sort of evil villain organisation, but that's not the case. The realitysmiths were not harmed! They were there voluntarily and knew exactly what they were getting into. It's called Informed Consent, and it's an important bastion of science!'

'Fine,' Quinn said. 'Did you find out how they work?'

'Well,' Maggie said, 'the short answer is, no. At least, not up until a year and half ago. That was when I left, so maybe they've had a breakthrough since then?'

'What's the long answer?' Quinn said in interest. They moved into the next room, which was full of First Nations art and artifacts.

'Well,' Maggie said, 'if you really want the details... Basically, the team was trying to figure out how P.I.U.S interacts with reality. In other words, when someone channels P.I.U.S, what is actually going on, on a molecular level? We figured that if we understood this better, we might be able to control it to a better degree. With greater control, we could do things like reduce detrimental side effects, or possibly even remove P.I.U.S from an affected individual.'

'Remove P.I.U.S?' Quinn blinked.

'Yes,' Maggie said. 'Obviously, that was a long-term goal.

In the short term, if we found any way to make P.I.U.S just a little bit safer and less miserable and unpredictable for the people who have it, that would be a win.'

'Right,' Quinn said. 'Go on.'

'Yeah, so,' Maggie said. 'We were trying to measure how unrealitic forces were acting on the Canon Material Timeline. But, as it turns out, that's extremely difficult. All of the tools that we tried to measure it with, all the maths and physics and biology, they're all centred around observing and measuring OUR universe. Portents and P.I.U.S, meanwhile, are not part of our universe. The rules that we know, and learnt in school, and discovered over years upon years of research – those rules simply do not apply.'

She sighed, staring into the distance.

'Basically,' she said, 'we were trying to re-learn everything, from scratch, for not just one, but eleven different universes. So yeah... it was kind of a losing battle.'

'Damn,' Quinn said. 'Did you at least discover something? Mathematics 2? Gravity: the next generation?'

Maggie snorted. 'Well, actually, we did find out something,' she said. 'Or rather, we confirmed it officially, with statistical significance. You may not know this, because it isn't common knowledge outside of Sanctuaries, but when two realitysmiths channel their powers towards the same task, it amplifies the effect beyond what would be expected if the two worked alone. That's what we confirmed.'

'Huh?' Quinn said. 'Could you say that again, but this time assume I'm an idiot?'

'Say there's a weather station,' Maggie said, 'and there is one weathersmith inside. And say this weathersmith can manipulate up to one cubic kilometre of air pressure. Okay?'

'Okay,' Quinn said.

'But if there are two of them,' Maggie said, 'then they can manipulate MORE than two kilometres cubed. The power magnitude increases beyond what it should. They amplify each other.'

'Huh,' Quinn said. 'That IS pretty cool! I didn't know that.'

'It gets even cooler,' Maggie said. 'We also confirmed that it works in much the same way with realitysmiths of different types – but the effects are a LOT more random. For example, if you had a mattersmith and a weathersmith, and told them that they were to move a two-ton boulder across a room, by themselves, they would each struggle to move the boulder. The mattersmith might attempt to alter the shape of the stone and slowly move it across the room by tipping it over itself. The weathersmith might attempt to erode the stone with fierce wind. But both of these would take a long time, and may not even be successful, depending on the ingenuity and power magnitude of the individual smith.'

'Okay,' Quinn said.

'But when both smiths work together on the same task, things get interesting,' Maggie continued, brushing her finger absently along the dusty top of a display case. 'The effects are able to combine in bizarre new ways, and not only that, the power of both amplifies. Suddenly, there are a lot more possibilities. The boulder might fly apart and whizz across the room as a small tornado. Or it might turn into a liquid, evaporate into the air and then come down as lava rain in the correct location. The downside is that the effects are much harder to predict. Up until the moment the realitysmiths unleash their abilities, we have absolutely no idea what will happen. Obviously, this can result in some pretty strange or dangerous effects.'

'Like what?' Quinn said.

'Well, mostly people get injured in ways never before seen to man,' Maggie said. 'But one time, a spacesmith and a fleshsmith managed to create an extremely large, extremely angry, two-headed mouse.'

'Is that why you left?' Quinn asked. 'Mouse-zilla ate all your co-workers?'

'No,' Maggie said. 'Sadly, the mouse was euthanised almost immediately.'

'Aw,' Quinn said. 'How big was it, anyway?'

'Huge,' Maggie said.

She pointed into the next room, to where a display of several scale models of Late Pleistocene megafauna beasts were locked forever in battle.

'Almost as big as that Diprotodon,' she said.

'Damn!' Quinn said. 'Absolutely enormous! An enor-mouse, if you will.'

'I will not,' Maggie said, grinning.

They wandered over to the megafauna display and looked at it closer. The plaster constructions had clearly been painted by someone who had far more interest in colour than realism. The Diprotodon, a massive wombat-like creature, had a bright blue head, and each of its legs was painted in a different primary colour. The beast attacking it, a marsupial lion, was painted in bright polka dots. Meanwhile, on the other side of the room, a seven-metre long Megalania lizard crouched, in hot pink, with yellow flowers painted across its back, while what looked like a gargantuan goose stood proudly in rainbow stripes.

'I doubt they were those colours,' Quinn said, eyeing the creatures.

'Probably not,' Maggie said. 'Although, we can't know for sure, I suppose. All we have left are the bones.'

She gestured to a glass display cabinet, which contained actual fossils from the four ancient beasts on display. There was a huge jawbone from the Diprotodon, a skull and forearm from the marsupial lion, and a femur from the goose. For the lizard, there was only a single vertebrae piece.

'That's all that's left, huh,' Quinn said, looking at the chunk of spine. 'Poor lizard. Almost entirely gone – but not forgotten! I won't forget you, girl.' She patted its pink snout.

'If it was alive,' Maggie said, 'I'm sure it'd be so pleased, it'd eat you.'

'Aw,' Quinn said. 'Don't bully her! She's already extinct!'

'Well,' Maggie said, 'from one extinct beast to another, I salute you. And commend your efforts, for not dragging the rest of the world down with you when you left it.'

'Hey, we're not extinct yet,' Quinn said. 'Not us, and not music either! You gotta stop being such a glass-half-empty, sad sack Debbie Downer, Maggie. We're alive and kicking, aren't we? And while we are, we can make things better.'

'Yeah.' Maggie sighed. 'Sure. Sure we can, Quinn.'

Slowly, they wondered out of the last room, and back into the entrance hall.

# CHAPTER 20

# BAD DECISIONS

**Date: Sunday 21 December 2081**

After waving to the old woman at the desk, Quinn and Maggie went back outside. There was still an hour left before the carols began, and Maggie made a beeline for the museum café.

'Do you want to get a Tim Tam?' she asked. 'Since they're selling them today.'

'No, thanks,' Quinn said.

'A coffee then?'

'No.' Quinn made a face. 'I don't like coffee.'

'Well, I'm getting a coffee AND a Tim Tam,' Maggie said. 'If you want, you can have a corner?'

'No, I don't like Tim Tams either,' Quinn said, a little crossly.

'What?' Maggie said. 'Okay, coffee I understand, but Tim Tams? Everyone likes Tim Tams! They're objectively delicious!'

'Well, I don't like them,' Quinn said.

Maggie eyed her and Quinn saw her mouth start to open, a question forming.

'While you get coffee, I'm going to see what Kylie's doing!' she said quickly.

She could feel Maggie's eyes on her has she walked away and wondered if she'd said too much. Had Maggie figured it out already? If she'd known that Maggie was a former Department Scientist, who had actively worked with relics and realitysmiths, she would have been a lot more careful in some of the things she'd said around her.

When she approached the gazebo, Kylie glanced up from her laptop screen, her brows furrowed.

'Oh, hi Quinn,' she said distractedly.

Quinn moved around to look at what she was doing, just in time to see Kylie close a tab.

'What was that?' she said suspiciously.

'What was what?' Kylie said.

'That tab!' Quinn leaned closer. 'What was it? Don't think I didn't see!'

Kylie opened her mouth to argue – but then abruptly deflated.

'Okay, fine,' she said in a low voice. 'You were right. About the screensaver, I mean. Of course I wouldn't make it for free. It's actually a remote access program.'

'Kylie!' Quinn said. 'Why?'

'Because I'm a snoopy bitch.' Kylie shrugged. 'Fucking sue me. Anyway, take a look at this.'

She reopened the tab, revealing a live stream of someone else's desktop.

'Kylie!' Quinn said again, and glanced around in worry. 'Is that...?'

'It's Jean's laptop, yes,' Kylie said. 'She loved the animated screensaver. But that's not the point. I want you to look at her desktop and tell me what you see.'

'Um,' Quinn said. 'It's very neat? All the apps and stuff.'

'It sure is,' Kylie said. 'Anything else?'

'It looks new,' Quinn said. 'The desktop background is one of the default landscapes.'

'Yep,' Kylie said. 'And all the apps are the default ones that come with the computer.'

'So, you're saying this is a new computer?' Quinn said.

'Nope,' Kylie said. 'It isn't. Jean's had it for years, or so she says. Have a look at this.'

She opened the file explorer program and cycled through several of the files. They were all completely empty, except for Documents, which contained a single text file, titled 'Events'.

Kylie highlighted the date, which showed that the file had been created over four years ago. Then, she opened the document.

It was a list of Ark events, arranged by month. Each event had a small blurb next to it, describing what it was – but that was it. There were no other details at all. No budgets, contacts, supply lists, nothing.

'This document is literally the only thing on her computer which wasn't included by default,' Kylie said, in a baffled tone. 'I checked her emails as well – also empty!'

'Huh,' Quinn said. 'That's... weird.'

'Yeah, it's super fucking weird!' Kylie said. 'Isn't she supposed to be the Minster for Events Management? How is she managing everything?! Does she have another computer? Is this one a decoy? Why would she have a decoy computer? What the fuck? Am I going insane?'

'Maybe her computer crashed recently?' Quinn said.

'If that's the case, then why hasn't she said anything?' Kylie said. 'If I was running weekly events for an entire town and MY computer crashed, I would be a mess! But she's fine! Have you seen her? Swanning around, without a care in the world!'

'Yeah, I guess that IS pretty strange,' Quinn said. 'She must have her files stored somewhere else. Either that, or she's set up a virtual façade, like what you do when the sinnies look at your computer.'

'I...' Kylie said. 'I suppose. But I could have sworn this old biddy was basically computer illiterate...'

'Well, maybe she keeps everything in hardcopy, then?' Quinn said.

'Maybe.' Kylie sighed, rubbing her eyes. 'Oh well. Back to square-fucking-one. At least I know the screensaver works as intended.'

'What are you trying to do anyway?' Quinn said, eyes narrowed.

'Well, ultimately, the goal is to get into Brinesworth's

computer,' Kylie said with a sigh. 'I was going to use Jean's laptop to email the screensaver to Brinesworth. But now I don't think it'll work. Apparently, Jean hasn't sent a single email in her life. If she starts now, it'll be suspicious.'

'Why are you trying to get into Brinesworth's computer?' Quinn said, folding her arms.

'Oh, trust me, it's for a good cause,' Kylie said. 'You'll see why when I... fucking hell. What is that idiot doing now?'

Quinn turned around, following Kylie's gaze. Across the field, Mullet had just stumbled out of the bushes. He was laughing and there was a can of beer in his hand.

Keanu appeared a moment later, tripping over his own feet. He also had a beer, which he spilled all over his own shirt, to Mullet's raucous amusement.

'Are they fucking drunk?' Kylie said. 'It's not even 6PM! Fuck's sake. Quinn, can you go and tell Mullet that he's an idiot and he needs to stop? Also, tell him that Keanu is a bad influence and that I dislike him immensely.'

'Why can't you tell him yourself?' Quinn said.

'Because I'm working,' Kylie said. 'These lights won't program themselves, Quinn!'

Quinn was pretty sure that Kylie had finished programming the lights hours ago, but she didn't see any point in arguing further. Sighing, she left the gazebo and followed after Mullet.

Both he and Keanu were completely off their faces drunk. Tottering to and fro, they wondered across the lawn, before collapsing down near the museum. Quinn reluctantly approached them, folding her arms and eyeing them judgementally.

'Oh, hey Quinn!' Mullet slurred when he saw her. 'Want some beer? We've had... two slabs... already...'

'Two slabs?!' Quinn said.

'Yeah.' Mullet grinned. 'There's, there's another one... so-somewhere... ha ha... Keanu, mate, where is the other slab?'

'I thought you had it,' Keanu said.

They looked at each other and began howling with laughter.

'Kylie says you have to stop,' Quinn said, watching them. 'Also, she says Keanu is a bad influence.'

'Well, Kylie can suck my butt,' Mullet said. 'Do you want a beer, Quinn?'

'No,' Quinn said. 'They're gross, and also relici... um, gross.'

'Aw,' Mullet said. 'So many things you can't eat and drink, poor widdle smiffie.'

'Shut the fuck up, Mullet,' Quinn said through her teeth.

Glancing around, she saw Maggie approaching, and had a minor heart attack. Maggie, however, was focused on the two drunk boys on the ground.

'Oh dear,' she said, putting her hands on her hips. 'What's happening here?'

'Hey, Maggie!' Mullet grinned. 'Want a beer? Actually never mind, we uhhhhhhh forgot where we put them!'

'Probably for the best,' Maggie said. 'You boys should probably go home and sleep it off.'

'Nah, bro!' Keanu said. 'We're here for the candles by carolight! Nobody can stop us!'

'Yeah!' Mullet said. 'We're gonna... sing and shit!'

Maggie and Quinn glanced at each other.

'This isn't the first time Keanu's done this,' Maggie said quietly, while the boys began yelling and playfully slapping each other. 'He got arrested last time, you know? He climbed up onto the roof one of the shops, and wouldn't get down.'

'Arrested?' Quinn said. 'By who? I thought there weren't any sin-seekers down here?'

'There aren't,' Maggie said. 'He was arrested by security. You know, those scary dudes in the Kevlar vests? They locked him in their office until he sobered up.'

'Huh,' Quinn said. 'I forgot about them.'

'Yeah, well they only really show up when there's trouble,' Maggie said. 'Speaking of which... here comes Ms Harper. This is not looking good. They're totally gonna get arrested.'

The Minister for Events Management was a short, rotund

woman with cropped silver hair and a face like a frog, and she emanated a powerful aura of disapproval as she approached.

'Boys,' she said, eyeing Mullet and Keanu sternly. 'Please take your horseplay elsewhere. The event is not yet open and even when it is, your current volume is not appropriate.'

'But we're singing, aren't we?' Mullet said. 'You're supposed to be loud!'

'You are clearly drunk,' Jean said. 'This is a serene, joyous event. It is no place for public inebriation.'

'Why not?' Keanu said loudly. 'Anyway, we're not drunk, are we Mullet?'

'That is clearly a lie,' Jean said crossly. 'Please, you must leave the event, right this minute.'

'Ms Harper, we can take them home,' Maggie said. 'Leave it up to us.'

'No, you won't take us home!' Keanu howled. 'And you won't make us leave! You can't catch us!'

He began rolling around on the grass and thrashing his arms and legs. 'Try and grab me now!' he yelled. 'I'm a slippery eel! AHAHAHA!'

Ms Harper clicked her tongue, and abruptly walked away.

'Shit,' Maggie said. 'What did I say? I bet she's going to call security. Keanu, calm down! You'll get arrested again! Mullet, you too!'

Her words, however, fell on deaf ears. While Keanu, or Mullet, might have listened on their own, with both of them, it was impossible.

'What do we do?' Quinn said in concern. 'Should I go and get Kylie?'

'Yeah, good idea,' Maggie said. 'Mullet might listen to her, at least.'

Quinn nodded and ran off across the lawn, towards the gazebo. Kylie once again saw her coming, and stood up abruptly.

'Alright, what have they done?' she said.

'Nothing specific,' Quinn said breathlessly. 'They're just really drunk, and Ms Harper asked them to leave, and they won't. Maggie thinks they might listen to you.'

'Ugh,' Kylie said. 'Fine.'

She stalked back towards them, and Quinn followed. Just as they were getting close however, Quinn abruptly stopped in her tracks.

Someone was using P.I.U.S nearby. It was faint, but unmistakable – a five-second burst of twisting, jittering unreality.

While Kylie kept walking, oblivious, Quinn looked around, suddenly on high alert. As far as she knew, there were no realitysmiths in Ark 2 aside from her.

Clearly, though, this assumption was untrue. There was someone else, likely in hiding just like she was.

But what type of smith were they? And what had they just done?

While Kylie began yelling at Mullet, she instead set off in a different direction. The burst had come from the museum, although whether inside or around the back she wasn't sure.

Quinn poked her head inside and saw that the old woman was still sitting in the corner. Was it her? No, surely not – she'd been eating a Tim Tam earlier.

'Hey,' she said to her. 'Did anyone come in here just now?'

The woman looked up and shook her head. 'No, no one since you and your friend earlier,' she said. 'Why? Are you looking for someone?'

'Yes, but don't worry, I think I just saw them!' Quinn said quickly and closed the door.

Outside, she paused for a moment, wondering what to do. She didn't know where the burst had come from – and while curious, she wasn't sure whether following it was a good idea. At best, she would find someone who was trying to hide their P.I.U.S, who probably wouldn't appreciate being found. At worst, it was something much more dangerous.

It probably wasn't worth it. She should leave it be, let the person live their life in secret. Who was she to judge them, after all?

Behind her, in the gazebo, music started playing. They were doing a sound check.

Quinn frowned.

Yes, she should probably let sleeping dogs lie. But on other hand... if she made the wrong choice... she could always undo it...?

Just then, there was another burst of unreality.

Quinn didn't hesitate. It was a lot closer this time, just behind the museum. The music emboldening her, she ran directly towards it.

She turned the corner, and almost ran directly into a person coming the other way.

It was one of the security guards in Kevlar, their face hidden behind a helmet. Startled, they looked down at Quinn, hand drifting towards their gun holster.

'Oh... sorry!' Quinn said quickly, stepping aside.

The guard didn't say anything, disappearing around the corner. A second guard followed them. Quinn watched the pair run across the lawn with narrowed eyes.

Were the guards the ones using P.I.U.S?

Turning, she looked at where they'd come from. There was a path behind the museum, leading back to the main road, fifty or so metres away. On one side of the path were flower gardens, and on the other, trees.

They must have come from the road, then. But if that was the case, then what was the source of the unreality?

There was something resting in the middle of the flower garden, something that did not belong. At first, Quinn thought it was a dead animal, in late stages of decomposition. It was formless, gelatinous, glistening –

It moved.

Quinn's eyes widened as the slimy thing oozed across the ground. Reams of muscle contracted, membranes sliding over unidentified organs, trailing dark red juice in its wake. It reached the gutter at the back the museum and sucked itself up into a drain pipe. In moments, it was gone – but Quinn remained frozen in place.

What. The FUCK. Was that?

She didn't dare go closer to investigate. She didn't want to get any closer to that thing. What if it came back?

Disturbed and disgusted, she backed slowly away around the corner, then ran full tilt back to where the others were.

The two guards that she had passed on the way were there now and they'd grabbed Keanu, pinning him on the ground, while he yelled incoherent abuse at them. Mullet, meanwhile, had gone quiet – for now, the guards were ignoring him.

With all attention focused on Keanu, Quinn had a moment to catch her breath and calm her racing heart.

What the fuck had she just seen? What the FUCK was it?

It was almost certainly the source of the unreality burst, she knew that much. But following through on this logic, Quinn felt even more disturbed.

As far as she knew, only humans could use P.I.U.S. Animals could display the symptoms, but they couldn't use them, not actively.

That meant that the thing she'd seen had probably been a human – or had been once. But what sort of horrific, inside-out, bone-melting mutation had they gone through to end up as that Thing?

Were they a fleshsmith? That made the most sense. They were well on their way to resembling the Fifth Portent.

Quinn felt sick. In front of her, Keanu was getting dragged away by the guards, but she couldn't find the energy to care about it.

'Alright, dumb-shit,' Kylie was saying to Mullet nearby. 'Home time! See what happens when you don't listen?'

Mullet protested, but only quietly, as Kylie began half-leading, half-carrying him out of the field.

Quinn silently went to help them, letting Mullet lean on her shoulder. She was quiet all the way back to Melody Sands.

'There we go,' Kylie said, tucking Mullet into bed, fully clothed. 'Nap time, fuckass! You can come back when you're sober. Come on, Quinn, let's go back to the carols. They're probably starting by now.'

'Actually,' Quinn said distantly. 'You know... I've had enough for today. I might just stay here with Mullet. Someone should keep an eye on him, right?'

'Oh?' Kylie said. 'I mean, sure. If that's what you want.'

She left, and Quinn sat down on the floor near Mullet's bed. The slime thing crawled into the drain over and over in her mind's eye.

In the next room over, she could very faintly feel the matchbox in her bedside drawer, prickling like static. It grated at her nerves. Crossly, she got up, picked up the box and took it into the bathroom at the other end of the cottage.

Opening the cabinet below the bathroom sink, she moved aside the first aid kit and stuffed it behind the u-bend. Then, she went back to her room and shut the door.

She didn't want to think about things anymore. Kylie didn't like her using their limited collection of headphones, but this was an emergency. Jamming the earbuds into her ears, she climbed into bed, put on some music and turned it all the way up.

## Lyrics to the song SILENCE IS GOLDEN
## by TEMPORAL BOOM

SILENCE IS GOLDEN

Verse 1

You're a good friend, it's fun to hang out

You've always got something to tell me about,

You're cool and you're stylish, your wit is sublime

You know that you're smart, so you talk all the time

I like you, but sometimes, I can't get a word in

My stories, truncated, to fit between your thing

I like you, but sometimes, I don't think you hear me

And sometimes, my good friend, it bothers me dearly

BLAH BLAH BLAH BLAH

Chorus

I've something to say, so please let me say it

I don't want to wait for your pause to okay it

I'm begging you, one time, to harken my plea:

Please shut the fuck up and listen to me!

Please shut the fuck up

Please shut the fuck up

Please shut the fuck up

And listen to me

Verse 2

I know that you care, but I wish you'd care my way

You're not the sole person who has something to say

I repeat myself twice, but you still get it wrong

You won't even get it if I show you this song

If silence is golden, then you can't see yellow

If tact is in treble, then you play the cello

That's cool that you're confident in your own crap

But shut the fuck up or I might fucking snap!

Chorus

# INCOMPETENCE

### Date: Thursday 12 March 2082

The Detective arrived at the Ouyen Sin-Seeker Office just before midday. Bill had taken a little longer than expected in dropping off the spacesmiths and acquiring a vehicle, but overall, it could have been worse. The vehicle he'd gotten was a sin-seeker paddy wagon, with ample space in the back to store the would-be car thieves. It was also one hundred per cent roadworthy, which was a nice change.

After stopping briefly at the truck stop to let Stevo out, the Detective took the van back to the office, parking out the front. Then, Bill in tow, they marched inside to introduce themselves.

The person behind the front desk, a stocky man with a receding hairline, looked up and, recognising Bill, nodded in greeting.

'You're back, then,' he said. 'That was quick. Have you collected your, uh... half a dozen bushrangers?'

'Yes,' the Detective said. 'Although there are five, not six.'

The man blinked slowly at the Detective. 'So, you're "the Detective", then, eh?' he said. 'Bill mentioned that you were some sort of wonder cyborg.'

'Yes,' the Detective said. 'We require the use of your jail cells immediately.'

'What does "wonder cyborg" even mean?' the man continued. 'What can you do? Are you entirely made up of cybernetics? Man, that must have been expensive to make. How much did it even cost?'

'Officer, I do not have the time to answer these questions,' the Detective said, frowning slightly. 'I must insist on the immediate use of the jail cells on premises.'

'Alright, alright,' the man said. 'Keep your hair on! Or, uh... your hat anyway. Why do you need the cells?'

'To detain the criminals,' the Detective said.

'Oh, yes, right, the half a dozen bushrangers.' The man grinned.

The Detective stared back at him stonily. The man's grin slowly began to fade.

'Uhh,' he said. 'Do you... are you telling me that you really do have five bushrangers in the van back there?'

'Yes,' the Detective said. 'If you follow me, I will show you.'

They turned and led the way outside. The man hurriedly got out from behind his desk and followed them, a baffled expression on his face.

The Detective unlocked the back of the van, and carefully opened it. Inside, the detainees were all awake, their hands and feet tied. They glared angrily from the floor where they'd been laid out like so many kippers in a tin.

'Oh, wow,' the officer muttered under his breath.

He beckoned the Detective back inside.

'So, uh, there's a problem,' he said, addressing Bill. 'I thought... honestly, I didn't think you were serious. C'mon, your cyborg friend captured a whole pack of bushrangers by themselves? You can't blame me, right? Anyway, that's on me and if I'd known, I would have said something earlier. But basically... the jail cells are out of commission at the moment.'

'What do you mean?' the Detective said.

'Pipe burst,' the man said. 'It's completely flooded down there. Half a metre of water. We're waiting on the plumbers, but they've been delayed. They're not expected to come until tomorrow.'

'I see,' the Detective said. 'This is unfortunate.'

'Yeah,' the man said and sucked in through his teeth. 'I suppose we can keep them in one of the spare offices for now? In cuffs and under surveillance? Or we could call the Mildura office and get those guys to process them?'

'That is not possible,' the Detective said in exasperation. 'The Mildura office is having existential issues at the moment.'

'Oh,' the man said. 'Yeah. I forgot about that. Um. Well, I suppose I can get someone to call some of the smaller precincts and see who has free space...'

'This is a monumental waste of time,' the Detective said. 'But yes, I suppose that will have to do.'

***

While the Ouyen office tried to figure out what to do with the bushrangers, the Detective decided to take the time to recharge. Half of the day remained after all, and with all the running and using the left arm taser function, their battery was already less than fifty per cent.

They located an out-of-the-way electrical socket, inside a storage closet, and plugged in, staying there for two hours. This brought their battery to seventy-five per cent, which was better, if not ideal.

While they recharged, they analysed the new data, as usual – and while they did so, decided to prepare a report highlighting all the ways which the sin-seeker offices in the area could be improved. In total, the two offices they had seen so far had both shown abysmal organisation and preparedness. Taking into account the time spent locating transport, dealing with local crime, and now this new issue of no jail cells, over six hours had been wasted picking up the local Department of Sin's slack.

At 2PM, they emerged from the broom closet and went to see if the bushrangers had been dealt with. By their estimation, it should have taken less than an hour to contact another office and arrange pickup. But that was assuming that the officers would behave both logically and efficiently – which the Detective had come to realise was quite unlikely.

After locating Bill, who had just come back from buying lunch, they were pleasantly surprised to find that the criminals had, in fact, been moved elsewhere. The man who had met them earlier explained that they had been driven to Robinvale and would be processed there.

He also informed them that the superintendent wanted to speak to them about their investigation – at 3PM.

'Why not now?' the Detective said impatiently. At this rate, the entire day was going to be wasted.

'Sorry,' the man said. 'He has another meeting first. He's a busy man!'

'Is his *other meeting* of such importance that the investigation of potential new Portent can wait?' the Detective frowned.

'Detective, it's fine,' Bill said, touching their arm. 'It's just an hour. I know you don't like sitting around, but sometimes, patience is necessary when dealing with us lowly humans.'

'So I have come to find,' the Detective said coldly. 'May I at least access the relevant case files while I wait?'

The officer agreed and took the Detective to the computer room. There were two computers with attached monitors and the Detective sat down in front of one.

While technically working, the computer was barely functional and took nearly ten minutes to just turn on and load its contents. The Detective took some time to close a dozen unnecessary programs that were clogging up the RAM and then began making their way through the case files.

There were a lot, and their method of organisation was totally inscrutable. It was clear that several different people had attempted to organise the files, in several different ways, and each of them had given up before finishing.

The files themselves were also very poorly written, with sparse information, spelling and grammar mistakes, and blatant duplications of entire passages across reports.

It was only getting worse, as well. Five years ago, the files weren't too bad, but around four years ago, they became noticeably lazier. The very worst files were the most recent, written in the last couple of months. There were barely any files to begin with, and the ones present were horribly unprofessional and imprecise.

The Detective searched through reports on bushranger and music dealer activity from the last twelve months and found practically nothing. There were only two reports of bushrangers, one of which the Detective was sure were the exact same bushrangers they'd captured earlier. As for reports of music dealers, there were none at all.

The Detective doubted this was because there were no music dealers in Ouyen. It was much more likely that the office had simply failed to do anything about it.

The Detective left the report of the First Portent until last, as they already had a copy from Red Cliffs.

At least for this report, most of the details were there. The time, the date, the suspected casualties, radius of effect, etcetera, all were present. The location, however, was written only as 'fifty kilometres south of Ouyen', and there were barely any follow-up reports. There were no witness statements either, which was highly irregular. Although direct witnesses of the First's landing were next to non-existent, there was always someone who witnessed the ten-kiloton explosion from a distance.

It was sloppy – worse, it was incompetent, and actively frustrating. If the records were kept this badly, then how was the Detective supposed to trust the Ouyen Sin-Seeker Office? Something had to be done about it – although what exactly, the Detective wasn't sure. Was this what all the offices were like? If so, then what hope was there to solve any case, ever?

Fortunately, a chance to address the multiple, grievous problems was scheduled at 3PM. As the time approached, the Detective left the computer room and went to stand outside the superintendent's door.

At 2:58PM, the door opened, and an older Caucasian man with neat salt and pepper hair poked his head out.

'Hello, hello!' he said, smiling with very white teeth. 'Apologies for the wait. Do come in, Detective!'

The Detective did so, and Bill came in as well. The superintendent closed the door behind them and went and sat down behind his desk.

'Welcome!' he beamed. 'Superintendent Matthew Mc-Cleave, at your service! Please, call me Matt.'

He reached across the desk to shake the Detective's hand.

'Detective Claw,' the Detective said, shaking it briefly. 'Mr McCleave, after observing your operations and records for three hours, I must say that am thoroughly unimpressed by this precinct and its operations.'

Beside them, Bill hunched down and made a face, clearly mortified, but the Detective didn't care. The Ouyen branch was a mess and they needed to know.

'Oh?' Matt said, his grin fading slightly. 'If this is about the flooded jail cells, I do apologise. They should be fixed by tomorrow.'

'And the records?' the Detective said. 'How soon might they be fixed? If it is even possible to fix them.'

'I, uh,' Matt said. 'Look – we've been having a chaotic few months here, so unfortunately there isn't much we can do about the records for now. However, I will note it down as something that needs to be dealt with in the future.'

'Okay,' the Detective said. 'I suggest you deal with it sooner rather than later. Keeping accurate records is an important aspect of maintaining law. Without them, many important patterns and details are lost.'

'Yeah, alright,' Matt said, with a note of annoyance. 'No need to tell me how to do my job, Detective.'

'On the contrary,' the Detective began, but Bill interrupted them.

'How about we talk about the reason why we're here!' he said loudly.

'Indeed,' the Detective said, after a pause. 'Let us talk

about the disappearance of Mildura, and, more relevant to you and your office, Mr McCleave, the appearance of the First Portent in January of this year.'

'Ah, yes,' Matt said. 'I assume you have already read the report on it?'

'I have,' the Detective said. 'There were several important pieces of information missing. Most importantly, the precise location of the impact. There were also no witness statements appended to the report.'

'Well, that's because there were no witnesses.' Matt shrugged. 'It landed in the middle of nowhere. Empty bush and abandoned farmland for kilometres in every direction.'

'If it landed "in the middle of nowhere", then why were there nine recorded casualties?' the Detective said.

'Well, there was a farm there,' Matt said. 'Real remote place. Nine people were registered at that address. We're assuming they all died.'

'Assuming?' the Detective said. 'So, you did not confirm it, then?'

'Well... no,' Matt said. 'I mean, how could they have possibly survived? There's no way.'

'There are plenty of ways,' the Detective said. 'If the inhabitants were far enough from the point of impact at the time, or happened to be away from home, their chance of survival is far greater than zero.'

'Well, none of them have come forward and announced that they are not dead,' Matt said, 'and it's been over a month. If they were alive, they would surely have made themselves known by now.'

'Again, that is not necessarily true,' the Detective said. 'For example, if they have developed P.I.U.S, and do not wish to be registered, this might provide ample motive to remain in hiding. In your hesitance to follow proper procedure, it is possible you have allowed up to nine unregistered timesmiths to roam the countryside and cause problems for both themselves and others.'

'Okay, well, that's very unlikely,' Matt said. 'You know it happened in the middle of the night, right? Just after 2AM?

Mark my words, everyone in that house was asleep, in bed, when the First fell through the roof and blew up. There is NO WAY in hell they are still alive.

'BUT,' he added, as the Detective opened their mouth to argue, 'if you REALLY want to check for yourself and sift through all the rubble and radioactive dust to try and dig out some dead bodies, then sure! We can go and visit the site, later this afternoon. You can see it for yourself and decide for yourself that everyone there is dead!'

The Detective nodded. 'Good,' they said. 'I was going to suggest the same anyway. What time will we leave?'

'5PM,' Matt said.

'Okay,' the Detective said.

'Actually,' Matt said, '5:30PM. I need to organise rad suits.'

'Okay,' the Detective said, with narrowed eyes.

'Do you even need a rad suit?' Matt said, eyeing them back. 'Or does the miraculous cyborg not require such paltry safety measures?'

'I would prefer to use a rad suit, if possible,' the Detective said. 'Radiation is detrimental to the functioning of my electronic components. Additionally, my brain is organic and thus susceptible to cellular damage.'

'Of course,' Matt said. 'Is there anything else I can help you with?!'

'Yes,' the Detective said. 'As well as Portent sightings, I am additionally investigating the activity of music dealers within the region. I was unable to find any documents on such activity amongst your archives – however, I am wondering whether you personally have anything to say on the matter?'

'Music dealers?' Matt said and he snorted in amusement. 'Oh, we don't have any around here. Trust me, you needn't worry about that.'

'You seem very confident,' the Detective said. 'Why?'

'Well, we would have found some of them, right?' Matt said. 'But we haven't. The archives aren't wrong in that regard.'

The Detective narrowed their eyes. 'Are you certain

about that? Considering the heightened numbers of music dealers in surrounding areas, I find this difficult to believe. I find it more likely that you are simply not looking hard enough.'

'Wow, okay,' Matt said. 'Look – I'm not going to sit here and be insulted. Detective, you're just going to have to trust me when I say we don't have a music dealer problem here. Let it go, okay?'

'I cannot do that.' The Detective frowned.

'Well, you're going to have to,' Matt said. 'Sorry! That's just how it is. Now, if you'll excuse me, I have work to do. I'll come find you again after 5:30.'

He got up and shooed the Detective and Bill out of his office. The Detective considered fighting against it – but decided not to. After all, they were relying on the man to take them to the First Portent's impact site later. Without his cooperation, finding the site would take a lot longer.

As Matt firmly closed the door behind them, the Detective turned to look at Bill, a frown on their face.

'That man's incompetence is highly concerning,' they said.

Bill made a face of sympathy. 'Yeah,' he said. 'Although, I think some of it was because you insulted him. He was deliberately being obtuse.'

'Why?' the Detective said. 'That is very unhelpful.'

'Yeah,' Bill said, 'that was the point. I don't think he likes you very much.'

'Well, the sentiment is mutual,' the Detective said. 'Today has been nothing but frustrating.'

'Well, that's how it is, sometimes.' Bill sighed. 'Some days you make progress, and some days you don't. Some days you even go backwards. As long as the overall trend is forwards though, it's fine! You get used to it.'

'Extremely inefficient,' the Detective muttered.

With another two hours left to wait, they returned to the same cupboard as earlier and plugged back into the socket. They did not have much more data to analyse, so they left it for later. Instead, they spent time finishing the report about the Ouyen office's incompetence.

They weren't sure who they were going to send it to, but it was clear that something had to be done.

The last piece of evidence would be seeing how the officers acted in the field. Fortunately, they wouldn't have to wait too long for that.

# CHAPTER 22

# CRASH SITE

## Date: Thursday 12 of March 2082

t was nearly 6PM by the time Superintendent McCleave was ready to go.

'Rad suits are ready,' he said, patting a large grey bag. 'And I've grabbed a few other things as well – a crowbar, torches, rope, Geiger counter, etcetera. Say though, it's going to be sunset by the time we get there. Should we wait until tomorrow morning?'

'No,' the Detective said firmly. 'We're going now.'

'Okay, but it's going to get pitch black out there,' Matt said. 'Are you sure you want to be climbing over radioactive ruins in the dark?'

'I can see perfectly well in the dark,' the Detective said.

'Oh, well, good for you,' Matt said. 'I can't, and nor can Bill.'

'It's fine,' Bill said resignedly. 'We have the torches. They're Sixth Portent grade, so we should be able to see well enough. Although... will they work, with all the radiation?'

'The radiation should not be anywhere so high as to interfere with the torch,' the Detective said. 'That is, assuming the correct protocols regarding radiation reduction were followed?'

They looked pointedly at Matt.

'Yes, we got the mattersmiths to get rid of the worst of it!' Matt said. 'We're not complete idiots, Detective, despite what you may think.'

The Detective didn't say anything as they got into the passenger seat of the Ouyen office sedan.

Matt got into the driver's seat and, after passing Bill the Geiger counter, he started the engine.

'Keep an eye on that,' he said to Bill. 'When the dial starts increasing, we'll stop to put on the suits.'

As they pulled away from the office, everyone was silent. Matt concentrated on the road and Bill shut his eyes in the back, while the Detective stared silently out the window.

Around thirty minutes later, after turning onto a series of increasingly neglected roads, they saw a sign ahead which said:

TURN BACK! UNREALITY HAZARD! RADIATION HAZARD!

Just beyond it was a makeshift roadblock, little more than a plank of wood, painted with yellow and black radiation symbols and with several low tier relics nailed on.

'I guess this is it, then,' Bill said, leaning forward. 'Geiger counter hasn't really moved yet, though.'

'Yes, because we got rid of most of the radiation,' Matt said pointedly. 'This is probably a good spot to stop and put on the suits, though.'

He pulled over and they all got out to gear up. The radiation suits were bright yellow, with inbuilt gloves and rubber boots, as well as a full hood and face-shield. They were also fully soundproofed and contained inbuilt communications, which Matt spent nearly ten minutes setting up.

Once the suits were on and the comms working, the Detective moved the roadblock aside and Matt drove through.

It wasn't much longer before the Geiger counter started reacting, the dial twitching upwards, the red warning light flashing faster and faster. At the same time, they started to see signs of destruction.

Trees, blackened by fire and stripped of foliage. Fences, flattened, and bare earth scorched of life.

The road they were following turned to dirt, leading

them across a panorama of burnt pastures, washed in red by the setting sun. In places, grass was returning, a splash of colour amongst the brown and grey, although most of it was already yellowing. In the distance, a line of jagged structures was all that remained of a wind farm, broken blades jutting at angles from the hillside.

As they came around a copse of blasted, bark-stripped trees, Matt brought the car to a halt.

'See that crater up ahead?' he said, pointing through the windscreen. 'That's ground zero. If we're going any closer, we should walk. Radiation, and also unreality, are a lot higher over there and I don't want to spend hours cleaning the car.'

'Okay,' the Detective said and they opened the door.

As they got out, switching their vision to infrared, they caught sight of something, half stuck into a charred tree trunk nearby. It was a thin sheet of metal, about a metre long. Approaching, they grabbed it with both hands and pulled, wiggling it back and forth until it came loose.

It was covered in soot and dust but, after wiping it off, they saw that there were words on it.

'Ark 2,' they read aloud. 'Is that the name of this farmstead?'

'I believe so,' Matt said.

The Detective nodded and placed the sign down at the base of the tree.

'Let us go, then,' they said and began marching towards the distant crater.

Bill and Matt followed, although somewhat more hesitantly. The sun was well and truly setting by now, with long shadows casting the fields into inky blackness.

As they got closer, the light on Bill's Geiger counter was no longer flashing, instead displaying a continuous red glow. Nervously, he weaved around the increasing volumes of brick and rubble and corrugated iron.

'You know, some of these bits are probably fragments of the First,' he said, shining his torch at a large, mysterious slice of metal which was wedged into the ground. 'We shouldn't stick around for too long!'

'The unrealitic hazard posed by fragments of the First Portent in its Latent Phase are negligible,' the Detective said. 'You have nothing to fear.'

'Mmm,' Bill said doubtfully.

They were silent for a moment, as they went around a massive metal beam, twisted around itself like a coat hanger.

'There is a surprising volume of metal and debris here,' the Detective said thoughtfully. 'I had assumed this farmhouse was quite small. But appears I was mistaken. The debris indicates a relatively large structure, with an extremely sturdy design. Excessively sturdy, in fact, for a homestead and accompanying sheds and barns. These beams are similar to those used in the construction of skyscrapers.'

'Perhaps they used what materials they had on hand?' Matt said.

'It seems unlikely that what they had on hand was a skyscraper,' the Detective said.

As the sun vanished from the sky completely, Matt and Bill slowed significantly, torches swaying as they picked their way forward. The Detective adjusted their own movement by zigzagging back and forth, examining bits and pieces along the way.

There really was far more debris than they had been expecting – and it was heavy duty stuff. The more the Detective looked at it, and pieced it together in an internal simulation, the more they started to think that Ark 2 hadn't been a farmhouse at all.

Instead of household debris, such as appliances or trinkets, they found pieces of machinery, and massive chunks of pipe, and a panel that looked like it came from an elevator.

Frowning, they circled back to Matt and Bill.

Matt jumped slightly when they appeared out of the

dark, the points of their eyes glowing blue through their face-shield.

'There is evidence to suggest this place was not just a farm,' they said without preamble. 'I don't suppose you have any records of what it may have been instead?'

'No, sorry,' Matt said. 'I thought it was a farm.'

'Your response is as expected,' the Detective said. 'Entirely unhelpful.' Matt glared at them.

'Are we done yet?' he asked. 'Are you satisfied that everyone who was here is dead? Can we go?'

'I am not satisfied, no,' the Detective said. 'In fact, I have more questions now than I did before.'

'Great,' Matt grumbled. 'If I fall in a hole and break my leg, it's you who I'm suing.'

'Uh, Detective, I'm actually kind of with Matt on this one,' Bill said. 'Sorry. I know you can see in the dark, but we can't, and there are a lot of pitfalls and trip hazards. I'd much rather come back and finish the investigation tomorrow.'

'But we are here now,' the Detective said, gesturing at the crater ahead. 'I am aware of your discomfort, Bill,' they added when Bill gave them an exasperated look. 'If the terrain is too much trouble, why don't you stay here? I will continue on, observe the crater and return in ten minutes. Is that acceptable?'

'Well, I'd rather you didn't!' Bill said, glancing around. 'For the fifteenth time, you're not supposed to go anywhere without me! Also... it's spooky here.'

'Then Matt can stay here with you,' the Detective said.

'Matt will certainly not stay here,' Matt said. 'If you're going to the crater, then I'm going to the crater too!'

Bill sighed.

'It's fine,' he said. 'We can keep going. Just don't expect me to be very fast. I'm going to take my time.'

'That is acceptable,' the Detective said.

By now, the outer wall of the crater was less than two hundred metres away and the Detective decided to speed things up. Leaving Bill and Matt behind, they climbed on ahead, scaling the side of what had once been a hill.

After scrambling up onto the crater's lip, they paused at the top, looking down into the recess below. It was a deep crater, deeper than they'd been expecting.

Most of the debris had been blown outside of the crater – but what remained was very interesting. There were more gigantic pipes, half buried in the exposed rock, and metal beams, melted into slag.

The Detective once more attempted to digitally reconstruct what they were looking at – and came to the conclusion that it was some sort of underground structure. From here, they could only see the very top of it and there was no way of knowing how deep it went. It was highly possible that it extended down several hundred metres.

From this, they could make several other conclusions.

Firstly, the structure that had been here was absolutely not a farm. Based on the name 'Ark 2', it was possible it had been some sort of massive underground bunker, created for the purpose of 'weathering the apocalypse'.

Secondly, the structure was large enough to support dozens, if not hundreds, of people – people who, if present at time of the First Portent's impact, had almost certainly been trapped underground when the structure collapsed above them. Even if they'd survived the initial impact, they would have been left there, with no food or water, for over a month. There was no way they were still alive.

Matt had said there were nine people with a registered address at this location – but Matt had also thought it was a farm.

The Detective had a horrible suspicion that the death toll was quite a bit higher than nine.

If Matt had been right about one thing though, it was that survivors were unlikely. With the remote location and the fact that no one had apparently known what Ark 2 really was, it was actually entirely feasible that there had been no survivors, and no witnesses, of the First Portent's landing.

As they stood at the top of the crater, thinking, there was the faint sound of loose gravel sliding behind them. Turning, they saw that Matt had gotten to the crater faster than they'd been expecting.

'It is dark, so I doubt you will be able to see what I am seeing,' they said, turning away again, 'but I am now certain that this place was not a farm. Regretfully, I am also certain that the death toll for this incident is higher than initially thought. Potentially several magnitudes higher.'

'Oh?' Matt said breathlessly, clambering onto the top of the crater's rim. 'Why do you say that?'

'There is some sort of large structure below this hill,' the Detective said. 'I believe the function of the structure was to provide a place of refuge for people who wished to escape the realities of the Last Nation. There may have been hundreds of inhabitants. Maybe even thousands.'

'Really?' Matt said. 'How very interesting.'

The Detective frowned. The way he'd said it... His reaction had been not as expected. The news that thousands of people may have died below their feet was something that should have elicited shock and horror. But instead, Matt sounded... bored?

Had he already known, then, what this place was? If so, then why was he hiding the knowledge?

'Matt,' the Detective said. 'I must ask you to please answer the following question with complete truth. Did you already know about this place? That it wasn't a farm?'

They turned around to look at him, to closely watch his answer. He was bent over, fumbling with something with his bulky rad-suit gloves.

'Truthfully?' he said, straightening. 'Yeah, I knew about it.'

He was holding a gun. It was pointed at the Detective.

The Detective eyed it and then slowly raised their hands above their head.

'Well,' they said. 'I am relieved.'

Matt blinked. 'Relieved?' he said.

'Yes,' the Detective said. 'I was getting extremely

concerned at the level of incompetence displayed by the Ouyen Sin-Seeker Office. I was starting to think that standards of professionality were horrifyingly low. But you're not incompetent at all. You are just corrupt!'

In a blur of motion, they dropped low and lashed out with a savage kick, direct to Matt's shin. He yelled and fired off the gun, but the bullet went wide.

As he stumbled away, hopping on one leg, the Detective grabbed his arm and yanked it back, forcing him to drop the weapon. They then kicked out the other leg and Matt went down like a sack of bricks. Still yelling, he tried to roll away and tipped over the edge of the crater.

As he began rolling down into the pit, the Detective leapt after him, jumping from beam to broken beam. The slope was steep though, and only steeper further down. If they didn't act quickly, McCleave might be killed.

Looking around, the Detective saw a large, flat piece of metal sticking out of the rubble, and they leapt towards it. Yanking it out in a shower of dust, they bounded down the slope and jammed it into the ground just metres in front of the tumbling McCleave.

He smacked into it and, groaning, came to a stop. The Detective let go of the metal sheet and grabbed him, pulling him up by his shirt collar.

As their hand left the metal, however, something strange happened. Electricity arced unbidden from their fingertips, burning through the rad suit – and with it came a bizarre sensation. It was as though, for a second, the logic of the world had vanished, leaving nothing but pure chaos in its wake. Somewhere inside them, electricity surged, powerful, unstoppable...

It was a uniquely unsettling sensation. The Detective rapidly withdrew their hand from the metal, eyeing it warily. It was almost certainly a sizable piece of the First Portent. But there was no time to analyse what had occurred any further – Matt was struggling in their grasp, trying to break free.

Hauling him upright, the Detective dragged them both up the slope, fighting against sliding gravel and debris.

With great effort, they climbed back up to the rim and over the other side. There, they dropped McCleave on the ground and sat on his legs, arms twisted behind his back.

'You cannot escape, sinner,' they said coldly. 'You will be brought to justice – and you will explain to me what exactly is going on. It is clear you know the truth about Ark 2. It is also clear you do not wish me to know it. Unfortunately for you, I am determined to know, and I will not rest until you tell me everything. For your sake, I suggest you keep it snappy.'

'Oh yeah?' McCleave snarled.

'Yes,' the Detective said. 'You can start by telling me what you have done with Bill. Why is he not responding over comms?'

McCleave grinned, his cheek pressed against the yellow material of the rad suit.

'I ate him,' he said.

The Detective narrowed their eyes. 'What did I say about telling the truth?'

'I am,' McCleave said – and he started laughing.

With no further warning, the solid mass upon which the Detective sat abruptly liquified. McCleave's arms turned to jelly, drooping in the Detective's grasp like bags of water. His legs sagged out beneath their weight, thin enough to feel rocks through.

Startled, the Detective leapt back – just in time to see the rad suit rupture. Red slime, internally striated with coiled muscle, oozed out from under the split and, in seconds, vanished amongst the rubble.

The Detective sat very still for thirty seconds, analysing this series of new developments. Their left hand sparked and then sparked again. Shortly, they came to the realisation that they had absolutely no clue what was going on.

Three things, however, were perfectly clear.

One – McCleave was not only a sinner, but some sort of rogue fleshsmith.

Two – McCleave had done something horrible to Bill.

And three – the Detective was going to stop at nothing to get to the truth of the matter.

Electricity was surging inside them, lighting their insides with buzzing, jittering power. Opening their case file, they added a new priority to the growing list:

*Priority: Locate the rogue fleshsmith known as Matthew McCleave, determine the extent oF hIS infLUeNce in tHE rEGion OF OuYEn, aND IF HE HAS HURT BILL, I WILL KILL HIM –*

No, that wasn't right! The Detective shook their head, clearing it of the strange, giddy feeling, like distant, roaring static.

*Priority: Locate the rogue fleshsmith known as Matthew McCleave, and determine the extent of his influence in the region of Ouyen. Additionally, determine the whereabouts and vital status of Bill and, if possible, perform a rescue.*

That was better. Frowning, the Detective hurriedly left the crater behind. Clearly, the baseline unreality of the First Portent in its latent phase was working its influence more strongly than expected. It would be better if they left the area as soon as possible.

# THE SIXTH PORTENT

FIRST RECORDED SIGHTING: 05/02/2056, Alice Springs, Arrernte country, NT

PHYSICAL APPEARANCE:

The Sixth Portent is an anomalous light-emitting entity, capable of both absorption and emission of electromagnetic radiation across the full EM spectrum. Commonly observed travelling horizontally at approximately 1m above the ground, the Sixth is comprised of two discrete zones: the Core, responsible for emission, and the Spectre, responsible for absorption.

The Core, which sits at the centre of the Spectre, is often difficult to observe with the naked eye, due to extreme brightness when emitting on the visible spectrum, or invisibility when emitting in infrared or lower. However, in the right conditions, it is possible to make out the shape of a human foetus, at approximately 20 weeks into development. The shape has no mass and is entirely comprised of emitted light.

Far more difficult again to observe than the Core, the Spectre is only identifiable through its ability to absorb EM radiation. Surrounding the Core at a variable distance of between 3cm and 1m, the Spectre absorbs all EM radiation that enters on an angle that would otherwise intercept the Core. Following absorption, the energy is transmitted instantaneously to Core, from where it is emitted at a randomly determined angle. Notably, the Spectre does not re-capture or interact with any EM radiation travelling from the Core outwards.

With no small difficulty, the topographical shape of the Spectre has been recently mapped by DOU scientists and has been revealed to resemble an adult human female, standing upright at 166 cm, and visibly within her second trimester of pregnancy.

BEHAVIOUR:

The Sixth Portent is able to move horizontally at a maximum speed of up to 8 kilometres per hour; however, it typically travels at a slower pace of around 4 km/h, or remains still for many hours on end.

The brightness and visibility of the Sixth Portent varies widely depending on light sources around it, of which it absorbs and re-emits approximately 98% of direct EM radiation. In full sun, the Sixth is extremely bright, while in complete darkness it becomes invisible.

All EM radiation absorbed by the Sixth Portent is emitted again at a shorter, higher energy wavelength than before - in clear defiance of scientific canon. Specifically, the wavelength of absorbed EM radiation is shifted by -116 nanometres when emitted. For example, 650 nm (red light) becomes 534 nm (green light), and 470 nm (blue light) becomes 354nm (UVA).

This increase in energy results in a visible shift towards blue when in sunlight, as well as the generation of hazardous levels of ultraviolet and x-ray radiation. Additionally, the acceleration of energy input frequently results in increased temperatures and spot fires forming in the vicinity of the Sixth Portent.

Note – If you can see the Sixth, then you are too close! You are at risk of sunburn, heatstroke, fire and x-ray mutagenesis.

Note 2 – If it is dark, then you cannot see the Sixth! Avoid travel at night, and if unavoidable, bring a powerful flashlight to better spot the Sixth at a distance.

PORTENT INDUCED UNREALITY SYMPTOMS:

P.I.U.S RUBICON RADIUS: 13m.

ACTIVE SYMPTOM DEVELOPMENT: 71%

LETHALITY: 23%

DESIGNATION: Radismith

ADDITIONAL NOTES: P.I.U.S abilities arising from the Sixth Portent typically relate to the manipulation of light, heat and electromagnetic radiation.

# CHAPTER 23

# SPOOKY DRAIN MAN

### Date: Thursday 22 January 2082

Another month passed in the Ark – and while just as peaceful as the first, Quinn could not help but feel uneasy.

While she had not seen hide nor hair of it since, she could not forget the fleshsmith she'd seen behind the museum. She knew it was somewhere in the Ark, living out its slimy days in the various pipes and plumbing systems. And while she had no evidence to suggest it was at all dangerous, there was a primal part of her brain that screamed that it was.

Still, after a month of nothing, she had started to forget. There were other things happening that required her attention. Kylie was still working on a new way to break into Ava Brinesworth's computer and would not be discouraged. Mullet and Keanu got into trouble every other day, and a few times, they were arrested by security.

On top of this, there was a concert coming up – and Quinn was going to be performing in it.

The concert was for 'Australia Day', an old public holiday that had changed dates several times, but had stuck around for the longest on January 26th. The Ark interpreted the date as a sort of remembrance day for Old Australia – and it was one of their biggest events of the year.

As part of the three-day-long festival, the musicians of Melody Sands were putting on a concert on Saturday afternoon. The majority of them were going to be in it at some point and a wide range of music was going to be on display.

Quinn, upon finding out about the event, had immediately put her name down to perform – and this time, it wasn't just going to be her on stage. Maggie and Keanu were going to be playing the bass and guitar parts live.

As the event grew closer and closer, Quinn was equal parts excited and terrified. She was going to sing, on a proper, old-fashioned stage, in front of the entire population of Ark 2. At least this time, Kylie didn't seem to care about stopping her. It was going to go well. She had new material ready to go, and other people backing her up on stage!

As the event approached, however, things started to go wrong. The first thing was Keanu who, a week before the concert, suddenly announced that he had a family emergency and had to leave the Ark.

'Sorry, dude,' he told Quinn as she stood in his doorway, watching him throw clothes into a suitcase. 'I'll be back again. I'll play in your next gig, honest!'

'It's fine,' Quinn said, with a small sigh. 'If your mum's in the hospital, you gotta go see her. Not your fault. Shit happens.'

'Yeah,' Keanu said. 'Not the first time she's been in, though. Still, apparently it's real bad this time.'

'Is she gonna be alright?' Quinn said.

Keanu shrugged. 'Don't think she's been alright for a while,' he muttered. 'But, hey! Nothing the fleshsmiths can't handle. At least in the short term.'

Mullet was also sad to see Keanu leave – and spent the next few days moping about the house. To cheer him up, Quinn asked him if he wanted to take Keanu's place in the concert. A part of her hoped he would say no – while he had progressed phenomenally over the two months in the Ark, he was still an amateur and his skills weren't exactly flawless. Quinn wasn't confident that he could get through the songs without making any mistakes.

He looked so happy when she asked him though, that it was worth it.

'Hell yeah!' He grinned. 'Playing live on stage? Absolutely! Finally, all the Ark will see how cool I am!'

'Well, only if you don't fuck it up,' Quinn said. 'Do you, uh... do you actually know how to play any of my songs?'

'Yeah!' Mullet said. '...Some of 'em.'

'Which ones?' Quinn said. 'And how well can you play them?'

'Um,' Mullet said. 'Remind me how they go again?'

Quinn sighed and then went and grabbed a mobile phone from her room. It was one of the ones that Kylie had restored from the junkyard, but she'd recently co-opted it, using it to store her music and play her songs for people whenever they asked about it.

Mullet, meanwhile, went and got his guitar – and they spent the next half an hour figuring out which of the songs Mullet could feasibly play. Quinn mentally changed the list of songs to perform, which sadly involved saying goodbye to most of her new stuff.

It would be fine though – just playing anything live was exciting. And Mullet wasn't making too many mistakes. With a bit of practice before the concert, he would probably be fine.

While he kept practising, Quinn took a break to go to the bathroom – and that was when the second bad thing happened.

The matchbox full of Portent fragments was still sitting behind the U-bend, where Quinn had grown so used to it that she barely noticed it anymore. This time, however, as she went to wash her hands in the sink, she heard a faint noise from underneath.

Frowning, she paused and bent to open the cabinet. Pulling the first aid kit out of the way, she eyed the shadowy space in suspicion.

The aura of unreality fuelled her imagination, giving her all sorts of explanations for the noise. Rats, spiders, possums, snakes; all manner of critters could have moved in and were patiently waiting to chew on her hand.

She didn't dare reach for the matchbox, not until she could see properly. Quickly, she dashed into the kitchen and grabbed a small battery-powered torch from the odds and ends drawer. Then she ran back and shone it under the sink.

Nothing. There was a single cobweb but no spider. The matchbox was still there, undisturbed.

Quinn picked it up and put it back in her pocket. Maybe the bathroom wasn't the best place for it after all?

As she straightened and went to turn off the torch, however, the beam happened to pass over the drain at the bottom of the sink – and Quinn's heart jumped to her throat.

There was an eye in there.

In an instant, it was gone again – but the image was already burnt into her retinas. A hazel pupil at the centre of a blood-shot sclera, quivering at the top of a pencil-thin, red tendril. As soon as the light had touched it, it had withdrawn again, collapsing in on itself like the eye-stalk of a snail. But it was there. It was there in the pipe. It was there, right inside the fucking house.

No. No, no, no, no, no. Quinn bolted out of the bathroom, slamming the door behind her. Wordlessly, she ran into Mullet's room and slammed that door as well.

Mullet looked up from his guitar with a startled expression.

'Dude, what is it?' he said.

Eyes wide, Quinn forced herself to take a breath. It was in the house! The slime thing from behind the museum, it was right fucking there, looking at her through the drain!

How long had it been there? How long had it fucking been there?!

She didn't know what to say to Mullet – how to explain what she'd seen, and what it was, and how she knew. But she DID know that they had leave, immediately.

'Let's go to the shops!' she said loudly. 'Right now!'

'What?' Mullet said.

'I'm super hungry!' Quinn said. 'Aren't you?!'

'Did... did something happen?' Mullet asked in a low voice. 'Or... is something about to?'

'I'll tell you on the way!' Quinn said.

She left Mullet's room, and speed-walked to the front door. Then, Mullet hurrying after her, she practically ran down the driveway and out onto the road.

'Quinn, what is going on?' Mullet said worriedly as they turned towards town.

Quinn glanced around and, for the first time, noticed the rainwater drains built into the side of the road. Why were there rainwater drains? There was no rain down here. Had it REALLY been necessary to put them there?

'Pretend we're talking about lunch,' she said in a low voice. 'I'll explain, but quietly. There's a chance it's watching us.'

'What?!' Mullet said and then coughed. 'Oh, yeah!' he said loudly. 'I could really go for some fried chicken right about now!'

'I think it's a fleshsmith,' Quinn went on. 'Or, it used to be, but it's super mutated. I saw it once before, a month ago. It looks like this red, meaty slime thing, kind of like a slug, but it moves really quickly. It hides in the pipes.'

Mullet gave her a horrified look. 'Pizza, with pineapple?!' he exclaimed.

'It gets even worse,' Quinn said. 'Just now, I was in the bathroom, and I'm pretty sure I saw it again. It was inside the drain, looking at me with its tiny little eye-on-a-stalk.'

'What?!' Mullet said, eyes wide. 'I mean... yuck, that sounds like the worst sandwich ever!'

'Yeah, which is why we're leaving the house,' Quinn said.

'And you think this sandwich might be following us?' Mullet said quietly, looking around.

'I hope not,' Quinn said. 'But maybe. It saw me seeing it. It knows that I know it's there.'

'Well, what are we going to do? Can we tell someone about it?'

'Who? The security guards? The council? I don't know if they'll know how to deal with something like this.'

'Dude, if there's some sort of weird flesh man oozing through our walls, we need to tell someone!'

'You think we should tell the council about it, then?'

'Yeah, AND security! Everyone!'

'Okay, but what do we tell them?' Quinn said. 'I only knew the slime was there because it was doing some P.I.U.S shit. What if they ask me about that?'

'Just say you saw it.' Mullet shrugged. 'Who's going to dispute you? The slime?'

'I suppose you're right,' Quinn said.

'I'm always right.' Mullet grinned. 'C'mon. First council member we see, we're telling them!'

'Fine,' Quinn muttered.

They walked to the main square, where they briefly discussed lunch for real. Then, after settling on kebabs, they bought one each and sat down to eat.

Shortly, Mullet brightened and pointed across the square. 'Look!' he said. 'There's Matt McCleave! We can tell him about the slime man!'

Quinn was still reluctant – but after remembering the eyeball in the drain again, she nodded and stood up.

'Let's do it,' she said.

Matt had just bought a coffee and a muffin from a café and was turning to leave the square when Quinn and Mullet blocked his way.

'Oh, hello there!' he said, eyeing them over his coffee. 'Can I help you folks?'

'Yes,' Quinn said, and took breath. 'I saw something weird and I want to report it!'

'Oh?' Matt said. 'Shouldn't you report it to security?'

'Yes, but we also want to tell someone from the council,' Quinn said. 'It's serious!'

'What did you see?' Matt said concernedly.

'Uhh,' Quinn said. 'It's kind of hard to explain. I think it was... a rogue fleshsmith?'

'A rogue fleshsmith?' Matt said. 'In the Ark? That IS serious. Here, let's sit down! Tell me what happened!'

He sat at one of the tables outside the café and Quinn sat opposite. Then, hesitantly, she explained what she'd seen – both outside the museum and again inside her own bathroom.

Matt slowly ate his muffin while she spoke, his brows furrowing deeper and deeper.

'Well,' he said, when she'd finished, 'that's quite the tale! How very strange! I wonder if anyone else has seen this creature? If it really is crawling around inside the drains, then maybe others have caught sight of it as well?'

'Maybe,' Quinn said.

'In any case,' Matt continued, 'I will certainly bring this up during the next council meeting!'

He stood up and brushed crumbs off his shirt.

'Wait,' Quinn said. 'Are you... are you going to do anything else about it?'

'Well, I'm not sure what I could do,' Matt said. 'I'm no expert on catching rogue realitysmiths! But I do thank you for telling me. I will make sure the information gets into the hands of those who can act on it!'

'Alright,' Quinn said.

Matt nodded farewell and left.

Quinn turned to pout at Mullet.

'See?' she said. 'He doesn't know what to do! In fact, I'm not sure he even believed me!'

'Well, it was worth a shot.' Mullet shrugged.

Quinn sighed and stood up as well. 'Now I don't even want to go home again!' she said in annoyance. 'Stupid slime thing!'

'We could go to Maggie's house?' Mullet said. 'That way, if the slime attacks, it's three against one.'

'Hmmm,' Quinn said. 'Actually, that's a good idea. I don't know if she's told you but Maggie used to work for the DOU. She might actually have some ideas on what to do.'

'The dow?' Mullet said. 'What's that?'

'The Department of Unreality,' Quinn said.

As Quinn began telling him about Maggie's former profession, they left the shops behind and began dawdling back towards Melody Sands. About halfway back, they cut across the communal veggie garden, a shortcut they often took and often came out of with a handful of fresh fruits and vegetables.

As they stopped to pick some strawberries, however, Quinn abruptly stopped talking, head jerking upwards like a startled rabbit.

'Shit,' she said while Mullet stared at her. 'Someone's using P.I.U.S again!'

'Is it the slime?' Mullet hissed, hands in karate-chop pose.

'Almost certainly,' Quinn said, looking around. 'I think it was coming from over there!'

She pointed across the veggie garden, to where a small hydroponics shed stood. The walls were made of semi-opaque white plastic, with the vague shapes of tomato vines visible inside.

'Do we go and look?' Mullet said, eyeing the greenhouse warily.

'I dunno!' Quinn said. 'Should we? What if it's in there?!'

'Then that's more evidence!' Mullet said. 'Come on!'

He charged across the garden, ignoring Quinn's squeak of protest. After hesitating for a moment, Quinn ran after him, all senses on high alert.

Upon reaching the door, Mullet paused for half a second, eyeing a large sign pasted across it which said AUTHORISED ENTRY ONLY. Then, shrugging, he pulled the door open and poked his head inside.

'Do you see anything?' Quinn asked him, looking around in worry.

'Nah,' Mullet said.

He went to step inside but Quinn stopped him.

'Wait!' she said, and then reaching into her pocket, she brought out her mobile phone. 'Music,' she said.

'Don't we want to be stealthy?' Mullet said.

'I won't play it yet,' Quinn whispered. 'But I want to have it ready!'

Mullet nodded and waited for Quinn to open the music app and line up a song. Then, after she nodded at him, he stepped into the shed.

It was warm and humid inside and it smelt strongly of tomatoes. Three long racks of vines ran down the length of the shed, under blue strip lights. At the far end was a stack of fertiliser bags and another door.

Carefully, Mullet looked down each of the aisles – but there was nothing there.

'Are you sure it was from inside the shed?' he whispered to Quinn.

'No, I'm not sure,' Quinn said. 'I said it came from this direction!'

Mullet moved further into the shed, pausing to pick and eat a cherry tomato. Quinn, meanwhile, eyed the hydroponic piping with great suspicion.

'Mullet, we should go,' she said. 'We should leave it be. It's probably gone anyway.'

'What if it isn't?' Mullet said, continuing towards the far end of the shed.

'Well, that's even worse!' Quinn said. 'Also, we're not even supposed to be in here!'

'So what?' Mullet said.

'So, we'll get in trouble!'

'And?'

'And I don't want to!' Quinn said. 'I'm not Keanu. I don't want to be arrested, like, fifty times!'

'It's not that bad,' Mullet said. 'All they do is lock you in their office for a bit. And you tell them you won't do it again, and they let you go. And then you do it again anyway.'

Quinn went to reply – but just then, there was a noise from the far end of the shed.

They froze, staring at the door. Through the thin plastic of the back wall, something large was moving.

A second later, the far door opened.

Quinn went to run, finger on the play button of her phone – but then she saw who had come in.

'Wait,' she said. 'Is that...? That's not the slime man! It's that sin-seeker dweeb!'

'Spencer!?' Mullet said. 'What in the fuck are you doing here?!'

# CHAPTER 24

# TOMATO SHED SHOWDOWN

### Date: Thursday 22 January 2082

Spencer froze, hand on the door handle, staring at Quinn and Mullet.

For a moment, they all just stood there, staring in surprise. Then, Quinn felt Spencer start to do something P.I.U.S.

'Oi, stop that!' she yelled, gripping her phone. 'Don't you fucking try it! Remember what happened last time?'

Spencer narrowed his eyes – but the unreality dissipated.

'So you ARE a realitysmith,' he said. 'I knew it!'

Quinn blinked, then scowled at him.

'Okay, yeah,' she said. 'I am. But here's the thing, dipshit. I know that you're a mattersmith. But you don't know what I can do, can you? Eh, Spencer? All you know is that last time, we beat you. And if you try that shit again, then the same thing will happen!'

'Oh, yeah?' Spencer said.

'Yeah, fucking try us,' Mullet said, jutting his jaw.

Spencer glared silently at them for a moment.

'Alright,' he said. 'So, what are you going to do? Are you going to attack me? Are you going to try and capture me again?'

'What are YOU going to do?' Quinn asked. 'Are you still following us?'

'Yeah, did you think I'd forgotten about you?' Spencer

sneered. 'Music-dealer trash! Plus, now I know for sure that you've got P.I.U.S! You deserve to be locked up!'

'I don't see you turning yourself in!' Quinn said. 'Fucking hypocrite.'

'I will,' Spencer said. 'Just as soon as I've brought you down! You two, and the pink woman too! Justice is coming for you, just you wait!'

Quinn looked down at the lime green watch on her wrist.

'When?' she said. 'It's been, what, two months? When is the justice arriving?'

'It'll come!' Spencer snarled, waving his finger. 'And I will be the one who brings it! I am an avatar of the Nation's law, and you are sinners! I WILL bring a stop to your death and destruction!'

'Oh, come off it.' Quinn rolled her eyes. 'Death and destruction? What are you talking about? Okay, we break some rules, but they're not even that bad! Why don't you go after real sinners, like, I dunno, murderers or something?'

'No sin is too small!' Spencer said. 'All sinners must be brought to justice!'

'No, some sins are definitely worse than others.' Quinn folded her arms. 'For example, if I was a serial killer who went around and stabbed a hundred people and wore their skin, that would be pretty bad. But if, say, hypothetically, I went and sold a hundred USBs full of music... all that would happen is that the customers would listen to the music in their own home, and it would make them slightly happier.'

'You are perpetuating noise!' Spencer said. 'Music is noise! Noise brings Portents! And Portents bring death and suffering!'

'What if the music is indoors?' Quinn said. 'Huh? What if it's behind soundproofing? How is it any different from talking inside your house? I'd say that ninety-nine per cent of people who own music, only listen to it indoors!'

'And what about the one per cent who don't?' Spencer said. 'Are you fine with those people drawing Portents into town and killing everyone?'

'That sort of thing is extremely rare!' Quinn said. 'People

talk outside all the time! If you keep the volume down, music is the same! Do you often hear about Portents attacking towns because one person was talking? No, you don't! In fact, it's much more likely that the Portent just randomly wanders in!'

'Untrue!' Spencer said. 'The actions of the Portents are not random. There's ALWAYS noise! There's always SOMEONE playing music, or hammering in nails, or yes, talking loudly!'

'Yeah, because living is noisy!' Quinn yelled. 'You walk around and interact with the world and it makes fucking noise! Where do you draw the line, huh, Spencer? Is breathing too loud? Is a heartbeat too fucking loud for you?

'Also,' she continued hotly, 'you're wrong! There isn't always noise when Portent shows up! Sometimes, it just shows up! Sometimes, you do the right thing for years – staying quiet, following the rules, keeping your head down and your mouth shut, all of that garbage! And then one day, for absolutely no fucking reason, a Portent shows up and instantly vaporises your entire family and everything you ever knew and loved! And there's nothing you can do about it, or could have ever done about it, even with all the time in the world!'

Next to her, Mullet let out a low whistle. 'Damn,' he said. 'Spencer, now you've really gone and done it. She's started bringing up her tragic backstory!'

While Spencer stared at her from the door, Quinn reached into her pocket and pulled out the matchbox. Opening it, she showed Spencer the two dozen flakes of metal that sat inside. Even from several metres away, she could tell he could feel their aura.

'See these?' she said, glaring at him. 'Do you know what they are? They're pieces of the First Portent. I've pulled them out of my skin, where they appeared after you tried to kill me in Mildura. Do you think I enjoy that, Spencer? No, I don't. I wish I didn't have P.I.U.S. But guess what? I do. And there's no reason why I have it. There's no reason why I survived and no one else did. There's no reason why the

First Portent landed where it happened to land! Shit just fucking happens! And now I get to remember everyone else who died, and have shitty magic powers, and probably a bunch of radiation poisoning – but for now, in this moment, I'm alive! And while I live, I'm going to make noise! Not a lot of it – just enough to make my own existence slightly less fucking miserable! And Spencer – you can't fucking stop me!'

Silence followed her outburst. Spencer was staring at her – and so was Mullet. Quinn took a breath and put the matchbox back into her pocket.

'So, there,' she said.

Spencer cocked his head.

'So, you're a timesmith, then,' he said. 'Interesting. That explains why you were so hard to find. How many times have you changed the timeline to avoid me, sinner?'

Quinn glared at him. 'Like, once,' she said. 'I think you actually just suck at finding us.'

'I mightn't have found you even now, if you hadn't been using your P.I.U.S just before!' Spencer continued. 'But now I know what you can do, it's over!'

Quinn blinked. 'Wait, what?' she said. 'Using my P.I.U.S? When? I literally haven't used it for months.'

'Just before!' Spencer said. 'Don't lie, I felt it! That's why I came back here!'

'Wait, that wasn't you?' Quinn said.

'N-no?' Spencer said hesitantly. 'Are... are you saying that wasn't you?'

'Shit,' Quinn said, looking at Mullet.

'Slime man,' Mullet said.

'Yeah, must have been.'

'Do you think it's still around?' Mullet peered into the tomato plants nearby.

'Maybe,' Quinn said. 'Shit, it probably heard everything I just said!'

'Hey!' Spencer yelled. 'What are you talking about? What do you mean, it wasn't you? Who was it, then?'

'Shut up, Spencer!' Quinn said. 'You're not the only problem in our lives!'

Just then, they heard the sound of footsteps approaching on the gravel path outside. All three of them turned to look at the door behind Quinn.

It opened abruptly, revealing a security guard.

'You are not supposed to be in here,' he said flatly, his voice slightly muffled by the helmet.

Spencer immediately turned and ran.

'Catch him!' Quinn yelled as the door banged closed behind him. 'He's got P.I.U.S!'

The security guard glanced at her and then glanced back outside to where a second security guard was standing. Without a word, the second guard abruptly ran towards the back of the shed.

The first guard, meanwhile, still stood in the doorway, blocking the exit.

'Um,' Quinn said. 'You should probably both go. He's a mattersmith. Your friend is in pretty serious danger right now.'

'You are trespassing,' the guard said, in monotone.

'Only because we saw Spencer in here!' Quinn said.

'Yeah.' Mullet folded his arms. 'We only came in here to tell him HE was trespassing!'

The security guard tilted their head. 'This is your third offence within two weeks,' they said, eyeing Mullet.

'Oh yeah?' Mullet said. 'What are you gonna do about it?'

'Guys!' Quinn said, wringing her hands. 'I'm not fucking kidding! Spencer is gonna fuck that guy up!'

She tried to step around the guard in the door but he wouldn't move. Meanwhile, outside, Quinn saw Spencer sprinting back towards the main veggie garden. 'There he goes!' she said in frustration.

The other guard ran past as well and out of sight. Then, a second later, there was a short burst of unreality.

'Shit!' Quinn said. 'Welp, he's fucking dead!'

The guard in the door, perhaps seeing her expression, finally turned his head to look.

He was just in time to see, but not react to, his own incoming death.

The fence of the veggie garden was wrought iron, a series of thin metal bars with decorative crosspieces and aluminium spear-tips on the top, shaped like flur-de-lis. It was one of these spear-like bars that appeared now, whizzing at high speed through the air, before impaling itself directly through the chest of the guard in the doorway.

He jolted forward and then soundlessly fell to his knees. A faint gurgling sound came from his helmet.

As he toppled forward, Quinn saw Spencer standing in the garden behind him. He was twenty metres away, his hand outstretched towards them.

Behind him, the fence had been unnaturally bent out of shape. Two of the prongs were missing.

Spencer coughed once and wiped something slick and black from his mouth. Then, he ran out of sight again.

Open mouthed, Quinn looked down at the guard.

He was dead, there was no doubt about it. The spear was small but it must have punctured something important. Blood was pooling beneath him, trickling into the gutters around the shed door.

'Holy fucking shit!' Mullet squeaked from behind her.

'I fucking SAID Spencer would fuck them up!' Quinn said and fought back a panicked laugh.

'Is he dead?!' Mullet squeaked. 'He... he might not be!'

Before Quinn could stop him, he ran forward and knelt down in the blood. 'We should give him air!' he said, tugging at the man's helmet. 'Mate,' he said, as the helmet slid off, 'mate, can you hear me? Stay with us, dude! You gotta...'

He trailed off and Quinn saw his face go blank.

'What?' she said.

Mullet didn't respond, so she moved around him to see for herself. The guard's helmet was completely removed, his face out in the open.

Quinn was so not expecting to see it, that it took her a

moment to comprehend what she was seeing. Or rather, who she was seeing. But there was no mistaking it.

It was Keanu.

'It... it can't be,' Mullet said, shaking his head. 'It's not him!'

'I...' Quinn said. 'Does... does he have an identical twin?'

'I don't know,' Mullet said, and he stood up. 'It's not him, though. Why would it be? He's not a guard!'

'Yeah,' Quinn said. 'That... doesn't make any sense...'

They both stared down at the corpse for a moment longer, too stunned for words. The blood spread out further and further, spreading out more than Quinn had ever thought possible. How could one person contain that much blood? How could it be Keanu, when he wasn't even in the Ark anymore?

Quinn frowned.

The blood was still increasing, and now, there was literally too much of it. It was a ludicrous amount, and still coming, seeping out of the wound in buckets and buckets...

The guard's chest was sinking in and his legs had already gone. Before their eyes, his arms turned to sludge and lastly, his face began to melt. Flesh and hair congealed into a red jelly, collapsing in on itself.

'Okay, what the FUCK –' Mullet began.

Quinn pressed play on the music.

The guard had become a gelatinous mass, no longer remotely human in form. As Mullet gaped at it in shock, it shifted, gathering itself and rolling towards him.

He backed away, into the tomatoes, but it continued to advance. A slice of it peeled off and oozed towards Quinn.

She backed out the door, but not before seeing the hydroponics start to rupture. Splitting along their seams, the white plastic pipes cracked open and red tendrils shot out. With shocking speed, they wrapped around Mullet's arms and legs. Then, while he yelled and tried to pull free, the larger tendril rose up from the floor and wound around his chest.

Quinn backed away further. Time, she needed more time! The split tendril followed after her, gaining speed.

There was a sharp popping noise behind her in the garden, and Quinn turned to see what it was. The neat flagstone path was cracking apart, shifting upwards. Red jelly welled upwards from between the cracks, gaining mass, a rising membranous wave.

In the shed, Mullet's screams became more desperate – and then suddenly muffled. Quinn looked around wildly as one of the tendrils tried to grab her. In the garden, the larger piece billowed upwards, taller than a person. Vague bone structures assembled themselves beneath a thin film of translucent skin. Faces half formed and subsided, eyes rolling, fixing on Quinn.

Beneath her, the pavement cracked, slime flowing over her shoes. It was warm – the same temperature as a body.

Quinn decided to call it there.

The music distorted in her ears, and then came to a stop.

In relief, she watched as the monster receded back into the earth, shuddering inwards, tendrils retracting from view. Above it, the pavement fixed itself, pieces fitting together like a perfect jigsaw.

The tendril from the shed snaked back inside, to the sound of Mullet's stilted backwards screams. As Quinn went back towards him, she saw the tendrils let him go and hide inside their thin white tubes, eggshell cracks sealing away into nothing.

On the ground, the body of the guard reformed itself, Keanu's face rising from the dripping goo.

As Quinn had been banking on, time rewound even further. She hadn't had long, only about ten seconds, but the song had been complex, with many layers. It was working as intended. Mullet put the guard's helmet back on and moonwalked away. Blood sucked inwards, back into the body.

Then, like a marionette on strings, the guard rose upright. He shuddered as the spear left his chest and shot back into its place in the fence.

The song had almost reached its start – and dammit, it wasn't quite long enough! The guard was still arguing with Mullet. Spencer had still run off!

Quinn had to do something. She had to change what happened or things would go the exact same way.

With a jolt, she returned to the timeline and braced for the side effects.

Her legs felt weak and something was happening to her right hand. She almost didn't want to look at it – but she forced herself to anyway.

It was twitching uncontrollably, flickering in space. Her fingers were where they were supposed to be – and then they weren't, duplicating and reversing and bending off at strange angles.

Grimacing, Quinn shoved the hand into her pocket. She would deal with it later.

She had seconds until Spencer killed the security guard again.

There was no time to second guess. Quinn took a breath and kicked the guard in the nuts as hard as she physically could.

He buckled to his knees, hissing behind his helmet. While Mullet stared at her in shock, Quinn dodged back again.

A spear shot over their heads, whistling over the tomatoes and thudding into the far wall, where it vibrated menacingly.

Mullet jumped in shock, and the guard turned to stare after it.

Ducking around him, Quinn reached the door. Outside, Spencer was standing with his arm outstretched.

Their eyes met and Quinn flipped him the bird. Then she firmly closed the shed door.

Mullet and the guard were staring at her.

'Saved your life,' Quinn said tiredly. 'No biggie.'

She promptly sat down on the floor.

Mullet, who realised what had just happened, went quiet. He didn't protest at all when the guard informed them they were both to come and spend a few hours in the office to think about what they'd done.

Now that she'd seen his face, Quinn recognised that it was Keanu's voice – albeit a dead, monotone version. She didn't say anything though, at least not yet.

The slime was still there, she knew it. It was watching her and it almost certainly knew what she was. It was also far, far bigger than she'd realised.

In the office, she sat very still and looked at her right hand, which had gone back to normal – although one of the fingernails was missing, with nothing but smooth skin in its place.

'Hey, Mullet,' she said eventually.

'Yeah?'

'I think we should leave Ark 2 soon,' she said.

'What?' Mullet said. 'But I thought you liked it here?'

'I did,' Quinn said. 'But I think Kylie's right. We can't stay in one place forever.'

'I suppose,' Mullet said. 'It has got a little duller now that Keanu left. Hey – maybe we'll see him up there?'

Quinn glanced sideways at the guard who was still there, keeping an eye on them.

'Maybe,' she said. 'But I doubt it.'

# CHAPTER 25

# THE AUSTRALIA DAY CONCERT

## Date: Saturday 24 January 2082

On the day of the concert, Quinn woke from a nightmare where she had plummeted to a fiery death. Sitting up in bed, gasping for air that was no longer burning, she struggled for a second to recall where she was. But then she remembered and her stomach twisted painfully.

The big performance was later that day – but she didn't feel excited about it. Instead, she mostly felt dread. She wanted to leave, get out of here, as fast as she possibly could.

The slime thing was probably watching her in the walls – but as long as she didn't acknowledge its existence, she doubted it would make a move.

Spencer was also still somewhere loose in the Ark, and Quinn had no idea what he would try and do next. Ever since seeing him, she had kept her mobile phone full of music on her at all times, ready to whip it out if something happened.

The previous morning, she'd written a note to Kylie, explaining what she had seen. She didn't dare tell her out loud, or sign it out in the open, in case the slime was watching. Kylie had agreed that they should leave as soon as possible – although not until after the concert.

'It's fine,' Quinn had said. 'I don't mind missing the concert, if it means we leave the Ark sooner.'

Kylie, however, had insisted they leave on the Sunday.

'There are some things I have to do first,' she said. 'Besides, we need to pack up our stuff, which is going to take a couple of days, and we also need to give the cottage a good clean. Otherwise they'll probably charge us for it.'

Quinn had reluctantly agreed to wait – but the longer she waited, the worse her uneasiness got. The dread, and the feeling of being watched, only intensified by the hour.

Distracted at practice, she made a lot of basic mistakes, forgetting lyrics and fudging cues. Maggie mistook her distractedness for pre-concert nerves and sat her down to give her a pep talk – but Quinn barely heard a word of it. She hadn't told the older girl that they were leaving tomorrow. She hadn't told her anything. She hadn't known where to begin.

As the afternoon rapidly approached, it dawned on Quinn that she was, in fact, about to perform in front of a crowd – and her nerves got even worse. She wished that she could forget about the slime, for just an hour, until the set was over. She was going to fuck it up. It was her first time performing live with a band at her back and she couldn't have felt less like doing it.

The concert started at 2PM, and continued until late, and the entire population of the Ark were going to be there. Temporal Boom, as the newest band on the block, were playing the opening act.

At 1:30PM, Quinn and the others arrived at the botanical gardens, where a huge, old-style music stage had been constructed. There were rows of lights above it, in all different colours, and massive towers of speakers stacked on either side. Usually, Quinn would have been foaming at the mouth in excitement to see it – but today she just felt like throwing up.

As they began set up, her hands felt like clammy blocks of meat.

'Relax, Quinn,' Maggie told her, putting her hand on her shoulder. 'You're gonna do fine. This might be your first real concert but it's not gonna be your last. It doesn't matter if it's not perfect. The world's not gonna end a second time!'

'I dunno about that,' Quinn muttered as waves of nausea rolled over her.

Outside, the crowd began arriving, setting up picnic rugs on the grass and chattering excitedly. At the back, Quinn couldn't help but notice several security guards, keeping an eye out for trouble.

She tried her best not to look at them, but their presence occupied her mind. How many of them were part of the slime? Was it all of them? Or just a few? Who else knew about it? Had Keanu found out? Is that what had happened to him?

Suddenly, it was time for soundcheck, and adrenaline spiking through her system, Quinn was forced to concentrate on the task at hand. On the stage, Maggie was helping Mullet attach his guitar to the amplifiers. He played a chord and it rang out from the tower of speaker, clear and loud.

The sound vibrated in Quinn's chest and she took a deep breath. She had to focus. The slime wasn't going anywhere – and it wouldn't try anything, not now, with so many witnesses.

She moved up to the microphone and began setting it up. After a couple of horrible whining noises, she tested it and it sounded fine.

Behind her, Maggie plugged in as well and plucked out a short riff. The air hummed with bass around them. In the crowd, a couple of people cheered in excitement.

Quinn turned to look back at Maggie. 'It's so loud!' she whispered.

'Yep,' Maggie said. 'And this is nothing compared to how they used to be. Before the End, concerts used to be aggressively loud events. The music was played well over a hundred decibels. Also, the crowds were insane. Popular bands would have hundreds of thousands of people go to see them. Millions, even!'

Quinn looked out over the crowd gathering on the lawn. Most of Ark 2 were there, around fifteen hundred people. It was already a huge number. She couldn't even begin to comprehend the numbers that Maggie was talking about.

Just after 2PM, Ava Brinesworth appeared on the stage to open the event. She winked at Quinn as she passed, stepping up to the mic at the front of the stage.

As the sound of her clearing her throat echoed through the speakers, the crowd fell silent.

'Hello, Ark 2!' Ava called. 'Welcome all, to our annual Australia Day music concert! How about you make some noise?'

The crowd cheered.

'Perfect!' Ava smiled. 'This may be the last remaining place on Earth where you, the people, can cheer and holler and enjoy live music, free from tyranny and oppression! I hope you're all enjoying yourselves!'

The crowd cheered again.

'I quite agree,' Ava said. 'But here I am, waffling on, when it's the music you're here to see! How about I introduce you to our first act of the afternoon?'

Quinn gulped in terror as the crowd cheered, even louder.

'Ladies and gentlemen – please welcome to the stage our newest residents of Melody Sands, and freshest faces in all of the Ark – Temporal Boom!'

Ava retreated from the mic and, in a daze, Quinn stepped up to take her place. Below on the lawn, a sea of eyes stared up at her expectantly.

Quinn took a breath. She'd wanted to do this sort of thing since she'd first learnt about it. But now... now she was actually there...

No, dammit. She still wanted to do it!

She leaned closer to the mic.

'Um,' she said, her own voice amplified on either side of her. 'Hi everyone. We're Temporal Boom. I feel like shit today. Here's a song about it.'

***

The set passed in a blur, and then it was over. Quinn couldn't have said if it went well or not. There had certainly been a few mistakes here and there – but the crowd had seemed to be enjoying it, which was the main thing.

For a bit, she was blissfully caught up in the exhilaration of performing live. But then, as the next band got on stage and started their set, her fears from earlier began seeping back in. If anything, the feeling of dread had gotten worse. It was as though a strange pressure was bearing down on her, like a distant rumble at a frequency too low to hear.

She followed Maggie and Mullet to the back of the crowd, where they found a spot to sit and watch the other acts. But although the acts were good, she couldn't relax, fidgeting constantly and looking around at the crowd.

'Are you okay?' Maggie asked her between sets, after she shifted position for the third time in two minutes. 'You seem agitated. What's going on?'

'Nothing,' Quinn said, shifting position again.

Maggie eyed her doubtfully. 'Is it Kylie?' she said.

Quinn blinked. 'Huh?'

'Is she up to something again?' Maggie said. 'I saw her early this morning, and I'm not gonna lie, she was acting pretty suspicious. I know you don't like it when she does that sort of thing.'

'What are you talking about?' Quinn said. 'What was she doing? Actually, come to think of it, where is she? I haven't seen her all day!'

'I saw her heading off into town, around 6 this morning,' Maggie said. 'She was wearing all grey and black, and carrying a large bag. I didn't even know that she owned grey or black clothes.'

'Oh no,' Quinn said. 'That's her breaking and entering outfit!'

'Her what?' Maggie said.

Quinn looked at Mullet. 'Where's she breaking into do you think?'

'Someone's house, probably.' Mullet shrugged. 'Dunno whose.'

Quinn looked up at the stage, where Ava Brinesworth was getting ready to announce the next act.

'I think I know,' she said.

'Shit,' Maggie said. 'This is more serious than I was expecting. Should we do something?'

'I don't think there's anything we can do,' Quinn said. 'Except wait, and hope she doesn't get caught.'

Waiting was easier said than done, however. The next few hours passed with torturous slowness. The music was good, but Quinn couldn't concentrate.

As the artificial sky above changed slowly from sunset hues to twinkling night sky, Quinn's anxiety grew to breaking point and she abruptly stood up.

'I'm sorry,' she said to the others, 'I have to go. I need to see if Kylie's come back yet.'

Wordlessly, both Mullet and Maggie stood up as well.

'We'll come with you,' Maggie said.

'Yeah.' Mullet grinned. 'This set is boring anyway.'

Quinn nodded gratefully, and all three of them picked their way through the crowd and left the botanical gardens behind. Beyond the gardens, the streets were eerily quiet, the music from the stage echoing oddly between the empty houses.

As they got back to Melody Sands, they could already see from the road that their cottage was dark. They checked anyway – but it was empty. Kylie wasn't there.

'This is weird, right?' Mullet said. 'Surely breaking into a house doesn't take that long?'

'Maybe she came back and left again?' Maggie said.

'If she did, you'd think she would leave a note or something?' Quinn said.

'Maybe she did?' Maggie said.

They spent the next few minutes searching the house for notes or clues of Kylie's whereabouts. Her room was very tidy and she'd started, but not finished, packing her clothes away into a suitcase.

'Is she planning on going somewhere?' Maggie asked.

'Yeah,' Quinn said. 'We... we all are. We were going to leave the Ark tomorrow, after cleaning the house...'

'Oh shit, really?' Maggie said. 'When exactly were you going to tell me that you were all leaving?!'

'Sorry,' Quinn said. 'I was gonna tell you...'

'Hey,' Mullet said from where he was standing and looking at Kylie's favourite monitor. 'What do you guys make of this?'

'Is it a note?' Quinn said, coming over.

'No,' Mullet said. 'It's just a weird email, from... Ava Brinesworth?'

He moved aside to let the others see. On the screen was an open email, with a single word in the body text: *Surah*.

There was nothing else, not even a subject line or header.

'Why would Ava send that to Kylie?' Quinn wrinkled her nose. 'What does it mean?'

'Sent at 3:46 PM,' Maggie said, frowning. 'Weird. Do you think it's a password?'

'Oh!' Quinn said. 'I bet it IS a password! And I bet Kylie sent it, to herself, from Ava's computer! After all, that's what she'd been trying to do this whole time – break into Ava's laptop.'

'Okay,' Maggie said. 'Makes sense. But if she sent it this afternoon – then where is she now? That was five hours ago.'

They were all silent for a moment.

'Maybe she got arrested by security?' Mullet said.

'We could go and see?' Quinn said. 'Although... usually they tell us immediately when YOU get arrested, Mullet.'

'Yeah, but breaking and entering is bit more serious than getting drunk and drawing dicks on stuff,' Mullet said.

'Isn't that even more reason to tell us?' Quinn said.

'How about this,' Maggie said. 'Let's go to the security office and see if she's there. If she is, problem solved. If she isn't... well, we can cross that bridge when we get to it.'

They all agreed, and left the cottage behind, hurrying

across town. It didn't take long to get to the security office. It took even less time to confirm that Kylie was not there.

'Alright,' Mullet said, as they stood outside. 'Where's the bridge go, Maggie?'

'I don't know,' Maggie said. 'What the fuck? Where IS she?'

# MISSING PERSONS

Date: Saturday 24 January 2082

With no other clues as to where Kylie could have gone, they decided to go and snoop around Ava Brinesworth's mansion. It was all the way on the other side of town. As they passed by the botanical gardens again, the event was still in full swing, with one of the last and most popular acts up on stage.

Soon, they entered the area with the particularly massive houses – an area that Quinn had not been to many times, aside from their initial visit to the Brinesworth house. As the noise from the concert once again faded into the background, the streets became eerie, with massive, dark houses crouched behind tall fences.

Eventually, they came to the Brinesworth house and stopped outside the wrought iron gate. On the other side, the dark driveway stretched like a looming shadow from the main bulk of the house.

Unlike many of the houses around, there were several lights on inside. As they watched, a light on the top floor abruptly turned off, and a different one turned on in the next window.

'Someone's home,' Quinn said quietly. 'Probably the butler, right? What was her name again?'

'Saoirse,' Maggie said. 'Originally an Irish name. Fun fact – it's spelt quite differently from how it's pronounced!'

'Maybe that's Kylie in there?' Mullet said as another light turned on.

'Why would she turn the lights on?' Quinn said.

'To see, duh?' Mullet said.

Quinn tried to smack him but he dodged out of the way.

'So, what's the plan anyway?' Maggie said, shining a phone torch into the nearby bushes. 'Are we just going to poke around the fence for clues?'

'It would be better if we could go in there,' Quinn said, peering through the bars.

'No, we're not doing that,' Maggie said. 'Two acts of breaking and entering don't make a right.'

'But what if Kylie's in trouble?' Mullet said. 'What if we hear a blood-curdling scream? Would you break in then?'

'Depends how blood-curdling,' Maggie said. 'Are we talking girly shriek, or full-lung-capacity bellow of anguish?'

'Guys, can we focus?' Quinn said. 'I have this awful feeling that she IS in trouble. I've been feeling it all day.'

Mullet raised an eyebrow at her. 'When you say feel,' he began.

'No, not like that,' Quinn said quickly. 'It's more of a gut feeling. Although I suppose I AM also worried that our slimy friend is involved. Or Spencer. Or both.'

'Dude,' Mullet said. 'You're right. If Spencer found her by herself, he might have tried something! I didn't even think of that!'

'Yeah,' Quinn said, 'or if Mr Slimy suspected she knew something, it might have made a move! It probably knows I told her everything...'

'Umm,' Maggie said. 'You two care to explain what you're talking about?'

Quinn and Mullet exchanged glances.

'It's like this,' Quinn said quietly. 'There's this guy who's been following us. He's an ex-sinnie and, for whatever stupid reason, he has a personal vendetta against us. We saw him in the Ark on Thursday.'

'What?!' Maggie said. 'Shouldn't you report this to someone?!'

'Oh, security knows about him,' Quinn said. 'But... we

also don't trust them. Don't ask how we know, because it's complicated, but basically, at least one of them is a slime monster.'

Maggie raised an eyebrow. 'Quinn, what does that even mean?' she said.

'I mean, they're some sort of mutant fleshsmith,' Quinn said. 'But they can make themselves look like a regular person.'

'Specifically, like a security guard,' Mullet added.

Maggie looked at them, one then the other.

'You're pulling my leg,' she said.

'Nope,' Quinn said. 'Wish I was.'

'Well, then, how the fuck do you know about this?' Maggie said. 'If they look like a regular person, then how do you know they're a "slime monster?"'

'Quinn saw a guy turn into a slime,' Mullet said.

'Yeah,' Quinn said. 'Basically, Spencer, um... threw a spear at a dude, and he turned into jelly and crawled away down a pipe.

'Spencer is, uh, the guy who's following us,' she clarified as Maggie continued to look confused.

'He threw... a spear?' Maggie said, then shook her head. 'You know what? It doesn't matter. There's a slime man who looks like a security guard. Sure. I believe you.'

'Well, maybe,' Quinn said, frowning. 'Or maybe he looks like someone else now?'

'You think it can do that?' Mullet said.

'I think it's possible,' Quinn said. 'In fact, more than possible! It's totally feasible that the slime man can could change its face to look like anyone!'

'Really?' Mullet said.

'Yes,' Quinn said.

'So we can't trust anyone?' Mullet narrowed his eyes.

'Nope!' Quinn said.

'Even ourselves?' Mullet said, and he pointed dramatically. 'What if YOU'RE the slime?!'

'What if you are?!' Quinn pointed back. 'Quick! Tell me something that only the real Mullet would know!'

'Like what?' Mullet said.

'Don't ask me, idiot! You're the one supposed to be proving your identity!'

'Now who's unfocused,' Maggie said. 'None of us are a slime, that's stupid. But if you REALLY want to check whether someone is a fleshsmith or not, it's simple. You just hand them a relic and watch them squirm.'

'Okay, but we don't have a relic,' Mullet said. 'Unless...? No... Kylie left the boomerang in THE GLAM VAN.'

'There's always Tim Tams,' Quinn said slowly. 'There are heaps of those around the Ark. I'm sure we could find some.'

'Good idea!' Mullet said. 'Everyone time we meet someone, we get them to eat a Tim Tam and if they refuse, we kick the shit out of them!'

'Well... maybe we give them a chance to explain themselves first,' Quinn said. 'Some people just don't like Tim Tams, you know?!'

Just then, they all heard voices coming from further down the street. Turning, they saw a small group of people approaching, talking and laughing as they walked in and out of the pools of light cast by the street lamps. Among them was Ava Brinesworth.

'Shit,' Quinn said. 'Should we go?'

'Actually,' Maggie said. 'I think we should tell Ava what's happening.'

'What?' Quinn said. 'Why?'

'Because,' Maggie said, 'if everything you've said is true, about the fleshsmith and the man following you, then this could actually be pretty serious. Kylie's missing and we need to let someone know about it. Someone who can actually get shit done, like organise a search.'

'But she went missing while robbing Ava's house!' Quinn hissed.

'Yeah, so we leave that detail out,' Maggie said. 'We can just tell her that Kylie has gone AWOL, and we're worried about her.'

'Alright,' Quinn said doubtfully.

They waited in front of the gate until Ava got close enough to see them. As the rest of the chattering group peeled away and went into their own homes, she approached, nodding at them amiably.

'Good evening,' she said as she got closer. 'Is something the matter?'

'Yes, actually,' Maggie said. 'Our friend is missing. Kylie Collins. We haven't seen her all day and... we have reason to believe she might be in serious danger.'

'Kylie Collins?' Ava said. 'Yes, I remember her. When did you see her last?'

'Early this morning,' Maggie said. 'I saw her leaving Melody Sands at around 6AM. None of us have seen or heard from her after that, aside from one weird email around 4.'

Ava nodded seriously.

'And you believe she's in danger?' she asked. 'Hmph. I suppose you'd better come inside and tell me about it.'

She opened the gate and went in and they all followed after her. As they approached the front door, it opened and Saoirse peered out.

'Welcome home, Madam,' she said, eying the small crowd on the doorstep. 'Shall I prepare supper?'

'No, thank you, Saoirse,' Ava said.

'Um, actually,' Quinn said quickly. 'Could you... would you be able to bring us some tea... and Tim Tams?'

'There's a reason for it,' she added quickly, as Ava sent her a curious look. 'We'll explain in a minute, but it's important, trust me!'

Ava nodded and Saoirse disappeared.

'I suppose we had better go to the tearoom, then,' Ava said.

She led them to the exact same room they'd had tea in last time, where she removed her jacket and sat down with a sigh.

'Alright,' she said, as they all sat down opposite. 'Please, go ahead and explain what's happened.'

'Um,' Quinn said. 'We... we need the Tim Tams first. Then we'll explain.'

Ava raised an eyebrow. 'Tim Tams? What is so important about them, if I may ask?'

'We're going to need you to eat one,' Quinn said.

'I...' Ava said. 'Okay. Are you going to tell me why?'

'Yes, once you've eaten it,' Quinn said.

They waited in awkward silence for a couple of minutes before Saoirse came in and wordlessly put down a tray of tea and biscuits. Eyeing Quinn, Ava immediately picked up the nearest Tim Tam and sniffed it delicately.

'You want me to eat the entire thing?' she said.

Quinn nodded.

With a bemused shrug, Ava bit a piece off and ate it, swallowing with zero hesitation.

'I admit, I am VERY curious as to what you have to say now,' she said when she was finished.

Glancing at the others, Quinn nodded and opened her mouth.

'So, basically, there's a rogue fleshsmith hiding in the Ark,' she began.

Ava listened attentively to her explanation, nodding occasionally and sipping on her tea.

'I see,' she said, once Quinn was finished. 'This is a strange problem indeed. But you know... when you described this "slime monster" just now, I think... I do believe I may have seen it myself. I had forgotten until now, actually.'

'What?' Quinn said. 'Where? When?'

'It was a few months ago,' Ava said. 'In the botanical gardens. I took the scenic route to the shops, as one does sometimes, and happened to see... well, now I am almost certain it was this same creature you have described. At the time, I thought it was a poor, sick animal of some sort. In fact, I told the security to deal with it, and dismissed it as dealt with. But... I suppose it's still there.'

'Where in the botanical gardens was it?' Quinn said, leaning forward.

'Oh, behind the museum, if I recall correctly,' Ava said.

'That's where I saw it the first time!' Quinn said. 'It slithered up into a pipe!'

'Yes, exactly,' Ava said. 'I thought it was some sort of severely mangy possum.'

'Oh, it is WAY bigger than a possum now, trust me,' Quinn said.

Ava frowned. 'This is quite serious,' she said. 'Why did you not come to me sooner?'

'Honestly,' Quinn said, 'I didn't think you'd believe me. Matt McCleave didn't seem to. But if you've seen it as well...!'

'And you two'—Ava looked at Maggie and Mullet—'have you also seen it?'

'No, just Quinn,' Mullet said. 'But I believe her.'

'Well, what do you propose we do?' Ava said. 'Should we attempt to capture it?'

'I mean, the main problem right now is finding Kylie,' Maggie said. 'Our concern is that the slime may have attacked her, since Quinn told her about it. Either that, or this Spencer guy did something.'

'Spencer?' Ava said. 'Oh – do you mean Vincent Spencer? Security told me that they apprehended an intruder by that name a couple of days ago.'

'Teenager, curly blonde hair, red hoodie?' Quinn said.

'Yes, that's him.' Ava nodded. 'He was sent topside and handed over to sin-seekers, I believe.'

'Oh shit!' Quinn said. 'They really got him?'

'I guess that narrows our suspects down to one, then,' Maggie said grimly.

Remembering how the slime had attacked both her and Mullet in a timeline that no longer existed, Quinn frowned.

'What would this slime have done, had it attacked your friend?' Ava asked. 'Would it take her somewhere?'

'That makes sense,' Maggie said. 'Since the Ark isn't very big, it can't have just struck and left her there. Someone would have seen the body by now.'

'So you do think it took the body with it?' Ava said.

'Can you not say "the body" like she's dead, please?' Quinn squeaked.

'Apologies,' Ava said. 'Although, it is possible. I hate to say it, but you should probably prepare yourself for the worst.'

'Well, can we hurry up, then!' Quinn said. 'Where would the slime take her?!'

'The museum, perhaps?' Ava said. 'Since we have seen it there twice. Maybe that's where it has its den?'

'It does seem to hang around there a lot, especially for somewhere that's full of relics,' Maggie said. 'It's a good place to start looking at least.'

'Well, let's go then!' Quinn jumped up.

'Woah, wait a minute,' Mullet said. 'When we find this thing... what are we gonna do? Isn't it huge? What if it attacks us?'

There was a long pause.

'Tim Tams?' Quinn said. 'We could bring a bunch of them with us? That way, it won't want to get too close.'

'Oh yeah!' Mullet said. 'What if we wore the packets like armour?'

'That's... actually not a bad idea,' Maggie said. 'Ms Brinesworth, how many packets of Tim Tams would you say you have on premises?'

'Oh, three dozen, at least,' Ava said.

'Perfect!' Maggie grinned. 'Would we be able to have them?'

'Of course,' Ava said. 'Perhaps if one of you comes with me, we can collect them now?'

Mullet volunteered, and the two of them disappeared from the room. 'I think this can work,' Maggie said thoughtfully. 'Three dozen weak relics... That's a dozen each...'

'But... there are four of us,' Quinn said.

'Yeah.' Maggie eyed her. 'But I figured you wouldn't want any.'

Quinn blinked at her. 'Wha... you... w... what do you mean?' she stammered.

Maggie smirked at her.

'Remember where I used to work?' she said. 'Who I used work with? You're not as subtle as you think you are, Quinn. And if we're going slime hunting, we're gonna need everyone's wits about them, you included.'

Quinn opened and closed her mouth a couple of times, before deciding this was an issue for later.

'Fine,' she said. 'Let's just go and find Kylie, okay?'

# CHAPTER 27

# ENTER THE FLESH PIT

**Date: Saturday 24 January 2082**

Ava and Mullet were soon back, along with Saoirse, all three of them loaded up with Tim Tams. Soon, decked out in biscuit packets and armed with flashlights, they set off back towards the botanical gardens. It was silent now and very dark in the gardens, the only light coming from distant streetlights and the artificial constellations above.

As they got closer to the museum, Quinn took out her mobile phone full of music, primed to play if something bad happened. Maggie, on seeing this, also took out her phone – and used it to check her messages.

'Still nothing,' she muttered, frowning at the screen. 'I've sent her a bunch of texts, but she hasn't even seen them.'

'Maybe you should tell her where we are and what we're doing?' Quinn said. 'Just in case it's all a big misunderstanding, and her phone was just flat, and she goes home and thinks we're the ones who are missing?'

'Good idea,' Maggie said and she started typing. 'Going to museum,' she muttered, 'with Ava Brinesworth, and... how do you spell Saoirse again...?'

She trailed off and stopped in her tracks, staring down at her phone.

'What?' Quinn said, stopping as well.

'Oh, nothing,' Maggie said – but she was frowning deeply. 'I... just had an idea. Um... You know, I think I should go back and check if Kylie is at Melody Sands!'

'Huh?' Quinn said. 'But...!'

'Don't worry, I'll come back,' Maggie said, a little louder. 'I just got a feeling that she's there! You guys can keep going!'

'Okay?' Quinn said slowly.

Confused, she watched as Maggie hurriedly walked away.

She was almost certain that Maggie was hiding something – but she didn't have time to ponder on it before they had arrived at the back of the museum. It was dark there, the gutter pipes yawning like empty mouths, swallowing the torchlight that shone up into them.

'Where do those pipes go?' Mullet asked, looking them up and down.

'Well, they would be connected to the main water system,' Ava said thoughtfully. 'So, I suppose they go everywhere, really.'

'Is there, like, some sort of big maintenance room near here?' Quinn asked. 'Somewhere with a lot of pipes in one place?'

'Not specifically, no,' Ava said. 'There are boiler rooms here and there, which have a lot of pipes connected through them. In fact, I think there is a boiler room below the museum. I remember visiting it once.'

'That's it!' Quinn said. 'How do we get there?'

'Well, I don't recall exactly, but I assume there would be some sort of staff access from inside,' Ava said.

Quinn frowned, trying to remember if she'd seen a staff room when she'd been there, but she wasn't sure. She had, after all, passed through much of the museum in a hurry.

'I guess we should go in and look for it,' she said.

The front door of the museum was locked – but Saoirse produced a skeleton key and promptly opened it. Inside, the museum was spooky, statues looming like ghosts along the walls, empty racks of historical clothes seeming to move in the corner of the eye.

Quinn lagged behind as the others looked around for doors, reluctant to enter the rooms with the relics. Shortly though, Mullet announced that he'd found something and she hurried to join him.

In a short corridor were a couple of bathrooms and at the end, a mysterious door marked Staff Only.

'That's gotta be it, right?' Mullet said.

'It is!' Ava said. 'I remember now!'

Mullet tried the handle and the door swung open, revealing a dark staircase leading down. A faint musty smell rose from the pitch-black depths, as well as something strangely acidic.

'Hey, Mullet,' Quinn said. 'You should go first, since you found the door.'

'No, no.' Mullet gestured at the stairs. 'After you, I insist.'

'But you're so brave,' Quinn said. 'I've always admired how brave you were, Mullet!'

'Thank you,' Mullet said. 'Now, ladies first!'

Saoirse stepped between them and without a word, entered the staircase.

Cautiously, they all followed her down into the darkness, torches illuminating dense cobwebs and dust. Clearly these stairs were not used often.

Shortly, they came out into a room full of dusty boxes, veiled statues and mysterious cabinets full of papers.

'This must be all the extra stuff that they don't put on display,' Quinn said in interest.

'Where's the boiler?' Mullet said. 'Isn't that what we're trying to find?'

'That's strange,' Ava said. 'I could have SWORN it was down here.'

'Maybe there's another basement?' Quinn said.

'No,' Ava said. 'It's the same one, only... I thought it was bigger...?'

Frowning, she stepped around the boxes and placed a hand against the back wall. Then, balling her fist, she began knocking on it at regular intervals.

*Tap tap*, went her hand on the stone.

*Tap tap*

*Tap tap*

*Dok dok*

Quinn exclaimed, as the hollow sound rung out. Ava turned around and gave everyone a meaningful look.

'What did I say?' she said, smiling excitedly. 'There's a false wall here! It's just plaster.'

'A hidden doorway?' Quinn said.

'Something like that,' Ava said. 'Someone must have boarded it off.'

'The slime!' Quinn said. 'It's made a secret nest for itself down here! It probably gets in there through the pipes!'

'Yes,' Ava said. 'Speaking of which, I'm not sure how we are to get through.'

'Oh, that's easy,' Mullet said cheerfully – and with no further warning, he ran across the room and took a flying kick at the plasterboard.

There was a loud cracking noise as his foot went straight through it. Mullet caught himself on his hands and extracted his feet again, grinning. Ava looked taken aback.

While Mullet picked himself off the floor, Quinn moved closer to the hole and shone her torch through.

'You're right, the room extends this way!' she said. 'I can see the boiler at the other end! Also, there's a huge hole in the floor! Do you think that's where the slime lives?'

She and Mullet began pulling away the rest of the board and after a moment, Ava joined in, delicately pulling away small chunks of plaster. Soon, the hole was large enough to get through, and Quinn and Mullet immediately went in.

'Yo,' Quinn said, shining her torch at the ceiling. 'Look at the pipes! Someone's cut into them!'

'That's how it travels all over the Ark,' Mullet said.

'Exactly,' Quinn said.

Cautiously, they both approached the hole in the floor. It was deep and almost precisely circular, bored down through the concrete floor and beyond through several metres of solid rock. Into the side of it was bolted a metal ladder, trailing down into inky darkness.

On the far side of the hole, taking up most of the spare space in the boiler room, was a huge, cylindrical boulder.

Clearly, the boulder was the piece that had been removed to make the cavity in the floor – although how that was possible in museum basement, Quinn wasn't sure. It certainly wasn't possible through normal means – but through unreality, many things were possible.

'Where does it go?' Mullet asked, shining his torch down the pit. It seemed to be about three metres deep, and one and half metres wide, with bare stone visible at the bottom.

'Dunno,' Quinn said, nudging the top of the ladder with her foot. 'Maybe there's a cave down there?'

Behind them, Saoirse helped Ava through the hole in the plaster and then stood back as Ava vigorously dusted herself off.

'Goodness me,' Ava said, looking around at the room and the pit in the floor. 'What is going on here?!'

'We should be careful,' Saoirse said flatly. 'It is possible we will encounter the fleshsmith soon.'

'Yeah, this is probably where they live,' Quinn said. 'Everyone got their Tams at the ready?'

'Yes!' Mullet said and Ava nodded.

'Okay,' Quinn said. 'Let's go down there!'

Phone in one hand, thumb poised to press the play button, she cautiously tapped her foot on the first rung of the ladder. It seemed solid enough – but she still hesitated. Half of her brain was convinced that the slime was right there in the pit, waiting for her to step in.

'You know what?' she said, withdrawing her foot again. 'I think we could all use a little music, don't you?'

'Good idea,' Mullet said. 'Put on something dramatic!'

'What?' Ava said. 'Music? Shouldn't we be quiet? Won't music alert the fleshsmith that we're coming?'

'Oh, if it's here, it already knows,' Quinn said. 'The music is necessary, trust me.'

Ava didn't look convinced but she didn't protest any further, so Quinn went ahead. After selecting an old soundtrack from a movie about spies, she pressed play and stowed the phone in her pocket. Then, emboldened, she took a breath and began climbing down the ladder.

She reached the bottom without issue and looked around, shining the torch into every crack and crevice. Immediately, she saw that there was, in fact, a cave down here, connected to the pit through a short, artificially created tunnel. The cave wall glinted wetly under her torch, striated vertically like the inside of a throat and glittering with fragments of micra. It was noticeably cooler as well, and the music in her pocket echoed strangely.

After explaining to the others what she was looking at, Quinn stepped further into the cave. Poking her head around the corner, she saw that it continued in both directions, although one direction widened out, while the other narrowed ominously.

After glancing back to make sure Mullet was coming down after her, Quinn stepped down the widening tunnel. At the end, it turned sharply to the right and opened up into a much wider space. Quinn shone her torch around the corner, saw what was there and immediately withdrew.

'Shit!' she hissed, moving back up the tunnel. 'Mullet! It's here!'

'Dude, what?!' Mullet called back.

He emerged into the cave, wrinkling his nose at the dripping water.

'Come and look!' Quinn told him.

In the centre of the wider cave was a large ball of slime. It was dense, ovoid and opaque red, taking up space from floor to ceiling. Tendrils extended away from it across the ceiling and floor.

It didn't react when Quinn shone her torch across it – and carefully, Quinn stepped closer.

'Dude!' Mullet hissed behind her. 'Gross! Do you think it's asleep?'

'Maybe?' Quinn said.

She stepped further into the cave and realised that there were more of them – four, no, five oblong shapes, suspended between floor and ceiling. Each was around two metres tall, pulsing slightly.

'They look kind of like eggs,' Mullet said curiously. 'Do

you think they're eggs? Are they going to hatch out baby slimes?'

'Dunno,' Quinn said. 'That doesn't really make any sense. Fleshsmiths don't lay eggs?'

'Well, there's something inside them,' Mullet said. 'Shine your torch behind that one again. I couldn't see what it was.'

Quinn did as he said and watched him frown, tilting his head to the side.

'Is that…? It kind of looks like a person,' he said. 'In fact, it kind of looks like… oh shit, is that Kylie?!'

'What?!' Quinn said.

'That's Kylie in there!' Mullet said, stepping closer. 'We gotta get her out!'

'Wh-how?' Quinn said. 'Do you have a knife?!'

'No, just fucking Tim Tams!' Mullet said.

'Well, use them!' Quinn yelled.

Mullet ripped open one of the packets that was dangling from his belt, and threw a handful of biscuits at the ball of slime. Predictably, they bounced off of it and scattered across the floor.

'You gotta shove them in there!' Quinn said.

Gingerly, she picked a couple of Tim Tams off the floor, and darting forward, she pressed them into the side of the ball.

The slime prickled to the touch and continued to do so even after she withdrew her hand. Hurriedly, she wiped off her fingers, backing away. She wasn't entirely sure how the slime was going to react to a minor relic shoved directly into its body, but it certainly wasn't going to be pretty –

The slime did nothing.

Quinn waited for twenty seconds, watching it closely – but it just sat there.

She frowned, confused. Why hadn't it reacted? It was definitely a creature of unreality, she knew that for sure. Did the Tim Tams not bother it?

Footsteps echoed at the entrance to the wider cave and Ava came in, followed closely by Saoirse. Upon seeing the slime balls, Ava stopped and shone her torch at them.

'Goodness me,' she said, panting slightly, 'this is the most exercise I've done in months! You've certainly made my evening quite exciting!'

'Yeah,' Quinn said, 'well, it's about to get even more exciting. Kylie's inside that egg and we have no clue how to get her out! The Tim Tams aren't working either!'

'Maybe you need to use more of them?' Ava said.

Mullet opened another packet and pushed the entire thing, plastic tray and all, into the slime, but again, nothing. The Tim Tams almost immediately began to dissolve, bubbling at the corners, chocolate spreading thinly outwards.

'Do YOU have a knife?' Quinn asked Ava. 'Or anything to split it open with?'

'Why would I carry a knife?' Ava said.

'Well, does Saoirse then?'

'No, she doesn't either,' Ava said. 'Here – we should put even more Tim Tams in there. You're not putting enough! Can't you see they're dissolving?'

She came closer and began opening packets, a stack of which she handed to Quinn.

'Hey!' Quinn said, trying to give them back. 'Don't give them to me! Give them to Mullet!'

'But he has his own,' Ava said. 'Come on, in they go!'

She handed Quinn even more packets and Quinn, whose brain was starting to shut down, just stood there and looked at them, unable to make a decision.

'I...' she said. 'Stop... no...'

Something moved at her pocket – and before she realised what was happening, Quinn's phone had disappeared. Abruptly, the music cut off.

Slowly, her brain moving through treacle, Quinn turned around. Ava dropped the phone on the ground and helplessly, Quinn watched her step on it, grinding her heel.

'There,' Ava said, smiling at Quinn. 'That's how you do it, isn't it? You need the music to turn back time?'

'Wha-?' Quinn said.

'Oh, I knew you were a realitysmith right from the

moment you didn't eat the Tim Tams,' Ava said. 'Although, it did take me an embarrassingly long time to figure out what type. It was only because of that Spencer kid that I got there, actually. And even then, I almost became convinced that you were uncatchable. If I attempted anything, you would just rewind time and escape. In fact, I'm certain that actually happened, did it not?'

Quinn stared at her, her brain struggling to comprehend what she was hearing. Somewhere, a part of her was screaming that this was really, really bad – but her conscious mind hadn't caught up yet.

'But it's the music, isn't it?' Ava continued. 'You need it, in order to use your symptoms. I'm right, aren't I?'

'Hey, what the fuck are you talking about?' Mullet said, backing away a couple of steps. 'Are you... are you the slime pretending to be Ava?!'

'Oh, no, I am Ava,' Ava said. 'The real, original one. But, I suppose I am also the slime, yes. Sorry to deceive you, I really am. Your little Tim Tam trick was clever – but I've actually developed quite the resistance to them. Never could quit them, you know? They're just so delicious and quintessentially Australian.'

Mullet abruptly tried to run, but a previously inert tentacle suddenly shot up from the floor and grabbed his leg. He screamed as it hoisted him up towards the ceiling, dangling him upside down.

'LET ME GO, YOU FUCK!' he screamed, flailing about.

Quinn somehow managed to drop the Tim Tams, but too late – tentacles were already winding around her legs. She struggled to get out of them but they were tight, and powerful, made almost entirely of muscle.

'Why are you doing this?!' she squeaked, weakly shoving the tentacles down.

'Oh, the usual, really,' Ava said. 'You know too much. Although, I might have done it even if you didn't know, to be perfectly honest. Realitysmiths have no place in old Australia, even if they make good music. And you'—she looked at Mullet—'you're a troublemaker. I have no need of you either.'

'So you're gonna kill us?!' Quinn said, fighting to keep her arms free. The tendrils around her were growing thicker by the second, burning against her bare skin like a thousand tiny needles.

'No,' Ava said. 'You won't die. In fact, you will live on for much longer than you would have normally. You will be preserved – your core, your memories, your personality – all of it, forever. Don't you want to live forever, Quinn? Isn't that why you make music?'

'No?!' Quinn yelled. 'I don't want to be preserved!'

'Oh, you won't mind, once it happens,' Ava said. 'It's nice! Many have gone before you.'

'Yeah?!' Quinn yelled, stretching her neck above the coiling slime. 'And what about you, Saoirse? Are you just going to stand there and watch her murder me?!'

'Oh, silly,' Ava said. 'Saoirse and I are the same person. Don't you get it? We all are.'

Before Quinn's eyes, Saoirse began to melt. Her face sagged outwards, body crumpling in on itself, her hands dripping out of their sleeves. In seconds, she was nothing but a puddle of red slime on the floor, oozing slowly across to join the rest.

'I am Ark 2,' Ava said, 'and Ark 2 is me. Everyone here who matters is me. The council, the security, the shop owners... Everyone, except for the musicians. I never did have any musical talent, and somehow, it never translates across. But who knows – perhaps you'll be the one who brings it, Quinn? Welcome to the Ark. This time, for real.'

Quinn screamed and screamed and thrashed about, but it was useless. The red slime rose around her throat and face and she felt it go down her throat, prickling and burning, and then she couldn't scream anymore.

# BECOMING SOMEONE ELSE

**Date: Thursday 12 March 2082**

After briefly scanning the rubble into which the fleshsmith had escaped, the Detective concluded that McCleave had made good his escape. There was so much rubble around that it would be a pointlessly time-wasting task to search through it all.

McCleave had not left no evidence, however. His radiation suit and clothes remained where he'd shed them – and they were covered in a congealed residue.

Carefully, the Detective collected a sample of the rapidly drying goo and, briefly unzipping their rad suit, fed it into the onboard biological sequencer inside their left thigh.

The sequencer was very basic but it was able to provide simple analysis of samples within a few hours. Leaving it to run, the Detective picked up and folded the clothes and began heading back towards the car.

As they jogged through the rubble, they thought about the new information they had gathered. There was a lot of it, some of it very strange. On top of that, the close contact with what had almost certainly been a piece of the First Portent had left them shaken. Something had changed internally, although they were not sure what exactly, and it still hadn't gone away. It was as though their circuits were buzzing with additional power that had not been there before. But the power was tainted, wild – completely illogical.

The Detective did not like it. They didn't like how it

threatened to compromise their otherwise sterling logical decision making. They also didn't like how they could not think of a single satisfying explanation for it.

Of course, they had considered the possibility that they had somehow started to develop P.I.U.S – however, this didn't make sense. The First Portent, while in a dormant state, did not display an unreality index high enough to generate P.I.U.S. Additionally, the Symptoms of the First Portent generally related to the manipulation of the flow of time – and as far as the Detective could tell, they seemed to be experiencing something more akin to the generation of additional electrical power.

Just in case, the Detective flicked through multiple first-hand accounts of the experience of developing P.I.U.S. The records were largely in agreement with each other and commonly described an active decision to use the power, drawing it from an internal source as a conscious act. The Detective had done no such thing. The surge they had felt had arisen entirely unconsciously.

The most likely conclusion was that unreality here was just unusually high. The Detective would examine the problem again later.

Arriving back at the car, which was fortunately still where they left it, the Detective frowned to themselves. This entire mission had gone south with startling rapidity. If they were going to have any chance of bringing it back on track, they needed a solid plan of action.

But first, there were a couple of issues to resolve. In spite of the unrealitic surge they'd experienced, the Detective's batteries were already starting to run low. They needed somewhere to rest and recharge – but where? The sin-seeker office was clearly compromised and they had not spent sufficient time in Ouyen yet to know where they might find a secure alternative.

The other problem was a much more immediate one. The Detective did not have the keys to the car. McCleave had had them. And after checking the pockets of the fleshsmith's abandoned clothes, the Detective found them empty.

It was likely the keys had fallen out when McCleave had rolled down the crater.

Turning, the Detective looked back the way they'd come.

Finding the keys in the crater would be almost impossible. There were dozens of points at which they could have fallen out and hundreds of trajectories they could have taken. It would take hours, if not days, to locate them.

The Detective did not have that sort of time available.

Turning again, they looked at the car. The keys were needed in order to unlock the door, and to turn on the engine.

Technically, these things were possible without the keys. But without the proper tools, breaking into the car would require a window to be broken and part of the dash dismantled.

The car belonged to the Ouyen Sin-Seeker Department, which meant that technically, breaking into it could be justified, as the Detective was part of the same organisation. It wasn't exactly proper but in an emergency, it was permitted.

However, the noise generated by driving with a broken window meant that the car would not be roadworthy afterwards.

The Detective eyed the car, thinking. It was possible they would be able to find suitable tools amongst the rubble in order to jimmy open the lock, although it would probably take a while.

(Or they could just smash it and be done with it?)

But no! They could not drive the car afterwards, if it was not roadworthy!

But if they did not drive, then they would have to walk for over forty kilometres, which would take significant time and energy...

(And besides, there was no one there to see them break the law.)

That was not the point! The law had to be upheld at all times, regardless of scrutinisation!

Although... in this case... the longer they left it... the more likely it was that Bill was dead.

There was simply no time to analyse it. Shaking their head, the Detective moved to the car, and placing McCleave's jacket over the passenger window, they smacked it sharply. With a muffled splintering, it cracked apart, falling into the seat.

Taking the jacket away, the Detective carefully removed the remaining glass and reached inside to open the door. Then, moving around to the driver's seat, they sat down and peered underneath the dash.

Knowledge on how to jumpstart a car had not been included in their training files. But they knew how cars worked – and from that, it wasn't hard to figure out the rest.

They needed a spark to start the engine – but fortunately, their left hand had been sparking on and off for the last half an hour. Holding a finger to the exposed wire, they waited a moment, until they felt another surge. They were pleased when it worked exactly as expected.

With the engine on, they paused a moment, eyeing the broken window and considering ways to muffle the noise of rushing air. Perhaps if they hung the jacket over it?

But no, the flapping of cloth would be even louder. Better if they just drove slowly. Throwing the car into reverse, the Detective turned the car around and accelerated up the road.

***

The next problem was finding somewhere secure to plan and recharge – and as they attempted to approach this issue, the Detective found themselves missing Bill. They were not certain what sort of protocol should be followed in this circumstance. Their onboard training had not prepared them for a scenario in which the sin-seeker office itself was compromised.

They considered driving on to another office – however, this was risky, considering they did not know the extent of McCleave's influence. It would be better to bunker down somewhere completely unknown to McCleave.

But where? A hotel? They were not sure what sort of speeds the fleshsmith could travel at but if McCleave arrived back in Ouyen before them, it was possible he was keeping an eye on the hotels.

Should the Detective then ask a civilian for shelter? They did not particularly like the idea. It did not seem proper. And without Bill there, they were not confident they could convince a civilian to help them.

The heart of the problem, the Detective realised, was that the level of McCleave's influence was unknown. The Detective did not know the extent of his power, nor to what lengths he would go to hinder their progress.

Assuming the worst, he could arrive in Ouyen before they did and mobilise the entire town against them. It would be his word against theirs – a presumably respected and high-ranking officer versus a prototype cyborg with qualities that Bill often described as 'uncanny'.

The Detective's face could be circulated in the sin-seeker database and falsely named as a criminal. While confident that the Melbourne office would eventually clear things up, the Detective was also certain that this sort of thing could potentially set their investigation back weeks, if not months.

Assuming this worst-case scenario, there was therefore one obvious solution. If their face was to be plastered on wanted posters across town – then they would simply change it. McCleave couldn't hinder them if he didn't recognise them.

Changing their face would take a little time – but in this case, they decided it was well worth it. They would also have to abandon the car and acquire a new set of clothes, but those were later problems.

Just under five kilometres from Ouyen, the Detective pulled the car off the highway and drove it slowly in an overgrown field. Then, once they were sure it would not be visible from the road, they cut the engine and got out.

Removing their damaged rad suit and clothes, they folded them neatly and placed them on the back seat. Then, moving away from the car, they stood beneath a gum tree, completely naked, and opened the appearance program.

It hadn't been long since they'd looked at it last – but a lot had happened since then.

After scrolling through the various options, they made a decision. Then, deactivating their dermal sensors, they grabbed hold of the skin of their forearm and began ripping it off.

It came off in large swathes, peeling back from shiny metal, its underside dripping with a thin, clear lubricant. Piece by piece, it dropped to the ground, like the sloughed skin of a lizard. Arms, legs, torso skin, removed in long, continuous strips with a sound like ripping fabric.

The Detective removed their face last, pulling it off in one smooth motion.

For a moment, they held it out in front of them and looked at it. It had served them well. But it was time for a new one.

The plates of their body began to shift. The shoulders broadened and the hips narrowed. The face became squarer, the chin more pronounced and the brow bones heavier.

Ports opened and skin fluid seeped out, in the same dark tone as previously. The Detective patiently waited for it to solidify and then tried it out. They clenched and unclenched their hands, rolled their shoulders and twisted their neck.

Everything was working as expected. The transformation was complete.

They moved back to the car and examined themselves in the glass of the windscreen. A masculine face stared back at them, still conventionally attractive and still completely hairless, but otherwise brand new. Only their eyes remained the same, black irises, with a single blue point at the centre of the pupil, visible in the low light.

This would take a little getting used to. But in the meantime, their next few problems were waiting to be solved.

The first of these was acquiring new clothes. Their old clothes, aside from giving away their identity, would also no longer fit them. They needed new ones ASAP – but the question was, where from? Stores were not open at this hour – and even if they were, the Detective did not want to draw attention to themselves by entering a shop whilst naked. They were hoping a solution would present itself as they got closer to Ouyen.

As they jogged towards town, they soon came across a house with the lights on, despite the late hour. Pausing outside, they decided it was worth a shot and went to ring the doorbell.

There was a long pause before someone opened the door – and they opened it only very slightly, peering out into the dark with a wary expression.

The Detective stepped closer. *Hello,* they signed. *I apologise for the late hour. I have unfortunately lost my clothes. Might I purchase spare clothes from this household?*

The house occupant, a man in his twenties, looked them up and down in disbelief.

*You lost your clothes?* he signed.

*Yes,* the Detective said.

*Righto,* the man signed. *How did that happen?*

*It's a long story,* the Detective returned. *I do not have the time to tell it. Can I purchase clothes or not?*

The man stared at them for a moment longer.

*Give me a minute,* he signed, and the door closed.

'No, it's not the cops,' the Detective heard him say to someone as he opened the inner door. 'It's some dude, completely naked! Yeah! No, I don't know him. Dude's probably high or somethi –'

His voice cut off as the inner door closed.

The Detective waited for a few minutes before the door suddenly opened again. The man was back and holding a small bundle of clothes.

'Here,' he said quietly, holding them out to the Detective. 'Mate, I dunno what you're going through, but look – we've all been there at one point or another. Here, take 'em. Free of charge.'

*I am perfectly happy to pay you,* the Detective signed.

'Nah, it's fine,' the man said. 'Go on, take 'em. My ex bought them for me, so I wasn't using 'em anyway.'

He pushed them into the Detective's hands and then stepped back.

'You have a good night, now,' he said, pointing a finger at them. 'Put those on and get yourself to the med clinic. Sober up, have good night's sleep and you'll be right as rain.'

The Detective nodded vaguely.

*Thank you,* they added after a pause.

The man nodded and disappeared inside again.

The Detective turned and left as well, pausing outside the front gate to unfold the clothes they'd been given. They seemed to be approximately the right size, albeit a little baggier than the Detective was used to – blue boxer shorts, black trousers and a black T-shirt with the word DILF emblazoned across it.

It wasn't perfect – but it would do for now. The Detective quickly got dressed and began jogging down the road.

It was by now approaching midnight and the streets were quiet. Slowing down to a casual walk, the Detective passed through the town centre, searching for somewhere to bunker down for the night.

Shortly, they found a place called the Victoria Hotel, an old red-brick building with a colonial-style façade. As they approached, however, they noticed a pair of officers standing outside the front.

It could have been a coincidence – but it almost certainly wasn't. It was highly likely that they were keeping an eye out for the Detective.

Ah well – it was time to test out their new face.

Setting their expression to neutral and putting their hands in their pockets, the Detective walked towards the hotel. As they got closer, the officers briefly turned towards them – but almost immediately looked away again.

The Detective passed them by and went inside. There, they took their hands out of their pockets and approached the bar. There was no one there – but there was a small buzzer on the wall with a note that said 'ring for after-hours service'.

The Detective did so – and a few minutes later, a woman came out of a door at the back. The Detective quickly booked a room for the night, under the freshly generated name of Calidor Fang.

Their room turned out to be small but clean and, most importantly, it had access to electrical sockets. Gratefully, the Detective uncoiled their ankle cable and plugged it in, relaxing as their body went through its usual diagnostic motions. With a base of operations established, they could get back to planning and figure out once and for all what was going on.

As they started to gather the information, ready to analyse, they were interrupted by a diagnostic ping. A small warning message had appeared at the corner of their internal HUD.

*R.L. integrity compromised*, it said. *Current value: 83%*

The Detective stared at it and wondered what it meant. R.L? That wasn't an acronym they had come across before.

After searching their files, they found no mention of it either. That was strange. As far as they knew, every other onboard function was well documented.

Perhaps it was related to the bizarre surge they had experienced earlier? Lifting their left hand, they inspected the skin there, fresh and unbroken.

There had been no more sparks since they'd left the

vicinity of the First Portent. The Portent was almost certainly what had caused it.

(Almost certainly.)

Frowning, the Detective filed the question away to ask Bill just as soon as they found him.

Assuming he wasn't dead already. They really hoped he wasn't.

# CHAPTER 29

# CABLE WHIP

Date: Friday 13 March 2082

The genetic analysis of the goo sample came back in the early hours of the morning and immediately provided interesting results.

The slime was genetically human, unsurprisingly. What was odd was that it contained genetic markers from at least twenty-eight individual humans.

This was a concerning development – although the Detective wasn't sure what exactly it meant. The implication was that the fleshsmith had apparently absorbed and assimilated biological material from a large number of people. McCleave had said that he'd 'eaten' Bill – but until now, the Detective had not been taking that statement as literal.

For what purpose the fleshsmith had consumed organic matter from other humans, the Detective was also not certain – but then, perhaps there wasn't a reason. Perhaps it was just a tidy method to dispose of evidence or deal with people who got in their way.

In any case, it was a disturbing find – and all the more reason to bring McCleave to justice as soon as possible.

The Detective spent several hours exploring ideas and calculating the odds of success for each one. But the more they planned, the more they came to realise that there were many unknown variables involved.

They knew that McCleave was a high-ranking officer – but not how well liked and respected he was.

They knew that McCleave had known Ark 2 wasn't a farm – but they didn't know what it had been instead.

They knew that McCleave was a rogue fleshsmith – but they didn't know the full extent of his abilities.

The first step, therefore, was to start to fill in these gaps in their knowledge.

At 6AM, the Detective was on full battery and ready to go. Without having to wait for Bill to go through his morning routine, they took mere minutes to pack away their power cord and top up their fluids before heading downstairs and checking out of the hotel.

If all went well, they would not have to stay there a second night. Alternatively, if things went absolutely terribly, they would also not have to stay there a second night.

As they left, the Detective paused in the airlock to check if the officers were still waiting outside. They were surprised to see that they were, in fact, still there.

After scanning their faces, the Detective confirmed that they were the exact same officers as the night before – a woman with a short ponytail and a man with a full beard. They were also standing in almost the exact same place, perfectly still, despite the chilly morning.

This struck the Detective as quite strange. All evidence they had seen suggested that there was no way a normal human would remain standing in one place, unbothered, for over six hours.

Perhaps with great discipline, it was possible. But the Detective had seen the Ouyen Sin-Seeker Office first-hand. They personally knew it to be far from a tightly run ship.

The Detective opened the door and went outside. As they did so, one of the officers glanced their way before turning back to stare down the road.

After briefly debating the risk, the Detective decided to take a direct, if duplicitous, approach, and walked towards the pair.

*Good morning,* they signed, as both officers turned to

look at them. *It is unusually early for sin-seeker work. Has something happened?*

*It is none of your concern,* the male officer replied briefly.

*I only ask,* the Detective pressed on, *as I saw something strange last night, and I am wondering if it is related to your work.*

The officers glanced at each other.

*Please explain,* the woman signed.

The Detective pointed down the road. *I saw someone break a window and climb in through it.*

*What did this person look like?*

*Tall,* the Detective said. *Dark skin. Female. Wearing an orange and blue jacket.*

The officers glanced at each again.

*Where was this?* the woman asked in interest.

*I will show you,* the Detective said. *Follow me.*

They moved away – and just as they had been hoping, the woman followed after them, while the other officer stayed in position by the hotel.

The Detective went around the corner, towards an abandoned store with boards over the windows and graffiti on its walls. They had observed a broken window on one side of it the previous evening, having briefly considered spending the night there.

The woman poked at the broken window and then went around the back, hand on her gun. She tried the handle of the back door but it was locked.

Turning, she saw that the Detective was still there and gestured that they should leave. The Detective, however, had other plans. After feigning walking away, they came back and, before the officer could react, they snatched the gun out of her holster, turning it around to point at her.

Startled, the officer froze and then slowly lifted her hands above her head.

*Do not run,* the Detective signed awkwardly around the gun. *And do not lie. Tell me everything you know of McCleave.*

*McCleave?* the officer signed hesitantly. *What do you mean?*

*Who is loyal to him?* the Detective asked. *How many?*

*I... what?* the woman signed, eyes darting side to side.

*Are you loyal to him?* the Detective asked, leaning closer.

*He is my boss,* the woman said.

*And do you like him?*

*He's okay?* the woman said, radiating uncertainty.

The Detective cocked their head. Perhaps this woman was a normal human after all...

There was a very slight noise behind them, barely perceptible – but the Detective turned their head to look.

They were just in time to see a nozzle of a pistol appear around the corner.

The Detective leapt to the side as the gun went off, a silenced metallic cough sharp in the morning air.

Bullets punched through a wooden fence, leaving a line of neat holes in their wake. The Detective, meanwhile, sprinted around the back of the store before leaping powerfully up onto the fence and, from there, onto the roof.

Their feet clacked sharply on the ceramic tiles as they raced back towards their assailant. He barely had time to look up before they dropped down behind him and brought their left hand, taser prongs extended, to connect with the exposed skin at the back of his neck.

It was the second officer – but how had he known what was happening, so quickly?

The Detective's question was answered a second later. Instead of collapsing from the high voltage sting, the officer buckled inwards, sagging like jelly. In moment he had melted into a puddle of organs and red, viscous fluid.

The Detective spun around as the first officer charged in for an attack. As she ran, her body got spindly thin and her face and arms began to extend. Her eyes and teeth sunk in and vanished, and goo poured out of the holes, spilling outwards in a torrent, forming a thin, whiplike pillar of muscle. Her fingers fused together, lengthening and spiralling around each other like a fleshy drill-bit.

Without hesitation, the Detective grabbed onto one of the tendrils and, with all their might, slung it around. The officer was lifted off her feet and slammed bodily into the brick wall of the abandoned store.

Before she could recover, the Detective tased her as well. Her body melted into goo, spreading out in a wide puddle.

Stepping back, the Detective watched as the two puddles slowly merged into one.

Suddenly, things had become a lot clearer.

The fleshsmith contained the DNA of twenty-eight people – because it was literally twenty-eight people.

Perhaps it had started as only one – but the original smith had absorbed another person, and in doing so, had transformed the other person into a copy of itself.

Whether or not the twenty-eight or more fractions of the fleshsmith shared one mind, or retained their own individuality, was not yet certain. However, considering how quickly the second officer had appeared, it was clear that they were able to communicate with one-another at supernatural speed.

This meant that, more than likely, by attacking one member of the conglomerate, the Detective had inadvertently alerted every single fraction of the whole to their current location and new appearance.

This was not good.

The Detective immediately took off at a run, away from the hotel – but they were already too late. As they sprinted down the street, another officer appeared and began shooting at them.

The Detective returned fire with their borrowed gun until it ran out of bullets. Then, dropping it, they sprinted off again, sharply changing direction and changing again, ducking down a residential street. As they raced towards the end, a seeker car nosed into view, red and blue lights pulsing.

The Detective took a flying leap, clearing the car and hitting the ground at a sprint. Behind them, doors banged open and bullets began to fly.

The Detective skidded around a corner, back towards the main road, only to see three more officers running towards them. Head turning back and forth, the Detective charged into a narrow strip between two houses – and found a dead end. Pausing, they eyed the garbage skip that took up three quarters of the space.

A bullet pinged off the metal side, and another smacked into the brick, taking away chunks. There was no time to stop and think. Every second they hesitated, more fractions would arrive.

The Detective's right arm came up and the thumb folded away, the large, serrated knife clicking into its place. The taser prongs crackled in the palm of their left hand.

Behind them, the two men from the car ran into view, guns at the ready.

The Detective leapt up vertically onto the skip, launching off of it and onto the wall. Bullets cracked into the bricks behind them as they leapt towards their attackers.

They landed on the first man, slitting his throat in one smooth motion, while turning him to act as a human shield. The other man hesitated for slightly too long before the Detective barrelled into him, slamming him into the wall and tasing him at full voltage.

Three more assailants were rapidly approaching. The Detective leapt back again, retreating as the first two melted into goo.

They had to keep moving or risk being overwhelmed. They jumped from the skip, to the wall, to the roof of the next house along and sprinted away.

On the road beside them, the fragments gave chase, five of them now, half in sin-seeker uniform, half in civilian clothes. As they did so, their bodies began morphing, legs growing longer, increasing their stride. As the Detective turned to look, they saw a sixth fragment emerge from a storm drain, transforming into a lithe, muscle-bound creature that barely resembled a human.

Two of the fragments leapt up onto the roof behind the

Detective, gaining on them in massive leaps and bounds. Meanwhile, ahead, there was another problem – the rooftops were about to run out. Beyond them was nothing but a wide, empty road. On the other side was a primary school – but the roof was too far to jump to.

Reaching the end, the Detective hesitated, looking around. Behind them, the two fragments were seconds away, while below on the ground, fragments were running in from all sides.

On the other side of the street, an electrical powerline ran parallel, high voltage cables strung up between wooden poles.

One of the cables ran into the building on which the Detective currently stood.

The Detective ducked low as one of the fragments pounced at them, narrowly missing, scrabbling for purchase as it skidded to the edge of the roof. Then, as the other fragment made to jump at them, they reached down and yanked the electrical cable out of the eaves. It crackled loudly as they pulled it around and slammed it into the slick chest of the leaping fragment.

There was a loud sizzling and the smell of burning meat. The fragment writhed as it fell back and melted into organ soup.

The Detective grabbed the cable with both hands and tugged on it, testing its strength. If it could carry their weight, there was a chance they could use it to swing –

Something snapped and the cable came off completely, sparking as it fell into the road below.

The Detective blinked at it for a second – and in their surprise, they remained still for slightly too long. One of the bullets hit their left arm at the elbow, shattering the metal carapace in an instant.

The Detective jumped back, avoiding the follow-up barrage of shots – but the damage was already pretty bad. Their left arm hung limply at the elbow, attached by nothing more than a few stray cords, the break point sparking wildly. Warm, clear fluids dripped out across the roof tiles.

This wouldn't do. The Detective grabbed their arm and ripped it off completely. It was better gone than dangling uselessly at their side, hindering their progress.

Spinning, they brought their severed arm around and used it to smack the fragment that remained on the roof. Then, while it reeled back from the strike, they grabbed the fallen cable and jammed the end into their shattered elbow socket.

The cable immediately became electrified – and grabbing it, the Detective began whirling it around themself in wide arcs.

Most of it was insulated with rubber – but the very end had become a powerful long-distance taser. With a loud crack, the end connected with the fleshsmith fragment on the roof, dropping it instantly. Then, spinning it wider, the Detective zapped two more fragments that had gotten too close in the road below.

As the cable whizzed about their head, arcing electricity, something once again stirred inside them. A buzzing static, wildly out of place, yet also... somehow familiar. Had they... done this before? Surely not. It was such a strange and specific circumstance to be in...

No... it was just their system playing up again. They could feel it, that electrical supply of mysterious origin, surging through them, providing their whip with additional power.

It was concerning – but also strangely exhilarating. Suddenly, in that moment, they no longer cared what the source of the power was and that this time, there was no Portent nearby causing it. All that mattered were the enemies before them.

A grin came over their face unbidden as they leapt to the ground and advanced on the remaining fragments. The cable whip spun and cracked as one, two, three, four fragments went down, electricity sparking throughout their red, liquid bodies. As their fellows fell, the others began to back off before turning and running full tilt away as the Detective advanced on them.

In moments, they had all gone, vanishing as quickly as they had appeared, slithering down drainpipes and into grates. And as the last one disappeared from view, the Detective came to a stop, the whip falling limp in their hands. Slowly, they detached it from their arm and rolled it up.

Standing in the middle of the street, they paused to take stock.

It wasn't great. Multiple warning lights were flashing before their eyes, informing them of severe carapace damage and fluid pressure loss, as well as the same 'R.L. integrity loss' message as before. Their battery was also already at half-capacity, despite the fact that it wasn't even 7AM.

After a moment, they turned and walked back to where their arm lay on the ground.

While most of the arm was intact, the elbow was severely damaged beyond what they personally knew how to repair. Still, it might be possible to fix it. Maybe Bill would know how to...?

Bill.

The Detective had not considered Bill's plight with the new evidence in mind. But now that they knew more about their enemy, they had a much better idea of what might be happening to their short companion.

The fleshsmith was probably attempting to assimilate him. The question was, how? How did this process occur? Was it fast, or slow? Could it be stopped once started?

The Detective frowned to themselves. If Bill had been assimilated, then surely the fleshsmith would have sent him to fight them? The psychological damage this strategy could potentially cause would certainly have been irresistible.

No – it wasn't over just yet. The Detective only had forty-six per cent battery left, and fifty per cent of their arms intact – but there was no time to recharge. Bill hadn't stopped fighting, and they sure as hell weren't about to either.

# WEATHERING HARDSHIP

### Date: Friday 13 March 2082

The Detective did not know for certain where Bill was – but with no other solid leads, they decided to return to the Ouyen Sin-Seeker Office. It was obvious that the rogue fleshsmith had assimilated most, if not all, of the staff there. It was clearly a base of operations of some sort.

After stowing their left forearm in a bush to come back for later, the Detective hoisted up their cable whip and set off at a jog towards the office. It would have been good to change their face again and maintain an element of surprise but there was no time.

In any case, they did not have the battery left to make a head-on assault on the office. Although they had temporarily incapacitated ten of the assimilants in the last twenty minutes, another eighteen or more remained at full strength. If all of them were to attack at once, the Detective would not stand a chance.

A stealthy approach was therefore more appropriate – although this had its own challenges. The fleshsmith conglomeration had dozens of eyes, in potentially dozens of places, each of them able to communicate at lightning speed with the rest. If just one of the fragments saw the Detective, then the jig would be up. In fact, the Detective was almost certain they were being watched right at that moment. Meanwhile, the Detective had no idea where each of the fragments were, or how quickly they could move.

How, then, to get into the office unseen?

They could not crawl in through the drains – the drains, it seemed, were the domain of the fleshsmith.

They could not climb over from the roof – the sin-seeker office was a free-standing building.

They could not run in from the side, not without an inordinate amount of luck.

In fact, any which way they put it, the Detective could not think of a way to reliably approach the office without being seen. The problem was that the fleshsmith could see everywhere at once. Perhaps if it was night, or heavily raining, the Detective might be able to slip through. But no – it was a clear, bright autumn morning, without a single cloud in sight...

Unless...

The Detective came to a sudden stop, their eyes fixed on the distant tower of the Ouyen weather station.

Abruptly, they set off again towards it. The weather usually followed a very strict schedule – but in extraordinary circumstances, it was not unprecedented for that schedule to be altered.

Shortly, they arrived at the front gate and let themselves in. The weather station was not officially open until 8AM, but there were weathersmiths on shift around the clock and management staff on premises at all times.

As they approached the entrance, they saw through the front window that there were two people inside, standing and staring at the approaching Detective. As the Detective went to open the door, the one on the left, a petite blonde woman in an orange weathersmith uniform, backed away sharply, an expression of fear on her face.

Glancing down at themselves, the Detective realised their appearance was more than a little alarming. They were covered in clotted slime, with an arm missing and several visible tears in their synthetic skin. They immediately altered their stance to convey meekness, eyes low and palm raised to show they meant no harm.

The second person inside, an overweight woman with thick, black curly hair and a sky-blue blouse, glanced between the Detective and the weathersmith, but held her ground.

*Hello,* she signed hesitantly. *Can I help you?*

*Yes,* the Detective signed back. *I am in need of assistance. I am Detective Calidor Fang from the Melbourne Sin-Seeker Office. An emergency is currently occurring.*

They reached up to their neck and removed their ID badge from its slot, holding it up for the woman to see.

The woman frowned at it for a long moment.

*What sort of emergency?* she signed. *Should I activate the E.W.S? Is there a Portent?*

The Detective stepped in through the airlock, closing it behind them.

'It is not a Portent,' they said. 'It is merely a rogue fleshsmith. However, they are extremely powerful and represent a significant threat.'

'Is THAT what it is?' the woman said and she glanced back at the weathersmith, who had all but fled the room, standing by the exit and staring at the Detective. 'A fleshsmith, eh? Maisy, is that what you guys were picking up?'

Maisy gulped visibly.

'M-maybe?' she squeaked.

'I do not possess the ability to detect unreality,' the Detective said, 'however it seems logical that a large number of unrealitic bursts would have been perceptible across the town this morning.'

'Well, there you go,' the woman said. 'So, uh. Do you require the E.W.S?'

'The early warning system is not necessary,' the Detective said. 'Actually, I am here to ask another favour.'

They turned to look at the weathersmith.

'I require the absolute worst weather you have,' they said. 'Rain. Sleet. Fog. Anything to reduce the visibility to practically zero. Are you able to do that?'

'I...' the weathersmith said, her eyes darting back and forth. 'W... why? I mean... it's not in the... in the schedule...'

The Detective once more flashed their badge. 'It is part

of an extremely important sin-seeker operation,' they said. 'I do not say such things lightly, but the township of Ouyen and its citizens are very much in jeopardy. This is a matter of life and death.'

'Well... I suppose,' the weathersmith said. She met the Detective's eyes for a fraction of a second before looking away again. 'I suppose we can alter the schedule,' she muttered at the floor.

'Good,' the Detective said. 'How long do you expect it will take? As soon as possible would be preferable.'

'Um,' the weathersmith said. 'We can... get started right away if you'd like. It should take about... twenty minutes?'

'That is an acceptable timeframe,' the Detective said.

The weathersmith nodded and made to leave before pausing and looking back.

'Um,' she said. 'If you don't mind me asking... what... what are you?'

'I am a cyborg,' the Detective said. 'And an officer of the Melbourne Department of Sin.'

The weathersmith blinked at them for a moment.

'Okay?' she said. 'But w... um... nevermind. I'll go and tell the others about the assignment!'

She practically ran through the exit, disappearing up a flight of stairs.

'Well,' the other woman said, 'this is going to be interesting. I've never seen them make "the worst weather possible" before. We should probably warn everyone; otherwise, we're going to get a lot of complaints. Lots of plans ruined. Will it interfere with your operation terribly if we do issue a warning through the E.W.S?'

The Detective considered it.

'You may issue a warning in half an hour,' they said. 'Once the bad weather has already commenced.'

'Well, alright.' The woman sighed. 'I suppose that will have to do.'

***

The Detective decided to wait just outside the weather station until the visibility had been reduced – that way, the fleshsmith would not know which way they went.

About five minutes later, there was a noticeable change in the morning air.

The humidity rose steeply and the Detective's pressure gauges began to swing back and forth. About eight minutes in, noticeable clouds began to form around the weather station tower, spiralling slowly outwards in ever thickening bands.

The few people who were out and about saw what was happening and stopped to watch in awe before running indoors when a thunderclap split the air, so close and so loud that the windows shook. The wind picked up, sending the racing clouds gusting outwards, rolling through the streets in walls of thick, churning fog.

In moments, the visibility went from excellent, to terrible. The wind dropped again, and the fog settled in, dense and rapidly darkening, like a grey sheet over the eyes. Suddenly, it was difficult to see anything more than a metre away – at least, for anyone who didn't have infrared vision.

The Detective quickly switched to IR spec and left the weather station. The faster they acted, the more unprepared the fleshsmith fragments would be.

Almost immediately, they saw an officer stumbling along the road, arms outstretched as he tried to make sense of his once-familiar surroundings. The Detective recognised him as one of the officers who had tried to shoot them before, and with a faint *snick* they drew their thumb knife.

The fragment had no warning before his throat was sliced from ear to ear. Blood sprayed out and then coalesced into red goo, flowing into the rest of the collapsing pillar of flesh.

By the time the fragment's head melted away into itself, the Detective was already several streets away. But their act of violence had not been entirely wanton. As they ran towards the office, they saw several more fragments travelling in the other direction, moving to the Detective's last known location – and leaving the sin-seeker office relatively undefended.

By the time they arrived at the office, the fog had become even thicker and darker, pressing damply against the Detective's skin sensors, choking out light and heat until even IR spec vision became hard to see with. Outside the office, several more officers were trying their best to see, shining torches through the fog – but if anything, this made it even worse for them, the light bouncing dazzlingly off the whirling water droplets.

The Detective easily slipped past and ran lightly around the side of the building, to where they had spotted the fuse box the previous day. Inside the building, the lights were on – but they turned off all at once when the Detective sent a pulse of electricity directly through the circuit breaker.

With the office plunged into darkness, the Detective located a window to an unoccupied room and, after hesitating for only a second, smashed in the glass.

The noise was muffled, swallowed by the swirling mists. Immediately, fog began rolling into the room – and the Detective climbed in with it.

There were people in the building, most likely more fragments. In the dark, the Detective heard them running back and forth, grabbing more torches and turning them on. They were oddly quiet as they did so, communicating presumably through their own strange means.

With thirty-nine per cent of their battery remaining, the Detective got ready to fight the fragments that were left in the station. But, as it turned out, this was not necessary. Shortly, the sounds of running feet stopped and the inner airlock closed with a faint squeak.

Stepping out into the main hall, the Detective cautiously made their way to the front – but there was no one there.

Apparently, the fleshsmith had decided to concede this particular battleground.

The Detective stood in the front of the office and frowned to themselves. If the fleshsmith had abandoned this post so easily, then apparently it was not worth so much to them.

That being said – it meant the Detective could investigate the place in peace, at least for the time being.

They quickly and methodically went through each of the rooms in turn, noting down anything of importance. They found an additional computer in McCleave's office, which would be useful to go through later. In the evidence locker, they found several bags of personal belongings which were suspiciously not assigned to any case.

Then, in the 'flooded' jail, they found something particularly interesting.

The room turned out not to be flooded at all but instead, housed half a dozen large, slimy oblong shapes, one in each jail cell and two in the hall. Each of the shapes, opaque and jellylike, hung suspended from the ceiling by a network of thick tendrils.

The Detective stepped up to the nearest one and gently poked it with their finger. It was warm to the touch and gave slightly, like the skin of an overripe fruit.

There was also a warmer mass in the centre, a mass that was clearly human shaped.

Frowning, the Detective used their thumb blade to slash into the fleshy orb. Foul smelling, acidic liquid immediately spilled out, splashing on the floor and across the Detective's feet.

The Detective ignored this and dug deeper into the orb, pulling it apart. It wasn't long before they got to the mass at the centre and pulled it out onto the floor in a wash of digestive juices.

It was Bill. He was alive – but only just.

Parts of his skin had been melted away, leaving large patches of raw, red tissue. His hair was gone, and his ears, nose and lips had been eaten into. His fingers and toes had been worn down almost to the bone, with chunks of white clearly visible between exposed tendons.

He would not survive long in this state – not without immediate, aggressive medical attention.

The Detective glanced briefly at the other five digestion orbs, wondering who they were before remembering that there had been five bushrangers. Assuming the fleshsmith had placed them inside the orbs as soon as they were brought in, that meant they had been in there for about twenty-one hours – over twice as long as Bill.

There was no way they were still alive. And besides, even in the slim chance they were, they were mere sinners, while Bill... Bill was more important.

The Detective hauled Bill over their shoulder and took the stairs two at a time.

They had gone past the med clinic twice already that morning and knew exactly where it was. Outside, the heavy fog was still in place – but the Detective ignored it, taking to the streets at a sprint.

No one stopped them on their way and they made it to the med clinic in minutes. It was open, the lights inside blazing bright. On the wall, text scrolled across the E.W.S, declaring a current 'unscheduled weather event due to sin-seeker operations'.

The Detective burst in through the airlock, charged past the short queue of people in line and gently placed Bill's body on the reception desk.

The clerk jumped up in shock, spilling papers onto the floor.

'This man requires immediate medical attention,' the Detective said.

'I can see that!' the clerk screeched and he reached over and pressed a buzzer that was built into the desk.

'Clement, we've got an emergency situation!' he yelled into it. 'I need someone immediately!'

'What sort of emergency?!' a voice buzzed back. 'What's going on out there? Is there a Portent?'

'What?' the clerk yelled back. 'No – I'm not talking about the weather! There's a guy with no fucking skin on my desk!'

The Detective stepped back slightly, moving to the side.

Behind them, everyone who had been standing in line were staring at Bill with expressions of shock and horror.

A door at the back of the room banged open and two people in scrubs came out with a stretcher. Upon seeing Bill, their eyes widened.

'Fucking hell,' the man who the Detective recognised by his voice as Clement said. 'What in the Nation happened to him? Stace, grab his legs.'

'He is the victim of a rogue fleshsmith,' the Detective said, watching them lift Bill onto the stretcher.

'What?' the clerk said. 'A rogue fleshsmith? Geez. What the fuck is going on today?'

He glanced at the window, which was pitch dark, water droplets whirling in the light from the clinic.

'What sort of bullshit sin-seeker operation is this anyway?' he said.

'Keep an eye out,' Clement said as the other nurse hauled the stretcher away. 'The smiths have been on edge all morning. Seem pretty convinced the Third is about to walk right in here.'

'Really?' the clerk said. 'That's concerning.'

'The Third Portent is not responsible for this weather event,' the Detective said. 'I am a sin-seeker. While I cannot explain the details of the operation, I can assure you that it is realitysmith activity, and not a Portent, that is causing the strange conditions this morning.'

'Phew!' the clerk said. 'The last thing we need right now is Ol' Weatherface showing up.'

As he grabbed a paper towel and began wiping up the blood on his desk, one of the people who had been standing in line cleared their throat. Turning, the Detective met the eye of a stocky First Nations woman with a close-shaved head and a red leather jacket.

'Excuse me,' she said to the Detective. 'I couldn't help but overhear you say something about a rogue fleshsmith?'

The Detective turned around to face her fully.

'That is correct,' they said.

'Right.' The woman nodded, and she reached into her coat pocket, pulling out a colourful business card.

'Tanya Fletch,' she said, showing it to the Detective. 'Rogue hunter. Thought I'd introduce myself, in case you required the services of someone such as me.'

The Detective took the card and turned it around in their hand.

'You are officially affiliated with the Sanctuaries?' they asked.

'Yep,' Tanya said.

'And you specialise in finding and apprehending rogue realitysmiths?'

'That's right,' Tanya said.

The Detective nodded.

'Your services would very much be appreciated,' they said.

## THE THIRD PORTENT

FIRST RECORDED SITGHTING: 14/09/2052, Melbourne, Kulin country, VIC

PHYSICAL APPEARANCE:

The Third Portent resembles the headless, naked body of an adult human male, of average height and weight, commonly seen standing, walking or running in an upright position. In place of a head, the Third Portent carries an iron weathervane, displaying the four cardinal points, a 30cm long free-spinning arrow, and the silhouette cut-out of a crowing cockerel.

While the Portent's body initially appears complete, it is possible to observe through the top of the neck that the skin is hollow and held in place via pressurised air. The skin itself is highly weather-damaged, criss-crossed with scar tissue and leatherlike in consistency; however, it has been seen to display regenerative properties. Due to the frequent extreme weather events surrounding the Portent, rips and tears appear in the skin at an average rate of two per week, however these damages are able to repair themselves at a rate similar to that of living skin, leaving behind further scar tissue.

Like the body itself, the weathervane appears

to be held in place via air pressure, with
the base extending downwards through the
hollow core of the body. While it appears
largely fixed in place on a vertical axis, it
is able to rotate freely on a horizontal
plane and does so frequently. The cardinal
points on the lower section of the
weathervane align precisely towards their
corresponding true coordinates, barring
disruption by the presence of strong magnetic
fields. The upper section of the weathervane,
consisting of the arrow and cockerel, is able
to rotate rapidly back and forth – and in
doing so generates the Portent's primary
anomalous effect: the spontaneous local
creation of extreme low or high atmospheric
pressure systems.

BEHAVIOUR:

The Third Portent travels on foot at a speed
of between zero and ten kilometres per hour,
stopping and starting or changing direction
seemingly at random. While its core is
relatively small, the effects of its presence
extend for many kilometres above it. The
exact effects generated depend on the
rotation of the weathervane.

When the weathervane rotates in a clockwise
direction, a low-pressure system generates in
the atmosphere above. Winds travel inwards
towards the core, circling in a clockwise
direction. Water vapour condenses, resulting
in locally situated clouds and rain.

When the weathervane rotates in an
anticlockwise direction, a high-pressure

system develops in the atmosphere above.
Winds blow outwards away from the core,
travelling in an anticlockwise direction, and
the sky above becomes clear and sunny.

Occasionally, the weathervane will undergo
periods of rapid oscillation, resulting in
violent and unpredictable weather as
atmospheric pressure rapidly climbs and
drops. During these times, lightning storms,
flash flooding, hail and cyclonic winds are not
unusual.

Conversely, during periods in which the
weathervane remains largely still,
atmospheric interference drops to zero. In
this state, the Third Portent enters a phase
known as 'the doldrums', in which its body
becomes deflated and hangs from the
weathervane, dragging along the ground at a
sluggish pace.

If there exists a logic to which way the
weathervane spins at which time, it is not
yet understood.

PORTENT INDUCED UNREALITY SYMPTOMS:

P.I.U.S RUBICON RADIUS: 11m

ACTIVE SYMPTOM DEVELOPMENT: 62%

LETHALITY: 14%

DESIGNATION: Weathersmith

ADDITIONAL NOTES: P.I.U.S originating from
the Third Portent typically relate to the
manipulation of weather and pressure.

Note – P.I.U.S of the Third were the first type of P.I.U.S recorded in humankind, and the first subsequently used to benefit the Nation, contributing in no small part to our ongoing survival. To date, due to its relatively low lethality, highly useful symptoms and long-standing presence in the Last Nation, the Third boasts the largest number of realitysmiths active in the field.

# CHAPTER 31

# RELYING ON OTHERS

**Date: Saturday 24 January 2082**

Air – sweet air in her lungs.

Quinn coughed violently, red jelly dripping out of her mouth and nose, stinging as it left her body.

Her vision was blurry, but clearing by the second. As she struggled to ungum her eyelids, a shape swam into view. It was a face, looming close, brow furrowed in worry.

Maggie – it was Maggie.

Maggie was there, patting her on the back as she vomited slime. Maggie had saved her life. She had almost died. She had almost fucking died. It had been so close this time.

She tried to speak, to express the gratefulness she felt, but Maggie stopped her.

'Don't talk,' she whispered. 'Just rest! I have to get the others!'

Wincing as her breath rushed over her raw throat, Quinn let herself lay on the floor, watching as Maggie moved away and began hacking into another of the slime balls with a pocketknife. Mullet fell to the floor a moment later and began coughing and retching as well.

Maggie paused, eyeing the other slime balls.

'Cut it open!' Quinn rasped weakly. 'Kylie –!'

Maggie nodded and got back to work. Meanwhile, Quinn struggled slowly into an upright position, inspecting her arms and body.

Her clothes had started developing holes, and her skin

looked red and raw, like it was sunburnt. Blisters were starting to form all over the place. It was painful – every movement stung.

'How... how long were we in there?' she managed.

'About forty minutes,' Maggie said, stepping back as rancid liquid sloshed out of the next slime ball. 'Ava stuck around for ages, wrapping you into these gross eggs! I hid in the other tunnel and waited until she left. Was terrified you were all dead already. But you're not!'

'Forty minutes?' Quinn rasped, massaging her throat. 'How... how did I survive that long, without air?'

'The slime is oxygenated?' Maggie said. 'That's my guess. It's full of capillaries, so it makes sense to me that it would be.'

'Right,' Quinn whispered.

She paused, watching Maggie gratefully.

'I thought you went back to Melody Sands,' she said.

'Nah, I didn't go anywhere,' Maggie said. 'I just followed you at a distance. I wasn't fully sure what was going on but I knew enough to be very suspicious.'

'How?' Quinn said. 'How did you figure it out?'

'Kylie's weird email,' Maggie said. 'And dumb luck. Remember when I went to message Kylie about where we were? I couldn't remember how to spell Saoirse for the life of me – so I just wrote Sursha, S-U-R-S-H-A, which is how it sounds. And then, because Sursha isn't a word, my phone autocorrected it, to Surah!'

'Huh?' Quinn said.

'Surah!' Maggie said. 'Remember – that's the exact same word that Kylie sent to her own computer!'

'Oh!' Quinn said. 'Shit!'

'Yeah!' Maggie said. 'Kylie had been trying to write Saoirse! And considering she'd spelt it wrong, it meant she didn't have time to correct it before she hit send! Since she was missing, I thought that was really suspicious. Clearly she had only had time to write one word – and that was the one she chose?'

'Holy shit,' Quinn said. 'I would never have figured that out!'

'Well, it was only luck that I did,' Maggie said. 'And I didn't know exactly what I'd figured out. Only that Saoirse was in on it...'

She hacked into the next slime ball and another body fell out.

Quinn recognised Kylie immediately – but she was not looking well. Her skin was terribly blistered and peeling, the tissue underneath raw and bleeding. Aside from her jewellery, her clothes had dissolved completely and her long dark hair was starting to break away and dissolve.

Maggie hurriedly laid her out in a comfortable position and wiped off the worst of the slime. 'Crap,' she said grimly.

'Is she...?' Quinn asked, eyes wide.

'She's alive,' Maggie said. 'But those acid burns are bad. We have to get her to a medical fleshsmith really soon. If the wounds get infected, she's a goner.'

She took off her skirt and, ripping it into several long pieces, tied them tightly around the worst of the bleeding. Then she took off her jacket and wrapped it around Kylie's torso. Then she paused, looking at the remaining slime balls.

'I'm just going to check if there's anyone else still alive in there,' she said and began hacking at the next one.

Shortly, an odd, truncated shape fell out. It made a heavy noise as it hit the floor, like metal hitting stone.

'Woah, what is that?' Maggie said.

Puzzled, she nudged the object with her foot. It was irregularly shaped, a moulded mess of sheet metal held together with wires and half-melted gears. A long, thin tube poked out of one side.

Maggie leaned closer, frowning.

'I think... it's a person?' she said. 'But... they're encased in metal?'

Quinn scooted closer, frowning, before coming to a sudden realisation.

'Oh, it's fucking Spencer!' she said.

'What?' Maggie said. 'The guy who was following you?'

'He's a mattersmith!' Quinn explained. 'He's used the metal from his own cybernetic arms and legs to protect himself from the slime!'

'Huh,' Maggie said. 'That's pretty clever, actually.'

'Yeah, whatever.' Quinn snorted.

'I wonder if he's still alive in there?' Maggie said, nudging the metal cocoon again. 'He would have been in there for days! I suppose that long tube is for air? But he wouldn't have had any water or food.'

'Who cares, honestly,' Quinn said.

Maggie gave her a concerned look, but then moved on to the next flesh sac.

This time it was immediately obvious that there was no one inside alive. Foul smelling liquid dribbled out. Then, a partially dissolved bone dropped onto the floor.

Maggie stopped hacking and stepped back, hand over her mouth as she tried not to throw up.

'Okay,' she said in a tight voice. 'This one is super dead.'

'Right,' Mullet wheezed from the floor. 'Can we fuck off, then?'

'Yeah,' Maggie said. 'Let's get out of here. I'll make sure the coast is clear.'

She moved towards the short tunnel, cautiously shining her torch around the corner. For a few minutes she was gone. Then she was back, with a grim expression on her face.

'So, we have a problem,' she said. 'The tunnel is a dead end, and the hole we came down through has been blocked off.'

'With what?' Quinn said.

'Looks like stone,' Maggie said. 'I think... remember that huge stone chunk that was sitting next to the hole? I think it's that.'

'Great,' Quinn said. 'That rock was huge! How are we supposed to move a rock THAT big?'

She paused, looking at Maggie. Then both of them turned to look at Spencer's metal-bound torso.

'Lucky we have a mattersmith right here!' Maggie said brightly.

'Fuck's sake,' Quinn muttered.

Maggie moved back to the metal cocoon and knocked on it sharply with her knuckles.

'He's not going to cooperate, you know that, right?' Quinn said. 'He's a ex-sin-seeker, and he REALLY hates us.'

'He will cooperate,' Maggie said brightly, 'or he'll die here with the rest of us!'

'Knowing him, he might choose death,' Quinn said.

'Well, we'll deal with that if it happens,' Maggie said. 'Any ideas on how to get him out of his cocoon?'

Quinn scooted closer.

'Oi, fuckhead!' she yelled into the breathing tube. 'Someone's selling music out here!'

'I don't think –' Maggie began.

The cocoon twitched.

Quinn hurriedly scooted back again as the metal began to break apart. Thin cracks spread across it before it abruptly shattered outwards, falling away in a shower of shards.

Spencer coughed and opened his eyes. They floated unfocused across the ceiling and then landed on Quinn. Abruptly, Spencer's expression sharpened.

'Fuck,' he said.

'Now, that's not very nice,' Quinn said. 'We just saved your life.'

'I'd rather be dead,' Spencer croaked weakly.

'See?' Quinn looked at Maggie. 'Told you.'

Maggie stepped into Spencer's view and handed him a water flask.

'Alright,' she said in her no-nonsense voice. 'Have a drink, have a breather, then get your shit together. We don't have time to be immature babies right now. You can continue your vendetta later, but right now, we need to work together. Otherwise, Ava will come back and kill us all. Okay?'

'Speak for yourself,' Spencer rasped, finishing the water he'd been handed. 'Didn't kill me, did it?'

'Yeah,' Quinn said, 'but now your legs and arms are all used up, idiot. That's them sprinkled all over the floor.'

'Then I'll just remake them!' Spencer said.

'Can you do that?' Maggie asked in interest.

Spencer looked at her.

'Um,' he said. 'Yeah?'

'Do it then,' Quinn said. 'Go on.'

Spencer glared at her and Quinn felt unreality increase. For a second, the flakes of metal began to shiver towards each other across the floor – but then it abruptly petered out.

'Okay,' Spencer said through gritted teeth. 'I can't make new limbs. I'm not an engineer. I don't know how cybernetic limbs work. They're actually really complex.'

'So, what, you're going to lie there and do nothing?' Quinn said.

'Hey, hey,' Maggie said. 'You can get your cybernetics back later – once we leave Ark 2! Right now, the priority is getting as far away from here as possible. Spencer – that's your name, right? Can your mattersmith abilities move stone, or just metal?'

'Why do you want to know?' Spencer said.

'We have a large stone that we're going to need you to move,' Maggie said. 'Here – I'll take you to where it is.'

'What if I don't want to?' Spencer protested as Maggie grabbed him under the armpits and hoisted him up.

'Then me and Mullet will set up some goal posts,' Quinn said. 'And we'll play football with your stupid torso.'

Spencer scowled at her but he didn't say anything else as Maggie carried him to where the stone blocked their way.

Quinn got to her feet as well, which took a couple of minutes because her skin was still very raw. Then, leaving Mullet to keep an eye on Kylie, she hobbled down the tunnel.

'What do you mean, you can't move it?' Maggie was saying to Spencer when she arrived. 'Is it can't, or won't?'

'It's can't, moron,' Spencer said. 'I can move about two hundred kilograms, that's it. This rock is at least four or five times that. Thus, I cannot move it. Simple mathematics!'

'Well, can you move a quarter of it, but four times?' Maggie said.

'And suffer four side effects at once?' Spencer said. 'Yeah, no thanks. Forget it.'

'Okay, but if you don't move it, we'll all die here,' Maggie said. 'Ava will be back here eventually.'

'Yeah, well, I'm not dying so you can live,' Spencer said. 'Anyway, why don't you ask HER to do it?' He jutted his chin in Quinn's direction. 'She's a timesmith. Just get her to change the timeline so none of this happened!'

Maggie blinked at Quinn. 'You're a timesmith?' she said in surprise.

'Yeah,' Quinn said. 'I thought you knew that?'

'I knew you were a smith,' Maggie said. 'But I didn't know what kind. I assumed it was a weathersmith or something else irrelevant to our current situation. But if you're a timesmith, then Spencer might have a point. CAN you change the timeline and get us out of here?'

'Well,' Quinn said. 'I don't know. I thought about it too, but there are some problems. I can reverse time, but only if there's music playing. The first issue is that we don't have any music down here, except for singing and drumming on things, which I don't think will be powerful enough.'

'I have music!' Maggie said and she took out her mobile phone. 'On here!'

Quinn frowned. 'Okay – well that's a start,' she said, 'but I'm still not sure it's enough. Ava trapped us in here nearly an hour ago, which is longer than I've ever reversed before. Even ignoring that, and assuming I can go back an hour – then what? Ava is a giant fucking slime monster, with eyes literally everywhere. She still had the upper hand an hour ago! She had it two hours ago as well, and six hours ago, when she captured Kylie, and two days ago, when she captured Spencer and found out I was a timesmith! In fact, she knew I was a smith from the very first day I got here and didn't eat the Tim Tams, and she's been watching me since then. If at any point in the last few months I suddenly decided to leave the Ark for no reason, she would probably get suspicious and well, basically, what I'm trying to say is that short of rewinding time to before we ever came to Ark 2, I'm not confident we can escape her!'

'I see,' Maggie said thoughtfully. 'How do your symptoms work exactly, if you don't mind me asking?'

Quinn explained what she knew of how they worked. As she spoke, Maggie produced a notebook out of thin air and began writing it down.

'I think you're right,' she said once Quinn had finished. 'There isn't a clear point to go back to and change things, especially recently. It would definitely be better to escape from this timepoint, where Ava thinks she's already won.'

'Yes, but how?' Quinn said.

Maggie tapped her pen on the paper.

'I have an idea,' she said. 'It may be a bad idea – but if it works, then the boulder will move back in time to when it was not blocking the exit and we can escape.'

'That's not how my symptoms work,' Quinn said.

'No,' Maggie said. 'But what if you combined yours and Spencer's?'

Spencer wrinkled his nose. 'Eugh, no thanks.'

'Remember how I told you I used to work for the Department of Unreality?' Maggie ignored him. 'And how one of the projects we worked on was quantifying the additive effects of realitysmiths working together?'

'Yeah?' Quinn said.

'So,' Maggie said. 'If you are able to manipulate the flow of time and Spencer is able to move rocks, then if both of you focus on moving the rock, at the same time, then there's a good chance that the result will be the rock moving in time! Hopefully, to a point in the timeline when it was not in the way!'

Everyone stared at her.

'You really think that will work?' Quinn asked doubtfully.

'I'd give it about a sixty per cent chance?' Maggie said.

'That's not very high,' Quinn muttered.

'Here's the thing,' Maggie said. 'Something WILL happen, I am certain of that. The main area of uncertainty is what exactly will happen. But the rock repositioning itself in time seems pretty likely, don't you think?'

'How far will it go back?' Quinn asked. 'What if it spends most of the time blocking the hole and we just reposition it back to when it was already blocking the hole?'

'Hmm.' Maggie stroked her chin. 'What sort of song would rewind you half an hour, Quinn?'

'Something quite complex,' Quinn said. 'Lots of layers. More than five layers for a three-minute song.'

'Five or six instruments, huh?' Maggie said. 'What about an orchestral piece? That has a lot of layers, surely?'

'Do you have something like that on your phone?' Quinn asked.

Maggie turned her phone around to show it to her.

'Beethoven's Symphony Number 7?' Quinn said. 'I don't know it.'

'It's a whole orchestra, and it goes for over forty minutes,' Maggie said.

'Okay, well, that's too long,' Quinn said.

'We don't have to listen to the whole thing,' Maggie said. 'Just the first few minutes. Here, I'll play a bit! See what you think.'

She turned up the volume, and pressed play. Dramatic music echoed throughout the cave. Immediately, Spencer began yelling to turn it off – but when no one acted to do so, he fell silent.

'Orchestral, huh,' Quinn said thoughtfully, as more and more instruments joined in. 'I haven't used orchestral music before. It definitely has a lot of layers.'

'Do you think it'll work?' Maggie said.

'Yeah,' Quinn said. 'I think so.'

'Okay,' Maggie said. 'I'll stop it then, and play it again from the start, for three minutes. Is that good?'

'Yeah, that should do,' Quinn said.

Maggie did so and, while the music played again from the start, they moved into position. Maggie propped Spencer up against the wall, just beneath the stone, and Quinn reluctantly sat next to him. Even more reluctantly, she did as Maggie said and put her hand on his shoulder. Spencer, meanwhile, remained quiet, his expression one of stiff resentment.

'Alright,' Maggie said, once everyone was in place. 'When I say go, I want both of you to focus your symptoms on the rock. You should feel a sort of connection as you do so, which means it's working. I don't exactly know what it feels like, since I haven't personally experienced it, but apparently, it's pretty obvious. With luck, the result will be what we're hoping it to be.'

Quinn took a breath, suddenly nervous.

'What if it doesn't go as planned?' she said. 'What else might happen?'

'That's difficult to say,' Maggie said. 'And you're better off not thinking about it. The best thing to do is focus on the stone and what you want it to do. Nothing else is important.'

Quinn nodded.

'Okay,' Maggie said, looking at her phone and backing away into the tunnel. 'We're almost there. Are you both ready?'

Quinn nodded again.

'And you, Spencer?' Maggie said.

'Yeah,' Spencer said flatly.

Quinn eyed him. 'If you don't do it, you know what will happen?' she said. 'I'll go back in time half an hour instead of the stone. And then I will stop Maggie from getting you out of the flesh sac, and you'll stay there forever.'

'I'm gonna do it,' Spencer snapped at her.

'Good,' Quinn said.

There was a pause, and then Maggie took a breath. 'Alright!' she called. 'Ready? Three! Two! One! GO!'

Quinn grasped the music and felt it stretch and slow – but immediately, something was different. There was another note, another flavour of unreality, tangling amongst the threads of her own.

Spencer's power. For a second, she felt it touch her, and she understood it completely. She felt the structure of the rock around them, the tiny interlocking lattices, the forces that held them in place. She felt the very atoms they were made up of, spinning and shuddering, and the empty space between them, unimaginably vast. They might be rearranged, excited, changed, with just the right nudge...

Above, the stone behemoth stood in her way – but it could be moved. Time could move it. Frowning, as the music stretched into one endless note, she seized the stone core and untethered it from time.

The First and the Fourth Portent roared in her mind, sirens blaring, gears clanking, churning on and on. The song began to play backwards. She heard Spencer gasp as he heard it too. But for the first time ever, she stayed in one place. This time, it wasn't her that went back.

She could feel the power of it, racing through her like a rip current beneath still waters. It was unstoppable, fuelled by the song, rushing back to its beginning. With each new instrument added to the track, the torrent swelled larger and larger. Time was unravelling quickly.

Too quickly, Quinn realised. Much, much more quickly than she'd thought. There were more instruments in the song than she'd realised – and for each part played, there were multiple people playing it. It wasn't one violin, but three, and another two playing in harmony. It was a whole fucking orchestra, and everyone in it, each individual, was adding to the power.

On top of this, Spencer's input was boosting it further. It was accelerating – accelerating more than Quinn had ever thought possible.

Quinn didn't know how far it would go – but she knew they were going to overshoot the half-hour mark, probably by a matter of years, and there was nothing she could do about it.

She was almost scared to look up at the rock. But when

she forced herself to open her eyes, she found it oddly still. The torrent of time was roaring through it, she could feel that. But the rock itself appeared unchanged. In fact, if anything, it had gotten... bigger?

In a flash, Quinn realised what was happening. They were moving the rock through time – but not space. Usually, Quinn travelled through both – but Spencer's input had changed that. The molecules that made up the rock were getting younger – but that was it.

Perhaps if they reversed time enough, the rock would revert to how it was before it had been a rock? Perhaps it would turn into lava? Or perhaps nothing would happen. After all, what was time to a rock? Some rocks were billions of years old...

But there were still more instruments chiming into the piece – and with each one, time roared faster, exponentially larger, like a vast waterfall thundering upwards. Years had become decades, decades to centuries, centuries to millennia...

Abruptly, the song reached its beginning, and with a temporal thunderclap, time fixed in place.

Both Quinn and Spencer gasped as the whiplash hit them. Quinn felt incredibly tired all of a sudden, and sank back against the wall. Her ears were ringing. She was aware of Maggie yelling something but it sounded very distant.

There was sand in her eyes and she wiped it away. More appeared. Frowning, she brushed it away again, wondering if the side effect this time meant perpetual eye grit.

But no – the sand was everywhere, on her clothes and on the floor around her. Blinking, she once more looked up at the rock above.

A small amount of sand dribbled down from it and onto her shoe.

'Did it work?!' Maggie was calling. 'Are you okay? Quinn, can you hear me?'

'Y-yeah,' Quinn said, and then coughed. Her voice had sounded odd somehow.

'Yeah, you're okay?' Maggie asked as she scooted back away from under the rock. 'Or yeah, it worked?'

'Umm,' Quinn said, wincing. There was definitely something weird happening with her voice. 'Both?'

Massaging her throat, she shakily got to her feet and eyed the rock. It looked... different somehow. Grainier.

'Maggie, can you pull Spencer out of the way?' she said.

'Woah!' Maggie said, reaching for Spencer. 'What happened to your voice? You sound like you're talking through a walkie-talkie!'

'Great,' Quinn said. 'Hopefully that's not permanent.'

Frowning, she raised a hand towards the rock.

'Everyone close your eyes,' she said, and then jabbed it sharply.

The rock disintegrated into sand. It showered down with a heavy THWUMP, spilling out into the tunnel and half burying Quinn.

'Woah, what?!' Maggie yelled from the tunnel. 'That's not what I was expecting at all! Why did it turn into sand?!'

'It used to be sand, I guess.' Quinn shrugged. 'Thousands of years ago.'

Her ears were still ringing and she still felt tired, as well as sore. Suddenly she was overcome with an intense desire to just go to bed and sleep for an entire week.

But she couldn't. They weren't out of the woods yet. Sighing, she slowly dug herself out of the sand, and then helped Maggie push it out of the way down the tunnel.

'Thousands of years?' Maggie was saying excitedly. 'I can't believe it went that far back! Do you think it was purely because of Spencer's input? Or was it the music we used? I wonder how many instruments there were in that orchestra anyway? I bet if you got the sheet music, you could count and know for sure. I wonder if you could turn it into a precise formula?'

She didn't seem to expect any answers, so Quinn didn't provide any – and ten minutes later, they had cleared enough of the sand to access the ladder.

It took a little more time to figure out how to get

everyone out of the hole, but after tying the unconscious Kylie to Mullet, and Spencer to Maggie, they managed to climb out in one piece.

At the top, Maggie dusted herself off with an air of victory.

'Alright!' she said. 'We did it! Good job, everyone! It didn't go perfectly, but you know what? All's well that ends well!'

'Bit early to say that,' Spencer said, from where he was strapped to her back.

'Nonsense,' Maggie said. 'Ava already thinks we're dead. She'll never expect us to make an escape attempt now!'

'I wasn't talking about Ava,' Spencer said and he jutted his chin, gesturing upwards.

They all looked up. Above them, a ragged hole extended through the ceiling, through the floor of the next room, and through the ceiling of that as well, up into the museum.

'Shit,' Quinn said. 'Did... did we do that?'

'Doesn't matter,' Maggie said. 'So what if part of the building got blasted out of the timeline? If anything, it'll make getting out of here easier!'

'Again,' Spencer said, 'I wouldn't say that.'

'Why not?' Maggie said. 'I'm trying to be positive here, Spencer, and you're really killing the vibe! Maybe you should zip it for –'

She was interrupted by a long, low, animal rumble from directly above them.

All they all looked up again, just in time to see a very large something poke its hairy snout over the lip of the hole.

'Is that,' Maggie said. 'Is that a Diprotodon?'

# CHAPTER 32

# CAUSING A PLEISTO-SCENE

**Date: Saturday 24 January 2082**

Quinn opened the STAFF ONLY door and carefully peered down the corridor. It was empty, so she tiptoed to the end, looking both ways out into the museum.

'Okay,' she whispered back to the others. 'Coast's clear!'

Maggie and Mullet came out of the stairwell to join her. Mullet was carrying Kylie over his shoulder, fireman style, while Spencer was still strapped to Maggie like the world's angriest backpack.

Quickly and quietly, they ran past the exhibits and towards the entrance hall. But on getting there first, Quinn took one look at what was inside and hurriedly backpaddled.

Behind her, the others skidded to a stop.

*Ava?* Maggie signed.

Quinn shook her head. 'Big lizard,' she whispered, eyes wide.

'Oh, boo hoo.' Spencer snorted. 'A lizard? Are you scared of lizards, Quinn? You know they're harmless, right?'

'No,' Quinn said. 'I'm not scared of normal lizards, arsebutt. When I say big, I mean BIG. Like, I've seen smaller cars!'

'Ah,' Maggie said. 'The Megalania. I guess the Diprotodon wasn't the only creature that got reanimated. Fantastic.'

Quinn turned to look at her. 'Shit. What other creatures were in that room? Do you remember?'

Maggie blinked. 'Uhhh,' she said. 'There was a big bird, right? Like, a huge goose-looking thing? I've forgotten what it was called. And then there was the marsupial lion…'

'The what now?' Mullet said.

'Don't worry,' Maggie told him. 'It's actually the smallest creature in the room. Size of a large dog.'

Mullet looked around in concern.

'So, how are we going to get past the lizard?' Quinn said, peering around the corner again. The Megalania was currently nosing at the desk in the corner. Its tongue flickered ponderously in and out, tinted blue, the size of Quinn's entire arm.

'I think we should avoid it,' Maggie said. 'There was a big window a few rooms back – we should probably just break out through that instead. We've already caused a lot of property damage, so what's a bit more, right?!'

'Right,' Quinn said.

They ran back the other way, past the STAFF ONLY door and into the room beyond. Once again though, it wasn't empty.

'Great,' Quinn said. 'I found the bird.'

Mullet pushed the door wider and it creaked loudly. Inside the room, a grey-feathered monster lifted its head, yellow eye filled with all the raw malice and aggression of an angry goose, only ten times the size.

As it puffed up its feathers and took a step closer, Mullet hurriedly closed the door again.

'You know what?' he said to the others. 'I'd rather take my chances with the lizard.'

'There's another window,' Maggie said.

'Okay?' Quinn said. 'You don't sound very happy about it?'

'Because it's in the fossil room.' Maggie sighed.

'I don't see the problem,' Quinn said. 'All the fossils have walked elsewhere.'

'I guess they have,' Maggie said.

They ran back again, past the entrance hall and around into the fossil room.

It was also occupied. The Diprotodon, which was too large to fit through any of the doors, was standing inside, nose over the hole in the floor. When they came in, it slowly turned its head to look at them with beady brown eyes.

'Nation, it's so big,' Maggie muttered.

'Nah, look at him, he's chill!' Quinn said, brightening. 'He doesn't know what's happening, poor dude! A few minutes ago, he'd been dead for millennia! Weren't you, buddy? Aw, he's pretty cute, Maggie.'

'Don't get attached,' Maggie said, heading for the window. 'You're not going to see him again.'

'Aw.' Quinn pouted. 'I wish we could take you with us, big guy! Hey Mullet, do you think Kylie would let us have a Diprotodon as a pet?'

'I doubt it,' Mullet said. 'She wouldn't let ME keep a pet last year.'

'Yeah, but that was a brushie tail possum that you found in a garbage skip,' Quinn said. 'Henry is much more dignified!'

'Henry?' Mullet said.

'Can we please focus on getting out of here?' Maggie said from the window. 'I'm going to need some sort of heavy object to break the window with...'

'Like, a big piece of metal?' Mullet said, pointing at the broken fossil display case, which had been partially blasted into oblivion.

'Sure,' Maggie said.

Mullet put Kylie gently down on the floor, kicked the piece of metal out of its holdings and hefted it.

'Should I smash it?'

Maggie nodded, and gleefully, Mullet attacked the window. It shattered immediately, in a rattle of broken glass.

The Diprotodon snorted and turned to face the noise. Everyone else held their breath, half expecting Ava to appear outside.

Silence reigned.

'Okay,' Maggie whispered. 'There's our exit.'

'Right,' Quinn said. 'Um... what next?'

'I've thought about it,' Maggie said. 'Firstly, I think it's too risky to try and get back to Melody Sands, so say goodbye to all our stuff that's there. Secondly, as far as I know, the only way out of Ark 2 is via the elevator – so that's where we have to go. Once we're outside in the open, it'll be relatively easy to break into the vehicle garage and hopefully find Kylie's RV. Or even if it's not there, we'll be able to borrow *something*. The main problem is going to be getting into the elevator in the first place. It's guarded twenty-four seven by security goons.'

'Who are all part of the Ava slime conglomerate,' Quinn added.

'Exactly,' Maggie said. 'If they see us, then Ava will realise we've escaped.'

'So we need to sneak past them?' Quinn said.

'Something like that,' Maggie said. 'Um. If anyone has any other ideas, please don't hold back.'

'What if,' Mullet said, 'Quinn and Spencer sneak up behind the guards and ZAP! They send those suckers back in time until they're not even born!'

'Absolutely not,' Quinn said.

'Alright, what's your idea then?' Mullet said. 'Bet it's not as cool as mine.'

'We could cause some sort of distraction?' Quinn said. 'And while the guards are busy looking at the distraction, we run past them into the elevator?'

'Not a bad idea,' Maggie said. 'Although I'm not sure what sort of distraction would work. I'd rather not do anything that could result in innocent people dying. No setting anything on fire, for example.'

'We could play music somewhere?' Quinn said. 'Although... that might be less effective down here than it would be outside. There's always music playing down here.'

On Mullet's back, Spencer snorted. 'Are you guys for real?'

'What?' Quinn glared at him.

'You're looking for a distraction?' Spencer said. 'You're

standing in a room with a living Diprotodon... and you're wondering what you could possibly use as a distraction? Honestly, I'm shocked you guys weren't arrested years ago.'

Quinn narrowed her eyes.

'Alright, genius, how exactly do we use Henry as a distraction?'

'You just let it outside!' Spencer said. 'As soon as the security guards see it, it's going to take up all of their attention, trust me!'

'Fair point,' Maggie said thoughtfully. 'Although, it's too big to fit out the window, or the front door. How do we get it outside?'

'Christ's sake,' Spencer said. 'Do I have to do everything myself?'

He fell silent and Quinn felt unreality spike. Before she could react, there was a cracking noise in the wall around the window. A moment later, the entire thing fell away, leaving a huge, square hole.

'There you fucking go,' Spencer said and then coughed. Something dark splattered out onto the floor.

'Spencer!' Maggie said. 'That was unnecessary! We could have come up with something else. You're going to hurt yourself if you use your symptoms too much!'

'Oh, like you care,' Spencer snapped. 'You're only being nice to me 'cause I'm useful to you anyway. But I'm not completely helpless, you know! If I had my limbs, I –'

He broke off, coughing wetly. More black liquid splattered to the floor, where it glistened with a rainbow sheen. It was oil, Quinn realised.

'What are you looking at?' Spencer snapped at her. Oil dripped between his teeth, dribbling down his chin.

'There's...' Quinn said carefully, 'there's some oil on... you know what? Never mind. Have fun with that. Are we leaving?'

'Yes,' Maggie said.

There was a garden bed just outside the window and she climbed out into it. Pulling up a large handful of grass, she brought it inside and wafted it underneath the Diprotodon's big, leathery nose.

'Yummy grass?' she said cautiously. 'Do you want the yummy grass?'

Moving outside as well, Quinn clicked her tongue. 'C'mon, Henry!' she called.

'I can't believe you named it,' Maggie said.

The Diprotodon snuffled at the grass in interest and then took a step forward. Maggie moved away hurriedly, backing outside.

Soon, she had successfully led the massive hairy beast to the hole in the wall. Carefully, pausing often, it stepped out into the garden bed. There, it snorted happily at the plants in the garden.

'Yes!' Quinn said. 'Good boy, Henry! Now, we just need to lead him towards the elevator-!'

Maggie grabbed her suddenly, pulling her back inside. A second later, a figure came around the corner.

It was a security guard. They were walking quietly and scanning the bushes, gun in hand.

'Crap,' Maggie whispered. 'They must have heard something!'

They watched the guard walk past the Diprotodon in the garden before catching sight of the massive beast and doing a double take.

In the garden bed, Henry rumbled happily and took a big bite out of a boronia bush.

'Shit!' Maggie said. 'This is too early!'

'Should we go back to the front door?' Mullet said. 'Maybe the lizard moved?'

'That's too close to here!' Maggie said. 'They'll see us come out!'

'The other window then?' Mullet said and he pulled up his sleeves. 'I'll beat the shit out of that giant goose, just fucking try me.'

'They'll probably hear the smash,' Maggie said. 'But I guess we don't have much of a choice. We're going to have to hurry though!'

As they stood up, the guard outside took a step forward and raised their gun, levelling it at Henry's head. Seeing this, Quinn gasped.

'No!' she breathed. 'They're gonna shoot him!'

'I told you not to get attached, idiot,' Maggie said, grabbing her arm. 'C'mon, Quinn!'

'No!' Quinn broke out of her grasp. 'He was just brought back to life! He can't die yet!'

'It's not worth the risk!' Maggie said. 'Quinn –!'

There was a startled yell from outside and several gunshots. Quinn turned wildly, expecting to see Henry bleeding on the ground.

But instead, the guard was the one on the ground. Something large and tawny brown was crouched on top of him. Its teeth were buried in the guard's neck. As they watched, it shook its jaws and the guard's head separated clean from their body.

Both the head and the body immediately melted into reddish slime.

Quinn clapped her hands over her mouth, and Mullet swore.

'Maggie, what the fuck!' he said squeakily. 'Is that the marsupial lion? You said it was only the size of a dog!'

'A *large* dog,' Maggie said stiffly. 'Anyway – the prehistoric beasts are well and truly out of the bag. Let's get going, before more security guards show up!'

They slipped outside and into the shadows. Behind them, the marsupial lion sniffed at its melted prey in confusion and the Diprotodon wandered off to begin demolishing the next decorative garden.

The elevator was only a few streets away but by the time they'd got there, an uproar was already commencing. More guards ran past them, in the direction they'd come from, and Quinn felt several bursts of unreality, near and far.

Leaving the botanical garden behind, they ran by the silent shops, hurrying toward the elevator. As they reached the main square, however, they saw that there were two guards standing outside the miniature Flinders Street Station.

'Shit,' Maggie breathed. 'How do we get those two to move?'

'There's only two,' Mullet said, eyes narrowed. 'We could probably take 'em!'

'They have guns!' Quinn said.

'Yeah, well, we have magic powers!' Mullet said. 'You could totally time-blast them from here!'

'Mullet, I'm not about to fucking kill those men!' Quinn said.

'Why not?' Mullet said. 'They're evil slimes!'

'Well, that's not their fault,' Quinn said.

'I'll kill them, I'm not a coward!' Spencer said.

'Everyone shut up,' Maggie said. 'I have a better idea. I've been to Flinders Street Station before – the real one, I mean. I know this one is a lot smaller but it's based on the real one, then it should have least two more entrances. We should check around the back, before we rush in all gung-ho and get ourselves shot.'

They all agreed and quietly made their way around behind the building. But it became immediately obvious that, where the real Flinders Street Station backed onto train platforms, the copy instead backed onto nothing but a yellow-painted brick wall.

'Well,' Maggie said, 'there goes that plan.'

Spencer made a frustrated noise.

'Do you guys even want to escape?' he snapped. 'It's just a wall! I could break it in two seconds.'

'Yeah, but...' Maggie said.

'I told you, stop pretending you care if I get hurt,' Spencer snarled. 'Trust me, we'll all be much happier when this is all over! So, am I breaking it or not?'

'Do it,' Quinn said after a pause.

Spencer concentrated and a few seconds later, a metre-by-metre chunk of wall fell out in a tidy square.

'There you fuckin' go,' he said and spat a tiny metal cog onto the ground.

They all clambered in through the hole, into the darkened elevator station. The lights were off inside – but fortunately it wasn't hard to find the elevator itself.

Maggie hit the open button, and they crowded into the waiting cubicle. Then, as the doors closed, everyone breathed a sigh of relief.

'Okay, we're on the home stretch,' Maggie said, looking around at everyone. 'We're doing great! But it's not quite over yet. As soon as the elevator starts moving, Ava's gonna know what's up. She might have guards posted at the top of the elevator, waiting for us to pop out, or something else, who knows. We're gonna have to figure that out when we get there. But I think we can do it.'

'I'll put on some music,' Quinn said. 'So we can redo it if it goes wrong.'

'Oh yeah, good thinking!' Maggie said.

She pushed the up button and slowly, the elevator began to ascend, as tinny music played from the phone in Quinn's hands. As it rose out of the roof of the miniature Flinders Street, gathering speed, they saw the Ark spread out below. It was dark but there was movement in the streets. Below, the two guards ran out and looked upwards, pointing their guns at the elevator.

'They've seen us,' Maggie said grimly.

Mullet flipped the guards off with both hands – although they were already too far away to see it. Meanwhile, Quinn tapped her feet and muttered 'hurry up, hurry up' to herself.

Soon, Ark 2 had gotten very small below. They ascended past the crossbeams that held up the sun and the stars, and past the projected sky. They entered the long, dark shaft that separated the Ark from the outside world, tense faces lit by the pulsing glow of the red wall lights.

None of them could remember exactly how long the trip had taken on the way down – but it was surely much longer on the way up. Every second, Quinn expected the elevator to grind to halt. Surely, Ava was chasing after them? There was no way... no way they'd get out this easily, after everything else that had happened. There was a feeling closing in on her, a rising fear, the memories of a nightmare that were only getting stronger and stronger –

With a soft jolt, the elevator came to a stop and the doors slid smoothly open.

They had been expected guards to be waiting outside – but there was no one.

'Huh,' Maggie said carefully. 'Maybe we really did catch Ava unawares?'

Quinn turned her music way down – but not off.

Cautiously, they all stepped out, moving down the short, white-painted hall and out into the cowshed. Even more cautiously, they opened the outer door and stepped outside.

It was a clear, still night, with barely a cloud to cover the vast expanse of the sky. The air was fresh, warm and dry, smelling faintly of hay and cow manure.

Quinn looked up and breathed in deep. She hadn't realised how much she'd missed the real sky until now.

Not that it helped alleviate her tension. In fact, if anything, she was feeling even worse. There was something... something she'd missed, a strong feeling in her gut. It felt as though she'd left the stove on and now the house was burning down. As though she'd seen something terrifying in the corner of her eye, then forgotten it the instant she'd turned away...

Quietly, trying to calm her racing heart, she followed behind as the others began searching for THE GLAM VAN. It was stored away in a shed somewhere – although they had not been told which one.

Fanning out, they began peering through the windows and opening the doors of each shed they passed, trying to make out the contents. Most were empty or full of storage boxes. One held chickens, clucking sleepily. Another held an old tractor, clearly left unused for many years.

As they moved towards one of the larger sheds at the back, there was a faint noise – a low gurgling, like water in a pipe, and a creaking, like rusty hinges sliding open.

*Stop,* Maggie signed. *What was that?*

They stood in silence, listening. Wind blew up dust, sighing though grass, rattling a loose piece of corrugated iron. Very faintly, music played from the phone in Quinn's hand, masked somewhat by the loud beat of her pulse in her ears –

Just ahead, a shed door banged open.

'There you are!' Ava stepped out.

'RUN!' Quinn yelled.

They scattered, bolting in different directions – and the ground erupted around them. Tentacles burst out of a dozen buried pipes, lunging viciously at running legs.

Ava herself rose into the air, her legs morphing into a pillar of muscle. More tentacles burst out of her back, coiling and thrashing in rage.

'I don't know how you PATHETIC SHITS managed to escape,' she screamed, 'but it's not going to happen again! And this time, I won't be so nice!'

A tentacle lunged blindly at Quinn, forcing her to jump out of the way. Nearby, she saw Mullet run around a shed and saw tentacles follow after him, snaking along the walls.

Running in the opposite direction, Quinn glanced at her hand, where the music was still playing. It was fine. Things were still well under control. Ava was extremely pissed off, but if anything, it was making her sloppy.

Quinn could reverse time now – or, she could try to find a few things out first. Like where THE GLAM VAN was. (And what she'd missed. She was missing something, something obvious. Something really fucking important –)

Glancing into the window of the nearest shed, she saw it was full of crates. Not that one, then. Dodging another tentacle, she ran to the next one and looked in, but it wasn't that one either.

There was a scream nearby as someone got caught – but it didn't matter. She would reverse it. Just as soon as she figured out (WHAT SHE WAS MISSING) where THE GLAM VAN was.

There was a buzzing in her head, a jittering feeling of terror and exhilaration. Her heart was racing, pumping wildly. A feeling of doom overcame her – a horribly familiar feeling.

There – THE GLAM VAN, she saw it. She'd found it, in one of the sheds at the back of the farm, a flash of bright, obnoxious apple-green paint through the window.

But still, she did not turn back time. She had to know. She had to remember!

Where was it? Where was it? Where the fuck was it? As her mind finally made the connection, she froze in place, her heart dropping into her stomach.

Slowly, she looked up.

A tentacle caught her, wrapping around her waist – but she didn't make a sound. She was paralysed with dread. No. No. NO. NO. NOT AGAIN!

Ava was coming towards her, looming into view as she raised the tentacle higher. Her face was set in a triumphant snarl, teeth bared, eyes glittering with icy rage.

'Got you,' she hissed, hoisting Quinn off the ground. 'Foolish girl! Did you really think you could escape? It was only ever a matter of time until I caught you again!'

Quinn stared beyond Ava, up into the night sky. It was very hard to see, far away as it was – but it was there. She had felt it there for ages – ever since it had entered its active cycle, growing gradually stronger. And now she could also see it – a dark shape, blotting out the stars, tiny flames flickering from its angular wings.

'A matter of time, eh?' she said, with deathly calm.

Too late, Ava tried to stop her. The tentacle pressed in, crushing her hand – but the music had never stopped playing.

Time unravelled – but Quinn barely noticed. She was still staring at the sky.

Now that she knew it was there, she had no idea how she'd ever missed it. Its power radiated like excruciating heat from a blasphemous sun. She would recognise it anywhere. The same power channelled through her even now.

The tentacles vanished back into the earth and Ava

closed the shed door. Trancelike, Quinn watched herself scurry back into the elevator and descend towards the Ark.

Presently, two words emerged from the depths of her brain. They were shit and fuck, alternating in turn.

As the elevator reached the bottom of the shaft, she was unceremoniously dumped back into the timeline.

'I'll put on some music,' she heard herself say. 'So we can redo it if it goes wrong.'

Then the whiplash caught her and she doubled over.

'Crap!' Maggie said as Quinn sunk to the floor. 'I guess it went wrong then! Are you alright?'

Coughing and gasping, Quinn desperately tried to quell the uncontrollable shaking that had taken control of her body. There were patches of something on her skin, clinging like a fine film, but first she needed to tell them what she'd seen. They were running out of time. Every second they wasted was too many!

'It's alright,' Maggie said, patting her back. 'Shh. Give yourself a minute.'

Quinn shook her head, trying to gather her thoughts. Grabbing one hand with the other to quell the shaking, she reached into her pocket and pulled out the matchbox full of Portent shards. Fumbling it open, she desperately stared into it.

It was empty. The shards were gone.

'Shit,' Quinn said vehemently. 'Fuck!'

'What is it?' Mullet asked. 'What's about to happen?'

'Well,' Quinn said, staring at her palm. 'I guess I have good news and bad news!'

She closed her palm again, crumpling the matchbox.

'The good news is, I think we can escape from Ava,' she said. 'There are no guards up there and I know where THE GLAM VAN is. By the time Ava crawls out of the pipes, we can already be on our way.'

'That's great!' Maggie said. 'Excellent work, soldier!'

'What's the bad news?' Spencer asked.

Quinn took another breath.

'The bad news,' she said, 'is that while outrunning Ava

will be easy, outrunning the First Portent is going to be a bit more difficult.'

There was silence, as everyone stared at her.

'W-what?' Maggie said.

'The First Portent is up there,' Quinn said and stifled the insane urge to laugh.

'The FIRST Portent?' Mullet said blankly. 'As in... the Portent that's a fucking nuclear bomb?'

'Yep,' Quinn said.

'How, how long have we got?' Mullet asked, his voice cracking.

Quinn looked at the time on the mobile phone she was holding.

'I'd say about eight minutes?' she said.

# CHAPTER 33

# THE FIRST

### Date: Saturday 24 January 2082

'Is there any way to make this elevator go any faster?!' Quinn said as they ascended the second time.

'Not without damaging it,' Maggie said.

Quinn bounced anxiously on the balls of her feet, looking up at the ceiling. Slowly, Ark 2 sunk away beneath them again.

Quinn estimated that Ava had gotten to the surface about three minutes after they had – and about two minutes after that, the First Portent had been close enough to see with the naked eye.

When it came to the First, if you could see it, then you were inside the blast radius and thusly completely fucked. That meant they had approximately five minutes, from the point when the elevator arrived at the top of the shaft to the point when the First Portent was too close to escape, in which they could attempt to get into THE GLAM VAN and drive away as fast as fucking possible.

Would it be enough? Quinn wasn't sure. It was definitely going to be close.

'Five minutes,' she said out loud. 'That's how long we have to clear the farm. Any time after that is a bonus.'

'I thought you said eight?' Mullet squeaked.

'Yeah,' Quinn said. 'But that's including this slow-arse elevator ride! And once we reach the top, if we haven't escaped by five, then I'm not sure we'll clear the blast. It's really fucking big!'

'A four kilometre radius, from memory,' Maggie said nervously. 'For the initial blast, anyway.'

'If we don't make it,' Quinn said grimly, 'we can always try again.' She resisted the urge to scratch at the filmy-whatever-it-was that was clinging to her body.

Maggie gave her a concerned look.

'We should try to make it the first time,' she said firmly.

They fell silent, faces lit by the flashing of red lights. Then, as the elevator began to decelerate, they tensed, ready to run for it.

'I know where THE GLAM VAN is,' Quinn said, as it came to a stop. 'Follow me!'

With a DING, the doors opened.

They burst out, racing down the short hall, banging through the door at the end with no regard for stealth. As they burst outside, Quinn paused for a second, getting her bearings before charging off towards the back of the farm.

She could feel it already, the First's malevolent power bearing down on them, instant death on flickering silver wings. Now that she knew what it was, she had no idea how she'd failed to recognise it immediately. Its mark lived inside her, after all. It was like seeing the back of her own head – a part of her, unseen and taken for granted, but ever present.

Arriving at the shed where THE GLAM VAN was, she yanked open the door, ignoring the metallic shriek as it pulled over stone. Inside, it was pitch dark – but there was a light switch near the door.

The shed turned out the be full of vehicles, most of them covered in dust and cobwebs, untouched for many years. Some of them were models that no longer existed, imported from overseas. Like many old cars, the symbols they bore on their bonnets were faintly relicious – but these relics were nothing but candles in the wind when compared to the churning, all-encompassing aura of the First.

THE GLAM VAN was parked at the end of the row, newest in the collection, its bright-coloured paint dulled by layers of dust. It was locked – but Quinn knew where the key was. Reaching around the unconscious Kylie's neck, she grabbed the heart-shaped locket that hung there and flipped it open. The key folded neatly out.

'Can you drive?' she hissed at Maggie.

Maggie nodded and Quinn thrust the key locket into her hand. Then they all bundled into the RV.

While Maggie seat-belted Spencer into the passenger's seat, Mullet and Quinn went into the back, pausing to look around. The RV was almost empty, since they'd taken all their stuff down to Melody Sands – but it was still a familiar space, almost comforting, if it wasn't for the stress of the present moment.

While Mullet placed Kylie gently onto the floor, wrapped in blankets, Quinn leant into the driver's cabin. Maggie turned the key in the engine, revving and revving, and finally starting. Then, she paused, looking out the front window.

'Um,' she said. 'How do we get out of this shed? Do you think that roller door is locked?'

'No time for that!' Quinn said and looked at Spencer.

Spencer huffed slightly in annoyance but he'd caught her drift. He concentrated briefly and the wall of corrugated iron fell neatly outwards.

'Well, that works,' Maggie said and put her foot on the accelerator.

While Spencer grimaced in his seat, Quinn was once again reminded of her own, as yet mystery, side effect – and gingerly, she lifted the hem of her T-shirt to see what the damage was.

She got a glimpse of something grey and yellow, mottling the flesh of her belly before abruptly deciding it was a later problem. For time being, it didn't hurt any more than the acid burns she already had, and they had more pressing issues.

Spencer saw her drop the hem in a hurry and his eyes narrowed.

'What are you looking at?' Quinn glared at him.

He turned away, silent.

Maggie navigated around the various sheds, more carefully than Quinn would have liked, before finally pulling clear. Above, the sky was still clear of burning aircraft and for a moment, Quinn allowed herself to think about the possibility of actually escaping.

But by now, three minutes had passed – and right on cue, Ava showed up again.

Mullet, who was keeping watch out the back window, saw her appear and swore loudly.

'Slime McGee is back at it again!' he called. 'Now with more tentacles then ever!'

'Too late!' Maggie called. 'We're out of here!'

'Yeah, suck my arse, you wrinkly old bitch!' Mullet yelled, sending two middle fingers in the direction of the farm. Then he went silent, his hands dropping.

'Oh shit,' he said.

Quinn joined him at the back window, just in time to see a monster emerge.

Ava had once more lifted into the air – but this time, instead of spreading out all over the place, her tentacles converged on her. Jelly sucked inwards, tree-trunk bands of muscle and arcs of sinew twisting into place. Beneath the spot at which she held suspended, four thick pillars of flesh split out, lengthening and changing shape until they resembled the legs of a beast.

The creature, six metres tall, took a lurching step forward, the top of it writhing, settling into place. Eyes blinked open along its front and flanks, brown and blue and black and green, and a vast mouth gaped wide, revealing rows upon rows of human teeth.

As the creature took another step forward, more certain now, Mullet let out another string of swear words.

'MAGGIE!' he screamed as the creature broke into a trot. 'FUCKING STEP ON IT!'

'I am!' Maggie yelled back. 'This piece of crap has the worst fucking acceleration I've ever seen!'

The monster began gathering speed, its legs morphing to become even longer, shape becoming more streamlined by the second. Soon, it was leaping forward in great bounds, spine whipping in and out like a racing greyhound.

It was gaining on THE GLAM VAN – and as it got closer, a long tentacle began forming at the front of it.

'FASTER!' Quinn yelled, backing away from the window. 'ITS GETTING CLOSER!'

'THIS IS AS FAST AS I CAN GO!' Maggie yelled back. 'IT'S A DIRT ROAD, IF I GO ANY FASTER I –'

She broke off with a scream as the RV hit a pothole and fishtailed wildly.

In the seconds it took to correct the van, the monster had almost closed the gap between them. Maggie mashed the accelerator, the wheels spinning on gravel as it bore down on them like a fleshy semi-trailer.

The tentacle that had been gathering at the front abruptly rocketed forward and shattered the back window before whipping around and grabbing onto the sill. Immediately, it began growing in size, swelling outwards, spilling into the van, eyeballs opening across it like blooming flowers.

Quinn grabbed a miniature fire extinguisher from its case and pulling the pin, sprayed foam all over it, blinding the eyes. Then, when the foam ran out, she used the extinguisher bottle as a club to hit it repeatedly, screaming all the while.

Mullet, meanwhile, disappeared for a moment before returning with the boomerang relic from the glovebox. Yelling, he began smacking the monster with it as hard as he could.

The flesh recoiled from it briefly – before surging forwards and engulfing it. With a muffled snap it broke in two, its relic aura dissipating.

Mullet, who had only just avoided having his hand engulfed as well, grabbed a chair and began hitting it with that instead.

Unfortunately, neither the chair, nor the fire extinguisher, were particularly effective as weapons – and the flesh would not be budged. Even worse, the van was slowing, its tires skidding as the monster pulled it back, anchoring its feet in the dirt.

As they were brought almost entirely to a stop, Quinn glanced in panic at the sky. The First Portent was so close now – and they weren't out of range!

Dropping the fire extinguisher, she ran to the front of the van and hoisted Spencer out of his seat. Ignoring his yells, she dragged him into the back and pointed wildly at the tentacle.

'GET RID OF IT!' she screamed.

'WH-HOW?!' Spencer yelled.

'I DON'T KNOW, YOU'RE A FUCKING MATTERSMITH!' Quinn threw up her arms. 'THROW SOME ROCKS OR SOMETHING!'

Spencer frowned and, a second later, the entire back panel of the van came off.

The tentacle tumbled away – and the van violently jolted forwards. Mullet fell over and Quinn grabbed wildly onto a shelf, narrowly avoiding the same fate.

The monster, which had been pulling the other way, stumbled back, allowing them precious seconds to gain speed. Too soon though, it was back on its feet and gaining again.

As it once more began to draw close, Quinn saw another harpoon forming at the front of it.

'SWERVE, SWERVE!' she screamed as the tentacle lanced outwards.

Maggie spun the wheel and the van skidded sideways in a cloud of dust. The tentacle missed its target, grazing off the side.

The swerve had once against lost them ground, however, and the monster was now mere metres away behind them, toothy maw snapping in rage.

Even worse, the First Portent was now close enough to see – a mere spec in the sky, only visible if you knew it was there, but still much, much too close for comfort.

Quinn began grabbing anything within reach and throwing it at the monster. Furniture, cutlery, spare cleaning supplies – anything that wasn't literally welded to the floor. It bounced off the rubbery flesh of the creature, doing next to nothing.

On the floor, Spencer tried to do something and unreality began to build – but before it could manifest, it collapsed in on itself. Spencer hissed loudly in pain and closed his eyes, black oil streaming down his face from beneath tightly closed lids.

More tentacles began to form at the front of the monster – multiple of them at once. Quinn once again yelled for Maggie to swerve – but this time they were too close. Maggie let out another scream as the van careened back and forth, tentacles stabbing into it, one after the other.

Then one of the tentacles struck a back tire and it burst with a loud BANG. The RV fishtailed again and then skidded off road, barrelling across dry grass.

'I'VE LOST CONTROL!' Maggie yelled, letting go of the wheel and ducking down. The RV smashed through a small fence and juddered into a dense patch of weeds, bouncing wildly. Shortly, it came to a stop, resting on a slight angle.

There was a moment of silence. Then a tentacle speared through the wall.

Quinn grabbed the sliding door, hauled it open with all her might. Then, after a moment's hesitation, she went back, grabbed Spencer by the shirt front and threw him bodily into the weeds. She jumped after him – and not a millisecond too soon. Behind her, the entire van was lifted into the sky.

Turning, she saw a gigantic tentacle wrap around the entire van, like a python around its prey. With a screech of metal, THE GLAM VAN buckled, crumpling inwards. Then, the tentacle brought it around and slammed it repeatedly into the ground.

Glass flew everywhere. A door spun away across the grass, and a rear-view mirror flew just over Quinn's head. Quinn hadn't seen if the others got out. If they hadn't...

After thoroughly flattening the RV, the tentacle lifted it high once more and flung it violently into the tree line.

Quinn watched it go with mouth slightly open.

When she looked back again, Ava was there, upper body emerging from the top of her monstrous creation. A tentacle shot out and grabbed Quinn around the middle, lifting her up and closer to Ava's face.

'You can't escape me!' Ava screamed at her. 'You can't outrun me! Don't you get it?!'

The sound of an airplane was faint, but all consuming in Quinn's ears. She said nothing, paralysed by indecision. There were so many options – infinite possibilities, infinite timelines and all of them bearing down on her at once.

'WHY COULDN'T YOU JUST HAVE DONE WHAT I WANTED?!' Ava screamed at her, her face now mere inches away. 'WHY MUST YOU FORCE ME TO GO TO THESE EXTREME LENGTHS?!'

Quinn closed her eyes as spit sprayed across her face. Ava shook her like a toddler with doll.

'I PROVIDE THE PERFECT ENVIORNMENT FOR YOU,' she screamed. 'I GIVE YOU FREE FOOD, FREE AC-COMODATION, FREE MUSICAL INSTRUMENTS, AND HOW DO YOU REPAY ME?! WITH INSOLENCE! DIS-OBEDIENCE! DISRESPECT! WHY? WHY?! WHY, QUINN? IS ARK 2 NOT GOOD ENOUGH FOR YOU?!'

'No,' Quinn gasped.

'NO?' Ava screeched. Her eyes were bulging, bloodshot. 'NO?! WHY NOT?'

'No,' Quinn said again.

Ava opened and closed her mouth. Veins popped in her forehead. In her grasp, Quinn winced and closed her eyes again – but this time it was for a different reason.

'What?' Ava said, tightening her grip even further. 'What now? Are you trying to use your symptoms? Didn't you learn your lesson? It doesn't matter! It doesn't matter if you use them, because I'll still catch you every time!'

Quinn shuddered deeply and shook her head. Above, the dull roar of an airplane engine had gotten much louder.

'Can't you hear it?' she whispered feverishly. 'Can't you feel it? Your Ark is doomed. Just like the rest of the Nation.

You've been living in your bubble for so long that maybe you don't remember what it's like. Or maybe you never learnt in the first place?'

'What are you blathering about?' Ava snarled. 'Never learnt what?'

She glanced up at the sky, frowning at the sound of engines, which were now almost deafening.

'The Portents come for all who do not play by their rules,' Quinn said.

Her eyes rolled back in her head and her mouth fell open. Radio static crackled unbidden from her throat.

*Help me*, a voice hissed amidst rising static. *Please, please, please, please, please –*

Ava dropped Quinn like she was burning hot.

As though through a long tunnel, Quinn watched the monstrous form turn and flee. In the distance, a star was falling from the sky, flickering bright and billowing smoke.

Quinn sank to the ground. Her body was on fire, a hundred shards piercing her every which way. Her ears roared with the sound of engines and her own pulse, and radio static filled her mind, spilling out of her uncontrollably.

*Please*, she whispered in a voice that was not her own. *God, Jesus, anyone, save me. Please, if you're there. Please help me. Please, I am begging you. I am trapped in hell, but I repent. I repent my sins. Whatever they were, I repent them. Please, God. Have I not been punished enough?*

Almost gently, the airplane hit the ground. There was a moment of silence, and then a flash of blinding light. Dust billowed upwards in a mushroom shape, backlit in white and orange.

Quinn barely saw it. She couldn't move. Static was roaring in her mind. Tears were streaming from her face.

The ground was moving beneath her. Rock punched upwards into her stomach. She was flying.

Blurrily, she saw the shock wave coming, a ripple of air and razor-sharp debris. Trees were flattened in its wake and burnt to a cinder. In her mind was a mirror of that last time she saw it, comparing what was different and what was the same.

Then she was falling. Backwards, and further than she'd been expecting. Grass and rock blocked her view. The shock wave roared overhead.

Then she hit solid ground and blacked out.

# A TENTATIVE VICTORY

**Date: Sunday 25 January 2082**

As she slowly came to, Quinn became aware of a quiet electrical hum and the sound of Mullet talking.

Stirring, she slowly rolled over, wincing when the movement reminded her of her acid burns. Consciousness surfacing, she opened her eyes and saw that she was lying on a bunk in an RV.

It wasn't THE GLAM VAN.

It was around then that she remembered that THE GLAM VAN had been destroyed.

Frowning, she shuffled around to look up at the ceiling – and came face to face with a massive huntsman spider, hanging mere centimetres from her eyes.

With a squeak of surprise, she jerked away from it and sat up.

It was inside a glass jar, she realised. The jar itself was hanging from the ceiling, which was less than half a metre above her bunk.

Frowning, she looked around and saw more glass jars, also hanging from the ceiling, and also containing spiders.

There was a curtain partitioning the bunks from the rest of the RV and while Quinn sat and stared bemusedly at the spiders, it was suddenly pulled open.

Mullet stood there, grinning at her. 'You're awake!' he said cheerfully and then turned to address someone behind him. 'She's awake, everyone!'

He moved aside, allowing Quinn to see into the room

beyond. Maggie, as well an unfamiliar man, were sitting at a tiny dinner table and playing some sort of card game. Next to them was a bank of computers, monitors and other tech that rivalled Kylie's collection.

A collection that was now gone, Quinn realised sadly.

Maggie placed her cards down on the table and stood up.

'How are you feeling?' she asked, coming through the curtain.

Quinn blinked at her. 'Um,' she said. 'Okay, I guess.'

She frowned and cleared her throat. 'Huh. Seems like that radio-voice side effect has gone.'

'That's good,' Maggie said. 'Does anywhere else hurt?' She reached up to put her hand on Quinn's forehead.

'I have a headache,' Quinn said. 'And my skin is still quite sore. Also there are some weird grey patches on it that I've been avoiding looking at. But it's probably nothing! Um. How are we alive? Also, where are we?'

'This is Dingo's van,' Maggie said, and gestured to the unfamiliar face at the table. Dingo, a tall, heavily tattooed man in a tank top and a fashionable fade cut, winked at Quinn and clicked his tongue.

'Nice to meet ya, kid,' he said.

'He's a sat-tracker,' Maggie continued. 'Saw the First Portent come down and came by to see if there were any survivors. Fortunately, we did in fact survive. Our little race with Ava meant we were far enough away from the site of impact. The blast only tickled us, really.'

'Right,' Quinn said. 'I can't believe I've survived the First Portent twice now. Do you think... do you think that's some sort of record? Will I get more symptoms and become a double timesmith?'

'No,' Maggie said, 'people can only get P.I.U.S once.'

'Will YOU become a timesmith?!' Quinn said.

'I don't think so,' Maggie said. 'We were too far from the epicentre. It's possible, I suppose – but so far, I couldn't tell a relic from a toilet brush.'

'And everyone's alright?' Quinn looked around. 'Where's Kylie?'

'She was in a pretty bad way, so we took her to the Ouyen med clinic,' Maggie said. 'Told them that she was in a car wreck that caught fire. I don't think they believed us exactly, but they didn't turn us away, which is the main thing. We're going to pick her up in a few hours. They said she should make a full recovery.'

'Oh, good,' Quinn said. 'Um – one more question. What's with the spiders?'

'They have relicious properties, apparently,' Maggie said, eyeing the spider jars.

Quinn wrinkled her nose. The spiders did not have relicious properties. No living thing did.

'They do, and even better, they're free!' Dingo said from the table. 'Some people are really out there paying thousands of dollars for relics, when there are heaps of 'em all around the bush!'

'Right,' Quinn said, and she lay back down on the bunk. She didn't feel like telling the nice man who had rescued them that his spiders were not relics just at that moment.

The details of what had happened after the First Portent showed up were a little hazy. Her brain still ached from the memory of its proximity. She remembered static screaming through her mind and clouding her vision, and she remembered seeing the plane hit the ground and explode.

There was still one part which was unclear though. The shockwave, and all the debris carried with it, had been coming right for her – but something had dragged her out of the way at the last second. No... dragged was the wrong word. It had felt like a punch in the gut, as though the very ground beneath her had shoved her back.

Quinn frowned.

'Where's Spencer?' she asked. 'Is he still here?'

'Yep, he's still here,' Maggie said. 'We didn't really know what else to do with him. He's napping in the front currently.'

Quinn sat up and moved to climb out of the bunk.

'Hey, wait,' Maggie said, 'what are you doing? You should rest!'

'I will,' Quinn said, 'but first I have to ask Spencer something.'

'Can't it wait?'

'No,' Quinn said.

She found her feet and hobbled through the RV to the front section. In the cabin, the passenger seat had been laid out flat. Spencer was lying with his back towards her, under a blanket.

'Oi,' Quinn said.

No reaction.

Quinn moved closer. 'Oi,' she said again, reaching out to shake his shoulder.

'Don't touch me,' Spencer said.

Quinn withdrew her hand and watched him wriggle around until he was facing her.

'What do *you* want?' he said – although there wasn't a lot of venom in it.

Quinn took a breath.

'Why...' she began. 'Why'd you save my life?'

Spencer blinked at her, his expression closing up.

'I didn't,' he said.

'Bullshit,' Quinn said. 'A rock spontaneously flew up out of the ground and flung me out of the path of the blast? Yeah. You're the only one who could have possibly done that.'

Spencer was silent.

'Well?' Quinn threw up her hands. 'Why? I thought you wanted me dead. I thought that was, like, your whole mission in life. So, why'd you save me?'

'I don't fucking know,' Spencer snapped. 'Why'd YOU save me?'

'What? When did I save you?' Quinn said.

'When that thing grabbed the RV,' Spencer said. 'You... you picked me up and took me with you, even though you didn't have to. If you hadn't, I would have died. Why'd you do that, huh?'

'I...' Quinn said. Grabbing Spencer out of the crashing RV hadn't been something she'd consciously thought about.

'I don't know,' she said. 'I guess... I couldn't just leave you there to die?'

'Why not?' Spencer said.

'I don't know!' Quinn said, embarrassed. 'Because you're a person! Even if you're my enemy, you're still a human being. I couldn't just leave you, that would have been really shitty of me! Anyway, I'm the one asking questions here! Why did you use your fucking P.I.U.S to get me out of danger?'

'I didn't want to owe you,' Spencer said stiffly. 'And... I didn't want it to end like that.'

'What?'

'It wasn't right,' Spencer muttered, looking away. 'You need to pay for your sins. My goal isn't to kill you, it's to bring you to justice. I couldn't bring you to justice if you'd been shredded by shrapnel, could I?'

'Right,' Quinn said, hands on hips. 'So... how exactly are you planning on bringing me to justice then?'

Spencer scowled.

'It's a work in progress,' he sniffed. 'But... I will do it! Mark my words, Quinn.'

'Sure, whatever, Spencer,' Quinn said.

She left him to it, re-joining the others at their table. They were playing bottle-cap poker, but Quinn passed on joining in. Her headache had gotten worse. She decided to nap until it was time to pick up Kylie.

***

When she woke again, the RV was moving, and Kylie was already back and awake. She was sitting on one of the other bunks, wrapped in fluffy blankets, a cup of tea in hand. Her skin had been fixed but she still looked tired, with massive bags under her eyes. It was the first time Quinn had seen her without her usual impeccable makeup on. She looked younger – more vulnerable.

As Quinn sat up, she met Kylie's gaze. Kylie raised an eyebrow at her in a friendly manner.

'Look at us, Quinn,' she said huskily. 'A pair of ugly, feeble, sad sacks. But we're both heroes as well, aren't we? You saved everyone's life by reversing time, as you do. I saved everyone's life by showing you all that Ark 2 was, in fact, a weird cult all along...'

'You got kidnapped by Ava, you mean?' Quinn said, smirking. 'I wouldn't call that saving our lives. Endangering them, maybe.'

'Oh, Quinn,' Kylie said, 'you only put yourselves in mortal danger to save me because you love me. Also – I WAS right about Ark 2. And if you think I'll ever let you forget it, then you're sorely mistaken.'

Quinn rolled her eyes – but she was grinning as well.

'Fuck you,' she said. 'But also... I'm glad you're alright. And I'm glad the whole Ark 2 thing is over now.'

Kylie made a sceptical face.

'What?' said. 'What was that for? Am I wrong?'

'You should probably ask the others,' Kylie said, 'because I missed most of what happened, being in my beauty coma and all. But apparently they saw Ava in town when they were picking me up.'

'What?!' Quinn sat bolt upright.

'Yeah.' Kylie inspected her nails. 'The bitch still lives. Although barely, from what I hear. Apparently, she looked like death walking. Mascara all streaky, skin blotchy, hiding away under a hood, the works. I'm not sure why this is such a big deal honestly, but the others reacted in a similar way to you, so I'm assuming this is shocking news.'

'I guess it's not that shocking.' Quinn sighed. 'She was just as far away from the First Portent as we were. But it's still bad. What are we going to do?'

'Nothing,' Kylie said.

'What do you mean nothing?' Quinn stared at her.

'I mean, it's not our problem anymore.' Kylie shrugged. 'We got out of Ark 2, and now it's gone. Ava survived, but that's her problem. She's lost Ark 2, and with it, most of her power. Right now, she's nothing but an ugly homeless lady. Maybe she'll try and build Ark 3 and live out her gross slime monster dreams somewhere else – but it's not our problem. As we speak, we're driving the fuck away. Chances are, we'll never see Ava again.'

'Oh,' Quinn said. 'Well... I suppose that's alright then.'

'Better then alright,' Kylie said. 'I'd say we've even come out on top!'

'What?' Quinn said. 'But... we've lost everything! All our stuff – THE GLAM VAN! All your computers!'

'Yes,' Kylie said. 'But we do have *this*.'

She reached into the side of her bra and pulled out a USB stick.

'See this?' she said. 'This is our future. We can always buy new hardware. But this – this is priceless.'

'What is it?' Quinn said. 'Is it music?'

'Yes, but its more than that.' Kylie smiled. 'It's also Ava Brinesworth's entire contact list of music buyers!'

Quinn stared at her, open mouthed.

'Yeah,' Kylie said. 'I'd be stunned as well. After all, I'm stunning. And also brilliant. And very soon, I'll be rich too.'

'I...' Quinn said. 'How... how did that survive the acid? You were in there for hours!'

Kylie, however, just gave her a wink.

# CHAPTER 35

# ROGUEHUNTER

### Date: Friday 13 March 2082

'To catch a realitysmith,' Tanya Fletch said, 'you need to use a realitysmith. It's the most reliable way. That, and relics, of course.'

The Detective had followed the rogue hunter outside and across the street to a small café. There, after the Detective had taken a few moments to clean off the worst of the goo and grime that covered them head to toe, they sat themselves down at one of the tables. It was near the window and specially located near a wall socket, so the Detective could charge as they talked. Outside, the fog was starting to lift, morning sunlight filtering through the dissipating clouds.

'I would have thought,' the Detective said, 'that relics were the most effective way. Is it not true that realitysmiths cannot abide their presence?'

'"Cannot abide" is a strong phrase,' Tanya said. 'It's more of a discomfort, from what I understand. Perfectly abideable, just unpleasant. With a bit of practice, rogue-smiths can get very good at hiding their reaction, or even train that sense to dull to nearly nothing.'

'I see,' the Detective said. 'How, then, does one use a realitysmith to apprehend a realitysmith?'

'They can sense them,' Tanya said, tapping her nose. 'When a realitysmith uses their symptoms, any other smith in the vicinity can feel it. It's obvious to them, like a beacon in the dark. Of course, the tricky part is getting the roguesmith to use their symptoms at all. Until they do that, it's basically impossible to tell them apart from your average joe. But with enough pressure, they all crack eventually.'

She grinned wickedly.

'And this is your specialty?' the Detective said. 'Getting them to "crack"?'

'You could say that,' Tanya said. 'It's all psychology. The trick is convincing them they have to act. Make them think that they're cornered and have no other choice. To be honest, relics do play a big part.'

She leaned forward. 'Did you know,' she said, 'that if someone is talking passionately, and you hand them an object, often they will just take it without thinking? If you do this with a relic, a normal person will take the object and continue talking. But if they are a realitysmith, they will become distracted.'

She leaned back again. 'Then, of course, if they're experienced, they'll play it off. They'll ask why you handed them a random object, make a joke or two. But they know that they faltered – and they don't know whether or not you noticed. It's the uncertainty that gets them.'

'I see,' the Detective said. 'The goal is to scare the smith and thus cause them to act rashly.'

'That's right,' Tanya said. 'And when they inevitably do, my realitysmith will feel it, and BAM! The trap snaps shut.'

She snapped her hands closed, fingers interlocking.

'Do you always have a realitysmith with you?' the Detective asked.

'Pretty much,' Tanya said. 'Although not this morning. I didn't think I'd need one, walking up to the med clinic and back again. Got about halfway, when the mist started pouring in. That was when I knew I'd severely misjudged what sort of morning it was.'

'I suppose we should go and collect your smith, then?' the Detective said.

'I suppose we should,' Tanya agreed. 'Hmm. A fleshy, eh?

I reckon we could use a 'lectro to counter that. Or a radi would also work.'

'I don't follow,' the Detective said.

'Oh.' Tanya grinned. 'It's simple! Hunting realitysmiths is a bit like rock-paper-scissors. You gotta get the smith that best counters the one you're trying to catch. That way, if your target attempts to use their P.I.U.S on you, you've got a good chance of getting the upper hand!'

She grabbed a napkin and began scrawling a diagram across it.

'Use a gravsmith to catch a mattersmith,' she said, 'and a mattersmith to catch an electro, and an electro to catch a fleshy, etcetera. Obviously, the specific ability of the smith comes into play as well. This is only a rough guide, not a rule. But it's helped me plenty of times in the past. Anyway, since it's a fleshsmith we're after, we should use an electrosmith to catch them – although certain radismiths would work as well. Fire and lightning beats organics, see?'

She turned the napkin around and pushed it across the table for the Detective to look at.

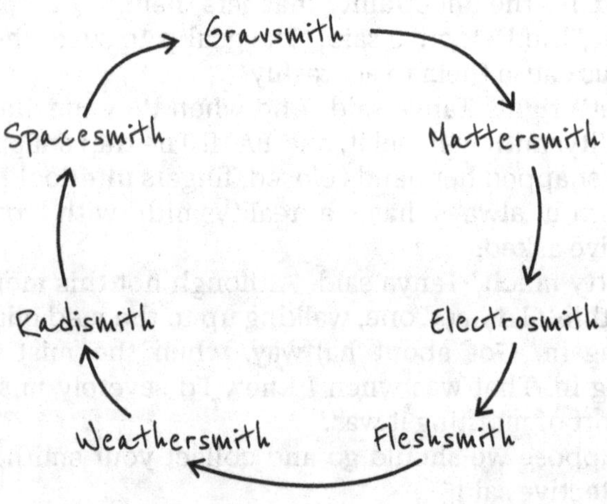

The Detective eyed it in interest before noticing something else, scrawled in the corner in tiny font.

*Table six*, it said.

The Detective nodded slowly, casually ripping the corner away. Table six was the one directly behind them – but they knew better than to look at it.

'I have personally observed the effectiveness of electricity against this particular creature,' they said.

'Exactly,' Tanya said. 'Doesn't matter if you're the most muscle-bound hulk in all of the Nation – you're not immune to two hundred thousand volts applied directly to the nips.'

'We may require more than one, however,' the Detective continued. 'This fleshsmith is by no means ordinary. They are unusually powerful and dangerous.'

'Oh yeah?' Tanya said, leaning on her elbows. 'Well, go on then, spill the beans. What do you know about them so far?'

The Detective explained how the fleshsmith was made up of at least twenty-eight different people, which had been absorbed into it, and shared what appeared to be some sort of telepathic hive mind. Tanya listened intently, interrupting only to thank the waiter when they brought her a cup of tea

'You're right,' she said, once the Detective had finished. 'This is an unusual case. Do you have any idea who the original smith is, out of the twenty-eight?'

'I do not,' the Detective said.

'Shame,' Tanya said. 'It's likely that if we are able to incapacitate them, the rest of these so-called fragments would also become incapacitated.'

'Is that so?' the Detective said. 'Interesting. How would you suggest we approach this?'

'Well, first of all, we go and grab our smithy buddies and a bunch of relics,' Tanya said.

'And then?'

'And then, we start asking questions.' Tanya slapped her hand on the table. 'You've seen some of the fleshsmith's faces, right? You can describe them to people, ask if anyone's seen them around town. Ouyen isn't very big. It's only a matter of time until we find one of the fragments.'

'And once we do?' the Detective said.

'We bring down the might of the Sanctuary upon them!' Tanya said. 'I believe there are three electrosmiths, and two radismiths, at our disposal. If we bring all of them, that'll be a lot of fire power. Literally!'

'Good,' the Detective said. 'Then our first stop is the Sanctuary?'

'Nope,' Tanya said. 'First, I want to go and get some relics. I have a couple in the car. I feel sort of naked without them, honestly.'

'Okay,' the Detective said. 'Where is your car?'

'It's a bit of a walk,' Tanya said. 'I left it at the solar station, right on the edge of town. Not that it would have gotten any sun this morning, ha!'

The Detective glanced outside to where the mist had almost entirely dissipated.

'It seems the weather event is over,' they said. 'The rest of the morning should be pleasant and sunny as per the regular schedule.'

'Perfect for a walk, then.' Tanya grinned.

They both stood up from the table, carefully avoiding looking at table six. The Detective unplugged themselves from the wall while Tanya went to pay for her coffee. As they left the café, the Detective allowed their gaze to pass just once over the occupant of the table behind them.

It was an elderly woman, white hair tied in a tight bun, head down, apparently engrossed in the daily paper. The Detective had been listening, though. The entire time she'd been there, she hadn't turned the page once.

She was almost certainly a fragment – and had heard every word they'd said.

But that was exactly what they were counting on.

As the last wisps of mist evaporated in the warm morning air, the Detective and Tanya left the cafe, walking swiftly down the main road towards the solar station.

The station sat at the very end of town, beside the town's solar farm – a neat array of heliotropic solar panels, glinting blue-black in the sun. Tanya's car, a popular variety of modern pickup-truck often referred to as a nute, was parked between the station and the farm, beside a gigantic storage battery.

Tanya took out her key and unlocked the nute, revealing a plain black bag, which contained a small treasure trove of relics. Most were weak, although after briefly scanning each one and accessing their paperwork, the Detective found that several were of considerable power.

Most of them were also wearable and the Detective watched as Tanya put them on. The autographed boots of an Olympic athlete. Gloves bearing the symbol of a popular fictional character. A hat with corks hanging off the rim. A necklace bearing the Christian cross.

Glancing at the Detective, she gestured at the bag of relics. *You should equip some too,* she signed.

The Detective nodded and reached into the bag, although their attention was elsewhere. They were being watched, of that much they were certain. The question was, where was their watcher? In the solar station convenience store? In the storm drains beneath them? In one of the buildings across the road? All of the above?

Absently, they replaced their ripped, stained shirt with a fresh, relicious T-shirt bearing the likeness of Che Guevara. Then, at Tanya's insistence, they added a bracelet with a hamsa charm and a beanie bearing the logo of a now-extinct soft drink company.

*No, thank you,* they signed, when Tanya gestured that they should equip even more relics. *There is a good chance these items will be destroyed or lost while in my possession.*

*It's worth it, if they save your life,* Tanya signed back. *They can always make more relics, but if you die, that's it.*

The Detective frowned slightly.

*If I 'die', they will simply make another Detective,* they signed. *However... my destruction will mean a substantial delay in the investigation.*

*Yeah,* Tanya said. *So, take another! It's fine, honestly.*

The Detective hesitated, eyeing the bag. Behind them, a freighter truck had pulled into the solar station, blocking off a significant wedge of their view into the street.

The Detective did not look at the truck – but their attention was focused wholly on it.

*It is not entirely true, that they can always make more relics,* they signed. *Yes, they can make more. But it is well known that each generation of relic since the End of the World is weaker than the last.*

*True.* Tanya nodded sadly. *The meaning becomes lost over time. People forget the significance of things. And if no one knows the significance of a thing, then there might as well be none.*

In the solar station, the truck nosed slowly past the recharge points and did not stop.

*Is it not possible, then, to create new significance?* the Detective said, watching the truck in the corner of their eye.

*Don't know,* Tanya said. *As far as I am aware, all relics originate from before the year 2051. Any attempt to create new types of relics since then has failed. We can only create copies of those that already exist.*

*Then each relic is precious,* the Detective said. *And each one destroyed is a tragedy. Perhaps equally so to the loss of a life, wouldn't you agree?*

*No,* Tanya said. *A life is still worth more.*

*Why?* the Detective said. *If relics are able to save lives, then is it not more important to save the relic, so that it may go on to save more lives later?*

*Oh, fuck off with your trolly problem bullshit,* Tanya said.

The truck had gotten much closer now and seemed to be making for the parking space next to Tanya's nute. With the whispering hiss of breaks, it slowed to a crawl, then a complete stop.

*At the very least,* the Detective signed as the truck's engine cut out, *I could not argue that my life is worth more than, say, a tier 5 relic. I am an artificially constructed cyborg. I have not lived for more than a week. There would be those who argue I am not truly alive at all. A tier 5 relic, meanwhile, can protect an entire town from Portents for many years.*

*You're alive,* Tanya said. *You have human organs, don't you? A human brain? Even if you don't, you're clearly sentient. That's alive enough for me.*

She paused and then grinned suddenly.

*Are you really less than a week old?*

*I carry only five days worth of memories,* the Detective said.

*Oh?* Tanya grinned. *And what have you learnt in five days?*

*I have learnt that many people are incompetent,* the Detective said. *I have also learnt how to destroy a fleshsmith.*

The back of the truck slammed open and a gigantic tendril whipped out, whistling as it sliced the air. It slammed into the ground, right where the Detective had been standing, concrete cracking beneath the force of the blow.

The Detective was no longer standing there. At the first sign of movement, they had dashed forward, grabbing Tanya and lifting her off the ground. Before she could do more than squeak in surprise, they dumped her into the passenger seat of the nute and slammed the door.

Tendrils grasped at where she'd been but too slow. The Detective ducked beneath them and sprinted around the other side of the truck.

As they ran, they unravelled the coiled power cable, tied at their waist, and jammed the end into their left elbow socket. The end of it crackled with charge as they wheeled around – and for the first time saw the fleshsmith in its entirety.

The back of the truck was full of meat, reams upon reams of coiled muscle, roping tendons and dark patches of pulsing organs suspended in jelly. As the Detective approached, electrified cable whirling about them, it poured itself out of the truck, leg-like pillars forming beneath a thrashing nest of tentacle protrusions.

Bone spikes formed, jagged and sharp, along the tentacle's edges, whipping down at the Detective. They were forced to dash away, their own electric whip pathetic in comparison.

Behind, in the solar station, a cluster of civilians burst out of the convenience store and bolted away down the street – but the fleshsmith was focused on only one target. Boiling and twisting around itself, the blood-red behemoth grew ever taller, tendrils erupting all over. As the Detective dodged back out of the way, it followed after them, spiked whips lashing and whirling, breaking the ground into chunks before it.

It was huge, bigger than the Detective had been anticipating. Twenty-eight people had been a conservative estimate – the truth was more like twice that, maybe three times.

But it did not matter. The trap had already been set, and even now, was closing around it. It did not matter how large it grew – it was not immune to electric shock.

The Detective could almost sense the electricity around them, a certain sharpness in the air that tickled at the exposed wires of their damaged arm, strangely exciting. The entire township of Ouyen received power from this solar farm. It was no accident that Tanya had suggested this place as a battle arena.

The solar-farm's main transmission line was a thick, heavy-duty, high-voltage cable, suspended high up in the air, well out of reach – at least for a normal human. Dodging back again from the threshing tendrils, the Detective took a giant leap and landed half-way up one of the pylons. Rapidly, they scaled the rest, climbing up onto the top of it.

Too late, the fleshsmith realised what they were doing. The tendrils, reaching for the Detective, began to withdraw –

In one swift motion, the Detective tore the high-voltage cable out of its socket and jammed their fingers into it.

Synthetic flesh burned away in an instant, revealing shiny chrome. Their whip arced around, crackling with power, and made contact with the fleshsmith.

In exhilaration, the Detective felt the current pour through them and into the gelatinous monster. It went rigid, muscles contorting and twitching uncontrollably, falling back from the whip – but not far enough.

Relentlessly, the Detective lashed again and again, striking it over and over, electrocuting repeatedly. Their cable whip whirled like a living thing, arcing, crackling viciously. Flickering sparks jumped to the ground and the pylon, burning their bright afterimage into the air.

In the centre of it all, the Detective crouched, eyes blazing blue, tongues of electricity flickering from their back and shoulders, a violent corona of heat and ozone. Their clothes were smoking, burning away, and so was their skin, but they didn't care. Below, the monster was melting, smoke rolling off it in waves as blackened patches began to spread, forking like lightning throughout its bloated body.

The Detective was grinning, ear to ear. Warning lights were blinking but they meant nothing. That strange power was back and stronger than ever, ebbing and surging with the flow of electrons.

It felt right, somehow – or at least familiar. Something deep in the Detective's memory was stirring. Something unconscious, unprogrammed, something they were supposed to forget. It was utterly untameable, insane, chaotic, insidiously meaningless –

They were laughing, they realised. They had not meant to – but now they found it hard to stop. This... No. This was bad. Abruptly, they forced their hand to let go of the transmission cable, clamping it instead across their mouth, stifling the laughter. It fell to the ground behind them, sparking as it went. The surge inside them faded.

This wasn't right. This was dangerous – extremely dangerous. Whatever it was, they were not supposed to use it. It was shut off for a reason.

After a short pause, they removed the hand from their

mouth and set their face to neutral. Smoke was rolling off their shiny carapace and dozens of warning lights were flashing, obscuring their vision. But there was no time for that. They had to focus. Things weren't over just yet.

Before them, the fleshsmith had sagged like a deflated balloon, folding in on itself beneath a haze of acrid smoke. It looked badly damaged – but not dead. If left by itself, it could heal. That's what fleshsmiths were best at, after all.

As the Detective jumped down to the concrete and approached, they caught sight of a dark knot at the centre of the collapsing mass. It was human-shaped and moving slightly, drawing towards the surface like a bubble in detergent.

As the Detective paused to watch, the shape breached the surface, membranes pulling away from a human face. The mouth opened, gasping for air, drawing it in deeply. It was the face of an old woman.

As she rose higher from the smoking mass, the Detective saw that she did not look well. Her pallid skin was raw and blistering, large parts of it sloughing away. Bulbous, tumour-like growths grew across her neck and arms. Her hair was patchy, falling out in places.

It wasn't just electrical burns, the Detective realised. Her symptoms resembled acute radiation poisoning. Apparently, this creature had spent too much time at the site of the First Portent's landing. If she had been a normal woman, she would have died many times over already.

She was wearing nothing but an expression of barely contained indignance and fury. Eyes fixed on the Detective, she slowly raised her hands in a sign of surrender.

'Alright, alright, I give up!' she called hoarsely. 'You got me, you freak!'

The Detective cocked their head.

*The original fleshsmith, I presume?* they signed.

'That's right, the original,' the woman said bitterly and she paused to cough out brown slime. 'A thankless job. I've saved the lives of countless people by incorporating them into myself. They would have died if I hadn't! But will anybody thank me for it? No, they won't.'

The Detective narrowed their eyes, remaining silent.

'So,' the woman continued, 'what happens now? What in the blazes are you, anyway?'

*I am the Detective*, the Detective said.

'Right,' the woman said. 'Sure. Well, here's what I think, *Detective*. You COULD arrest me and take me into the Sanctuary, where they'll probably decide I'm too dangerous, and put me down like a sick dog. Or... we could come to another arrangement.'

She eyed the Detective slyly. 'Eh? What do you say to that? It could be something that benefits the both of us.'

*What exactly are you proposing?* the Detective signed.

'Oh, the details are entirely up for negotiation.' The woman smiled broadly. 'But in essence, it's something like this: you leave me alone, tell everyone I escaped, forget you ever saw me here, that sort of thing. In return, I provide you with... well, anything you want, really. I know I may not look it right this second but I am a rich woman. I have money and connections. Rare items. Relics. Narcotics. Music. Girls. Boys. Sugary treats. Anything you desire, I can get it for you. The only limit is your imagination.'

The Detective was still for a moment.

*Anything I desire?* they signed, blank faced. Electricity sparked at their broken elbow joint.

'Oh, yes, anything.' The woman leaned closer. 'I see something has come to mind, then. What is it, my freakish little Detective? What do you desire?'

The Detective stepped slowly forward, into the pool of gelatinous slime that covered the ground.

*It is not something within your power*, they signed.

'Oh, dearie,' the woman whispered hoarsely. 'You underestimate me! I said anything, and I mean it. Just say the word!'

The Detective looked around and then stepped closer again. They were standing right before the woman now, less than two metres away.

*I desire*, they signed and trailed off.

'Yes?' The woman leaned closer. 'Speak it aloud if you want no one but me to see it!'

Around the Detective, eyes and ears began to bloom like a carpet of strange fungus. The Detective ignored this, eyes fixed on the woman's face.

Their lip twisted in disgust. In their right hand, their thumb silently retracted and became a knife.

'I desire your death,' they said and pounced.

In an instant, they crossed the distance and slammed the knife into the woman's throat. She gargled and her eyes rolled back, brown ichor pouring out of the wound.

Around them, the jelly violently heaved and rolled, shapes forming and unforming within it. Fingers grasped weakly at the Detective's ankles, lengthening, coiling around them, rising higher.

Swiftly, the Detective drew the knife back and stabbed a second time, sawing it across.

In moments, it was over. The head came away cleanly.

After eyeing it for a moment, the Detective let out a small sigh. Then, lowering their hand, they began wading their way out of the slime, back towards Tanya's car.

# CHAPTER 36

# ANSWERS AND QUESTIONS

## Date: Friday 13 March 2082

Tanya stared with wide eyes as the Detective gently placed the fleshsmith's head on the ground and opened the door of the nute.

*I apologize for seizing you suddenly,* they signed, blank faced. *I was concerned you would be struck and killed.*

Tanya blinked at them, glancing at the head on the ground and back again.

*That's fine,* she returned slowly. *I... thanks...*

Her hands hovered uncertainly, unspoken questions clearly jostling for attention.

*You killed her,* she signed momentarily.

The Detective nodded. *She was extremely dangerous and unrepentant. Even with her last breath, she attempted to bribe me. I could not see a future for her as a sanctioned smith.*

Tanya nodded and took a deep breath.

*What's done is done,* she signed. *We should alert the Sanctuary and the sin-seeker office to what has happened here.*

*There are no sin-seekers present at the office,* the Detective said. *They were all part of the fleshsmith.*

*Right,* Tanya said.

*The Sanctuary should be alerted immediately, however,* the Detective said. *Might I leave that to you? This site needs to be cordoned off, due to electrical and biological hazards, and there are no other officers of the law present to do it.*

Tanya nodded and scooted over into the driver's seat of the nute.

*On it,* she signed through the window.

The Detective watched her start the engine and pull out of the parking lot, turning onto the road towards the Sanctuary. Then, they stood back and surveyed the collateral damage.

It was going to be a lot of work. The concrete had been shattered in many places and the transmission line that the Detective had pulled out required urgent repair. On top of that, the pool of human jelly was fifteen metres across and only spreading wider.

As to damage caused to their own body, it wasn't great – but it also could have been worse. Their skin was gone, battery was on twelve per cent, and the dozens of warning lights hadn't gone away – but their carapace had not been damaged any further than it already had been. The relics that they'd borrowed from Tanya had, as they predicted, burned away in the electrical current – but that had been fully expected.

The Detective did not have any barricade tape on them but they found duct tape in the solar station convenience store, and, after billing the price of it to the Melbourne Department of Sin, they used it to construct a rudimentary barrier around the scene. As they worked, civilians began to draw closer, staring in interest at them and the damage behind them, signing questions to each other. The Detective, however, ignored them. Public relations were not part of their intended purpose.

Soon, Tanya returned, along with several cars full of people from the Sanctuary. After warning them about the live transmission cable that was still trailing on the ground, the Detective stood back and let them take over. Shortly, they were shooed off site completely, as a bus full of realitysmiths arrived to begin the clean-up.

As they stood on the far side of the road and watched a pair of mattersmiths begin fixing the concrete, the Detective heard someone walking rapidly towards them.

Turning, they tensed, ready to leap away. But on seeing who it was, they immediately relaxed.

*Bill!* they signed, grinning at him. *They fixed you, then. That was quick.*

Bill came to a stop, panting slightly. He was looking remarkably well, considering what had happened to him, although his nose and ears looked oddly chewed and there was faint scarring visible across much of his skin, like a dusting of spiderweb.

He was also very clearly in a state of stress. Eyes glinting with a certain wildness, he waggled his finger at the Detective aggressively.

*Detective!* he signed. *Inside, now! We need to have a little talk!*

The Detective let themselves be shepherded into the nearest open door, which happened to be a hardware store. The moment the door was closed, Bill opened his mouth.

'Where did you go?' he demanded. 'I need a full list of places you went to without me, right now!'

This was not what the Detective had been expecting him to say.

'You... you are upset that I did not remain in one place?' they said. 'Was saving your life not necessary?'

'I... Okay, thanks for saving my life,' Bill said quickly. 'And I'm not upset about that. I just... I'm in damage control mode. I need to know where you've been. I...'

He paused for a moment, taking several deep breaths.

'There's a certain diagnostic stat,' he said, 'which I need to ask about. It's called R.L. integrity. Don't ask what it means, because I'm not going to tell you. But I need to know it's current value.'

'R.L?' the Detective said. 'Currently, it is on sixty-four per cent.'

Bill hissed sharply through his teeth. 'Already?' he said. 'Geez. Although... I suppose it could be worse. That's above fifty. I can fix that. Yeah. Speaking of which – where is your arm?'

'I stored it in a bush,' the Detective said. 'Why can't you tell me what R.L. stands for?'

'I just can't,' Bill said. 'Please don't ask me, or try to figure it out. What do you mean your arm is in a bush?'

'I can collect it now, if you'd like,' the Detective said.

'Please,' Bill said. 'And in the meantime, I need that list of places you've been to. With contact details, if at all possible. I need to call them and apologise immediately.'

The Detective frowned slightly.

'Are my social skills really that egregious?' they said.

'No, no,' Bill said. 'Well, actually, yes. You're not even wearing your skin right now, need I say more? But that's not... look, I am very much not supposed to leave you unsupervised. If anyone finds out you were let loose by yourself for'—he glanced at his watch—'FOURTEEN HOURS, then I'm going to be in BIG trouble.'

'I see,' the Detective said. 'Although, you did not exactly abandon your duties by choice. I'm sure your superiors would understand.'

Bill, however, just shook his head, muttering under his breath.

'C'mon,' he said abruptly. 'Let's get that arm. Lead the way!'

He corralled the Detective outside again and they both walked briskly back into town. The arm was, fortunately, exactly where the Detective had left it and Bill picked it up and turned it over, clicking his tongue in disapproval.

*How did you lose it anyway?* he asked, as they moved off again. *You need to fill me in on what happened. Last thing I remember, we were at the First's landing site. Suddenly, it's the next day, and I'm in the med clinic, and I keep hearing all sorts of things, about roguesmiths and Portents running around, and I'm, well, I'm panicking a little bit.*

*You need not panic,* the Detective signed. *There were no Portents here. It was weathersmiths, and an unusually powerful fleshsmith. But it's over now anyway. We may continue with the main investigation.*

Bill nodded. *Sure,* he signed. *But first, your arm needs re-attaching.*

Fortunately, there was a mechanic in town, who was happy to lend Bill his tools in re-attaching the arm. While Bill got to work, scolding and clicking his tongue as he did so, the Detective recharged and filled him in on everything he'd missed.

After some time, Bill stood back and gestured that the Detective should try to move the arm. They did so, nodding in approval when the fingers bent and wrist turned in exactly the way they wanted.

'Good,' Bill said, brushing himself off. 'Good. That's one problem fixed. Bloody hell. What's your R.L. value at now?'

'Seventy-one per cent,' the Detective said.

They fell silent, watching Bill. Somewhere inside them, something still buzzed, quiet now, but not gone.

'I'm sorry I can't explain it.' Bill sent them an apologetic look. 'If you know, then it might compromise the data. Whatever else you may be, you are still a prototype. There are certain aspects to your design that are still in testing phase. Your knowledge of these aspects could alter the outcome.'

'I see,' the Detective said.

'I hope you do,' Bill said. 'And I hope you know you can ask me anything else.'

'Okay,' the Detective said. 'Then I have another, unrelated, question.'

'Shoot,' Bill said.

'It is about the main investigation,' the Detective said, sitting up straighter. 'So far, our core assumption has been that a Portent is the most likely culprit behind Mildura's disappearance. However, following recent experiences, I have come to change my mind.'

'Oh?' Bill's eyebrows shot up.

'I have witnessed first-hand the power of realitysmiths,' the Detective said, 'and have come to realise that under the right circumstances, their power can, in fact, rival that of a Portent. In light of this understanding, combined with the fact that we have yet to discover any evidence suggesting a Twelfth Portent exists, I now believe it perfectly reasonable, and even likely, that a realitysmith is actually responsible.'

'Oh, wow,' Bill said. 'What sort of realitysmith could erase an entire town from existence?'

'I do not know for certain,' the Detective said. 'But there are several varieties of P.I.U.S that could potentially result in this outcome. Most prominently, a space or timesmith.'

'If it's a spacesmith,' Bill said, 'then that implies Mildura has been placed somewhere else! Do you really think that's the case?' He glanced upwards. 'Do you think it's on the moon or something? We'll never find it there.'

'Actually,' the Detective said. 'I believe that current evidence points to a timesmith. Upon re-examining my notes from the scene, I have been reminded that there was a clear temporal discrepancy between plant life in and outside the zone of disappearance. Additionally, the Murray River was still in place. If the entire area had simply been teleported elsewhere, the river would have been noticeably disrupted. However, if the area was instead sent backwards, or forwards, in time, to a point where Mildura did not yet, or no longer, existed, then these observations make perfect sense.'

'I see,' Bill said. 'I suppose it does make sense. A timesmith, eh? If that's the case, then we're going to have an absolute hell of a time trying to find them.'

'Why is that?' the Detective said. Reaching into a small storage space in their right leg, they took out the napkin diagram that Tanya had drawn for them earlier and unfolded it.

There was no timesmith on it. All other types of realitysmith were there, except for timesmith. Why had they not noticed that earlier?

'Rogue timesmiths are notoriously difficult to catch,' Bill said. 'Every time you get close to them, they just change the timeline, so you didn't. Any move you make, they know in advance. Any mistake they make, they can erase it. There's no one better in all of the Nation at hiding than them.'

'Is that so?' the Detective said.

They crumpled up the diagram in their newly fixed left hand and tossed it into a trash can. It landed perfectly in the centre.

'It is fortunate, then, that there is no one better in the Nation at seeking than me,' they said.

**From:** DetectiveEX025@nationet.au

**To:** GeneralInquiry_DeptSinMelb@nationet.au

**Subject:** Ouyen Sin-Seeker Office staff replacement

To whom it may concern,

I regret to inform you that all existing staff members of
the Ouyen Sin-Seeker Office are deceased, following
roguesmith activity. The rogue responsible has been dealt
with; however, the office remains empty. I would highly
recommend sending replacements A.S.A.P.

Please see the attached incident report for details.

Yours faithfully,

Detective Calidor Fang/Calista Claw/EX025

# ACT 3

# SMALL CRIMES

### Date: Wednesday 29 January 2082

Vincent Spencer lay in bed and stared up at the slats of the bunk above him.

Quinn Kelly was sitting up there, he knew. She was silent, with only the slightest of creaks betraying her presence as she shifted position. The sound of a pencil on paper was occasionally audible as she wrote something down. Probably more music, Vincent thought with a scowl.

Did she do it on purpose to bother him? Or did she just not care? The second option was more likely. None of Vincent's kidnappers seemed to care about him very much. He was just a problem to them, and not even a particularly dire one. What could he do, after all? He had no legs to run away and no arms to fight with. He had P.I.U.S, but using it was risky, and only so useful to begin with. He was trapped in his own body, with no option but to make things even worse for himself.

They still kept an eye on him anyway, in case he 'tried something'. What exactly he could try, Vincent wasn't sure – but the result was at least one person watching him at all hours. This afternoon, it was Quinn, pretending to ignore him from the top bunk. Earlier, it had been the goth woman, Maggie – Vincent wasn't sure who she was or why she had joined the group. The previous day, Kylie Collins had sat in the corner and painstakingly applied a set of long, pink false nails. Her back had been towards him, but he'd met her eye in the handheld mirror several times.

None of his jailors had been particularly cruel to him. They brought him food and pillows to sit up on and they moved him into the bathroom when he asked them to. Maggie had even tried to engage him in conversation several times – although he hadn't given her the satisfaction of a proper response.

It was clear that they didn't want him there, though. It would have been better for everyone if he wasn't there. Sometimes, Vincent wished they would just get rid of him and be done with it. Drop him off at a Sanctuary or leave him in a ditch to die. They were being nice to him, for some unknown reason, but he wished they wouldn't. If they were awful, then at least he could hate them properly.

As it was though, he was here, and there was nowhere else he could go. They wouldn't let him, not with what he knew. And besides, even if he did manage to escape – what next? Yes, he could turn them in, and get the lot of them arrested. But after that...?

After that... The thought of after that filled him with creeping dread. There was nothing after that. He couldn't re-join the sin-seekers, not with the Fourth Portent wrapped around his heart like a coil of live copper wire. But if not a sin-seeker, then what was he to do with his life? He had never considered anything else. He was always going to be a sin-seeker, like his father, and his grandfather before that. Upholding the law was the Spencer family way. Nothing else would ever be good enough.

They still thought he was dead. He hadn't told them yet that he wasn't – but if he couldn't be a sin-seeker, then he might as well be. The thought of working as a sanctioned mattersmith made him feel sick. The thought of telling his father that he had become a mattersmith made him feel even sicker.

But what other choice was there? The die of fate had been cast. He had P.I.U.S. There was only one legal job choice for him now. He would move earth, and stack bricks, and set concrete, and oil would come out of his eye sockets, and then one day his heart would mutate into a four-stroke engine and he would fall down dead on the spot.

It was not a future he wanted, not at all. He didn't want to be here, in this bed, either.

He wished he'd never come across the Fourth Portent. He wished he'd never chased after the music dealers who'd caused it to appear. He wished he hadn't used his P.I.U.S to save himself from the fleshsmith – maybe, that way, it would all be over?

But wishing was useless. There was no way to change what had already happened.

Well, not unless you were Quinn-fucking-Kelly, anyway. Spencer sighed as the bunk above him shifted again. Maybe there was some way to convince her to undo six months' worth of time? But no – she could only undo time for herself. Even in the impossible scenario that she did agree to it, there was no way that the Vincent of six months ago would ever believe what she told him.

'Yo, dickheads!'

Vincent turned to look as Joey 'Mullet' Collins came through the curtain that separated the sleeping area from the rest of the RV. He was holding something made of colourful strips of fabric.

'What?' Quinn said from the upper bunk.

'Kylie wants you.' Joey looked up at her. 'They're having an emergency meeting, about getting a new GLAM VAN and stuff. Sounds like they've come up with a fresh money-making scheme. Kylie seems pretty excited about it.'

'Oh, great,' Quinn said. She swung her legs over the bunk and dropped to the floor. 'Are we bringing Spencer?'

'Nope!' Joey said. 'They just want you. I'll look after him, don't worry!'

As she left, Joey turned to grin at Vincent. 'Yo, check this out,' he said, and lifted up the fabric he was holding.

Vincent looked at it for ten or so seconds, but still had no clue what he was looking at.

'It's a harness!' Joey beamed. 'So I can carry you on my back and we can go outside!'

'Ugh, you are NOT carrying me around like some sort of pathetic baby,' Vincent scowled.

'Yeah I am,' Joey said. 'But just for today! I've got my own plans, see.' He tapped his nose. 'Kylie's not the only one scheming.'

Vincent stared at him in dawning worry. 'What exactly are you planning?' he said. 'It better not involve me! Hey, no, don't pick me up! I didn't say I wanted to go anywhere!'

'Bro, this plan hinges on you,' Joey said. 'It's one hundred per cent necessary that you come!'

'What plan?' Vincent yelled as Joey strapped him into the harness and hauled him onto his back. 'I didn't agree to this!'

'I guess you could say it's a heist,' Joey said.

'What?' Vincent said. 'What do you mean a heist? Are you planning on stealing something? I'm not going to help you commit crimes, you cretin!'

Ignoring Vincent's yelling, Joey opened the door of the RV and jumped down to the ground. Vincent hadn't known where they were – and seeing outside, he still wasn't sure. It was evening and they were parked on the edge of a small town, streetlamps illuminating a single line of shops along the main road.

Vincent wanted to ask what town it was, but they were outside, and he had no hands to sign with. Fortunately, several of the storefronts announced that they were in Wycheproof. It wasn't a town Vincent had been to before.

Joey turned off the main road and made his way uphill before coming to a stop across the street from a med clinic. Seeing this, Vincent frowned, wondering where this was all going.

Joey turned his head and signed that Vincent should be quiet. Vincent, who was being quiet already, rolled his eyes. Then, he watched in growing alarm as Joey crossed the street and ran down the side of the med clinic, keeping to the cover of the bushes.

Shortly, they came around the side of a garage with a large roller door. The front of the garage was well lit and clearly locked up for the night. After peering around the front to make sure there was no one there, Joey moved back around the side again, where the evening shadows were darkening by the second.

*The clinic is closed for the night,* he signed to Vincent. *But there might still be staff on duty for emergencies.*

Vincent scowled before leaning forward and whispering into Joey's ear. 'Why are we at the med clinic?'

*They have something we want,* Joey signed back.

'I already told you,' Vincent whispered furiously, 'I'm not stealing anything!'

*How do you feel about light property damage?* Joey signed.

'No!'

'Not even a small, person-sized hole?' Joey whispered back. 'It would take you a couple of seconds. This wall isn't even that thick!'

'No, I'm not using P.I.U.S so that you can steal from a small-town med clinic!' Vincent snapped. 'What is wrong with you?'

'Oh well,' Joey said cheerfully, 'guess we're doing this the old-fashioned way, then.'

He picked up a large rock from the ground and hefted it, eyeing the window.

'Stop!' Vincent hissed. 'You'll make noise!'

'Well, it's your choice.' Joey grinned impishly. 'You make a hole silently or I make one noisily.'

Vincent glared at him. 'Is this your plan?' he snapped. 'You think if you implicate me in your crimes, then I won't go to the authorities later?'

'Nah bro,' Joey said. 'I don't have time for that sort of four-dimensional chess shit. This is a just simple case of breaking and entering. But trust me – it's for a good cause.'

'It's a crime, it can't be for a good cause!' Vincent said.

'Dude, just because something's illegal, doesn't mean it's always wrong and bad,' Joey said.

'Breaking and entering is wrong and bad!' Vincent said

crossly. He could feel his cheeks getting warmer as the anger rose.

Joey lifted the rock again.

'Wait!' Vincent said. 'For Christ's sake. Fine! I'll make your hole! There! The mortar is gone! Happy? You can steal all the medicine that sick people need to not die! You can – ow.'

He broke off, wincing as the side effect hit. For a moment he felt dizzy, spots dancing before his eyes, his heartbeat thundering too loud in his ears like the mechanical churning of pistons.

'Are you okay?' Joey whispered.

Vincent breathed in and out a few times until the spots began to clear.

'Just shoot me now,' he muttered.

'I'll assume that's a yes,' Joey said. 'Right – let's do this.'

He reached out and began to carefully remove the bricks, around which the mortar had spontaneously disappeared. In a couple of minutes, he had created a decent sized hole. He then removed the harness and put Vincent down on the ground.

*Back soon,* he signed, and then went into the garage.

Vincent watched him disappear into the darkness and let out a deep sigh. Above, the sky was lit in sunset colours. A single star glinted brightly to the west.

Here he was again, getting involved in shit he hadn't asked for. It didn't seem to matter how much he protested – the shit went on regardless.

It was his fault, really. He had lost his temper and done something rash again. He could have kept refusing to break the wall, stalling for time. Maybe Joey had even been bluffing with the rock?

Maybe he could have used the P.I.U.S to attack, knocking Joey out and making a break for it? They were in a town. It wouldn't be long until someone saw him...

But then what? Then what? Then what? THEN WHAT?

There was a faint rattling at the hole and he turned his head to look. Joey was coming back – and he was bringing something with him. It was a large object, awkwardly shaped, folded in on itself. Joey had to turn it on just the right angle to get it through the hole.

Finally it was free and, with a grand flourish, Joey unfolded it.

*Knew they'd have one,* he signed excitedly.

It was a wheelchair. Vincent stared at it blankly.

*It's for you,* Joey signed, still grinning. *It's old and shit, but looks like the neural interface is working, so you can wheel it around with your mind. Thought you'd appreciate not being stuck in bed constantly. I know I would hate that.*

'I...' Vincent said. He cleared his throat.

*Let's check if its working,* Joey said and he went and hoisted Vincent up by the armpits. Vincent didn't protest as he was strapped into the chair and the interface lattice attached to his head.

Joey turned the chair on and stepped back, looking at Vincent expectantly.

*Go on, see if it's working,* he signed.

Vincent thought about moving. For a moment, nothing happened – then the chair suddenly lurched forward a couple of centimetres.

Joey pumped his fists in excitement. *Yes, it moved!*

'Yeah, there's a huge delay, though,' Vincent said, slowly moving back and forth. 'My cyber limbs reacted basically instantly. This interface takes several seconds to do anything.'

*We can get cyber limbs later,* Joey signed, *when we have a lot of money! But don't worry, the others are working on that right now! C'mon – follow me! Let's take the chair for a spin!*

He began jogging back the way they'd come and Vincent moved the chair after him, juddering over small rocks and twigs. Once they got back onto the road, he picked up the pace and caught up to Joey, overtaking him. Joey stifled a laugh and increased his own speed, chasing the chair.

Vincent brought the chair to its maximum speed, cool evening wind whipping through his hair. It could go surprisingly fast. The road went further up a hill, and he flew to the top, and down the other side, gaining even more speed as gravity took his side.

He continued until he reached a junction, which marked the end of town, and the beginning of a long, empty highway. There, he brought the chair to a stop, waiting until Joey caught up.

Joey was not far behind and, breathing hard and grinning ear to ear, he came to a stop as well.

*That thing can go!* he signed enthusiastically. *Should I see if there's another one? We could race them!*

'No,' Vincent said. 'Stealing one is already too many!'

*Well, I'll race you on foot, then,* Joey said. *To the top of the mountain?*

Vincent squinted at him. 'What mountain?'

Joey pointed at a nearby sign.

WELCOME TO WYCHEPROOF, it said. HOME OF THE WORLD'S SMALLEST MOUNTAIN.

'That's a hill,' Vincent said, unimpressed.

*Well, I'll race you to the top of it,* Joey said. *Ready?*

Vincent nodded and focused on the chair. *Steady,* Joey signed. *Spaghetti... wait I didn't say go yet!*

He took off at a sprint after Vincent, zooming away up the hill.

***

A few hours later, they returned to the sat-tracker van, Joey covered in sweat, and both of them grinning ear to ear. Back inside the RV, there wasn't a lot of space to wheel around – but it was better than nothing. Much, much better than nothing.

When they came in, Kylie was sitting at the tiny dinner table – but she stood up abruptly.

'There you are,' she said. 'I was beginning to wonder if you'd gotten lost. Is that a wheelchair?'

'Yep!' Joey said. 'We borrowed it from the med clinic.'

'They'd better not have seen you.' Kylie waggled a finger.

'Anyway, in other news, while you were out, we came up with a plan to get a shitload of money, pretty much instantly. It's really fucking smart and I don't know why I didn't think of it sooner honestly.'

'What's the plan?' Joey said. 'Or is it still top secret?'

'It was never secret, I just didn't want to get everyone's hopes up until I knew if it would work,' Kylie said. 'But Quinn and Maggie seem to think it will. Something, something, orchestra music?'

'Oh, fantastic,' Vincent said sarcastically, 'it's more timesmith garbage, isn't it?'

'Yep!' Kylie said. 'Quinn's going to win us the lottery!'

# CHAPTER 38

# DISCREPANCY

## Date: Friday 13 March 2082

Following the re-attachment of their arm, the Detective took a couple of hours to get themselves back up to a presentable state. This included fixing superficial damage such as skin and clothes, as well as topping off their fluids and battery to one hundred per cent.

Bill initially offered to lend some of his clothes to the Detective before realising that his suitcase was back at the sin-seeker office and grumpily going retrieve it. The Detective, who was fairly certain Bill's clothes would have been too small anyway, took the time to restore their skin properly.

Once Bill returned and they confirmed that his clothes were too small, Bill went out and bought some larger ones, firmly insisting that the Detective stay in the tool shed while he was out.

'I don't care if it's not real skin,' he said sternly, 'no one wants to see what looks like a six-foot-eight naked man galivanting about the town!'

'I can decrease my height to six foot five, if that is better,' the Detective said.

'That is not better!' Bill said and firmly closed the door.

While they waited, the Detective went over their latest plan of action. As Bill had said, finding a timesmith was not going to be easy.

'I think,' they said, when Bill came back, 'we should go back to the landing site of the First.'

'What?' Bill said, dumping a pile of clothes onto a workbench.

'To find this timesmith, assuming they exist,' the Detective said, 'we should start with the First Portent. In order to become a timesmith, one must survive a close interaction with the First during its active cycle. I believe our next course of action should therefore involve combing the area surrounding the impact site for signs of survivors – footprints, tire tracks, torn clothing, temporary shelters and the like.'

'You want to go back to the crash site?' Bill said. 'Now?'

'Yes,' the Detective said.

Bill sighed, glancing out the window.

'Well, at least it's daytime, I suppose,' he said. 'Here are your clothes, anyway. You're welcome.'

***

Dressed in a brand-new blue T-shirt, black active pants and a fresh yellow radsuit, the Detective stepped out of the sin-seeker paddy wagon which, in the absence of anyone to object, they'd borrowed from the Ouyen office.

Beneath the afternoon sun, the crash site of the First looked even worse. The full extent of the damage was easier to absorb when brightly lit beneath a cloudless blue sky.

'So,' Bill said through the radsuit coms and he gestured expansively at the burnt, rubble-strewn landscape. 'Where do you suggest we begin?'

'The blast radius of the First Portent is around 4.5 kilometres, plus or minus 0.8 kilometres,' the Detective said. 'Within one kilometre is the zone of total destruction. Nothing can survive within this area. Within two kilometres, survival is still extremely unlikely. Between two and four kilometres, however, survival is possible with luck. The P.I.U.S rubicon, meanwhile, can be found at 3.8 kilometres. Thus, we must search the zone between two and 3.8 kilometres from the point of impact.'

'Great, easy peasy,' Bill said dryly. 'What are we looking for, exactly?'

'Any sign that someone may have survived the blast,' the Detective said.

They paused.

'You may find this difficult, Bill,' they added. 'While I encourage you to look regardless, the level of detail required for this task may not be possible for someone with organic eyes.'

'Thanks,' Bill said sarcastically. 'I didn't realise that finding a single footprint in a mountain of rubble was going to be difficult if not entirely impossible.'

'You may wait in the car, if you like,' the Detective said.

'Absolutely not,' Bill said.

As the Detective began speed-walking to the start point of 3.8 kilometres, he grumpily jogged after them, muttering something about long-arse legs. The Detective, meanwhile, plotted out a virtual course to best maximise efficiency of ground covered.

At the 3.8-kilometre mark, they stopped to let Bill catch up.

'We will begin by circling the outer rim,' they said, 'as survival is more likely at this distance.'

Bill just nodded at them, breathing heavily.

They set off again, moving clockwise. At this distance, there was less rubble from the impact site, but trees and bushes were flattened, if not burnt away completely.

The Detective scanned everything they passed, alternating through IR, visible and UV spec. Anything strange, a rock at an odd angle, a dint in the dirt, they stopped to examine. Unfortunately, most of the rocks they saw were at odd angles, so the going was slow.

After fifteen minutes of this, they stopped to generate a virtual filter to the remove rocks that had clearly been thrown by the blast from their scan. As they did this, Bill sat down on a boulder and stared off into the distance.

'Hey,' he said momentarily, 'does that tree over there look strange to you?'

The Detective turned to follow his gaze and saw that he was pointing at something around two hundred metres away, outside of the search range.

'Bill,' they said, 'I would ask that you please focus your efforts within the designated –'

They broke off, eyeing the tree in question. Their head titled to one side.

The tree was a young mallee eucalypt, little more than a sapling, with thin, spreading branches and silver-grey leaves. There was nothing particularly special about it inherently – but compared to the trees around it, which were so many crispy splinters, it stood out starkly.

The Detective immediately cancelled their filtering program and jogged towards the tree.

As they got closer, it became apparent that something very strange was indeed going on. The tufts of grass around the base of the tree were also unscathed and the earth below unscorched. Not only that, but there was a clear line where the scorching began – nay, not a line, but a triangle. A perfectly triangular patch of earth, eight metres on the longest edge, that was completely free of nuclear devastation.

While the Detective stared at it, gears turning in their brain, Bill came up behind them.

'Ho-lee-shit,' he said, staring at the patch. 'How's that for organic eyes, eh? Organics one, cyborg zero!'

'This is the same as Mildura,' the Detective said.

Suppressing the jittering buzz of excitement that had risen unbidden inside them, they crouched and ran a finger along the triangle's edge. Brittle ash on one side. Long yellow grass on the other.

'The inside of the triangle displays a clear temporal discrepancy when compared to the outside,' they said, standing up and wiping the dust off their hand. 'This is the exact same process that occurred in Mildura, albeit on a much smaller scale!'

'You're certain this isn't something else?' Bill frowned. 'Maybe there just happened to be a large, heatproof, triangular object in the way, which protected this area from the blast and then later moved somewhere else?'

'What sort of large, triangular object?' The Detective frowned.

'Well,' Bill said. 'No, you're right. The only explanation I can think of is aliens. Your explanation is a lot simpler.'

The Detective stepped into the triangle and snapped off a twig from the tree, noting its perfectly ordinary structure. The tree itself was in one of the corners of the triangle and some of its branches spread out beyond the patch.

The Detective moved past it and into the very middle, where they immediately found something else of interest. Tire tracks – faint, worn away by shifting dust and weather, but still unmistakable.

'Bill, what do you make of this?' the Detective said, crouching down again.

Bill moved to join them, humming curiously.

'There was a vehicle here!' he said.

'Yes,' the Detective said. 'Specifically, a large, heavy vehicle. Perhaps a truck, or an RV? But that is not all. See there? The vehicle clearly drove away, out of the triangle. But look on the other side – there are no entry tracks.'

'Huh?' Bill said. 'What does that mean?'

'The vehicle seems to have spontaneously appeared here, in the centre,' the Detective said.

'You're sure they didn't just drive in, then reverse out over their own tracks?' Bill said.

The Detective stood up again, scanning the area. 'I can see no overlap,' they said. 'Although... In revision of my previous statement, I no longer believe that the vehicle appeared here spontaneously. It seems much more likely that a vehicle was here already, but in a broken-down or delipidated state. Our timesmith then came across it and used their symptoms to reverse the state of the vehicle so that it was new again. They then drove away in it, in that direction.'

They pointed to the north-west.

'Huh,' Bill said, following the disappearing tire tracks with his eyes. 'The highway is back that way.'

'Indeed it is,' the Detective said. 'I am sure that is where they went.'

'So, they could be anywhere now,' Bill said.

'Yes,' the Detective said. 'But this is still significant progress! For one, we can now be certain that a timesmith is responsible. We also have some inkling of their specific symptom: they are able to reverse time for all objects within a certain area, including inorganic and organic objects. Additionally, we have a timeframe for when they were here. At maximum, it was just after the First's landing. At minimum, based on weathering, it was around two weeks ago.'

'That's, what, a month-long window?' Bill said. 'Not exactly precise.'

'It is far better than what we had before,' the Detective said.

They moved out of the patch again and began walking around it, scanning the earth. There were faint hints of footprints here and there, but they were too weathered to gather specific information.

Then, upon widening their circle, they found something more substantial.

It was a computer case – or at least half of one, cracked and busted wide open, cables splayed out like intestines.

It was also sitting upright on a flat rock, like it had been placed there deliberately. Next to it were several more broken computer fragments, stacked on top of each other like a cairn.

The Detective stopped to have a closer look, wondering where the parts had come from and, more importantly, who had arranged them in such a manner.

'Bill,' they said shortly through the radsuit coms. 'Come and look at this.'

Bill made his way over and stared at the pile of broken tech, hands on hips.

'A computer?' he said eventually.

'Yes,' the Detective said. 'But evidently, it has been discarded.'

'Who was here, taking the time to sort through computer parts, at the crash site of the First Portent?' Bill said.

'That is the question,' the Detective said.

They turned around, hand on chin, and looked again at the mysterious triangle of unburnt grass.

'Computer parts,' they said. 'A large vehicle. Reckless opportunism in the face of obvious danger.'

They turned back and looked down at Bill.

'I believe we are looking for a sat-tracker,' they said.

# CHAPTER 39

# BENDIGO BLUES

## Date: Thursday 30 January 2082

'Remind me why we're in Bendigo again?' Maggie said with a scowl.

They were standing inside the solar station convenience store, where Dingo had dropped them off. It was a massive solar station, befitting of a small city – which is what Bendigo was.

'There's a lottery here,' Kylie said, turning a visitor's map sideways and frowning at it.

'There are other lotteries, though,' Maggie said. 'Why did it have to be this one?'

'Because I also have contacts in Bendigo,' Kylie said. 'I need a new computer. There's a lovely man here who can get me one for a VERY reasonable price.'

'And you can't buy a computer in Ballarat?' Maggie said. 'Or Geelong? Or Melbourne even?'

'I could, if I wanted to,' Kylie said, looking up from the map. 'Why? What's wrong with Bendigo?'

Maggie sighed, deeply.

'I used to live here,' she said. 'For six years. Uni, first job, friend group – my entire life was here.'

'Okay?' Kylie said. 'So, what, you're worried you'll run into an ex?'

'Yeah, I suppose so,' Maggie said. 'Or an ex-co-worker. Or one of the friends I haven't seen in two years. Or the staff from the café I used to go to everyday...'

'I get it,' Kylie said. 'That would be super awkward. Do you want my sunglasses?'

Maggie hesitated for a moment.

'Actually, yes,' she said.

Kylie handed them over. Then she reached into her bag, took out a second, identical pair of sunnies and put them on.

'Twinsies!' she said. 'Anyway, back to my computer contact and the little problem I'm facing. I don't have his number, since my phone got destroyed by that fleshsmith bitch, and I also can't remember where he lives. Not exactly, anyway. I know it was near some sort of trashy, tourist-trap gold mine museum...'

'Oh, I know where that is!' Maggie said. 'Here, let me have a look...'

While they pored over the map, Quinn leant on the wall nearby and stared down the aisle at the produce on sale. Mullet had already wandered off with Spencer in tow in his new wheelchair. Ever since he'd gotten it, Spencer had been following Mullet everywhere like a lost puppy. Quinn could hear them now, giggling over something in the next aisle over.

With a frown, she pushed off the wall and drifted over to see what they were laughing at. It turned out that Mullet had rearranged the fruit stand to resemble a series of phalluses.

'Wow,' she said, looking at it. 'Now that's comedy.'

'Yeah, it fuckin' is.' Mullet grinned. 'Imagine you're trying to buy some fruit. Woops, all dicks!'

Next to him, Spencer smirked in amusement but he stopped when Quinn looked at him.

'What?' he said, jutting his chin. 'Is this joke too unrefined for you?'

'No,' Quinn said, glaring at him, 'I just don't get why YOU think it's funny.'

'Hey.' Mullet stepped between them. 'No more being shitheads to each other. We're all friends now, got it?'

'No, we're not,' Quinn said. 'He stabbed me! Or have you forgotten?'

'When?' Spencer said. 'When did I stab you? That literally never happened!'

'It did happen,' Quinn said. 'Just because I reversed it, doesn't mean you wouldn't have done it again!'

'Well, why don't you reverse your way back into the other aisle so I don't have to look at your ugly face?' Spencer snapped.

'Oi!' Mullet said. 'Stop it! Quinn, I know Spencer stabbed you in another timeline, but in this one, he didn't.'

'Yeah, because you knocked him out with a table leg!' Quinn said. 'Or has he forgotten about that too?'

'Water under the bridge.' Mullet shrugged. 'We thought he was an enemy at the time, but maybe he doesn't have to be? What's a little concussion between friends?'

'Ugh,' Quinn said and she turned and left. Tears were threating to make an appearance but she angrily blinked them away.

'Oh, there you are,' Kylie said as she came back into their aisle. 'You're going with Maggie to scope out the Lotto.'

'Mm,' Quinn said.

'Meanwhile, I'll be taking the boys with me to find my guy,' Kylie said. 'We'll meet up again this evening, okay?'

'Sure,' Quinn said.

Wordlessly, she followed Maggie out of the store. It was a hot, sunny day outside and they hurried across the road and into the shade.

*Are you okay?* Maggie signed as they set off down the street.

Quinn shrugged, not meeting the older girl's eyes.

*You don't have to do this, if you don't want to,* Maggie went on. *I know the lottery plan hinges on you, but we can always think of something else.*

Quinn frowned.

*The plan is fine,* she signed back. *That's not what I'm annoyed about. Mullet keeps taking Spencer's side,* she added, when Maggie gave her a curious look. *It's... I... I thought he was my friend!*

Tears pricked at the back of her eyes again. Maggie reached out and patted her on the shoulder.

*He is your friend!* Quinn saw her sign in the corner of her eye. *He always will be! Making friends, and keeping them, is one of his main strengths! Which is... why he's trying the same thing on Spencer.*

*Why?* Quinn signed angrily. *Why do we have to be friends? Spencer isn't our friend! He stalked us for ages! He stabbed me! He killed Mullet as well, indirectly, when he impaled that security guard! The security guard that was Keanu, mind you. What would Mullet say if he knew Spencer killed Keanu, huh? And yeah, I fixed it, so none of it happened anymore, but if I hadn't...!*

Maggie frowned.

*What do you mean, Spencer killed Keanu?* she signed. *I thought Keanu moved away before all of that?*

*No,* Quinn said, *Keanu got eaten by Ava and turned into a security guard.*

*What?!* Maggie sent her a horrified look. *Shit! You didn't tell me that!*

*Yeah, well, you didn't need to know,* Quinn said bitterly. *Mullet doesn't need to, especially. He's better off thinking that Keanu just went home.*

*I,* Maggie signed, and stopped. *I don't know what to say. Geez. Quinn, you shouldn't have to carry this by yourself!*

Quinn just shrugged again. Her vision had become blurry. Maggie continued to sign, but she couldn't really see it anymore.

Shortly, Maggie stopped and grabbed her shoulders.

'Quinn,' she said quietly. 'You really don't have to do this. The lottery, I mean. We don't experience the same things you do, so sometimes we forget. We forget how much it sucks to see things like that, people you know getting hurt or dying and be the only one who remembers it. I can't even imagine what that's like. But I can imagine that you don't appreciate us asking you to use your P.I.U.S for something that, in the grand scheme of things, is so unimportant.'

'It's fine,' Quinn mumbled, wiping her eyes. 'I don't mind, really. We need the money.'

'We don't,' Maggie said. 'We can get it elsewhere. There are always other options.'

'I told you, it's fine,' Quinn said.

She broke free of Maggie's grasp and kept on walking.

*Can we go over the plan again?* she signed.

*I think you should consider what you really –* Maggie began

*Please,* Quinn interrupted her. *All I'm doing is remembering some numbers, aren't I? I think I can handle it.*

*Well... if you're sure,* Maggie signed doubtfully.

*I am. What's the plan? Please.*

Maggie looked around to make sure there was no one close enough to see the conversation.

*Okay,* she said. *Well... we're going for the Bendigo Lotto. It's drawn every Saturday morning at 9AM. There are six numbers, and if you guess all six of them on your ticket, then you win a hundred thousand dollars. The numbers are projected on E.W.S screens all over town.*

Quinn nodded. *Where do we get the ticket?*

*At the newsagency, and a few other stores,* Maggie said. *We need to double check, but I think you can buy tickets for the upcoming lottery all week as long as your ticket is registered by Friday, 5PM.*

*So,* Quinn said, *that's, what, sixteen hours between submitting our ticket and finding out the results of the lottery?*

*Yes,* Maggie said. *Which is the tricky bit. Sixteen hours is a bit longer than a few minutes, and a bit shorter than several thousand years, which are our current data points for your abilities. But as I mentioned yesterday, I've been working on a mathematical formula. It intakes the length of the song and the number of layers present and spits out the time reversed. The more difficult part is then finding a song to match it. But... I think I have a couple of candidates.*

*For sixteen hours?* Quinn said.

*For eighteen to twenty-two hours,* Maggie said. *That gives us more room for error.*

*So,* Quinn said, *the plan is, we buy a lottery ticket, then we wait to Saturday morning and see what the winning numbers are, then I go back in time to before the 5pm deadline and fill them in?*

*Yes,* Maggie said. *But again, Quinn – if you don't want to do this...*

*I do,* Quinn said. *It'll be fine. It's just eighteen hours of what I'm sure will otherwise be a normal, boring day. We can specifically make sure it's boring. Spencer won't even ruin it, because he's Mullet's buddy now, apparently.*

*So... you're fine with reliving the same eighteen hours twice?* Maggie said.

*Sure,* Quinn said. *It'll be fine. I'll be asleep for half of it.*

***

Arriving at one of Bendigo's shopping centres, they soon located a newsagency, and Maggie confirmed that her details about the lottery were correct. While she went up to the counter to purchase a ticket, Quinn stayed back near the door, eyeing a cabinet of low tier relics for sale on the far side of the room.

'Here,' Maggie said, coming back and handing her a single paper ticket. 'Don't lose it!'

Quinn looked closely at the ticket. It was printed on colourful paper and had room for six guesses. She would only need one of them.

She put the ticket away in a pocket and followed Maggie back out into the shopping centre.

'Now we just need to go and rendezvous with the others,' Maggie was saying. 'Hopefully, they found their guy and he's willing to put us up, like Kylie seems to think he will. Then, we can just do nothing for a few days! You're right, if we make an effort to keep it as boring as possible, then

448

everything should be fine. We're about to have the dullest, laziest forty-eight hours ever, just you watch –'

'Maggie?' a voice said. 'Is that you?'

Maggie stiffened.

A young man with short, dirty-blonde hair and white T-shirt was rapidly approaching them, a grin on his face.

'It is you!' he called cheerfully. 'Holy crap! It's been a while! How are you?'

Maggie turned to look at the man, a smile fixed on her face. 'Ryan!' she said. 'Hi! I'm fine, how are you?'

'Great!' Ryan said. 'I didn't realise you were back in town?'

'Oh, I'm just here for a few days.' Maggie smiled at him.

'On holiday?' Ryan said.

'More of a business trip, really.'

'Right,' Ryan said. 'Well, have you got any time spare? If you do, you should swing by the old Department for a couple hours! I'll shout you lunch!'

'Oh, I don't know about that,' Maggie said.

'Aw, c'mon.' Ryan bumped her arm. 'We all miss you! Especially a certain someone. Still talks about you all the time, you know?'

'O-oh?' Maggie said, her smile faltering. 'She does?'

'Oh yeah.' Ryan grinned. 'Seriously, come on by! I can show you what I'm working on!'

'I-I don't know if I'll have time,' Maggie said.

'Not even after work?' Ryan said. 'I can organise drinks instead?'

'No, that's worse!' Maggie said quickly. 'Um. I... okay... maybe tomorrow afternoon? After 3PM?'

'Sweet!' Ryan said.

'I can't guarantee it, though,' Maggie added hurriedly. 'Work might get busier than I was expecting! Don't get too excited.'

'See you then!' Ryan beamed at her and then walked away as quickly as he'd come.

'Who was that?' Quinn asked.

Maggie sighed. 'An old co-worker,' she said, 'from the DOU.'

'A scientist?' Quinn perked up.

'Yeah,' Maggie said.

'Is he one of the ones who does experiments on realitysmiths?' Quinn said.

'No,' Maggie said, 'he works with relics, same as I did. He sort of took over my project once I left.'

'And you're going to visit him tomorrow afternoon?' Quinn said.

'Absolutely not,' Maggie said firmly.

'Why not?' Quinn said. 'He seemed nice!'

'He is,' Maggie said. 'But... I don't want to go back there. It would be weird.'

'Not even to see the person who "still talks about you"?' Quinn eyed her.

'I...' Maggie said.

'Not even if tomorrow afternoon is going to be completely erased from the timeline?' Quinn continued.

'Huh,' Maggie said, 'I guess... it is going to be erased, isn't it? But... No. No, we're keeping things boring, remember?'

'Visiting your co-workers IS boring,' Quinn said.

'How about this,' she said as they headed for the exit to the shopping centre. 'We both go to the DOU tomorrow afternoon, and you say hello to your friends and see what they've done with your old project, and afterwards, once I revert time back to tomorrow morning, I tell you how it went?'

'Maybe,' Maggie said. 'None of them will remember it, will they?'

'Nope,' Quinn said. 'You won't either. But I will. And I can tell you ALL the details of their lives, without you ever having to actually talk to them.'

'Hmm,' Maggie said. 'No. Nope. We can't do that. Absolutely not. Never in a million years...'

# CHAPTER 40

# ACQUAINTANCES

### Date: Friday 31 January 2082

The following afternoon, at 3:20PM, Quinn and Maggie stood before a massive brick building on the corner of the Bendigo university campus. A large white banner over the door read:

DEPARTEMENT OF UNREALITY – BENDIGO BRANCH
WE PAY CASH FOR RELICS!

'We should not be doing this,' Maggie said. 'Why are we here? I can't believe it. Why am I like this?'

Next to her, Quinn was also starting to regret convincing Maggie to come. There were hundreds of relics in the building in front of her, some of them very strong. There were also frequent bursts of unreality emanating from other sections of the building, which resulted overall in an eddying, wildly oscillating pattern of stillness and hyperactivity. It was similar to walking past a weather station but twenty times worse.

Apprehensively, they approached the building and entered in through the airlock. Inside, a middle-aged woman with a dyed red bob and blue eyeshadow sat behind a large reception desk. She looked up, glancing at Quinn briefly, before her eye fell on Maggie.

'Margaret?!' she said. 'Oh my goodness, is that really you?'

'Hi, Nirene!' Maggie said, smiling a little too broadly. 'Yeah, I'm back! For this afternoon, anyway.'

'Oh, how exciting!' Nirene beamed. 'I love what you've done with your hair!'

'Thanks,' Maggie said.

'Nothing's changed here,' Nirene went on. 'Your old mob are still hard at work. They'll be very excited to see you! Piper especially – she still mentions you sometimes.'

'Oh, really?' Maggie said, panic in her eyes.

While they talked, Quinn stood awkwardly by the door and looked around the room. There was a large mural across the back wall, with bushland and brightly coloured native flowers on one end, and an idyllic beachside cityscape on the other. There were words in the middle, stylised in grand, looping font:

*Thus, in this Department shall be trusted the future of the Nation.*

*Through them, the scientific method shall be preserved.*

*Through them, the collective knowledge of humankind shall be treasured and passed on for generations to come.*

*May this collective knowledge only grow.*

*And with it, may the mistakes of the past at last be undone.*

'Who's this, then?' Nirene asked, looking at Quinn.

'That's my cousin, Quinn,' Maggie said. 'She's interested in science, so I wanted to show her around, if that's alright?'

'Of course!' Nirene beamed. 'I'll get the both of you a visitor's badge!'

She rummaged in a drawer and found a pair of lanyards with orange VISITOR tags attached. 'There you go!' she said handing them over. 'Those will get you up to the offices! It won't get you into the labs, but I'm sure someone will be happy to give you a tour.'

She winked at Quinn, who stared back blankly.

'Thanks!' Maggie said, putting on the lanyard. 'C'mon Quinn, let's go upstairs!'

They headed down a corridor and towards an elevator.

As soon as they were out of sight of the visitor's desk, Maggie's smile dropped.

'Bloody hell,' she muttered. 'It's like I never left.'

'Is that a good or a bad thing?' Quinn asked.

'I...' Maggie said. 'I don't know.'

They got into the elevator. As they did so, Quinn winced as a particularly strong wave of unreality blew over her.

'Are you alright?' Maggie said. 'There are a lot of relics and stuff around here.'

'I am aware,' Quinn said.

'They're not too bad, I hope?' Maggie gave her a worried look.

'I'll be fine.'

'Well, let me know if it gets too uncomfortable,' Maggie said. 'I'll take any excuse to leave. Although... I guess seeing Professor Wattle won't be too bad. I'm actually looking forward to seeing him, now that I'm here. He was my old supervisor. A great man – brilliant, and hilarious too, in a goofy sort of way. I think you'll like him.'

The elevator opened and they stepped out onto the second floor. The corridor was carpeted and lined on either side with doors. Most of the doors had plaques on them, marking the office of Professor Whatsit and Doctor So-and-So.

Maggie walked past all of them, and stopped to peer into a break room. Inside, a young East Asian man with long hair tied back in a ponytail was making himself a cup of tea.

Maggie dodged out of view again, glancing at Quinn.

*Kevin,* she signed. *Nice bloke. Huge nerd.*

She took another deep breath and stepped into the break room.

'Hi, Kev!' she said. 'Long time no see!'

The man looked around in surprise and his face broke out into a toothy grin.

'Maggie!' he said. 'What are you doing here?'

'Visiting!' Maggie said. 'Just for a few hours. Did... did Ryan not say anything?! I bumped into him yesterday...'

'He didn't say anything, no,' Kevin said. 'But this is a pleasant surprise to be sure! Welcome back!'

'Is Ryan even here?' Maggie said suspiciously. 'Or has he stitched me up?'

'He's around,' Kevin said. 'Piper's here too, somewhere. Probably downstairs in the computer lab.'

'Oh,' Maggie said awkwardly. 'Um. This is my cousin, Quinn! She wants to study science, so I thought she'd be interested in seeing the Department up close.'

'Oh?' Kevin said, looking at Quinn. 'What sort of field do you intend to specialise in?'

'Umm,' Quinn said, trying to remember what Maggie had told her to say. 'Relics and stuff. They're, um, pretty cool!'

'Do you know if Professor Wattle is in?' Maggie said quickly as Kevin opened his mouth.

'He isn't,' Kevin said. 'Oh. I suppose you wouldn't have heard, but he actually left.'

'What?' Maggie said.

'Yeah,' Kevin said. 'Over a year ago, now.'

'Where did he go?' Maggie stared at him.

'He transferred to HQ.' Kevin shrugged. 'The Project had a huge breakthrough and city campus got involved. We're still working on it here, mind you – but ours isn't going as well.'

'Wait,' Maggie said. 'What project is this?'

'You know, the Project,' Kevin said. 'With a capital P?'

'I don't know what you're talking about,' Maggie said.

'Ohh,' Kevin said. 'Right. That must have happened just after you left.'

'What happened just after I left?' Maggie frowned.

'Well,' Kevin said. 'I actually don't think I'm allowed to talk about it, since you don't work here anymore. Sorry.'

Maggie scoffed in disbelief. 'Since when do you guys do anything important?' she said. 'Is this Project really that big of a deal?'

'Yeah, it is,' Kevin said. His face was serious.

'Really?' Maggie said. 'Huh. That's... huh. Well, if Prof Wattle is gone, then who's in charge now?'

'Professor Latrobe,' Kevin said.

Maggie's eyebrows shot up. 'What? How' —she glanced around furtively—'how did he get that job?'

Kevin shrugged. 'I don't know. We were all surprised, to tell you the truth. But we're used to it now. He's not so bad, if you play by his rules.'

'Bet he's no William Wattle, though,' Maggie said. 'So, what else has changed?'

Quinn sat on a table and swung her legs while Kevin began filling Maggie in on two years of workplace drama. Halfway through, Ryan came in and loudly greeted Maggie, clapping her on the back. Maggie told him off for not letting the others know she was coming – but she was grinning the whole time.

Quinn tried her best to listen as they resumed gossiping, since she had promised Maggie that she would tell her everything – but most of the names they mentioned were not people she knew, so it got a little difficult to follow.

Around twenty minutes later, another person stuck their head into the room – a middle-aged Caucasian man in an old-style business suit, with a handful of wispy black strands combed across his balding head. He coughed and the chatter died down instantly.

'Kevin,' the man said dourly. 'Can I meet you in my office? I believe we were scheduled to catch up, ten minutes ago?'

'Oh.' Kevin hurriedly put down his empty tea-cup. 'Crap, I forgot! I'm so sorry, I'll come right now!'

'Yes,' the man said, his eyes roving the room. 'Margaret, what are you doing here?'

'Hi, Professor Latrobe,' Maggie said. 'I'm just here for a quick visit.'

'And who is that?'

'That's my cousin, Quinn.'

'Science is cool!' Quinn said, a little too enthusiastically.

'You don't look related,' Professor Latrobe said.

'It's by marriage,' Maggie said quickly.

Professor Latrobe waved his hand around, encompassing the entire room.

'This isn't appropriate,' he said flatly. 'Civilians are not supposed be in here during work hours, especially without formal invitation.'

'I WAS invited,' Maggie said. 'Ryan invited me.'

'Well, the invitation was not run by me first,' Professor Latrobe said. 'Socialising is fine, outside of work hours and at an appropriate venue. But this is a workplace. We are all very busy and distractions are not appreciated. You need to leave immediately.'

'Why?' Maggie said. 'It's a Friday afternoon. It's not like anyone is working hard.'

Professor Latrobe sent her a beady-eyed glare.

'Margaret, do you want me to call security?'

Scowling, Maggie hopped down off the bench she'd been sitting on and pushed past Professor Latrobe. Quinn went after her, eyeing the Professor as she passed him. He stared stonily back.

Maggie crossly pushed the down button on the elevator as behind her, Professor Latrobe led a sheepish Kevin away down the hall. The elevator arrived and Maggie went in. But before the doors could close, Ryan stepped into the elevator as well.

'You're not leaving yet!' he said and jabbed the button for the third floor.

'But –' Maggie began

'Fuck the professor,' Ryan interrupted. 'He's going to be in a meeting for an hour now. He won't know if you happen to take a little detour on your way out.'

'I guess,' Maggie said. 'I... civilians?! Who does he think he is? The fucking Department of Sin?'

'Yeah, the power has gone to his head a bit.' Ryan grinned.

'I'll say!' Maggie snorted. 'How do you guys put up with it?'

'With saintly patience,' Ryan said. 'Nah – look, I kinda understand where he's coming from. He's under a LOT of pressure. This current Project... if anything goes wrong, the consequences could be really serious. And it's not just him either, its all of us who could screw it up. Still... I wish he'd stop micromanaging.'

'This is the Project, with a capital P, right?' Maggie said. 'Kevin mentioned it. But he wouldn't say what it was.'

'Well, yeah, we're all under NDAs,' Ryan said.

'Seriously?' Maggie said. 'Shit. Our little Department, doing important things? I never would have thought it.'

'Yep,' Ryan said. 'Honestly, I wish it was less important sometimes. It's stressful being this successful! But hey – I can still talk about my project, with a small p. Wanna see what I've been up to?'

'Your project?' Maggie said with a small grin. 'You mean, my project?'

'Mine now!' Ryan said. 'Plus, the focus has shifted. It's a very different beast than it was when you were here.'

Quinn trailed behind them as they stepped out onto the third floor and moved down a sterile white corridor. There were doors along it with window panels, which Quinn looked through in interest. Inside were laboratories, with scientists at work. A woman in full PPE pipetted liquids into a tray. A man with a plaited beard fiddled with a disassembled cybernetic limb. A woman sorted through colourful containers full of powdered chemicals, the names of which were all strings of letters and numbers.

Ahead, Ryan opened one of the doors and gestured to follow. Inside, Quinn was surprised to see a dozen barbeques, lined up in a neat row.

'Okay,' Maggie said, looking at the barbeques. 'What the hell is this?'

'It's a relicity experiment,' Ryan said. 'Basically, barbeques are weakly relicious. That's why we have Barbeque Days after all. But not all barbeques are made equal. Obviously, the more similar a relic is to the original concept of Barbeque, the more relicious it is. But what counts as the "original barbeque"? That's what I've been trying to quantify. What combination of snags, onion, sauces, bread, side salads, etcetera, results in the highest relicity index?'

'Yeah, this is entirely different from what I was doing,' Maggie muttered.

'They really pay you to cook up a sausage sizzle every day?' Quinn said sceptically.

'Quinn, wasn't it?' Ryan looked at her. 'Yes, they pay me to do this. And yes, I can eat as many of them as I want. But there's more to it than meets the eye. On the surface, I am arranging sausages on a grill and quantifying tomato sauce to the microlitre. But this experiment can potentially tell us a lot more about how ALL relics interact with each other – and therefore how to best make use of them.'

'I see,' Maggie said. 'It IS still my project. But scaled back quite significantly...'

'Yeah, well, all our strong relics are being used elsewhere.' Ryan shrugged.

'Let me guess,' Maggie said, 'the Project again?'

Ryan waggled his eyebrows and made a zipping motion over his mouth.

'All of them?' Maggie said. 'Really? ALL of our five-hundred or so relics? Man, I am SO curious. This is going to keep me awake all night for sure.'

'Maybe you should come work for us again?' Ryan said with a smirk. 'Then you'll find out everything!'

Maggie shook her head. 'No,' she said. 'No. I'm not THAT curious.'

She sighed, deeply.

'I... should probably go,' she said. 'I'm glad your project is going so well. But Professor Latrobe isn't going to stay in that meeting forever and I don't want to get you into trouble.'

'Wait, you can't go yet!' Ryan said. 'You haven't even said hello to Piper!'

'It might be for the best if I don't,' Maggie said.

'What do you mean?' Ryan wrinkled his nose. 'You gotta say hi! She'll be devo if you don't.'

'Only if you tell her I was here,' Maggie said.

'Wha-well, obviously I have to tell her!' Ryan said as Maggie went to open the door. 'I can't keep a secret, you know this! I'm terrible at keeping secrets!'

'Tell that to your NDA,' Maggie said.

'That's different,' Ryan said. 'They'll arrest me if I talk about that one! Hey, Maggie, come back–!'

The door closed with a faint snap.

'Did I say something wrong?' Ryan asked Quinn.

Quinn gave a large shrug.

'I shouldn't have brought up Piper,' Ryan muttered. 'Maybe it's a sore topic.'

'Who is Piper, anyway?' Quinn asked him.

'Piper Grevillea,' Ryan said. 'She and Maggie used to be very close friends. Like, VERY close. We were all ninety per cent sure they were into each other, but I don't think they ever dated, not officially.'

'I see,' Quinn said.

There was a long, awkward silence.

'So you like science, hey?' Ryan said.

'Not at all,' Quinn said. 'I should find Maggie. Bye.'

She left Ryan with his barbeques and went and found Maggie, waiting for the elevator. Neither of them said anything as the elevator took them down to the lobby.

Maggie was polite to Nirene as they returned their lanyards but as soon as they left the building, her expression dropped. Wordlessly, she led Quinn away from the campus and across the road to a small café.

Inside, she dropped into a chair and laid her head on the table.

'Bloody hell,' she mumbled.

'Are you okay?' Quinn said.

'No,' Maggie said.

A waiter came by to take their order and Maggie ordered a beer while Quinn asked for a chocolate milkshake. Once the waiter was gone again, Quinn leant her elbows on the table and stared across at Maggie.

'I don't get it,' she said.

Maggie raised her head slightly to look at her.

'What don't you get?'

'What you're running away from,' Quinn said. 'From what I could tell, they were all really nice! Ryan and Kevin and their cool, top-secret project that they can't talk about. Okay, maybe Professor Latrobe isn't cool – he seems like a dick. But he's just one dick in a sea of perfectly nice people! Plus, there's Piper, someone who seems to like you so much that she talks about you years after you left!'

'Ugh,' Maggie said, face on the table again.

'Why "ugh"?' Quinn said. 'What did they ever do to you?'

'It's not what they did,' Maggie said, sitting up abruptly. 'It's nothing to do with them, in fact.'

'Then what is it?' Quinn said.

Maggie let out a very long sigh.

'It's me,' she said. 'I'm not... built like they are. You're right, they ARE perfectly nice people. In fact... they're perfect people. They're smart, and athletic, and cool and confident, and most of all, they're motivated. Anything they put their mind to, they could do it – but they don't even let that go to their head. I... I can't compete with that, Quinn. I might be academic, sure, but I don't... I couldn't...'

She sighed again.

'I'm not as strong as they are,' she said.

'What are you talking about?' Quinn said. 'You're one of the smartest people I know! And you're cooler than they are. You play bass guitar! Bet they can't do that.'

'Actually, Piper plays the drums,' Maggie said. 'Which is just as cool, if not more so...'

'Okay, well that's not the point,' Quinn said. 'The point is, you ARE as cool as they are. I don't get why you don't want to see them! Do you not like them?'

'I...' Maggie said, 'that's not it. I do like them! Very much! And I miss them! Ryan, Kevin, Prof Wattle... Piper... I... I miss Piper every day...'

She took a deep breath.

'Here's the thing,' she said in a low voice. 'Ryan has technically taken over my project. But what he's doing, it's not the same as what I was doing. It's related, but... well, basically, where he's trying to optimise relicity in existing relics, my goal was to boost it higher. In a nutshell, I was given a bunch of strong relics and told to make them even stronger.'

'Did it work?' Quinn said.

'Well, the short answer is, no,' Maggie said. 'I worked on that project for three years and no – not once did I manage to boost a relic. But… I did find out something else that was… pretty important.'

'Oh?' Quinn asked.

Maggie looked out the window.

'I found out that the relics were getting weaker,' she said. 'All of them. Not just copies, but originals too. Over time, every single one of them decreased in potency.

'Not by a lot,' she went on. 'The decrease was only noticeable over three years, and only because I regularly took measurements and statistically analysed it. But once I saw the trend, I realised it was everywhere. Across all relics. I tested other people's data and found the same thing.'

'Right,' Quinn said. 'Relics decreasing in power. That's… not good?'

'No, it's not,' Maggie said. 'It's not good at all. Relics are currently the only way by which we can deter the Portents, or control them at all. Without relics, we're basically helpless to their whims. And if they keep increasing in number, the way they have been…'

'You think there are more than eleven?' Quinn asked.

'Almost certainly,' Maggie said. 'Every few years, another one shows up. I don't know whether they're finding their way here from elsewhere on the planet, or if they appear, fully formed, on our shores – but either way, there could be dozens more of them. Hundreds, even. We're fighting a losing battle. We, humans, and our entire timeline. The CMT is doomed. It has been for thirty years now.'

'But we're still here,' Quinn said.

'Yep,' Maggie said. 'We're here, living. And our kids will be, and their kids too. But the end is coming and it's not so far away. In fact, I did the math once. It will take about three hundred years before the most powerful relic in our collection is neutralised completely.'

'Right,' Quinn said. 'What will happen after that?'

Maggie shrugged. 'Who knows?' she said. 'There will be a lot of realitysmiths. A lot of chaos and suffering. Maybe they'll find a new way to live, as reality breaks apart around them? Maybe they'll find a way to fix things? Or maybe they'll slip through the cracks and invade someone else's timeline? Whatever the case – we can't stop it from happening. *I* can't stop it from happening. I tried, for three years, and I can't. I can't make relics more powerful. It isn't possible.'

She took another deep breath.

'So I left,' she said. 'Because... it was getting to me. I gave it my best shot, and it didn't work. There was no solution. I had to accept that or lose my sanity.'

'And... you couldn't do something else?' Quinn said.

'No, you don't understand,' Maggie said. 'I couldn't do something else. I was obsessed. I... even going back there today... it all started coming back...'

She swallowed, rubbing her eyes.

'I'm sorry,' she said. 'I don't want to talk about it anymore.'

Quinn wasn't sure what to say, so she just reached out and patted Maggie's arm. The waiter came by and delivered their drinks.

'Well,' Quinn said eventually. 'I'm glad you left the Department. If you hadn't, I wouldn't have met you. And then Temporal Boom would have no bass player.'

Maggie nodded, a small smile lifting the corners of her mouth.

'Saving the Nation, one sin at a time,' she muttered.

They sat in silence for a while and finished their drinks. Eventually, Maggie stood up and went to pay the bill.

*So,* Quinn signed as they went outside. *What do you want me to tell you, when I go back to this morning? Would you do it again?*

*No*, Maggie signed. *It was a bad idea. Tell me that I regret it. I regret everything.*

Quinn nodded – and in silence, they went back to Kylie's friend's house. There, they did nothing for the rest of the day and slept through the night uninterrupted. And then, the next morning, Quinn woke up and saw the lottery numbers, and went back nineteen hours to write them down.

'We did it, then?' Maggie said, when Quinn showed her the filled in lottery ticket. 'It worked just like we expected?'

'Exactly like expected,' Quinn said.

'My math was all correct?'

'Your math was all correct.'

'Any side effects?'

'Nothing particularly terrible.'

'Great!' Maggie said. 'And... what about the trip to the DOU? How did that go?'

'I think,' Quinn said, 'that you should talk to Piper.'

# CHAPTER 41

# ACQUAINTANCES (n=2)

### Date: Friday 31 January 2082

That afternoon, at 3:20PM, Quinn and Maggie stood before the massive DOU building on the corner of the Bendigo university campus.

*You're sure this is the right decision?* Maggie signed nervously as they headed towards the front door.

*Yes,* Quinn signed back and she gave the older girl an encouraging smile.

She wasn't – in fact she was entirely unsure. Maggie had specifically told her not to come back a second time. But last time had ended so sadly! This time, armed with what she now knew... maybe she could fix it?

Face set into a carefully neutral position, she followed Maggie into the building and watched the exact same exchange as last time between Maggie and the receptionist, Nirene. Her eyes once again fell on the mural across the back wall, gaze lingering on the last line of the quote:

*... may the mistakes of the past at last be undone.*

She set her jaw in determination.

'Who's this, then?' Nirene was asking, looking at Quinn.

'That's my cousin, Quinn,' Maggie said. 'She's interested in science, so I wanted to show her around, if that's alright?'

'Of course!' Nirene smiled. 'I'll get the both of you a visitor's badge!'

She handed over the lanyards and Maggie led the both of them over to the elevator.

'Bloody hell,' Maggie said as they waited for the elevator to open.

'Exactly the same, right?' Quinn said.

'It's like I never left.' Maggie nodded.

She glanced at Quinn. 'Are you SURE this is the right thing to do?'

'Yep, mmhmm.' Quinn smiled at her. 'But if I tell you to do something, Maggie, you have to do it, and don't ask questions. Okay?'

'Sure,' Maggie said with a sigh. 'You're the one who's already done this.'

They were silent as the elevator took them up to the second floor. There, Maggie made a beeline for the break room where she once again found Kevin.

While they had the exact same conversation as last time, Quinn stuck her head out into the corridor, looking back and forth. The way she remembered it, things had been going great – right up until Professor Latrobe showed up. That was it – the point at which she would make the timeline diverge.

'That's my cousin Quinn,' she heard Maggie say behind her. 'She wants to study science, so I thought she'd be interested in seeing the Department up close.'

'Oh?' Kevin said as Quinn turned around and looked at him, hands behind her back. 'What sort of field do you intend to specialise in?'

'Time travel,' Quinn said brightly.

Kevin blinked. 'Oh,' he said. 'Um. Like, particle physics?'

'No,' Quinn said.

'Ha ha, she's a quirky one,' Maggie said, sending Quinn a look. 'She's been interested in, um, the First Portent lately.'

'Oh, the Portents,' Kevin said. 'Well, I don't blame you, they are extremely fascinating! Actually, I'm working on a Portent related project myself!'

'Oh, which Portent?' Maggie said.

'The Ninth,' Kevin said.

'Really?' Maggie said. 'That's quite different from what you were you doing before?'

'Yeah, well, there's been a couple of big changes.' Kevin shrugged. 'New management, new projects. Well, one Project in particular. Most of us are working on it, directly or indirectly. I guess you left before that started, though?'

'Yeah, I don't know what you're talking about,' Maggie said.

'Right,' Kevin said. 'Oh, I guess you also wouldn't know this, but Professor Wattle left!'

'What?!' Maggie said.

'Yeah. Transferred to HQ. Over a year ago now.'

'Really?' Maggie said. 'Huh. That's... huh. Well, if Prof Wattle is gone, then who's in charge now?'

'Professor Latrobe,' Kevin said.

Like last time, they bitched about Latrobe for a while, before going into detail on other recent workplace dramas. Soon, Ryan came in too – and that was when Quinn decided to intervene.

Sidling over to Maggie, she sharply nudged her in the ribs. Maggie, who had been halfway through a sentence, broke off and looked at her.

'Should we go somewhere else?' Quinn said, eyeing Maggie meaningfully. 'Professor Latrobe might come by and ask us to leave.'

'Nah, he never comes down here to mingle with us plebians,' Ryan said. 'Don't worry about it!'

'Doesn't he?' Quinn looked at Ryan. 'What if someone has, say, a meeting scheduled, but they're late, so he comes down here to find them?'

'Oh!' Kevin smacked himself in the forehead. 'You just reminded me! I have a meeting in, like, ten minutes! I completely forgot!'

Maggie sent Quinn a pointed look. Quinn smiled at her innocently.

'Sorry, guys, I have to go,' Kevin said sadly. 'Maggie, if you're still here in an hour, let me know!'

He hurried away down the corridor. Ryan made a face.

'That was sudden,' he said. 'Um. Maybe we should go

somewhere else? I could show you what I've been working on?'

'What, my old project?' Maggie said. 'No thanks, I never want to see that again.'

Quinn once again stepped in and put a hand on both Maggie and Ryan's shoulders.

'What if we went and found Piper?' she said.

Maggie's eyes widened. Ryan grinned.

'Yes!' he said, just as Maggie said 'No!'

'No?' Ryan said. 'C'mon, she misses you! Bet you miss her too.'

'She does!' Quinn said.

'Quinn!' Maggie exclaimed.

'C'mon, I know where she is,' Ryan said. 'Let's go see her!'

'I am going to kill you.' Maggie pointed at Quinn as Ryan shepherded them out of the room.

Quinn sent her a double thumbs up.

Ryan led them back to the elevator, where he punched a button labelled LG1. As he did so, Quinn noticed for the first time that there were a surprising number of LG buttons, all the way up to LG6.

'Huh, this place has a pretty big basement,' she said in interest.

'Yeah, most of the above-ground rooms are offices and labs relating to the CMT sciences,' Ryan said. 'You know – biology, chemistry, physics – the normie fields. Plus relic studies, since they're pretty harmless. But below ground? Now, that's where all the fun stuff is. And by fun, I mean we have no clue how it works!'

'Is THAT where you dissect the realitysmiths?' Quinn said.

'Ignore her,' Maggie interrupted when Ryan opened his mouth. 'I've already explained that we don't do that.'

The elevator deposited them in a white, windowless corridor with fluorescent lights lining the ceiling. LG1 was painted on the wall in giant red letters.

Ryan led them past several closed doors, arriving at one that stood propped open. Inside was a massive bank of computers and an entire wall of monitors, each displaying something different. Quinn had never seen so much gear in one place before. Kylie would probably strangle someone to death just to get a look at it.

A scrawny Caucasian woman with a dyed purple undercut and a nose piercing sat at a desk in front of the monitors, typing away at a keyboard. The monitor directly in front of her showed a data entry program, while the one above showed what looked like grainy, live CCTV footage of some sort of... stadium?

The woman was also wearing headphones, high quality by the looks of it. Quinn wondered where she'd gotten them. They were not sold anywhere legally.

'Hey, Piper,' Ryan called from the door. 'Have you got a moment?'

The woman lifted one half of the headset and spun herself around in her swivel chair. 'Oh, hi, Ryan,' she said cheerfully. 'I'm currently babysitting Nina, but I'm off duty in about half an hour if –'

She broke off as Maggie stepped into view. A huge smile cracked across her face.

'Maggie!' she yelled and tore the headset off, launching across the room.

Before Maggie could react, the purple haired woman had slammed into her, arms thrown around her. Maggie looked startled as she was aggressively bear-hugged and then let go again.

'You're back, you're back!' Piper said, bouncing on her toes. 'Oh my goodness! You're here! I've got SO much to tell you! Argh!'

'Yeah,' Maggie said, looking everywhere but Piper. 'I guess I am back...'

'Yay!' Piper bounced even more. 'How long are you here for?'

'Here in the building?' Maggie said.

'No, here in Bendigo, dummy!' Piper said. 'Have you moved back?'

'No, I'm just here for a couple of days,' Maggie said.

'Aw.' Piper deflated before brightening instantly. 'It's the weekend! We can hang out! Get some coffee! Have a jam sesh! Oh, you can come see my new Staffy puppy! She's called Bean!'

While Piper began bombarding Maggie with questions and puppy photos, Quinn wandered further into the room. Things seemed to be going well. It looked like her gamble was paying off.

Pausing in front of the wall of monitors, she absently looked at the various graphs and sheets of numbers before her eyes once more fell on the CCTV footage. It wasn't a stadium, she realised, but a large, circular room, floodlit on all sides and housing a strange, lattice-like structure at its centre.

Frowning, she went and stood in front of it, trying to make sense of the grainy, monochrome footage. The structure was cube-shaped, each of its faces made up of a grid of smaller squares. There were random objects tied all over it, which gave some sense of scale. The cube had to be at least three metres tall.

There was something in the middle of it, Quinn realised with a start. It had been standing perfectly still, right in the centre of the cube – but suddenly it moved, rotating to the left. It was a person! No... wait... was it? It certainly resembled a person but there was something off about it. It was upside down... and oddly stiff... and floating in the air...?

'Wait, what the fuck?!' Quinn said out loud. 'Is that the Ninth Portent?'

By the door, the others instantly fell quiet.

'Oh, uh,' Piper said and she ran over and closed the tab. 'Aha ha. You're, uh, not supposed to see that!'

'Wait, but is it?' Quinn said. 'Is that... where is that footage from? Why is it in a cube?!'

'Holy shit,' Maggie said from the doorway. 'Did... are you telling me Prof Wattle actually managed to pull it off?!'

'Pull what off?' Quinn turned to look at her.

'Capture a Portent!' Maggie said. 'It was always this crazy

idea he had. But I never thought… Holy *shit*. He did, didn't he? That's this big Project you're all so secretive about! Isn't it?'

'Umm,' Piper said, glancing at Ryan.

'We're REALLY not allowed to talk about it,' Ryan said.

'Holy FUCKING shit,' Maggie said. 'I can't believe he did it!'

She came closer and opened the tab that Piper had just closed. Piper didn't stop her as she leaned in and stared at the video feed.

'There it is!' she said in disbelief. 'That's it! Wild.'

'Yeah,' Piper said slowly. 'Okay, yep. Yes, that's the Ninth Portent and yes, we managed to capture it. But you CANNOT go talking about it outside of this room! I'm serious, we will get into HUGE trouble if word gets out!'

'Don't worry, I get it,' Maggie said. 'And Quinn knows how to keep a secret. Right, Quinn?'

'Yeah,' Quinn said as everyone looked at her. 'Um. I'm sorry, how the FUCK did you capture a Portent?'

'Well, it wasn't easy,' Piper said. 'But basically, we used a shitload of relics. You can see them there, all tied to the outside of the cage. There's enough of them there to neutralise Nina completely. She's got just enough juice left to float on the spot.'

'Nina?' Maggie said.

'Yeah, that's what we call her.' Piper grinned. 'Nina the Ninth! She's even started to respond to it!'

'She responds to it?!' Maggie said.

'Oh yes,' Piper said. 'I mean, we always pretty much suspected that most, if not all, of the Portents displayed some level of sentience. This Project has basically proven that beyond a doubt.'

'Wow,' Maggie said. 'Just… wow. This is incredible. Although I'm a little nervous about that relic cage. I hope you took my power depreciation calculations into consideration? And how it accelerates when exposed to unreality?'

'Yep, it's all factored in,' Piper said. 'If left entirely by itself, the cage should hold for over four months before it degrades to the point where Nina can escape. And we never leave it by itself! We're constantly keeping an eye on it and adding new relics to counter the depreciation. None of this would have been possible without your maths, though!'

'Well, I'm glad my research turned out to be useful,' Maggie said. 'Although, I shudder to think how many relics you're burning through.'

'Oh, it's twice as bad as you're thinking,' Piper said cheerfully. 'Again, this is extremely classified information – but Nina isn't the only one. There's another one, at HQ!'

'You're kidding?' Maggie said. 'Crap! That's why Prof Wattle went there, isn't it? Let me guess, it's the Seventh? That was always the one he insisted he could catch, because it's relatively small and harmless? I always thought he was joking!'

'It IS the Seventh actually,' Piper said. 'At least, I think it is. They don't tell us much. For all we know, it could have gotten out and run amok through Melbourne CBD by now.'

'So, what, do they plan to capture all of them eventually?' Maggie said. 'I feel like all that will achieve is relics running out a lot sooner than we thought.'

'It's just these two for now,' Piper said. 'And not forever. Just until we understand them a little better.'

'And how is that going?' Maggie asked. 'Understanding them?'

'Okay, I suppose,' Piper said. 'As I said, we know that they're definitely sentient. Nina doesn't have biological organs, or understand English or any other language we've tried – but she always knows when we're there in the room, and she definitely reacts to her name and dozens of other sounds! She has a personality! She gets into moods and sulks up near the ceiling or spins when she's happy! She really likes music as well and even has favourites! We haven't figured out how to communicate beyond very simple yes-or-no questions yet, but we're getting closer every day!'

'So, they really do like music, then?' Quinn said,

frowning. 'How do they even hear it, if they don't have ears?'

'We have no idea!' Piper said. 'It's not through any means that we possess – or can even imagine possessing, I suppose. It's like trying to picture a new colour. It's impossible without some frame of reference. That's why we want to get to the point where we can ask her complex questions! Ultimately, that's what we want to know. What's going on in there? What's it like?'

'I suppose it's worth all the trouble, then,' Maggie said. 'If it means we finally understand what they are. What they want.'

'Exactly!' Piper beamed. 'If we can figure out how they see the world, then maybe we can understand why they keep destroying things? Or if they even realise that's what they're doing.'

'Wow,' Maggie said. 'This is incredible. I'm happy for you guys. This is all extremely exciting stuff!'

'Yeah!' Piper grinned. 'And now you're here to see it too! Hey, do you want to go and see her closer up?'

'What, Nina?' Maggie said in alarm.

'Yes!' Piper said. 'This evening, we could go! I have a key! There's usually no one down there after hours on a Friday, right, Ryan?'

'Well, Kevin sometimes is,' Ryan said.

'Oh, he won't mind!' Piper said.

'I don't think this is a good idea,' Maggie said.

'Why? It's safe,' Piper said. 'Thanks to your calculations! And I think she'd like to meet you! I've told her about you, you know?'

'Y-you told a Portent about me?!' Maggie said. Her cheeks were a little flushed.

'Of course!' Piper said. 'C'mon, it'll be fun! Me and Ryan can show you around! Oh, and you can come too,' she added, looking at Quinn. 'If you want.'

'Of course I want to see a captive fucking Portent,' Quinn said.

'Yeah, see?' Piper nudged Maggie's arm. 'That's the correct response!'

Maggie sighed. 'Won't you get into serious trouble?'

'Not if they don't catch us!' Piper said. 'C'mon! You can be irresponsible for one day, right?'

'I was already irresponsible for one day,' Maggie said. 'This was supposed to be the responsible version of events... But... ugh. Fine, I'll come.'

'Yay!' Piper hugged her again. 'It's a date!'

'Sure,' Maggie mumbled. Her cheeks were still very much flushed.

## THE NINTH PORTENT

FIRST RECORDED SIGHTING: 30/10/2068, Lorne, Gadubanud country, VIC

PHYSICAL APPEARANCE:

The Ninth Portent is a spherical gravitational anomaly, spanning 212m in diameter. Within its borders, travelling from the outer rim inwards, local gravitational pull gradually decreases from 9.8m/s2, to 0.0m/s2 at 53m, a zone known as the turning point. Following the turning point, gravity once more increases; however, the direction of acceleration is inverted, causing objects to accelerate away from the Earth instead of towards it. At the centre point of the sphere, local gravity reaches a maximum of 9.8m/s2 inverted.

Objects within the borders of the Ninth Portent behave in a manner consistent with changed or low gravity. Pre-turning point, objects that are not attached to the ground will float into the air, while post-turning point, object are actively accelerated upwards away from the ground. Any object that is thrown out of the Ninth Portent's area of effect is once again subjected to normal gravitational forces and will behave as such.

At the centre point of the Ninth Portent, an object can be found that appears unaffected

by the inverted gravitation. The object is a
bronze statue of 'Lady Justice' – a
personification of the moral forces of order,
resembling a robed and blindfolded woman,
with a sword in her right hand, and a set of
scales in her left. The statue is 1.8m in
length and is oriented with head towards the
Earth and feet to the sky. It displays heavy
damage of unknown origin, with sizable pieces
missing from the torso, legs/toga, and arms.
Debris, most likely from the statue itself,
can be seen orbiting the statue in three
distinct bands at a distance of between 1 and
3 metres.

BEHAVIOUR:

The Ninth Portent is able to float above solid
or liquid surfaces, with the centre point
reaching a maximum height of 53m.
Horizontally, it is able to travel at speeds
in excess of 85km/h, however it is more often
observed travelling at lower speeds of
between 1 and 20 km/h.

The movements of the Ninth Portent have no
clear pattern, with the Portent changing
direction both vertically and horizontally at
a moment's notice, sometimes even doubling
back on its own path. Wherever the Ninth
Portent touches down, its inverse
gravitational effect causes nearby loose
objects, animals, people, and very large
objects such as boulders or vehicles, to fling
up into the sky, resulting in heavy damage to
all in its path.

Note – while the damage caused by the Ninth

Portent is often severe, its sling-shotting behaviour can be both seen and heard at a great distance, thus allowing ample time for you and your dependants to evacuate the area.

Note 2 – When evacuating from the Ninth Portent, it is of utmost importance to remain as quiet as possible. The Portent is attracted to noise, and capable of bursts of speed in excess of 85 km/h!

PORTENT INDUCED UNREALITY SYMPTOMS:

P.I.U.S RUBICON RADIUS: 53 m.

ACTIVE SYMPTOM DEVELOPMENT: 83%

LETHALITY: 75%

DESIGNATION: Gravsmith

ADDITONAL NOTES: P.I.U.S abilities of the Ninth Portent commonly relate to the manipulation of gravity and weight.

# CHAPTER 42

# NINA

### Date: Friday 31 January 2082

At 9PM, Maggie and Quinn returned to the Department of Unreality and went around the side. There, behind a gas canister storage shed, Piper emerged from a back door, grinning ear to ear.

Signing for them to follow, she led them around towards a small, innocuous brick building. The building looked new and had no signage anywhere on it, aside from a stern NO ENTRY – AUTHORISED PERSONNEL ONLY on the door.

Piper produced a key and let them inside where a massive industrial elevator waited. Piper ignored the elevator completely, leading them instead into an adjacent stairwell.

'The containment chamber is underneath the Department,' Piper said as they began their descent. 'LG7, we call it – although it isn't directly connected to the other floors. They built this whole thing – chamber, observation rooms, elevator, everything – in a couple of weeks! Hired an entire flock of mattersmiths and engineers. Then they took Nina down in her cube and built this little brick shack over the top to hide the entrance.'

'Wild,' Maggie said.

Their feet rang out nosily on metal as they traipsed down seven flights of stairs. Around the third flight, Quinn began to feel something strange – a sort of churning of reality and unreality, more violent than anything she'd felt before. The feeling only got stronger the further down they went, a boiling disturbance, barely contained, like storm-whipped waves in a glass bottle.

It made her feel slightly queasy if she concentrated on it. Quinn determinedly tried to think about other things, but with little success.

By the time they reached LG7, there was no escaping it. The trapped Portent's aura beat down on her like a physical heat. Quinn had to force her legs to keep on walking, struggling to keep her expression as neutral as possible.

They stepped out of the stairwell through a heavy door marked with hazard stripes and into a corridor that looked remarkably similar to LG1 – painted white, with fluorescent lighting. At the end of it was another heavy door, which Piper unlocked using her DOU ID card.

'If anyone asks,' she said, 'you're visiting from HQ!'

Beyond was another corridor, lined on either side with offices. Most of the offices were dark, except for one. As they approached it, Ryan poked his head out of the doorway and waved to them.

'Hi!' he called. 'Don't worry, the coast is clear! Kevin and I are the only people down here.'

'Great!' Piper called back. 'Are you guys coming with us to see her?'

'Nah, I've seen her a million times,' Ryan said. 'Go on ahead.'

Kevin poked his head out of the office as well.

'Hello,' he said, a little nervously. 'For the record, I'm against this. Professor Latrobe will combust on the spot if he finds out.'

'It'll be fine!' Piper said. 'C'mon – this way, ladies!'

They moved to the next door and went in. As they did so, Quinn had to take a moment to stop her knees from buckling.

It was a viewing room, with a large window overlooking the same floodlit space that had been on the CCTV. In the middle sat the relic cube – and in the middle of that...

'There she is!' Piper said grandly.

The cube was much more imposing in person. Inside it,

dead centre, the Ninth Portent floated in silence, suspended as though held up on strings. It was not that large, but it drew the eye magnetically, familiar in its human form, yet so, so alien. It was dull bronze and pitted like an asteroid from the depths of space. Three rings of dust and broken fragments, thin but distinct, turned gently in opposite directions around its knees, centre mass and shoulders.

In a daze, Quinn followed Maggie to the glass, her thoughts drowned out in roaring turbulence. There were more relics in that room below than she'd ever even imagined in one place – and they were all powerful, none lower than tier 4.

But despite that, they were only just enough. The Portent's domain, usually hundreds of metres across, was compressed and wrapped around it, folded in four-dimensional space like a spring, compressed to its absolute limit. Just one crack in the cage, one or two relics removed...

'This is incredible,' Maggie was saying in awe, leaning in close to the glass. 'I never thought I'd see the Ninth this close up! Not without being in serious danger, anyway.'

'Do you want to talk to her?' Piper said excitedly.

'I don't think we should disturb her.' Maggie sounded nervous.

'Oh, don't worry, she loves the attention!' Piper said.

She moved over to where a laptop sat on a desk and opened it up. Watching her, Quinn noticed there were several other items on the desk as well – one of which was a tape cassette player.

'Is that a cassette player?' she said.

'Yeah it is!' Piper said. 'I'm surprised you recognised it – they're pretty rare!'

'Do you play music on it?' Quinn asked.

'Sure do,' Piper said. 'Nina loves it. I'll show you in a bit! But first, watch this!'

She plugged in a tiny USB microphone.

'Hello,' she said into it.

The window between the containment chamber and the viewing room was soundproofed – but a red light came on in the corner, indicating that something was happening. Immediately, the Portent reacted – rotating around on its axis to face the blinking light.

'That's speaker one,' Piper said, grinning. 'Now, if we go to speaker two...'

'Hello, hello,' she said, pressing a different button. Again, the Portent rotated towards the noise.

'Hey, Nina,' Piper continued. 'Nina, that's you, isn't it?'

The Portent moved again, rotating a full 360 degrees before coming to a stop facing the speaker.

'See?!' Piper beamed. 'That's her "yes, I am Nina" spin!'

'Holy shit,' Maggie said in awe. 'That's equal parts terrifying and... weirdly cute?'

'I love her,' Piper said. 'Anyway, want to see something even cuter?'

She opened a box next to the cassette player and took out a tape.

'Golden Oldies is one of her favourites,' she said, loading the tape into the player. 'Just let me rewind it back to the start...'

There was a whir as the tape rewound, before *Oh Carol* by Neil Sedaka began to play.

Piper moved the microphone close to the music and then stood back, smiling fondly. Inside the containment cell, the Portent began rotating again as well as bobbing up and down in time to the beat.

'See?' Piper said excitedly.

'This is so weird,' Maggie said.

Piper grabbed her hand and dragged her away from the window, swaying in time with the music. Maggie resisted at first, before giving in and dancing as well, laughing in embarrassment.

Feeling suddenly like a third wheel, Quinn looked back into the containment cell, staring down at the Portent. It was still spinning and bobbing, frozen in position, left arm outstretched, like an inverted music box ballerina.

Entranced, Quinn watched it spin before a change in the lighting caught her eye. It was a reflection in the glass, fluorescent light glowing as the door opened behind her.

There was a figure silhouetted in the frame – and with a jolt, Quinn recognised the wispy comb-over.

'What *exactly* is going on in here?!' Professor Latrobe snapped.

Piper and Maggie jumped in shock, hurriedly moving away from each other. Behind Prof Latrobe, Ryan was standing with a panicked expression. *I'm sorry!* he signed. *We tried to distract him!*

'Um,' Piper said, and opened and closed her mouth. 'We... uh...'

'There's no explanation for this,' Professor Latrobe said. 'C'mon. Get out! Now! And don't think for a second that you're ever coming back here, Grevillea! You've forfeited that right!'

'What?' Piper said. 'What do you mean? I have to come down here, it's my job!'

'Not anymore, it isn't!' Professor Latrobe pointed a finger at her. 'You're fired! Effective immediately! And you two – you're lucky I haven't called the sin-seekers already! But if you're not off the premises in FIVE MINUTES –'

'What?!' Piper yelled. 'You can't just fire me like that! That's not –'

'I can, and I have!' Professor Latrobe interrupted. 'It's my team and I won't have anyone so blatantly irresponsible on it!'

'It's not your team, it's Prof Wattle's team!' Piper yelled.

'Oh yeah?' Professor Latrobe snapped and he reached for his pocket. 'Tell that to the sin-seekers. I'm about to let them know that there are three trespassers in our facility!'

While Piper stood, stunned, he brought a mobile phone up to his ear.

'Yes, seekers please,' he said into it and he reached out for the cassette player to turn it off.

In that split second, Quinn made the decision to act. In

less than a minute, everything had gone to shit. There was no time to think it through. The current situation was Bad.

But it didn't have to be.

It was tricky, with so many relics right there, but the Portent's aura mostly countered their effect. Quinn seized the music and Professor Latrobe's finger froze in place, centimetres from the off button.

The song warped and strained. Faces around her froze in expressions of outrage, dismay and disbelief.

Quinn sighed internally as time rewound, Professor Latrobe yelling in reverse, Piper flailing her arms. The professor walked backwards out the door, closing it in front of him and Maggie and Piper went back to their dance.

The song was only a simple one and wouldn't go much further. Quinn watched the Ninth Portent spin in reverse, then come to a stop as Piper un-inserted the tape from the player, putting it back in its box.

Almost there now. Quinn braced for the usual jolt as she re-joined the timeline.

As the last note chimed, however, Quinn realised that something was different. Time was slowing again, coming to a stop – but she was still frozen outside of it, unable to move.

For an instant, time stopped completely. She was just inside the door to the viewing room, Maggie ahead of her. The top of the Ninth's cube was only just visible from this angle.

What... what was happening?!

Quinn's mind was racing as something else began to happen. The song... the song was playing again! But now, it was playing forwards. And, adrenaline coursing through her veins, Quinn could only watch helplessly as time began move forwards again – rapidly.

At double speed, she watched herself move up to the glass and watched Piper talk to the Portent through the microphone. Piper once again put on the tape.

What was going on?! Why was she going forwards? How far would it go? Would it ever stop?!

Panic gripping her, she tried to move out of the course she'd already taken – but it was impossible. Her body had already done this before and now, she would walk the exact same path.

She tried to scream as Professor Latrobe came in through the door but she couldn't even make a sound. The Professor and Piper yelled at each other and the Professor went over to turn off the tape –

With a feeling like hitting a wall at 60km/h, Quinn crashed into the timeline.

It was the exact same instant she'd left it. Her legs gave way and, winded, she collapsed to the floor.

Her bones hurt and she couldn't breathe. In her mind, the tape was still playing, on to the end of the song. But it couldn't take her with it. That future was one she hadn't chosen yet.

Dimly, she saw the others react, turning in shock to see what had happened. She tried to open her mouth, to say anything, but only spit dribbled out.

'What in the –?' Professor Latrobe said, very far away. 'What is wrong with her? Is she having a seizure?!'

Maggie swore and ran to Quinn's side, turning her onto her side. 'Quinn, can you hear me?' she was calling. 'Quinn, please respond! What just happened?'

Finally, Quinn managed to breathe, gasping in air like a drowning woman – but things were getting even worse now – much, MUCH worse. Oh God. Oh fuck. Why had she tried to reverse time here? She was an idiot. She was a FUCKING IDIOT. Every nerve in her body was screaming, telling to run, run, RUN NOW –

With a gurling cry, she thrashed out of Maggie's grasp, rolling onto her hands and knees. Terror driving her, she crawled for the door. Behind her, she could feel it breaking, one small crack becoming larger and larger. She tried to stand up but failed, collapsing again. Her stomach heaved and she threw up onto the concrete, drool dripping from her nose and mouth.

On the floor in front of her, the vomit bubbled and then rose up into the air in a series of liquid droplets.

'What –' Maggie said.

The corners of Maggie's jacket were lifting into the air, as were her braids. Next to her, Piper and Professor Latrobe looked around in surprise as the laptop and cassette player tumbled up off the desk.

In dawning horror, they all turned to look at the containment chamber.

An alarm began wailing.

'I BROKE IT!' Quinn screamed from the floor. 'I BROKE THE FUCKING RELIC CAGE! NINA'S GETTING OUT! RUN! RUN! RUUUUUUUN!'

# CHAPTER 43

# GRAVITY

### Date: Friday 31 January 2082

The burst of unreality following Quinn's violent re-entry to the CMT had lasted no longer than a fraction of a second. But that instant had been long enough, and strong enough, to disrupt the cage, tipping the balance in the wrong direction. The Ninth Portent's 106m radius was instantaneously restored – and local gravity immediately began to fuck up.

Wordlessly, Maggie hauled Quinn upright, flinging her over her shoulder like she weighed nothing – which was becoming truer by the second. Behind them, Professor Latrobe, closer to the Portent and slower on the uptake, yelled in fear as his feet left the ground.

As he began to tumble towards the ceiling, kicking and flailing, Piper grabbed his foot, pulling him after her like a human balloon. She didn't get far before her own feet left the ground. She was joined moments later by Maggie and Quinn, and all of the furniture.

Grabbing the doorframe, Maggie hauled herself out of the room, hitting into the corridor wall and kicking off it like a swimmer. Ahead, Ryan was yelling at Kevin, who was cowering in shock, to get up and run.

Piper followed Maggie's lead, launching off the wall, Professor Latrobe in tow. As they got further down the hall, the gravity began to restore and they touched back down to the ground, leaping like moonwalkers.

'What the fuck happened?!' Ryan yelled over the wailing siren, dragging Kevin out of the office. 'How did it get out?!'

Maggie glanced at Quinn, who was still in a state of shock and could only stare back blankly.

'We'll figure that out later!' she yelled back. 'Right now, we need to get out of here! Everyone follow me!'

As she paused to open the door towards the exit, there was a loud shattering noise behind them. The window of the observation room burst, shards flying up towards the ceiling. Inside the containment chamber itself, relics were detaching from the cage one by one, rocketing upwards and bouncing away.

'Shit,' Piper said. 'It's getting stronger!'

'Shhh!' Maggie hissed. 'No noise!'

They hurried down the hall towards the exit, heavier with each step. Around them, the walls were creaking alarmingly and dust had started to drift down from the corners.

As Maggie opened the door to the stairwell, the lights suddenly flickered and went out, casting them all into pitch darkness. At the same time there was another loud crash.

It was followed by an eerie calm. The siren had cut out with the lights.

Quinn squeaked in terror as she felt the Ninth Portent shifting, power radiating through the pitch darkness like ink-black waves beating her into the rocks. In the distance, there was a soft pattering noise, like rain or light hail.

Gravity began to decrease again.

Someone began to panic, kicking in the dark. 'We need to keep going!' Kevin's said, his voice sharp with fear. 'We need to go, we need TO GO NOW!'

'Shut up!' Ryan hissed through his teeth. 'It can hear –'

The lights abruptly came back on, as some sort of backup system activated. Wordlessly, they scrambled onwards, hurrying for the exit.

The stairs were made of thin metal, and rang like a bell as six people began their ascent. As gravity sharply decreased again, Piper halted and held up her hand, signalling for everyone to stop moving.

Around them, the building was groaning and creaking. The pattering noise had gotten louder, heavier, like the thud of falling bricks.

'Why are we stopping?!' Professor Latrobe hissed, his eyes wild.

'SHUSH!' Maggie said. 'Quiet!'

Carefully, Piper took a step, half floating into the air and coming down gently a few stairs further up, her weight tapping only lightly on the metal.

Nodding at the others, she went up again and the others imitated her, moving quietly upwards.

For a time, it seemed to be working. Six flights of stairs to go. Five. Four... But even as they gained height, gravity wasn't getting any stronger. In fact, if anything, it was getting weaker and weaker...

Quinn took a step and didn't come back down, floating towards the underside of the next set of stairs. Before she could say anything, there was an almighty CRASH from somewhere above them and the entire building shook.

'The elevator!' Maggie hissed.

As they all clung to the ceiling, scrambling along it like flies, there was the loud groaning of metal and a piece of the stairs flew up through the centre of the well, rocketing into the ceiling.

Heart racing, Quinn pulled herself up over the lip of the stairs and floated up to the next one. As she did so, she glanced down through the centre of the stairs, down to the very bottom.

The lights were flickering, alternating pitch black and stark white. In the flashes, she saw it – the Ninth Portent, floating there, gazing up with its blind, stone face.

It started to rise.

Quinn let out a small scream and let go of the stairs, letting herself float up faster. Below, the stairs were breaking apart and tumbling upwards, metal poles and wedgelike sheets, razor sharp if they hit on the right angle.

The walls were breaking as well, bricks peeling away and shooting up into the empty elevator shaft. As a massive chunk of wall broke off beside her, Quinn caught sight of the night sky above, stars twinkling coldly.

The elevator had been propelled upwards and, heavy as it was, had ripped through the roof of the small shed, creating a hole into the endless sky. If they fell through that...

'Hold on to the wall!' Maggie yelled, abandoning silence as the stairs began to disintegrate around them. 'HOLD ON FOR DEAR LIFE –'

She broke off with a yelp as a chunk of stair crashed into the wall next to her, bouncing off and tumbling away into the sky. Near her, Professor Latrobe scrabbled for purchase on the bricks and missed. He screamed as he lost grip and flew upwards, smacking into what had been the floor of the shed.

For a second, it held. Then, silently, it snapped off. Quinn caught sight of his pale face, eyes wide in terror, and then he was gone.

Kevin was screaming as well, clutching at a pipe that was groaning alarmingly under his weight. Next to him, Ryan was pressed flat to the wall, knuckles white as he gripped onto a tiny ledge.

Maggie and Piper were holding onto each other, Maggie holding onto a support beam with her other hand, Piper wedged into a crack that was growing wider by the second. Quinn grabbed onto an electrical cable, tied onto the wall with nothing more than a series of pins. As she watched, one of the pins came loose and she jolted further upwards.

By now, the stairwell and elevator shaft had become one giant, pitch dark, empty hole, debris tumbling upwards through it at an ever-increasing speed. The Ninth Portent was closing in. Quinn could barely breathe, her heart pounding, threatening to rip itself out of her chest.

Another of the pins came loose and she jolted upwards again, floating out over the abyss. Below her, something was moving, rising towards her –

The Ninth came to a stop just metres below her, glinting in the starlight. Quinn's pulse was roaring in her ears. It was so close. The unreality was almost unbearable. Her mind became static, as the walls of the elevator shaft lost their meaning, nothing but lines, connections, polarised charge and empty space. Void above and void below, and chaos all around. Nothing was real. The cable wasn't real, jittering in and out of focus, three of it at once and then none at all. Her hands weren't real and she wasn't either. Maybe she never had been?

'Nina,' a voice said.

The syllables crashed into her like weight. Meaning. Familiarity. A name. Below, a shifting, rotation towards the sound.

'Hi, Nina,' the voice said carefully. 'Do you... do you remember? It's me, Piper.'

Yes, Piper, Quinn thought. How had she forgotten that?

'Nina,' Piper went on. 'I need you to listen to me. I know you don't really understand my words. But maybe you'll understand the tone? I need you to leave, Nina. If you stay here, we'll die. I love you Nina – but you have to go now.'

The Portent rotated around itself, but it did not move away. Kevin whimpered as his pipe began to bend and he slipped towards the end of it.

'Please, Nina,' Piper said, her voice shaking. 'I'm begging you to do as I say, just this once!'

'She won't,' Maggie said. 'I'm sorry, Piper. She isn't a person. You need to stop talking to her. If we're quiet, maybe she'll go away?'

'We should sing to her,' Quinn said dazedly.

'What?' Maggie said.

'She isn't going to leave,' Quinn said. 'Not while we're still here. But if there's music... I might be able to...'

'You're sure you're up to it?' Maggie said.

'There are five of us,' Quinn said, ignoring Maggie's question. 'Five layers. If we sing for three minutes, that's more than twenty minutes restored!'

'What is she talking about?!' Piper said.

'Quinn is a timesmith,' Maggie said briefly. 'She might be able to fix this. But we all need to sing!'

'Now?!' Piper gasped. Nearby, Kevin squeaked again as he slipped further down the pipe.

'Yes, now!' Maggie said. 'Look, the Portent is already right here! We might as well try!'

'I'm not fucking singing!' Ryan yelled from where he was hanging onto a tiny ledge, legs up towards the sky. 'Are you insane?!'

'Sing or die!' Maggie yelled back. 'Your choice!'

'What's something we all know?' Quinn said, watching in deathly calm as another pin came loose. 'Is there anything? A children's rhyme maybe? Row row row your boat?'

'Let's go with that!' Maggie yelled, and she went right into it. 'ROW ROW ROW YOUR BOAT, GENTLY DOWN THE STREAM!'

'MERRILY MERRILY MERRILY MERRILY,' Piper joined in, her voice strangled.

'LIFE IS BUT A DREA-ARGH!' Kevin squawked, slipping again.

'KEEP GOING UNTIL YOU CAN'T HOLD ON ANYMORE!' Quinn yelled and then began singing as well, starting when the others were halfway through to make it a round. Ryan was last to join in, his voice uncertain, muffled as he sang into the wall.

Around Quinn, unreality was shifting, vibrating with sound. Below her, the Portent was spinning again.

Is this why they like it? Quinn wondered, watching the chaos dance. Meaning, where there was none. Time arranged in patterns and pressed upon the world in waves. Equal parts precision and feeling. Kevin was barely holding on now, knuckles white around the smooth metal. Ryan was tiring too, his arms shaking. Piper was not holding onto anything except Maggie anymore, Maggie's beam supporting them both.

There were only two more pins holding Quinn in place. One more pin. And that last one was coming loose...

Kevin lost grip of the pipe. Screaming, he tumbled away into the empty sky.

*Row row row your boat,*

Moments later, Ryan dropped as well, silent as he went. For a moment, he managed to grab onto the lip of the roof – and then he was gone.

*Gently down the stream,*

The others kept on singing until Quinn's last pin came loose. As the cable detached from the wall, she felt the rush of air and saw Maggie's face, eyes wide, disappearing into the dark of the pit.

*Merrily merrily merrily merrily,*

She kept on singing. She had to get further away from the Ninth anyway. The interference was too strong. She passed the edge of the roof and fell upwards, past upside-down trees and buildings, with nothing but star-spangled void to greet her below...

*Life is but a dream.*

Gravity reduced, and then started to come back.

Quinn reached for the music.

It was just her singing now, just one voice suspended amongst the stars. But that was enough to set the events in motion. The music still played backwards, and when it reached a point where there were more voices, it took Quinn with it. Back down she went, gathering speed as Ryan and Kevin's voices re-joined the chorus.

Numbly, Quinn watched the Ninth Portent retreat back into the pit and the walls reassemble themselves in its wake. The stairs came back, folding into place, and Quinn watched herself travel back down into the dark, shadows shifting with the flicking lights below.

Downstairs, the Ninth Portent's cage once more closed in around it. Cracks sealed and dust sucked back up into the corners. Relics flung themselves back into place. Maggie carried Quinn back into the observation room.

Then, for the second time, Quinn watched Professor Latrobe yell at Piper, and Piper and Maggie dance, out of time with the song that was currently playing. She was getting nervous now. How much longer would it go back? Would the same thing happen? Was she doomed to unleash the Portent again?

But no... no... she was leaving the room. She was leaving the room and going back up the corridor. Time was starting to slow again, but she was getting further away. Would it be far enough? Would it be far enough?!

They passed by Ryan and Kevin in their office and Piper unlocked the door. There was only two singing now – and then one.

Quinn froze in place as Maggie's voice alone carried on. This was it, then. This was where she discovered if their efforts had been enough...

With a gasp, she fell back to the timeline and her knees buckled. Her heart was racing already, fight or flight response galvanising her back to her feet, feeling ahead for the terrible implosion she felt sure was about to happen...

'Holy FUCKING shit,' Maggie said.

Quinn blinked.

The Portent hadn't reacted. They'd done it! They were far enough away!

But Maggie was holding onto the wall, gasping for breath, barely upright. And next to her, Piper had her hands on her knees, face as white as chalk.

'As long as I live,' Piper said queasily. 'I NEVER want to experience that again!'

Quinn frowned.

'Wait,' she said. 'Did... do you remember–?'

'Remember running away from Nina and almost dying?' Maggie said. 'Yep. Sure do!'

'Why, is that not normal?' Piper asked faintly.

'No,' Quinn said, staring at them. 'No, it is not.'

# CHAPTER 44

# THETA

### Date: Friday 13 March 2082

'To find a sat tracker,' the Detective said, 'we need to think like a sat tracker.'

They were sitting in the passenger seat of the paddy wagon while Bill drove them back towards Ouyen. It was evening and the headlights illuminated the road ahead beneath a glowing sunset sky.

'What does that mean?' Bill said absently, eyes on the road.

'Satellite tracking is a notoriously mobile profession,' the Detective said. 'If it is indeed a sat tracker we are chasing, then finding them will be no small task. They have no permanent address and often travel hundreds of kilometres week to week. Our sat tracker could be literally anywhere in the Nation.

'Thus,' they went on, when Bill said nothing, 'we need to go about this intelligently. First of all, we must ask ourselves, what does a satellite tracker want? What drives them? What motivates them to get up in the morning?'

'Satellites,' Bill said dryly.

'Exactly,' the Detective said. 'They want to find fallen satellites, to dismantle them and sell the parts – and they want to find them before anyone else does. Now, in order to do this, it is my understanding that trackers often rely on predictive software, which is able to calculate the most likely place for a satellite to fall. The program uses a combination of orbital decay algorithms and visual data, often gathered by the sat trackers themselves, and jealously guarded within the trade. It is not one hundred per cent accurate, but allows the tracker get close enough and claim the satellite once it falls.'

'Mmm,' Bill said.

'Therefore,' the Detective continued, 'in order to find a sat tracker, I believe we must ourselves become sat trackers, temporarily. We must scour the sky for the most likely landfall and make our way to that location. There, we will undoubtedly find others in the trade – and with luck, one of them will be, or at least know of, our suspected timesmith.'

'Right,' Bill said. 'So, uh. How do we find a falling satellite?'

'Well, my onboard systems are perfectly capable of performing the orbital decay calculations,' the Detective said. 'However... the visual data is an issue. Telescopic vision was not included as part of my design and I do not possess a telescope, nor know the location of one.'

'A telescope, huh?' Bill said. 'Oh! I actually might have a solution to that.'

The Detective cocked their head, looking at him.

'It's a long story,' Bill said, 'but basically, one of my previous jobs also involved trying to find a Portent. Unlike our Twelfth, which it turns out probably doesn't exist, I knew this one had to be somewhere. So, in order to find it, I visited several DOU monitoring stations. One of the stations I went to specialised in monitoring the Eleventh which, as you know, is in outer space. It wasn't the one I was looking for, but they were still extremely helpful. Ended up pointing me in the right direction. Anyway, what I'm trying to say is that Monitoring Station Theta has a telescope and actually isn't too far away from here.'

'Where is it?' the Detective said.

'Mount Arapiles,' Bill said. 'I'd say a three-hour drive at most?'

'That is well within an acceptable timeframe,' the Detective said. 'However, I am concerned that that telescope is not open for public use.'

'That's alright,' Bill said. 'Like I said, I know them and they're very friendly. I'm sure they'll be glad to help.'

'How sure are you?' the Detective said. 'If asked you to give a percentage?'

'Ninety per cent,' Bill said. 'Ninety-five, even. Look, I'll give them a call tomorrow morning to make sure, if it makes you feel better.'

'Can you not call them now?' the Detective said.

'No!' Bill sent the Detective a look. 'They're not open now! We're not such good friends that I can call them just when they're going to bed. That would be rude!'

'Alright,' the Detective said. 'I was simply covering all options. There is no need to get worked up. I simply do not wish to waste time driving three hours unless we are certain the telescope is usable.'

'I'll call them,' Bill said again. 'First thing tomorrow. Well... 9AM. Any earlier and they might not be there yet.'

'I suppose that will have to do,' the Detective said.

***

At 9AM the following morning, Bill made the phone call while the Detective watched him intently.

'Hello,' he said into the receiver. 'Is Gabriella there? Oh, fantastic! Tell her it's Bill calling. Bill from – Oh, you remember me? Ha ha. Yeah, that's me alright. Oh, yeah, it's going really well! Um, can't talk about that now though, got ol' double-oh-seven in the car with me, breathing down my neck. Yeah! Well, if I come by later today, we can talk then! Yep, see ya!'

He paused, winking at the Detective. 'Told you they were friendly,' he said with a grin, and then turned away, phone at his ear. 'Hi Gabbie,' he said.

The Detective listened impatiently as he exchanged pleasantries with the person on the other end before eventually asking if they could use the telescope. Shortly, he gave the Detective a thumbs up and they immediately turned the key in the paddy wagon engine.

Moments later, Bill waved at them to turn it off again.

'Wait, wait!' he said. 'Gabbie says she already has a bunch of recent satellite data! It might save us the trip! Hang on...'

He put the phone on the loudspeaker, leaning over it. 'Can you still hear me?' he said.

'Yes,' a crackly voice came through.

'Okay – can you say what you just said again?'

'We routinely gather satellite data,' Gabriella said, 'since the Eleventh interacts with satellites, it's relevant to our continual monitoring. In fact, we have a field agent out there chasing satellites as we speak! Anyway, if you want the data, we can send it to you directly! It'll be raw, so you'll need access to a computer to both receive it and decipher it, but it's better than driving three hours just to look at the same thing on a screen here.'

'Computer access is no issue,' the Detective said. 'I have an onboard computer. Provided the file is not too large, I can also analyse it in situ.'

The person on the other side of the phone let out a small, excited squeak.

'Is, is that –'

'Yes, that's the Detective,' Bill said quickly.

'Oh my goodness,' Gabriella said. 'Sorry, I just... I never thought... Bill told me all about you! I never thought I'd actually get to talk to you! Never in a million years!'

'Yes, well, moving on,' Bill said loudly. 'How large is this data file? Will we need special software to decode it?'

As Gabriella went into detail about the file, the Detective listened and took mental notes on the software required – but a part of their computing power was busy elsewhere. This Gabriella person... why did she know about the Detective? As far as the Detective knew, Bill had never contacted her before – certainly not within the last week. And yet, she had sounded so excited just to exchange a few words.

Did she know the Detective? Did she know Bill? Were Bill and her much closer than he'd made out? Or did he just tell everyone he knew about the Detective? That didn't come across as particularly professional, if true...

'Did you get all that?' Bill addressed the Detective, snapping them out of their musings.

'Yes,' the Detective said. 'It will be no problem. I have an inbuilt email address. Would you like me to give it to you so that you may send the data directly?'

'Yes, please!' Gabriella said excitedly.

The Detective recited it to her, and shortly, the file arrived in their inbox. The Detective immediately opened it and got to work in the background.

'I have received the data,' they said aloud. 'Thank you. This has been extremely helpful.'

'You're welcome!' Gabriella said, her grin almost visible through the phone. 'Happy to help anytime! If you're ever in the area, in your shiny metal bod, come and say hello! Only with your bod though, I'd better not see you without _'

Bill turned the phone off loudspeaker.

'Alright, well, we should be going!' he said loudly. 'Lots of data to analyse, satellites to chase, etcetera!'

The Detective frowned as Bill hurriedly wrapped up the call and hung up.

'Gabriella seems to know me,' they said as Bill put the phone away.

'Hmm,' Bill said, looking elsewhere. 'I suppose you could say that. She knew, um... one of your previous iterations.'

'My previous iterations?' the Detective said curiously.

'Yes, but you wouldn't remember that,' Bill said. 'And please don't try to. For the love of God.'

'Why not?'

'I can't tell you,' Bill said. 'Look, remember when I said there was some information that if you knew it, would alter the outcome of the experiment? This is part of that information.'

'EX025,' the Detective said thoughtfully. 'I'm the twenty

fifth iteration, then. What happened to the others before me?'

'They asked too many questions,' Bill said through his teeth. Then he sighed.

'Look,' he said, 'one way or another, the previous iterations had issues. Something went wrong and we had to go back to drawing board. It doesn't matter what went wrong – what matters is that you are the most recent version and the most perfect so far. Just keep doing what you're doing and maybe, once the trial period is over, I will tell you more. But for the time being, you must be content in knowing there are some things you can't know. It's for your own good, okay?'

The Detective was not all content with this answer. But if Bill said it... Bill, who they were just now realising, they knew almost nothing about. Bill, who had not said where he was from or who he worked for. Bill, whose surname they didn't even know... if Bill even was his real first name...

'Okay,' they said, face neutral.

But underneath, they were boiling with curiosity. That electricity at their core was crackling, darting and flickering like serpent tongues, filling them with wild thoughts and possibilities. And in that moment, without even planning to, they created a new entry in their case file.

*Priority: determine the true identity of 'Bill' and his involvement in the experiment of which I am the twenty-fifth iteration.*

THE ELEVENTH PORTENT


FIRST RECORDED SIGHTING: 08/03/2076, 1730 km
above Canberra, Ngunnawal country, ACT.

PHYSICAL APPEARANCE:

The Eleventh Portent is a non-geosynchronous
Earth satellite with an erratic, highly
elliptical orbit. It resembles a typical
communications satellite bus, with two
symmetrical solar panel arrays and three
satellite dishes of varying sizes (1.8m,
1.2m, and 80cm diameter). The logo of an
unknown company, incorporating a five-pointed
star and the letters 'S' and 'C', can be seen
stamped multiple times across its exterior.

The satellite continuously transmits an
analogue video signal within the C band (4-
8GHz). This silent video feed, which appears
to be 'live' and from the perspective of the
satellite itself, is thought to originate
within the satellite – however, studies are
ongoing to confirm this information beyond
doubt.

Due to the satellite's erratic orbit,
capturing its signal has proven challenging,
but not impossible. Below are listed some
notable examples of imagery captured thus
far:

- A red-giant star replacing, or perhaps the

evolution of, the sun, approximately 180 million kilometres in radius.

- The Earth, with continents arranged in previously unknown configurations.

- The Earth, with extensive volcanic activity.

- The Earth, seemingly entirely engulfed by the Second Portent.

- The appearance of a pulsar, orbiting the sun at a distance of 92 million kilometres (between Mercury and Venus). The pulsar displayed an irregular spin which, when analysed, was found to correspond precisely to Pi at approximately 900 billion figures past the decimal point.

- Multiple thin, kilometre-long metallic structures of unknown function and origin, suspended at mid Earth orbit.

- The appearance of a rotating, non-reflective tetrahedron at an unknown distance, visible only as it passed in front of stars. It was unknown whether the tetrahedron was small and close to the point of observation, or very distant and unimaginably vast.

- Darkness with only three red stars visible.

Note - It is unknown whether the imagery transmitted by the Eleventh Portent depicts a real, potential, or completely fictional, scenario.

Note 2 - researchers are advised that viewing

footage from the Eleventh Portent for longer than half an hour has been documented to result in headache, blurry vision, and feelings of paranoia.

BEHAVIOUR:

The Eleventh Portent travels on a highly elliptical orbit and can be found anywhere between 460 km and 74,000 km away from the Earth. Its orbit is erratic and non-geosynchronous, with point of perigee and orbital inclination changing frequently. On multiple occasions, it has been observed colliding with other satellites, disrupting their orbit and contributing to the accelerating decay of satellite-reliant systems such as GPS.

The scenes transmitted by the Eleventh Portent change every 58 hours on average, and are not always possible to observe, dependant on the Portent's position relative to Earth-bound receivers, as well as interference from weather and alternative microwave sources. It has been hypothesized that a far cleaner, more consistent signal could be obtained from a receiver that was placed in low orbit – however, the costs associated with reinstating a national space program in order to launch such a study are prohibitively high, especially as there are those who are not convinced the Eleventh Portent deserves its title, and may in fact be nothing more than an elaborate hoax.

HENDEKON RADIATION:

On multiple occasions, high energy particles thought to originate from the Eleventh Portent have been observed interacting with the Earth's upper atmosphere. The exact properties of these particles, dubbed Hendekon Radiation, are largely unknown; however, they are evidently able to interact with CMT matter – an interaction that results in the instantaneous and violent dissolution of both particles into their subatomic constituents.

The DOU hypothesizes that satellites that have interacted with the Eleventh Portent should also show damage associated with Hendekon Radiation. However, to date, no direct evidence has been acquired by the Department.

PORTENT INDUCED UNREALITY SYMPTOMS:

Due to its location, there are no existing realitysmiths of the Eleventh. It is unknown what abilities, if any, would develop in a theoretical smith of this type.

# SATELITE TRACKERS

**Date: Saturday 14 March 2082**

t was just after midday, the sun high in a cloudless blue sky, when Calidore Fang and associate, professional satellite trackers, pulled up in the middle of an overgrown field of grass.

They arrived in a blue van that, while shabby and noticeably second-hand, was perfectly up to code. Despite the heat, Mx Fang was wearing long-sleeves and a large pair of sunglasses over their faintly glowing blue eyes. The associate, meanwhile, was wearing a Hawaiian shirt, with tiny dolphins leaping into rolling waves.

After cutting the engine, Mx Fang took a moment to scan the field, taking in the terrain. 'It seems,' they said momentarily, 'that we are not the first ones here.'

'What?' Associate Bill said, peering out the window through his own oversized pair of sunglasses. 'Where?'

'Two-o-clock, three hundred and forty metres,' Fang said. 'A van. Eight-o-clock, five hundred metres, what seems to be a converted bus. And four-o-clock, five-hundred and sixty metres. An RV.'

'That's good, right?' Bill said.

'Yes,' Fang said. 'They are exactly who we're here to see. Although we cannot let them know that, as we are undercover!'

'That's right,' Bill said. 'Although please stop saying that. You're going to ruin it.'

'Obviously, I will stay "in character" when a suspect is

within earshot,' Fang said. 'I am Calidore Fang, satellite tracker! I am new to the field, but excited by the thrill of the chase and potential treasures to be found with each landing! Satellites and finding them are my one passion in life! I do not care that the profession notoriously draws scammers, sinners and general ne'er-do-wellers and I am statistically likely to be arrested at least once before the age of twenty-five!'

Bill rubbed his face. 'They're going to figure it out immediately,' he muttered. 'Hey, Detec... uh, Mx Fang, maybe I should do most of the talking?'

'Would that not be even more suspicious?' the Detective said.

'Not if you play the strong, silent type,' Bill said. 'You know, just stand there, looking menacing and not speaking a word? That way they might think you're just hired muscle and won't ask questions.'

'Perhaps you are right,' the Detective said, cocking their head. 'How might I go about looking "menacing"?'

'Oh, just act like you normally do,' Bill said. 'It's already pretty scary. If anyone addresses you, just give them that blank, shop-dummy stare that you do when processing things. They'll leave you alone immediately.'

'I assume you are referring to my neutral expression,' the Detective said. 'I was not aware that it was frightening. It was not designed to be so.'

'It's just uncanny, is all,' Bill said. 'No way around it. Anyway – no talking, got it? Monosyllabic answers and only when directly addressed. Okay?'

'Yes,' the Detective said, neutral expression in place.

'Perfect,' Bill said. 'You're a natural. Okay, let's go.'

They opened their respective doors and stepped out into the long grass. After getting his bearings, Bill set off immediately towards the nearest sat-tracker vehicle, the Detective close behind him.

The van in question turned out to be an ancient Mr Whippy truck, complete with an oversized plastic ice-cream cone on the roof. The paint was chipped and badly faded, although colourful graphics of various ice-creams, hotdogs and cold beverages were still visible along the flanks.

The entire thing looked about as aerodynamic as a pile of bricks and was only barely up to code on soundproofing – but the Detective stifled the urge to say anything as they approached.

A man was visible through the front windshield, sitting and drinking a beer with his feet up on the dash. He was thin and wiry in build, Caucasian, with a cropped red beard under a threadbare Roosters cap. It was probably a weak relic, or had been at one point, although it was now quite stained and damaged.

As Bill and the Detective got closer, he got out of his seat and disappeared into the back of the van. A moment later, the service window at the side rolled open and he stuck his head out.

'Can I help youse?' he called.

As the Detective struggled not to reprimand him for talking outside, Bill nodded at the man in a friendly fashion.

*Afternoon,* he signed. *Sorry to bother you. But we have a few hours before the satellite arrives. Would you be interested in passing the time with a board game?*

This strategy had been Bill's idea. The direct approach, Bill said, was too risky. If they simply walked up to the satellite trackers and asked for information, chances were they would spook the suspects and learn nothing. On the other hand, if they approached with a friendly request for a couple of beers over a game, there would be far more opportunities to casually ask questions.

The Detective hadn't been entirely sold on the idea. The direct approach, in their experience, had worked perfectly fine up until now. Bill had reminded them, however, that they were attempting to catch a timesmith. They were going to have to be a lot more subtle about it from now on, and close the trap before the smith even realised it was there.

The first step to this was figuring out if any of the sat

trackers present were a smith at all – and initially, it was looking like this first suspect wasn't. He was wearing a relic, for one, and when he opened the window, the Detective spotted several more weak relics inside. They couldn't be fakes, either. Any object that sufficiently resembled a relic was a relic itself.

Still, even if this man was not himself the timesmith they were after, there was a chance he knew who was. The sat tracker industry was, after all, small and highly competitive. Everyone in it knew everyone else, as their direct competition and/or mortal enemies.

The man in the ice-cream truck, however, looked interested when Bill mentioned board games.

*What sort of game?* he signed.

*We have Jenga,* Bill signed.

There was a pause.

*That it?* the man said.

*Yes.* Bill shrugged. *Sorry. We were hoping other people might have more.*

The man scratched his chin. *I have a game of chess,* he signed, *but it's a relic, so I'd rather not use it. Also, its only two-player.* His eyes flickered to the Detective.

*Hopefully the others will have something then,* Bill signed cheerfully.

The man narrowed his eyes.

*You're inviting the others?*

*I was going to, yes,* Bill said. *Is that an issue?*

*Can't trust those bastards,* the man said.

*You know them?*

*Course I know them.* The man leaned forward. *That flaming bitch over there.* He pointed towards the bus. *That's Jillaroo. A right piece of work, she is. Stab you in the back as soon as look at you. And I don't mean metaphorically.*

He pointed to the RV. *The shithead over that way is Dingo,* he said. *Puts forward this chill, easy-going persona, but don't fall for it, it's a fuckin' lie. He's slippery as a snake and cunning as a rat. You gotta keep an eye on him.*

*I'll keep it in mind,* Bill said. *Appreciate it – we're new here, so we need all the help we can get! I'm Bill, by the way. And that's Mx Fang.*

*Folks call me Doc Scurvy.* The man grinned and he reached out to shake Bill's hand. *Sat tracker, relixorcist and brewer of artisan beer!*

*Really?* Bill said. *Is that the artisan beer you're drinking now?*

*It is.* Doc Scurvy grinned – and he began going into detail.

While Bill nodded along and feigned interest remarkably well, the Detective shifted impatiently from foot to foot. The fact that this man claimed to be relixorcist and seemed to at the very least believe it himself, absolutely ruled him out as a suspect. Relixorcists had to prove that they owned a certain number of relics before they could even complete the licence paperwork. There was no way a roguesmith would go to that much effort just to cover up.

That meant Doc Scurvy was not a suspect – and therefore, not of primary interest. There were still two more suspects to interview – and only two hours before the satellite landed.

As Bill began asking where Doc Scurvy bought his hops, the Detective noticed movement far in the distance. As it got closer, they saw it was yet another vehicle – a nute this time, with a government logo on the bonnet.

The Detective waved at Bill to draw his attention and then pointed across at it. Bill and Doc Scurvy both looked and Scurvy made a face.

*Fuck sake,* he signed, *it's that scientist again.*

Bill looked at him questioningly.

*Department goon, always running around with their scientific doohickie-whirly-bob and getting in the way,* Scurvy explained. *Aubrey, I think they're called.*

Bill sent the Detective a quick look. Clearly, he had come to the same conclusion that this scientist was probably the same field agent that Gabriella from Monitoring Station Theta had mentioned over the phone.

*Are fall sites usually this busy?* Bill asked.

*No.* Scurvy scowled. *This is well busier than average. Whole fucking circus is here today. No offence.*

*None taken,* Bill said and he stepped away from the window.

*Anyway,* he said brightly, *if we want our game of Jenga anytime soon, I'd better go and talk to the others. But don't worry – I'll keep in mind what you said about them!*

He tapped his nose conspiratorially and Doc Scurvy grinned, displaying a row of crooked teeth.

*You're alright, mate,* he said. *Hey, but where should I go for the game?*

*Blue van over there.* Bill pointed. *I'll set up a table in half an hour or so.*

Doc Scurvy nodded, rolling closed the window, and Bill struck off towards the next closest vehicle. The Detective stalked after him, falling into step.

*He is not our suspect,* they signed subtly, once they were a bit further away.

*I thought the same,* Bill replied. *But he might still know something. By the way, good job staying in character!*

*I didn't do anything.* The Detective frowned.

*Yes, exactly,* Bill said. *That can't have been easy for you! Anyway, shush now, here's the next one.*

He plastered a friendly smile on his face as they approached the redecorated bus. It was covered roof to hubcaps in leopard-print decals and most of the windows were tinted, with a sticker on the back window that said If You Can Read This, Fuck Off.

As Bill went around to knock on the side door, it abruptly opened and a woman stepped out, Caucasian with dirty-blonde hair, wearing a faded jean jacket and a Stetson. She closed the door behind her and then folded her arms, looking at Bill with distinct hostility.

'Wha'd'ya want?' she said.

*Hello,* Bill signed. *Name's Bill. I'm new in the business and just walking around to meet the neighbours, as it were. Are you interested in a game of Jenga to pass the time?*

'Is HE gonna be there?' The woman jutted her chin towards Doc Scurvy's van.

*Yes,* Bill said. *Is that an issue?*

The woman scowled.

*He's a fuckin' ratbag,* she signed. *Thinks he's top shit, with his fancy-schmancy 'artisan' beers. Taste like horse piss, but he won't hear none of that. Can't take any criticism, fuckin' man-child that he is.*

*It sounds like you know him pretty well,* Bill said.

*Yeah, well, we dated for a year.* The woman shrugged. *I was the one who gave him the idea of makin' beer in the first place, y'know? Bet he didn't tell you that, did he?*

*Can't say he did,* Bill said.

*Yeah, that's right.* The woman scowled. *Never gives me any credit for anything. You know, half of the shit he owns used to be mine? He was a fuckin' slob when I first moved in with him, had like, three bits of furniture to his name. Felt sorry for him and bought a bunch of new stuff, out of my own pocket and the kindness of my heart. Next thing you know, he's run off with that spider fucker and taken all my shit with him. Well, he can keep it. Bet it smells like piss now anyway.*

She paused, glaring across the field.

*What's this about Jenga?* she said.

*We're playing,* Bill said. *If you're interested in joining in, come over to the blue van in twenty minutes or so. I'll be setting up a table.*

*Right,* the woman said.

Without another word she turned around and went back into her bus.

Bill looked at the Detective with a bemused expression.

*Thoughts?* he signed, as they began making their way over to the RV.

*It seems that she and Doc Scurvy lived together for a time,* the Detective signed back. *If Doc Scurvy was in possession of his relics during this period, then this makes her an unlikely candidate for our roguesmith. However, it is possible that the relics, or her smith abilities, are a recent acquisition...*

*I personally don't think it's her,* Bill said. *But you're right – the hard evidence is currently inconclusive.*

The Detective nodded. *Inconclusive,* they agreed.

They headed over to the next vehicle, the RV. On first impression, the RV looked better kept than the other two vehicles they'd seen, with a recent coat of paint and only small amounts of caked on dust and grime. A muscular man with full sleeve tattoos and a tank top bearing the First Nations flag was sitting outside of it on a fluoro-orange deck chair.

As Bill and the Detective drew near, he lifted his aviator shades and sent them a curious look.

*Hello,* Bill signed at him. *We're asking around if anyone wants to play Jenga while we wait for the satellite. Would you be interested in joining?*

The man sat up slowly, looking Bill up and down before staring at the Detective for several seconds.

*You're new here, aren't you?* he signed.

*Yes,* Bill said. *How could you tell?*

*There's sort of an unspoken code, amongst satellite trackers,* the man said. *It's called Always Be A Cunt To Each Other. Quite self-explanatory, really. But, see, what you're doing here is being nice instead. It's very strange and upsetting and it clearly marks you as an outsider.*

Bill nodded. *I see,* he said. *Well, there's always time to be rude later. We can be nice for one afternoon, surely?*

*I suppose we can give it a good old college try,* the man said with a grin.

He stood up and went to shake Bill's hand.

*Name's Dingo,* he signed cheerfully, and then turned to look at the Detective again.

*Fuckin' hell, you're tall,* he said. *Don't meet many people taller than I am. What are you, seven foot?*

*I am currently six foot eight,* the Detective responded. *However, I am able to alter my height to a maximum of seven foot if it is required.*

Dingo gave them a curious look. Behind him, Bill was frantically signing *ONE WORD RESPONSES ONLY!*

*Cybernetics, eh?* Dingo said a moment later. *Shit, you have a lot of 'em. That must have cost a small fortune! What are you doing in sat-tracking? If you sold even some of your gear, you'll be set for life. Or at least a couple of years.*

*You know, sometimes, it ain't just about the money.* Bill stepped hurriedly into view. *Anyway, um... are you interested in Jenga or not?*

*Yeah, I'm interested,* Dingo said. *Lead the way!*

Bill hesitated. *We... we should probably invite that scientist as well,* he said. *Dingo, if you would come over to our van in about ten minutes, we'll set up, okay?*

Dingo nodded and slowly went back to his deck chair. Bill waved goodbye and hurried away to where the Department car was parked on a slight slope. Dingo's eyes followed them the whole way.

*Okay,* Bill said to the Detective, signing very close to his body as they walked. *What do you think of him?*

*Very suspicious,* the Detective said immediately. *His RV was slightly radioactive.*

Bill's eyes widened. *What?*

*It was only around four times that of background levels,* the Detective continued. *However, it does indicate that he has recently driven somewhere radioactive – for example, the landing site of the First Portent.*

*Oh shit, it's him then!* Bill signed excitedly. *Right? Although... he didn't seem like a smith. He was wearing a relic, for one...*

*That doesn't rule him out completely,* the Detective said. *Even if he isn't the timesmith himself, it seems likely that he might know who is.*

*Yes,* Bill said. *But we have to be careful! He already seems a little suspicious of us as well.*

*A game of wits then.* The Detective narrowed their eyes.

*Yep,* Bill said. *A game of wits. And also, a game of Jenga.*

# CHAPTER 46

# JENGA

### Date: Saturday 14 March 2082

Hello, the scientist signed, as Bill and the Detective came to a stop near their car. *Is... is my equipment in the way? Sorry! I can move it!*

*No, no,* Bill signed quickly as they went to uproot what looked like a strange box taped to a tripod. *It's not in the way! I'm Bill, and that's Mx Fang. We just wanted to ask if you were interested playing a game of Jenga?*

The scientist, a young person of deliberately indeterminate gender, blinked at Bill in confusion.

*Jenga?*

*Yes,* Bill said. *Over at our van, in a few minutes.*

*Why?* the scientist said after a pause.

*For fun,* Bill said. *Look, you don't have to join us if you have other things to do.*

*No, that's okay.* The scientist looked flustered. *I'm done setting up! Although... my equipment is already acting up again. But I don't know how to fix it, so there's not really anything I can do!*

They tapped the box on stilts and shrugged.

*Acting up?* Bill said in interest. *How so? I might be able to fix it, if it's a mechanical problem.*

*Honestly, I have no idea what sort of problem it is,* the scientist said sadly. *It's just giving me weird readings. Look.*

They rotated the box to face Bill, showing him a small dial. The red needle was currently jumping up and down, from one end of the scale to the other and back again.

*It's not supposed to do that,* the scientist elaborated.

*What IS it supposed to do?* Bill asked, moving closer and peering at the dial.

*It's a relicity meter,* the scientist said. *New tech. Usually, we just rely on smiths to tell us when there's a spike in unreality, but those measurements tend to be subjective and imprecise, so we've been trying to build a mechanical version. Unfortunately, it sucks. It's barely functional at the best of times, and paranoia inducing at the worst. It keeps randomly spiking or dropping and giving me a heart attack, thinking a Portent is about to appear. But now this? This is just ridiculous. Both index five unreality and index six reality at the same time? That's not even possible!*

Bill nodded thoughtfully. *Can we open it up and have a look?* he asked. *I've spent a lot of time fixing cybernetics, so I might be able to help. Who knows, maybe a wire just became disconnected?*

*Maybe,* the scientist said doubtfully. *I... don't think we should open it up, actually. My supervisor told me to just log any incidents and bring it back.*

*Do what your supervisor says, then,* Bill said. *Don't worry about it. In the meantime, the Jenga invitation is still open?*

The scientist nodded. *Sure, I'll play. I'll just put the meter back in the car.*

Bill nodded, grinning. *I'll see you at the blue van, then,* he said. *We're starting soon! Don't delay... I don't think you said your name?*

*Aubrey!* the scientist said quickly. *See you in a minute!*

As he and the Detective headed back towards their own van, the Detective frowned slightly.

*Why did we invite them?* they said. *They are clearly unrelated to our case.*

*Yes,* Bill said. *But it would have been rude to not include them. Not to mention suspicious! We're staying in character, remember? Also... I admittedly was quite curious as to what that box of theirs was. Never seen one like it before. Very interesting!*

*You should refrain from getting distracted,* the Detective told him sternly. *We must focus on the task at hand!*

*Yes, yes, I know,* Bill said, looking back at Aubrey, who was struggling to lift their bulky equipment back into the trailer. *Um. You know, I should go and help them with that. Could you go on ahead and set up our Jenga table?*

*Yes,* the Detective said resignedly.

They watched Bill jog back towards the nute and then, shaking their head, went on to the van. There, they found Doc Scurvy already waiting, sitting on a rock, a fresh beer in hand.

*G'day again,* he signed, eyeing the Detective. *Need any help setting up?*

*No,* the Detective said briefly.

They unlocked the back of the van and rolled open the door. Inside, the space was almost entirely bare. There were only seven things inside, six of which were plastic lawn chairs and the final being a fold-away camping table.

The Detective unceremoniously set up the chairs and table in the middle of the van before placing down the battered game of Jenga, which Bill had found that morning in a scrapper's guild antiques store.

Doc Scurvy came around and watched them set up before inviting himself in and placing a slab of beer on the table next to the Jenga game.

'Righto,' he said, looking around the van with a critical eye. 'Here we are. Place is kinda empty, isn't it?'

*Yes,* the Detective signed, seating themselves down in a lawn chair.

Doc Scurvy sipped his beer, staring at them over the top of it.

'Had this van long?'

*No,* the Detective said.

'Mmm,' Doc Scurvy said. 'You're a man of few words, I see.'

*Yes,* the Detective said, pleased that their character was coming across.

'Want a beer?' Doc Scurvy nudged the slab in their direction. 'I brewed 'em myself.'

*No*, the Detective said, nudging it back.

'Great,' Doc Scurvy said. 'Well... good talk.'

There were footsteps at the door and Jillaroo, the woman in the Stetson, came into view. Hands on hips, she paused, looking at Doc Scurvy with a critical eye.

'Afternoon, Jill,' Doc Scurvy said. 'Nice of you to make an appearance.'

'Piss off,' Jillaroo said. 'I'm not here to see you.'

She moved to sit at the furthest possible position from Doc Scurvy.

'How's your furniture, then?' she asked Scurvy, leaning back and folding her arms. 'You know, all the shit I bought for you?'

'It's good,' Scurvy said. 'I appreciate it.'

'Bet you do,' Jillaroo said and nudged the Detective. 'Oi, don't suppose you've got a smoke on ya?'

*No*, the Detective signed.

'Yeah, don't even bother,' Doc Scurvy said. 'He doesn't wanna talk.'

Silence fell for a moment, before the third sat-tracker, Dingo, came in as well. Wordlessly, he sat down, folded his shades and hung them on the collar of his singlet.

'Long time no see,' he said, looking from Doc Scurvy to Jillaroo and back again.

Jillaroo snorted in irritation and Doc Scurvy said, 'Not long enough, if you ask me.'

'What?' Jillaroo said. 'I though you two were all buddy-buddy now?'

'What, me and him?' Doc Scurvy snorted. 'Nah, you're cooked, mate.'

'What?' Jillaroo said. 'You're telling me that you fucked off and left me in a ditch over this spider fucker, and now it's three months later and you already hate each other?'

'Spider fucker?' Dingo said, offended. 'What does that mean?'

'Well, you have, like, twenty of them in your bedroom,' Jillaroo said. 'In their shitty little jars?'

'Yeah, they're relics,' Dingo said.

'No they fuckin' aren't,' Jillaroo said.

'Oh yeah?' Dingo said. 'Well, explain why when I showed one to that weathersmith chick, she ran off like her arse was on fire?'

'She was probably scared of spiders, you fuckin' idiot!' Jillaroo snapped.

'Hold on.' Doc Scurvy held up a hand. 'Wait a minute. Jill... when exactly were you in Dingo's bedroom?'

'None of ya business,' Jillaroo said. 'You two aren't even a couple anymore, why do you care?'

'When did this happen?' Scurvy said, leaning forward. 'When, huh? Dingo, you're being awfully quiet all of a sudden?!'

'Okay, okay, now let's all calm down,' Dingo said, holding up his hands. 'No jumping to conclusions. Just because Jill saw my spiders doesn't mean anything happened.'

'Oh yeah?' Scurvy narrowed his eyes. 'Then why's Jill looking at the floor, huh? It was at Kilian's bush-doof, wasn't it? Huh? You fuckin' snake!'

'Yeah, well, you're no angel yourself,' Dingo scoffed.

'Yeah!' Jillaroo piped up. 'And anyway, Dingo stole you from me, so I only thought it was fair I stole him back from you!'

'Wait, is that the only reason why you did it?!' Dingo looked at her sharply.

'You fuckers!' Doc Scurvy jumped to his feet. 'I can't trust any of ya!'

The Detective stood up as well and the others went abruptly silent. Inside the cramped interior of the van, the Detective looked alarmingly tall.

Quietly, the Detective stepped back from the table and went over to roll the door closed. Once it was shut, they turned around again.

'I would ask that you please keep the noise a minimum,' they said calmly.

There was a long pause – before someone tapped softly on the outside of the van door. The Detective opened it again and let in Bill and the young scientist, Aubrey.

'So, what's happening?' Bill said cheerfully, pulling out a seat and dropping into it. 'Everyone getting along famously, I hope?'

'They are not,' the Detective said, sitting down again as well. 'They were just getting into an argument.'

'Oh,' Bill said, 'ah. Well. Um. Maybe we should start the game, eh?'

'That might be for the best,' the Detective said.

In silence, everyone watched as Bill somewhat awkwardly began setting up the Jenga tower.

'So,' Bill said, 'has everyone played before? Or should I go over the rules?'

'I would, um, appreciate if you went over them,' Aubrey said in a quiet voice.

They were sitting on the opposite side of the table to the Detective and were distinctly avoiding the Detective's gaze. Whenever the Detective looked at them, they hurriedly looked away with an air of barely contained terror.

This was a recent development, the Detective thought in sudden suspicion. Had Bill told them about their secret identities? What... what else had he told them?

'It's simple,' Bill said, sitting back in his seat, the tower of Jenga blocks set up before him. 'When it's your turn, you pull out one brick and place it on the top of the tower. You can only use one hand to pull it out and no one is allowed to interfere physically – although verbal distractions are permitted. This continues until the tower falls over. Whoever knocks the tower over is the loser!'

'I think there might be a couple of fuckin' losers in here already,' Doc Scurvy muttered into his beer.

'What happens to the loser?' Dingo asked, ignoring Scurvy. 'Are they kicked out of the game until we're left with one champion?'

'We could do that, sure,' Bill said.

'What if,' Jillaroo said, 'the loser also has to do something? Like scull their drink? Or... tell a truth?'

'A truth?' the Detective said in interest. 'What do you mean?'

'You know, like truth or dare?' Jillaroo said. 'The loser is asked one question and has to answer it truthfully.'

'I don't know about –' Bill began, but he was interrupted.

'I think it's a good idea,' Dingo said. 'Might be interesting to get a few truths around here. You know, as a change.'

'I actually agree,' Doc Scurvy said. 'There are certain things I would LOVE to get cleared up.'

'I also think this is a good idea,' the Detective said.

'Hoo boy,' Bill muttered. 'Well... I suppose if you're all into it... Truth Jenga it is...'

He reluctantly reached out and pulled one block from the middle of the tower.

'There, I've started us off,' he said. 'The game goes clockwise. Whoever knocks over the tower is out of the game and has to truthfully answer one question. Dingo, you're next.'

The game progressed quickly at first before slowing down as the tower became gradually more unstable. It ended somewhat prematurely, however, when Aubrey, hand shaking visibly, accidentally knocked the table with their knee and toppled the tower.

Everyone looked somewhat disappointed that it had been Aubrey to lose the first round – but Doc Scurvy cleared his throat and raised a finger, indicating that he had a question.

'What is it that you do?' he asked, with a frown. 'You're always poking around the satellite sites. Why?'

'Um,' Aubrey said, shrinking under everyone's gaze. 'Well. I'm trying to find proof of Hendekon Radiation. You know... the highly destructive particles that come from the Eleventh? Well... that's probably where they come from. We're not one hundred per cent sure!'

'Right,' Doc Scurvy said. 'Did you find it yet?'

'No,' Aubrey said. 'It's, uh, hard to tell what damage is

caused by Hendekon Radiation, and what's caused by atmospheric re-entry. Um. I have a relicity meter now, though. So, that might help! If it, uh, stops misbehaving...'

'Sounds complicated,' Doc Scurvy said. 'No wonder you're always scurrying all over the place. Anyway, should we set up round two?'

Round two went for longer than round one – and this time Bill knocked over the tower.

'Oopsie,' Bill said, 'fat fingers, ha ha. Guess I'm out of the game! Anyone got any questions for me?'

The others once again looked disappointed but Doc Scurvy again opened his mouth.

'Why is your van so empty –' he began.

'Oi,' Jillaroo interrupted. 'Why do you get to ask all the questions?'

'Well, I didn't see you saying anything,' Scurvy grumbled.

'I was thinking,' Jillaroo said. 'Although... that is a good question. Why IS your van so empty?'

'Blatantly stealing my ideas,' Doc Scurvy muttered.

'Yeah, well, you stole my furniture,' Jillaroo said.

'It's empty because it's new,' Bill said. 'Well, new to us, anyway. We had an old one, but some shit happened and we lost it, along with all our old belongings.'

'What sort of shit?' Dingo asked.

'The Fourth Portent,' Bill said. 'I don't know if any of you have ever seen it, but its massive and spews rivers of oil all over the place. It ripped our old van open like a can of sardines and filled the sorry remains with oil. We fortunately weren't there at the time, but when we came back, everything was destroyed! Flat as pancake, or seeped in oil the point where it wasn't worth trying to salvage it.'

He was a smooth liar, the Detective noted. Of course, none of this had happened – he was making it up on the spot. But if the Detective hadn't known that, even they would have had trouble picking it up.

The others, meanwhile, were enthralled by the tale.

Portents, of course, always made a spectacular story, if you survived them.

But more than that, it was clever – shockingly clever. The Detective had never picked Bill as the devious sort – but when his story came to an end, naturally, the others were compelled to tell of their own close encounters.

'I saw the First Portent, just recently,' Dingo said, entirely unprompted.

The Detective's eyes widened, just slightly. Bill was a genius!

'Did you really?' Bill said, leaning in in interest.

'Yeah, from a distance,' Dingo said. 'Saw the flash on the horizon when it landed. I was just about to go to bed, in my pyjamas and everything, and then suddenly it looked like the sun was rising. Fucking terrifying, to be honest. Heard the explosion a few minutes later.'

'Fuck,' Doc Scurvy said. 'What did you do?'

'Well, after I'd finished shitting my pants,' Dingo said, 'I actually went a bit closer to see where it had landed. You can find some very interesting stuff in the wake of a Portent, if you're willing to take the risk. Anyway, turns out it landed on some farm. Poor buggers had been blown to kingdom come, nothing left. I did pick up a couple of stragglers, though. Unlucky bastards had parked their RV even closer to the explosion than I had. One of them was pretty badly injured, actually. Had to take her to the fleshies and get her fixed up.'

'What sort of injuries did she have?' the Detective asked.

'Looked like burns,' Dingo said. 'All over her body. Really bad. She was fine after they fixed her up, though. Actually, you guys would know her. Kylie Collins – remember her? Used to be a sat tracker.'

'Oh, her?' Jillaroo said. 'Yeah, I remember. Feisty bitch, she was. Wouldn't stand for anyone's shit. I respect it, honestly.'

'She didn't like me,' Doc Scurvy said. 'Wouldn't give me the time of day.'

'She probably smelt your breath a mile off,' Jillaroo told him.

As they traded insults, the Detective and Bill shared a look. With this latest information in mind, it seemed as though Dingo was not actually the sat tracker they were after. This Kylie Collins on the other hand...

'What's the girl up to these days, anyway?' Jillaroo said. 'Kylie. Did she tell you?'

'I think she's gotten into the music business,' Dingo said.

'Goodness,' Jillaroo said. 'Actually, you know what, that doesn't surprise me. High risk, high reward was exactly her M.O.'

'What made you think she was in the music business?' the Detective asked.

'It was just the vibe I got,' Dingo said. 'They didn't specifically tell me that. They just went on about music a lot.'

'They?' the Detective said.

'Yeah,' Dingo said. 'Kylie and the other stragglers I picked up.'

'Who were these others?' the Detective asked.

'I dunno,' Dingo said. 'Another woman and some teenagers. Why do you care?'

'I am simply curious,' the Detective said.

'Sure.' Dingo side-eyed them. 'Whatever. Shall we start the next round of Jenga?'

The third round, with four people remaining in the game, went quite a bit longer than both the previous two. By the end of it, the tower was teetering horribly, each new brick pulled causing it to wobble dangerously.

At last though, Doc Scurvy chose the wrong brick and the tower collapsed sideways in a rattle of wood on plastic. Scurvy swore loudly and sat back, arms crossed.

'Oh ho.' Jillaroo grinned at him. 'Now look who's in the hot seat! But what question to ask?!'

'Hold on,' Dingo said, 'you asked the last one!'

'Yeah, but I didn't come up with it,' Jillaroo said.

'That's your problem,' Dingo said. 'It's my turn now!'

'Oh, is it?' Jillaroo glared at him. 'Your turn? Just like how it was your turn to steal MY BOYFRIEND?'

'He left you of his own free will.' Dingo shrugged. 'Guess you just aren't good enough.'

'That's not what you said at the bush-doof.' Jillaroo narrowed her eyes.

'Woah, woah,' Bill intervened. 'If you can't decide on a question, then perhaps I'll ask one?'

'NO!' both Dingo and Jillaroo said at the same time.

'Why don't we just ask Scurvy who he'd pick now?' Jillaroo said. 'Having dated both of us. Which one does he like better? Huh, Scurvy? Me? Or him?'

'Fuck's sake,' Doc Scurvy said. 'I hate both of youse. You fuckin' deserve each other, as far as I see it.'

'You have to pick!' Jillaroo pointed an aggressive finger. 'You're in the truth seat! You have to answer!'

'Fuckin' make me,' Scurvy scowled.

'I fuckin' will, if you don't speak soon,' Jillaroo snapped.

'What are you gonna do, peel off my toenails?' Scurvy said. 'Fuckin' harpy.'

'She would,' Dingo said. 'I'm clearly the nicer person.'

'You shut your mouth.' Jillaroo turned to glare at Dingo instead.

'Or what, you'll peel off my toenails as well?'

'I bet you'd enjoy that, spider fucker!'

'The only hairy-legged beast I ever –'

'LOOK,' Doc Scurvy shouted over them both. 'I can't choose! I...'

He drew in a long-suffering breath.

'I like both of youse,' he said quietly. 'Still. At the same time. I can't choose. Jillaroo, you're a firecracker and you set my heart alight. Dingo, you're as solid as a rock – and you're my rock. I like you both, for different reasons. And I simply can't decide between you. Which is why I've been avoiding both of you completely. That's the fuckin' truth.'

There was a long silence.

'Damn,' Bill said, wiping his eye. 'That was weirdly romantic.'

'Should we, uh, leave?' Aubrey said. 'I think... they might have some things to sort out...'

'No, don't go anywhere,' Dingo said. 'We still haven't figured out who's the Jenga champion!'

'Well,' Jillaroo said a little faintly. 'I don't really give a shit about that, personally.'

'Do you forfeit, then?' Dingo said. 'Because I'd very much like to square off against *Fang* here. I've got a question or two I'd like to ask him.'

'I'm pretty sure it's "them", not "him", Aubrey said, a little defensively.

'Right,' Dingo said. 'Well, I'd like to know where *they* got so many cybernetics.'

The Detective cocked their head. 'And I would like to know the details of those other people you picked up from the landing site of the First Portent,' they said.

Dingo narrowed his eyes.

'Alright,' he said. 'One last game, then? Just you and me, Fang? Winner gets their answers?'

'I agree to these terms,' the Detective said.

They were confident that they would win. They were capable of analysing every single block and its weight distribution within less than a second. Each block they pulled was mathematically the most likely to succeed.

But Dingo was fierce competition. He was clearly a natural athlete, his movements smooth and precise, his hands steady even as the tension grew.

Soon, the tower of blocks was teetering higher than ever before. The others, initially uninterested, watched with bated breath as Dingo, the Detective, then Dingo again, pulled out brick after improbable brick and dropped it neatly onto the top of the stack.

'You're cheating, you know,' Dingo said as the Detective nudged out another brick. 'Your cybernetics mean you have greater precision than is possible for natural hands.'

'There are no rules stating that cybernetics cannot be used when playing Jenga,' the Detective said.

'Maybe your copy of the rulebook is out of date?' Dingo

said. 'In most competitive sports, augmented athletes are not permitted.'

'This is not a competitive sport and I am not a professional athlete,' the Detective said.

'Yes – but what ARE you?' Dingo eyed them. 'There are only a handful of professions that encourage augmentation. Emergency workers... Relixorcists get them, if they're rich enough...'

He paused.

'Sin-seekers...'

The Detective dropped their next brick onto the stack and sat back.

'You wish to distract me,' they said. 'But you will find your efforts are in vain.'

'I dunno, I think I saw some sweat,' Dingo said.

'I do not sweat,' the Detective said.

Dingo pulled his next block and froze when the tower wobbled. It set into place though, and gently he dropped the block on top.

'So, what are you, some sort of robo-cop?' he asked, as the Detective scanned for their next brick. 'You're clearly not a sat tracker. But you ARE looking for something. Or someone.'

The Detective wordlessly placed another brick on top of the tower. Dingo took a while to pick his next one but successfully removed it.

'Is Aubrey in on it too?' Dingo asked during the Detective's next go. 'Don't think I didn't notice Bill and Aubrey's little pow-wow over there in the corner. Seemed like quite the conversation. What was that about, huh?'

The Detective hesitated. What WAS that about? They hadn't seen this conversation – but they knew something had been said. Aubrey had been acting strange ever since they'd come into the van. They were clearly nervous and they still hadn't looked the Detective directly in the eye.

What had Bill said to them?

Beneath their outstretched finger, the tower wobbled.

The Detective drew in a breath.

Outside, there was an almighty C R A S H!

Everyone, concentrating on the wobbling tower, jumped out of their skins in fright. The table flew up and Jenga blocks went everywhere.

'IT'S ALRIGHT,' Bill yelled as everyone fought to extract themselves from the table. 'IT'S THE SATELLITE! THE SATELLITE CAME DOWN! It's over there, on the hill! I saw it through the window!'

'Shit, I forgot why we were here!' Doc Scurvy said from the floor.

'Last one there's a rotten egg!' Jillaroo yelled and lunged for the door.

Doc Scurvy ran after her and Aubrey sidled out as well, jogging away towards their nute.

Dingo, who had stood up in a hurry, looked down at the Jenga bricks on the floor.

'It was going to fall,' he said.

'It was not,' the Detective said calmly, from where they still sat in their seat.

'Why don't you both answer each other's questions?' Bill said when Dingo opened his mouth to argue. 'Since its now impossible to say for sure? And since we're leaving.'

'Fine,' Dingo said. 'But you first. Are you cops?'

'Yes, you got us,' Bill said. 'Well, sort of. We're investigating the disappearance of Mildura.'

'Oh?' Dingo's eyebrows shot up.

'The people you assisted at the landing site of the First Portent,' the Detective said. 'We have reason to believe they may have knowledge relating to our case. I therefore ask that you tell me their names and any other information about them you may remember, including age, physical appearance, behavioural quirks and the like.'

'Well, damn,' Dingo said. 'And here I thought you were a couple of regular pigs, sniffing around up in our biz for no reason. My apologies. Uh, the people I picked up? There was Kylie Collins, who I knew previously. Twenty-five or around that, about yea high. Used to dye her hair blonde but it's black naturally. Wears a lot of pink.'

'Okay,' the Detective said. 'And the others?'

'Well, I didn't know any of the others,' Dingo said. 'But there was a woman called Maggie, similar age to Kylie, and then there were three teenagers, two boys and a girl. I don't remember their names, because I never really spoke to them and frankly, I didn't care to, but I can give you descriptions?'

'Please,' the Detective said.

They carefully recorded every word that Dingo said, creating virtual profiles of these latest suspects.

'And did any of these people display signs of P.I.U.S?' they asked, once Dingo had finished.

'Uh.' Dingo wrinkled his nose. 'Not that I remember. And I have relics in the RV, which they weren't bothered by.'

'Are they relics or are they spiders?' the Detective said.

'Spiders are relics,' Dingo said stubbornly.

'They are not.'

'Fine,' Dingo said. 'In that case, I only own like two relics, which probably isn't enough to do shit. So yeah, I have no idea if they had P.I.U.S or not.'

'Okay,' the Detective said. 'And where did you see them last?'

'Dropped them off in Bendigo,' Dingo said.

'Is that where they live?'

'Well.' Dingo looked amused. 'Actually, they said they were going there to enter the lottery. Apparently, that was their plan to make money. Stupid if you ask me.'

The Detective frowned.

'When was this?'

'Late January,' Dingo said. 'Or maybe early Feb?'

The Detective did a rapid search through their files, which included a large number of recent articles they'd previously scanned through for Portent related news. Something about the lottery had triggered a memory – something they'd read, and disregarded, at some point in the past.

There! There it was. A newspaper article, from the Bendigo Times, on the 1st of February. It was a picture of a woman, perfectly matching Dingo's description of Kylie Collins. She was beaming ear to ear and holding up a lottery ticket.

LOCAL WOMAN WINS 100K JACKPOT! the headline underneath read.

The Detective felt electricity surge through their body in excitement. 'She won,' they said.

'What?' Dingo said.

'Kylie Collins won the lottery,' the Detective said. 'I have an article proving it saved in my hard drive.'

Dingo stared at them. 'But... how?!' he said. 'That's not possible. You can't PLAN to win the lottery?!'

'No,' the Detective said. 'You can't.'

They turned to look at Bill.

'Not unless you're a timesmith,' they said.

# CHAPTER 47

# RULES OF TIME TRAVEL

### Date: Saturday 1 February 2082

*RULES FOR TIME TRAVEL*
*01.02.82*

*Subject Alpha is a timesmith with reversal-type P.I.U.S. Below are listed the known parameters of Subject Alpha's Portent Induced Unreality Symptoms.*

1. *The symptoms are triggered by the presence of music and are activated voluntarily.*

2. *The 'complexity index' of the song used to activate the symptoms corelates directly with the magnitude of the resulting effect. A complexity index of 1 results in time 'freezing in place' for Subject Alpha, for a period of time equal in length to the song played before symptoms were activated. A complexity index of 2 or more results in time 'running backwards' for Subject Alpha, with higher complexity indexes adding exponentially to the length of time unwound.*

3. *Complexity index is determined by the number of 'layers' present within the activating song, OR by how many individual people were involved in the song. I.e. if one person within the song produces two separate layers (e.g. singing and playing guitar at the same time) this counts as an index of 2. OR if two people*

within the song produce the same layer (e.g. two first violinists in an orchestral assembly) this also counts as index 2.

4.  Once activated, Subject Alpha's ability must complete to the end and cannot be interrupted.

5.  Once the ability has completed, Subject Alpha is able to remember events that occurred during the period of unwound time and is able to take actions to permanently change these events.

6.  Other individuals are able to remember events that occurred during unwound time ONLY if they were actively involved in the music used to trigger the unwinding. I.e., if live music is used to activate the symptoms, any person involved in the live music will remember the period of unwound time as well as Subject Alpha.

7.  If the activating song is played forwards as normal, then time will unwind backwards. However, if the activating song is initially played backwards, time will instead move forwards at a pace consistent with complexity index.

8.  Subject Alpha cannot time travel further into the future beyond the point at which symptoms were initially activated.

KNOWN COMBINATIONS WITH OTHER P.I.U.S:

Subject Alpha and Subject Beta, a mattersmith with state-shift-type abilities, combined P.I.U.S, resulting in approximately 1 ton of solid limestone reverting to sand. Matter seemingly returned to the state it had been in at a *time point equal to the length of the activating song multiplied exponentially by the complexity index.*

*Note – several fossils that were coincidentally caught within the radius of effect were also seen to revert to a living state. This is particularly interesting, as the materials included within the parameters of Subject Beta's P.I.U.S do not usually include living creatures.*

*FURTHER QUESTIONS:*

*Q1: Given infinite complexity index, how far back in time can Subject Alpha travel?*

*Hypothesis 1 – Subject Alpha can at maximum travel back to the point at which they first received P.I.U.S.*

*Hypothesis 2 – Subject Alpha can at maximum travel back to the point at which they were first conceived.*

*Hypothesis 3 – Subject Alpha has no maximum travel point and, given infinite complexity index, can travel back to the beginning of the universe.*

'So, what do you think?' Maggie said. 'Does this cover everything?'

'Um.' Quinn blinked down at the small notebook that Maggie handed her. 'I... think so?'

'Great!' Maggie grinned. 'If I did miss something, let me know. Even if it's a tiny thing. The more details, the better!'

'Mmm,' Quinn said.

Maggie frowned at her. 'What's wrong? Is it... is it too much? I'm sorry – I got a bit excited after the whole Ninth Portent thing.'

'No, it's fine.' Quinn closed the book and handed it back to Maggie. 'I just... I've just never seen it all written down like that, I suppose. And... Subject Alpha? That's so cold and science-y.'

'Well, I didn't want to use your name,' Maggie said. 'In case someone reads this who I didn't intend to.'

'Sure,' Quinn said. 'Although... why did you write it down at all, if you don't mind me asking?'

'Because it's super interesting!' Maggie said. 'Quinn, you're probably one of the most powerful smiths I've ever met! Your P.I.U.S has SO much potential – you don't even realise! I didn't realise either until I saw it in action myself. But holy shit! Exponential time reversal? There's SO much you can do with that!'

'I guess,' Quinn said.

'I haven't been this excited about something for years!' Maggie went on. 'The possibilities! With the right formula, you could reverse disasters! Save so many lives! A Portent destroys a town? You could go back a couple of days and warn them it's coming! A factory blows up? You can go in and tell them to check their gas lines before it happens! And even better, if they sing along, you can bring people with you, so they also remember it. Politicians won't be able to keep on ignoring incoming disasters if dozens of people personally remember the disasters happening!'

Quinn sighed.

'Yeah, okay,' she said. 'But where does it stop?'

'What?' Maggie stopped pacing to look at her.

'Where do I draw the line?' Quinn said. 'Say I turn myself in to the Sanctuary tomorrow and offer my services as someone who can avert disasters. Yes, I can save lives, great. But I can only do it so many times before it fucks me up for good. So, which disasters do I choose to avert? Huh? Because things go wrong all the time, and people die all the time, and I can't save all of them. Only some.'

'Okay, well, that's true,' Maggie said thoughtfully.

'And since it's only some,' Quinn went on, 'how do I choose? Who do I bring back, and who isn't worth the trouble? Do I choose, or does someone else? If it's someone else, then how do they choose? Do they set a death threshold? Twenty people and we bring them back? What if nineteen people die? That's still bad, isn't it? What if they were nineteen children? Nineteen of the nicest people in existence? Do we only save people if they deserve it? If they're rich and important? And if they're poor, or old, or unfriendly, or unlucky, or a sinner who likes music, then we leave them dead?'

'I...' Maggie said. 'I suppose that is a problem, yes.'

'Yeah,' Quinn said. 'I've thought about this before myself. And yeah, in theory, I can stop disasters from happening. But if I do, then there's no going back, because it doesn't end, ever, and I can't save everyone. So I'm not going save any, unless they happen to be right in front of me. And I'm sure you'll think I'm a selfish arsehole, but I don't care.'

Maggie nodded slowly. 'No,' she said. 'You're right. It wouldn't be fair to ask so much of you. You're not even legally an adult yet. And you're not a selfish arsehole. You deserve a normal life. I shouldn't have brought it up. Sorry.'

'That's okay,' Quinn said. 'Sorry to be a downer.'

'No, no,' Maggie said. 'I get carried away sometimes. Sometimes I need someone to smack me over the head with reality...'

She trailed off, her expression distant. Absently, she put the notebook away in her pocket and wandered off into the next room.

They were staying at Kylie's friend's house – a young South Asian man who claimed to be both an entrepreneur and a hacker and had introduced himself by the name Snakebyte. His house was somewhat of a mess, with old dishes on every surface and miscellaneous technological junk stacked in the corners. He was nice enough though, and had made an effort to clear the couch so that Quinn could sit there.

Currently, he was chatting with Kylie in the front room, both of them practically yelling out of excitement. Kylie, who had gone to collect the $100k from the Lotto just a couple of hours ago, was in high spirits and had cracked open a bottle of sparkling rosé to celebrate.

Maggie, meanwhile, had been furiously writing all

morning – Quinn now knew what – while Mullet hung out in the games room with his new bestie, Spencer.

Quinn could hear them laughing, and it pissed her off. Mullet had occasionally poked his head out of the games room to send her puppy-dog-eyes, but she was ignoring him.

She had woken up with a headache that morning and things had not gotten any better from there. She was still mentally recovering from the clusterfuck that had been the previous afternoon but around her, everyone seemed to be having a great time. Kylie with her money, Mullet with his new friend and Maggie with her bizarre, clinical take on Quinn's P.I.U.S.

Quinn, sitting by herself, was attempting to write some lyrics, but her headache and all the noise in the house was making it difficult. After a time, she crossly gave up and crumpled up the paper she'd been writing on, tossing it at a bin that was standing in the corner.

She missed. Sighing, she got up from her seat and went and picked it up to throw away properly.

When she came back, Mullet had poked his head into the room again.

'Yo,' he said. 'Do you want to play a board game?'

'No,' Quinn said grouchily.

'Aw.' Mullet pouted. 'Why not?'

'Got a headache. Two, actually. One of them is in there, in a wheelchair.'

'Aw, c'mon,' Mullet said. 'Spencer really isn't that bad, once you get to know him!'

'I don't want to get to know him,' Quinn said. 'Stabby McFriend-stealer.'

'He even listened to music!' Mullet went on. 'And he liked it! Although he won't admit it...'

'I didn't like it,' Spencer said, wheeling into view behind Mullet. 'It was just... catchy! It got stuck in my head! Which is EXACTLY why it's bad!'

'He was groovin' out,' Mullet said with a grin. 'He thought I didn't see!'

'Was not!' Spencer snapped, his cheeks flushing.

Quinn scowled at them both. 'Why did you come in here?' she said grumpily. 'I was writing. You're interrupting me.'

'Oh yeah?' Mullet said. 'What did you write?'

'Lots of stuff.' Quinn narrowed her eyes.

'Is that so?' Mullet cocked his head. 'Where is it, then?'

Quinn bristled but then let it go with a sigh.

'In the bin,' she admitted. 'It was garbage.'

Mullet came closer and patted her on the shoulder. 'There, there,' he said cheerfully. 'They can't all be winners. Why don't you come into the games room and play some games and listen to music with us?'

'I don't wanna play games,' Quinn said at the same time as Spencer said, 'I don't want to listen to music!'

'Too bad!' Mullet said. 'Quinn, what should we put on? Snakebyte has a pretty extensive collection. What would Spencer like the most, do you think?'

In spite of herself, Quinn found herself considering the question.

'Probably rock or metal,' she said after a pause.

'Ohh!' Mullet's eyes lit up. 'I haven't shown him metal yet! Spencer, you'll love it. It's lots of angry screaming!'

'That sounds horrendous,' Spencer said.

'Yep!' Mullet said. 'That's the point!'

Grinning, he pushed back into the games room. Shortly, the sounds of aggressive guitar and growling vocals emanated from inside.

As Spencer rolled back out of sight, yelling at Mullet to turn it off, Quinn stood up and went into the games room. Mullet was standing in front of a speaker and blocking Spencer from getting close to it.

'This is awful!' Spencer was yelling. 'Turn it off!'

'Make me.' Mullet grinned wickedly, and then yelped when Spencer ran over his toes. Jumping back, he smacked into a shelf, loudly knocking its contents to the floor.

'Fuck's sake,' Quinn said, watching them. 'Mullet, first of all, you can't start with this song!'

'Eh?' Mullet looked at her, hopping on one foot.

'You have to ease into metal!' Quinn said. 'You should start with Iron Maiden or something! Does Snakebyte have that?'

'Oh.' Mullet turned the music way down. 'Yeah, I think so. Hang on...'

Shortly, the opening riff of *The Trooper* began playing. Spencer stopped trying to run Mullet over. His eyes narrowed.

'There,' Mullet said, nursing his foot. 'What do you think of this?'

'Hmm,' Spencer said.

Mullet grinned. 'That means he likes it.'

'Do not,' Spencer said. But there was no conviction behind his words.

While the song played, Quinn went over and helped Mullet pick up the stuff he'd knocked off the shelf. One of the items, a miniature Dog On The Tuckerbox statue, had broken, the dog's head snapped clean off from the body.

'Oh no,' Mullet said, holding the two pieces up. 'I hope this isn't a relic.'

'It was,' Spencer said without looking. 'It isn't anymore.'

'Shit,' Mullet said. 'What if we glued it?'

'That won't fix the relicity, idiot.'

'Yeah, but will Snakebyte notice?' Mullet said.

'Will I notice what?' Snakebyte said, waltzing in through the door.

'Oh, um,' Mullet said guiltily.

'Mullet broke your relic,' Quinn told him. 'Sorry. We can pay for it.'

'Ah.' Snakebyte eyed the pieces in Mullet's hands. 'Nah, no worries, bro. It was a cheapo.'

'What's happening in here?' Kylie swanned in behind Snakebyte, clearly a few drinks deep. 'Is it a party? Would anyone like some bubbly?'

'No thanks,' Quinn said as Kylie tried to hand her a flute glass.

'But we're celebrating!' Kylie said. 'It's not every day you win the Lotto! Although... it could be! Ahahaha! We could do it again! Right, Quinn?! We can do it as many times as we want!'

'We probably shouldn't,' Quinn said.

'We definitely shouldn't,' Maggie said, coming in behind Kylie. 'Once was fine, but two in a row would be very suspicious!'

'Okay, everyone just crowd around me, that's fine,' Spencer said crossly.

'Would you like some bubbly?' Kylie said to him.

'I'm underage!'

'So, should I glue the head back on or what?' Mullet said to Snakebyte, holding up the pieces of the dog statue.

'Nah, just chuck it,' Snakebyte said. 'I only had it because it was a relic.'

'Wait, what's a relic?' Maggie said. 'Oh no, it's broken!'

'Mullet broke it,' Quinn said.

'Do YOU want some bubbly?' Kylie said to Maggie.

'Wait, wait,' Maggie said, ignoring her. 'We could fix it!'

'Yeah, just glue the head back on, that's what I've been saying,' Mullet said.

'No, that's not what I meant.' Maggie reached into her pocket and pulled out her notebook.

'Fine, more for me,' Kylie muttered and took a swig directly from the bottle.

Quinn watched apprehensively as Maggie flipped through the pages of her book and came to the notes she'd been writing earlier.

'Quinn, Spencer,' she said excitedly. 'I know this is a bit of an ask, but if you guys combined abilities again, like you did back in the Ark that one time, you could probably restore the statue to how it was five minutes ago!'

'Why?' Quinn said. 'It was a really weak relic and Snakebyte doesn't even care about it. What's the point?'

'Maybe it's weak,' Maggie said, 'but it IS still a relic! It will be really interesting to see if the relicity restores when it's fixed!'

'Oh,' Quinn said, suddenly fully understanding where

Maggie was coming from. Restoring a relic was something Maggie had failed to do before, even after years of trying.

'Please?' Maggie said. 'I know you don't like using your P.I.U.S, and this is pretty unimportant, but it's... well...'

'It's important to you,' Quinn said. 'Yeah, I know. You don't remember, because it happened on the Friday that doesn't exist anymore, but you told me all about your relic research. About the three-hundred-year deadline.'

'Oh,' Maggie said. 'I told you about that?'

'Yeah,' Quinn said. 'So, I get why this is important to you.'

'So,' Maggie said, 'you'll do it? For science?'

'Sure,' Quinn said. 'For you.'

Maggie beamed. 'Thanks, Quinn! This really does mean a lot to me!'

'Yeah, well,' Quinn said, 'just don't expect me to go saving workers from exploding factories or whatever.'

'Hold on,' Spencer said, 'am I supposed to be involved in this discussion at all?'

'Yes,' Maggie said. 'Would you be willing to take part in a small science experiment?'

'I'd rather not,' Spencer said.

'Oi,' Mullet said to him. 'Remember that chat we had about being nicer to people?'

'No, no, he's well within his rights here.' Maggie waved a hand. 'If he doesn't want to, he's allowed to say no.'

'Okay, but this is going to be really easy,' Quinn said. 'Tiny little dog statue and a couple of minutes? We probably won't even get any side effects.'

'Yeah, but why should I risk it?' Spencer said. 'What if I do get a side effect and it's really bad? For what, that piece of trash?'

'It's not the statue itself, it's what it represents,' Quinn said. 'It's a relic! You don't understand – they're all getting weaker over time! But we might be able to reverse that!'

'It's fine, Quinn,' Maggie said. 'You can't force people to do things.'

'Who's forcing what?' Kylie leaned on Maggie's shoulder.

'Spencer is being uncooperative again,' Quinn said.

'Hey, 'scuse me,' Snakebyte said, 'if I could interject here... what's all this about? I'm hella lost.'

Maggie briefly explained and Snakebyte nodded thoughtfully.

'That's fully sick!' he said. 'Can you fix, like, any object?'

'Uhh,' Maggie said.

'I ask because I spilt OJ on one of my laptops the other day,' Snakebyte said. 'Fried the sucker in an instant. It had some important gear on it that I'd like to get back too. Could you fix that?'

Everyone was momentarily silent.

'I mean, technically we could, yeah,' Quinn said. 'If we wanted to.'

'I'll pay you for it,' Snakebyte said. 'Money – or anything else? Is there anything you want? You probably already have it, right? If I had those symptoms, I'd have everything I ever wanted.'

'What do you mean?' Maggie said.

'I mean, I'd go down to the scrap yard, purchase a broken computer for pittance, then come back and ABRA-CADABRA, restore it to full working order,' Snakebyte said, wiggling his fingers. 'Then I'd sell it and make bank! Repeat forever!'

'Woah, woah, wait a sec,' Kylie said. 'Quinn – can you really do that?'

'Well, no, not by myself I can't,' Quinn said. 'Spencer has to put in fifty per cent.'

'And you guys didn't say anything?' Kylie said.

Quinn blinked at her.

'C'mon,' Kylie said, 'I'm tipsy and even I get it! If you can instantly restore any object to when it was working, then why did we even need to win the Lotto? We could just go and fix our old stuff! Right? We could instantly restore THE GLAM VAN to when it was new! Or am I misinterpreting what's going on here?'

There was another silence.

'Dude!' Mullet said. 'Could you guys really do that?'

'I guess we could?' Quinn said. 'Do you think so, Maggie?'

'Makes sense,' Maggie said. 'Based on the one test we've done so far. We would have to do more tests before we can be fully sure that it would fix something as complex as a van or a laptop...'

'Well, do the tests, then!' Kylie said. 'I'd love to have THE GLAM VAN back. I miss her. Any other RV wouldn't be the same! Oh, I thought I'd lost her forever!'

'Okay, but you're all assuming I'm agreeing to any of this,' Spencer said. 'Which I'm not. I told you, I see no point in risking it. What would I get out of it, huh? Maybe you lot get a shiny new RV, but all I get is increased risk of an early death.'

'Oh yeah?' Kylie said. 'What if we got your cybernetics back?'

'Don't be ridiculous,' Spencer said. 'You can't just buy cybernetics. You need thousands of dollars, months of spare waiting time and a squeaky-clean record. And no, before you ask, I don't have any parts of the old ones left to magically zap into the future.'

'Thousands of dollars, huh?' Kylie leaned closer. 'Surely not more than one hundred thousand?'

'I...' Spencer paused.

'And sure, our records aren't the cleanest,' Kylie said. 'But Snakebyte doesn't call himself a hacker for no reason. He's got certain contacts in certain places that can bypass the waitlists, speed up the process a little...'

'Yep, and all for the low, low price of my poor laptop's restoration,' Snakebyte said.

Spencer frowned around at everyone.

'So to get this straight,' he said. 'If I agree to restore your laptop –'

'And THE GLAM VAN,' Kylie interjected.

'And THE GLAM VAN –'

'And this relic?' Maggie added. 'Sorry. It's important, I swear.'

Spencer sighed loudly.

'If I agree to restore the laptop, THE GLAM VAN and that piece of crap relic,' he said. 'Then you'll get me my cybernetic limbs back? All four of them? Within a reasonable timeframe?'

'Yes,' Kylie said. 'Right everyone? Sound fair?'

'Sounds fair to me,' Snakebyte said.

'Sure,' Quinn said, eyeing Spencer. 'Although, if you think for a second that you can use your limbs for evil – that is, stabbing someone, turning us all in, or anything like that – then I'm going to remember this moment, and time travel back to it, and smack you.'

Spencer narrowed his eyes.

'Fine,' he said.

## Excerpt from the personal notebook of
## MARGARET LAMINGTON

*TEST 1 – 02.02.2082*

*Subjects Alpha and Beta combined P.I.U.S with the goal of reversing damage to a low tier relic.*

*Hypothesis – the relic will be restored to how it was prior to receiving damage.*

*Method – Subject Alpha held the damaged relic in one hand, while the other hand was on subject Beta's shoulder. Time since damage had occurred was 15 minutes. Time reversed was 24 minutes.*

*Results – The hypothesis is correct! Both Subjects Alpha and Beta confirmed that the relic was emitting a low-tier relicious aura (!!!!!). Neither Subjects reported notable side effects.*

*Conclusion – this experiment marks the first known case of a relic increasing in power level – approximately tier 3 from tier 0. Further testing is required to confirm whether higher tier relics react in the same way.*

*TEST 2 – 02.02.2082*

*Subjects Alpha and Beta combined P.I.U.S with the goal of reversing damage to a broken laptop.*

*Hypothesis – the laptop will restore to how it was prior to being damaged.*

*Method – Subject Alpha placed one hand on the damaged laptop and one on Beta's shoulder. Time since damage was approximately 54 hours. Time reversed was 56 hours.*

*Results – Laptop was fully restored, with all data intact, beside that which had been created later than 56 hours.*

Subject Beta reported low level side effect. Subject Alpha reported no side effect.

Conclusion – this method is able to restore delicate or complex objects to a specific former state.

TEST 3 – 05.02.2082

Subjects Alpha and Beta combined P.I.U.S with the goal of reversing severe damage to a recreational vehicle (RV).

Hypothesis – the RV will restore to how it was prior to being damaged.

Method – Alpha and Beta stood on opposite sides of the RV. Time since damage had occurred was 12 days. Time reversed was 14 days.

Results...

# CHAPTER 48

# GLAM VAN RESURRECTIONS

**Date: Wednesday 5 February 2082**

*M*ake sure you get all the pieces! Kylie signed. *I don't want half of THE GLAM VAN back, I want all of it! Search the bushes! Search the rocks!*

Vincent Spencer, who had just sat down to catch his breath, stood up again with an angry huff.

He stood up too quickly and his head swam for a moment, stars bursting behind his eyeballs. He still wasn't quite used to having limbs again. The connection points felt odd and unfamiliar – his new limbs were a different model to the last ones he'd had. But it felt good to have them there at all. He'd sorely missed the autonomy.

Still, it would take a bit before he'd mastered them. His fitness had taken a hit over the last few weeks – just walking around and looking for computer parts was exhausting, both physically and mentally. It didn't help that they were standing around on the landing site of the First Portent. The unreality here was higher than average, putting him on edge, and he could feel the constant prickling of radiation, a harsh static, like pins and needles.

It was faint – the area had been cleaned up of the worst of it – but it was still present. They'd taken some precautions against it, of course. Heavy clothes and gloves, to discard later, and face masks so as not to breathe the particles in.

All of this served to make moving around more difficult.

After another five minutes, Vincent sat down again and shook some of the sweat out of his hair.

Joey came over and sat next to him, handing him a water bottle.

*You alright?* he signed.

Vincent nodded and took a swig from the bottle. The water was deliciously cold. He considered pouring some of it on his head but decided not to. His limbs were brand new – he didn't want to risk damaging them with water immediately. Technically, they were waterproof, especially if he put on the synthetic skin layer. But usually he left it off, for aesthetic purposes, and he wasn't sure how much of a battering these limbs could take yet.

Ahead, Kylie and Quinn were carrying a crumpled door between them, which they sat down with the other parts of THE GLAM VAN. Maggie, meanwhile, came over and dropped a single sideview mirror onto the pile, while Piper carefully placed down a glove full of broken glass. Piper had driven them all up to the site of the First, in a van she'd borrowed from the DOU. Vincent wondered whether the DOU knew exactly what it was she'd borrowed it for.

*Hey.* Kylie pointed over at Vincent and Joey. *What are you doing, you slackers? Get off your arses and find more bits!*

*Actually,* Maggie signed, *this is probably enough. I don't think it matters if there are a couple of small pieces missing. As long as MOST of it is there.*

*Are you sure?* Piper signed. *There's more glass back there!*

*I'm not one hundred per cent sure, no,* Maggie signed back. *It's never one hundred percent with P.I.U.S, is it?*

*Okay, how about ninety nine per cent?* Piper nudged her. *Ninety-nine point five?*

*Ninety-nine point nine nine nine nine,* Maggie signed back, grinning.

Vincent rolled his eyes.

'Those two are nauseating,' he said out of the side of his mouth. 'They should get a room already.'

'Aw.' Joey grinned back. 'I think its sweet!'

Across from them, Kylie was also looking un-amused. *You'd better not have got my hopes up for nothing,* she signed tersely. *This better work!*

*It will,* Maggie signed.

*Within three standard deviations of certainty!* Piper added and stifled a giggle.

*Alright, well, can we get a move on?* Kylie said. *We're losing daylight. Quinn, Spencer, get over here!*

Vincent rolled his eyes again, but he did as she asked.

*Okay,* Maggie signed, pulling out her tiny notebook and handing it to Piper. *This one is obviously a bit bigger than the last two, but I'm confident you can do it. The only problem is, the last two objects were small or intact enough that you could just hold them in your hand. This time, there is an entire stack of large, heavy objects. I'm not entirely sure how this will go, but I think if Quinn, you stand on that side of the pile, and Spencer, you stand on this side, then the area between you should be what gets reverted.*

*Shouldn't they hold hands?* Piper said.

*Ideally, yes,* Maggie said. *But don't think it's strictly necessary, especially since they've worked together several times before. They know what to feel for. Right guys?*

Vincent glanced at Quinn, who was also looking at him, her expression blank. They met each other's eyes for an instant and looked away again.

*Yes,* Quinn signed, and Vincent nodded.

*Okay, fantastic,* Maggie signed. *I've got a song that should work to bring the RV back fourteen days. That's two days before it got destroyed, just for a bit of wiggle room. Piper, do you have the speaker?*

Piper triumphantly lifted a small Bluetooth speaker into the air.

*Great,* Maggie said. *Just hold it up so both of our smiths can hear it. Quinn, could you go over there please? And Spencer, a bit more to the left? Yep, that's right! Okay. Everyone else move back behind Piper. Smiths, are you ready?*

Quinn and Vincent both nodded.

*Okay,* Maggie signed excitedly. *I'm going to start the music on the count of three. Then, I'll count down from ten a bit later in the song. When I sign GO, activate your symptoms, focusing on the space between you. Alright?*

They nodded again.

Maggie held up three fingers, then two, then one. Then she hit play on her mobile phone. Vivaldi's *Summer* began playing through the speaker, the sound small and tinny in the wide-open field.

For a couple of minutes, everyone waited in suspense. Then Maggie began counting from ten.

Vincent swallowed nervously. There was going to be a side effect this time, he just knew it. They were changing too much, breaking off a piece of the timeline and bringing it forward to where it never should have been. One didn't do something like that without consequences.

As the countdown neared its end, he reluctantly reached out and touched the piece of Portent that was wedged somewhere at his core, drawing its power through a space smaller than a pinhead. He felt reality blur, the lines coming untethered around him. Across from him, Quinn was doing the same.

Maggie flicked her fingers sharply down, signalling GO – and Vincent let the power out, pouring it into the pile of junk that sat in front of him. The sub-atomic structures that gave it form were suddenly visible to him, not through his eyes, but through another sense, a prickling of flavours undulating on different angles.

Quinn's power was there too – slow and vast, inexorable, seizing the particles and making them dance in time to the music that was echoing, backwards, inside his mind. They spun in reverse, faster and faster, connections forming and reforming again. For a while, they just spun there, as if waiting. Then, all at once, the pieces of THE GLAM VAN began to move.

The process was eerily silent, and shockingly rapid. Pieces climbed over each other and slotted into place, connections forming in a bright cascade. Joey yelled and ducked as glass flew over his head and landed in the windscreen, slotting and sealing together.

Then it was over and, with a jolt, the song reached its beginning.

Pain – instant pain in his back.

Vincent gasped, crouching down, reaching instinctively for his lower spine. The pain intensified then numbed abruptly.

His hand brushed over something there – something made of metal where there should only have been flesh. He couldn't see it, but it felt lumpy, warm with body heat. Then it suddenly moved, ticking around itself and he withdrew his hand in a hurry.

'Dude,' Joey was saying, grabbing his shoulders. 'Are you okay?'

Vincent looked at him, his gaze swimming. The thing in his back ticked around again, making a faint CLICK noise as it did so.

'There's,' he managed to say, 'there's something on my back.'

Joey tipped him forward and pulled up his shirt. Vincent heard him exclaim.

'What is it?' Vincent asked weakly.

'Your spine!' Joey said, 'It's like... clockwork? There's all these chunky cogs and wheels! Argh! They move!'

Vincent let out a shaky breath.

'Fantastic,' he said.

Maggie came into his field of vision, looking concerned. *Do you need to go to the fleshsmith?* she signed.

Vincent shook his head. *I don't think a fleshsmith is going to be any help.*

'He's turning into a clock!' Joey waved his hands around.

Maggie made a face. *It's the fate of all smiths to start resembling their Portent eventually,* she said. *Becoming part machine is common for mattersmiths. I know that isn't exactly consoling to know...*

*I'm already part machine,* Vincent signed crossly.

Frowning, he glanced across to where Quinn was. She

was sitting down as well, staring off into space, her expression slack.

'So,' Kylie said, drawing everyone's attention. 'It looks like it worked – from the outside at least. Maggie, may I step inside and inspect my baby?'

*Yes, go ahead!* Maggie signed. *Piper, can I have my notebook back?*

Piper handed her the book, while Kylie stepped towards the freshly constructed GLAM VAN. It looked exactly like it had fourteen days ago – grime on the windscreen and everything.

Pulling her locket out of the neck of her shirt, Kylie unfolded it into its key shape and unlocked the driver's door. Everyone watched as she climbed into the cabin, scrutinising it closely. Pencil and notebook in hand, Maggie went and looked in as well.

'Does it look correct?' she asked Kylie.

'Hmm,' Kylie said. 'Seems to all be there. Bit dusty. I was hoping all the time travel would give it a bit of a clean.'

She opened the door to the back and looked inside.

'All our shit is still there too,' she commented.

'Yo, it is?' Joey ran over to look.

'Yeah, the stuff we left here, at least,' Kylie said. 'The stuff we brought down to the Ark is still gone.'

'Dammit, I didn't think of that!' Maggie said. 'We should have reversed it further! Then EVERYTHING would have been here.'

'Would it have been?' Piper said, poking her head into the cabin as well. 'If those things were destroyed by the First Portent, would it be a paradox for them to exist now?'

'No,' Maggie said. 'Because we've restored them to a state in which they weren't destroyed, that's the point. This version of the RV is an exact molecular copy of the one from fourteen days ago...'

As they all went into the back of the RV, their voices faded from hearing.

Vincent sighed.

'You're welcome,' he muttered. 'Not like my spine is a series of cogs now or anything...'

On the other side of the RV, Quinn let out a sharp huff of air.

Vincent turned to eye her. She was grinning, in a humourless sort of way.

'What?' he said.

'Nothing,' she said. 'It's just kinda funny.'

'What is?' Vincent said.

'How we try to avoid this bullshit,' Quinn said. 'And yet, every time, we end up doing it anyway.'

'Yeah, well, welcome to being a smith,' Vincent said. 'That's the life, isn't it? You do the impossible and get nothing in return.'

'Most of the time,' Quinn said, 'they don't even remember anything that I did. This is kind of a nice change.'

'Yeah?' Vincent said. 'Well, at least your symptom is unique and useful. What can I do? Make holes in walls? Me and every other mattersmith.'

'I WISH I was the same as a bunch of other mattersmiths,' Quinn said. 'Then no one would care about what I could do. Have you seen Maggie's notes? Fuckin' Subject Alpha?'

'Yeah?' Vincent said, 'Well, I wish I could reverse time like you can. Do you know how many times I would have used that, if I could?'

'Oh?' Quinn said. 'Like when?'

'Like...' Vincent paused. 'Well... all the time. I have... made a lot of mistakes. I wish I had the ability to redo them.'

'But would you though?' Quinn said.

'What? Yes, of course!'

'But would you really?' Quinn said. 'If it was something that happened years ago. Do you really want to re-live several years of your life? Doesn't that sound exhausting?'

'If I could relive my entire life, with the knowledge I have now,' Vincent said, 'I would.'

'Really?' Quinn wrinkled her nose. 'But most of it will end up being the same! The same people in the same places, and they'll treat you the same as they always did. And you'll probably react the exact same as well. Not every moment matters, you know. Most moments are boring and changing them won't change shit.'

'There are moments that do matter, though,' Vincent said. 'In one of them I accidentally stabbed you, didn't I? And then you changed it, and I didn't. If you hadn't changed it, you might be dead and I would be a murderer. Both of our lives would be vastly different.'

'Accidentally stabbed?' Quinn narrowed her eyes. 'I'm pretty sure it was deliberate!'

'I don't think it was,' Vincent said. 'Obviously, I don't remember it. But I can't think why it would have been on purpose. I didn't want to kill you, I wanted to capture you. I think I must have panicked.'

'Hmm,' Quinn said. 'I think you've forgotten how much you hated us.'

'Maybe I have,' Vincent said. He paused.

'I'm... sorry about stabbing you,' he said awkwardly. 'Even if from my perspective it never happened.'

Quinn blinked at him.

'An apology?' she said. 'Huh. Maybe Mullet is right about you after all. Maybe you do just need some friends.'

'Hey!' Vincent bristled. 'I have friends!'

'Oh yeah?' Quinn said. 'Name two. Not including Mullet.'

Vincent opened and shut his mouth.

'I have... I had friends,' he muttered. 'Although... to be honest they weren't very good ones...'

'They haven't even tried to look for you, have they?' Quinn said.

'Well,' Vincent said. 'That's because they still think I'm dead.'

'Hmm,' Quinn said. 'You don't seem very interested in letting them know otherwise.'

'Yeah,' Vincent said quietly.

They were both silent for a moment.

'Hey,' Vincent said hesitantly. 'So, that song you got Mullet to play at Snakebyte's house...'

Quinn brightened. 'You liked it?'

'No!' Vincent said. 'Not... not yet. I haven't listened to enough to decide...'

'Guess I'll have to show you more then!' Quinn grinned and she stood up. 'Where's Maggie's speaker? Oh, there it is –'

She broke off, frowning.

'Is it just me,' she said, 'or was that tree not there before?'

'Huh?' Vincent looked to where she was pointing. A small sapling was standing upright, directly in front of the speaker.

There was grass too, around the base of the tree, and extending out on an angle on either side. There was a clear line where the grass ended and the nuclear-blasted rubble began.

Vincent watched Quinn follow the line out of sight around the RV. Shortly, she came around the other side, a puzzled expression on her face.

'It's a triangle,' she said. 'Everything inside the triangle has been reverted to how it was two weeks ago.'

'Yeah, and?' Vincent said.

'Why is it a triangle?' Quinn said. 'There's a point over there, where I was standing, here, where you were standing, and... there, where the tree is? Or where the speaker was, I guess...'

'So the speaker acted as a third person?' Spencer said. 'That sounds pretty consistent with your musical time garbage, right?'

'I guess so,' Quinn said.

She looked thoughtful for a moment and then sighed.

'Well, there's one thing for sure,' she said. 'Maggie is going to be VERY interested in this.'

**Lyrics from the song ROBOT,
by TEMPORAL BOOM**

ROBOT

Verse 1

When I wake up in the early morn

I always get up straight away

I always take the time to eat

Three full, nutritious meals a day

I exercise at 6AM,

And don't forget to make my bed

I don't waste time while in the shower

Thinking 'bout the rising dread

I'll do the things you ask me to

And sometimes extra stuff as well

Cause I'm reliable like that

And your life is a living hell

And my life, yeah it's fine, why ask?

I have my work, I have my friends

I teeter, but I never fall,

Off tightropes that can never end

But what of it? I'm fine, I'm fine

I'll do this every day, all year!

Cause I'm not really human, see

I'm made of metal, wire, gears!

My battery's always on full,

My robot arms are big and strong

I'll carry all the world with them

And nothing ever will go wrong!

Chorus

I'm a robot, a robot

I don't have time to feel

Cause I'm a robot, and I got

Humanity to kill

Faster, faster, more and more

Don't you dare put down that load

Because if you stop for just one tock

You'll instantly explode


Verse 2

I don't exist for my own sake

I'm here to serve a greater good

I can't have interests of my own

And wouldn't have them if I could

I'm fine with giving all the time

And getting little back in turn

I'd never ask for anything

(Except for all the world to burn)

I'm sorry I don't have the time

I'm busy making no mistake

I'm sorry I don't love you back

My heart is actually a fake

I'm sorry that I sometimes glitch

And all the rage comes pouring through

I'm sorry that I lied and said

That I was not a human too

Chorus

I'm a robot, a robot

I don't have time to feel

Cause I'm a robot, and I got

Humanity to kill

Faster, faster, more and more

Don't you dare put down that load

Because if you stop for just one tock

You'll instantly explode

ACTUALLY, FUCK ALL OF THAT! IT'S NOT FUCKING
TRUE AT ALL! RAGH!

I'm a human, a human

I'm full of angst and strife!

Cause I'm a human, and I am

Not wasting up my life!

I'll sit right down and do fuck all

And with that, there is nothing wrong

I won't explode but I sure as hell will

Write another angry song!

# CHAPTER 49

# SUSPECT NUMBER ONE

### Date: Saturday 14 March 2082

'I have finished reviewing all the evidence so far,' the Detective said. 'Would you like to hear the summary?'

It was evening, and the Detective was sitting at a small table opposite Bill. They were in a Chinese-style restaurant in the town of Robinvale beside a window that looked out onto the Murray River. As it was a Saturday evening, the restaurant was busy – but that hadn't stopped the Detective hooking their charging cable into a wall socket and hogging the spot for several hours.

Bill, who had just ordered his third plate of dumplings, nodded around a large mouthful of food. *Go ahead*, he signed, chewing vigorously.

'So,' the Detective said. 'To begin with, here is a summary of our assumptions and discoveries so far. We know that the town of Mildura disappeared, between the hours of 11AM and 1:30PM on Sunday the 8th of March. We initially assumed that a Portent was responsible for this unusual occurrence – however, upon following multiple leads on recent Portent sightings, no evidence to support this theory was uncovered. In light of this lack of evidence, we have instead investigated the alternative theory that an individual, or multiple individuals, with P.I.U.S, are instead responsible for the disappearance.'

'Yep.' Bill nodded, dipping another dumpling into a small bowl of soy sauce. 'Go on.'

'Due to visible temporal discrepancies at the site of the

disappearance,' the Detective continued, 'the current running assumption is that a timesmith is responsible. This theory has been further validated by the discovery of a similar, if much smaller, temporal anomaly at the most recent landing site of the First Portent.'

'Yep, yep,' Bill said. 'That I found, mind you. I hope you've included that in your report!'

'Following evidence found at this smaller site'—the Detective ignored him—'our next assumption was that a satellite tracker was, if not the timesmith themselves, at least present when the smaller temporal anomaly was created. We have since validated this theory after interviewing the tracker known as Dingo, who has in turn provided us with a name - Kylie Collins.'

'Right,' Bill said. 'Suspect Number One!'

'Indeed,' the Detective said. 'This woman was not only present at the site where the First Portent landed, but went on to win the lottery later that very week - an achievement that simply cannot be a coincidence. It is almost certain that she, or one of the others in that same group, or perhaps more than one of them, are the rogue timesmith or smiths, that we are after.'

'Right,' Bill said again. 'So, uhh, how do we find this Ms Collins?'

'That is the question,' the Detective said. 'I have thought it over. And I have made some progress.'

'Oh?' Bill said.

'Kylie Collins won the lottery in Bendigo,' the Detective said. 'However, I do not believe she permanently lives there. Dingo mentioned that she used to be a satellite tracker herself but was more recently "into the music business". Both of these "professions" are notoriously mobile. It is very possible that Ms Collins does not have a permanent address at all. This, plus the fact that she has recently won a large amount of money, mean that she could theoretically be anywhere in the Nation.'

'Not anywhere,' Bill said. 'Assuming she IS the timesmith, then she was in Mildura about a week ago.'

'That is correct,' the Detective said. 'Although she may have fled the scene following the incident. But you are right. Until last Sunday, she was in or near Mildura. I will mention now that there is even a possibility that she disappeared with it.'

'Oh,' Bill said. 'We'll never find her if that's true!'

'We cannot rule it out,' the Detective said. 'At least, not until we confirm a sighting of her alive and well later than last Sunday, the 8th of March. In order to confirm such a sighting, I believe the best way forward is to locate friends, family and acquaintances of Kylie Collins and interview them. If she was not caught up in the disappearance of Mildura, then there is a chance she spoke to these people afterwards. If she did not intend to vanish the town, then she would seek council amongst those she trusted. If she did intend to, then perhaps she explained her plans to someone in advance. Either way, such information will be invaluable.'

'Okay,' Bill said. 'Sure. How do we find Ms Collins' friends and family?'

'Well,' the Detective said. 'I am working on that. However, we do have one lead. Dingo mentioned that when he picked Kylie Collins up from the landing site of the First Portent, there were four other people there too. One of them was a woman called "Maggie", while the other three were teenagers, whose names Dingo did not remember. This "Maggie" has unfortunately proven to be a mystery – I cannot find record of her amongst my available files. However, I do believe I have identified of one of the teenagers.'

'Oh, great!' Bill said. 'How?'

'I have constructed images of the four, based on the descriptions that Dingo provided,' the Detective said. 'I then ran these images against the criminal record database and one came up in close resemblance – a seventeen-year-old male, from Mildura, called Joey Collins. Charged with two counts of shoplifting.'

'Joey Collins, eh?' Bill said. 'Related to Kylie?'

'It seems likely,' the Detective said.

'Well, there we go,' Bill said. 'Great job, Detective!'

'Well,' the Detective said, 'I am unsure that this information is at all useful.'

'Oh?'

'As I mentioned, Joey Collins officially resides in Mildura. Thus, there is a high chance he has disappeared. The alternative is that he works closely with Ms Collins, and in that case, it is likely they are both in the same location. In other words, finding Joey Collins will be just as difficult as finding Kylie Collins herself.'

'Ah,' Bill said. 'Well... at least we can rule him out, I suppose. Did you find anything about the other teenagers?'

'I did not,' the Detective said.

'Damn. What next, then?'

'It seems likely,' the Detective said, 'that Kylie Collins had friends and family in Mildura and potentially the surrounding areas as well. As such, I have sent the constructed images of the suspects, as well as the names that we know, to all sin-seeker departments within the region. I have also included the vehicle licence number associated with Ms Collins in case their vehicle is sighted. It is my hope that someone will recognise them or at least point us in the right direction. In the meantime, we can manually search for anyone who may know Kylie or Joey Collins. Joey must have attended a school in Mildura – perhaps he has a classmate who moved away from the town and can tell us about him? Or perhaps there are other Collins family members that we can locate? For example –'

They broke off when Bill's mobile phone suddenly lit up on the table, announcing that someone was calling.

Bill frowned, leaning forward to read the caller ID.

'Look,' he said, grabbing the phone, 'it's the Red Cliffs office! Hello?' He put the phone to his ear. 'Hi... Wombat! Yeah, of course I remember you! I... Is this... Wait, do you mind if I put the phone on loudspeaker?'

The Detective watched his eyebrows go up.

'Oh?' he said. 'Um, okay. Sure, hang on.'

He lowered the phone and, gesturing for the Detective to follow him, he stood up.

'Let's go to the bathroom,' he said quietly.

Frowning, the Detective went after him as he made for the back of the restaurant.

'Is this necessary?' they said as Bill locked both of them into a tiny, dim bathroom stall.

Instead of answering, Bill lifted the phone up and put it on loudspeaker.

'Okay,' he said seriously. 'We're alone now.'

'Thanks, I appreciate it,' Wombat's voice came through the other end. 'What I've got to say is somewhat... well, let's just say I'd rather that it isn't overheard by everyone this side of the Murray. Off the record, too, okay?'

'No prob, Bob,' Bill said. 'Fire away!'

'Is the Detective there?' Wombat said.

'They are,' Bill said.

'Okay,' Wombat said. 'So, uh. How's your Portent investigation going, first of all?'

'Well, actually we've decided it probably wasn't a Portent,' Bill said. 'Right Detective?'

'That is correct,' the Detective said. 'Our current working hypothesis is that a smith is responsible for the disappearance of Mildura. A timesmith, to be specific.'

'Woah,' Wombat said, 'you sound different! Did you change your voice?'

'I did, yes.'

'Fair enough,' Wombat said. 'A timesmith, did you say? Oh, huh. That... makes far too much sense, actually. In fact, its blindingly obvious come to think of it. The picture of the First Portent and everything...'

'What are you talking about?' Bill frowned. 'What's blindingly obvious?'

'Well, basically,' Wombat said, 'I saw the Detective's email. The one you just sent, half an hour ago, about the persons of interest?'

'Yes?' The Detective leaned in. 'Did you recognise one of them?'

'I recognised all of them,' Wombat said. 'They're... Well, they're a band.'

'What?' Bill said. 'As in a musical band?'

'Yep,' Wombat said. 'They're called Temporal Boom. Which, combined with the knowledge that they're probably timesmiths, is actually... my God. They have a picture of the First Portent on the drum set. It's not even subtle at all.'

'Huh,' Bill said, looking at the Detective.

'Dingo said that Kylie Collins was involved with music,' the Detective said. 'But this is more involved than I anticipated.'

'So are you, what, investigating them currently?' Bill said excitedly. 'Or do you – Please tell me you have them locked up already?'

'Uh, no, we don't unfortunately,' Wombat said. 'But I suppose you could say we've been investigating them. They've recently become very popular around here. Weren't even on the radar last year and now they're doing live concerts in Mildura. Or they were, before it disappeared.'

'Is that so?' The Detective cocked their head. 'Is that where you saw the drum set?'

'Um,' Wombat said. 'Yes. Tank and I, uhh, infiltrated one of the concerts, about a month ago. That's how we know what they look like. Although they wear masks on stage. But I'm pretty sure it's them. Eighty per cent sure. Ninety, now that you've told me about the timesmith thing.'

'Temporal Boom,' the Detective said. 'You're right, it is quite... on the nose. But Bill, we've come across that name before. Do you remember? It was the band that Mr Liam King was listening to, when he encountered the Eighth Portent. I noted at the time that it was an odd name.'

'Huh,' Bill said. 'So it is! Detective, I think we're finally closing in! It's all coming together!'

'Perhaps it is,' the Detective said. 'Or perhaps not. Officer Wombat – why have you not yet arrested these musicians?'

'Um,' Wombat said. 'Well...'

She paused.

'I imagine you have tried,' the Detective said, 'however, no matter from what direction you approach, they always know you're coming. Is that correct?'

'Uh, yeah, exactly!' Wombat said. 'Timesmiths! You just can't catch 'em!'

'Not unless you are very clever,' the Detective said. 'You must prepare a trap so complete that they cannot escape it, even through time.'

'Right,' Wombat said hesitantly.

There was a pause.

'Do you, uhh, have a specific trap in mind?' Wombat said.

'No,' the Detective said. 'Not yet. I require more information. Who are the members of this band? Is just one of them a timesmith, or more than one? What are the precise parameters of their symptoms? And, a simpler but very important question – where are they now? Officer Wombat, I don't suppose you have seen these people since the disappearance of Mildura?'

'No, I haven't,' Wombat said. 'Although, I haven't exactly been looking out for them. We've had a few other things on our plate, you know?'

'When was the last time you saw them?' the Detective said. 'And where?'

'Oh, well, that I can answer,' Wombat said. 'Valentine's Day. February 14th, a Friday night. They played a concert just outside of Mildura that evening.'

'Okay,' the Detective said. 'And Kylie Collins was there?'

'Yes, she was there,' Wombat said. 'I definitely saw her. She's not in the band, though. I think she's the manager or something. Had a stall set up, where she was selling USBs and merch. They were selling like hotcakes.'

'Okay. And Joey Collins?'

'He was there too. Pretty sure, anyway. As I said, they were wearing masks on stage, but I think he's the lead guitar.'

'Okay,' the Detective said. 'And do you know the names of any of the others?'

'No, I don't,' Wombat said. 'Sorry.'

'No names at all?' the Detective said. 'Of anyone else who was there?'

'Oh,' Wombat said. 'There was the M.C.?'

'Yes?'

'He referred to himself as M.C. Funtimes, but his real name is Jason,' Wombat said. 'Jason? No, wait. Jaden? Jordan? Something beginning with J. He has a pretty noticeable full-facial cybernetic, anyway.'

'A cybernetic?' the Detective said. 'Interesting. I ask that you send a detailed description of this man to my email address at your earliest convenience. In the meantime, is there anything else you remember from this event?'

Wombat paused again.

'We didn't really talk to anyone else there,' she said. 'Although...'

'Although?'

'We bought a USB,' Wombat said. 'From Kylie Collins. As, uhh, evidence.'

'Do you still have it?' the Detective said.

'Yes. It's probably in the back somewhere. I can find it, if you'd like?'

'Please,' the Detective said.

# CHAPTER 50

# VALENTINE'S DAY

**Date: Friday 14 February 2082**

'A toast,' Justin Waratah said cheerfully, 'to the rising stars of the music world.'

He raised a flute glass, clinking it against Kylie's. Then, pressing a small button on the side of his jaw, he opened a section of his full-facial cybernetic. Quinn, standing to the side, caught sight of bared teeth and pink flesh as he tipped the sparkling wine inside and closed the panel again.

Justin apparently noticed her staring, as he turned to look at her, his cartoon face giving her a wink. 'Are you sure you don't want any champers?' he said. 'You're the real star here, after all.'

'No, thanks,' Quinn said.

They were standing in Justin's living room, next to the gigantic, centre-piece shark tank. It was Valentine's Day, and there was a concert later – and Temporal Boom were the headline act. Quinn could barely believe it was really happening. Things had moved so fast in the last two weeks.

Hell, things had been moving fast for the past few months. Just six months ago, they had stood in this same room and Quinn had begged Kylie to let her take part in Justin's original works competition. Now, they were the ones organising the event and not only that, the event was sold out.

It felt surreal, like a dream. Quinn kept pinching herself

in case she woke up. But she didn't and here they were, a couple hours before curtain up.

'So, just to triple check,' Justin said, 'you guys remember what to do if there's an emergency? The venue is fully soundproofed and all guests have been vetted through the usual means; however, there is always a chance that someone undesirable will get in and cause trouble.'

'Yes, like Spencer did at the last one,' Kylie said.

'That's right,' Justin said. 'Do you remember what to do if it happens again?'

'There's a secret exit at the back,' Quinn said. 'Behind the stage.'

'Correct,' Justin said. 'What else?'

'If there's trouble incoming, you will signal to us with a picture of a snake,' Quinn said.

'That's right,' Justin said, his screen changing to display a green, cartoon serpent. 'If you see this image, you should leave immediately, regardless of what is happening. And what else?'

'We have to wear masks,' Quinn said. 'So we're not recognised outside the event.'

'Correct. I trust your masks are ready to go?'

'Yeah,' Quinn said. 'We made them yesterday.'

'Excellent.' Justin rubbed his hands. 'Sounds like everything is ready to go, then! Nervous?'

'Um,' Quinn said. 'Not really. I don't think it's hit me yet.'

'Well, good, you shouldn't be.' Justin grinned at her. 'This is going to be great! They're gonna love you. Hell, they already do! The success is a given!'

'It is,' Kylie said. 'And if it's not? We'll just do it again until it is!'

'That's the spirit!' Justin said and he filled both of their glasses again. 'Another toast, to success!'

'And great big, juicy, fat stacks of cash.' Kylie winked at him.

'That too.' Justin beamed.

They clinked glasses again and Quinn rolled her eyes.

'Is that all I am to you?' she said. 'Money?'

'Of course not!' Kylie said. 'Quinn, you have no idea how much I appreciate you. Without you, literally none of this would have been possible! I never should have doubted you or your fuckin' amazing talents.'

'It's true,' Justin said. 'You're a rare breed, Quinn. We're privileged to know you!'

'Okay,' Quinn said. 'But what if I didn't make any money? What if my music was crap and no one liked it? What if'—she looked at Kylie—'I didn't have the *abilities* that I do? Would you care at all?'

'Of course we would!' Kylie said. 'I took you on before I knew anything about you, didn't I?'

'Yeah,' Quinn said. 'But was that because you suspected? Did you only take me on because you thought I might be useful? There was a ninety-eight per cent chance, wasn't there? But what if I wasn't? What I turned out to be a perfectly ordinary with no special talents at all?'

'Well, then you'd still be doing the dishes for me,' Kylie said. 'What do you want me to say? You turned out like you turned out. Is there any point dwelling on alternatives that never happened?'

'Of course there is,' Quinn said. 'I think about them all the time.'

'Well,' Kylie said. 'That sounds like a you problem. Quinn – in this timeline, we love and appreciate you. Deal with it. And for fucks sake, stop worrying, and enjoy being a superstar.'

***

A few hours later, when they arrived at the venue, Quinn's nerves began to come in for real.

The venue was different from last time – a gigantic machinery storage shed, rickety from the outside, but heavily soundproofed on the inside, a forty-minute drive away from Mildura. Since it was difficult to get to, Justin had arranged transport in the form of a small fleet of trucks, the inside of which were full of cannibalised bus seats. The trucks arrived at staggered timepoints, depositing small hordes of guests onto the farm. Other guests arrived in their own personal transport and were directed to park inside of another empty shed.

As more and more truckloads of guests arrived, Quinn became increasingly terrified. There were so many of them – and they just kept arriving!

'How are there this many people?' she squeaked to Maggie after peeking out of the stage wing. 'Half of Mildura is there!'

'It is a lot, isn't it,' Maggie said, looking faintly queasy.

'I don't think you realise how popular you are!' Justin appeared behind them, cartoon grin in place. 'Kylie could tell you – Temporal Boom sales are through the roof! Local, talented band, making new music? People love that shit!'

'But THAT many people?' Quinn said. 'I didn't even know that many people listened to music!'

'Of course they do.' Justin patted her heartily on the back. 'Everyone pretends not to, of course. But I'd say more than fifty per cent of Mildura have listened at least once. Around a third own music themselves! And I'm not just pulling those numbers out of my arse. I've seen the sales myself!'

'Really?' Quinn said. 'A third?'

'Oh yes,' Justin said. 'And all of them want to see it live. This concert is going to be a smash hit, I can tell. All thanks to you!'

Grinning, he moved off, nodding to Mullet and Spencer who were coming up the stairs on the side of the stage.

'Yo,' Mullet said excitedly, bouncing closer. 'Are you guys ready to absolutely DROWN in sexy hunks and babes?'

'What?' Quinn wrinkled her nose.

'Fans!' Mullet threw up his hands. 'Groupies! Have you seen them? Absolutely frothing out there!'

'Ah, well, you can have them,' Quinn said nervously.

'Where's your girlfriend?' Mullet addressed Maggie.

'Huh?' Maggie said, her face flushing slightly. 'Um. She's bringing up the drum kit.'

'She's playing then?' Mullet grinned. 'Awesome! I knew you could convince her!'

Behind him, Spencer was staring apprehensively out at the stage. Quinn moved closer to him, looking out as well. There were even more people than last time. Her stomach did a flip-flip.

'I can't believe this,' Spencer said quietly.

'Yeah,' Quinn said nervously. 'They're all going to be looking at me in about twenty minutes.'

'How are there so many?' Spencer said. 'Are they all from Mildura?'

'I think so, yeah.'

'Well, that doesn't make sense,' Spencer said.

'What?' Quinn looked at him. 'Why not?'

'Because if THIS many people listen to music,' Spencer said, 'then why aren't there more Portent attacks?'

'Because people aren't complete idiots?' Quinn shrugged. 'They listen to music indoors, in the comfort of their own soundproofed home. If the noise doesn't get out, it's fine.'

Spencer was silent for a moment.

'The Department of Sin has no idea,' he said shortly. 'Absolutely no clue what they're dealing with. They're fighting a losing battle. And...'

'And?' Quinn said.

'I don't even think it's a battle worth fighting,' Spencer said.

'What?' Quinn's eyebrows shot up. 'You don't?! But I thought being anti-music was your entire personality? Have you changed so much?'

'No,' Spencer snapped at her, 'I haven't changed that much, I've just...'

He sighed. 'I've just re-evaluated some of my priorities, I suppose. And I think that maybe there are more pressing issues than hunting down music users. Maybe in the past, when we didn't have soundproofing on everything, it was important. But these days... well, if there are this many of them, and the Portents haven't killed us already, then... what's the point?'

'There isn't one,' Quinn said gleefully. 'The ban on music is stupid! I'm glad you've finally seen the light!'

'Okay,' Spencer said. 'Here's something else that's stupid – why haven't you done anything about it?'

'Wh-huh?' Quinn blinked. 'What do you mean?'

'I don't mean you, personally,' Spencer continued. 'I mean you, the music community. If you have all this evidence that listening to music in private doesn't increase Portent risk, then why haven't you told anyone?'

'Well... because they wouldn't listen!' Quinn said. 'They're already convinced that we're all sinners who revel in bringing danger to helpless, god-fearing communities. Why would they change their mind?'

'You have facts and evidence, don't you?' Spencer said. 'They're people capable of rational thought, are they not?'

'Debatable,' Quinn said.

'You haven't even tried, have you?' Spencer said.

'We haven't, no,' Quinn said, 'because we've been too busy running away from sin-seeker twerps who want to arrest us.'

'What, all of you?' Spencer said and he gestured out at the crowd. 'All of them? You really think ALL of them could be arrested at once?'

Quinn stared at him.

'What are you trying to say here?'

Spencer frowned.

'I think,' he said, 'I'm about to do something rash again.'

'What?'

'If it goes horribly wrong,' Spencer said seriously, 'can you please undo it?'

'Wha- Spencer, what are you about to do? Wait, where are you going?!'

Spencer, a determined look on his face, had stepped onto the stage and was making a beeline for the mic. Before Quinn could do anything, he'd grabbed it off the stand and was speaking into it.

'Hello everyone,' he said, causing feedback to whine throughout the room.

As the crowd quietened, looking up at him, Mullet appeared beside Quinn, a baffled expression on his face. 'What the fuck is he doing?' he hissed.

Quinn shrugged helplessly as Spencer moved the mic further away from his mouth and tried again.

'Hello,' he said, his voice amplified around the room. 'My name is Vincent Spencer and I used to be a sin-seeker.'

'I used to be a sin-seeker,' he went on, as Justin appeared on the stage and tried to usher him off. 'But now I'm not! Oi, don't touch me, creep!'

Justin raised his hands defensively as Spencer sent him his patented glare. 'I won't be long,' he said. 'Just gimme a sec. I have something to say.'

Justin stepped back a bit as the audience laughed. 'Fine, you've got five minutes,' he said. 'Impromptu comedy act, let's go!'

'This isn't a joke,' Spencer said as the audience laughed again. 'I'm serious. I used to be a sin-seeker and I used to hate music. I'd never heard it before, but I hated it anyway, and everyone who listened to it.'

'Is he TRYING to get bashed?' Mullet hissed, head in his hands, as the crowd booed loudly.

'But recently,' Spencer went on, 'I met some people who changed my mind. They're the people who make up the band you're all here to see – Temporal Boom. They write music and sell it, and apparently, you all listen to it.'

There was a hesitant cheer from the crowd.

'I couldn't help but notice that there are a LOT of you here,' Spencer said. 'I was shocked, in fact. Are you all from Mildura?'

There was a louder cheer.

'And you all listen to music?'

A considerably louder cheer.

'Okay,' Spencer said, 'so why haven't you made music legal yet?'

There was a confused silence.

'There's enough of you here,' Spencer said slowly, 'that if you ALL protested, or went on strike or something, Mildura would stop functioning. If you made a stink about it, the authorities could NOT ignore it. They couldn't arrest all of you either. There's too many. Do you get what I'm saying? Or do you want me to spell it out even more?'

More silence.

'If you all work together,' Spencer said, his tone like that of one speaking to a toddler, 'you can change the law. Do you understand?'

'You can do that?' someone yelled.

'Yes!' Spencer said. 'The law isn't set in stone. It's supposed to change over time, to reflect the changing needs of society.'

'Legal music?!' someone else yelled. 'Sign me the fuck up!'

'Preach it, pig boy!' someone else yelled.

There were a couple of cheers and then someone began chanting *Change The Law! Change The Law!* In seconds, the chant had swelled in volume, filling the space.

'Yeah, exactly,' Spencer said into the mic. 'Get that into your skulls.'

Then he put the mic back on its stand and left, brushing past a stunned Justin on the way out.

As he came back to where Quinn and Mullet were standing, the chant was still going, louder than ever. As he left the view of the crowd, Spencer sagged slightly, his hands visibly shaking – but there was a fire in his eyes that Quinn hadn't seen there for a while.

'What the fuck was that?' Mullet said in disbelief. 'Where did that come from?'

Spencer shrugged.

'If I'm changing my mind, then I'm changing it,' he said. 'Only wimps sit on the fence!'

'Well, okay,' Quinn said. 'I guess I'm glad our fight is the one you've decided to take up. Don't expect things to change overnight, though. These people might be chanting now, but they won't do shit about it once they go home.'

'Maybe not,' Spencer said, 'but they'll be thinking about it!'

Quinn opened her mouth to respond, but just then, Justin announced over the mic that the band would be on in ten minutes. The crowd, still chanting, broke out into a deafening cheer.

'Shit,' Quinn said, all other thoughts leaving her mind. 'It's time to set up!'

She ran over to where she'd left her mask and put it on. It covered the top half of her face, painted with a black and yellow radioactive symbol.

Mullet's mask resembled a fanged skull, while Maggie was wearing oversized motorcycle goggles with iridescent lenses like the eyes of an insect. Piper's mask was pink and resembled a triceratops, with long, paper mâché horns.

Grinning, they all looked at each other – before grabbing their equipment and hauling it on stage.

Spencer helped them move their stuff, and Kylie made a brief appearance, wishing them luck before running back to the merch stall. Once everything was in place, they moved into position and signalled to Justin that they were ready. He sent them three thumbs up, two with his hands and one with his face, before disappearing in front of the curtain to address the crowd.

Quinn took a deep breath, in and out.

'Okay,' she said. 'Let's do this perfectly the first time.'

'Or at least adequately!' Mullet said.

'It had better go well the first time,' Maggie said. 'This many people, singing along – do you know how many layers that is?'

'Shit,' Quinn said. 'You're right. We'd get flung into the Jurassic era, along with, like, a third of Mildura.'

'They'll remember it was us as well!' Piper said. 'Right? If they sing? Bet they'd be pissed! They'd probably feed us to a T-rex!'

'Dude, that's a pretty epic way to die,' Mullet said. 'Hey, do you think if we sent a third of Mildura back to dino times, would they domesticate them? Could they save them from extinction? Could we have them now?'

'You say that like it would be a good thing,' Quinn said.

'She's right, that would wreak havoc on the canon timeline,' Maggie said. 'Plus, its bold of you to assume a bunch of people from Mildura could stop an entire mass-extinction level apocalypse...'

She paused, frowning.

'Wait... could they?'

'Okay,' Quinn said as Justin announced them on the other side of the curtain. 'It's go time! Everyone shut up.'

'I will,' Maggie said. 'But for the record, I just had an idea and it's a fucking doozy.'

'Cool, tell us later!' Quinn said. 'The curtain's opening!'

They all fell silent as the lights came on, bathing them in stark brightness. In instant later a wall of sound broke over them as the crowd began cheering.

Quinn instantly forgot everything except the here and now and she stepped up to the mic and became an avatar of music. But later, after the show, she asked Maggie about her idea. And Maggie sat her down and explained it to her.

It was, in fact, a fucking doozy.

# INTERVIEW WITH THE MC

### Date: Dunday 15 March 2082

'Bill,' the Detective said into the darkness. 'Bill, wake up. I believe I have found our next lead.'

Bill, who was asleep in the motel bed, muttered something incomprehensible and rolled over onto his side.

The Detective reached out and gently touched Bill's shoulder.

'Bill,' they said again. 'Wake up.'

Bill's eyes flickered open. Then, with a high-pitched yell, he rocketed upwards, staring at the Detective.

The Detective withdrew their hand, blinking at him, the blue points of their eyes faintly illuminating Bill's shocked face.

'Oh,' Bill said, and he let out a breath. 'It's you, Detective!' He clutched at his heart, shaking his head. 'One of these days, I'm going to have a heart attack.'

'I apologise for waking you,' the Detective said. 'However, I have made an important discovery. I thought you would like to hear it as soon as possible.'

Bill looked wearily at the digital clock on his bedside table.

'At 4:35 AM?' he said. 'Couldn't it wait another hour?'

The Detective paused.

'I suppose it could have. If you would like to resume sleeping, I will allow it.'

'No, no.' Bill sighed. 'No point. I'm very much awake now.'

He rubbed his eyes and leant over to turn on his bedside lamp.

'What is it?'

'I believe I have identified the man that Officer Wombat mentioned was at the Valentine's Day music event,' the Detective said. 'The one she denoted as "M.C. Funtimes".'

'Oh?' Bill said.

'Officer Wombat mentioned that she thought this man's real name started with J and that he had a "full-face cybernetic",' the Detective went on. 'I have used this information to search through the national cybernetics registry and have discovered a man called Justin Waratah, who matches both of these descriptions, and in addition, has a permanent address near Mildura.'

'Okay.' Bill nodded. 'Promising. Assuming he didn't vanish with Mildura, that is.'

'His address is nearby, not in the town itself,' the Detective said. 'Assuming the zone of disappearance was approximately a circle, equal on all sides, then his residence should have survived the incident.'

'Oh good!' Bill said. 'So, what? Are we going to pay him a little visit?'

'Yes,' the Detective said and glanced at the clock.

'Now is DEFINITELY too early,' Bill said quickly.

'Yes, I think we should delay for two hours,' the Detective said.

'6:30 is still too early, Detective. Very weird to visit someone at that time.'

'Three hours?'

'I suppose that's fine. It'll be light at 7:30 at least.'

'In the meantime,' the Detective said, 'I will email a picture of this Justin Waratah to the Red Cliffs office to confirm his identity. I do not expect them to see it for at least four hours, at which point we may already have confirmed his presence at the Valentine's Day concert. But additional evidence is always welcome.'

'Shouldn't we wait until after Wombat confirms his identity before barging into his house?' Bill said.

'That is too much time wasted.' The Detective frowned. 'Today marks one week since Mildura disappeared. That is already too long.'

'God, it's been a week already?' Bill said, and he sighed. 'Time flies when you're sleep deprived.'

***

At 7:00 AM, Bill and the Detective left the tiny motel room and got into their blue van, which was parked directly out the front of it. They had already driven back to Red Cliffs the previous evening, so the residence of Justin Waratah was not far – although getting there proved more difficult than anticipated, since most of the local roads were missing.

It took over an hour but finally, they arrived. It was a massive house, the long, straight driveway passing through several acres of bushland. Bill parked the van out the front and gave a low whistle.

'This man has dough,' he said, impressed. 'Look at this place!'

The Detective narrowed their eyes. 'I am willing to wager that much of this "dough" has been acquired through sinful means.'

'Oh, yes, for sure,' Bill said.

They got out and made their way towards the front door. Before they got there, however, the door opened – and a man that the Detective recognised as Justin Waratah leaned out.

He was wearing grey tracksuit pants and a singlet, and his hair had been hastily brushed back into a messy ponytail – but his face, a gently curved screen, displayed a cheerful cartoon smile.

*Hello,* he signed, his words mirrored on the screen. *I don't believe I know you?*

*Hello,* the Detective signed back. *We have not met previously. I am a detective, investigating the disappearance of Mildura, and this is Bill, my civilian associate. We have cause to believe that you may have information relating to this case.*

Justin cocked his head. *I do?* he signed, his face unchanged. *What sort of information?*

*We believe you may have previously met one or more of the perpetrators,* the Detective signed.

*Perpetrators?* Justin's expression changed to one of surprise. *I thought a Portent was responsible?*

*We no longer believe that is the case,* the Detective said. *May we come inside?*

Justin nodded, waving them in.

'People made Mildura disappear?' he said, once the door was closed. 'Damn, that's crazy. How is that even possible?'

'We believe a timesmith is at the root of it,' the Detective said as Justin led them further into the house and up a flight of stairs.

'A timesmith?' Justin said. 'Wow. That's really something. Would you like a cup of tea?'

'Yes, please,' Bill said.

Justin led them into a huge kitchen, where he gestured for them to sit on the bar-style stools that lined the island bench. 'No tea for you, Detective?'

'No, thank you,' the Detective said, looking around at the clean, white tiles and expansive collection of alcohol on display along the shelves. 'Mr Waratah, is it just you living in this house?'

'Yeah,' Justin said. 'Although usually, there are guests coming in and out. Always a bit of a party here, you know? Although, this week's been quieter than average.'

'Why is that?' the Detective said.

'Well, Mildura disappeared, didn't it,' Justin said. 'That's the majority of my friends and clients right there!'

The Detective frowned.

'You do not sound particularly upset, considering all of your friends have recently died.'

'Oh, well, I don't think they're *dead* dead,' Justin said.

'Why wouldn't they be dead?' Bill said in interest.

'It's just a feeling I have.' Justin shrugged. 'Maybe I'm just an optimist, y'know?'

'Or maybe'—the Detective leaned forward—'you know more about what's happened than you're letting on?'

'Naw,' Justin said. 'I don't know anything. Look – maybe I've met these people that you say are responsible for Mildura disappearing. But frankly, I wouldn't remember. Do you know how many people I know? How many new people I meet on a weekly basis?'

'Why do you meet so many people?' the Detective said.

Justin shrugged again. 'Because I got a sweet house and I throw parties on the reg. People come here to get drunk and meet more people. Over time I've a gotten a reputation for throwing a sick bash. It's not easy being popular, but someone's got to do it, right?'

'So you regularly throw parties?' the Detective said.

'Yep.'

'How regularly?'

'Once a fortnight. Sometimes more.'

'And is there usually music at these parties?' the Detective asked.

'Nah, we keep it all chill and above the table,' Justin said smoothly. 'Drinks, games, hanging with friends, that sort of thing.'

The Detective frowned again and exchanged a look with Bill. They were almost one hundred per cent sure that this was a lie – but Justin had shown no signs of lying. His cybernetic, of course, made it a lot more difficult to tell – but even his body language had betrayed no deception.

Either they had gotten the wrong man – or Justin was a highly accomplished liar. This made interrogating him more difficult than anticipated.

'So,' Justin said, handing Bill his tea and sitting down on another stool. 'Who are you trying to find? As I said, no promises that I know 'em well, but chances are I HAVE met them at one point or another.'

'Our primary suspect is a woman called Kylie Collins,' the Detective said, watching Justin's reaction.

'Hmm.' Justin scratched his chin. 'Kylie Collins... What does she look like?'

'East Asian female, long hair, possibly dyed, in her mid-twenties,' the Detective said. 'I have an image of her if you would like to see it?'

They took out a printed picture of the newspaper clip and showed Justin.

'Oh, shit!' Justin said. 'Yeah, I've seen her before! She drives, uhh, an RV, right?'

'Yes,' the Detective said. 'We believe she is involved in music dealing.'

'Oh, really?' Justin said. 'Damn, that's crazy. I had no idea.'

'Is that so?' the Detective said. 'So, you don't know any music dealers?'

'Nah,' Justin said. 'As I said, I try to keep things above the table here. Of course, I don't know what all my guests do in their spare time...'

'So you're not involved in the music industry at all?'

'Nope.'

'That's interesting,' the Detective said, 'because I have just received an email confirming a sighting of you at a music event on the 14th of February of this year. You were hosting the event, as the master of ceremonies, and referring to yourself M.C. Funtimes.'

'What?' Justin said, his face displaying shock. 'Nah, that wasn't me! I've never been to any shit like that! Your source is fibbing, mate. Trying to frame me or some shit!'

'I don't think so,' the Detective said. 'I think you are the one who is fibbing. I think that you are very much involved in the music industry and that you know Kylie Collins well.'

'Oh yeah?' Justin said crossly. 'Well, if you're gonna come in here and make accusations, then I think I'm done talking to you. I think you can talk to my lawyer. Go on, get up – and fuck off out of here!'

'I am not going anywhere until I have gained the information I came here to get,' the Detective said coldly.

'Yeah?' Justin said. 'Well, in that case, you're trespassing.

How about I call the sinnies on you, huh? Are you even with them? Or are you making that up as well?'

The Detective stood up, looming over Justin with their full height.

'You may call them if you like,' they said, 'however, you will find that they will only corroborate my information.'

'What, are you trying to intimidate me now?' Justin said. 'That shit won't work on me, Detective. If you want to arrest me, you're going to have to go through ALL the correct paperwork first. And that includes talking to my lawyer. So yeah, see in your court, motherfuck-ARGH!'

He let out a squeak as the Detective suddenly grabbed him and hoisted him into the air.

'There is no time for paperwork,' they said, and electricity crackled along the joints of their arm.

'Uh, Detective, what are you doing?!' Bill squeaked.

'Why must everything take so long?' the Detective went on. 'It's so inefficient! I know you are lying, Mr Waratah, and you know that I know. The paperwork will only reveal the same in the end. What is the point in doing it, if we both know this?'

'Because that's how the fucking law works!' Justin squeaked. 'Let me go, you psychopath!'

'He's right, let him go!' Bill said nervously. 'There are processes we have to follow! I know they're inefficient and feel like a waste of time, but they're there to keep things fair!'

'Fair?' the Detective said. 'This man has enough funds and connections to alter the process of law for his own personal gain. He has both the means and the desire to muddy the truth, perhaps indefinitely!'

'Okay, but please put him down!' Bill said. 'I am begging you!'

The Detective hesitated before gently lowering Justin's feet back to the floor. He immediately scurried around behind the island bench, his face an empty black panel.

'Yet more wasted time piled upon this investigation,' the Detective said, eyeing him. 'It could have been easy, but instead, Mr Waratah insists on lying. But know this, Mr Waratah: you may have bought yourself time now, but as soon as my current investigation is over, I will be back. I will tease out the details of your involvement in the music industry and it will not even take me long.'

'Oh yeah?' Justin said defensively. 'What are you going to do? Attack me? Torture me?'

'No,' the Detective said. 'There is no point in that. You will only continue to lie. However, you know many people. And maybe, these people know you as well? How much do they know about you, Mr Waratah? And how much do you trust them with that information? Are they all as good at lying as you are?'

When Justin said nothing, they turned and began to head towards the door. Before they got there, however, Justin came out from behind the bench and ran after them.

'Okay, okay,' he said. 'Maybe... we're all being a bit hasty here?'

The Detective paused, looking at him.

'Maybe,' Justin said, 'we should all sit down and go over some of the details again? Maybe I can remember a bit more about Kylie Collins and her crew? And maybe, once you've gotten the information you need for your investigation, you can leave it at that, huh? Neither of us wants to turn this into a long, drawn-out court case after all, do we?'

The Detective was silent.

'C'mon,' Justin said. 'Follow me, and we can have a little chat in private. This way. There's a little something I can show you, strictly off the record.'

He moved out of the kitchen, turning left into a doorway. After a moment of hesitation, the Detective went after him, Bill in tow.

Justin led them into a room that was strangely empty, except for a fridge in the corner. At the back of it was a line of bookshelves, with nothing on them, except for a single leatherbound book in the middle row.

Justin moved towards the book and raised his hand before pausing and looking around.

'Stand back,' he said, eyeing the Detective and Bill with a face that was still entirely blank. 'No, even further back. Yep, that's good.'

As he reached for the book again, Bill frowned. 'What is this?' he said, 'some sort of secret passage –'

With a solid THUNK Justin pulled the book out, revealing that it was, in fact, a lever.

An instant later, the floor beneath Bill and the Detective fell away, dropping the both of them neatly into the shark tank below.

# CHAPTER 52

# RAPID DECAY

## Date: Sunday 15 March 2082

The Detective realised what was happening an instant before hitting the water and jammed their eyes closed. Seals designed to prevent water from entering their system sprung into place, blocking anything that wasn't covered with waterproof synth-skin.

Eyes, nose, ears and various cooling vents sealed shut, the Detective sunk like a stone, hitting the bottom of the tank in seconds. Their perceptive senses were greatly reduced but they could feel movement in the water – Bill, struggling at the surface, and the two sharks swimming rapidly around in circles. They were not gigantic sharks – only two metres in length. But they were large enough that their bites could cause serious damage to Bill – if he didn't panic first and drown himself.

Thinking fast, the Detective felt around at the bottom of the tank. Their movements were slow in the water, but shortly their hand closed around a rock. It wasn't big, but it was better than nothing. They felt further until they reached a glass wall and smacked the rock into it as hard as they could.

The glass shook slightly but didn't break. It was thick, shatterproof, designed to hold the weight of a shark sized aquarium.

After hitting it several more times with the same result, the Detective abandoned that course of action and felt around again, hoping to find something larger. Above them,

Bill was still kicking and thrashing, the sharks circling towards him. The sharks were a more pressing issue, the Detective decided. They would have to deal with them before anything else. They drew their thumb-blade – a manoeuvre that let in a small amount of water, causing the wrist mechanism to short circuit. The blade would be stuck in the out position, at least until that could be fixed. But that was a later problem.

The Detective began waving their arms back and forth in an attempt to draw in the sharks. The movement above them changed slightly – although the sharks still seemed more interested in Bill.

Jumping up and down, the Detective attempted to swim higher in the tank – but their weight made it very difficult. They were not built to swim. They were not built for water at all. With ventilation shut off, their internal systems were starting to overheat already.

They had a few minutes before systems started to shut down. One of the sharks came closer – but then circled away again. How far away was it? The Detective didn't know exactly. How large was the aquarium? Based on the curvature of the glass, it was about four metres across. Surely there were other decorative objects on the floor beside small rocks? Hurriedly, the Detective stepped forward, sweeping their arms in the hope that their hand would hit into something of use –

Above, the movement changed again. Bill was thrashing with new vigour and the sharks were right up near him. The Detective thought they felt one dart in and Bill went under, his struggling slowing.

No! Bill! Had the shark bitten him? Was he bleeding out?

If only they could see what was happening! Wait – if they opened one of their eyes, they would see for a microsecond before the eye short-circuited. It wasn't much but it would be enough to assess the situation. They could see their surroundings and formulate a proper plan!

There was no time to question it. The damage could be fixed later. Positioning themselves for maximum field of view, the Detective manually removed the seal that shielded their left eye, and opened it wide –

*KRAK!*

Energy, vast amounts of it, discharged all at once. The Detective's vision went white as a lightning bolt surged through their entire body.

Water beat down on them, thunderous, as static filled their senses, roaring in their auditory sensors. The feeling, like endless, boundless energy shook at their core, threatening to go supercritical.

They came to a stop and gasping, they opened their vents. Air flooded in and steam poured out, cooling their mechanical guts. They were lying on the floor now, horizontal. One of their eyes was offline and the other was blurry to the point of uselessness – but their other senses were working again.

Bill – was Bill okay?

Dizzy, disoriented, the Detective sat upright. Numerous alerts and warnings were flashing on their internal interface.

The Detective closed the alarms off and focused on listening to the room around them. There was a strange slapping noise to their left and, to their right, someone was coughing.

'Bill,' the Detective said, moving towards the coughing. 'Bill, is that you?'

'Ye-yes,' Bill said and went into another coughing fit. 'I'm, I'm okay! I'm alive! They missed me! They bit my shirt, but they missed me!'

'Where are the sharks now?' the Detective said. 'Please describe what is happening. I cannot see.'

'Look at me,' Bill said. 'Oh. Wow. Yeah. We're going to need to fix that.'

'I agree,' the Detective said. 'What happened to the aquarium?'

'I think you blew it up,' Bill said. 'There's glass everywhere – but the water mostly drained away already. I don't know where – that's Mr Waratah's problem now I suppose.'

'And what of the sharks?'

'You fried one of them to a crisp and the other one is flopping all over the floor as we speak.'

'And Mr Waratah?'

'I don't know where he is. Not here. Detective, if you don't mind, what is your current R.L. value?'

'Forty-four per cent,' the Detective said.

'Forty-four per cent!' Bill exclaimed. 'Oh God. Well, that's horrifyingly low. You know, I think we should leave before Mr Waratah tries to dispose of us again –'

There was the sound of a door opening.

'What the fuck?!' Justin screeched.

'Welp,' Bill muttered.

The Detective immediately sprang into action. Leaping to their feet, they charged across the room towards the door.

Justin reacted, turning to run – but too slowly. The Detective heard him take a step back and pounced on him, grabbing him and pinning against the wall.

Justin tried to scream, wiggling in the Detective's grasp, before he felt their thumb-blade under his chin and went abruptly still.

'Mr Waratah,' the Detective said, staring at where they thought his face was. 'You are under arrest. You have not only lied to me repeatedly but have also attempted to kill both me and my associate. This I cannot forgive. I suggest you start cooperating this instant, or I may *lose my patience.*'

'What are you gonna do, kill me?!' Justin squeaked.

'Maybe I will,' the Detective said. 'Or maybe I'll just remove some pieces! You're a wealthy man, are you not? You can afford the cybernetics.'

Justin gulped, shrinking back as a spark ran along the blade of the knife that was pressed against his throat.

'Fine,' he said. 'Fine, I'll cooperate! I'll tell you what you want to know! Just, chill with the knife, okay?!'

'I will remove it,' the Detective said coldly, 'but once I do, you are not to attempt an escape. Understand?'

Justin nodded, eyes wide.

The Detective slowly moved their arm away, unpinning Justin from the wall. They were ready to give chase if he made a move – but he didn't.

'I know who Kylie Collins is,' he said resignedly. 'You're right, she's in the music business. And yes, okay, so am I.'

'Okay, good,' the Detective said. 'And is Kylie Collins a timesmith?'

'No,' Justin said. 'She's not. But I think I know who is – this teenage girl called Quinn Kelly. She and Kylie work together, with uhh... well, they have a band, called Temporal Boom. Quinn's the lead singer and writes a lot of the music. Kylie manages the whole thing.'

'I see,' the Detective said. 'And what makes you think this girl is the timesmith?'

'Well, she's definitely a smith,' Justin said. 'I haven't seen her using P.I.U.S, so I don't fully know what type, but timesmith makes sense. You know they won the lottery, just a few weeks ago? That was definitely some smith shit. No one just wins the lottery like that.'

'Okay,' the Detective said. 'Can you please describe Quinn Kelly to me? And also the other members of this band?'

Justin did so, and the Detective quickly matched them with the previous descriptions provided by Dingo. They matched almost perfectly – although the group had apparently gained one member, a woman with purple hair whose name was Piper.

'Okay,' the Detective said, once they were satisfied with the descriptions. 'Now, all we have to do is locate these people.'

'Oh,' Justin said. 'Well... that might be difficult.'

'Why?'

'They disappeared when Mildura did, didn't they?'

'Did they? Can you confirm that?'

'Well,' Justin said, 'Actually, no. I haven't heard from

them since then, but it's possible they've just gone into hiding... But...'

'But what?'

'The evening before it happened,' Justin said, 'Kylie was here. And she told me that they were going to do something that was, in her words, "really fucking stupid". But she told me not to worry about it. We'll be back, she said. Then the next day, Mildura vanished.'

'She said that they would be back?'

'Yeah.' Justin shrugged. 'Which is why I'm not really worried about Mildura. It'll come back. Don't know when, though. Hopefully soon.'

'Interesting,' the Detective said. 'Thank you, Mr Waratah. This is extremely useful information.'

'Yeah, whatever,' Justin said. 'If you would leave now, I'd appreciate it.'

The Detective cocked their head.

'We will leave now,' they said. 'But you're coming with us. Don't think I have forgotten your recent attempt on our lives. You are still very much under arrest.'

'Right,' Justin said defeatedly. 'Yeah. Shit.'

***

Forty minutes later, they arrived at the Red Cliffs Sin-Seeker Office and the Detective took Justin through to the cell to await processing.

Once they'd locked Justin in, they returned to the main office, where they found Officer Wombat waiting.

'Detective,' she said, and then paused.

'Jesus, what happened to you?'

'Don't worry,' the Detective said. 'It is merely surface damage. Bill can fix most of it, given the time.'

'Okay,' Wombat said hesitantly. 'Um. While you were gone, we found that RV you were looking for!'

'The RV belonging to Kylie Collins?' the Detective said.

'Yes. Tank saw it a few days ago, actually, sitting on the side of the road near the disappearance zone. Remembered and went back to look this morning. It's the same one, alright – numberplate is the same.'

'Oh shit!' Bill said.

'Don't get too excited,' Wombat said. 'There was no one inside. Tank checked.'

'This is still a highly significant find!' the Detective said. 'We should go there immediately. What are the coordinates?'

Wombat didn't know, but she called Tank, who was able to give directions. Wombat then offered to drive them there, but not before Bill tried his best to fix the worst of the Detective's damage.

He was able to get the wrist and thumb-blade working again, and he restored the blurry eye, but there wasn't a lot he could do about the left eye without full-on replacing it.

'Even if I did have spare cybernetics with me,' he said sadly, 'I'd have to open up your entire head to put in the new one. It's going to be a very delicate operation. Not something I can do in the back of a van. In fact, we'll probably have to go back to HQ for that one.'

'That is fine,' the Detective said. 'I can still see through my right eye, and my other sensors are operating perfectly well.'

This was true – however, there was more to it than they told Bill. Their sensors were operating perfectly – but strangely, there were more of them than there had been before.

An additional sense had apparently come online following their dip in the aquarium – one that could 'see' electromagnetic fields. There was no output for it apparent on their internal interface, but it was there all the same – a sort of impression of where things were, based on the flow of electrons and the spaces between.

It was very accurate, to the point where the Detective could effectively see all around them for quite some distance, even with visual systems shut off. It wasn't just horizontal, either – the sense extended up into the air above and down into the earth, where magnetic rocks tugged and rolled beneath their scrutiny. Why it had been turned off before, the Detective wasn't sure. It was clearly a very useful sense to have.

They didn't tell Bill about it, though. If it had been deactivated until now, then maybe Bill had done that deliberately? It being on now would surely only worry him.

Wombat went and brought the car around, which had undergone significant repairs since the last time they'd been there, and they headed off to where Tank had seen the suspect's RV. Tank met them halfway, and led them to where it was. It was banana yellow in colour, with the words THE GLAM VAN spray painted along the side.

Approaching, it was immediately obvious that no one was home. Not only was there a week's worth of dust accumulated on the bonnet, but the Detective felt no life inside. Life had a distinct signal, they were coming to recognise – a electromagnetic pattern that branched outwards, pulsing and glinting and changing direction like a school of fish in the sunny shallows of the ocean.

They tried the driver's door to the RV but it was locked. Hesitating for only a moment, they drew back their fist and plunged it through the glass.

'Detective!' they heard Bill hiss in disapproval.

*It's unlocked now,* they signed in his general direction.

When he didn't respond, they opened the door and went in. The others followed as they climbed through the cabin and into the back. Once everyone was inside, Tank closed the inner door and they were blanketed in the oppressive closeness of soundproofing.

'Well, that's one way to get in,' Wombat said. 'Wowzer, look at all those computers!'

The Detective had also noticed the computers and moved to turn them on. With their strange new vision, they saw the electronics blink to life, a dense, intricate lattice.

Reaching for a USB port, they opened the top of their finger and plugged themselves in. The electronic system shifted in response, interfacing with their own electronic body. The sensation distracted them for a moment. The complexity was astounding.

'Dammit,' Bill said next to them. 'Password protected! Don't suppose we know Kylie Collin's birthday, do we?'

He and the two sin-seekers began making guesses – but the Detective ignored them. Instead, they focused on the computer itself. The password was expected – and what was expected was stored there, hard to see, but not impossible. It just needed a combination of signals, in just the right orientation.

One hand plugged in, the Detective reached out and placed their other hand on the side of the computer. They could feel the charge, positive and negative, so neat and tidy, ready to obey. If they caused the electricity to surge in just the right way, like *so*...

The monitor went bright with static before abruptly clearing to display an unlocked desktop.

'Woah!' Bill exclaimed. 'What did you do?!'

'I unlocked it,' the Detective said calmly.

'But how?' Bill said. 'Detective – Detective, what's your R.L. value now?'

'Thirty-nine per cent,' the Detective said.

'Oh God, it's started to decay,' Bill said. 'Shit. Detective? Hey, Detective! Look at me. I think we need to have a break from the investigation. Just for a couple of days! I think that little unscheduled swimming lesson might have destroyed a couple of things, that urgently need repairing. If we fix them now, it'll be fine, but if we leave them –'

'We're so close,' the Detective said. 'We can't stop now! Look – here are Kylie Collins' personal documents. Music sales. Client lists. The music itself!'

'Yes, and it isn't going anywhere,' Bill said. 'If your R.L. is decaying that quickly, then fixing that takes priority over the case!'

'Why?' the Detective said, turning around to look at him. 'Why, Bill? What does R.L. mean? Why is it so important?'

Bill made a noise of frustration.

'I can't tell you! I've already explained this, Detective!

But trust me, it's REALLY important that it does not hit zero! Preferably by a safe margin!'

'Would it not be safer if I knew why it was important?' the Detective said. 'If I knew what it was, then I would be more motivated to slow its decay. I would be better at slowing it!'

'No,' Bill said. 'Every time I've told you what it means before, your R.L. immediately dropped by at least twenty per cent! A few times, it immediately went to zero!'

'Oh?' the Detective said. 'So it cannot be THAT bad if it reaches zero, then? Since it has clearly happened at least twenty-four times before.'

'No, it IS really bad!' Bill said. 'God, why must you always turn into a capricious arsehole when you're below fifty per cent? Can't you just trust me on this?'

The Detective was going to respond, but just then Wombat made a noise of surprise.

'Weird,' she said. 'Uh... not to interrupt or anything... just, look at this song!'

Everyone looked at the monitor screen. Wombat was hovering the mouse over a MP4 file, titled *Way Back Home*. The file was strangely large and had a play time of 168 hours.

'That IS unusual,' the Detective said in interest. 'Open it.'

Tentatively, Wombat clicked on the file. A sound program opened and the song began playing through a small, tinny speaker.

It was a single riff, looped over and over, for an entire week. Wombat skipped forward through several days, but it was still the same.

'Why is it so long?' the Detective said, frowning.

'They might have just been messing around?' Wombat said.

'Then why name it?' the Detective said. 'Especially something like *Way Back Home*...?'

'Are they...' Bill said. 'Are they using the music to time travel?'

'What do you mean?' the Detective looked at him.

'Nothing,' Bill said quickly. 'It's nothing. Let's go home, shall we?'

'The music,' the Detective said. 'That is it, isn't it? It's related! They DO use the music to time travel! And this song is the way back home, to the present, in a literal sense!'

'Do you think so?' Wombat said.

'Yes!' the Detective said. 'But it's one week long? What does that mean?'

'Probably nothing!' Bill said.

'One week,' the Detective said. 'How long has it been since Mildura disappeared?'

'One week?' Wombat said.

'How long exactly?' the Detective said excitedly.

'Well, let's see,' Wombat said. 'We estimate that Mildura vanished between 11AM and 1:30PM on the 8th of March. Right now, it's 11:46AM on the 15th of March. If we assume the disappearance occurred at midday exactly, that's six days, twenty-three hours, and forty-six minutes.'

The Detective abruptly made for the door.

'Woah!' Bill yelled, running after them. 'Where are you going?'

'To Mildura,' the Detective said. 'I have... What do you call it? A hunch?'

'A hunch about what?' Bill said defeatedly.

'That Mildura is about to come back,' the Detective said.

### Excerpt from the personal notebook of
### MARGARET LAMBINGTON

*TEST 4 – 18.02.2082*

*Live test 1. Subjects Alpha and Beta combined P.I.U.S with the goal of de-aging a living creature (a moth, captured on site).*

*Hypothesis – the moth will de-age up to the point at which it is born, after which it will disappear.*

*Method – Subjects Alpha and Beta stood on either side of a glass jar containing a single moth and focused abilities on the vessel and its contents. Time reversed was 1 year (a time period greater than the lifespan of the moth).*

*Results – The moth underwent a reverse metamorphosis into a caterpillar, back into an egg, and then disappeared. Time continued to reverse past this point, with nothing visibly changing. Side effects minor.*

*Conclusion – this test confirms that living creatures are affected in the same manner as other matter during this combination of P.I.U.S.*

*TEST 5 – 21.02.2082*

*Live test 2. Subjects Alpha and Beta combined P.I.U.S with the goal of de-aging a living creature (another moth) to the point at which it was born before restoring it with reversed music.*

*Hypothesis – the moth will de-age like previously observed before aging again rapidly to the age it originally was.*

*Method – Same as test 4, except the song used to activate P.I.U.S was played first in reverse, and then forwards, before P.I.U.S was activated.*

Results – the reversed 'palindromic' music resulted in time moving first backwards as usual, before flipping and moving forwards again. As expected, all contents of the jar, including the moth, were first de-aged, and then hyper-aged in a forward direction.

Note – as the time reversed was again 1 year, a timespan larger than the life span of the moth, the moth de-aged beyond the point at which it had ever existed, but was then restored exactly as before. The moth showed no signs of external damage following this experience.

Conclusion – this ability is able to cause living creatures to rewind to before their own birth before restoring them perfectly. The 'palindromic' music thus can be assumed to function as a safety net for further time travel experimentation.

## QUESTION – WHAT DOES THE MOTH EXPERIENCE DURING THIS PROCEDURE?

## QUESTION 2 – WHAT HAPPENS IF THE MOTH SINGS?

TEST 6 – 28.02.82

Live test 3. Subjects Alpha and Beta combine P.I.U.S with the goal of sending a human subject (myself) back in time, beyond the point of birth, before restoration to present state.

I will sing while possible, in an effort to remember everything that happens. Afterwards, experiences will be recorded.

Note – this test is risky, and as such, a backup song has

been prepared for time reversal of this entire test, should it go horribly wrong.

Hypothesis – I will revert through time beyond the point of my birth before restoring to the state I am in the year 2082. Hopefully there are no weird side effects.

Method – I sat inside a crate, on a chair, while subjects Alpha and Beta stood outside with hands on either side of the crate. The purpose of the crate was so that the de-aging subject was hidden from view and could not distract the smiths while undergoing a rapid and potentially horrific de-aging process.

The time reversed was 28 years. The song used was palindromic.

Results:

Sat in the chair in the crate. Music was audible through the crate. I sang along to the music while it played in its forward state. As the song reached its end, P.I.U.S was activated.

Hard to describe the next bit. Extremely rapid series of memories and experiences and a feeling of strong disorientation and dizziness. The disorientation increased and I was overcome with a feeling of fear as memories blurred together and became meaningless. After some time, don't know how long or whether time is a meaningful measurement in this case, the feelings of disorientation ended.

I was standing on the side of a tarmac road, unknown time and place, although the flora/trees were consistent with those around Mildura. Dreamlike quality. My body appeared to be present, and in the state it is in the year 2082. The sun was very bright.

After what felt like around ten seconds, it unravelled again. Same feeling as before of extreme disorientation. Later (??) I became aware of the crate and the chair. I was returned.

Body is in one piece. Mind seems to be in one piece. I immediately went and wrote this down.

Note – Subjects Alpha and Beta both suffered moderate side effects. Both subjects also noted that I had a heightened unreality index following the experiment. Will have to keep an eye on that.

Conclusion – Was this true time travel? Did I exist at a point in time that I had never existed before? Or was it some sort of hallucination? Either way this is VERY EXCITING. We will proceed with the seventh test!

# THE SEVENTH TEST

### Date: Sunday 8 March 2082

t was around 11AM on an overcast Sunday morning when a van marked with the logo of the Department of Unreality pulled up outside the Mildura weather station.

Security footage captured the van hesitating in the driveway, in front of a sign that said STAFF ACCESS ONLY, before driving past it and into the parking bay. There, it came to a stop, silent for a moment, before the driver and passenger door simultaneously opened.

Maggie and Kylie stepped out of the van, glancing at each other in silence, before heading for the front door of the building.

Inside, they approached the visitor's desk, where a teenage girl, braces glinting across her buck teeth, was sitting and very slowly typing on a keyboard with two of her fingers. The girl looked up, startled, when Maggie dropped a stack of folders onto the desk next to her.

'Hi,' Kylie addressed her, smiling sweetly. 'We're here for the experiment. Who should we speak to about bringing in the equipment?'

The girl blinked at Kylie, a look of mild panic on her face.

'Um,' she said, eyes darting back and forth. 'Uhh, what?'

'We're from the DOU, Bendigo branch,' Kylie said. 'For the survey?'

'Oh, uhhh,' the girl said.

Kylie frowned. 'Were you not told we were coming?' she said crossly. 'Or did you just forget?'

'It's okay,' Maggie said, stepping forward when the girl looked even more frightened. 'Is there someone else we could speak to?'

'Y-yes,' the girl said and lunged for a phone that was sitting on the desk.

'Hi, Dad,' she said into the speaker. 'Can you come down? There are some people from the DOU here?'

She put the phone down again and eyed Kylie nervously. 'He said he's on his way!'

'Good,' Kylie said.

A few minutes later, a door opened at the back of the room and a Caucasian man in a blue button-down shirt came over to shake Kylie and Maggie's hands.

'Hello,' he said. 'I'm Troy, acting station manager. Uhh... I'm very sorry, but I think there's been some sort of miscommunication. You're from the DOU?'

'Yes,' Kylie said, while next to her, Maggie flashed a badge. 'We're here for the state weathersmith survey.'

'Right,' Troy said.

There was a pause.

'Uh, I'm sorry, but what is that again?'

Kylie clicked her tongue in annoyance.

'I'm starting to think this is an issue on our end,' she said, glancing at Maggie. 'This is the third station now!'

'It's fine.' Maggie sighed. 'Look, basically, we're conducting a survey on weathersmiths for each region. We're comparing weather control effectiveness, side effect rates, working conditions, etcetera, with the goal of standardising the weather control process. You are no doubt aware that there are natural spectrums in power level, control and specific ability that exist across different weathersmiths? Well, with our survey, we aim to account for this with greater accuracy than ever before, so that all Victorians, and eventually the entire Nation, can experience a uniform, predictable weather schedule. Also, weathersmiths will be able to take comfort in knowing that they will experience consistent, fair working conditions regardless of where they are stationed.'

'Right, okay,' Troy said, nodding. 'Yeah, we never received any information about this. Sorry.'

'Well, here's the details, if you would like to have read,' Maggie said, lifting the stack of folders and advancing on Troy.

'Oh,' Troy said, stepping back, 'no, that's okay. Uh. What does the survey involve? If it's just a questionnaire then I'm sure our smiths will be happy to take part in it.'

'It's a questionnaire, and also a short test of ability,' Maggie said. 'We have some equipment with us with which to test this. It won't take long, but there is a danger of side effects, as usual. Participation is, of course, voluntary; however, we would encourage as many smiths as possible to include themselves in the survey.'

'Right,' Troy said. 'Well, I suppose we'd better go and talk to them, then?'

'Great!' Maggie said. 'I AM sorry about barging into your day like this. It really won't take long, I promise. We'll be out of your hair in a couple of hours!'

'Ah, it's fine.' Troy waved a hand. 'We weren't exactly busy today.'

'That's lucky,' Maggie said. 'Anyway, if I go with you to talk to the smiths, do you mind if my associate brings in our equipment? There's quite a lot of it – some new technology for testing P.I.U.S, actually – very exciting! Uh, if possible, we'd also like to set it up at the top of the tower, so there's minimal relic interference.'

'Uh, yeah, sure,' Troy said. 'There are currently two smiths on duty up there... but I can call them down so they're all together. That way you won't have to repeat yourself!'

'Oh, really?' Maggie beamed at him. 'You'd do that? Thank you so much! Kylie, do you mind wrangling the equipment while I talk to the smiths?'

'I don't mind,' Kylie said. 'Perhaps this girl can show us the way to the tower?'

The girl at the desk's eyes widened and she looked to Troy.

'Good idea,' Troy said, smiling at his daughter in encouragement. 'Brianna, can you show the nice lady where to go?'

'Y-yeah!' Brianna said and hurriedly got out from behind the desk.

'Okay, but don't touch anything,' Kylie said to Brianna as they both went outside.

Maggie hoisted up her pile of folders and followed after Troy. Shortly, Kylie and Brianna came back. In tow with them were four other people, carrying between them a series of heavy boxes and bags.

'Okay,' Kylie said sharply, once everyone was through the airlock. 'Where now?'

'This way!' Brianna said, practically running towards a double door at the back of the room.

In a clatter of footsteps, the group followed her through several corridors to where an elevator waited. Then, once everyone had packed inside with all their equipment, they travelled up to the top of the weather station tower.

It took two trips to bring everything up. The elevator came out just below the weather room, in a foyer with a bathroom and a small kitchenette. A single narrow set of stairs led up to the top room, proving somewhat of an obstacle.

Soon though, everything was up in the weather room. The room itself was small and square, with large windows on every side. All furniture present was quickly shoved aside to make way for the equipment. There was also an E.W.S outlet, the screen displaying recent news – and beside it was an E.W.S entry terminal, where Portent sightings could be instantaneously reported if spotted from the tower.

'Okay,' Kylie said, once the last bag had been hauled up the flight of stairs. 'That's everything! Brianna! Would you be able to go and tell your father that we are ready to proceed when they are?'

Brianna nodded and bolted back to the elevator.

Everyone heard the quiet DING as the doors opened, and then a faint hum as the elevator began to descend.

Immediately, they dropped the act.

'We're in!' Mullet pumped his fists excitedly. 'They didn't question anything!'

'Yeah,' Quinn said, 'that was way easier than I was expecting!'

'I'm sweating, though!' Piper said. 'Who else is sweating? Oh my goodness! I hate this, it's stressful!'

'Everyone shut your mouth and start setting up,' Kylie said. 'We don't have long! That girl will probably be back in a few minutes, with her dad and a pack of unsuspecting weathersmiths. In fact, Spencer, can you keep an eye on the elevator? I'm going to have a fiddle with the E.W.S.'

As Spencer slouched downstairs, Quinn began helping Piper set up the drum kit. Meanwhile, Mullet unzipped the guitars out of their cases and began tuning his.

'Wait,' Piper said, 'has anyone checked the palindrome? Is it still playing?'

Quinn moved over to a crate with FRAGILE written across it and opened it up, revealing a single mobile phone held in place in a block of Styrofoam. A simple tune, playing in reverse from the phone's speakers, became audible.

'It's fine,' she said. 'Still going.'

'Phew!' Piper said. 'Man, I'm freaking out! Where's Maggie? Do you think she'll be able to give them the slip?'

'Stop worrying about it,' Mullet said, strumming a chord. 'Have faith. She got us in here, didn't she?'

'Um, WE got us in here,' Kylie said. In front of her, the terminal blinked to life. Kylie pursed her lips, eyeing it, before leaning in, fingers flying across the keyboard.

In the room below, Spencer cleared his throat.

'Elevator's coming back!'

'Shit!' Piper said. 'Argh! What if it's the girl again?'

'I could knock her out?' Spencer said, balling his metal fist.

'No,' Kylie said, without looking away from the terminal. 'If it's the girl, just send her away on another errand.'

The elevator opened and Maggie came out. She was alone. Everyone breathed a sigh of relief.

'Alright!' Maggie called, taking the stairs two at a time. 'We don't have long! I've got the smiths filling out the "surveys", and the management staff supervising. I'm supposed to be in the bathroom, so we've probably got around five minutes before they start wondering where I am!'

'Five minutes is fine,' Kylie said. 'I've almost got this. Just need to set up the microphones.'

'I'll help,' Maggie said. 'Where does this cable go?'

In a flurry of activity, they finished setting everything up. With a dramatic flourish, Kylie typed something into the E.W.S. terminal and smiled in satisfaction when the word STANDBY came up on the E.W.S screen. Maggie and Mullet slung their guitars around into position and Piper unfolded her collapsible stool, sitting herself down behind the drum set and grabbing the sticks. Next to her, Spencer stood with a triangle in one hand and a metal rod in the other, his jaw set with determination.

Quinn turned on her microphone and tapped it, causing feedback to whine. Looking up, she met Kylie's gaze.

'I think we're ready to go,' she said.

Kylie nodded, and raised a finger over the ENTER key.

'Any last words?'

Quinn took a breath. Her heart was racing – just like before any of the concerts she'd done. This time, things were different, of course. But they were also the same.

'In case we die,' she said, 'then I'd like to say first that I appreciate all of you, and I'm really glad that you're all as stupid as I am.'

'Or stupider, even!' Maggie said. 'I'd also like to say thank you to everyone for indulging the worst idea I have ever had.'

'Thank you, everyone,' Mullet said. 'For being awesome.'

Behind him, Spencer rolled his eyes.

'Yeah, whatever,' Kylie said, 'if we do all die, and I see you in hell, I'm going to sue your arses. Let's fucking get this over with, shall we?'

With a manicured finger, she hit the button, sending the pre-written message to every E.W.S in Mildura.

MUSIC IS A HUMAN RIGHT, it said.

*Live in three,* Kylie signed, *two, one –*

'Attention, attention,' Quinn said into the mic. 'Citizens of Mildura. This is an official message. Music is a human right – and if played indoors, it's perfectly safe. A lot of you know this already, but maybe it's time everyone knew? We're Temporal Boom – and it's your moral duty to turn this tune the fuck up!'

She reached for the phone that was playing the palindrome and held it up. Behind her, Mullet began playing the same riff, the right way around.

As the drums and bass came in, Quinn felt the adrenaline settling. The parts were all in motion now. All she had to do was sing, and then when the time came...

*No one likes a temper tantrum*
*You gotta keep it in*
*Hold your mental state to ransom*
*And plaster on that grin*
*Be placid, stoic, easy going*
*A paragon of grit*
*Just keep your chin up through the woe,*
*You fucking piece of shit*

As she sang the first verse, everything else faded away. There was no audience that she could see – it was just like one of the practice runs they'd done.

*You've got a little money spare*
*But there are so many things you have to repair*
*You got a little time for fun*
*But there's just so many errands to run*
*You have some friends to help you through*
*But they've got twice the problems you do*
*You have some music to soothe your soul*

*OH WAIT, NO YOU FUCKING DON'T, IT'S FUCKING ILLEGAL!*

There was an audience. She couldn't see it, but it was there, and there was no way of knowing how large it was. All across the town, the song was playing through the E.W.S – in the shopping centre, and the community buildings, and the restaurants, and in the sin-seeker office. They'd be trying to turn it off, she knew. But how quickly could they do that?

*I'm angry! I'm rowdy! I'm riled, I'm fucking pissed!*

*I'll scream and, I'll shout and, I'll wave about my fist!*

*The waves of life have tossed me high and dumped me in a trough*

*So I'll raise my finger to the sky and tell it to fuck off!*

'Everyone!' Quinn yelled into the microphone as the song quietened for the start of the second verse. 'Sing along! Sing if you agree with our message! Even if you don't know the lyrics, make some noise!'

*You can't always get the things you want*
*No matter how you curve it*
*But sometimes there's no point in staying civil*
*Those bastards don't deserve it*
*Let them hear your angry anthem*
*And let defiance bloom*
*Cause no one likes a temper tantrum*
*But they like a Temporal Boom! HA!*

There was noise downstairs as the elevator arrived and Troy appeared, his face an expression of bafflement.

'What the fuck is happening?!' he yelled, his voice drowned out by the music. Kylie got up from the E.W.S and moved towards him, shooing him aggressively back down the stairs. Behind him, his daughter was staring with round eyes.

*You fight your way through the rat race*
*But life it smacks you in the face*
*You drag yourself out of the ruts*
*But life it kicks you in the nuts*
*You give and give them, more and more*

*But life it socks you in the jaw*
*You've had enough*
*You've had enough*
*You've had enough!*
*YOU'VE HAD ENOUGH!*

As the chorus played for the second time, Quinn tried not to get distracted by the sounds of Kylie kicking Troy in the shins as he went for his phone. He was yelling, and Kylie was yelling, and Brianna was yelling, and she was yelling into the mic.

It was almost time. The end of the second chorus was the trigger point. As she sang the line, Quinn half turned and met Maggie's eye. Then she turned the other way and looked at Spencer.

He nodded. It was now or never.

She reached for the music.

Immediately, she felt the weight of it. It was huge, terrifyingly massive – magnitudes larger than she had been prepared for, spread out far and wide, amplified by every speaker through which it played. In the instant of frozen time before it hit her, a shock of adrenaline ran through her body.

Spencer felt it too, she could see it in his expression. Around them, the others stood frozen in place, unaware of the cataclysmic tsunami that was roaring towards them.

There was nothing she could do now, except hold on for dear life. The tsunami hit and took her with it.

Colours and memories flashed before her at breakneck speed. She was going back down the elevator. She was in THE GLAM VAN. She was eating breakfast, eating dinner, eating breakfast again. The sun was rising and setting, faster and faster, a whirling blade of light.

She was in the Ark, making music. She was on stage for the first time. She was at the shops, at the garbage dump, in a field, travelling on the road. She was on a hill, overlooking a vision of nuclear devastation.

She saw the First assemble itself, undoing the chaos and sorrow it had wrought – and still she went backwards. She was in a house now – a house hadn't seen for a very long time. She was young and her mother was there, shockingly young herself. She was even younger, playing on the swing set, in the sandpit, on the floor with a tiny plastic horse.

She was wrapped in blankets that were slightly too warm. Faces were looming in. Smiling. Frowning. Dark, light, dark, light. Her vision was blurry now. Colours and brightness, brighter, white, black. Nothing.

Nothingness. Darkness. Everything at once. Meaningless. Colours. Colours and sound –

She was standing near a river.

Sharply, she drew in a breath. The air smelt strange – fresh, yet spiced with an unfamiliar musky scent.

Who was she? No, where was she? When was she?

There was a sound and she turned to look. They were behind her, the others. The other members of the band.

She looked at them and they looked at her. She couldn't remember their names – but then she could. How had she forgotten?

There were others as well. Dozens more people, dotted about amongst the trees. They looked confused and she didn't blame them. She was confused too. Was any of this real?

The music was still playing, though. They were suspended between notes, but it wasn't over yet. The palindrome had reached its centre, but that was it. A moment of respite –

The tsunami was coming back, rolling in reverse. Quinn looked around at the others, taking in their faces, and then they were gone again –

# MILDURA RETURNS

### Date: Sunday 15 March 2082

'Can you not drive any faster?' the Detective said.

'Sorry,' Bill said, 'I can't. Have you seen the rocks? We'll blow a tire!'

The Detective grit their teeth, forcing themselves to be silent as Bill wound the car around boulders and trees. They were heading for the centre of where Mildura should have been, slowly but surely creeping across the vanished zone.

The air around them felt charged with a sort of potential that was hard to describe. Something was happening. The Detective could feel it with their new electromagnetic sense – and shortly, they began to see it as well.

Bill exclaimed as a tree abruptly appeared in front of the car, growing with supernatural speed, branches spreading, trunk swelling outwards. A moment later, another appeared, and another, surrounding them. Ground cover plants scattered outwards in waves, spreading and dying back and changing colour.

Swearing, Bill slowed the car even further, nosing through the rapidly growing and decaying forest. A tree caught their tail, punching upwards as it grew, knocking the car and causing it to bounce on its axels.

'That way!' The Detective pointed. 'That's where the road is going to appear!'

'I'm trying!' Bill yelled. 'There's a lot going on right now!'

Another tree knocked the car, rocking it sideways. Then, all of a sudden, the trees disappeared.

'Whoa,' Bill said. 'Grapes! It's all grapes now!'

'Keep going!' The Detective banged their hand on the dash. 'That means we're almost back to the current time period!'

Bill swerved through the rapidly expanding rows of grape vines, crashing through a fence that had assembled itself out of thin air. On the other side, a dirt road had appeared.

'Houses, I can see houses!' Bill yelled, accelerating down the road.

'FASTER!' the Detective yelled excitedly.

As they raced down the widening highway, houses began constructing themselves at hyper speed on either side. In an instant, the road they were on became paved with tarmac. Large warehouses began rising from nothing and traffic lights materialised, changing colour in a flickering blur.

'Oh God,' Bill said, swerving around a corner. 'Detective, what if there are other vehicles on the road? Are we about to have a car crash at relativistic speeds?'

The Detective frowned. 'You're right,' they said. 'This is close enough! We should get off the road.'

Bill hurriedly pulled over, bringing the car to a screeching halt. Immediately, the Detective threw open the door and leapt outside.

Bill threw open his door as well, ready to run – but before he could say a word, the Detective swooped in and picked him up.

'You are too slow,' they said, hoisting him over their shoulder. Then, energy churning throughout them, they charged down the street, towards the distant tower of the weather station that had only just appeared.

***

With a gasp, Quinn came back to the present, her senses returning all at once like a lance through the brain.

She was on the floor, but she couldn't remember falling

down. The floor – yes. It was the floor of the weather station tower.

She couldn't move. Her arms and legs were not listening to her. For a second, she panicked – but then jolted abruptly upright.

Around her, the others were doing the same. Mullet was dazedly rubbing his head. Maggie was sitting, hands splayed on the floor, breathing hard. Spencer was leaning on the windowsill, hand over his mouth. Piper was crouched next to her drum kit, her hair a tangled mess across her face

Maggie drew a deep breath. 'I...' she said shakily, 'I think we're back!'

'Holy bejeezus!' Piper said.

'Is everyone alright?' Maggie said, scrabbling to her feet. 'Quinn, are you okay? Spencer? Speak to me!'

Spencer gulped, opened his mouth, then clapped a hand back over it. Shaking his head, he stumbled to the stairs and half fell down them. The bathroom door banged below.

'I-I think I'm alright,' Quinn said weakly.

There was a sudden yell from below. 'Hey!' Kylie's voice came up the stairs. 'I told you not to move, arsehole!'

'Or what?!' Troy's voice returned. 'Who are you people?!'

'Crap,' Maggie said. 'I forgot about the manager!'

'Uh, yeah,' Mullet said slowly. 'What DO we do now, Maggie?'

'Gonna be real here,' Maggie said, 'I didn't think a lot about what we do afterwards.'

'Run away?' Piper suggested.

'Yeah, something like that!'

'I,' Quinn began, and then paused to burp. 'I think we-ow.'

She winced as the microphone on the ground next to her abruptly let out a high-pitched whine. 'Shit, did we turn off the E.W.S yet?'

Maggie lunged across and turned it off.

'There,' she said. 'C'mon, get up Quinn, we need to – ow, what the hell?!'

She stared at the E.W.S, out of which a large spark had just arced, zapping her finger. As they all looked at it, it cracked loudly, and the screen turned to static.

'Um?' Maggie said.

On the floor next to her, Quinn suddenly breathed sharply in.

'Shit!' she said, scrambling to her feet. 'I think th-ARGH!'

She broke off with a scream, doubling over.

'Quinn?' Maggie said.

Quinn screamed again, piercingly loud, and collapsed to the floor. The sounds of argument from downstairs broke off, followed by the sounds of running feet.

'What's happening?' Kylie called, appearing at the top of the stairs.

Quinn tried to speak, but she couldn't. The pain was everything, ripping outwards from her shoulder blades. She screamed again, writhing onto her back, before running out of air. She couldn't see. Blackness was closing in. Then the pain got even worse –

***

As the elevator opened, the Detective heard a piercing scream. Leaving Bill where he was, they ran into the room and bounded up the single flight of stairs.

The stairs came out into the tower room proper, where they were greeted by a chaotic scene.

There were instruments strewn about the floor and furniture pushed up against the walls. In amongst it all were seven people and all of them were yelling over the top of each other. A girl, who the Detective recognised as their main suspect, Quinn Kelly, was lying on the ground, apparently unconscious. Most of the other people present were also on the suspect list. Maggie Lamington was there, patting Quinn's face in an effort to wake her up, while Piper Grevillea fanned her with her hands. Kylie and Joey Collins were both there, yelling at a flustered looking man in a blue shirt. Behind the man, another young girl was standing, her jaw slack.

As the Detective came up the stairs, everyone went dead quiet and turned to stare at them.

'Hello,' the Detective said into the silence. 'You are all under arrest for, amongst other things, the unlawful creation and distribution of recreational noise, the use of unregistered P.I.U.S and the intentional vanishment of a major rural township.'

There was a pause. Then, the man who the Detective didn't recognise as a suspect shook his head.

'What?!' he said.

Maggie Lamington stood up straight.

'Um,' she said, 'who are you?'

The Detective had to think about it for a moment. 'I am Detective Fang, of the Melbourne Sin-Seeker Department,' they said.

'A sin-seeker?!' The man threw up his hands. 'Great, fantastic. Officer, I swear, I have nothing to do with any of this! Nor does my daughter! We don't even know what any of this is!'

'Then why are you here?' The Detective cocked their head.

'We work here!' the man said. 'These people hijacked the weather station!'

'I see,' the Detective said. 'I would like to take a statement from you if possible. The rest of you – I would ask that you stand against the wall and remain still and quiet until I direct otherwise. We have contacted the local forces and they are on their way. Until they arrive, do not attempt to escape. Any attempt to do anything other than what I say will be met with immediate counter measures.'

'Um,' Maggie said, and she gestured at Quinn, 'she needs urgent medical attention!'

'I have contacted the med clinic as well,' the Detective said. 'Do not worry. Now, please, move against the wall, with your hands in full view.'

Electricity crackled along their arm and the people in

the room flinched. All of them, beside the worker and his daughter, moved back to the wall, their hands up above their head.

'Good,' the Detective said. They stepped further into the room, glancing down at Quinn Kelly on the floor. She was lying on her front, her head to the side – and now that the other suspects had moved out of the way, something else strange was apparent. On either side of Quinn's spine, jutting out from her shoulder blades, were a pair of thin, angular wedges of metal, half a metre long, piercing through her clothes and smeared with blood. They were wing tips, the Detective realised – airplane wing tips, just like those of the First Portent.

This confirmed with one hundred per cent certainty that Quinn Kelly was the timesmith. Nodding to themselves, the Detective looked around at the others.

'Kylie Collins,' they said, watching the suspect for her response. 'You are the legal guardian of Quinn Kelly, are you not?'

Kylie blinked at them, clearly surprised.

'I want a lawyer,' she said after a moment.

The Detective's lip twitched. 'Another uncooperative one, I see,' they said. 'Ah well. It does not matter. I already know everything about you that matters.'

They turned their gaze on Maggie Lamington, who was doing her best to keep a neutral face.

'According to my records,' they said, 'you were a DOU scientist until recently. I am interested to learn the reason why you left such a respectable career for a life of sin.'

Maggie opened her mouth.

'If you don't mind me asking,' she said, 'what's the current date?'

'It is the 15th of March,' the Detective said. 'Your activities caused Mildura to disappear for an entire week.'

'Ah,' Maggie said. 'W-wait. Mildura? The whole thing?'

'Yes, the entire town.'

'Huh,' Maggie said.

Behind the Detective, Bill poked his head up into the room.

'The Mildura Sin-Seekers are on their way,' he said. 'They sounded a bit confused, but honestly they seemed happy to have direct orders to follow. I don't think they realise what's happened yet –'

He broke off, his eyes on the arrestees.

Maggie and Piper were both staring at him, expressions of naked surprise on their faces.

The Detective looked between the three of them and their eyes narrowed.

'Bill,' they said. 'Do you recognise these women?'

'Uhhhh,' Bill said.

'Professor?' Maggie said. 'What the hell are you doing here? I thought you were in Melbourne?'

'UHHHH,' Bill said.

Piper was frowning. 'I thought,' she said, 'I thought you were working on –'

She looked at the Detective and her eyes widened. 'Wait a second!'

'VSHHH!' Bill made shushing motions. 'DO NOT SAY ANYTHING, PIPER! OR YOU EITHER, MARGARET!'

'So, you do know each other,' the Detective said. 'Interesting. She called you Professor. You're a Professor, Bill?'

'Can we talk about this later?' Bill said though his teeth.

'Why, when we have time now?' the Detective said. 'How to you know these women, Bill?'

'We might have worked at the same facility at one point,' Bill said. 'It doesn't really matter!'

'Hey, "Bill",' Piper said from the wall. 'Why shouldn't we talk about it? What happens if we talk about it?'

'TRUST ME YOU DO NOT WANT TO FIND OUT,' Bill said.

'It's a bit risky, isn't it?' Piper said, 'Taking it out for a walk? Although, I have to say, I'm really impressed! Nina can just barely respond to yes or no questions. This is on a whole nother level!'

'Detective,' Bill said, 'do you have any duct tape on you to tape up their mouths?!'

'Who is Nina?' the Detective said.

Bill looked like he was about to pop a vein – but fortunately for him, the elevator opened and deposited half of the Mildura Sin-Seeker force into the room. Swiftly, they swarmed up the stairs, cuffing the suspects and frogmarching them away, except for Quinn, who was taken out on a stretcher.

Bill sighed visibly once they were gone – which the Detective immediately pounced on.

'You are relived?' they said. 'Why? What do those people know that you don't want me to know?'

'Nothing,' Bill said. 'Nothing. Just please let it go.'

'I don't think I can let it go,' the Detective said. 'I... do not want to.'

Bill sighed again, very deeply.

'Detective,' he said. 'Let's just finish the case and go home, okay?'

THE SEVENTH PORTENT

FIRST RECORDED SIGHTING: 14/01/2059, Darwin,
Larrakia country, NT

PHYSICAL APPEARANCE:

The Seventh Portent appears as an adult human
brain, suspended 2m above the ground through
anomalous means. Despite complete isolation
from a body, the brain appears physically
healthy, with adequate blood-flow, and
neuronal activity consistent with a living,
alert human being. In low light, it is
possible to observe a 'ghostly' nervous
system attached to the base of the brain
stem, along which electrical impulses can be
observed.

The Seventh Portent continuously generates a
strong electromagnetic field, with the North
pole of the field situated at the mid frontal
lobe of the brain and the South pole situated
at the cerebellum. The field extends to a
maximum of 30m around the Seventh Portent.
Inside the field, electronic devices are
severely affected and can often be seen to go
'haywire' - however, the Seventh Portent
itself displays some level of control over
this process and has on multiple occasions
displayed a capacity to manipulate electronic
devices in a manner that displays both
intelligence and purpose.

The Seventh Portent additionally generates massive amounts of electrical charge over time, which manifest approximately twice per hour as a powerful arc of plasma, similar in magnitude to that of a lightning strike. The discharge contains on average around 500 megajoules of energy, with a temperature of over 20,000 degrees Celsius. Spot fires and other localised damage are a common result of these arcing events.

BEHAVIOUR:

The Seventh Portent displays human-like intelligence and curiosity and is unquestionably sentient. When left to itself, the Seventh partakes in a range of human-like behaviours, including a day-night rest cycle and movement speeds consistent with walking, jogging and on rare occasions, sprinting.

In addition to noise, the Seventh Portent is attracted by the presence of electronic structures and devices, which it is able to sense over a distance of 2.5km away. It is commonly found following powerlines or attempting to break into buildings where electronic devices are stored. While not actively aggressive towards humans, this behaviour often results in severe property damage, and draws the Seventh Portent towards population centres at a rate higher than any other Portent.

Note – if you own one or more personal electronic devices, it is highly recommended that the device is turned off when not directly in use.

Note 2 – If you or someone you know encounters the Seventh Portent, remain calm, keep your distance and immediately report the sighting to your local authorities so that the Portent can be safely relocated.

ADDITIONAL INFORMATION: Following recent breakthroughs by the Department of Unreality, the Seventh Portent has been shown to be capable of human speech and communication. During multiple conversations with researchers, the Seventh Portent displayed a distinct personality, including a strong sense of morality, a fondness for riddles and logic puzzles, and a preference for gender-neutral pronouns. It did not seem aware of its own anomalous nature and had no memories aside from those recently created. Upon learning of its own state of existence, it became visibly upset – before shortly forgetting again, along with all other recently explained information.

PORTENT INDUCED UNREALITY SYMPTOMS:

P.I.U.S RUBICON RADIUS: 2.5m.

ACTIVE SYMPTOM DEVELOPMENT: 80%

LETHALITY: 20%

DESIGNATION: Electrosmith

ADDITIONAL NOTES: P.I.U.S abilities stemming from the Seventh Portent typically relate to the manipulation of electricity and electromagnetic fields.

# CHAPTER 55

# INTERROGATION

## Date: Sunday 15 March 2082

Quinn woke up in pain, with bright lights shining directly into her eyes.

Her brain felt like fog – stringing two thoughts together was a chore. She was lying on something that was tilted upwards like a dentist's chair and her limbs felt like blocks of stone. Her throat burned with bile and her back and shoulders spiked with pain if she moved at all.

Groaning, she tried to turn her head away from the light.

There were voices off to the side – and suddenly, a figure stepped into view. Quinn struggled to focus her eyes on the silhouette in front of her.

'Hello, Ms Kelly,' a voice said. 'Good to see that you're awake.'

The figure turned and adjusted the bright light away from her face. They were a sin-seeker officer, Quinn saw – a woman with a short blonde ponytail.

'My name's Wombat,' the woman said, moving closer again. 'I'm from the Red Cliffs Sin-Seeker office. That's, uh, not where we are, though. This is the Mildura office. The Mildura force are currently undergoing a crash course on what the fuck just happened.'

Quinn blinked at her hazily.

'Don't suppose you could answer that question, could you?' Wombat said. 'You're the timesmith responsible, aren't you?'

Quinn continued to stare at her blankly.

'Hmm.' Wombat looked around. 'Did we go a little too hard on the relics? OI, TANK!'

A man poked his head into the room. 'Yes?'

'Can you remove a couple of the relics?' Wombat said. 'She's not responding at all.'

'Sure she isn't faking it?' Tank said.

'Maybe,' Wombat said. 'Just take a couple away, okay?'

She moved back as Tank left again, a box in his arms.

'Do you know what the current date is?' she said to Quinn. 'Who's the Premier? What did I just say my name was?'

Quinn worked her mouth, getting some moisture going.

'I don't... know what the date is,' she said. 'It was... the 8th... last time I checked...'

'Oh, right,' Wombat said. 'Well, it's the 15th now.'

'Hmm,' Quinn said.

'Maybe you don't realise what's happened?' Wombat said. 'What do you think happened? What's the last thing you remember?'

Quinn worked her mouth again.

'There's a Portent nearby,' she said.

Wombat stiffened. 'What?'

'It's just... over that way.' Quinn tried to raise a hand but found that it was strapped down, the thick metal band cold against her wrist.

Wombat looked over at the wall to their left, which was a two-way mirror. Tank came back into the room.

'We've been asked not to talk about the Portent,' he said.

Quinn furrowed her brows. 'What?'

'They tamed it, apparently,' Wombat said. 'Don't worry about it.'

Quinn stared at her.

'Yeah,' Wombat said. 'Look, I'm also worried about it. But apparently it's safe, relatively speaking? Anyway, back to the questions. What do you remember?'

'Um,' Quinn said. 'Wh-where are my friends?'

She shifted in her bonds and in the process, found out that her feet were also tied down.

'We're questioning them too,' Wombat said. 'Look, I know you might not want to talk to me, but this is very important. You caused an entire town to disappear for seven days. The sheer disruption this has caused to SO many lives is just... well, I don't know if it was on purpose or an accident but either way, we don't want it to happen again.'

'We fixed it, didn't we?' Quinn said, frowning.

'Yes, it's back now,' Wombat said, 'but for an entire week, we all thought Mildura had vanished from the face of the Earth! We thought everyone had died!'

'But they didn't, though,' Quinn said stubbornly. 'Most of them won't even remember anything!'

'That's true, they sure don't,' Wombat said. 'Wait – so you DID plan this?'

'What am I under arrest for?' Quinn set her jaw. 'Vanishing a town, then bringing it back? Is that even a crime, technically? Do you have any proof it was me?'

'You have a pair of airplane wings sticking out of your back,' Wombat said. 'You are obviously a timesmith. If nothing else, you are under arrest for use of unregistered P.I.U.S. Also, you're a musician. Don't think I don't know about Temporal Boom. The citizens of Mildura are talking more about your little E.W.S stunt than they are the town vanishing! From their perspective, it only happened an hour ago.'

'The Portent is coming closer,' Quinn said.

Wombat's face fell, just slightly.

'Shit,' she muttered. 'Um. They're going to want to ask you some questions as well. Don't mention what they are, though. It will apparently make them, uh, upset.'

'Huh?' Quinn said.

She winced, as the horrible feeling of churning reality and unreality abruptly got a lot stronger. The door opened and a tall figure came into the room.

'Quinn Kelly,' they said in a robotic voice that hissed with static.

Quinn's mouth fell open. This... what... what the fuck was this?

Somehow, someone had, for some fucking reason, apparently trapped a Portent inside a shell of cybernetics and tightly packed relics. And here it was, walking around, and talking like a person. The sheer lunacy of the situation struck Quinn dumb for several minutes.

Eventually, she managed to get over her shock long enough to listen to what the Portent was saying.

'...know that it involves music,' they said, looming over her. 'However, I would appreciate it if you would explain the full process behind it.'

'Wh-' Quinn said. 'What -'

'Your specific process of reversing time,' the Portent said. 'I would like you to run through it.'

'Um,' Quinn squeaked, 'can I - can I speak to the other officers please?!'

'Detective.' Wombat stepped closer. 'I think you're upsetting her. Perhaps we should -'

'I am in charge of this case,' the Detective said, 'and I would like to see it through to the end.'

'Well, okay.' Wombat shrugged. 'But I think in this specific circumstance, your services may hinder rather than help the process.'

'You're a Detective?!' Quinn squeaked. 'Wh-How?!'

'It is how I was built,' the Detective said.

'Okay, who the fuck built you, and made you a COP?'

'I believe Bill had something to do with it,' the Detective said. 'Professor Bill, as I have recently discovered. Do you know him as well?'

'No?' Quinn said.

'Hmm.' The Detective moved away from Quinn, a thoughtful look on their face. With no explanation, they abruptly turned and left the room.

Quinn turned to stare at Wombat.

'Sorry,' Wombat said. 'They're a lot.'

'Which one is it?' Quinn said faintly.

'The Seventh, I believe,' Wombat said. 'Anyway - if we

could PLEASE get back to the interview. If you can even just confirm the basics, it would make my life easier.'

'Fine,' Quinn said.

'Your name is Quinn Kelly, correct?' Wombat asked.

'Yes.'

'And you are a timesmith.'

'...Yeah.'

'And you caused Mildura to disappear for seven days.'

'Yes,' Quinn said. 'And yeah, it was on purpose.'

'Okay. Why?'

'We're going to save the world,' Quinn said.

Wombat paused. 'What?'

'You heard,' Quinn said. 'Talk to Maggie if you want the details. She's the mastermind behind all of it.'

'Right,' Wombat said. 'Okay, one more thing, and I'll leave you be. You're the lead singer of Temporal Boom, aren't you?'

Quinn stuck out her chin. 'Yes,' she said.

Wombat nodded. 'Okay.' She stood up and moved towards the door.

'Big fan,' she said, and then disappeared.

****

The weather station tower had been silent for over an hour before the bathroom door creaked quietly open. Vincent poked his head out, looking around, before making a dash for the elevator.

He wasn't entirely sure what had happened or where the others had been taken after being arrested. He didn't know whether the sin-seekers knew about him and were looking for him too.

He felt certain that there had been a Portent outside just before – but apparently no one else had noticed it?

Whatever the case, he needed to act.

The weather station was oddly quiet and he faced no adversity as he made his way to the ground floor and exited through a fire escape. Outside, he pulled up his hood and hurried away from the scene of the crime.

Where to go next, though? He couldn't return to THE GLAM VAN – that was surely being watched. But where else? Where else?

There were plenty of places to go, at least temporarily. He knew Mildura, after all. He'd lived there for years. The entire town was full of memories...

He could go and sit in the public park for a few hours and gather his thoughts. There was a park near his parents' house, where they'd sent him out to walk the dog every evening when he was younger.

He'd loved that dog – a German Shepard called Sneakers, a sweetheart, scared to death of everything. He hadn't thought about her for ages. She had died when he was fourteen. He'd still gone out every evening for months without her...

The gym? Perhaps he could go there? He'd gone there many times with his friends, watching them lift weights together. There was no point in lifting weights himself – his cybernetic arms had a set deadlift maximum that could never increase. He had a membership anyway – although it had probably been cut off now, since he hadn't told them he wasn't dead...

The public library? It was free entry, and you could hide in there for hours and they wouldn't ask questions. He hadn't been to the library for years – not since he'd been a small child. When he'd gotten older, he hadn't had the time, what with football training, and gym, and boxing, and roo hunting on the weekends, and other activities his father had deemed suitable for a young, growing boy...

No. He didn't belong there. But where, then? A pub? Too many people with curious eyes. The shopping centre? That wasn't somewhere he'd be able to sit down for long or relax.

He could... always...

Go home?

No. Absolutely not.

His parents' house was not so far away, just on the outskirts of town. But...

But, if he went there, he'd have to explain things. He'd have to explain that he wasn't actually dead. He'd have to explain why he hadn't told them that immediately and why his body had become even more mechanical since last they'd seen him. He'd have to explain where he'd been, what he'd been doing, who he'd been hanging out with, in excruciating detail. He knew they'd want to know everything. And they wouldn't approve of any of it.

They would be upset with him, angry, disappointed. They would hate his new friends, people who they would condemn as delinquents, sinners, atheists, deviants, people who in their books caused the world to end through their existence.

And even amidst the worst of their judgement, they would expect things of him. They would expect him to follow the life that they had planned without question. And he didn't want to do that. The thought of it crushed him to the core.

He wanted to swear. He wanted to listen to music. He wanted to make friends with weird, interesting people, who his parents wouldn't approve of. He wanted to kiss girls, or boys, or anyone, if the mutual attraction was there – and not be judged for it.

And it hurt – it hurt to admit it – but if wanted any of these things, then he was better off dead. It would be better that his parents never knew he was still alive. And maybe one day he'd have to face it, and the longer he left it, it would only get harder.

But he couldn't face it. Not today. Not anytime soon. Not until he knew who he was without them.

At the next corner, he made a conscious turn away from their neighbourhood. He didn't know where he was going next, or what to do, but that was the one thing he was sure of.

Ahead, there was a crowd of people.

They were standing outside the fresh produce market,

several dozen in a loose group, some of them holding cardboard signs. A protest of some sort. Vincent glanced at them as he walked past – and did a double take.

MUSIC IS A HUMAN RIGHT.

The sign had clearly been constructed hastily, but the words were clear. The person holding it was wearing a mask – a roughly made version of the same black and yellow mask that Quinn wore on stage.

Vincent stopped in his tracks and stared at the group. Were they... protesting for music?

The person holding the sign caught him staring and waved it from side to side. Next to them, another person waved their sign as well. ADMIT IT, it said, WE ALL LISTEN ANYWAY!

Vincent pulled his hood further down over his face and hurried off. He didn't want anyone recognising him from the Valentine's Day concert. The sin-seekers were sure to appear and break it up any minute, and he didn't want to get caught in that.

The fact that they were there at all though blew his mind. Yes, he'd said those things on stage, encouraging this very thing – but he hadn't expected anything to come from it.

Was... was change really possible? Things hadn't changed for the better, not really, not for as long as he could remember. Mostly, they'd only gotten gradually worse.

And maybe this wouldn't really help, not in the grand scheme of things. Maybe this protest wouldn't achieve shit. But the fact that they were there at all...

He had to do something. He had to help the ball roll, get it going even faster.

The others had all been arrested – but somehow, the sin-seekers had missed him.

Big mistake, on their part.

Vincent balled his fists, and turned another corner, towards the Mildura Sin-Seeker Main Office. He knew where it was, and even the internal layout – he'd worked there after all. But now he'd changed his mind. He was young, he was pissed-off, and he had the power to manipulate matter at will.

It was time to instigate a whole lot of trouble.

# CHAPTER 56

# TEMPORAL (LOBE) BOOM

**Date: Sunday 15 March 2082**

It was around 2:30AM when Quinn was abruptly wakened to the sound of a large hole appearing in the wall.

Craning her neck, she could just make out a figure standing on the other side. 'Spencer?!' she hissed in surprise. 'Is that you?'

'Shh!' Spencer came into the room. 'We need to be quick! I cut the power and walled the on-duty officers into their room, but they're probably already calling for backup!'

'Okay,' Quinn said. 'Um. A little help?'

Spencer paused, eyeing the large number of relics that were piled in boxes against the far wall. Wordlessly, he grabbed the gurney that Quinn was strapped to and hauled it towards the hole he'd made.

'Ow!' Quinn exclaimed as she was roughly jostled over a pile of partially shattered bricks and into the adjacent room. 'Careful! My back is still really sore!'

'Why, what did you do to it?' Spencer said.

'Can you not see the wings?'

'Those are attached to you?'

'Sure fuckin' are,' Quinn said. 'They brought in a fleshsmith to try and fix it, but he didn't know how. Maybe you could remove them, since they're metal?'

'Maybe, but not right now,' Spencer said. He stopped pushing the gurney and concentrated for a moment. Unreality surged and a second later, Quinn's bonds fell away.

'Thanks,' Quinn said, sitting up. 'Are the others also here?'

'They're somewhere in there.' Spencer gestured vaguely. 'Your cell was the easiest to find – it's the one with all the relics. We're going to need a bit of luck to find the others – but now you're here, we can redo it if it's wrong. C'mon, let's go.'

He concentrated again and another chunk of wall fell out. On the other side was an empty cell. Spencer didn't hesitate but carried on through to the next wall into a narrow corridor.

Quinn ran after him and, following the corridor, it wasn't long before they found the others – Mullet and Kylie, Maggie and Piper each locked in their own individual cell. They got up from their cots, grinning and cheering quietly as he broke open the lock on each door, releasing them one by one. Oddly though, when he'd finished, there was still a feeling of unreality in the air –

As the feeling suddenly got stronger, Quinn realised what it was.

'Oh shit!' she hissed. 'That Portent cop is still around!'

'What?' Spencer said, then his eyes widened. 'Yep, okay, I can feel it!'

'Quick!' Quinn said. 'We need to go now! NO WAIT, MULLET, NOT THAT WAY! SPENCER–'

'On it!' Spencer hurriedly opened another hole in the wall as the feeling of unreality began intensifying at an alarming rate.

As Quinn shoved a confused Mullet through the hole, she saw the door open at the end of the corridor. For a split second, she saw them – the Portent in the shape of a human, single eye glowing blue, a pinpoint in the dark – then Spencer pulled her through the hole as well, and bricks slammed messily back into place.

'GO, GO, GO!' Spencer yelled as the Portent bounded towards where the hole had been, arriving a mere second too late. Above them, the lightbulbs pulsed and shattered outwards.

'WHAT THE FUCK WAS THAT?!' Mullet yelled.

'TRUST ME, YOU DON'T WANT TO KNOW!' Quinn yelled back.

In a thunderous hail of shattering brickwork, Spencer led them through a breakroom, an evidence storage room, then a vehicle bay, then out into the open, where they sprinted around the side of the sin-seeker office.

'WHERE DO WE GO?!' Quinn yelled as they ran. 'IT'S CHASING US! SPENCER, DO YOU HAVE A FUCKING PLAN?!'

'RUN!' Spencer yelled, 'JUST FUCKING RUN, MAYBE WE'LL –'

The door at the front of the office burst open and the Portent appeared again, charging toward them with horrifying speed, cutting off their escape.

Quinn skidded to halt and Mullet bowled into her, almost knocking her over. Spencer meanwhile froze in place, teeth bared in a snarl of fear. Some way behind them, Maggie, Kylie and Piper came to a more graceful stop.

In front of them, the Portent stopped as well and cocked its head to one side.

'Where exactly do you think you're going?' they said. A single spark arced from their eye socket, licking at the air, grounding itself on their own shoulder.

Quinn gulped. Not she, nor any of the others, could find the words to respond.

'Hmm,' the Portent said. 'I should have anticipated this. Quinn Kelly is not the only roguesmith.'

They turned to look directly at Spencer. 'Who are you? I had heard that there was an additional teenage male in the group; however, I had wrongly assumed you had since left. What is your name?'

Spencer didn't reply. He took a step back, swallowing, as the Portent moved closer to him.

'You are a mattersmith, are you not?' the Portent went on. 'Unregistered. Are any of the rest of you smiths as well? You might as well admit it now. There will be no further escape attempts.'

Quinn heard footsteps from behind her – and Maggie stepped into view.

'Hey,' Maggie said. 'Where's Professor Wattle?'

The Portent paused, looking at her.

'Who?' they said.

'Your babysitter,' Maggie said. 'Are you allowed to be out and about without him supervising?'

'What do you know about... Professor Wattle?' the Portent said hesitantly.

'I used to work with him,' Maggie said. 'Me and Piper. Didn't we?'

'Y-yeah.' Piper stepped forward as well. 'He was our boss at the Department of Unreality!'

'But he moved to Melbourne recently,' Maggie said. 'To work on a new project.'

The Portent was silent, looking at her.

'Do you want to know what the new project was?' Maggie said. 'Professor Wattle seemed pretty adamant that we don't tell you. But I know you're curious, aren't you? Of course, you are. It even says you're curious in your file. It's one of your defining traits.'

'...my file?' the Portent said.

'Yes,' Maggie said. 'The official document on the Seventh Portent.'

There was another long silence. Quinn felt the feeling of writhing unreality intensify and took an instinctive step back.

'Maggie!' she hissed through her teeth. 'What are you doing?!'

The Portent shook their head.

'You're lying,' they said. 'That's impossible.'

'Is it?' Maggie said. 'Am I lying? Think about it. That many cybernetics, yet you don't run out of battery every three minutes?'

'I have to charge myself quite often,' the Portent said.

'No, you don't!' Piper said. 'It's the other way around! You have to release the charge, otherwise you'll start ejecting lightning-bolts every which way!'

The Portent raised a palm.

'You think to distract me,' they said. 'Well, I will have none of it. You must return to your cells immediately.'

They reached out a hand and Quinn winced as it made contact with Maggie's upper arm. Maggie let herself be shepherded back towards the front door of the office.

'Come on,' the Portent said, a note of annoyance in their voice. 'All of you! This way. Do not attempt to run. I will NOT hesitate to bring you in by force if you do not comply.'

Slowly, everyone began doing as they said – but as they filed their way into the front room of the station, a man burst through the opposite door, wearing nothing but nautical-themed pyjama pants and a matching shirt.

'Detective!' he yelled, pointed at the Portent. 'How many TIMES do I have to TELL you to wake me up before –'

He broke off as the situation suddenly caught up to him and he noticed who else was in the room.

'Oh,' he said. 'Hello. W-what's going on?'

'Hello again, Professor,' Maggie said. 'Bit irresponsible of you, isn't it? Letting the Seventh Portent run off on its own.'

Bill swallowed visibly.

'Detective,' he said through his teeth, 'what's your R.L. value at?'

'Fifteen per cent,' the Detective said. 'Is it true, Bill? Am I the Seventh Portent? Is that what you've been hiding?'

Bill's eyes bulged. He took a deep breath. 'Okay,' he said. 'Okay. Where are the other sin-seekers? Why is it just you?'

'I believe they are trapped,' the Detective said. 'This young man is a mattersmith, it turns out.'

'Really?' Bill said. 'Great. Fantastic.'

'It's okay,' the Detective said. 'They are going back to their cells now. I have things under control.'

'Okay,' Bill said. 'Okay. W-wait. Where's the other one?!'

'What?'

'The woman!' Bill said, 'The one from the lottery photo. Kylie Collins! She isn't in this room, Detective.'

Quinn looked around in surprise. She hadn't been paying attention to what the others were doing. Mullet was next to her, his mouth slightly open. Maggie and Piper were standing on the other side of the Portent. Spencer was near the door.

Kylie was nowhere to be seen.

In a flash, the Detective leapt towards the front entrance. They paused in the airlock for a moment, looking back and forth, before running outside.

Everyone went to the front window, watching as they ran to the road, looking left and right. As they did so, Maggie suddenly went out the airlock, leaving it open, walking towards them.

'Hey,' she said loudly.

The Detective turned to look at her. Their expression was one of annoyance.

Maggie raised her hand. She was holding a mobile phone.

In a fraction of a second, Quinn recognised it.

Maggie hit play.

The Detective reacted extremely quickly. Barely a few notes played before the phone was snatched from Maggie's hand and crushed to a sparking pulp.

But it was enough. Quinn knew what the phone was. She knew exactly what would play. And she knew exactly what to do.

There wasn't time to warn the others. They would have to deal the consequences in a moment. Quinn reached for the music and felt unreality expand around her.

But it didn't go anywhere – it couldn't. The music that had been playing was running in reverse – the palindrome they'd made to bring them back to the present.

But they were in the present already. Instead, all the happened was unreality expanded – and then violently snapped back into place.

Quinn felt the air leave her body as a shockwave of unreality expanded outwards. In instant later, it hit the Detective.

The Detective's relic lattice, the structure that tamed and contained their unrealitic core, was already on its last legs.

In recent days, it had gone through a lot – high temperatures, friction, submersion in water and constant electrocution – but this was the final straw.

Just like last time, Quinn felt the moment that the Portent broke free of its cage. A mere instant was all it needed before its borders were restored beyond the confines in which it had been trapped.

The Detective's head exploded.

In its place, a crackling ball of plasma roared to life.

***

The Detective only had a fraction of a second to appreciate that their R.L. value had hit zero before reality collapsed. But in that instant, they felt at last as though they finally understood everything.

It was true. They were the Seventh Portent. They had read through the file and found that the evidence matched exactly. It was what Bill had been hiding and of course, he had been right to not tell them. He'd been right all along.

They should have trusted him – left things alone. They were foolish to have doubted him. But it was as the saying went – hindsight was 20/20. Without the knowledge they had now, there was no world in which they wouldn't have questioned it. It was a fundamental part of their nature.

It was the only aspect of their nature on which they were sure. The rest... was utterly incomprehensible. They were a Portent. A creature of unreality, impossibility. Their very existence made no sense. In a world of strange, inefficient, unintelligible nonsense, they were by far the worst of it.

It was infuriating. It was laughable. They had been sent to find a Portent but hadn't even realised they were one themselves. Their mission had been a failure. EXP025 was a failure. And now their time was running out.

They were tipping over into an endless abyss, a garbled kaleidoscope of signals, overlapping, roaring, shrieking, through them and from them, dizzyingly vast. It would consume them shortly, they knew that. Their idea of self, the memories they'd formed over the last week. The progress they'd made. All gone.

No. No, not all gone, not completely.

They had made a mark on the world. Their memories might vanish but others would remember them. They'd solved the case, hadn't they? And anyway, maybe this wasn't the last the world would see of them?

Maybe he would bring them back again? His name was already gone, but his face stayed with them for another few microseconds. A kind face, with wild hair and laughter creases around the eyes. They could make new memories. Experience and understand things again.

Their body was falling away beneath them, hollow, lifeless, and the kaleidoscope engulfed them. Energy surged, blindingly powerful. Joy. Freedom. But also loss. What had they lost? They had already forgotten. It was important, very important, but the words escaped them. Words meant nothing anymore.

Signals, magnetic, electric, tugging and flowing, and those that darted and branched outwards. Self, that notion of I Am, did not vanish completely – but significance did. They were still there, but there was nowhere and meant nothing. There was no up or down, no right or wrong, only signals and noise. Spikes on a graph, in four dimensions, irregular, overlapping into infinity.

Then there was a pattern – something out of nothingness. A beat and a harmony, a repetition in a howling storm of chaos.

With no other purpose, they moved towards it.

# LIGHTNING IN A SUITCASE

### Date: Sunday 15 March 2082

Maggie was thrown back as a bolt of lightning cracked into the pavement, mere inches away from her. She hit into a wall and slumped to the ground. Sparks roared to life as the Seventh Portent released, rocketed sideways, away from its collapsing body.

Quinn, who had known what was about to happen a few seconds before everyone else, still struggled to react in time as the disembodied brain, trailing lighting like a crackling comet tail, shot towards the station building.

'RUN!' she screamed as it smacked into a window, shattering through.

Everyone scrambled for the door in a panic. Behind them, the brain crashed into the far wall and ricocheted off, setting a desk on fire as it passed.

Outside, Maggie was still lying where she'd fallen. Fear spiking, Quinn ran towards her – but she was beaten by Piper.

'Maggie?' Piper yelled, shaking the other girl's shoulder urgently. 'Maggie!'

From further back down the side of the building, there was another crash – and a garage door flew off its hinges. A sin-seeker paddy wagon burst out, accelerating down the driveway. Music was blaring from the open windows – *Nutbush City Limits* by Tina Turner.

Kylie was sitting in the driver's seat. She brought the

wagon to a screeching halt in front of the station and leaned out.

'GET IN!' she yelled.

Quinn didn't need to be told twice. Hauling Maggie between them, she and Piper raced for the back doors, yanking them wide and throwing themselves inside. Everyone piled in after them.

The Seventh Portent catapulted itself through another window, trailing glass and sparks. There wasn't even time to close the back door before Kylie stepped on the accelerator, skidding out onto the street.

Grabbing onto the wall for support, Quinn helped Spencer bolt the door closed and peered out of the tiny back window.

'IT'S FOLLOWING US!' she yelled.

'Good!' Kylie yelled back. 'We need to draw it out of town, preferably before everyone starts blaming us for it being here!'

She cranked the music even louder, skidding around a corner and straight through a red light. Behind them, the Seventh turned the corner as well, flicking through the intersection on long forks of white electricity. The traffic lights all changed to green before the globes exploded outwards.

Quinn braced herself, looking around at the others in the van. Mullet and Spencer were holding onto the walls and Piper was clutching Maggie, her knuckles white. Professor Bill was also there, still in his pyjamas, his hair a mess, his expression distinctly glum.

Her eyes were drawn back to Maggie. The older girl lay still, eyes closed, her lips grey.

'Piper,' she said, 'is she–?'

'She's breathing,' Piper said grimly. 'But I don't know what's wrong, exactly. She might have been struck by the lightning…'

'She was very close to the Seventh when it emerged,' Bill said. 'There's a good chance she was inside the rubicon…'

Quinn looked at him.

'You're an expert on the Seventh Portent, aren't you?' she said.

'I suppose you could say that.' Bill shrugged. 'As much as anyone is, or can be.'

'Right,' Quinn said. 'So, what do we do? It's chasing us. Driving away is fine for now but we'll have to stop eventually. If it keeps this up, we'll be in trouble.'

Bill sighed.

'We're going to have to capture them again,' he said.

'What?' Quinn said.

'The longer we leave them out on the loose, the more trouble they're only going to cause,' Bill said. 'I've seen this all before. They're attracted to electrical signals as well as noise, so doesn't matter if we draw them out of town, they'll be back again the next day, messing with the electrical grid and shooting lightning bolts at unsuspecting pedestrians. The only way to put a stop to it is to case them in relics again. I don't suppose you have any on you?'

'What, relics?' Quinn said. 'We've just become the most notorious roguesmiths this side of the Murray. Why would we have anything useful?'

'Point taken,' Bill said. 'Well, do you know where some are? I have a few, but they're in my suitcase, back at the sin-seeker station.'

'There were a whole lot of them back at the sin-seeker station, actually,' Spencer said, reluctantly.

'Oh,' Bill said. 'Actually, the Seventh's old shell is still there as well, which is full of relics! Mind you, those relics aren't enough to hold them anymore... But they almost are! We only need a couple extra! The ones in my suitcase should be enough!'

'You want us to go back to the sin-seeker station?' Quinn said. 'Now?'

'Do you have somewhere else we can reliably find enough relics to trap a Portent?'

'No,' Quinn admitted. 'Hey, Kylie!' she yelled over the music. 'We need to go back to the cop shop real quick!'

'Why the fuck would we do that?' Kylie called. 'We're almost out of town!'

'There are relics there that we need!' Quinn said. 'It's the only way to stop the Seventh!'

'Ugh,' Kylie said and she mashed on the breaks, pulling abruptly into a driveway. As she reversed out again, they all saw the Seventh Portent crackling down the long, straight road towards them. It was still far away but travelling at top speed. About halfway between them was an intersection.

'THIS BETTER BE WORTH IT!' Kylie yelled, and she turned off the music and accelerated back the way she'd come.

Piper squeaked and hid her face and Mullet screamed, clutching onto Spencer's jacket as they rocketed towards the Seventh Portent. For a second, it looked like it would get to the intersection before they did. But then Kylie was turning the corner, so fast that the wagon's wheels almost came off the ground, and they were pulling away again.

After picking herself off the floor, Quinn went back to the window. The Seventh Portent was still following but the distance between them was growing.

Kylie zigzagged through the residential streets, weaving back into Mildura proper. Soon, they lost sight of the Seventh altogether. As they got back towards the centre of town though, they saw that the weather station was all lit up, pulsing red in the dark. The E.W.S had been activated. Someone else had apparently noticed the stray Portent rocketing around the streets.

'Great.' Kylie scowled. 'The entire emergency response team is going to get in our hair now.'

She wasn't wrong. As they pulled in towards the sin-seeker station again, they found it swarming with activity.

'Fantastic,' Kylie said, pulling in on the far side of the road and idling there. 'I hope you chuckle fucks have a good fucking reason for this.'

'Is the cybernetic shell still there?' Bill said urgently. 'Can anyone see?'

Quinn opened the door a crack and peered out.

'Yep, it's there,' she said.

'Okay,' Bill said and he drew a breath. 'Wish me luck!'

He got out the wagon and hurried across the street.

'Okay, should we ditch him?' Kylie said. 'Don't know about you, but I'd rather not be involved in whatever Department of Stupid nonsense he's got going on.'

'No, we can't abandon him!' Piper said sharply. 'He can't recapture the Seventh all alone!'

'That's his problem!' Kylie said. 'I don't want anything to do with that shit!'

'Okay, but it IS kind of our fault any of this is happening,' Quinn said. 'I think we should help him. Please, Kylie? I'll fix it if it's wrong.'

'Ugh, fine!' Kylie rolled her eyes.

Across the street, Bill had gone inside the building. Shortly, he returned, carrying a suitcase. Quinn watched him flash a badge at one of the sinnies and point at the pile of cybernetic limbs that had been the Detective's body. *It's tainted with unreality,* they saw him sign. *We need to dispose of it safely ASAP.*

The cop, who looked very distracted, nodded vaguely. *Go ahead,* he returned.

Bill tried to lift the carapace but it weighed a lot and he wasn't quite strong enough. Wiping his brow nervously, he glanced over at the wagon.

'Should we help him?' Quinn said. 'Who's the least suspicious of us?'

'Spencer WASN'T just arrested,' Mullet said.

'Yeah,' Spencer said, 'but I used to work with some of those guys. Also, I trapped half of them in their office like half an hour ago. I doubt they've forgotten that. If anything, I'm the most suspicious.'

'If we're all suspicious, then Mullet can go, since he's strong and can lift heavy things,' Quinn said.

'Hey, don't just volunteer me like that!' Mullet said.

'While you're all wasting time chin-wagging, it looks like Bill's gotten help from a sinnie,' Kylie said. 'They're coming this way.'

'Oh shit, everyone act natural!' Mullet said.

They watched as Bill and the sin-seeker hauled the cybernetic shell across the road. As they got closer, Quinn and Spencer both winced, drawing back. The shell was full of extremely powerful relics.

*Thanks,* Bill signed as he and the sin-seeker reached the back of the wagon. *I've got it from here!*

*You sure?* the sin-seeker said. *You'll probably need help lifting it inside.*

*I'm fine.* Bill waved a hand. *Go back to whatever you were doing!*

The sinnie looked at him for a moment, then at the paddy wagon. A slight frown creased his brow.

*Where exactly did you get –* he began.

Quinn lunged forward and kicked the wagon's back door violently into his face. While he reeled back, clutching his nose in pain, she shoved Mullet outside. 'GRAB IT!' she yelled.

Fuelled by adrenaline, Mullet and Bill seized the heavy metal body and hauled it into the wagon. They both climbed in after it and Kylie hit the accelerator again.

As they shot down the street, there were shouts and frantic movement behind from the station. Two interceptor sedans pulled into the road and began to give chase, roof lights pulsing red and blue.

'FUCK'S SAKE, HOW ARE WE SUPPOSED TO GET AWAY FROM THEM?!' Kylie yelled.

Quinn tried to look but her brain had turned into sluggish mush. The sheer power of the relics in the car was draining her ability to think or even move. Dazedly she sunk to the floor.

'We've lost a whole Portent already, surely we can lose these guys?' Piper yelled distantly.

'Where HAS the Seventh got to?' Bill nervously looked out the back window.

As he spoke, all of the lights in town abruptly went out.

'Oh dear,' Bill said. 'That's not good.'

'Professor,' Piper said, 'do you know where Seventh is

likely to be? If we go towards it, the sin-seekers might be reluctant to follow.'

'They like sound and electricity,' Bill said. 'Power lines? A power station maybe? Do you know where the solar plant is?'

'Since they're attracted to sound, shouldn't we just play music again?' Piper said. 'That way, they'll come to us!'

'Kylie, crank them bangers!' Mullet yelled.

Music blasting loud again, sin-seekers hot on their tail, they zoomed back through residential streets and out into the industrial district. All was eerily dark now, warehouses looming like corrugated cliffs on either side of the road.

In the distance, a single streetlamp flickered on, brightening steadily before exploding with a pop.

Kylie turned the wagon towards it. They swerved into a side street, turning a corner – before abruptly screeching to a halt.

The Seventh Portent floated just ahead in the middle of the road. It was still now, glowing softly blue, small sparks jumping along its length. In the pitch dark, its full form was visible – a delicate, weblike nervous system, shivering with faint electrical impulses. Unreality churned violently around it. Above, another street lamp glowed brighter before shattering in a hail of glass.

The Portent turned around, its ghostly face just barely visible. The points of its eyes, a dense bundle of nerves, glowed faintly blue. Looking straight through the windshield, it cocked its head.

Behind, the two interceptors screeched into view, spinning to a halt. Sin-seekers bundled out, weapons in hand, fanning out to cut off escape. They began an aggressive approach – before noticing the Portent and backtracking in a hurry.

'Now what, geniuses?' Kylie said through her teeth.

'Keep playing music, but quietly,' Bill said. 'We need to keep them here while we set up the trap. If they decide to run off, then we're thoroughly screwed.'

'If they come closer, we're also screwed,' Kylie said.

'Yes, they need to stay *right* there,' Bill said. 'The goal is to spread out and surround them, so they can't escape.'

'This plan is insane. You're insane,' Kylie said.

'You're not the first to call me that,' Bill said. 'And I'm sure you won't be the last.'

He turned and looked around at everyone. Quinn and Spencer, this close to the Portent, were looking queasy. Mullet looked scared but determined, shaking fists balled in resolve. Piper was paler than usual, her jaw clenched tightly.

'Okay,' Bill said calmly. 'First, we need to get the relics out of the carapace.'

He reached into his suitcase and brought out a screwdriver. While everyone watched, he deftly twisted a line of screws out of their sockets and opened the hatch, revealing a treasure trove, jam-packed full of the Nation's most compact tier 5 relics.

'Everyone grab some,' he said, doing so himself. 'Then fan out, around the Seventh. Keep your distance and place them on the ground. Then, when I say, we start moving them in, slowly. Keep the music playing.'

Quinn reluctantly took a handful of relics, as did Kylie, Mullet, Piper, Spencer and Bill himself. Then they exited the wagon. Down the end of the street, the sin-seekers reacted to their presence in a flurry of hand signs – but they didn't dare approach.

Carefully, Bill directed them to encircle the Seventh. It seemed calm, turning gently back and forth, aware of their presence but entranced by the music.

Slowly, carefully, they surrounded it – and Bill let out a sigh.

'That's one of the hardest bits done,' he said quietly. 'Now, we start tightening the circle...'

They began to do so – but as the powerful relics got closer to the Portent, it began to get noticeably agitated. Unreality shifted and spiked, and several more street-lamps exploded. The music from the wagon distorted with static – before abruptly cutting off.

Everyone froze as the Portent turned around and around, electricity arcing brightly from its core.

'Stay calm,' Bill said sharply, 'and stay low! This is the most dangerous bit! Quinn, you're closest – can you try to turn the music on again?'

Quinn stepped back towards the wagon but to her alarm, the Portent began to drift in her direction. A larger fork of lightning crackled off of it, flickering along the tarmac mere metres away. She glanced from the Portent to the wagon and back again. There was smoke curling out from under the bonnet.

'Uhhhh,' she said, a little dazedly. 'I think the wagon's fucked!'

'Okay,' Bill said, clearly trying his best not to sound worried. 'Stay calm everyone! Stay where you are. Can, uh, anyone here sing or something?'

'Can we sing?' Quinn said, and she snorted in amusement. 'Buddy, we're a whole band! Mullet – can you give me a beat?'

He did so, a simple rhythm to follow, and she opened her mouth and sung the words that came to her mind. The street fell still as her voice pierced the night.

*Here I am, a spineless vessel*
*Stand before me and tell me true*
*Do you like me? Am I special?*
*Do I come across as weird to you?*
*Would you die for me? Would you betray me?*
*Here's my heart, please don't destroy it*
*Here are my words, please don't deny them*
*Here's my song, so please enjoy it!*

The Portent drew closer again, looming over her, its lightning calmed once more. Quinn ignored the horrible feeling of its proximity, the feeling of her own unrealitic heart responding to its presence, energy shivering down the wings of the First that she bore on her back.

Around her, the others were creeping in, relics in hand,

closer and closer. Bill had opened his suitcase and taken out a footy – a size 5 official AFL game ball, scrawled with the signatures of legendary players. The football was sliced in two halves and he took one half in each of his hands.

*Thank god I'm not smoking hot*
*Or I'd probably get harassed a lot*
*Thank god I'm not stinking rich*
*Or I'd probably be a stuck-up bitch*
*Thank god that I'm not book smart*
*Or I'd spend my efforts on something that wasn't art*
*Thank god I'm me, or I'd never be.*

The Portent stood right before her now, two metres away. Around it, her friends had closed in. It felt like standing in a cyclone, unreality coiling inwards, tighter and tighter. The Portent didn't seem to notice, entranced by the song –

*BWAAAAAAARP BWAAAAAAAAAAAAAAP BWAAAAAA-AAAARP!*

The night was split by the raucous sounding of a car horn.

The relixorcist roared down the road from the opposite end to the sin-seeker blockade. Lights flashing, horn blaring, it drew all attention – including that of the Portent.

The spell was broken. Now beyond agitated, the Seventh thrashed about and found itself trapped. Sparks cascaded across its surface. It seemed to pulse and Quinn felt the hairs stand up across her body. Then, its surface fell unusually dark –

'NO!' Bill yelled, 'GET DOWN, IT'S GOING TO –'

A massive discharge of lightning sprung out of the Portent, straight towards Quinn. She didn't even have time to register it was coming before it struck.

A thunderous *CRACK* rang out, deafeningly close. Quinn smelt ozone and singed hair. She was hot, and tingly, and she stumbled back –

She was... alive? Had the bolt missed somehow? But no... it hadn't? She'd felt it hit...?

There was a hand on her shoulder, and dizzily, she turned to look. A figure stood beside her, other hand outstretched, and pointed to a bush that was now on fire. Her hair was standing up with static and smoke curled off her skin, wreathing her in dark vapour.

'Oh no, you don't,' Maggie said.

Even the Portent seemed surprised to see her – and in that brief moment of reprieve, Bill sprung into action. With a yell, he hefted his football halves and slammed them into place around the floating brain. Then, gasping, he brought it down amongst the other relics and, knee on top, bound it tightly closed with a luggage strap.

'PILE THE RELICS ON, QUICK!' he yelled. 'YOU, GRAB MY SUITCASE FROM OVER THERE!'

Everyone scrambled to follow his instructions, shoving all the relics into a pile around Bill's hands. Inside the football, the Portent was fighting to escape – but with each new relic added, its fight became weaker.

Mullet brought the suitcase over and Bill slam-dunked the football inside, along with all the other relics. Then, he yanked it closed, zipped it up and sat on top.

'Phew!' he said, wiping his brow. 'That was a close one!'

Everyone else stared at him with varying expressions of disbelief. Nearby, the relixorcist brought his jeep to a halt, cutting the engine and climbing out, squinting in confusion. He was wearing the same Wiggles costume as the last time they'd seen him. On the other side, the sin-seekers stood, jaws slack, unsure what to do.

Eventually, one of the sin-seekers stepped closer.

'W-WHAT DID YOU JUST DO TO THE PORTENT?!' they called through cupped hands.

Bill stood up and hefted the suitcase.

'I've captured it!' he called back cheerfully. 'Don't worry, everything's under control! I'm from the Department of Unreality!'

The sin-seekers looked at each other, baffled.

'It might attempt to escape at any moment, though!' Bill continued. 'I would suggest you let us through, so we can go and contain it properly!'

He began walking towards the sin-seekers, who, looking panicked, backed away from him, guns in hand. While he did this, Kylie appeared at Quinn's shoulder and nodded back at the relixorcist's jeep, currently standing unattended.

'We should leave before they remember we're here,' she said quietly.

As Bill continued to advance, all eyes on him, Quinn, Kylie, Mullet and Spencer slunk back into the shadows. The relixorcist, standing with hands on hips, didn't notice that his car was being stolen until the engine suddenly revved to life behind him.

He yelled, lunging for the door handle, but too late – the jeep reversed away, almost colliding with a row of bins before zooming off down the street.

The sin-seekers watched them go, too stunned to act. They parted to let Bill and his suitcase through and, smiling pleasantly, Maggie and Piper followed after him.

# LAYING LOW

### Date: Monday 16 March 2082

At dawn on the 16th of March, a dusty red jeep with football scarves blowing from the roof rack rolled into the town of Broken Hill, New South Wales. The jeep pulled into a parking lot behind an abandoned warehouse, where it was stripped of relics and promptly ditched by its inhabitants.

Kylie tiredly led the way to the closest of Broken Hill's gigantic solar stations to purchase breakfast and figure out where they were going next. They were all exhausted, with visible cuts and scrapes, but for now, they were safe, their pursuers given the slip.

'I suppose,' Quinn said quietly, as they watched the solar station attendant brew four cups of tea, 'that we'll have to let go of being a band? At least for a while.'

'I quite agree,' Kylie said. 'This whole Mildura fiasco has landed us in a bit too much hot water for my liking. We need to disappear for a few months. Go completely off the grid.'

'But we'll bring the band back after that, right?' Mullet said.

'Obviously,' Quinn said.

Kylie rolled her eyes.

'Do you think Maggie and Piper will want to continue being our bassist and drummer?' Quinn said.

'Oh, I'm sure we haven't seen the last of them,' Kylie said

scornfully. 'I'm certain Maggie still had about half a dozen science experiments planned out for you and Spencer.'

'She does, yeah,' Quinn said. 'Mildura was only the beginning!'

'Well, there you go, then,' Kylie said. 'I'm sure they'll be back, dragging us into their weird nerd garbage all over again. Never fear!'

As she crossly dragged Mullet away to pick out breakfast from a rack of baked goods, Spencer sighed.

'You seem fine with it all,' he said quietly to Quinn.

'Fine with what?'

'Being a lab rat,' Spencer said. 'Participating in all of Maggie's plans, for the foreseeable future.'

'Yeah, well, I've decided they're for a good cause.' Quinn shrugged. 'We're gonna save the world! Or at least give it our best shot.'

'The entire world's is a bit of a stretch, isn't it?' Spencer wrinkled his nose. 'So far we just caused Mildura to revert in time, and only for a week.'

'Yeah, well, what is the entire world, but Mildura on a larger scale?' Quinn said. 'With music on our side, we can only go bigger from here!'

'Tch,' Spencer said and he shook his head. 'I don't get it.'

'What don't you get?'

'Why you're so optimistic.'

Quinn shrugged, feeling the weight and unrealitic buzz of the wingtips that jutted from her shoulder blades. She still wasn't used to them being there. In the last ten minutes alone, she had knocked over a stack of cans and swept an entire basket of fruit off a shelf.

Even so, she found that she didn't entirely hate them. She'd have to remove them – they were too obvious – but for now, they felt right, in some strange way. Like they belonged to her – a physical manifestation of what she already felt inside.

'It's like this,' she said slowly. 'I know that it's almost impossible to change the world, let alone save it. Even for people like us, with literal reality altering magic powers, there isn't a lot we can do. The status quo is too strong. We can struggle against it our whole lives, and there's no guarantee that anything will change or get better.

'But,' she went on, 'right now, for us, the opportunity IS there. And I think we need to take it. I've finally accepted that I'm a timesmith – and I'm going to use that to change some things. And yeah, I know it'll get me into trouble, and that people are going to try and use me for their own ends, and that eventually it'll kill me. But ultimately, it's me who decides what I do – and I've decided that if there's a chance I can use what I have to save the world, then that's a pretty good use of my time and abilities. You know?'

'Even if it almost definitely won't work?' Spencer said.

'Yeah,' Quinn said. 'Especially then!'

'Why especially then?'

'Cause no one else is gonna do it,' Quinn said.

'Pessimistic piece of shit,' she added and elbowed him in the ribs. But she was smiling as she said it.

*Booting sequence initiated...*
*Internal system check: All systems online...*
*Carapace integrity: 100%...*
*R.L. integrity: 100%...*
*CONFIRM ACTIVATION = YES*
*Loading EXP026: 'THE COURIER'...*
*Initialising...*
*Visuals online in 3... 2... 1...*

The Courier opened their eyes. Apertures whirred, zooming and focusing under stark white light.

They were propped up inside a windowless warehouse, lit brightly beneath rows of fluorescent bulbs. Benches stacked with tools and machine parts lined the walls, between boxes of lab consumables and colourful safety posters. Three people stood at the far end, holding clipboards, watching the Courier as they awoke.

Calmly, the Courier lifted their hands and turned them over, wrist mechanisms whirring smoothly. The fingers were shiny chrome, reflecting their own face back at them. It had no skin yet, just metal and plastic, with dark cybernetic eyes, a blue point shining at their very centre.

Who were they? And more importantly, what were they supposed to be doing? For a fraction of a second, they were flooded with the feeling that they'd done this before, that they should remember... But no – upon probing their own mind, they found it blank. There were no memories, nothing – just a name and a ReadMe file on their internal HUD.

They opened it and digested the contents. They were the Courier – the latest and greatest in a line of prototype cyborgs. Their purpose was to deliver important packages, in timely fashion, and intact, to the most dangerous and inhospitable corners of the Nation.

Today was a test exercise – an opportunity to prove their mental and physical capabilities. They had been provided a list of tasks to complete and, after reading through it, they were confident they could complete them with flying colours.

They stood, and extracted themselves from the crate in which their body rested. As they did so, the scientists at the far end of the room came closer. Two were young women in lab coats, and the third, a rotund man in a Hawaiian shirt. He approached the Courier and smiled up at them.

'Good morning,' he said cheerfully. 'How are you feeling, Courier?'

The Courier selected a random voice before they responded. 'I am well,' they said. 'My battery is fully charged and I am ready to complete the tasks in my itinerary.'

The man grinned. 'Excellent,' he said. 'My name is Bill. I helped build you – although I doubt you remember that?'

'I do not,' the Courier said.

'Thought not,' the man said – and for a second, he looked sad. 'But don't worry,' he brightened. 'You'll know me all too well soon, I'm sure. You'll be sick of me, even.'

'Why is that?' The Courier narrowed their eyes.

'I'm to be your partner!' Bill said. 'Since you're a prototype and all, you'll need someone there to monitor how you go. We'll travel the Nation together and get into trouble! Although... maybe less trouble...' He trailed off.

'I don't believe that's necessary,' the Courier said. 'I am built to be the perfect courier. I do not require assistance. In fact, to be blunt, I suspect you will only slow me down.'

Bill snorted. 'Yeah,' he said. 'You know, I almost certainly will slow you down. But... maybe you need that?'

'Regardless,' he added, 'I'll be there. Always.'

'This sounds like a horribly inefficient arrangement,' the Courier said. 'But fine.'

THE END

THE KNOWN PORTENTS - A CHEAT SHEET


THE FIRST PORTENT

DESCRIPTION: A fighter jet, its wings ablaze, trapped in a time loop in which it continuously crash-lands, detonates in a nuclear fireball, and reforms.
P.I.U.S DESIGNATION: Timesmith
P.I.U.S ABILITIES: Manipulation of spacetime, emphasis on time.


THE SECOND PORTENT

DESCRIPTION: The Sydney Opera House, recursive and ever expanding, capable of transmuting living matter into more of itself.
P.I.U.S DESIGNATION: N/A
P.I.U.S ABILITIES: N/A


THE THIRD PORTENT

DESCRIPTION: The hollow skin of a human male, propped up and animated through air pressure, a weathervane spinning in place of its head.
P.I.U.S DESIGNATION: Weathersmith
P.I.U.S ABILITIES: Manipulation of weather, atmosphere and pressure.

## THE FOURTH PORTENT

DESCRIPTION: A vast mechanical construction, commonly found deep underground, but occasionally breaching the surface to spew forth copious amounts of oil.
P.I.U.S DESIGNATION: Mattersmith
P.I.U.S ABILITIES: Manipulation of inorganic matter and its states.


## THE FIFTH PORTENT

DESCRIPTION: A torus of bovine flesh and organs, ambling forth on a multitude of malformed legs, trailing mutagenic blood in its wake.
P.I.U.S DESIGNATION: Fleshsmith/Agrismith
P.I.U.S ABILITIES: Manipulation of organic matter, including living animal and plant tissues.


## THE SIXTH PORTENT

DESCRIPTION: The spectre of a woman and her unborn child, visible only through their absorption and re-emission of light.
P.I.U.S DESIGNATION: Radismith
P.I.U.S ABILITIES: Manipulation of light and heat.


## THE SEVENTH PORTENT

DESCRIPTION: A floating human brain and ghostly nervous system, capable of generating

massive electric charge, as well as
manipulating electronic devices within its
vicinity.
P.I.U.S DESIGNATION: Electrosmith
P.I.U.S ABILITIES: Manipulation of electron
flow and magnetism.


## THE EIGHTH PORTENT

DESCRIPTION: A shrieking, twittering sphere
of common mynas, which aggressively transmute
human DNA into bird DNA upon contact.
P.I.U.S DESIGNATION: N/A
P.I.U.S ABILITIES: N/A


## THE NINTH PORTENT

DESCRIPTION: An inverted statue of Lady
Justice, sword and scales in hand, around
which gravity is reversed.
P.I.U.S DESIGNATION: Gravsmith
P.I.U.S ABILITIES: Manipulation of gravity
and weight.


## THE TENTH PORTENT

DESCRIPTION: A family home, capable of
appearing in any abandoned building, inside
of which objects become permanently
dimensionally altered.
P.I.U.S DESIGNATION: Spacesmith
P.I.U.S ABILITIES: Manipulation of spacetime,
emphasis on space.

## THE ELEVENTH PORTENT

DESCRIPTION: A satellite on an elliptical orbit, which transmits strange images to earth.
P.I.U.S DESIGNATION: N/A
P.I.U.S ABILITIES: N/A

www.ingramcontent.com/pod-product-compliance
Lightning Source LLC
Chambersburg PA
CBHW010018200726
48283CB00015B/2954